A
DAY
OF
FALLEN
NIGHT

SAMANTHA SHANNON

BLOOMSBURY CIRCUS
LONDON · OXFORD · NEW YORK · NEW DELHI · SYDNEY

For my mother, Amanda

BLOOMSBURY CIRCUS
Bloomsbury Publishing Plc
50 Bedford Square, London, WC1B 3DP, UK
29 Earlsfort Terrace, Dublin 2, Ireland

BLOOMSBURY, BLOOMSBURY CIRCUS and the Bloomsbury Circus logo
are trademarks of Bloomsbury Publishing Plc

First published in Great Britain, 2023

A catalogue record for this book is available from the British Library

ISBN: HB: 978-1-5266-1979-2; TPB: 978-1-5266-1976-1; EBOOK: 978-1-6355-7793-8;
EPDF: 978-1-5266-1977-8; WATERSTONES SIGNED: 978-1-5266-6128-9;
WATERSTONES EXCLUSIVE: 978-1-5266-6129-6; GOLDSBORO: 978-1-5266-6166-1

HB: 2 4 6 8 10 9 7 5 3
TPB: 4 6 8 10 9 7 5

Typeset by Integra Software Services Pvt. Ltd.
Printed and bound in Great Britain by CPI Group (UK) Ltd, Croydon CR0 4YY

MIX
Paper | Supporting
responsible forestry
FSC
www.fsc.org   FSC® C171272

To find out more about our authors and books visit www.bloomsbury.com
and sign up for our newsletters

Contents

Maps   vi

Prologue   xi

I   The Twilight Year (CE 509)   25
II   As the Gods Slept (CE 510)   183
III   Age of Fire (CE 511)   351
IV   The Long-Haired Star (CE 512)   697

Epilogue   809

The Persons of the Tale   847
Glossary   861
Timeline   863
Acknowledgements   867

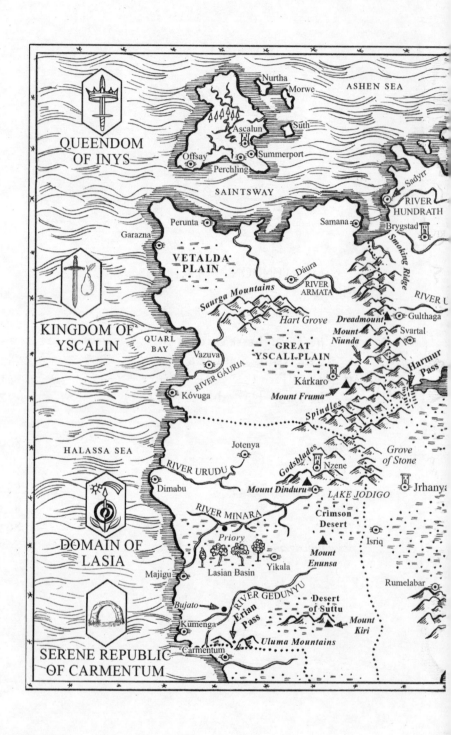

QUEENDOM
OF INYS

ASHEN SEA

Nurtha
Morwe
Ascalun
Suth
Offsay
Summerport
Perchling

SAINTSWAY

Sadyrr
RIVER
HUNDRATH

Perunta
Samana
Brygstad

Garazna

VETALDA
PLAIN

Smoking Ridge

RIVER U

Dáura

RIVER
ARMATA

Saurga Mountains

Hart Grove

Dreadmount
Gulthaga

KINGDOM OF
YSCALIN

QUARL
BAY

Mount
Niunda
Svartal

GREAT
YSCALI·PLAIN

Harmur
Pass

Vazuva

Kárkaro

RIVER GÁURIA

Mount Fruma

Kóvuga

Spindles

HALASSA SEA

Jotenya

Grove
of Stone

RIVER URUDU

Godsblades
Nzene

Dimabu

Mount Dinduru

Jrhanya

RIVER MINARA

LAKE JODIGO

DOMAIN OF
LASIA

Crimson
Desert

Priory

Isriq

Mount
Enunsa

Majigu

Lasian Basin

Yikala

Rumelabar

Bujato

RIVER GEDUNYU

Desert
of Suttu

Kumenga

Erian
Pass

Mount
Kiri

SERENE REPUBLIC
OF CARMENTUM

Carmentum

Uluma Mountains

Eldyng

Vattengard

Skelsturm

**KINGDOM OF
HRÓTH**

Aptan Forest

RIVER RINNA

MENTENDON

Spilda

INTH

GULF OF EDIN

THE ABYSS

Fratāma

Padāviya

WAREDA
VALLEY

Drayasta

Desert of
the Unquiet
Dream

Desert of
Queens

N

W   E

S

am

Little
Mountains

**THE
BURLAH**

Bardant

WHITE WASTE

Sarras
Mountains

Apata

THE ERSYR

QUEENDOM OF INYS

HOUSE OF BERETHNET

ASHEN SEA

Werstuth

Calthorn

THE FELLS

Strathurn
Castle

Drouthwick
Castle

RIVER LITHSOM

Nurtha

Befrith
Castle

HALLOW
LAKE

Queens'
Lynn

Morwe

Langarth

THE
LAKES

Madenley

HAITHWOOD

Yelden
Head

Goldenbirch

Cenning
Moor

THE FENS

Caddow
Hall

THE
LEAS

RIVER WENT

Cuthyll

Suth

Glowan
Castle

Arondine

Ascalun

Merroworth

THE
MARSHES

RIVER
TYRNAN

Selverpit

THE DOWNS

RIVER
LIMBER

Stilharrow
Deep

Summerport

Offsay

SAINTSWAY

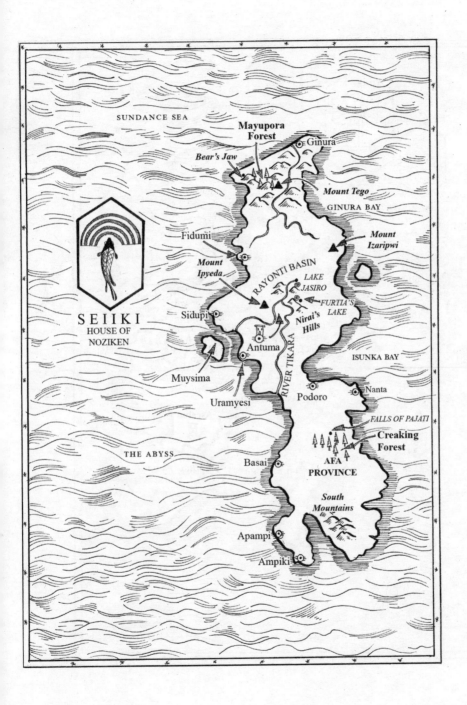

SUNDANCE SEA

Mayupora Forest

Bear's Jaw

Ginura

Mount Tego

GINURA BAY

Fidumi

Mount Izaripwi

Mount Ipyeda

RAYONTI BASIN

LAKE JASIRO

FURTIA'S LAKE

Nirai's Hills

Sidupi

Antuma

ISUNKA BAY

Muysima

RIVER TIKARA

Uramyesi

Podoro

Nanta

FALLS OF PAJATI

Creaking Forest

THE ABYSS

Basai

AFA PROVINCE

South Mountains

Apampi

Ampiki

SEIIKI
HOUSE OF
NOZIKEN

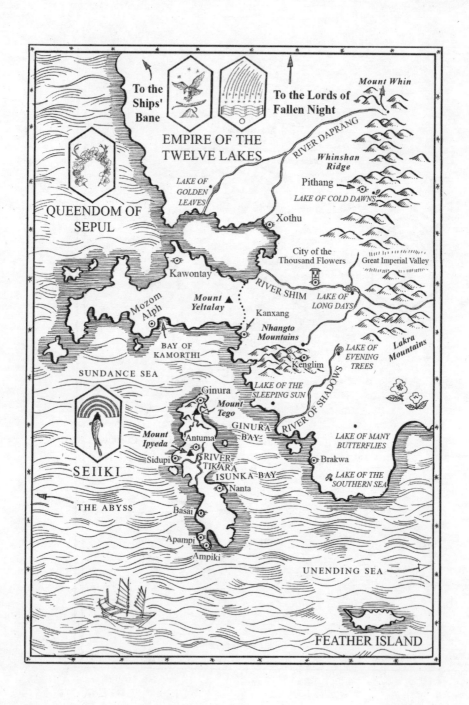

To the
Ships'
Bane

To the Lords of
Fallen Night

Mount Whin

EMPIRE OF THE
TWELVE LAKES

RIVER DAPRANG

Whinshan
Ridge

Pithang

LAKE OF
GOLDEN
LEAVES

LAKE OF COLD DAWNS

QUEENDOM OF
SEPUL

Xothu

City of the
Thousand Flowers

Great Imperial Valley

Kawontay

RIVER SHIM

LAKE OF
LONG DAYS

Mozom
Alph

Mount
Yeltalay

Kanxang

Nhangto
Mountains

Lakra
Mountains

BAY OF
KAMORTHI

LAKE OF
EVENING
TREES

Kenglim

SUNDANCE SEA

LAKE OF THE
SLEEPING SUN

RIVER OF SHADOWS

Ginura

Mount
Tego

Mount
Ipyeda

GINURA
BAY

Antuma

LAKE OF MANY
BUTTERFLIES

SEIIKI

Sidupi

RIVER
TIKARA

Brakwa

ISUNKA BAY

LAKE OF THE
SOUTHERN SEA

Nanta

THE ABYSS

Basai

Apampi

Ampiki

UNENDING SEA

FEATHER ISLAND

Prologue

Unora

Her name was Dumai, from an ancient word for a dream that ends too soon. She was born in the last glow of the Sunset Years, when every day poured soft as honey in the city of Antuma.

One spring, a young woman stepped through its gate, brought there by a forbidden wish.

She claimed to remember nothing of her past – only that she was called Unora. No one could have guessed, from her dusty clothes and callused hands, that her father had once held the power to set the whole court fluttering in his wake.

No one could have guessed what she was in the capital to do.

****

In those years, it was hard to farm the dry interior of Seiiki. Since the gods' retiral, long droughts had afflicted the island. Away from its shrivelled rivers, the ground thirsted.

Had the Governor of Afa been like other men, he would have lamented his post in a dust province. Instead, he laboured every day to channel water to its fields. Each time he returned to court, Empress Manai deemed him more inventive and hardworking. She gave him a mansion in the capital, where he placed his daughter, Unora, under the care of a nursemaid.

But Empress Manai had long been unwell, and her ailment did not ease. She renounced the throne before her time and retired to Mount Ipyeda, leaving her only child to be enthroned.

Though Prince Jorodu was still young, he had learned from his mother. In his first act, he summoned the Governor of Afa and made him River Lord of Seiiki, overlooking all others in his favour. For a year, he was the most trusted and beloved of the boy emperor.

So it shocked no one when he was suddenly banished, accused of having roused a god to make his province thrive. One family surrounded the emperor, and they allowed no one else close. Not for long.

****

Their servants found Unora and flung her into the dark street. At nine, she was left a destitute orphan. Her nursemaid stole her back to Afa, and for ten long years the world forgot them.

Unora worked the fields once more. She learned to bear the sun. Without her father, water no longer flowed. She planted millet and barley and wheat, folding seed into dry earth. She lived with a burning throat and a dull ache in her bones. Each night, she walked to the shrine on the hill, the shrine for the dragon Pajati, and clapped.

One day, Pajati would wake. One day, he would hear their prayers and bring rain to the province.

Over time, she forgot her days in the capital. She forgot what it was like to hear a river, or to bathe in a cool pond – but she never forgot her father. And she never forgot who had destroyed them both.

The Kuposa, she thought. *The Kuposa undid us.*

In her twentieth year, death came to the settlement.

The drought lasted for months that year. The fieldworkers pinned their hopes on their well, but something had tainted the water. As her old nursemaid vomited, Unora stayed at her side, telling her stories – stories of Pajati, the god they all willed to return.

The villagers took the body away. They were next to die. By the sixth day, only Unora was left. She lay in the stubble of the crop, too thirsty to fight, and waited for the end.

And then the sky opened. Rain touched the ground that had long been a deathbed – a patter that became a downpour, turning the dry earth dark and sweet.

Unora blinked away droplets. She sat up and cupped the rain in her hands, and as she drank, she laughed for joy.

The storm left as suddenly as it had come. Unora stumbled towards the Creaking Forest, soaked in mud from head to foot. For days, she sipped from leaves and puddles, finding little she could eat. Though her legs shook and an old bear stalked her, she kept on following the stars.

At last, she came to the right place. Behind the trickling remains of a waterfall, the white dragon Pajati slumbered – Pajati, guardian of Afa, who had once granted wishes to those who paid a price. Unora sought the bell that would wake him, faint with hunger and thirst.

Now she would leave her fate to the gods.

Deep was their slumber in those years. Most had withdrawn into undersea caverns, beyond human reach, but some had gone to sleep on land. Though Seiiki grieved their absence, disturbing them was the highest of crimes. Only the imperial family had that right.

Unora found she had no fear, for she had nothing left to lose.

The bell was taller than she was – the bell that would wake the guardian, not to be touched on pain of death, green staining the bronze. Unora approached it. If she did this, she could be killed. If she failed to do this, there was only sickness and starvation.

I deserve to live.

The thought came like a thunderclap. She had known her worth since the day she was born. Exile had beaten her into the dust, but she would not stay there. Not one day more.

She struck the bell. After centuries of silence, it tolled the night in two.

Pajati answered its call.

As Unora watched, the god emerged from the cave, all the many coils of him. He was white all over, from his pearly teeth to the gleaming pallor of his scales. She let her knees give way and pressed her forehead to the ground.

'The star has not yet come.' His voice rushed like wind. 'Why do you rouse me, child of earth?'

Unora could not sign her words. No one could. When Pajati offered his tail, she grasped it with shivering hands. His scales were like wet ice.

It was not for her to ask gifts of the gods. That was the privilege of empresses, of kings.

'Great one, I am a woman of your province. I come from a village stricken by drought.' She clung to her courage. 'I beg you for rain, king of the waters. Please, send us more.'

'I cannot grant that wish. It is not time.'

Unora dared not ask him when the time would come. It had already been too long. 'Then I ask for a way to enter the shining court of Antuma, so I might beg the emperor to save my father from exile,' she said. 'Help me move the Son of the Rainbow to mercy.'

Pajati showed his teeth. He was the brilliance of the moon, his scales the milk and tears of night.

'There is a price.'

It was no small price to pay, where water and salt were so precious and rare. Unora closed her eyes. She thought of her father, the dead in her village, her solitude – and even though her lips were cracked, her temples light from thirst, a drop seeped down her cheek.

Snow Maiden wept for the great Kwiriki, and he understood humans had goodness in them, her nursemaid had told her. *Only when she wept for him could he know that she had the sea in her, too.*

The warning from her childhood beat within her. It urged her to accept the death that waited in her wake. But the god of her province had already spoken:

'One turn of the sun it will last, and no more.'

He gave her a tear in return, dropping it into her palm like a coin. She lifted the silver glow to her lips.

It was like biting into the blade of a sickle. That drop swept a decade of thirst from her throat, utterly quenching her. Pajati took her tear with the tip of his tongue, and before he could tell her the whole of the bargain, Unora fell to the ground in a faint.

The next day, a messenger found her still there. A messenger from the shining court.

****

The women of the palace looked nothing like her. Their hair trailed almost to the floor, the fishtails of their robes some way behind them. Unora shrank from their stares. Her own hair was cropped to sit on her shoulders, her hands roughened by a decade of toil. Whispers chased her to the Moon Pavilion, where the Empress of Seiiki waited in a wide, dark room.

4

'I dreamed there was a butterfly asleep beside those falls,' she said. 'Where did you come from?'

'I don't remember, Your Majesty.'

'Do you know your name?'

'Yes.' Her name was all she had left in the world, and she meant to keep it. 'I am called Unora.'

'Look at me.'

Unora obeyed, and saw a pale woman about her own age, with eyes that put her in mind of a crow, curious and shrewd beneath a crown of whelks and cockles. Two crests adorned her outer robe. One was the golden fish of the imperial house, her family by marriage.

The other was the silver bell of Clan Kuposa.

'You are very thin,' the Empress of Seiiki observed. 'You have no memory of your past?'

'No.'

'Then you must be a butterfly spirit. A servant of the great Kwiriki. They say his spirits fade if they are not always close to water. Your home must be here, in Antuma Palace.'

'Your Majesty, my presence would shame you. I have nothing but the clothes I stand in.'

'Fine garments, I can have made. Food and drink, I can provide. What I cannot give is the wit and talent of a courtier,' the empress said with a wry smile. 'Those things must be learned with time, but that I can give, too. In return, perhaps you will bring my family luck.'

Unora bowed to her, relieved. This Kuposa empress had no inkling of who she was. If she was to reach the emperor, she would have to ensure that none of them did.

****

Unora bided her time. Time had been a rare gift in Afa. The courtiers spent theirs on poetry and hunting, feasts and music and love affairs. These arts were unknown to Unora.

But now she had all the food she could eat, and all the water she could drink. As she healed from the long chew of poverty, she grieved for those left in the dust, while the nobles soaked in private baths, helped themselves to water from deep wells, and rode in pleasure boats along the River Tikara.

She meant to make things better. Once she reached her father, they would find a way.

Everyone at court believed Unora was a spirit. Even when the handmaidens ate together on the porch, when it was impossible not to discuss the beauty of Mount Ipyeda, only one of them – a kind poet, round with child – ever spoke directly to her. The others just watched, waiting for evidence of powers.

The loneliness ached most on summer nights. Sitting in the corridor, the handmaidens combed their hair and spoke in low voices, skin kilned by the heat. Empress Sipwo would often beckon Unora, but she always shied away.

She could not ask a Kuposa for succour. Only Emperor Jorodu could help.

Summerfall came and went. As autumn reddened and gilded the leaves, Unora waited for the emperor, who seldom emerged from his quarters in the Inner Palace. She needed to speak to him, but only once had she caught a glimpse, when he came to visit his consort – a flash of collar against black hair, the dignified set of his shoulders.

Unora kept biding her time.

Empress Sipwo soon grew bored of her. Unora could not sew with cloud or spin a handsome prince from sea foam. Pajati had given her no power she could touch. She was sent to the other side of the Inner Palace, to a cramped room with a leak. Though a servant kept her brazier full, she could not shake the cold.

In Afa, people had danced to keep warm in the winter, even when their bodies protested. It was time to start again. The next day, she rose before dawn and walked to the roofed balcony that enclosed the Inner Palace. The north side faced Mount Ipyeda.

Unora stood before it, and she danced.

The Grand Empress had gone to that mountain. Unora craved the same escape. If she failed to reach the emperor, she would have to find some other way to save her father – but she had no idea where to begin. For the time being, she would escape into this, her winter dance.

Now change had come, it would not stop. One night, a note slid under her door with two white leaves from a season tree, both impossibly perfect.

Sleepless, I wandered before sunrise
hopeless and forlorn, before I saw
a maiden spun from moonlight, dancing.

Entranced, I dream and walk past nightfall
waiting for first light, when I still hope
to glimpse her as she dances, laughing.

Someone had seen her. It should have been embarrassing, but she was so lonely, and so cold. She told the messenger to return, asking for an inkstone, a brush, a water dropper.

Water could not be squandered on ink in the provinces. It still filled her with guilt to use it, but her father had taught her to write, scratching characters into the earth. Her brush mirrored the ebb and flow of the first poem, and she found that it was effortless.

Restless, I dance before each sunrise,
cold within my skin. I never saw
my witness in the shadows, writing.

Haunted, I shy away from morning
wondering who sees, yet I must still
go dancing in the snowfall, smiling.

When it was done, she tucked her poem under the door, and the messenger took it away.

At first there was no answer. Unora resolved not to think of it, but the longing, once woken, was hard to press down – longing for someone to see her. A second poem rewarded her patience, the evening before the Day of the Sleepless. Unora held it to her lips.

Snow fell over the city. More poems arrived, often paired with gifts: fine brushes, a gold comb adorned with a seashell, fragrant wood for her brazier. When two of the handmaidens passed her new lodgings, smiling at her apparent misfortune, Unora smiled back without bitterness, for she knew that love papered the floor of her room.

When he came to her, she invited him in. From the way he was dressed, he could have been anyone. She led him across the room, to

7

where moonlight fell across the floor. His slender hands, untouched by toil, made short work of her sash. When he felt her eternal chill, he tried to warm her fingers with his breath. She smiled, and he smiled back.

That was the first of many times. For weeks, he came to her at night, tracing verses on her skin. She showed him how to foretell the weather. He read her tales and travellers' writings, an oil lamp wavering between them. She taught him how to stitch and weave, sang him work songs from her village. They lived in shadow and by firelight, never seeing each other in full.

He kept his name a secret. She called him her Dancing Prince, and he called her his Snow Maiden. He whispered to her that it must be a dream, for only in dreams could such joy exist.

He was right. In the story, Dancing Prince had dissolved after a year, leaving Snow Maiden alone.

The morning before Winterfall, the servant set a meal before Unora. She lifted the bowl of hot soup to her lips, tensing before it could touch them. The steam carried the scent of the black wing, a leaf that grew wild in her province. She had tasted it before, by choice.

It stopped a child from taking root, or hollowed out the womb.

Unora held her stomach. She had been exhausted and tender of late, and retched over her chamber box. Someone else had guessed the truth before she had known it herself.

There was only one man whose children could pose a threat to the way of things. Now understanding dawned on her, he was away from court. It was too late to ask him to pardon her father. It was too late for anything. All she could do was protect their child – the child she decided, in that bittersweet moment, that she was going to keep.

She poured the soup quietly into the garden and smiled at the servant who came for the bowl.

****

That night, Unora of Afa left court. She walked towards the sacred mountain, taking nothing but a gold comb and her secret. If anyone had seen her, they would have said she was a water ghost, grieving something she had lost.

8

Sabran

She was named Glorian to strengthen her dynasty, in Ascalun, Crown of the West. That had once been the eke name of the city – until the Century of Discontent, when Inys suffered three weak queens.

First came Sabran the Fifth. Queen since the day she was cut from her mother, she loved that her existence kept the Nameless One from rising. In her eyes, it was only fair that she spent her life rewarding herself for that service.

The Virtues of Knighthood had no hold on Sabran. There was no temperance in her greed, no generosity in her hoarding, no justice in her want of mercy. She doubled taxes, her treasury bled, and within a decade, her queendom was a shadow of itself. Those who dared question her were pulled apart by horses, their heads set on the castle gates. Her subjects called her the Malkin Queen, for she was to her enemies as the grimalkin to the mouse.

There was no revolt. Only whispers and fear. After all, the Inysh knew her bloodline was the great chain on the Nameless One. Only the Berethnets kept the wyrm at bay.

Still, with only foulness to inspire them, the people lost all pride in their capital. Hounds and rats and swine ran wild. Filth choked and slowed the river, so the people renamed it the Lumber.

In her fortieth year, the queen remembered to fulfil her duty to the realm. She wed a noble of Yscalin, whose heart gave out not long after the ceremony. Her councillors prayed she might die in childbed, but she strode triumphant from the birthing chamber, a plump baby girl squalling in her wake – a new link in the chain, binding the beast for the next generation.

The queen made a sport of mocking the child, seeing in her daughter a feeble imitation of herself, and Jillian, in turn, grew hard and bitter, and then cruel. Whatever her mother gave, she returned, and the two pecked at each other like a pair of crows. Sabran married her to a drunken fool, and soon Jillian had a girl of her own.

Marian was a fragile soul, afraid to raise her voice above a whisper. Her relatives ignored her, and she thanked the Saint for it. She lived quietly, and wed quietly, and quietly got with child.

Into this decaying house, a third princess was born.

Sabran was her name, to please the tyrant. No sound escaped her, but a crease rumpled her tiny brow, and her bottom lip poked out.

'Saint, poor lamb,' the midwife said. 'How stern she looks.' Marian was too weary to care.

Not long after the birth, the Malkin Queen deigned to visit, shadowed by the crown princess. Marian shrank away from them both.

'Named after me, is she?' The white-haired queen laughed at her. 'How you flatter me, little mouse. But let us see if your bantling amounts to more than you, before we draw comparisons.'

Not for the first time in her life, Marian Berethnet wished the earth would crack open and swallow her.

****

Like every other woman of her house, Lady Sabran grew to be tall and striking. It was a well-known fact that each Berethnet queen gave birth to one girl, who came to look just like her. Always the same black hair. Always the same eyes, green as southern apples. Always the same pale skin and red lips. Before old age changed them, it could often be hard to tell them apart.

But the younger Sabran did not have her mother's fear, her grandmother's spite, or the tyrant's cruelty. She carried herself with purpose and dignity, never rising to a taunt.

She kept her own company as much as she could, and the company of her ladies, who she trusted above anyone. Her tutors educated her in the history of Virtudom, and when she excelled in those lessons, they taught her to paint and sing and dance. They did this in secret, for the queen hated to see other Berethnets happy – and to see them learn to rule.

For ten years, the entire court watched the youngest of the four.

Her ladies were the first to hope that she might be their saviour. They saw the line that never left its seat between her brows. They walked with her to the castle gates, where she took stock of the rotten heads, her jaw clenched in disgust. They were there when the Malkin Queen tried to break her, the day she first woke to blood on her sheets.

'I was told you are ready to make a green-eyed bairn of your own,' the old queen said. 'Fear not, child ... I shall not let your beauty wither on the vine.' Her face was like the skin on milk, powder sunk into its creases. 'Do you dream of being queen, my lamb?'

Lady Sabran stood at the heart of the throne room, in sight of two hundred courtiers.

'I dare not, Your Grace,' she said, her voice quiet yet clear. 'After all, I could only be queen if you were no longer on the throne. Or, Saint forbid ... if you were dead.'

The court rippled.

It was treason to imagine the death of the sovereign, let alone speak of it. The queen knew this. She also knew she could not kill her granddaughter, for it would mean the end of the bloodline and her power. Before she could reply, the child left, followed by her ladies.

By that time, the Malkin Queen had held the throne for over a century. For too long, no one had been able to imagine a world free of her, but from that day on, hope was reborn. From that day on, the servants referred to Lady Sabran – always in whispers – as the Little Queen.

The tyrant died, aged one hundred and six, in her bed of finest Ersyri silk, Lasian gold on every finger. Jillian the Third was next to sit the marble throne, but few rejoiced in earnest. They knew Jillian would take all that her mother had denied her.

Not a year after her coronation, a man slipped into the hall where Queen Jillian was dining. The late queen had ordered him tortured to madness. He stabbed her daughter in the heart, thinking she was his tormentor. She was laid beside the tyrant in the Sanctuary of Queens.

Marian the Third wore the crown as if it were a poisonous snake. She refused to see petitioners who sought help from their sovereign. She feared even her councillors. Sabran pressed her mother to demonstrate more strength, but Marian was too afraid of Inys to control it. Not for the first time, there were rumblings – not just of discontent, but rebellion.

Blood averted blood, for war awoke in Hróth.

11

****

The snowbound North had ever been strange to the Inysh. Some years Hróth had offered trade, while in others, raiders had come in their boar ships to burn and ransack Inysh towns.

Now, across ice cascades and deep forests, the clans took up arms and marched to the slaughter.

It began with Verthing Bloodblade, who lusted after Askrdal, largest of the twelve domains. When its chieftain refused an alliance, he killed her, taking her land for his own clan. Those who had loved Skiri Longstride sought vengeance, and soon the feud had all Hróth in its grip.

By midwinter of that same year, as blood continued to soak the snow red, violence flared again, to the south, in the peaceful land of Mentendon. A devastating flood had struck its coast, sinking entire settlements, and Heryon Vattenvarg, the Sea King, hardest of all Hróthi raiders, attacked in its wake. With Hróth still at war, he had gone seeking greener lands and found one floundering. This time, he meant not to sack, but to settle.

In Inys, Sabran Berethnet listened to the Virtues Council bicker over what to do. At the head of the table, her mother was gaunt and silent, hunched beneath her crown.

'I agree we should not interfere with the war in the North,' Sabran told her in private, 'but let us help the Ments oust this Vattenvarg in exchange for their conversion. Yscalin could lend them arms. Imagine how the Saint would smile – a third realm sworn to him.'

'No. We must not provoke the Sea King,' Marian said. 'His salt warriors slaughter without pity, even as the Ments reel from this dreadful flood. I have never heard of such wanton cruelty.'

'If we don't assist the Ments now, Vattenvarg will crush them. This is no ordinary raider, Mother,' Sabran said, losing her patience. 'Vattenvarg means to usurp the Queen of Mentendon. If victory emboldens him, he will come for Inys next. Do you not see?'

'Enough, Sabran.' Marian pressed her temples. 'Please, child, leave me. I can't think.'

Sabran obeyed, but bridled inside. She was sixteen and still had no sway.

By summer, Heryon Vattenvarg had most of Mentendon, ruling from a new capital, Brygstad. He claimed the land for Clan Vatten.

Weakened by flooding, famine and cold, the Ments ceased their fight and knelt. For the first time in history, a raider had taken a realm.

Two years after the conquest of Mentendon, the war in Hróth came to an end. The chieftains had pledged to a young warrior of Bringard, who had won their loyalty with his sharp mind and tremendous strength. It was he who had slain Verthing Bloodblade, avenging Skiri Longstride, and united the clans, as none ever had. Soon Inys heard the news that Bardholt Hraustr – bastard son of a boneworker – would rule as the first King of Hróth.

He would also sail to meet the Inysh queen.

'This is a fine state of affairs,' Sabran said curtly, reading the letter. 'Now two nearby countries are ruled by heathen butchers. If we had aided the Ments, it would only be one.'

'By the Saint. We are doomed.' Marian wrung her hands. 'What does he want from us?'

Sabran could guess. Like the wolves that stalked their forests, the Hróthi could smell wounded things, and Inys was a realm still bleeding.

'King Bardholt fought long for his crown. I am sure he wants no further hostilities,' she said, if only to soothe her mother. 'If not, Yscalin is with us.' She rose. 'I have faith in the Saint. Let the bastard come.'

****

Bardholt Battlebold – one of his many names in Hróth – came to Inys on a black ship named the *Helm of Morning*. Queen Marian sent her consort to meet him. All day, she paced the throne room, plaits swaying. She wore a deep green overgown on ivory, which swamped her. Sabran countered her with absolute stillness.

When the King of Hróth appeared, shadowed by his retainers, the whole court turned to ice around him.

The Northerners wore heavy furs and goatskin boots. Their king dressed like the rest. Sabran was tall, but if she had stood on her toes, she doubted her head would have reached his chin. Thick golden hair coursed to his waist. His arms strained with muscle, and his shoulders seemed as wide and sturdy as a dowry chest. She thought he was in his early twenties, but he could also have been her age, weathered by the toll of war.

That war was etched into his tanned and well-boned face. A scar carved from his left temple to the corner of his mouth; another marked his right cheekbone.

'Marian Queen.' He raised a giant fist to his heart. 'I am Bardholt Hraustr, King of Hróth.'

His voice was low and somewhat coarse. It drove a chill through Sabran, as did his crown. Even at a distance, she could see that it was pieced together from splinters of bone.

'Bardholt King,' Marian said. 'You are welcome to Inys.' She cleared her throat. 'We congratulate you on your victory in the Nurthernold. It brings us joy to know the war is over.'

'Not as much joy as it brings me.'

Marian twisted her rings. 'This is my daughter,' she said. 'Lady Sabran.'

Sabran straightened. King Bardholt gave her a fleeting glance, then looked again, his gaze nailed to her face.

'Lady,' he said.

Without breaking his gaze, Sabran curtseyed, the pale sleeves of her gown caressing the floor. 'Sire,' she said, 'this queendom offers its esteem. Fire for your hearth, and joy for your hall.'

She spoke in perfect Hróthi. He raised his eyebrows. 'You know my tongue.'

'A little. And you know mine.'

'A little. My late grandmother was Inysh, from Cruckby. I learned as much as felt needful.'

Sabran inclined her head. *It would not be needful if this king had no interest in Inys.*

King Bardholt returned his attention to her mother, but throughout their exchange of courtesies, it drifted back to Sabran. Beneath her sleeves, her wrists and fingers warmed.

'Be at ease,' he said. 'The violence in my land will spill no farther, now Bloodblade is dead. I have all of Hróth – and I will have Mentendon, once Heryon Vattenvarg swears his allegiance to me, which he must, as a man of Hróth.' He smiled with a full set of teeth. Sabran thought that must be a fine rare thing after a war. 'I only wish for a friend in Inys.'

'And we accept your friendship,' Marian said, her relief so potent that Sabran could almost smell it. 'Let our realms live in perfect peace, now and always.' Since the danger seemed to have passed, she was steadier. 'Our castellan has prepared the gatehouse for your retinue. I am sure you must return to Hróth very soon – though if you wish to stay to celebrate the Feast of Fellowship, which falls a week from now, it would be our honour.'

'The honour would be mine, Your Grace. My sister and chieftains will manage in my absence.'

He bowed and strode from the throne room.

'Saint. He was not supposed to accept the invitation.' Marian looked sick. 'It was a courtesy.'

'Your courtesies are hollow, then, Mother?' Sabran said coolly. 'The Saint would not approve.'

'Nay, the sooner he leaves, the better. He will see the treasures of our sanctuaries and want them for himself.' When the queen rose, one of her ladies took her by the arm. 'Guard yourself well in the days to come, daughter. I could not bear you to be taken for ransom.'

'I should like to see them hold me,' Sabran said, and left.

****

That night, after her ladies had finished the long task of washing her hair, Sabran sat beside the fire and pondered what the King of Hróth had said. The words that had betrayed the truth.

There has been enough bloodshed for now.

'Florell, you know all secrets.' She glanced up at her closest friend. 'Is King Bardholt promised?'

'Not as far as I've heard.' Florell combed her hair. 'I've no doubt he's taken lovers, looking the way he does. They don't follow the Knight of Fellowship there.'

'No,' Sabran said. 'They do not.' A log in the fire crumbled. 'Is he a man of faith?'

'I've heard the Hróthi worship spirits of the ice, and faceless gods that dwell in the forests.'

'But you have heard nothing of *his* faith.'

Florell slowed as she worked on a stubborn knot. 'No,' she said thoughtfully. 'Not a whisper.'

Sabran reflected on that. As the idea formed, she said, 'I need a private audience with him.'

In the corner of the room, Liuma lowered her needlework. 'Sabran, he has taken many lives,' she said in Yscali. 'He has no place in Halgalant. Why would you want to speak with him?'

'To make him a proposal.'

Only the crackle of the fire broke the stillness. When Liuma realised, she drew a sharp breath.

'Why?' Florell said, after a silence. 'Why him?'

'It would bring another realm under the holy shield – two, if Heryon Vattenvarg kneels to him,' Sabran said softly. 'The Sea King would have to submit if Bardholt stood with us.'

Florell sank into a chair. 'Saint,' she said. 'He would. Sabran, you're right.'

'Your mother would never agree,' Liuma whispered. 'You would plot this behind her back?'

'For Inys. Mother fears her own shadow,' Sabran said darkly. 'You must see what will happen next. Either Bardholt or Heryon will claim this queendom, to show his strength over the other.'

'Bardholt said he would not attack us,' Florell reminded her. 'I hear the Hróthi take oaths seriously.'

'Bardholt Hraustr is not cut from the same ice as his ancestors. But I can make sure he poses no threat.' Sabran turned to them. 'It has been over a century since the Malkin Queen sowed the rot in Inys. That rot has set too deep for us to win a war against the heathens. I will be a peaceweaver. I will save the House of Berethnet, and make sure it rises stronger than ever – the head of four realms sworn to the Saint and the Damsel. We will rule the Ashen Sea.'

Florell and Liuma held a wordless conversation. At last, Florell knelt before Sabran and kissed her hand.

'We will see to it,' she said, her voice resolute. 'My lady. My queen.'

****

Just before dawn, Sabran slipped from her bedchamber, dressed for riding, leaving Florell and Liuma to conceal her absence. She stole into the castle grounds, through the wildflowers and oaks. Never, in her eighteen years, had she gone this far without her guards.

It might be folly. So might her idea – her dangerous and wild idea, curled within her like an adder, ready to sink its teeth into a king. If she could convince him, she would change the world.

Saint, give me strength. Open his ears.

The sun had almost risen by the time Sabran beheld the lake, and the heathen who bathed in its shallows. When he saw her, the king scraped his hair from his eyes and waded towards her, stripped to the waist. Loaves of muscle shifted under his many scars.

When he reached the shore, her nerve almost failed. He kept just enough of a distance for her to face him without craning her neck.

'Lady Sabran,' he said, 'forgive my undress. I always swim at dawn, to spur my blood.'

'If you will forgive me,' Sabran said, 'for inviting you here as I did, without ceremony.'

'Boldness is admirable in a warrior.'

'I am no warrior.'

'Yet I see you came armed.' He nodded to the blade at her waist. 'You must fear me.'

'I heard some call you Bearhand. Foolish to face a bear with no blade.'

For a tense moment, he only looked at her, still as a beast before the pounce. Then he chuckled low in his throat. 'Come then,' he said, folding his huge arms. 'Speak your mind.'

Water glistened on his chest. His voice polished her senses. She smelled the sweetness of bedstraw and grass, felt the hammered gold of her bracelet where her wrist had warmed it.

'I have a proposal,' she said. 'One I must make in confidence.' She took a step towards him. 'I am told the snowseers have not yet declared a religion for the new Kingdom of Hróth.'

'They have not.'

'I would know why.'

His gaze held steady. This close, she saw his eyes were hazel, more gold than green.

'My brother,' he said, 'was murdered during the war.'

Sabran had not grieved for her grandmother, and she doubted she would mourn her parents for too long. Still, she imagined the loss of a loved one would hurt like an arrowhead lodged in the body. Life would grow and twine around it, but it would remain, always hurting.

'When I found him, crows were feasting on his eyes,' King Bardholt said. 'Verthing Bloodblade had slit his throat and cast him off like an old pelt. My young nephew only escaped the same fate by cutting off his own hand.' His jaw worked. 'My brother was a child. An innocent. No god or spirit worth my praise would have allowed his death.'

The only sound between them was the fissle of the nearby trees. If Sabran had been born a heathen, she might have thought that something in those oaks had heard his treachery.

I must strike now, with force, or not at all.

'In Inys, we no longer answer to such things. We honour the memory of a man – my own ancestor – and live according to his Six Virtues,' she said. 'Like you, the Saint was a warrior in a land of small and feuding kingdoms. Like you, he united them all beneath one crown.'

'And how did he do this, your Saint?'

'He slew a vicious wyrm, and so won the heart of Princess Cleolind of Lasia. She forsook her old gods to stand at his side.' The wind spun long strands of hair from her circlet. 'Inys and Yscalin are united in praise of him. Join us. Swear Hróth to his Virtues of Knighthood. With two ancient monarchies at your side, you will leave the Sea King no choice but to kneel.'

'Heryon will kneel regardless,' was all he said.

'Winning his loyalty by force would mean another war. Many would die. Even children.'

'You appeal to my heart.'

'More than you think.' Sabran raised her eyebrows. 'You cannot have me unless you convert.'

That made him smile. It was a baleful thing, that smile, and yet it did hold warmth.

'What makes you think I would have you, Lady Sabran?' Her name was a dark thrum in his throat. 'How do you know I don't already have a consort in my own kingdom?'

'Because I saw how you looked at me in the throne room.' (He had not said *no*.) 'And how often.'

King Bardholt offered no reply. Sabran stood tall before him, for she was not her mother.

'I think,' she said, 'that you are a man familiar with having what you want. This time, you need not seize it with blood and force. I offer it all to you. Be my consort.'

'Your religion began with a love story. Am I the heathen in this tale, or the great slayer?'

Sabran only held his gaze. She imagined herself as a hook in water, still enough to lure a circling fish.

'I have heard the Berethnet queens bear only one child. Always, as far back as the songs go,' he finally said. 'I will need an heir for Hróth, to consolidate the House of Hraustr.'

'You have a sister. And she has a son,' Sabran said. 'With Virtudom behind you, your new house will be unassailable.' She lifted her chin. 'I know you will need to convince the snowseers to embrace the Saint. I know the Six Virtues are yet strange to you – but your realm is weeping, Battlebold. So is mine. Marry me, so all wounds may be knit.'

It was some time before he moved, reaching for her waist. Her heart beat thick and heavy as he slid her small blade from its sheath.

He could stab her where she stood, and Inys would be his to conquer.

'I will consult the snowseers,' he said. 'If we choose your way, I will swear it with your blade, in my blood.'

He walked back to the castle with her knife. As Sabran watched him disappear, she knew she had already won.

****

On the first day of midsummer, the Issýn, highest of the snowseers of Hróth, emerged from her cave to share a vision. She had dreamed of a chainmail that covered the world, and a sword of polished silver, passed from a long-dead Inysh knight to the new King of Hróth.

In the new capital of Eldyng, King Bardholt declared that Hróth, like Cleolind of Lasia, would abandon the ancient ways and follow the everlasting light of Ascalun, the True Sword.

In Inys, Sabran Berethnet received a letter, smeared with the blood of a king, saying only one word: *yes*.

In the weeks after they announced their betrothal, Heryon Vattenvarg made an announcement of his own, declaring loyalty to the King of Hróth, who named him Steward of Mentendon. Heryon converted. So did his subjects. Within a year, the King of Hróth wed the Princess of Inys, and across the realms pledged to the Saint, there was revelry and song.

Inys, Hróth, Yscalin and Mentendon – the unbreakable Chainmail of Virtudom.

Queen Marian yielded the throne before long. Having had more than her fill of court, she retired to the coast with her companion. The day Sabran the Sixth was crowned before her subjects, her Northern king was at her side, grinning as if his face would crack.

An heir did not arrive at once. Bardholt spent most summers in Inys to escape the midnight sun, while Sabran sailed across the water in the spring, but duty always stole between them. Their lands were still too fragile to abandon in the darker, harder months.

On her island, Sabran ruled alone. There was time for an heir, and she wanted as much of it as possible alone with her court, and with her consort, whose passion for her was ever strong.

One year, a few months after Bardholt had left Inys, Liuma afa Dáura found she could no longer lace the queen into her gown.

The next year, as the woodruff bloomed, Sabran bore a daughter, who screamed loud enough to bring down the Great Table. The attendants threw the shutters open for the first time in a month. As Florell sponged the sweat from her brow and Liuma nursed the baby, Sabran felt as if she was taking the first easy breath of her life. It was done, all of it.

She had made the world new.

When he heard the news, King Bardholt left Eldyng and boarded a ship with a handful of retainers, disguised as a seafarer. Five days later, he reached Ascalun Castle, fear gripping him harder than it ever had during the war. It faded when he found Sabran waiting for him, alive and well. He took her in his arms and thanked the Saint.

'Where is she?' he asked her hoarsely.

Sabran smiled at his excitement, placing a kiss on his cheek. Liuma brought the child.

'Glorian,' Sabran told him. 'Her name is Glorian.'

Bardholt gazed in wonder at their child as Sabran was dressed for the day. When she emerged on to the royal balcony at Ascalun Castle, with her consort beside her and their black-haired daughter in her arms, a hundred thousand people roared in welcome.

Glorian.

Esbar

A princess for the West. One lost in the East. In the South, a third girl was born, between the other two.

This girl was not destined to wear a crown. Her birth did not stitch the wounds in a queendom, or gift her with any right to a throne. This birth took place deep in the Lasian Basin, out of sight of the eyes of the world – because this girl, like her birthplace, was a secret.

Her many sisters waited as she crowned, some calling their encouragement, the room lit by their flames. Among them, Esbar du Apaya uq-Nāra panted in the last throes of delivery.

The day before, she had felt the first twinge while she bathed in the river, two weeks early. Now it was almost sunrise, and she was hunkered on the birthing bricks, wishing slow death on Imsurin for causing this, even though she had been the one to invite the man to lie with her.

'Almost there, Esbar,' Denag told her from the floor. 'Come, sister – just once more.'

Esbar reached for the two women who flanked her. On her right, her birthmother prayed aloud, soft and calming. On her other side, Tunuva Melim kept both arms around her shoulders.

'Courage, my love,' Tunuva whispered. 'We are with you.'

Esbar landed a shaky kiss on her temple. She had said the same words over a year before, when it was Tunuva who laboured.

When their eyes met, Tunuva smiled for her, even if her lips shook. Esbar tried to reply – only for another shooting cramp to rip the words away. *Let it be now*, she thought, through the fog of pain. *Let it be done.*

Gathering what remained of her courage, she fixed her gaze on the statue of Gedali and willed herself to be as strong as the divinity.

She bore down on the bricks, as if she meant to bestride the world. Her throat scorched with her scream. Her insides roiled. In a slippery rush, the child slid free, straight into the waiting arms of Denag, and Esbar slackened, as if she had pushed her bones out as well.

Denag turned the child, clearing a tiny nose. There was silence – a deep shared breath, unspoken prayer – before a thin wail shivered into the chamber.

'The Mother is with us,' the Prioress declared, to cheers. 'Esbar has given her a warrior!'

Apaya let go of her breath as if it had been caged for hours. 'Well done, Esbar.'

Esbar could only laugh in relief. Tunuva held on to her, keeping her from slumping off the bricks. 'You did it,' she said, laughing with her. 'Ez, you did it. Thank the Mother.'

Shuddering, Esbar pressed their foreheads together. Sweat trickled down both their faces.

Gentle chatter filled the chamber. Esbar lay on the daybed, and Denag placed the newborn on her chest – slathered in birthing wax, soft as a petal. She fidgeted, cracking her crusted eyes open.

'Hello, strong one.' Esbar stroked her brow. 'You were in a hurry to see the world, weren't you?'

The afterpains would begin soon. For now, there were prayers and smiles and good wishes, and more love than her heart could hold. Esbar brought the child to her breast. All she wanted now was to be still, and to savour what it was to only house one life within her.

Apaya brought a basin of boiled water and a cold poultice. 'Watch over Tunuva,' Esbar said to her quietly, while their sisters milled around. 'Promise me you will do this, Apaya.'

'For as long as it takes.' Apaya unsheathed a knife. 'Rest now, Esbar. Recover your strength.'

Esbar was only too glad to oblige. Her birthmother severed the cord, and at last, the child passed from the womb to the world.

****

Once the afterbirth had come, Apaya took her to her sunroom, still with the child against her heart. They stayed that way until Imsurin arrived.

'I told you we'd make a fine match,' Esbar reminded him. 'Ready to lose sleep for a while?'

'More than ready.' He leaned in to place a chaste kiss on her forehead. 'You honoured the Mother for both of us, Esbar. I can never repay you for bearing this gift to her.'

'I'm sure I'll think of something. For now, just keep her safe and happy while I sleep.'

And sleep she did. As soon as Imsurin had tucked their birthdaughter in his arms, Esbar fell into a blissful drowse, and Apaya was there to tend her.

It was almost noon by the time the Prioress came, accompanied by Tunuva and Denag. As they entered, Esbar woke in a spill of warm sunlight. Apaya helped her sit up with the child.

'Beloved daughter,' the Prioress said, touching Esbar on the top of her head, 'this day, you have made an offering to the Mother. You have given her a warrior, to guard against the Nameless One. As a descendant of Siyāti du Verda uq-Nāra, you may bless her with two names, in the way of the northern Ersyr – one for herself, and one to guide her.'

The child nosed at her breast, snuffling for milk again. Esbar placed a kiss on her scalp.

'Prioress,' she said, 'I name this child Siyu du Tunuva uq-Nāra, and entrust her, now and always, to the Mother.'

Tunuva grew very still. The Prioress gave a grave nod.

'Siyu du Tunuva uq-Nāra,' she said, anointing her head with the sap of the tree. 'The Priory bids you welcome, little sister.'

I

The Twilight Year

CE 509

This world exists
as a sheen of dew on flowers.

— Izumi Shikibu

I

East

First, the waking in the dark. It had taken her years to become her own rooster, but now she was an instrument of gods. More than any change of light, it was their will that roused her.

Second, immersion in the ice pool. Fortified, she returned to her room and dressed in six layers of clothing, each made to withstand the cold. She tied back her hair and pressed down every strand with wax, to keep it from blinding her in the wind. That could be deadly on the mountain.

She had caught a chill from the pool the first time – shivered in her room for hours, runny-nosed and red of cheek. That was when she was a child, too fragile for the tests of worship.

Now Dumai could endure it, as she endured the elevation of the temple. Mountain sickness had never touched her, for she was born into these lofty halls, higher than most birds were hatched. Kanifa had once joked that if she ever went down to the city, she would keel over, breathless and faint, as climbers did when they ventured this high.

Earth sickness, her mother had agreed. *Best stay up here, my kite, where you belong.*

Third, writing down the dreams she remembered. Fourth, a meal to give her strength. Fifth, stepping into her boots on the porch, and from there to the courtyard, still mantled in night, where her mother waited to lead the procession.

Next, the lighting of the woodfall, sweet bark from logs that had lain on the seabed. It burned with smoke as clean as fog, and a scent like the world in the wake of a storm.

In the gloom, wide awake, the bridge that crossed the gap between the middle and third peaks. Then the long climb up the slopes, chanting in the ancient tongue.

Onward to the shrine that stood at the summit, and then, at the first glow of dawn, the ritual itself. Ringing the chimes before Kwiriki, dancing around his iron statue – calling out to the gods to return, as Snow Maiden once had. Salt and song and praise. Voices raised together, the song of welcome golden in their throats and on their tongues.

That was how her day began.

****

Snow glared under a clear sky. Dumai of Ipyeda narrowed her eyes against the dazzle as she picked her way down to the hot spring, taking a long drink from her flask. The other godsingers trailed far behind.

She rinsed herself before she slid into the steaming pool. Eyes closed, she sank up to her throat, savouring the heat and quiet.

Even for her, the climb was hard. Most visitors failed to summit Mount Ipyeda, and they paid for the privilege of trying. Sometimes they became headsick or blind and had to admit defeat; sometimes their hearts gave out. Few could breathe its thin air for long.

Dumai could. She had breathed nothing but this air since the evening she was born.

'Mai.'

She glanced over her shoulder. Her closest friend had appeared, carrying her clothes from the shelter. 'Kan,' she said. It was not one of his climbing days. 'Are you joining me?'

'No. A message came from the village,' Kanifa said. 'We'll have guests by nightfall.'

Strange news indeed. There was a window of opportunity in early autumn for climbers, but this late in the season, when deep snow filled the lower pass and the wind blew strong enough to kill, the High Temple of Kwiriki did not expect guests. 'How many?'

'One climber and four attendants.' Kanifa laid her clothes beside the pool. 'She is from Clan Kuposa.'

There was a name to banish exhaustion – the name of the most influential clan in Seiiki. Dumai rose from the water.

'Remember, no special treatment,' she said, drying herself with a length of cloth. 'On this mountain, the Kuposa stand at the same height as others.'

'A good thought,' he said mildly, 'for a different world. They hold the power to close temples.'

'And why should they use it?'

'Let's not give them a reason.'

'You're growing as nervous of court as my mother.' Dumai picked up the first of her layers. 'All right. Let's prepare.'

Kanifa waited for her to dress. She tied fur warmers over her sleeves and trousers, pulled on her heavy black coat, secured her hood under her chin, snugly wrapped her feet and covered them with her deerskin boots, fastening her ice spikes to the soles. Last came her gloves, sewn to fit her. On her right hand, only the forefinger and thumb were whole, the others shortened with hot steel. She slung on her pelt and followed Kanifa.

They walked down to the sky platform, Kanifa with a small frown. At thirty, he was only three years older than Dumai, but the deep lines carved around his eyes made him seem older.

The platform creaked underfoot. Ahead lay Antuma, capital of Seiiki, built at the fork of the River Tikara. It was not the first capital; likely it would not be the last. Sunlight daubed its rooftops and sparkled on the frosted trees that stood between it and the mountain.

The House of Noziken had once ruled from the harbour city of Ginura. Only when the gods had withdrawn into the Long Slumber – two hundred and sixty years ago – had the court had moved inland, to the Rayonti Basin. Now its home was Antuma Palace, an impressive complex at the eastern end of the Avenue of the Dawn. If Antuma was a fan, that avenue was its central rib, a clean line from the palace to the main gate of the city.

Often, Dumai would look out and imagine what Antuma had been like when dragons roamed. She wished she had been alive in that time, to see them watching over Seiiki.

'Here they come.' Kanifa eyed the slope. 'Not yet frozen.'

Dumai followed his gaze. Far below, she made out a line of figures, specks of ash on the blinding white. 'I'll prepare the Inner Hall,' she said. 'Will you instruct the refectory?'

29

'I will.'

'And tell my mother. You know she hates to be surprised.'

'Yes, Maiden Officiant,' he said solemnly. Dumai grinned and gave him a push towards the temple.

He knew she had only two dreams. The first was to set eyes on a dragon; the second was to one day succeed her mother as Maiden Officiant.

Inside, she parted ways with Kanifa. He made for the refectory, she for the Inner Hall, where she built five screened enclosures for the climber and her servants, each with its own stove and bedding. By the time she was finished, hunger had rubbed her stomach raw.

She fetched a meal from the refectory: yolks steamed and beaten into a smooth yellow cream, poured over slices of skinned chicken and mushroom and speckled with dark salty oil. As she ate on one of the roofs, she watched for the sorrowers that nested in the crags above the temple. Soon their young would hatch and fill the evening air with song.

When she had cleaned her bowl, she joined the others for the midday prayer. After, she chopped firewood while Kanifa scraped ice from the eaves and gathered snow to melt for drinking.

It was dusk by the time the party appeared. They had survived the treacherous steps that led from the first peak to the second. First came their armed guards, hired to drive off the bears and bandits that stalked the wooded foothills of the mountain. They followed a guide from the nameless village on the lower slopes, the last waystop before the temple.

The climber came next, wrapped in so many layers that her head looked too small for her body. Her attendants huddled around her, heads bowed against the screaming wind.

On the porch, Dumai exchanged a look with Kanifa, who glanced over his shoulder. The Maiden Officiant was supposed to receive visitors, but Unora was nowhere to be seen.

'I will greet them,' Dumai finally said.

The snow was thick and swift, so heavy she could hardly see for the flakes on her lashes. Her hood kept most of her hair in place, but loose strands whipped free and caught on her lips.

She had barely reached the steps when a hand grasped her wrist. Expecting Kanifa, she turned – only to find her mother beside her, wearing her headdress of silver butterflies.

'I'm here now, Dumai,' she said. 'Is everything ready?'

'Yes, Mother.'

'I knew I could rely on you.' Unora touched her shoulder. 'Rest. You've worked hard today.'

She retreated, knowing better than to stay. Her mother was different when courtiers visited, especially the Kuposa – tense and distant in a way she never was elsewhen.

Dumai had never fully understood it. Though Clan Kuposa had enormous influence at court, they had only ever supported the High Temple of Kwiriki. They had financed crucial renovations, sent beautiful gifts, even paid for a distinguished artist to paint the Inner Hall. Still, it might be wise to tread with care around a family with such power.

On her way to bed, she cracked open a door. In the highest quarters of the temple, Osipa of Antuma was peering at a scroll through a water stone, feet perched on a hot brick.

'Osipa,' Dumai said, 'can I bring you anything?'

Osipa squinted at her. 'Dumai.' Her voice was clotted. 'Thoughtful of you to offer, but no.' She raised her grey eyebrows, still groomed in the old court style. 'I saw you working cracks into your hands again. Have you tried the balm I gave you for Summerfall?'

'I need them tough for climbing,' Dumai reminded her. Osipa shook her head, then coughed into her sleeve. 'Are you not well?'

'A chill.' Osipa dabbed her nose. 'I envy you, child. You weather the cold as well as the mountain.'

'Let me get you some ginger. It will help.'

'I know by now that nothing will.' She hunched over her scroll again. 'May your dreams be clear, Dumai.'

'And yours.'

Osipa had always hated the dark months. A loyal handmaiden to the Grand Empress, she alone had followed her mistress to Mount Ipyeda. Decades later, she had yet to settle.

Night plunged the temple into darkness. Dumai made her way to her room, finding a meal waiting on a tray, and the shutters locked against the wind. Once she had sanded her calluses, she undressed and slotted her legs under her blanketed table, where a box of coals smouldered.

As the wind moaned, she ate, warm as a nestling. Only when every dish was spotless did she open her prayer box, taking out a strip of paper, her brush, and a jar of cuttlefish ink. She wrote her wish – always the

31

same – and dropped the paper into her dream bowl. It thinned as it floated, the water absorbing her words, drinking them into the gods' realm.

Tiredness came rushing over her, like the sea she had never seen. She moved the coals next to her bedding, blew out the lamps, and laid her head on her pillow, falling asleep in a heartbeat.

****

First, the waking in the dark. Parched mouth, fingers slurred. They slid out from the bedding, finding the floor too soft, too cold.

Dumai swam up from the sea of dreaming. Shivering, her nose like ice, she tried to think why her face was damp, why there was snow under her fingers. Nearby, sounds fought to be heard over the wind. A squeak, a rattle – then a dreadful *crack* that jolted her upright.

One of her shutters had blown open. Left to clatter, it would wake the whole temple.

Her legs were slow to move. She groped her way to the window and reached out, fingertips hooking into the shutter.

Something gave her pause. She looked straight ahead, into the black roar of night, towards the lantern at the top of the stepway, protected from the wind. By its light, she could make out a shadow. Kanifa had always said she had sharper eyes than a bird of prey.

A bandit. Or a sleepless ghost. Something that did not belong. She remembered tales of teeth like arrowheads, of flesh rotting on bone, and suddenly she was a fearful child again.

She was also a godsinger, ordained before the great Kwiriki. Resolve hardened her spine.

The floor creaked as she carried a lamp from her room, down the stairs, past the softly lit doors of the Inner Hall. She had learned to walk in these corridors, knew them just as well in darkness as she did by day. On the porch, she put on the first boots she found.

The figure was still beside the lantern, so hunched against the wind it looked as if it had no head. Dumai walked towards it, grasping one of her ice sickles. She had never used it as a weapon, but she would try if necessary. When the figure turned, a face came into relief.

Not a bandit. This man wore the muddled garb of a saltwalker. He looked at Dumai with watering eyes, then coughed out a fine spray of blood and collapsed into the snow.

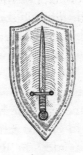

2

West

The first time Glorian saw her own blood, she was twelve years old. It was Julain who had spotted the smear, stark on her ivory shift. So splendid were the stories of Berethnet blood, Glorian had almost expected it be molten gold, for her blood kept a great wyrm shackled in darkness. Instead, it had been a dull, rusty brown.

It is less than I thought, she had remarked, and *less* had carried a few meanings. Julain had left to fetch a clout and tell the queen.

The second time Glorian saw her own blood, she was fifteen and a half, and the end of a bone had knifed through her skin, between the shoulder and the elbow.

This time, Julain Crest was less composed.

'Fetch the Royal Surgeon,' she shouted at the guards. Two went running. 'Quickly, quickly!'

Glorian stared down at her bone. It was a small piece that poked through, not much longer than a tooth – and yet it was somehow lewd, naked when it ought to be covered.

The night before, while the fire burned low, Helisent had shared a tale from the north. People there believed that oak galls – growths like apples on those trees, used in the making of ink – could hold signs of the future. If a bumblebee had nudged inside, the next year would be joyful. If a gallfly was there, caught in a thing of its own making, the year would be stagnant or riddled with blunders. Whatever was inside, there was some fate attached.

Heathen talk, Adela had muttered. Such tales stemmed from the days before the Saint, but Glorian had found it both charming and harmless. At sunrise, she and her ladies had ridden out in search of fallen galls, only for her horse to take a sudden fright and throw her.

A rush of pain snatched her back to the present. She must have fainted, for suddenly there was a flock of people, and the Royal Surgeon was staring at the chip of bone, and the horse, Óvarr, gave a terrified whinny. A groom was trying in vain to calm her.

'Lady Glorian, can you hear me?' the Royal Surgeon asked her. She nodded, dizzy. 'Tell me, now, do you feel your legs?'

'Yes, Doctor Forthard.' Glorian blew out a breath. 'Though I ... feel one of my arms more keenly.'

Grave faces crowded around her. She was strapped on to a length of wood and lifted by four guards.

Strong hands kept her head in line with her backbone as they marched her through the queenswood, past the lake, towards Drouthwick Castle. Above the south gate, the Berethnet standard proclaimed that Queen Sabran was in residence. Pain struck Glorian like an axe on a shield. When she tried to look at the wound, she found her head still trapped.

As soon as they entered the gloom of the keep, a familiar voice called her by name, and then Lady Florell Glade was at her side, flaxen curls tumbling from their net.

'Glorian,' she said, aghast. 'By the Saint, Doctor Forthard, what is this?'

'Her Highness fell from her horse, my lady,' Sir Bramel Stathworth said.

'The heir to Inys,' Florell said hotly as she kept up with the board. 'You are duty-bound to protect her, Sir Bramel.'

'The palfrey was calm all morning. Forgive me, but we could never have stopped it.'

'Please,' Doctor Forthard said, 'don't touch the princess, Lady Florell. You could sully the wound.'

Florell had seen it by now. She stared down at the place where the bone peeked through, her face ashen. 'Sweet child,' she said hoarsely, 'do not fear. The Saint is with you.'

The flagstones swallowed the sound of her flight. Glorian let her eyes close again, and all was shadow for a time, the tilt and sway of the board like a cradle.

34

Next she woke, she was in her own bed, and her left sleeve had been cut away to show the mess of her arm – white skin, red blood, that fang of bone. Doctor Forthard was soaping her hands in a basin of hot water, accompanied by two strangers: one in the brown herigald of an apprentice sanctarian, the other in a red tabard, a white tunic beneath.

A bonesetter. Her father paid a small army of them to crack his neck and back. This one stood with their hands tucked into their sleeves, as if to avert the imagination from the agony they were about to inflict.

'Lady Glorian.' The apprentice came to her. 'Drink this. It will dull the pain.'

He held a wineskin to her lips, and Glorian drank as much as she could. The wine left a meaty aftertaste of sage. 'Doctor Forthard,' she said, 'what must you do?'

'We must draw the two halves of the bone together, Highness,' Doctor Forthard said, 'so they may knit back into one. This is Mastress Kell Bourn, a member of the Company of Bones.'

'Your Highness,' the bonesetter said, low and calm. 'Please, stay as still as you can.'

Sir Bramel prayed under his breath. Glorian tensed as the strangers moved towards the bed. The apprentice sanctarian stood by her feet, while the bonesetter appraised her arm. 'I want banewort,' Glorian said. 'Doctor Forthard, please, I want to sleep.'

'No,' Dame Erda Lindley said firmly. 'None of your herbs or potions, Forthard. Queen Sabran forbids it.'

Doctor Forthard ignored the guard. 'Highness, even a spoonful of banewort can kill the drinker. It is a gentle poison,' she said, 'but poison, nonetheless.' She turned back to the bed. 'And you are the great chain upon the Nameless One.'

Glorian did not feel like a chain, great or otherwise. She felt like a child with a broken arm.

'Please,' she forced out, 'be quick, if you cannot be kind.'

Without replying, Doctor Forthard held Glorian by the shoulders. The apprentice sanctarian pinned her ankles to the bed. The bonesetter exhaled like an archer before they grasped her arm, brown hands big and firm as stirrups. The last thing Glorian heard was her own shriek.

****

When she woke, her flesh was ablaze, a heat so strong it stoppered her throat. Her upper arm was enveloped in plaster and fixed to her side with a leather strap.

Glorian had not often had to endure pain. Thimbles protected her for needlework, bracers when she drew a bow. Pain had been rare headaches, a bruised knee, her courses. All she could do now was escape into sleep.

'Glorian.'

Her eyes snapped open. 'Florell?'

Florell Glade had served Queen Sabran since their childhood, and was now her First Lady of the Great Chamber, tall and lovely as a sunflower. Hearing her voice was such a salve that Glorian almost wept.

'Hush, hush. It's all right.' Florell kissed her forehead and smiled at her, but shadows underlined her blue eyes. 'Doctor Forthard sewed the wound. The Saint is good.'

Glorian wished he could have been good enough to stop her mount unseating her in the first place. She knew better than to express this out loud.

'May I have a drink?' she said instead.

Florell brought a cup of ale. 'I feared you might take fever,' she said. 'Not long before your birth, my father put his kneepan out of joint. He never woke when they tried to right it.'

'I'm sorry.'

'Thank you, sweeting. Queen Sabran was generous enough to pay for his entombing.'

'Has she come to see me?'

'Her Grace asked me to watch you in her stead. She is in council.'

Though Glorian tightened her jaw and swallowed, fresh tears clouded her eyes. She had hoped her mother would make her excuses to the Virtues Council, just this once.

'She knows you aren't in danger,' Florell said in soft tones, seeing her face. 'It is urgent business.'

In answer, Glorian could only nod. There was always business more urgent and important than her.

Florell guided her back to the bolsters and stroked her damp hair. Queen Sabran had sometimes done the same, when Glorian was still young enough to lose her teeth. Those memories glinted, bright and distant – coins spent in a well, sunk too deep to pluck back out.

She took a closer look at her arm, sheathed in a cast from shoulder to just below her elbow. Beneath it, her skin itched. 'How long must I wear this?'

'Until your arm heals. However long that may be,' Florell said gently. 'Doctor Forthard made sure to purge the wound well, and the air is sweeter this far north. You are already mending.'

'I won't be able to ride.'

'No.' When Glorian sighed, Florell took her by the chin. 'We must always be careful with you, Glorian. Of all the people in this queendom, you are the most precious.'

Glorian fidgeted. Florell smoothed her hair once more before she went to stoke the fire.

'Lady Florell,' Glorian said, 'where is Julain?'

'With her mother.'

'Did they not let her stay with me?'

'I think she would have been permitted.' Florell looked at her. 'She blames herself, Glorian.'

'That's silly. It was the palfrey, not Julain.'

'Lady Julain is mindful of her duty. One day, she will be to you what I am to Her Grace – not just your friend, but your sister in all but blood, your protector. She will always fear for you, as I feared for your mother when she stood before the Malkin Queen.'

Glorian turned her cheek into the pillow. 'Send her to me in the morning.' She glanced back at Florell. 'Will you fetch my poppet, the one Father sent for my birthday?'

'Of course.'

Florell took it from the chest in the corner and folded it into her hand. Glorian held it close – a tiny figurine of a warrior girl, whittled from bone. She pressed it to her heart and slept.

****

The next day, Doctor Forthard brought her a dish of chopped fruit and insisted she drink a pungent tonic. 'To cool and fortify you, Highness,' the physician said. 'Apple vinegar, garlic, cropleek, other goodness.'

Glorian suspected it was her visitors who would need fortification. At dusk, after prayers, Florell came with a comb and a jug of lavender water.

'I asked for Julain,' Glorian said, while Florell coaxed the knots from her hair. 'Will she not see me?'

'She must if you command it, Glorian.'

After a moment to consider, Glorian said, 'I do command it.'

Florell smiled faintly at that. When she had finished combing, she left, and Glorian sat up in bed, wincing at the pain. At least now she smelled of lavender as well as vinegar and garlic.

After a time, the door cracked open. 'Lady Julain Crest,' her usher said, and in stepped her friend, garbed in a russet gown with a green bodice. Her dark hair hung in a single plait.

The door shut behind her, leaving them alone. Julain looked at Glorian, at her bound arm.

'Why did you not come earlier?' Glorian asked, a little hurt. Julain clasped her hands in front of her and bowed her head. 'Jules, Óvarr threw me suddenly. What could you have done?'

'I don't know,' Julain said thickly. 'It scared me that I didn't know.' When she looked up again, Glorian saw with surprise that her face was tearstained. 'You could have died. I thought you would. What if you were in danger again, and I couldn't save you?'

'I don't need anyone to save me. All I ever ask is that you not abandon me.'

Julain sniffed. 'I swear it.' She dabbed her face once more, then drew back her shoulders. 'I swear it, Glorian.'

'Very well.'

There was a pause before they both broke into relieved giggles, and Julain brushed her cheeks.

'Talk to me a while, before I fall asleep again.' Glorian patted the bed. 'I reek of garlic, so that can be your punishment for blaming yourself for my arm, and not a foolish horse.'

Julain used her stepstool to reach the bed, while Glorian moved a bolster to make room. 'Goodness, you do smell of garlic.' Julain wrinkled her nose. 'And ... cropleek, I think.'

'And lavender,' Glorian insisted. Julain wafted a hand. 'Oh, you're right. I can't drink any more of this before my commendation, lest I knock Mother from her throne with my breath.'

That made Julain stop smiling. 'Has Her Grace come to see you?'

Glorian looked away. 'No.'

Julain nestled up to her. It was a wordless and familiar comfort. Glorian clasped the hand she offered, trying to ignore the hollow, gnawing ache of envy. If Julain had taken such a grave fall, her parents would have sat with her all night, just to make her feel better.

Glorian wanted that from her mother. She also feared her coming, for she knew exactly what Sabran would say: that it was time for the larks of her childhood to end.

It was time for Glorian to learn what it meant to be the future Queen of Inys.

3

South

'S iyu, get down from there!'

The orange tree sighed in the breeze. Its gnarled trunk was always warm to the touch, as if there was sunlight trapped in its sapwood. Every leaf was polished and fragrant, and even deep in autumn, it bore fruit.

Not once, for however long it had stood here – since the dawn of time, perhaps – had anyone defiled its branches. Now a young woman crouched among them, barefoot and out of reach.

'Tuva,' she called down, her voice spiced with laughter, 'it's wonderful. I swear I could see all the way to Yikala!'

Tunuva stared up in dismay. Siyu had always been headstrong, but this could not be dismissed as youthful folly. This was sacrilege. The Prioress would be outraged when she heard.

'What is it, Tunuva?' Imsurin came to stand beside her, following her line of sight. 'Mother save us,' he said under his breath. He glanced back down at her. 'Where is Esbar?'

She barely heard him, for Siyu was climbing again. With a last flash of sole, she ventured into the higher branches, and Tunuva started forward, a strangled sound escaping her.

'You mustn't—' Imsurin began.

'How do you suppose I would?' Tunuva snapped. 'I have no inkling of how *she* got up there.' Imsurin raised his hands, and she turned back to the tree. 'Siyu, please, enough of this!'

The only answer was a sparkling laugh. A green leaf fluttered to the ground.

By now, a small crowd had gathered in the valley: sisters, brothers, three of the ichneumons. Murmurs spiked behind Tunuva, like the hum from a nest of spindle wasps. She gazed up at the orange tree and prayed with all her might: *Keep her safe, guide her to me, do not let her fall.*

There was no way to conceal what had happened. A place kept secret for centuries could not afford secrets within its own walls.

'We should find Esbar. Siyu listens to her,' Imsurin said, with certainty. 'And to you,' he added, a clear afterthought. Tunuva pursed her lips. 'You must get her down, before—'

'She will not hear any of us now. We must wait for her to come to us.' Tunuva pulled her shawl around her shoulders and folded her arms. 'And it's too late. Everyone has seen.'

By the time Siyu reappeared, the sky had flushed to apricot, and Tunuva was both rigid and atremble, like a plucked harpstring.

'Siyu du Tunuva uq-Nāra, come down at once,' she shouted. 'The Prioress will hear of this!'

It was a craven thing, to invoke the Prioress. Esbar would never have been so weak. Still, her anger must have found its mark, for Siyu looked down from the branch, smile fading.

'Coming,' she said.

Tunuva had assumed she would come down the same way she had climbed up, whatever that had been. Instead, Siyu stood and found her balance. She was light and small, and the bough was strong, yet Tunuva watched in dread, thinking it would crack beneath her.

Not once had she feared the tree before this day. It had been guardian and giver and friend – never an enemy, never a threat. Not until Siyu ran along the bough and leapt into open air.

In unison, Tunuva and Imsurin rushed forward, as if they had any hope of catching her. Siyu plummeted with a shriek, arms wheeling, and disappeared into the crashing waters of the Minara. Tunuva cast herself down at the riverbank.

'Siyu!'

Her chest was so tight she could scarcely breathe. She flung off her shawl, and would have dived in – had Siyu not surfaced, black hair slicked across her face, and let out a laugh of pure delight. Fanning her strong arms, she kicked against the flow of water.

'Siyu,' Imsurin said, his voice hard and strained, 'do not tempt Abaso's rage.' He reached for her. 'Climb out, please.'

'You always said I swam beautifully, Imin,' came the overjoyed reply. 'The water is bracing. Try it!'

Tunuva looked to Imsurin. Decades of knowing him, and never once had she seen fear on that raw-boned face. Now his jaw shook. When Tunuva lowered her gaze, she found her hands were quaking.

It's all right. She's all right.

Siyu grasped one of the roots and used it to drag herself from the river. Tunuva released her breath, the tension pulled from her at once. She wrenched Siyu into her arms and kissed her sodden hair.

'Reckless, foolish child.' Tunuva clasped the back of her head. 'What were you thinking, Siyu?'

'Do you mean to tell me no one has ever done it?' Siyu said, breathless with exhilaration. 'Hundreds of years with such a tree, and no one ever climbed it? I am the very first?'

'Let us hope you are the last.'

Tunuva retrieved her shawl and draped it around Siyu. Autumns were mild in the Lasian Basin, but the River Minara stemmed from the northeastern mountains, far beyond the natural heat that warmed the land around the tree.

When they stood, Siyu nudged her, smiling. Tunuva alone saw their sisters' flinty gazes. She curled an arm around Siyu and walked her across the cool grass of the vale, to the thousand steps that would take them to the Priory.

****

More than five hundred years had passed since its founding – since Cleolind Onjenyu, Princess of Lasia, had defeated the Nameless One.

The orange tree had decided that battle. When Cleolind had eaten its fruit, she had become a living ember, a vessel of the sacred flame, giving her the strength to defeat the beast. The tree had saved her from his fire and graced her with its own.

42

One day, he would return. Cleolind had been sure of that.

The Priory was her legacy. A house of women, raised as warriors, sworn to defend the world from the offspring of the Dreadmount. To listen for any whisper of his wings.

The first sisters had discovered a honeycomb of caves in the steep red cliffs that walled the Vale of Blood. In the decades that followed, they had dug further and deeper, and their descendants had continued their work, until there was a hidden stronghold in the rock.

It was only in the last century that beauty had been kindled there. Shale and pearl mantle inlaid the columns, and the ceilings were mirrored or painted in styles from across the whole of the South. The first hollows scraped out for lamps had been shaped into elegant arches, each lined with gold leaf to heighten the candlelight. Fresh air whispered into the caves from above, flowing through carven latticework doors, laced with the scents of the flowers the men grew. A strong wind might add the fragrance of oranges.

There was still a great deal of work to be done. When Esbar was Prioress, she meant to oversee the construction of a skygazing pool, with stove-heated water and pipes, and to use a clever arrangement of mirrors to bend daylight into the deepest caves. Esbar meant to do many things when the red cloak fell upon her shoulders.

Every day, Tunuva thanked the Mother for their home. This place had sheltered them from the avaricious eyes of the world. Here, there were no monarchs to force them to their knees, no coin to make them rich or poor, no tolls on their waters or tax on their crops. Cleolind had renounced her own crown to build a place where there was no need of them.

Siyu spoke first. 'Will the Prioress punish me?'

'I imagine so.'

Tunuva kept her tone flat. Siyu bristled. 'There was no harm in it,' she said, thorns in her voice. 'I've always wanted to climb the tree. I don't see why everyone must be so—'

'It is not my place to teach you right from wrong, Siyu uq-Nāra. You ought to know it well by now.' Tunuva looked sidelong at her. 'How did you reach the branches?'

'I threw up a length of rope. It took a month to knot one long enough.' Siyu gave her a coy smile. 'Why, Tuva – would you like to try it?'

43

'You have been enough of a fool today, Siyu. I am in no mood for jests,' Tunuva said. 'Where is this rope now?'

'I left it on the branch.'

'Then someone will have to recover it, and the tree will be defiled a second time.'

After a pause, Siyu said, 'Yes, sister.'

She had the sense to hold her tongue for the rest of the long walk.

At the age of ten, Siyu had been moved from where the infants and young children slept. Now she was seventeen and lived on the level below the initiates. Though she was old enough to join them, the Prioress had not yet deemed her worthy of the flame.

Tunuva opened the door to the right chamber. The lamps had all been lit, herbs left on the pillow. The men took special care to freshen the inner chambers, where sunlight never reached.

She conjured a small flame and let it drift away from her palm. Siyu drew the shawl closer as she watched it flicker above them, her long dark eyes reflecting its light. It sank towards the stove and caught the tinder. Bright flames leapt and burned without smoke.

Siyu peeled off her drape and knelt on the rug by the fire, rubbing her arms. Only when she ate of the fruit would she know how it felt to be warm all the way through. Tunuva had hoped that day would come soon. Now it seemed farther away than ever.

'Where is Lalhar?' she asked Siyu shortly.

'I thought she might bark if she saw me climb. Yeleni said she could sleep in her room.'

'Your ichneumon is your responsibility.' Tunuva stripped a layer from the bed. 'Yeleni knew your plans, then.'

Siyu snorted. 'No.' She raked her fingers through the ends of her hair. 'I knew she would stop me.'

'One of you has sense, at least.'

'Are you very angry, Tuva?' When Tunuva only wrapped the heavy woven mantle around her, Siyu watched her face. 'I frightened you. Did you think I would fall?'

'Did you think you would not?' Tunuva straightened. 'Arrogance does not become a future slayer.'

Siyu stared at the stove. A ripple of dark hair clung to her cheek.

'You could speak to the Prioress,' she said. 'She might not be so hard on me if you—'

'I will not defend what you have done, Siyu. You are not a child any longer.' Tunuva picked up her damp shawl. 'Allow me to offer you a piece of advice, as one whose name you carry. Reflect on what you have done, and when the Prioress summons you, accept your punishment with grace.'

Siyu clenched her jaw. Tunuva turned to leave.

'Tuva,' Siyu said suddenly, 'I'm sorry I scared you. I will apologise to Imin, too.'

Tunuva glanced back at her, softening. 'I will … ask him to bring you some buttermilk,' she said, feeling a stab of frustration at herself. She left the room and walked back down the corridor.

Half a century she had served the Mother. By now, she should be folded steel, each year making her stronger, harder – yet when it came to Siyu, she bent like sweetgrass in the wind. She took the stairs to the open side of the Priory, where torches fluttered in a breeze.

Before she knew it, she was in the highest corridor, tapping on the highest door. A hoarse voice bade her enter, and then she was standing before the woman who presided over the Priory.

Saghul Yedanya had been elected Prioress when she was only thirty. Her head of black curls had long since turned white, and where she had once been among the tallest and sturdiest women in the Priory, her chair of polished wood now seemed too large for her.

Still she sat upon it proudly, hands clasped on her stomach. Her face, mostly brown, was dappled with pallor, which also flecked her fingertips and formed a tilted crescent on her throat. Deep lines were carved across her brow. Tunuva envied such discernible wisdom – when every year could be read on the skin, laid out like the rings of growth in a tree.

Esbar sat opposite, pouring from a gold-rimmed jar. Seeing Tunuva, she arched an eyebrow.

'Who comes at this hour?' Saghul asked in her deep, slow voice. 'Is that you, Tunuva Melim?'

'Yes,' Tunuva said. Clearly they had not heard what had happened. 'Prioress, I came from the vale. One of our younger sisters has … climbed upon the tree.'

Saghul tilted her head. 'Who?' Esbar asked, perilously soft. 'Tuva, who has done this?'

Tunuva braced herself. 'Siyu.'

At once, Esbar was on her feet, expression thunderous. Tunuva moved to block her, or try, but Saghul spoke first: 'Esbar, remember your place.' Esbar stopped. 'If you wish to serve me as munguna, calm and comfort your sisters. This sight must have disturbed them.'

Esbar collected her breath, pouring sand on the fires within. 'Yes, Prioress,' she said curtly. 'Of course.'

She touched Tunuva on the arm and was gone. Tunuva knew she would still make her wrath known to Siyu.

'Wine,' Saghul said. Tunuva took the empty seat and finished serving it. 'Tell me what happened.'

Tunuva did. Better that it came from her. Saghul never touched the wine as she listened, gazing towards the opposite wall. Her pupils were grey instead of black, a condition that clouded her sight.

'Did she disturb the fruit?' she finally asked. 'Did she eat when it was not given?'

'No.'

There was silence for a time. Somewhere above, a bay owl called out.

'Siyu is spirited and adventurous. A hard thing in a world as small as ours,' Tunuva said. Saghul conceded with a grunt. 'I know she must be reprimanded for this desecration, but she is still young.'

'Does she regret it?'

It was a moment before Tunuva said, 'I believe she will. Once she has reflected.'

'If she does not regret it now, she never will. We impress a deep respect for the tree on our children, Tunuva. They learn it before they learn to write or read or fight,' Saghul pointed out. 'There are two-year-olds among us who know they cannot climb upon its branches.'

Tunuva was at a loss for a counterstroke. Saghul walked her fingertips towards the cup of wine, finding its base.

'I fear this is only the beginning,' she muttered. 'There is a rot at the heart of the Priory.'

'Rot?'

'More than five centuries since the Mother vanquished the Nameless One in this valley,' Saghul reminded her, 'and there has been no sign that he will ever return. It was inevitable that some among us would begin to question the need for the Priory.'

Tunuva drank a small measure of wine. It did nothing to solve the drought in her mouth.

46

'What Siyu did, profane though it is, is only a sign of the decay. She does not respect the tree any longer, because she does not fear the beast from which it shielded Cleolind Onjenyu,' Saghul said grimly. 'The Nameless One is a fable to her. To all of us. Even you, Tunuva, who are so loyal to our house, must have asked yourself why we remain.'

Tunuva lowered her gaze.

'When I first left,' she confessed, 'I walked in the Crimson Desert, the sun beating down on my skin, and I understood how wide and glorious the world must be; how many marvels it must hold. I did question, then, why we choose to hide in a small corner of it.'

She remembered it so clearly. Her very first journey beyond the Vale of Blood, Esbar riding at her side. Saghul had sent them to harvest a rare moss that grew on Mount Enunsa – a task that would take them away from their home, but not to any settlements.

Growing up, Tunuva had always found Esbar intimidating, with her sharp tongue and her indestructible confidence. Esbar had thought Tunuva prim and joyless. Still, they had always known they would take their first steps beyond the Priory together, given their closeness in age.

The year before the journey, all had changed when Tunuva was chosen to duel Gashan Janudin. Since they were children, Esbar and Gashan had been rivals, each determined to one day be Prioress. So intense was their competition, their certainty that no one else could match them, that Gashan had not concealed her disdain when Tunuva approached.

Before then, Tunuva had always underplayed her skill with a spear, seeing no need to show off to her sisters – but suddenly, she had felt weary of Gashan and Esbar, two suns overlooking the bright stars around them. She had slammed all her years of dutiful study into her weapon, and before Gashan had quite seen the danger, Tunuva had disarmed her.

That night, Esbar had found her on a balcony, stretching to keep her body limber. *You*, Esbar had said, sitting down uninvited, *have finally caught my attention.* She had come bearing wine, and poured two cups. *When did the quiet conformist nurture such a talent with a spear?*

You call it conforming; I call it surrender to the Mother. Tunuva had joined her on the steps. *And you might find me less quiet if you had ever paused to speak to me.*

Esbar had taken her point. They had spent that night getting to know one another, finding an unexpected warmth. By the time they went their separate ways, the sun had risen.

After that, they were far more aware of each other. Esbar would catch her eye in corridors, find reasons to pass her room, stop to talk when their paths crossed. And then they were both twenty, and the day had come for their first steps outside.

For a moment, Tunuva was lost in the past. The cruel beauty of the desert. How small her existence had seemed in the face of it. How the sand had sparkled like shattered ruby. They had left their ichneumons by a panhole and continued the approach on foot. She had never seen so much dazzling blue sky, unbounded by trees or the slopes of their valley. They were without their sisters, alone in a sea of sand, and yet anyone could find them.

She and Esbar had looked at each other in wonder. Later, they realised they had both felt it: a sense not just that the world had changed, but that they, too, were new. It must have been that feeling that had made Esbar kiss her. Breathless with laughter, they had embraced on the soft warmth of the dune, the sky almost too blue to bear, sand running like silk beneath their bodies, breath catching fire.

Thirty years had passed, and still Tunuva trembled at that memory. She was suddenly conscious of her drape against her breasts, and a richening ache in the base of her belly.

'Why did you return?' Saghul asked, drawing her back. 'Why not stay in the wide and glorious world for ever, Tunuva?'

Esbar had asked the same question that day, when they lay in the shade of a rock. They had both looked as if they were freckled with blood, covered in those glistening red grains.

'Because it made me understand my duty,' Tunuva said. 'It was laying eyes upon the world, being part of it, that made me appreciate the importance of protecting it. If the Nameless One does return, we may be the only ones who can – so I will remember. I will remain.'

Saghul smiled. A warm, true smile that creased the corners of her eyes and served to deepen her beauty.

'I know you still think Siyu too callow to eat of the fruit,' Tunuva said. 'I know the grave risk in making her an initiate before the time is right. I also know this ... error of judgement, this foolish violation, cannot have convinced you of her maturity, Saghul.'

48

'Hm.'

'But Siyu may need to fall in love with the outside, as I did. Let her ride to the golden court of Lasia and guard Princess Jenyedi. Let her taste of the wonders of the world, so she may understand the importance of the Priory. Let her never think of this place as her cage.'

Silence stretched wide between them. Saghul took a long drink from her cup.

'Sun wine,' she said, 'is among the wonders of the ancient world.'

Tunuva waited. When the Prioress of the Orange Tree told a story, it always had meaning.

'It costs a great deal to bring it here from Kumenga,' Saghul went on. 'I ought not to risk it, but if I have no supply on hand, I find it seeps into my dreams, and I wake with the taste of it on my tongue. To me, nothing but the sacred fruit is sweeter. And yet ... I leave half in the cup.'

She placed it between them. The sound of ceramic on wood rang loud in the still room.

'Some have the restraint to taste of worldly pleasure,' she said. 'You and I are among them, Tunuva. When I found you with Esbar the first time, I feared you would lose yourselves to your passion. You proved me wrong. You knew how much of the wine to taste. You knew to leave some in the cup.' This time, when she smiled, there was no warmth in it. 'But some, Tunuva – some would drink of the sweet wine until they drowned.'

With one knotted finger, she tipped the cup. Sun wine spilled across the table and dripped like watered honey to the floor.

4

East

The stranger had been asleep for two days. By the time Dumai towed him from the snowstorm, blisters had bubbled up on his fingers, and the cold had bruised his nose and cheeks.

Unora had gone straight to work. After so many years on the mountain, she knew how to save any part of the body that had not yet died. She had redressed the stranger and slowly warmed his frosted skin.

The cough was mountain sickness. In the summer, he would have been taken back down, but until the snow passed, he would have to endure. So would their Kuposa guest, who Dumai had glimpsed only twice, from a distance. Unable to attempt the summit, she kept to the Inner Hall.

Dumai wished she could welcome her, but her mother had taught her to never approach visitors from court. *The palace is a twisted net, snaring even the littlest fish. Best you stay free of its tangles,* Unora had warned her. *Keep your mind pure and cast your thoughts high, and one day, you will stand in my place.*

There was sense in that. Court was all gossip and artifice, according to everyone who had been there.

After her chores, she decided to check on Unora, who had been with the sick traveller ever since his arrival. Dumai had led the procession in her stead. On the porch, she took off her boots and replaced them with slippers, then went to the room where the stranger lay.

Kanifa was on his way out, carrying a cauldron. 'How is our guest?' Dumai asked him.

'He stirs now and then. I think he'll wake soon.'

'Then why do you look worried?'

The line between his eyebrows was deeper than usual. He glanced down the corridor. 'Our guest from court,' he said in a low voice. 'Apparently she's been asking questions about the Grand Empress. How she finds life at the temple. Whether she ever plans to return.'

'She did rule Seiiki. Climbers are always curious about her.'

'This one is an ambitious Kuposa. She may be trying to curry favour with the Grand Empress, or involve her in some intrigue,' Kanifa said. 'I mean to keep an eye on her.'

'Yes, I'm sure you would be happy to keep a close watch on a beautiful woman.'

Kanifa cocked a heavy eyebrow, a faint smile on his lips. 'Go to your mother, Dumai of Ipyeda.' He continued down the corridor. 'She will cleanse you of such earthly thoughts.'

Dumai screened her grin behind her hair as she stepped into the room. She teased him, but in truth, Kanifa had never expressed interest in anyone. The mountain was his only love.

The traveller lay on a mat, covered to his chin with bedding, feet snug in a heat trap. He was about sixty, grey woven through his thick hair, which framed a brown and solemn face.

Unora was nearby, watching a kettle. While there were guests in the temple, she was obliged to wear the grey veil of the Maiden Officiant, even outside the rituals she led.

The Maiden Officiant acted as the understudy and representative of the Supreme Officiant. While the latter was always a member of the imperial family, the former was usually not of noble birth. Her veil symbolised the waterline between the earthly and celestial realms.

'There you are.' Unora patted the floor. 'Come.'

Dumai knelt beside her. 'Have you found out who he is?'

'A saltwalker, from his collection.' Her mother motioned to a dish, full of shells of rare beauty. 'He woke for long enough to ask me where he was.'

For a saltwalker, he was curiously unweathered. They were wanderers who tended to the ancient shrines – only ever washing in the sea, dressing in what they found on its shore.

'And the climber?' Dumai said. 'Did you learn why she came so late in the year?'

'Yes.' Unora took the steaming kettle from the pothook. 'You know I can't share her secrets, but she made a choice she fears may cause a scandal at court. She needed to clear her mind.'

'Perhaps I could talk to her, give her some comfort. I think I am about her age.'

'A kind offer, but it was my counsel she sought.' Unora tipped the boiled water into a cup. 'Don't concern yourself, my kite. Your life is on this mountain, and it needs your full devotion.'

'Yes, Mother.'

Dumai glanced at the saltwalker. A chill grazed her spine. Not only was he now awake, but his gaze was hard and stunned on her face. He looked as if he had seen a water ghost.

Unora noticed, stiffening.

'Honourable stranger.' She moved between them, the cup between her hands. 'Welcome. You have come to the High Temple of Kwiriki. I am its Maiden Officiant.' The man did not utter a word. 'Mountain sickness ... can shadow the sight. Can you see?'

Dumai was starting to feel nervous. Finally, the man said, 'I have a thirst.'

His voice came deep and rough. Unora held the cup to his lips. 'Your head may be very light for a time,' she told him as he drank, 'and your stomach may feel smaller than usual.'

'Thank you.' He wiped his mouth. 'I dreamed the gods called to me from this mountain, but it seems I was too weak to answer.'

'It is the mountain's will, not your weakness, that prevents you climbing any higher.'

'You are kind.' As Unora took the cup away, he looked back towards Dumai. 'Who is this?'

'One of our godsingers.'

Dumai waited for her to be more specific. Unora only served more of the steeped ginger.

'I apologise,' the saltwalker said to Dumai. 'I thought you resembled someone I knew.' He rubbed his eyes. 'You are right, Maiden Officiant. It must be the mountain sickness.'

A creak sounded in the corridor. 'Ah, here is Kanifa,' Unora said brightly. 'He has dressings for you.' Her face turned back towards Dumai. 'Will you help Tirotu cut some more ice?'

Slowly, Dumai rose, meeting Kanifa on her way out. She brushed straight past him, making him look after her.

****

'What did you dream?'

Dumai kept her eyes closed. She was kneeling on a mat, hands resting on her thighs. 'I dreamed I flew again,' she said. 'Above the clouds. I was waiting for the night to fall.'

'For the sun to set, and the moon to rise?'

'No. It was already night, though moonless.' Dumai reworded it: 'I was waiting for the stars to descend from the sky. Somehow I knew they were supposed to come to me.'

'And did they?'

'No. They never do.'

The Grand Empress nodded. She rested on the kneeling stool she often used in the cold months.

Once, she had been the shrewd and beloved Empress Manai – until some unknown malady had left her frail and confused, baffling her physicians. When she could no longer work around her decline, she had seen no choice but to abdicate in favour of her son and withdraw to Mount Ipyeda, to take the vacant post of Supreme Officiant of Seiiki.

Her illness had mysteriously faded on the mountain, but by then, her ordainment had precluded her from returning to court. It was she who had welcomed a destitute and friendless Unora when she came to the temple, swollen with Dumai, and asked for sanctuary.

Since her abdication, the boy left on the throne had grown into a man. Emperor Jorodu had never once visited the temple, though he did occasionally write to his mother.

The Grand Empress watched the woodfall breathe in the brazier. White streaked her short grey hair, as if she had combed snow through it. Dumai longed for hers to be the same.

'Did you have a sense of what would happen,' the Grand Empress said, 'if the stars did *not* fall?'

Dumai pressed her hands flat, remembering. In the shapeless place between sleep and waking, she had dreamed her sweat was silver.

'Something terrible,' she said. 'Far below, there was black water, and in it, there was doom.'

53

The Grand Empress tucked in her lips, her face creasing. 'I have thought long on these dreams,' she said. 'Kwiriki is calling you, Dumai.'

'Am I called to be Maiden Officiant?' Dumai asked her. 'You know this is my only wish.'

'I do know it.' The Grand Empress laid a hand on her head. 'Thank you for sharing your dream. I will continue to dwell on them all, in the hope I can unravel the message.'

'I wonder if … I might ask for your guidance on another matter. It has to do with my mother.'

'What of her?'

Dumai wrestled with herself. It was not for a child to question a parent. 'It is a very small thing,' she finally said, 'but earlier, she chose not to tell a stranger that I was her daughter. She referred to me simply as a godsinger. I know it is uncommon for a Maiden Officiant to have children, but … there is no shame in it.'

'You speak of the man who arrived in the night.'

'Yes.'

The Grand Empress seemed to consider.

'Unora brought you into this world. Our parents' love can take strange forms, Dumai,' she said. 'See how the sorrower pricks her own breast, feeding her young with drops of her blood.'

Dumai had already seen. It was why she held such affection for sorrowers.

'As my representative, Unora must guide and comfort the climbers. You are not yet prepared for her role,' the Grand Empress said, 'but if they knew you were her daughter, they would likely see you as a way to her. Unora wants to keep your mind free of the ground … until you have spent long enough on the mountain that you can resist the allure of the earth.'

'I have been on this mountain for almost as many years as my mother. I have never stepped from it. How can I be tempted by something I have never seen?'

'Precisely.'

Dumai digested this. Like stones on a board, pieces shifted in her mind, forming a clear line, unbroken by doubt.

'Thank you, Grand Empress,' she said, rising. 'Your wisdom clears my eyes.'

'Hm. Sleep well, Dumai.'

Dumai slid the doors shut behind her. A visit to these quarters always eased her mind.

The Grand Empress was right, of course. Unora had lived away from the mountain, before Dumai was born; she knew the distractions and hardships below. It made perfect sense that she would want to separate Dumai from all of that, to protect her.

Dumai turned to leave the corridor. When she saw the woman in the gloom, she startled.

'Forgive me.' A soft voice. 'Did I scare you?'

The guest stood as still as the walls, wearing the dark robe the temple offered to all guests. Its plainness only served to call attention to her face, pale and fine-boned against her black hair, which was drawn into a scallop tuck, the simplest of the courtly styles.

'My lady,' Dumai said, recovering. 'I'm sorry, but guests are not permitted on this floor.'

'I apologise.' Her eyes were large, a bright brown that reminded Dumai of copper. 'I was looking for the refectory, but I must have taken a wrong turn. How thoughtless of me.'

'Not at all. The temple can be confusing.'

The woman regarded her with clear interest. Dumai lowered her chin, so her hair moved to conceal some of her face. The people of the ground shared a habit of looking too hard.

'I take it you are a godsinger,' the woman said. 'What a fulfilling life that must be.'

'I find it so, my lady.'

'I wish I could see the summit myself, but it seems the snow has trapped me here.'

'I hope that does not disappoint you too much, and that you will still find some peace among us.'

'Thank you. It has been some time since I last had peace.' The woman gave her a radiant smile. 'Do you have a name?'

Dumai had never seen a face like hers, one side precisely the same as the other. Kanifa said that was how you told a butterfly spirit from an ordinary woman.

She was about to answer truthfully when she paused. Perhaps it was the way the saltwalker had stared at her, but a sudden, unnerving sense of danger prickled at her nape.

'Unora,' she said, trusting it. 'And you, my lady?'

'Nikeya.'

'Please, follow me. I was going to the refectory myself.'

'Thank you, Unora.' Nikeya cut her gaze towards the doors. 'You are too kind to this poor guest.'

They walked to the bottom of the stairs and along the corridor, the old floorboards creaking under their slippers. Nikeya took in her surroundings with open curiosity. Dumai had expected her to be withdrawn, given her troubles at court, but she was the picture of ease.

'I hear the ordained who serve in this temple never eat of the sea,' Nikeya said. 'Is that so?'

'Yes. We believe the sea belongs to dragonkind, and we should not eat what is theirs.'

'Even salt?' She laughed a little. 'How can a person live without salt?'

'There are Lacustrine merchants who send it to us from Ginura. Theirs comes from salt wells on the mainland.'

'What of pearls and shells?'

'Shells can be found on the shore,' Dumai pointed out. 'Climbers often leave pearls at the summit for the great Kwiriki.'

'So you believe the emperor and all his courtiers – myself included – to be thieves, since we *do* eat of the sea?'

Dumai dropped her gaze. Already her foot was caught in the fishnet. 'That was not what I meant, my lady,' she said. 'We all serve the gods in whatever manner we think best.'

Nikeya laughed again, light and misty. 'Very good. You would make a fine courtier yourself.' Her smile waned. 'You were with the Grand Empress just now. Do you attend on her?'

'No.' Dumai governed her expression. 'Her Majesty has just one attendant, who came with her from court.'

'Tajorin pa Osipa.'

'Yes. Do you know Lady Osipa?'

'I know of her, as I know of many people. Including you now, Unora.'

They soon reached the refectory. At this time of night, it was always thick with templefolk, their voices drowsy after a long day of work and prayer. Nikeya turned to Dumai.

'It was a pleasure, Unora,' she said. 'In a short time, you have taught me a great deal.'

Dumai inclined her head. 'I wish you a pleasant stay, my lady.'

'Thank you.'

With another charming smile, Nikeya went to join one of her attendants, who had already finished her meal.

Across the refectory, Kanifa was serving bowls of buckwheat, the sleeves of his tunic fastened at his elbows, baring his lean brown forearms. Dumai caught his eye. He followed her gaze to the two women, then gave her the smallest nod.

Nikeya should not have been anywhere near the Grand Empress. Kanifa could yet be right in his suspicions. He would make sure she was escorted straight back to the Inner Hall.

Dumai decided to check on the saltwalker. In his room, she found the shutters flung wide, letting in thick flurries of snow. Hurrying to the window, she stared into the night.

A trail of footprints led away from the temple.

'Come back,' she cried. 'It's too dangerous!'

Only the wind answered, burning her cheeks. Little by little, Dumai made out a shape, a darkness on the snow. No sooner had she realised what it was than she was running.

She rushed through the temple, down the stairs and along the corridors. Tirotu was quenching the lamps.

'Leave them,' Dumai called as she ran past. 'I need the light!'

Tirotu stopped at once and came after her.

On the porch, Dumai flung a pelt over her shoulders. Her boots ripped into the deep snow outside. She trudged away from the temple, holding up a naked hand to shield her eyes.

Do not goad the mountain, Dumai.

A gale whistled in her ears, making them ache. She was still within reach of the lamps, still on snow painted with light, and she knew this ground well. Going much farther would be a risk, but it might also save a life.

When she reached the crumpled form, she went to her knees and cleared the snow from their head, expecting to find the saltwalker. Instead, she saw a face she had not seen in days.

'Mother,' she croaked. Unora was cold and ashen, her lashes frosted, breath weak. 'Mother, no. Why did you follow him?' She turned her neck and screamed towards the temple, 'Help me!'

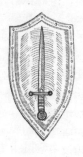

5

West

The sea crashed into Inys like a fist, spelks of white spray flying where it struck ancient rock. Beneath a clean blue sky, gulls filled the air with brabbling, striped sails billowed and snapped in the wind, and Wulfert Glenn watched golden sunlight flit between the waves.

Ahead, Inys waited.

The bowsprit pointed at the firth that would take the *Longstride* inland. Wulf drank in the cliffs that flanked it. Looming in both directions as far as the eye could see, they stood straight and black as iron swords, rusted with lichen, proud custodians of the queendom.

A humpback breached close to the ship. Most of the crew were hardened to the sight of whales, but it still made Wulf smile to see its fin rise, as if in welcome. He clasped his hands on the side and kept watching. Pine tar was bedded under his nails and the tang of sweat clung to his undershirt, but every housecarl could thole such discomforts.

Soon, for the first time in three years, he would be home.

Boots thumped across the deck. Regny came to stand beside him, smelling of damp wool, like everyone on the ship.

'Home at last,' she said. 'Ready?'

'Aye.' Wulf glanced at her. 'You're not.'

'You know Inys bores me. No offence.'

'None taken.'

She patted his back and strode on, her braid swinging from the intricate knotwork that overlaid it at the base of her skull.

The *Longstride* forged past a fire tower. By the time the ship reached the cliffs, the sun had more gold than silver in it.

'Wulfert.'

A booming voice snapped him to attention. He had been so immersed in the sights, he had failed to hear the king approach.

'Sire.' He touched a fist to his chest. 'I hear we're almost to Werstuth.'

Bardholt stepped up to the wale with a grin and placed his enormous hands on it. Wulf was tall and strong, but the King of Hróth was a mountain, enlarged by the white pelt he wore.

'A fine voyage. The Saint is good.' His golden hair lay oiled and heavy on his shoulders. 'Did I not swear upon his shield that I would see my daughter's commendation?'

'You did, my king.'

'I have missed Glorian terribly. My queen gave me a perfect daughter.' He spoke Hróthi with a deep rural accent. 'While we celebrate, you shall be my cupbearer, Wulfert.'

Only the most trusted and respected members of the household ever received such a privilege. Wulf breathed out. 'Sire,' he said, 'it is too great an honour for your humble retainer.'

'Honour is an axe with two blades. Should anyone try to poison me, you'll be the one to ascend to Halgalant.'

Wulf cracked a smile at that. King Bardholt clapped him on the back, with such vigour it almost knocked him overboard.

'You must visit your family, while we're here,' he said. 'Are they all still at Langarth?'

'Aye, my king.'

'Good. Stay for the commendation, then go to them for a day or two. Regny will pour my wine in your absence – by the Saint, she can outdrink us all.'

'That is true.'

'Is it also true that you've been trysting with her?'

Wulf looked slowly at the king, silenced by trepidation. Bardholt raised his thick eyebrows.

'Certain people keep me abreast of the small intrigues that unfold in my household. Even in the coops,' he said. 'Someone reported you, Wulf.'

Saint, when he kills me, grant me the mercy of a swift and painless death.

'I never knew you were fond of gossip, my king,' Wulf said, once he could speak.

It was a dangerous move, but it paid off. Bardholt respected boldness.

'Even a king can grow weary of politics,' he said, the corner of his mouth flinching. 'I was young once, Wulf – I understand – but that was before I knew the Saint. My housecarls must set an example, to ensure all Hróthi respect the Six Virtues. Before you bed anyone else, a love-knot ring must be on their finger. And you know you cannot put one on hers.'

Wulf glanced towards Regny. She was leaning against the mast, hair windblown, sharing a horn of wine with Eydag.

She was the heir of the late Skiri Longstride – Skiri the Condoler, who had welcomed Bardholt and his family when they were forced to flee their village, and whose murder had started the War of Twelve Shields. When Regny was wed, it would be to a fellow chieftain.

'It set with the midnight sun,' Wulf said quietly. 'On my oath, it won't happen again, sire.'

'Good man.' Bardholt gave him a last pat on the back. 'We shall talk again soon. Find a sanctuary, clear your conscience with the Knight of Fellowship, and let us feast and sing.'

He strode towards Regny, who remained expressionless. As the rightful Chieftain of Askrdal, she would receive a sterner reproach, though Bardholt would forgive her.

Wulf looked back at the sea, but his sense of peace had deserted him. With a sigh through his nose, he steepled his fingers on the wale and watched for the first sight of the city on the cliffs.

****

Glorian had not expected to be formally introduced to the world with one arm in plaster, but at least it saved her having to dance with every noble stripling in the West. She let her broken arm hang out of the water, feeling rather like a doll.

Her bathing chamber was her favourite part of the castle. It overlooked the queenswood of the Fells, the only province in Inys with real mountains. The shutters had been opened, letting in golden sunlight and a breeze, and water steamed in the wooden tub, which was lined and tented with white linen. It had been a gift from King Bardholt, made from snow pine, so Glorian could pretend she was basking in the hot pools of Hróth.

'I can't bear this wretched thing.' She rubbed at her cast. 'When will the itching stop?'

'Next time, try not to fall off a horse,' Julain said.

'Is that the sort of counsel you mean to give me when I'm queen?'

'I mean to always tell you when you do foolish things.'

Outside, a wren twittered. The linen shaded Glorian, while a small fire kept the chill away. Julain kneaded her scalp. Adela pared her nails. Helisent cleansed her face with rose oil. When she was Queen of Inys, they would be her Ladies of the Great Chamber.

Julain Crest – the eldest – had been her playmate when they were children. The holy descendants of the Knight of Justice, the Crest family had always held enormous influence as courtiers. Queen Sabran was one of the few rulers who did not have a Crest as her First Lady.

Helisent Beck was heir apparent of the Dowager Earl of Goldenbirch. The Becks claimed descent from Edrig of Arondine, closest friend and mentor of the Saint. She was sixteen and as tall as Glorian.

Youngest of them, at fifteen, was Adeliza afa Dáura, daughter of the Mistress of the Robes. She was minor Yscali nobility, her mother the eldest child of a hereditary knight.

'We should test your knowledge,' Julain said to Glorian. 'Who is the Decreer of Carmentum?'

'Carmenti leaders conceal their true names when they run for election, both to protect their families and to ensure their campaigns are based only on their politics,' Glorian said, making Julain nod her approval, 'but her tenure name is Numun. She will bring one of her advisors, Arpa Nerafriss, who often serves as her envoy.'

'I am never going to understand why Queen Sabran would invite a pair of *republicans*,' Adela said crossly.

'Precisely because the Carmenti are dangerous.' Julain poured from a jug, rinsing the suds away. She had such careful hands that Glorian never had to blink. 'A country that breaks the rudder of monarchy will swing wildly and crash into others, hurling all into disorder.'

'Aye,' Helisent said. 'Her Grace must think it best to keep close watch on their folly.'

'Well, I think they will spoil the commendation.' Adela trimmed another nail. 'We should refuse to receive them until they send *tribute* to the House of Berethnet, which shields them from the Nameless One.' Another slice took the white clean off. 'They should be grateful we don't crush them, as King Bardholt crushed the Northern heathens.'

'The Knight of Courage has lent you his lance today, Adela,' Glorian said, amused. 'I think you would march to war with Carmentum.' She took her hand back. 'And that, in your passion, you might relieve me of a finger.'

'Indeed,' a new voice said. 'Be cautious, Adeliza. My daughter is already injured.'

Julain dropped the comb into the water with a gasp. She stepped down to stand beside Helisent and Adela, and they all curtseyed, heads low.

'Your Grace,' they chorused.

The Queen of Inys stood in the doorway, arrayed in an elegant black gown, cut to show off a pair of white undersleeves. 'Good morning, ladies,' she said, gentler. 'Leave us, please.'

'Your Grace,' they said again, Adela with a furious blush. As they filed out, Julain reached up to grasp the handle and pull the door closed in their wake, shooting Glorian a look that said *courage*.

Glorian sank up to her neck, wishing she could draw her arm under. There was something absurd about the way it hung from the bathtub, proof of her failure to stay on a horse.

'Glorian,' her mother said. 'I am sorry to disturb you while you bathe. I am in council for the rest of today, making final arrangements for your commendation. Now is the only time we can speak.'

'Yes, Mother.'

'Doctor Forthard has kept me abreast of your condition. I trust you are not in much pain.'

'A little,' Glorian said. 'At night, especially.'

'It will pass. Doctor Forthard tells me you will only need to wear the cast for a month or two.'

Queen Sabran gazed out of the window. The sunlight turned her eyes to raw emerald. Glorian hunched deeper into the water, hiding behind her black curtains of hair.

In every conversation with her mother, there were snares. Each time, she leapt headfirst and trapped herself. Her first mistake had been confessing the pain. Her mother did not like admissions of weakness.

'I will be well for tomorrow,' Glorian said quickly. 'I will dance one-handed, Mother, if you wish.'

'And what would people say of the Queen of Inys if she forced her daughter to dance with a broken arm?'

There was her second mistake. 'That she was cruel and unfeeling,' Glorian said, cheeks hot. 'Like the Malkin Queen.'

'Precisely.' At last, her mother deigned to look at her. 'I will be frank. Tomorrow is not only your introduction as an eligible princess, but a display of strength and unity. For the first time, our country will host a delegation from a so-called republic.'

'Carmentum.'

'Yes. The Carmenti must see that absolute monarchy remains the only true and righteous way to govern a country. We cannot allow Inys, like Carmentum, to be thrown like fodder to the people, who will tear it apart with their conflicting opinions. There can only be one will that governs – the will of the Saint, who speaks through us.'

'Yes, Mother,' Glorian said meekly. 'I will not disappoint you.' She hesitated before asking, 'Why did you invite the Carmenti here?'

'Arpa Nerafriss sent me a letter, asking if I would consider opening trade negotiations. The Carmenti are athirst for our support. They want older, stronger countries to recognise their rule.' Queen Sabran raised her chin. 'Inys is small. We must remain open to the world. Through Yscalin, Mentendon and Hróth, we trade with the Ersyr, with Lasia – even with the Easterners across the Abyss, whose ways are unknown to us.'

The Abyss. The great black sea, so wide and full of monsters that few had crossed it and returned. King Bardholt had sailed on it before, but not far. Even he was wary of it.

'In any case,' Queen Sabran continued, hauling Glorian back to her own side of the world, 'the Carmenti have no power against the Chainmail of Virtudom. Your commendation seemed a fitting time to show them.'

Glorian felt a surge of admiration then. It was thanks to her mother that Inys would stand firm against the tide of republican feeling in Carmentum. Before her parents' marriage, there had only been two countries pledged to the Saint. Now there were four.

'I need not tell you, Glorian, that you will also meet potential consorts at the dance,' Queen Sabran said. 'There will be representatives of noble families from across Virtudom. We must keep our links strong.'

63

A chill squirmed in Glorian, as if an adder had crept down her throat and curled up in her belly.

'I don't want—' When Queen Sabran looked at her, Glorian drew her knees up to her chest. 'Must I marry so soon?'

'Of course not. Fifteen is not old enough to be wed,' her mother reminded her, 'but we might arrange a suitable precontract. You must be gracious and courteous towards every suitor, even if dancing is out of the question. You must behave like the blood of the Saint.'

'Yes, Mother. I promise I will be a credit to him.' Glorian peeked up at her. 'And to you.'

For a fleeting instant, her mother almost softened. Her lips parted, her brow smoothed, and she started to lift a hand, as if to touch Glorian on the cheek.

Then she clasped her fingers again, and she was once more a statue, a queen.

'I will see you on the morrow,' she said. 'And Glorian … we will speak about your riding soon.'

She left without a backward glance. Glorian rested her brow on her knees and wished herself all the way to the East.

6

South

The incense burner was shaped like a bird. Smoke curled from the openwork across its breast and folded wings. Taking in its scent, Tunuva closed her eyes as Esbar pleasured her.

Red light needled through a lattice, patterning their limbs. Tunuva steadied herself on her elbows. In a haze, she looked down at Esbar, drinking in the sight of her, the sun catching in her cascade of black hair. It made Tunuva tighter still, her body like a drawn arrow.

Since her blood had started to come less, her fires burned low on some days. The path to release was longer and steeper. Esbar knew it. They were of an age, Esbar half a year older – her body was changing, too. Her blood came heavier of late, soaking right through her cloths.

But on nights like this, when they were both sleek with desire, Esbar rose to the occasion as she did to all things, with tireless resolve. Tunuva tilted her head back as sweetness flared between her legs, tended by a tongue like fire and hands that knew exactly where and how to touch.

She gripped the sheet, her breaths fraying. Just as she reached the horizon of release, Esbar slid on top of her in one smooth movement so their hearts were aligned.

'Not yet,' she whispered. 'Stay with me, lover.'

Tunuva embraced her with all her limbs, smiling into their kiss. Esbar was quick in many things, but in this, she had always taken her time.

They drifted to the cool side of the bed, and now it was Esbar who reclined, and Tunuva who took the lead. Esbar reached up to hold her by the waist, fingertips pressed into skin. Tunuva held still, gazing down at her.

Esbar raised an eyebrow. 'What?'

Tunuva brushed their lips together, then their foreheads.

'You,' she said, leaning her hips forward, feeling Esbar firm her grasp. 'Always you.'

She made her slow way downward, caressing as she went. Esbar watched, each surge of breath coming a little sooner than the last. On the wall, their shadows were seamless, the candlelight melting them into one.

By the time they were sated, sweat bathed them both. Tunuva lay beside Esbar and rested her head against her breastbone, so she could feel the solid drumbeat of her heart.

'Exhilarated though I am,' Esbar said, 'I wonder what brought on such a surge of lust.'

Tunuva placed a kiss on the dark tip of her breast. 'Saghul asked me if I had ever questioned our purpose,' she said, her voice low. 'I told her that I had, and I told her when.'

'Ah, *that* day.' Esbar shifted to face her, hooking a warm thigh across her waist. 'It was not so long after that,' she said softly, 'that I knew what it was to miss you for the first time.'

Tunuva pressed close and kissed her. Even now, she never liked to relive that brief parting.

It had been two months after the Crimson Desert. In her memory, those days were a burning dream, as if she had spent the whole time with a fever. She would wake at dawn with an ache in her body, and it had been all she could do to pray and train before she could fling herself at Esbar. Desire had been a madness in her, grounded by a love that had filled her like breath – as if it had always been meant, written on her soul when it was just a seed.

The day the Prioress had found them, they had been laughing and entwined in the spicery, sprawled among sacks of rose petals and nutmeg and cloves.

At twenty, Esbar had already been the boldest of the sisters, outspoken even to her elders. Tunuva had never broken a rule. It had stunned her when Saghul banished them to separate ends of the Priory with no explanation.

Conception was one thing. In a closed society, bloodlines had to be carefully watched, but Saghul had never stopped unions that posed no risk of a child. At last, when Tunuva had thought she would lose her mind, Saghul had summoned them both to her sunroom.

Is this an affair of the body, she had asked them, *or of the heart?*

Tunuva had hesitated to answer, afraid that whatever she said could see her torn from Esbar. *I could never speak for Tuva,* Esbar had finally said, *but, Prioress, must one preclude the other?*

Saghul had been elected for a reason. From one glimpse, she had known theirs was not a passing attraction, one that would erode with time. It was two hearts meeting at a crossway, and deciding to go on together.

You are my daughters. I trust your judgement – but know this, both of you, she had warned. *You cannot allow any love to overpower your love of the Mother. Nothing comes above our calling. If duty takes you from each other, as I did these past few days, then you must bear the separation. Whatever comes, you must endure. Be together, if you wish, but remember you are a bride of the tree.*

'No wonder she was so vexed,' Tunuva murmured when their lips parted. 'All those cloves.'

'That was you, as I recall,' Esbar said, giving her a light slap on the hip. 'Always the quiet ones.'

'Not so quiet,' Tunuva said drily.

They both chuckled. Thirty years later, when either of them smelled cloves, they would still exchange a look.

Esbar kissed her once more before she sat up and raked back her hair, which tumbled to her waist in loose black curls. Tunuva folded her arm behind her head.

'Tell me,' she said, 'how long did it take you to disobey Saghul?'

'I resent your accusation. As munguna, I did precisely as the Prioress asked. Calmed and comforted our sisters.' Esbar reached for the wine jar. 'And then I went to Siyu and told her just what I thought of her reckless stupidity.'

Tunuva shook her head and smiled.

'Shake your head and smile all you like, Tunuva Melim. Saghul may not like it, but I grew Siyu. I laboured for a day and a night to give her life, and I will tell her outright when she shames me. Or you.' Esbar poured two cups of straw wine. 'It's your name she carries.'

67

'Has Saghul decided on a punishment?'

'Confinement for a week. For a month after that, she will not be allowed to go into the forest.'

Tunuva was silent, accepting the wine.

'You're too soft on her, Tuva,' Esbar said, unyielding. 'You know she has done wrong.'

'We were young and foolish once.'

'You and I spilled a few cloves. We would never have climbed the tree.'

It was true. Even at seventeen, Tunuva would sooner have cut off her own foot than place it on the sacred branches.

Esbar set a dish of fruit between them and chose a honeyed date. Tunuva took a butter plum.

'Hidat retrieved the rope. She has been at prayer all day, asking forgiveness of the Mother,' Esbar said. 'I doubt Siyu has been so devout.'

'Siyu hates to be confined. This will be a hard punishment for her.'

Esbar made a sound that could have been an agreement or a dismissal.

'I asked Saghul to send her out into the world. To let her taste it,' Tunuva said. 'I thought she might do well as a handmaiden to Princess Jenyedi. Saghul did not seem to agree.' She glanced at Esbar. 'Am I such a fool?'

'No.' Esbar took her hand. 'I do understand your outlook, Tuva. I also understand what Saghul fears. I am not persuaded that Siyu would behave at court.' She breathed out. 'Imsurin must have been the wrong choice. I am steel, he is stone, and together, we made a spark. No matter where she lands, she will burn something to the ground.'

'A spark can be coaxed into a bright flame, if given the chance.'

'And who would chance a spark in their own house?'

Tunuva bit into her butter plum. Esbar picked another date.

The matter had no end. Siyu was trapped in quicksand – unable to grow without the world, not trusted in the world until she grew. Whatever she did, Esbar would feel it reflected on her, so she would err on the side of caution. Tunuva resolved to go back to Saghul.

The air was as mild as if it were summer. They shared a flatbread with pounded fig and goat cheese, listening to the familiar sounds that drifted into the chamber. A red-throated wryneck called as it flew. Elsewhere, one of the men played a calming tune on a harp. When

Esbar had eaten her fill, she relaxed into the bolsters and swirled her straw wine.

She was as striking at rest as when she fought. Candlelight feathered across her dark golden skin, limning the thick muscle in her thigh. Except for the lines around her eyes and mouth and the grey strands in her hair, she looked almost the same as she had at twenty.

When Tunuva was young, she had never dreamed that she would know a love as passionate as this. She had thought her life would be devoted above all to the tree, and her ichneumon, and the Mother. Esbar had come as a surprise. The fourth string to her lute.

No, she had not expected Esbar uq-Nāra. Or the fifth string. The one that had come later. The thought drew her gaze downward, to the scars where her body had stretched – like ripples in sand down her belly and sides, dark on the warm brown of her skin.

'When did you last think of him?'

Esbar was looking at her face. Tunuva drank.

'When Siyu leapt from the tree.' The wine had no taste. 'I never thought his name or pictured his face, but … he was with me, in that moment. I would have hurled myself in after her.'

'I know.' Esbar laid a hand on her knee. 'I know you love her. But as munguna, you know what I must say.'

'She is not my daughter, nor yours. She belongs to the Mother.'

'As we all do,' Esbar confirmed. When Tunuva gazed at the ceiling, Esbar heaved a sigh. 'Comfort her this once if it will ease you, after you see the Mother. Imin will let you in.' When they kissed, Tunuva tasted dates. 'And then come back and love me one more time before we sleep.'

****

There were few titles in the Priory. Two loose ranks – postulants and initiates – but few titles, for the Priory was not a court or an army. *Prioress* was one title; *munguna* was another.

Then there was a third, the tomb keeper. On her fortieth birthday, Tunuva had received that title, and with it, the honour of guarding the remains of Cleolind Onjenyu, the Mother, slayer of the Nameless One and founder of the Priory, who had once been Princess of Lasia.

Few are more faithful than you, Tunuva. You will make her a fine warden, Saghul had said. *Guard her well.*

Tunuva had not failed. Each night, while the Priory quietened, she descended to the burial chamber to perform the final rites of the day. As usual, Ninuru prowled at her side, a white shadow.

Ninuru had been the smallest in her litter. Now she was near as tall as Tunuva and loyal to a fault, as ichneumons always were to the first person who fed them meat. They imprinted on that person for life.

They had also imprinted on the Priory. Centuries ago, a pack had come to the Lasian Basin to serve the Mother, whose handmaidens had taught them to speak. They had smelled the Nameless One in Lasia, marking him as their enemy, and ever since, there had been an alliance. They resembled mongooses in the way that a lion resembled a cat.

At the door, Tunuva set her lamp beside the chest and used one of her three keys to unlock it. Inside lay a mantle. Five centuries after Cleolind had worn it, the dye was still rich, a deep fig purple. Tunuva unfolded it with care and draped it around her shoulders. For years she had feared it might unravel between her fingers, this remnant of the Mother.

Her second key opened the door to the burial chamber. She walked its edge, using her own flame to light one hundred and twenty lamps, each a life the Nameless One had ended when he came to Yikala. Once the chamber was aglow, she turned to the stone coffin and illuminated the final lamp, held by a sculpture of Washtu, high divinity of fire.

Tunuva poured from a jar of precious wine, made with resin from the tree. Only the titled were permitted to taste of it. She knelt before the coffin, drank half of the wine, and observed a silence for the hundred and twenty.

Once she had recited their names, she sang out a long prayer in Selinyi, her throat warmed by the sound of worship. The language was that of the lost city of Old Selinun, from whence had come the prophet Suttu, and from her line, the House of Onjenyu.

Finishing the wine in one swallow, she stood. These days, the floor was hard on her knees – she would have to bring a mat next time. She placed a hand on the tomb.

'Mother, be still. We are your daughters,' she said softly. 'We remember. We remain.'

****

Outside the burial chamber, she locked the mantle back into its chest, leaving the oil lamps to burn through the night. At sunrise, she would return to replenish them and say the morning prayer.

The third key was cool under her drape. It was made of bronze, its bow shaped like an orange blossom, each petal enamelled in white. In ten years, Tunuva had never used it. *All you need do is carry and guard this*, Saghul had told her. *As to what it opens, that is not for you to know.*

At the top of the stairs, Tunuva turned to her ichneumon. 'Did you find it?'

Ninuru sloped into a hollow in the wall. Tunuva heard a scuffling before she returned with a woven bag in her mouth.

'Thank you.' Tunuva took it, then gave her a rub between the ears. 'Shall we ride soon?'

'Yes.' Shiny black eyes fixed on hers. 'Siyu is in disgrace. You should not give her gifts.'

'Oh, not you as well.' Tunuva tapped her pink nose. 'Esbar has already upbraided me.'

'Esbar is clever.'

'Perhaps you would sooner ride with clever Esbar tomorrow, then.' Tunuva scratched her under the chin. 'Hm?'

'No,' the ichneumon said. 'You are often stupid. But you fed me.'

She licked Tunuva clean across the face before she prowled away, tail brushing the floor behind her. Tunuva smiled and went in the opposite direction.

She found Imsurin sitting at his bench, embroidering the collar of an ivory tunic. When she approached, he looked up, eyebrows raised. They had turned grey over the past year.

'I want to see her,' Tunuva said. His mouth pressed into a line. 'Please, Imin.'

'You should not comfort her this time. Esbar would agree.'

'It is my name Siyu carries.' She came to stand in front of his bench. 'Let her have a little comfort tonight. After that, I will give her time to reflect.'

'And if the Prioress learns of this?'

'I will answer for it.'

Imsurin pinched the bridge of his broad, freckled nose. His eyesight had been failing him for years, giving him headaches. 'Go,' he said, 'but be quick, for both our sakes.'

Tunuva pressed his hand before she passed. He shook his head and returned to his needlework.

Siyu lay on top of the covers, one arm tucked under her head, hair swept over her face. Tunuva sat beside her and brushed a few dark strands behind her ear. She had slept this way since she was a child. Stirring, she opened her eyes and blinked up at Tunuva.

'Oh, Tuva.' She sat up and embraced her at once. 'Tuva, Imin says I must stay in here for a week. And that I may not go beyond the valley at all, for a whole month. Is it true?'

'Yes,' Tunuva said, feeling her back heave with sobs. 'Hush, sunray, hush. Imin will make sure the men keep you busy. It will feel as if no time is passing.'

'But I *can't* stay here,' Siyu said, frantic. 'Please. Will you ask the Prioress to forgive me?'

'She will, in time.' Tunuva drew back and frowned at her tear-stained face. Her skin was a deeper brown, her hair still black all the way through, but otherwise she was the picture of Esbar. 'Siyu, you must know this punishment is lighter than it could have been. The men do good work, important work. Is it so bad to help them for a few weeks?'

Siyu met her gaze. Something flickered in those thick-lashed eyes.

'No,' she said. 'I just hate to be trapped inside. And I'm ashamed.' She drew a scuffed knee to her chest. 'I suppose Esbar didn't want you to see me. She told me I disgraced you both.'

'Esbar loves you with her soul, as we all do.'

'She loves the Mother more.'

'As we all must – but Siyu, I was there when Esbar gave birth to you. You have made her so proud over the years. This mistake is a small part of your life. It does not define it.'

Swallowing, Siyu managed a nod. Tunuva reached into her overskirt and took out the pouch.

'For you. So you can smell the forest, at least.'

Siyu undid the tie. When she saw the delicate blue petals in the pouch, she drew out the bloom and held it to her cheek, tears running again. She had always loved dayflowers.

'Thank you.' She sank against Tunuva. 'You're always so good to me, Tuva. Even when I'm a fool.'

Tunuva kissed the top of her head. Even as she did, she remembered that Esbar could never be so tender with Siyu. She and Imsurin did not have that freedom.

'I would like something in exchange,' Tunuva said. 'I would like you to tell me a story.'

'What story?'

'The one that matters most.' Tunuva stroked her hair. 'Come. The way Imin used to tell it to you.'

With a tiny smile, Siyu shifted across the bed, so Tunuva could lean into the bolsters. 'Will you do the fire?' Siyu asked her.

'Of course.'

Siyu wiped her face once more, nestling close.

'There is a Womb of Fire that roils beneath the world,' she began. 'Centuries ago, the molten flame within it rushed together, taking solid form. And that form was terrible indeed.'

With a twist of her fingers and a flick of her wrist, Tunuva conjured a bright flame and tossed it into the stove. It ignited the dry wood and tinder in a rush. Siyu shivered, toes curling.

'Lava was its milk, and stone its flesh, and iron were its teeth.' Her eyes collected the flickering light. 'It drank until even its breath caught fire. This creature was the Nameless One, and in his ever-burning heart blazed one eternal need. The need for chaos.'

Tunuva remembered Balag telling her this story. How she had delighted in the chilling voices he would use, the shadows the men would make on the walls with their fingers.

'Though the Womb of Fire is deeper and wider than any sea, it was not enough for the Nameless One,' Siyu said, her voice strengthening. 'He thirsted for the world above. He swam up through the molten fire and broke the very mantle of the earth, and his terrible form emerged from the Dreadmount. Fire streamed in a river down its slopes, consuming the city of Gulthaga, and smoke blackened the morning sky. Red lightning struck and struck again, and as the sun disappeared, the Nameless One took wing.'

In the stove, the flame burned hotter.

'He sought the warmer climes to the south,' Siyu said, 'and so his dread shadow fell upon Yikala, where the House of Onjenyu ruled over the great domain of Lasia. He settled beside Lake Jakpa, and with his breath and the wind of his wings came a plague that poisoned all before him. The people sickened. Their blood ran hot, so hot they screamed and brawled and perished in the streets. The Nameless One beheld humankind, and he detested what he saw. He resolved to turn their world – this world – into a second Womb of Fire.'

'As below, so above,' Tunuva said.

Siyu nodded.

'Selinu Onjenyu ruled Lasia in those days,' she said. 'He watched as Yikala descended into chaos. Its water reeked and boiled. First, he sent warriors to kill the beast, but the Nameless One melted their flesh and scattered the shore of the lake with their bones. Next, the farmers surrendered their sheep and goats and oxen. And when there was no livestock left, Selinu saw no other choice. He stepped from his palace and gave the command that every day, the people must cast lots, and one would be the sacrifice.'

One hundred and twenty names.

'Selinu made a great oath,' Siyu said. 'He could not risk his own life, but the names of his children would be among the lots. When it came to the hundred and twenty-first day, it was his daughter – Princess Cleolind – whose name was plucked from the crock.

'Cleolind had spent her days in torment. She had seen the people suffering, seen even children go to their deaths, and swore to fight the beast herself, for she was a skilled warrior. Selinu had forbidden it. Yet when Cleolind was chosen, he had no choice but to send her to her doom. For this, they would for ever call him Selinu the Oathkeeper.

'On the day Cleolind was to die, a man of the West rode into Yikala, seeking glory and a crown. With him he carried a sword of rare splendour, the sword named Ascalun. He claimed it was enchanted, that he alone could slay the creature – but it was not kindness that moved him. In exchange for his blade, the knight of Inysca had two conditions. First, he would see the people of Lasia convert to his new religion of Six Virtues. And second, when he returned to his own country, he would have Cleolind as his bride.'

Siyu stopped to clear her throat. Tunuva passed her a goblet of walnut milk, which she drank.

'And what then?' Tunuva asked her. 'What did Cleolind say?'

When Siyu lay back down, she rested her head against Tunuva.

'She told her father to banish the knight,' Siyu said. 'Desperate though their city was, she would not see her people on their knees for a foreign king – but when she went to meet her death, the knight followed. And when Cleolind was bound to a stone, and the Nameless One emerged from the foul water to claim his payment, the knight faced him.

'But Galian Berethnet – that was his name – was a coward and a fool. The fumes and fire overcame him. Cleolind took up his sword. From the acrid shore of Lake Jakpa, deep into the Lasian Basin, she fought the Beast of the Mountain, tracking him to his lair. There, Cleolind was astonished, for in the valley grew a befruited tree, taller than any she had ever seen.'

That image appeared on many walls in the Priory. The tree, its golden oranges, the red beast twined around its trunk.

'They fought,' Siyu said, 'for a day and a night. At last, the Nameless One set Cleolind afire. She cast herself beneath the tree – and though the beast was drawn to it, his fire could not burn anything that lay within the shadow of its branches.

'As Cleolind began to die, the orange tree yielded its fruit. With the last of her strength, she ate, and all about her, the world brightened. She could hear the earth, feel its heat in her blood, and suddenly, fire was at her command, too. This time, when she confronted the beast, she drove the sword between its scales, and at last, the Nameless One was vanquished.'

Tunuva released her breath. No matter how many times she heard the story, it moved her.

'Cleolind returned the sword to Galian the Deceiver, so he would never come back for it,' Siyu said, 'before she banished him from Lasia.' Her voice was slowing. 'She renounced her claim to the throne, and with her loyal handmaidens, she withdrew from the world to guard the orange tree, to stand in wait for the Nameless One, for he shall one day return. And we, who are blessed with the flame, are her children. We remain.'

'For how long?' Tunuva asked.

'Always.'

Her breathing deepened. Tunuva closed her own eyes, and against her will, she remembered someone else falling asleep against her, long ago. The thought held her in place until Imsurin came and led her away.

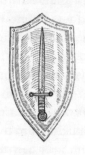

7

West

The day of her commendation. Glorian Hraustr Berethnet stared in expectation at her canopy, waiting for maturity to shine on her from Halgalant.

She had prayed for a sense that she was ready for her life. She had wanted the Saint to whisper to her, acknowledge her as his descendant. She had hoped she would finally long for her betrothal to a complete stranger, and her belly to puff with the next heir to Inys.

In short, she had prayed, hoped and expected to feel less of an imposter. Instead, she was drained from another painful night, she still had no interest in consorts, and the only puff she fancied in her belly was the sort that came from a good helping of blackberry pie.

Julain woke at cockcrow and slipped away to dress. Glorian snuggled into her pillows. She could have just a little more peace before she was scraped and trussed like a goose – at least, she thought she could, until Helisent flumped on to the bed beside her.

'Time for you to meet the world.' She threaded her arms around Glorian, making her smile. 'How are you feeling?'

'Sore.'

'About your commendation. You could be betrothed.'

'I could have been betrothed since my birthday.' Glorian looked at her. 'Did you feel different?'

Helisent considered. A small ruby hung from her circlet, sparkling in the middle of her brow.

'No,' she admitted. 'Every year, I expect to suddenly feel the way Florell and Queen Sabran look, as if I could say anything and be convinced I was right, and not terrified that someone will peck holes in my words. As if I've . . . set, or been kilned into shape. Still, I never do.'

Glorian sighed. 'I hoped you wouldn't say that.'

'Sorry.'

A rap on the door, and Florell herself was there, adorned with amber. 'Good morrow, young ladies,' she said brightly. Julain and Adela came after her. 'Oh, Glorian. Your commendation! I remember when you were so tiny, I thought I'd lose you in my sleeves. Now look at you – so tall and beautiful.' She patted Glorian on the cheeks. 'Come, let's get you dressed. We have a busy day ahead.'

****

Three miles from Drouthwick Castle, a rooster cawed over the drowsy settlement of Worhurst. In exchange for their silence about his arrival, Bardholt had opened his coffers and casks to its astonished inhabitants.

Wulf woke to rough blankets and the scent of a hayloft. Thrit slept beside him, head resting on a muscular arm, and Eydag snored nearby. Careful not to wake them, Wulf sat up and found his boots. As his footsteps creaked away, Thrit stirred, lashes flickering.

Outside the barn, Wulf secured a belt over his wools and stepped into a copse of oaks and golden birches, over their fallen leaves. Light dripped between the branches like watered beer, prancing on the stream they had crossed on their way into Worhurst. In the near distance, bells made a merry clangour for the Feast of Late Autumn.

He knelt beside the stream to shave his stubble from the crossing. On the other side, a swineherd whistled as she walked beside her hogs, letting them root through the acorns and beechmast. Wulf scrubbed his face clean and inspected his reflection in the water.

This day, he would serve as cupbearer to the greatest king the world had ever known. He could not let that opportunity slide from his grasp. Since he was fourteen, he had served as a housecarl. If he kept to the virtuous path, he might achieve his dream of knighthood.

To succeed, he would have to needlebind his heart, so no one could slip into it again. He had been a fool to return that first kiss, and not crush the bud before it could flower.

'What did he say to you?'

Wulf glanced over his shoulder. Regny stood beside a slumping willow, already groomed and armoured.

'Enough.' He used his shirt to dry off. 'Was he hard on you?'

Regny lifted a shoulder. 'Chieftain I may be, but I'm not old enough to rule in my province. Youthful folly can be excused and buried. Bardholt understands this more than anyone.'

'Any idea who told him?'

'A healer gave me certain herbs. I assume her tongue slipped.'

'I should have gone for you. Forgive me.'

'You wouldn't be the first to forget the need for such things.' Her cool gaze followed him as he joined her. She wore the silver collar of a chieftain, its ends decorated with the tree of Askrdal. 'Let me guess. You've sworn off vice for the rest of your days because our king gave you a slap on the wrist.'

'He never slaps on the wrist. Always the back.'

'Yes, I think he dented mine.'

'And my place at his side is more fragile than yours. I have to be careful, Regny.'

'You know full well that Bardholt favours you,' Regny said, 'but I respect your wishes.' The sunlight tempted out the auburn notes in her plaited brown hair. 'Don't lock your heart too fast, Wulfert Glenn. I happen to know someone else in the household has taken a liking to you.'

Wulf raised an eyebrow. 'Who?'

'I'd say you'll find out, but I'd rather make a sport of counting all the signs you miss.' She wrapped an arm around his waist. 'Come. Bardholt needs us to be his eyes in the Old Hall.'

****

Drouthwick Castle was almost as large as that of the royal stronghold of Ascalun. Its Great Hall stretched on for ever. Several fires crackled, warming its walls. Not that it needed much warming, for a tremendous number of people had filled it for the Feast of Late Autumn.

Glorian had never expected so many guests, or so much food. Elderflower cheesecake, golden as a windfall, served up with boiled cream or gooseberry butter; hot griddle bread and rosehip pudding; red pears simmered in honeyed wine. And such meat: goose stuffed with apples, spit-roasted chicken, charred sausages thick with pine nuts.

Her crimson gown was cut in a fashionable Yscali style, with a tight waist and hanging sleeves, altered to cover her cast. Florell had taken six pieces of hair and woven them into a virtue braid, leaving the rest loose down her back. With that and her gold coronet, she was unbearably hot.

She ate three more helpings of cheesecake. Applause resounded as the harpist plucked the first notes of 'A Royal Quarry' – a ballad about Glorian the Second, known to history as Glorian Hartbane. It was after that famous queen, whose marriage to Isalarico the Benevolent had brought Yscalin into the arms of the Saint, that Glorian had been named.

White banners draped the walls, showing the True Sword. It represented Ascalun, the enchanted blade the Saint had used to rout the Nameless One, and it surrounded the Carmenti.

The republicans sat with the Virtues Council. Grandest of the delegation was Numun, the Decreer – a tall and narrow-shouldered woman with a long, bare neck, unadorned by jewellery. Her sleeveless dress pleated at the waist before sweeping to the floor.

Her face was calm beneath her greying black hair, which was tightly braided and arranged at the top of her head. The only clear sign of her authority was a circlet of gold leaves. She had brought a pronged Southern utensil, which she used to spear each morsel.

Beside her sat her advisor, large and observant, wearing the same rich purple, with a white layer draped over his enormous shoulder. They were both dark of eye and brown of skin, Arpa Nerafriss a little paler than Numun. Glorian had yet to understand how they had reached their positions, or what those positions involved. It all sounded very complicated.

'What is that on their crest?' Helisent asked over the din. It showed a pale archway on lavender.

'The Gate of Ungulus,' Glorian said. 'The end of the world. Liuma told me.'

'The world has an end?' a flushed Julain said, frowning. 'With a gate?'

'Well, it has to end somewhere, doesn't it?'

Helisent tilted her head. 'Does it?'

'I hear Numun has two companions,' Julain said, hiding her mouth with her hand. Helisent snorted in amazement, while Glorian finished her third (or perhaps fourth) cup of wine. 'Yes, it must have caused a scandal in Halgalant. A marriage of three. Oh, wonderful, crispels!'

Glorian looked down the table with a grin. 'You there,' Helisent called, 'pass those here for the princess!'

'Her Highness,' people shouted, cups lifted. 'Lady Glorian!'

'To our magnificent princess,' Florell laughed from her place near the queen. 'Joy for her hall!'

Queen Sabran wore her mantle low, showing the creamy skin of her shoulders. She raised her own cup and favoured Glorian with a rare smile.

'Beloved daughter. Princess of Inys and Hróth,' she said, her voice ringing clear. The chatter died away while she spoke. 'May the Saint bless and keep you in this, your fifteenth year.'

Cheers went up around the hall. *She does love me*, Glorian thought, and the wine felt even warmer in her belly. *She is proud of me.*

A platter came her way, laden with pastries as thin as parchment, fried in butter and honey. She ate several in a row and licked the sweetness from her fingers.

Glancing up, she saw her mother looking at her, eyebrow arched. Glorian took the next crispel with more care, eating in tidy bites.

Conciliated, Queen Sabran returned to her conversation with Robart Eller, the Lord Chancellor of Inys, who sat on her left. Even as he spoke, he watched the hall, his blue eyes discerning. He was Duke of Generosity, and as such, he had paid for most of this feast, even providing spiced wine from Yscalin, where grapes could sweeten under a far warmer sun.

Beholding her mother, so poised and strong, Glorian was glad that she was such a poor imitation. She was born to be a shadow, and all shadows had to do was walk behind.

Out of nowhere, agony seared through her arm. 'You fool,' Julain gasped, sober at once. 'Have you tuns for feet?'

Glorian blinked needles from her eyes, trying to work out what had happened. One of the servants – a boy, a page – had tried to restock her cup, and instead knocked her broken arm.

'Highness.' He was shaking with fear. 'I'm sorry. Did I hurt you?'

'It's nothing.' Glorian could hardly speak. 'Excuse me.'

Suddenly it was too much – the heat and noise, the pain. When she stood, so did those closest to her. She fanned their concern away. Hopefully they thought she just needed the close stool, which she did. If her instinct was right, she was about to be horribly sick.

Drouthwick Castle had many odd crannies and in-between places. One of them was the long musicians' gallery that overlooked the Great Hall. Glorian ran up the stairs, past the hanging that guarded it – and crashed into something large and solid. Her arm screamed. She lurched and almost stumbled, just catching herself on the wall with her good hand.

Her first wild thought was that the gallery must have been walled up. Then the hanging was drawn back, and a stricken face appeared, cast into shadow.

'Who in Halgalant are you?' Glorian demanded.

Pain and embarrassment sharpened her voice. She had not thought to see anyone up here. The man – a young man, not much older than her – stared back at her in shock.

'My lady.' Recovering, he lowered his head. 'Your pardon. Are you hurt?'

His accent was a flinty burr. She could have sworn it had the rime of the North on it.

'Hurt?' Glorian snapped. 'I am vexed, by your presence. Why are you lurking up here in the dark?'

He seemed at a loss for words. She knew she was being rude, but she needed him to get out of the way, before she fainted on him. Her bone hurt so badly it made her sight prickle.

A second face looked out from behind the young man. A woman, about the same age, brown hair plaited over her pale forehead. When Glorian realised what she must have interrupted, she flushed.

'Unless you two are wed, you should not be trysting.' She drew herself up to her full, considerable height, her arm throbbing. 'Off with you, or Queen Sabran will hear of this.'

'We weren't—' the woman started, but the man cut her off.

'Aye, my lady. Forgive us.'

He ushered his friend away, and they were gone. Glorian waited until their footsteps had faded before she doubled over, painting the floor with vomit and bramble wine.

Somehow, she thought gloomily, just as her guards caught up, *I suspect Mother would have handled this better.*

****

Half an hour later, she sat at the high table in the Old Hall. Three hundred of the most important guests, including the delegation from Carmentum, had been invited to the more intimate chamber.

Her guards had summoned the bonesetter, Kell Bourn, who had fastened her arm to her chest. Now Glorian felt steadier, though her body ached. She had chewed on some catmint to freshen her breath, and a mantle hid the slender leather strap from the Carmenti.

Her fourth suitor was beside her. The first had been too shy to do anything more than whisper his name; the second had been odd ('Lady, your eyes are as green as two smooth toads'), and the third, heir to an olive region in Yscalin, had not even managed to meet her gaze.

This one was Magnaust Vatten, elder son of the Steward of Mentendon. His eyes were steely grey, and his white face was a picture of disdain. Where the Inysh were a blaze of autumn reds and golds, he wore sealskin and black tooled leather, defiant in his severity. He drew wary looks from all over the hall, this son of the man they had once called the Sea King.

Glorian, daughter of a real king, was unimpressed. Magnaust had done little but complain while he sawed his way through a dish of baked swan, and had yet to let her get more than a word in edgeways.

At least she had been spared from dancing. She could never get the timings quite right, though she loved the spectacle. Fifty people were performing the zehanto, a circle dance from Yscalin.

'And of course,' her ostensible suitor continued, 'the Ments might not openly speak ill of us – cowards, all – but I've no doubt they wag their forked tongues in private.'

'Terrible,' Glorian said absently.

'We pour our wealth into their cities. We defend them from free raiders. We showed them the way to Halgalant itself, yet they glower as if they would see us all shipwrecked.'

They both spoke in what was called High Hróthi – the language as it was spoken in Eldyng, rather than the dialect that had blossomed in Mentendon. Glorian wondered if he even spoke Mentish. Wanting very much to be elsewhere, she looked back at the zehanto.

Florell spun with consummate grace, the skirts of her russet gown swirling. She joined hands with Arpa Nerafriss, who looked quite taken with her, while Helisent danced with Sylda Yelarigas, the future Countess of Vazuva, who was visiting from Yscalin.

'Looters, they call us. Sea wolves,' Magnaust Vatten sneered. 'When I rule, I will root out the ingrates and burn them alive. They'll like that. The Nameless One rose from their vile mountain, after all.'

'Oh, indeed,' Glorian said, even more distracted, for the dance had come to an end, and applause thundered. To her right, her suitor gave a raw cough. 'Are you well, my lord?'

He was turning puce. She was wondering if she ought to slap him on the back when he reached into his mouth and dug out a bone. He threw it down on his plate in disgust.

'Your Grace,' the Decreer called in her sonorous voice, ending any further opportunity for conversation, 'among our company is a consort of the finest musicians of Carmentum.' At her gesture, they stepped forward and bowed. 'They would be pleased to play the thinsana, a dance of Gulthaga, for your daughter's commendation.'

'We would be honoured if you would join us in friendship,' Arpa said, standing beside her. 'And if the thinsana is strange to you, it would be my pleasure to teach you its steps.'

Glorian considered this. The offer could be honest, or a golden opportunity to make the Queen of Inys look a fool. If the dance was difficult, her mother might stumble in public. It could even be perceived as an insult, to expect a monarch to be schooled before her court.

It was also difficult for her to refuse without appearing pettish or aloof. All of this made Glorian nervous.

To her surprise, however, Queen Sabran was smiling again, faintly. She glanced towards the gallery, which had filled with figures. The harpist gave a signal.

'It is a very generous offer, Decreer,' Queen Sabran said, 'and it pains me to decline on this occasion. I have heard of the splendour of the thinsana.' She placed her hands on the arms of her seat. 'Regrettably, I have saved the next dance for my companion.'

For a moment, Glorian thought she had misheard, or that her mother had drunk more wine than her steady voice implied – until the clean note of a horn blasted out, the Inysh musicians struck up a welcome, and in poured a procession, bearing the crest of the House of Hraustr.

Queen Sabran rose as the King of Hróth appeared like a giant of old in the doorway.

'Father,' Glorian breathed in disbelief.

Happiness welled in her chest as gasps and chatter swept across the hall and everyone rose to bow. The Carmenti party exchanged unreadable glances before doing the same.

'My king,' Queen Sabran said, warm and clear. She descended to the floor and held out a hand. King Bardholt went to one knee before her.

'My queen,' he said in his thick Inysh. 'I believe I have this dance.'

'I believe you do.'

King Bardholt brought her knuckles to his lips. Glorian grinned as he turned to smile at her, so wide his hazel eyes crinkled. He had come. In the dark half of the year, he had come.

He strode to the high table and extended a hand for hers. Once she had given it, he bowed low, as though she, too, were a Queen of Inys.

'Daughter,' he said, and raised a fist to his chest. 'For this, your commendation, I have crossed the sea.'

The hall erupted into cheers and applause. Glorian threw her good arm around him, her heart floating up to the ceiling, her pain and the Vatten boy quite forgotten.

8

South

Ninuru cut through sheaves of sunlight, muscle pitching beneath fur. In the saddle, Tunuva ducked to avoid a branch. Hidat Janudin rode not far behind.

Ahead, a white-tailed longhorn smashed through the undergrowth. Its hooves were made for this wet ground, but an ichneumon could outrun anything.

The Lasian Basin could not be mapped, or so it was whispered throughout the South. Even the most gifted poets had never been able to capture the vastness of the forest, for none had laid eyes on its depths: its endless trees, their unthinkable heights, the layers built up over thousands of centuries.

Nothing grew alone. Nothing was bare. Moss enrobed the roots; the trunks wore vines. It was thick with the memory of its former selves.

No one had charted the Lasian Basin, but Tunuva knew her way.

Ninuru sprang off a fallen tree and landed in front of their quarry with a growl. Above, Esbar appeared on an arching root, enthroned on Jeda, who let out a fearsome roar. Frightened and snorting, the longhorn thundered off again, its sides lathered with sweat.

'The glade,' Esbar shouted. Tunuva was already chasing their prey.

The ichneumons broke into a glade matted with moss. Sunlight blazed through breaks in the canopy. Not far ahead, the trees drew close as lovers. Tunuva swung her bow from her back and notched an arrow to the string. Though her magic burned low, her eyesight was as sharp as ever. The arrow whipped across the clearing, the longhorn stumbled, and she pulled back, letting Hidat ride in front.

Jeda rushed past them both. Tunuva swallowed her shout – Esbar was already too far ahead. Hidat slowed, and they both watched as Esbar sprang off Jeda. A flash of steel, a huffing, and the beast collapsed into the grass. Jeda gripped its neck between her teeth.

Tunuva rode towards them, reaching the longhorn just as it slumped, the moss drinking its blood. Jeda let go of it and growled. Her fur was sleek black, and she had the amber eyes of most ichneumons, the pupils lying fessways.

'A good hunt.' Esbar rose and wiped her blade clean. 'Fortunate it brought us here – the men tell me we're low on moss. Small wonder, since I seem to be bleeding for three.'

'I'll gather some.' Hidat slid out of the saddle. Beads tapped at the ends of her braids. 'Does it hurt, Dartun?'

'No,' her sandy ichneumon said. The longhorn had gored his flank. 'Ichneumons do not lose to slow cattle.'

Jeda and Ninuru rumbled their agreement. Tunuva smiled and patted Ninuru, while Hidat tore up a wad of moss and pressed it to the wound, making Dartun knead his paws in contentment.

'Hidat,' Tunuva said, 'are you all right?'

'Fine. Dartun took the brunt of it.'

'I don't mean the hunt.' Tunuva touched her shoulder. She had mentored Hidat for several years, and knew when something was wrong. 'You removed the rope from the tree.'

Hidat glanced at her. Even when she was young, she had always been a woman anchored in herself, difficult to rattle. Now her dark eyes held a candid doubt.

'You are among the wisest of us, Tuva,' she said. 'Is it foolish to fear that it might never gift its fruit to me again?'

'It makes Siyu twice the fool,' Esbar muttered, 'for planting that thought in your mind.' She sheathed her hunting knife. 'It was good of you to do it, Hidat. I'll ensure Siyu makes amends.'

'Peace. It's done.' Hidat gave Dartun a reassuring stroke. 'Come, then, pup. Time for a drink.'

Leaving Ninuru to guard their kill, they walked until the trees thinned again, giving way to the River Minara. In this part of the Lasian Basin, it was almost two leagues wide.

Sunlight flashed off the rushing golden waters. While Hidat led her ichneumon to drink, Esbar shed her riding coat and wrung the blood from its sleeves.

'You have that look in your eye,' she said to Tunuva. 'Is it what I said about Siyu?'

Tunuva sat on a fallen tree and worked off her boots. 'No. I only hoped you would let Hidat kill the longhorn,' she said, dipping her feet into the shallows. 'It might have restored her confidence, to remember her skill.'

Esbar looked at her face for a time, then said, 'A kind thought.' She spread her coat on a rock before she joined Tunuva. 'Forgive me. You know how I relish the chase.'

'Which is why you're munguna.' Tunuva patted her knee. 'There's nothing to forgive.'

Esbar clasped their fingers. Tunuva traced the sunspots on the back of her hand. Both their hands had changed over the years: the knuckles thicker, the veins bolder.

'Tuva,' Hidat called. 'I nearly forgot – the Prioress wishes to speak to you.' She was up to her knees in the water. 'Go to her now, if you like. We can handle the longhorn, can't we, Ez?'

'I should think so.' Esbar glanced at Tunuva, lowering her voice. 'If this is about Siyu—'

'I will tell you.'

Tunuva kissed her and stood. Esbar tipped her face into the sunlight.

The shade of the forest folded back over Tunuva. Boots in hand, she retraced her steps to the glade, her bare feet making little sound. For some, the tree granted both the sacred flame and the silence of shadow.

She rode Ninuru back to the Priory, past its hidden wardings. Each time she crossed one, the mage who cast it sensed her coming.

The entrance lay between the thick and spreading roots of a giant fig tree, impossible to find by chance. She slid into the tunnel and walked until the earth rusted and gave way to smooth tiles. Once they reached her sunroom, Ninuru slunk off to doze on the balcony while Tunuva changed.

Saghul took her meals in her own sunroom, the Bridal Chamber. Tunuva found her picking at a platter of steaming rice, wood-smoked goat, and prawns simmered with leaves and groundnut butter.

The Wail of Galian thundered just beyond her balcony. The waterfall poured into the Vale of Blood, becoming a branch of the Lower Minara, which ran southwest to join the sea.

'Prioress,' Tunuva said, 'may I join you?'

'Tunuva Melim.' Saghul waved her into a seat. 'Sit. Eat. You must be famished.' Tunuva washed her hands in the basin before she served herself. 'Was your hunt successful?'

'A longhorn buck. It should yield fine meat.' Tunuva used the butter to roll a ball of rice. 'Hidat said you wanted to speak to me.'

'Indeed. I have no intention of staying awake longer than it takes me to finish this repast, so I shall be quick.' Saghul swallowed. 'I have considered your proposal that Siyu uq-Nāra be sent into the world.'

'I thought you had already come to a decision on that front, Prioress.'

'I merely voiced a thought on sun wine.' Saghul drank a little. 'Siyu will go to the court of Nzene. She will be an initiate.' She speared a prawn at the end of her knife. 'Gashan can instruct and counsel her.'

Tunuva hardly dared believe it.

'Prioress,' she said, relieved beyond measure, 'thank you. Siyu will make you proud.'

'Do you know why I chose Esbar as my successor?'

'Because she commands respect from the Priory. Because she is decisive, inspiring, high-minded. Because she is a great mage.'

Saghul grunted. 'All of those things, to be sure.' She chewed the prawn. 'But most of all, it was because of your influence on her. Your calming guidance. Your reason. When I am dead, yours may be the only counsel she will truly heed.'

'Saghul, she loves this family. She will listen to everyone.'

'Did Esbar slaughter the longhorn today, or did she let troubled Hidat strike the blow?'

Tunuva dropped her gaze.

'The former,' she said.

'A Prioress must do more than listen. She must not only look, but see,' Saghul said. 'If all of us are flames, Esbar is the flame at the head of an arrow. So long as she found her mark, she would miss the world catching fire in her wake. That unswerving nature is both her great strength and her weakness.' She laid down her knife. 'You saw what Hidat needed, even if she never told you. You did the same for Siyu, as you always have. You are the flame that warms, Tunuva Melim. The flame that seals a wound.'

Tunuva ate the rice ball she had just made. Every private talk she had with Saghul made her feel strange – unsettled and consoled at the same time.

'You honour me, Prioress,' she said. 'May I visit Siyu, to tell her of her posting?'

'You may. I cannot let her out at once – I will not encourage further desecrations – but as soon as she has served her punishment, we shall hold her kindling.' Saghul raised her eyebrows. 'Your own siden burns low, tomb keeper. Go to the valley this night, and be satisfied.'

****

At sundown, she took the thousand steps down to the valley floor. The night was cool. A few of the men talked and chuckled together, sharing a jar of wine by the river. Seeing Tunuva, they made themselves scarce.

Every sister ate alone – except, of course, for the first time, when she ate before her family. Tunuva had worn the white cloak of an initiate that day. With every step towards the tree, she had feared she was unworthy, that it might withhold its fruit from her.

Decades later, she was still an initiate – ready to fight, but never called. There were no other ranks, for there was nothing yet to slay.

She let her cloak fall and knelt between two of the roots. The oranges flickered like candles on the boughs. One tumbled with a flutter of petals, straight into her waiting hands. Light shone through its rind, stemming from the heart in its core.

Siyāti uq-Nāra had believed the whole fruit should be eaten, to ensure that no magic was lost. Later Prioresses had revised the rule, since one bite seemed to be enough. For her part, Tunuva removed the peel first, setting it aside to bury.

The orange broke under her teeth. Siden poured forth like molten sunlight – magic of the deepest earth, enriching her with its power again. She let herself be set on fire.

For a time, she was an impossible candle, her wick renewing as it burned. It was night by the time the magic settled. She lay still, aware of every wingbeat and blade of grass, the heavy scent of blossoms that had thickened almost to a taste. The stars gleamed sharp as arrow points, and all the world thrummed in her skin.

She glanced down to see a glow in her fingertips. That golden light would fade; so would the heavy calm. Her skin would be tender and feverish by morning. She would be hungry: for food, for touch.

Before all that could strike, she rose, and pressed her hot brow to the tree in gratitude.

****

In the initiates' quarters, Imsurin was singing one of the younger girls to sleep in his deep, soothing tones. Tunuva waited in the doorway until he noticed her.

'Imin,' she said in an undertone. 'The Prioress has allowed me to visit Siyu.'

He drew a blanket over the child. 'Why?'

'To tell her she is to be kindled.'

His mouth twitched. She could tell he was pleased, but he took all good news with a pinch of reserve.

'It's past time,' he said. 'Though I wish it had not taken this to move the Prioress.' He blew out the nearest lamp. 'Siyu has not been feeling well. She will be pleased to see you.'

'What troubles her?'

'I suspect a spindle wasp. If she doesn't improve, I will consult Denag.'

Tunuva nodded. It was rare for initiates to fall ill, but for now, Siyu was still a postulant.

The sting of the spindle wasp brought on a deep exhaustion. For that reason, Tunuva expected to find Siyu asleep. Instead, she was on her knees by the stove, retching over a pot.

Tunuva shut the door and crouched next to her, drawing back her long hair while she shuddered. Once Siyu had emptied her stomach, she sat back to catch her breath, and Tunuva brought her a cup of water, brushing a moth from the jug. Siyu drank thirstily.

'What is it, sunray?' Tunuva felt her brow. It was cool. 'Is it your bleeding pains again?'

'No.' Siyu wiped her mouth. 'I have not bled for ... some time.'

Tunuva frowned. As Siyu met her gaze and swallowed, all the warmth that had just filled her seemed to disappear.

'Siyu,' she said faintly. 'How long?'

Siyu glanced at the door and pressed a hand to her belly. 'I've missed two bleeds,' she said. 'Promise not to tell the Prioress. Swear it on the Mother, Tuva.'

Tunuva could hardly speak, let alone swear an oath.

'Siyu,' she finally managed, 'you know, you *know* the rules on childbearing. You're too young, and not yet kindled. What were you thinking?' When Siyu started to breathe faster, she collected herself. 'We can solve this, but I must know. Who was it?'

Siyu looked at her, fear dawning in her eyes.

'He isn't from the Priory,' she whispered. 'He is from outside.'

9

East

Steel chipped into ancient rock. Dumai gave her ice sickle a tug, ensuring it was fixed in place. She bent her right leg, her muscles burning with exertion, and drove the spiked toe of her boot into the snow. Not too far below her, she could hear the same *tap-crunch* from Kanifa.

They were more than halfway up the second peak of Mount Ipyeda. The only way to reach its summit was to climb, and only those who looked after the Queen Bell ever tried it.

Kanifa had been its caretaker for years. Unlike Dumai, he had been born on the ground. His parents had brought him to the temple when he was thirteen, hoping to save him from the wildfires in their province, and the Grand Empress had taken him in, given the convenient timing. The bellkeeper was growing old, and there was need of a successor.

For years, Dumai had watched Kanifa learn the way. It had fascinated her to see him on the middle peak, which seemed, to her, to scrape the sky. Finally, he had noticed her looking. *I want to go up there*, she had said. *Mother calls me her kite. I promise I'm strong.*

She had been only twelve years old, but Kanifa had believed her.

In secret, he had crafted her a pair of ice sickles. She had worked out how to keep her grip firm with her shortened fingers; how to secure her tool in such a way that she could drive its blade with her wrist, if needed. Then he had started imparting his knowledge.

The day Unora caught them, she had been too shaken to speak.

Mother, Dumai had entreated her, *before you stop me, watch us. Look.*

Unora had granted her that. Only when she had truly looked, and seen how they were climbing – tied to one another with a length of braided rope – had she allowed Dumai to continue.

I see you are set on this, but be careful, Dumai. You could be hurt.

So could Kanifa, but not any more. Now I can catch him if he falls.

Dumai had never shared the fear her mother had betrayed that day. No sweat dampened her palms. No wings swooped in her stomach. Descending could be hard, but she always had the comfort of the rope around her waist.

It's still a risk, Kanifa had warned her the first time, his fingers working up a tight and complex knot. *We might be able to stop each other falling – or we could pull each other down.*

So be it. If we fall, we fall together.

Now she steadied her boot on a fist of ice, tightened her grip, and looked east. From here, she could see all the way across the Rayonti Basin, the palace a smudge in the distance.

As she hung there to catch her breath, she wondered if the saltwalker had reached the city alive. The villagers had sent word that he had passed through, staying only long enough to eat and warm his feet and hands, looking as if a ghost was behind him.

Not a ghost. Just Unora. Dumai needed to understand why her mother – her wary, footsure mother – had tried to follow him at night, without so much as a hood to protect herself.

As the sun rose, they made it to the top, where the Queen Bell hung in a stout open tower. Most prayer bells had been cast from bronze in the Kuposa foundries on Muysima, but this giant was a rare wonder of ironwork. Its heavy wooden striker waited to be swung.

There was thought to be no larger or older bell in Seiiki, yet it bore no mark to reveal who had cast it. Its shoulder was engraved with stars. The templefolk had always cared for it – washed and oiled it, scoured the rust off, dried it after the worst storms. Only an inscription on the waist gave any clue as to its purpose:

TO HOLD THE RISEN FIRE AT BAY

UNTIL THE NIGHT DESCENDS

It was forbidden to sound the bell, except in circumstances known only to the Supreme Officiant. Death was the punishment – a rare thing in Seiiki, where most crimes were answered with exile.

Dumai sat in the tower to rest. Kanifa offered his flask to her before drinking.

'I thought you might not want to climb today, with Unora as she is,' he said.

'Osipa is with her.' Dumai gazed at the distant city, strands of hair lashing free of her hood. 'The chores must still be done.'

'It was madness for the saltwalker to leave during the night.'

'And madness for her to have followed him,' Dumai said, exasperated. 'Imagine if I had done that, Kan. Mother would be furious, and rightly so. How could she forget our rules, after all her years here?' She held up her right hand, snug in its glove. 'After this?'

The corners of his mouth puckered. He had nicked his jaw while shaving, leaving a small cut.

'She'll explain,' was all he could say.

'I hope so.'

They unpacked their tools and set up a stove, melting snow into a pot. Once they had warmed themselves, drunk some water, and finished the broth they had brought, they began.

Dumai cleaned inside the bell, chanting into its cavernous mouth. She always felt a sense of life from the dark iron – as if the bell was awake, trying its best to sing with her. Kanifa oiled the striker and tightened the yoke. They shinned up a rope to the rafters, where they searched for any trace of rot, filled a crack, and checked the joinery held strong.

Once they were satisfied, they sat at the very edge of the peak, watching the sun engolden Antuma – a city in another world, which would only ever glance off theirs, like rain blown from a roof.

****

Unora was still asleep when Dumai placed a tray of fresh embers beside her. For the first time in days, she was unveiled, so Dumai could see her freckled brown cheeks and sharp chin, the shadows inked under her eyes, and a crushed plum of a bruise on her temple.

There was very little in the room. Unora had brought nothing with her from her fishing village – nothing but Dumai, tucked up in her womb. The rest of their family was gone, she said, lost to a violent storm.

We took from the sea. The sea claimed its due.

A tiny sound escaped her now. 'Mother.' Dumai covered one of her hands. 'Can you hear me?'

Unora blinked at her. 'Dumai.'

'Why were you in the snow?' Dumai said, smoothing her short hair. 'You could have frozen.'

'I know.' Unora sighed. 'Osipa said you brought me inside. Thank you.' She gave her bruise a gentle press, testing its depth. 'I must have stumbled.'

'But why would you go out in the dark, without anything to keep you warm?'

'I was foolish.' She sounded tired. 'I panicked, Dumai. I remembered the storm that froze your fingers, how many died on the mountain that night. I didn't want to lose anyone else.'

'There are rules for survival,' Dumai said, her voice straining. 'You taught me that.'

'I know.' Unora drew her breath. 'Dumai, how would you feel if we moved to a different temple?'

Dumai frowned. 'What?'

'The South Mountains have beautiful temples. Or we could go west, to the coast,' Unora said, almost feverishly. 'Would you not like that, my kite, to swim in the sea – to see more of the world?'

'Our home is enough.' Dumai was unnerved. 'Mama, you're tired and hurt. You don't mean this.'

She stopped when Kanifa slid the door open, sweat on his brow. 'The Kuposa lady is gone.'

Unora stared at him, her face bloodless. 'She, too?' She sat up with trembling arms. 'When did she leave?'

'Tirotu went to wake them at sunrise and found their footprints. I came as soon as—'

'Stop her,' Unora barked, making Dumai flinch in surprise. 'Follow their tracks.' When Kanifa and Dumai exchanged a bewildered look, she spoke through clenched teeth: 'Kanifa, you can overtake her. You're faster and stronger than any of the others. No matter what her protests, bring that woman back. Do not let her reach Antuma.'

With little choice, Kanifa left. Dumai made to follow him, but her mother caught her arm, steel in her fingers.

'Kanifa will manage,' she said, quieter. 'You stay here with me, Dumai.'

****

95

By evening, Kanifa had not returned, but Dumai knew he would have taken shelter in the mountain village. He would never be fool enough to try to climb back up the steps in darkness.

While she waited, she looked after her mother, bringing her meals and icing her ankle. Unora moved little and said less. Each time the wind shook the shutters, or the temple gave one of its placid creaks, her eyes would snap open, her gaze darting to the corridor.

After a time, she dozed off, her forehead crinkled even in sleep. When Tirotu came with hot wine, Dumai whispered, 'Will you send word to the village tomorrow, to see if Kanifa arrived?'

'Of course,' they said. 'I'm sure he's fine, Dumai. Don't worry.'

'I'll try.'

Tirotu slid the door shut, and Dumai lay close to her mother, wondering why Unora would ever want to bring a guest back to the temple by force – and how she meant to keep her there.

****

The next day broke like ice, cold and clear. As Dumai walked to the sky platform, she noticed the snow had shallowed, and the frozen spines on the eaves were dripping. Strange in the darker half of the year.

She watched the slopes for a long time. At the sight of the tiny figure in the snow, the tension in her chest finally eased. Kanifa was on his way.

He was also alone.

By the time Dumai padded upstairs, Unora had woken. 'Dumai,' she said, 'I'd like to bathe today.' When she tried to put weight on her ankle, she grimaced. 'Are they back?'

She would worry if she knew. 'Not yet.' Dumai slipped an arm around her. 'Lean on me, Mama.'

They made their laboured way outside. At the edge of the hot spring, Unora stopped, frowning deeper lines into her brow. Dumai helped her shed her robe and step into the pool.

'Thank you,' Unora murmured. 'I'm sorry I am … not myself. My mind is full.'

'Clouds are often full. And then it rains.' Dumai kissed the top of her head. 'Call when you want to get out.'

While Unora sank into the heat, Dumai wandered back to the sky platform, arms folded against the wind. Below, the figure had vanished. Kanifa was on the steps that led up the first peak.

A sharp cry pierced the quiet. Dumai spun towards it. Steam was fuming from the spring – too much, a pot churning in fury.

The water bubbled and spat. As Dumai broke into a run, Unora crawled from the billows, wet and flushed, groaning in agony. Dumai pulled her away from the burning spray and the steam that scalded her face.

'Mother,' she gasped. She tore off her own coat and wrapped it around Unora. 'Hush, hush. I have you.'

Unora trembled with shock. Dumai took in her burnt skin, livid red below the waist. 'It has ... boiled once before,' Unora said, chest heaving. 'Centuries ago. But never since.'

They both stared at the seething water.

'We need to cool the burns.' Dumai spoke more to herself than her mother, trying in vain to steady her breathing. 'The ice pool. Hurry.'

Unora obeyed, walking on her parboiled legs, knowing they had to act. As they stumbled through the snow, all Dumai could think, through the clamour in her head, was that nothing had been quite right in her world since Lady Nikeya had come to the mountain.

She helped her mother sit beside the ice pool. 'Too cold,' Unora managed. 'We must warm the water a little.'

Dumai ran for a pot and tinder. She dug out a firepit beside the water and struck her kindling ablaze, hands sure even in her fear. While the flames crackled, she filled the pot from the pool, and once it had warmed enough to be tolerable, she carried it to Unora.

'Hold still,' she said.

She tipped some of the water over the enraged flesh. Unora seized, her neck cording.

'Dumai?'

Her head snapped up. Kanifa stood in the snow, staring at them both – Unora, dazed and shaken, and Dumai, soaking her. His cheeks were ruddy from the climb, strands of hair stuck to them. Dumai had never known anyone to scale the stepway so quickly.

He must have run.

'What happened?' he asked, kneeling beside them. 'Unora—'

'The spring, it—' Dumai stopped when she saw his face. 'What is it?'

Kanifa swallowed. 'We have to prepare,' he said, looking between them. Unora stared unblinking at him, lips aquiver. 'Emperor Jorodu is coming here. He's coming here now.'

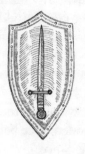

IO

West

Glorian spent every moment she could with her father, basking in his attention. He always made time for her in the mornings, when they broke their fast together on his balcony, and at supper, she had a place of honour by his side. She was so overjoyed she feared she might burst.

As the days passed, the guests from her commendation returned to their own provinces and countries. The Carmenti were last to go. On their final day at court, Queen Sabran invited them to dine once more with the royal family and the Virtues Council.

The Old Hall was dim at midday, shuttered against the sun. Glorian worked her way through a spiced beef pie while her father told her of his latest adventures. Like most Hróthi, he was a remarkable story-teller. She had yearned for his life for the whole of her own – the winter swims, the tests of strength, the late hunts beneath the glow of the sky lights.

He still attacked his food like a starved bear. While they talked, he tore through hocks of salted ham and goose legs dripping fat and honey, making sure her plate was always piled high, too. Ever since she was small, he had taught her that a warrior should eat well.

'Tell me about your suitors,' he said in his thick Inysh. 'Did Magnaust Vatten impress?'

Glorian gave him a look. 'Which one was he?'

Her father boomed a laugh. 'Uninspiring gallants, then.' He took a great swallow from his goblet. 'The elder son of Heryon Vattenvarg. I'm told he is well-read and devout, with fine grey eyes.' When Glorian snorted, he leaned in close to her. 'Ah. I see I must sharpen my axe.' She grinned. 'Tell me, what offence did he commit?'

'Had I sat a mommet in my place, I doubt he would have noticed,' Glorian said. That made him frown. 'And he seems to have no affection for Mentendon, the country he will rule.'

Bardholt grunted. 'Common among the Vatten. They were made to sack cities, not rule them.' He drained his cup. 'They grow too proud in Brygstad. He should have paid you more respect.'

Magnaust had already gone back to his father. Glorian wondered if he had given her a second thought. Hopefully not.

'Come,' Bardholt said, nudging her. She found a smile. 'Let us drink to you, daughter.' He beckoned his cupbearer, and the young man stepped forward to fill his goblet. 'Glorian, this is Wulfert Glenn. I thought it was time he came back to visit his homeland.'

'Lady,' the cupbearer said, and bowed with perfect form. 'An honour.'

Glorian recognised that voice. The man she had encountered in the gallery. Like all the retainers who protected her father, he wore a mail shirt under a leather surcoat, boots that reached his knees, and a bone-handled sax on his belt.

Now the light was better, she took the measure of him. Thick hair fell in curls so dark as to be almost black. He wore it short for a housecarl, only to his nape. His eyes were large and just as dark, his skin a warm golden brown.

He was not quite as tall as her father – no one was – but he was taller than Glorian, which was no small feat. She and her mother towered over almost everyone at court.

'Master Glenn,' she said, wondering why his face gave her pause. 'Good day. Whereabouts in Inys are you from?'

Too late, she remembered not to ask questions. A queen only made statements. Then again, she was not yet a queen.

'The Lakes, my lady,' he said. 'I'm the younger son of the Barons Glenn of Langarth.'

'And have you been knighted?'

'No, Highness.'

A younger son without the spurs. A peculiar choice for a cupbearer. 'He will be. I am confident of that,' King Bardholt said, with a proud smile. 'Wulf has greatness in his future.'

The odd sense of familiarity rose. Wulfert Glenn regarded her, a small crease in his brow.

'I wondered if you'd remember.' King Bardholt gave a hearty chuckle. 'You were playmates as children. Whenever I visited Inys, the two of you would chase one another through the gardens and orchards, soak each other in the fountains, all sorts of mischief to vex your minders.'

The cupbearer had been schooled in restraint, but his eyes told Glorian he remembered, and now so did she. Suddenly he was a touch shorter, with pimples and a breaking voice.

'Of course,' he said. 'Your Highness.'

Glorian strained her memory, finding impressions, pressed like a scent into fabric, like a seal into wax: the flower maze in bloom, the taste of plums, the cloying haze of the high summer.

Queen Sabran finally lured her consort into conversation with the Virtues Council. Wulfert Glenn swithered, staying near Glorian. She offered him a reassuring smile.

'So,' she said, so only he could hear, 'who was the mysterious woman in the gallery?'

He gave her father a cautious look, but the king was already enmeshed in an intense discussion. Keeping his voice low, he said, 'Truly, my lady, we weren't trysting.'

'It's all right. I'm just curious.'

'She's the head of my lith. Regny of Askrdal, niece of Skiri the Condoler.'

'Skiri Longstride,' Glorian said, intrigued. 'Her murder began the War of Twelve Shields.'

'Aye.' Gaining confidence, he filled her goblet. 'One of her brothers was the only surviving member of the clan. He died a few years ago, so Regny – his daughter – is already Chieftain of Askrdal.'

'She must be formidable, with such a heritage.'

The corners of his mouth lifted. 'She is.' He wiped the pitcher with a cloth. 'King Bardholt sent us to watch over the feast, so he knew when he could make his entrance.'

'I see.' Glorian hesitated. 'Do you really remember me, Master Glenn, or were you being courteous?'

His gaze fastened on hers. 'Yes,' he said. 'I remember.'

'I didn't at all, at first. You look quite different.' Glorian used her good hand to pick up the goblet, now heavy with sweet black mead. 'May I ask how old you are now?'

'Eighteen, or thereabouts, I think.'

'Surely you know for certain.'

'Not quite. A long story, Your Highness.'

'I'd like to hear it. Tomorrow, perhaps?'

'Surely Her Highness has a great deal more to do than speak with a humble retainer.'

'Her Highness has little to do but watch the trees grow, since her arm is in two pieces.'

'Ah. I wish you swift healing. I broke my leg as a boy.'

'Not when we were having forgettable chases through the grounds of Glowan Castle, I trust.'

'No. I was fool enough to walk on the ice without my cleats. A mistake I never made again.' He returned her smile. 'Kind as your invitation is, I leave for the Lakes at dawn. I've not seen my family since the last time I was here.'

'Of course. Safe travels to you, Master Glenn.'

With a bow, he retreated. Glorian finished her sweet curds and propped her head on her knuckles.

Temperance was not a virtue her father had ever cultivated. He drank twice as much as he ate. By the time the final course arrived, his face had flushed red as raw mutton.

'Tell me, Numun of Carmentum,' he called in his stentorian voice, 'how should one address a person of your ... standing?'

Across the Old Hall, conversations tapered away.

'*Decreer* will suffice, Your Grace,' Numun said. Today she wore an elegant cream robe, pinned with a brooch at her shoulder. 'My principal duty is to decree the will of the Carmenti.'

'And what is it that these people know of politics, that they decide who steers a realm, and how they steer it?' Bardholt said. 'My grandfather was a seafarer, Decreer. He would not have let just anyone choose the captains of his ships, for they knew nothing of the sea.'

'We officials trust those who elect us,' Numun explained, 'because we are confident they understand the world in which they live. Carmentum has several halls of knowledge, dedicated to rigorous study and debate, inspired by those in Kumenga and Bardant.'

'All this without the guiding hand of the Saint.'

'The Carmenti are free to follow any religion, but saints and gods do not govern us.'

Glorian glanced at her mother, who had been silent throughout this exchange. As she drank from her goblet of wine, Glorian remembered one of her early lessons in temperance. *A queen should learn the ways of watching. Like a falcon, she waits for her moment to strike. She also knows when she need not strike at all – when her shadow, her presence, is more than enough.*

'Monarchs do not govern you, either. It seems we are useless relics to you,' King Bardholt said, with a terrifying smile, 'and yet here you are, asking for trade in the court of a queen.'

'We respect other ways, and the people of Virtudom,' the Decreer said, still calm, 'but we ourselves do not see blood as high or low. It is commitment and talent that matters – a belief I thought you of all people would share, King Bardholt.'

A chill stole over the benches.

'Me,' he said, his expression fixed. 'Of all people.'

If he had spoken to Glorian that way, she would simply have sailed west and never returned, but the Decreer decided to give the bear another poke: 'You were born to a bone carver, not a king. Surely you must agree that blood is of no true importance.'

No one dared speak. King Bardholt was holding his goblet so hard that Glorian feared it might snap in his grasp.

A clear voice disturbed the stillness. 'We must both disagree on that, Decreer.'

Heads turned. Queen Sabran put down her own cup, its slight clink like a thunderclap.

'You see, here in Virtudom, we know the House of Berethnet is the chain upon the Nameless One. King Bardholt has long seen this truth.' She covered his hand with hers. 'It is my blood – the Saint's blood – that chains the Beast of the Mountain. As a Southerner, you understand the violence *he* would unleash if that blood were no longer in the world.'

Glorian looked at her parents' interlocked hands. The queen's fingertips were white.

She had waited for the trap to form, and then she had sprung it. With no choice but to concede or risk the room's anger, Numun inclined her head and returned to her meal.

Not long after, dinner was over.

With her arm broken, Glorian was bored out of her wits. All she wanted was to be outside, hunting and sparring with her father, for the short time he would be in Inys.

On the day the Carmenti left, she was playing cards with her ladies when a messenger appeared. 'Highness,' he said with a bow, 'Queen Sabran would like you to join her for supper tonight.'

'Thank you,' Glorian said, sinking back into her settle. He retreated. 'I wonder what Mother wants.'

'Perhaps to discuss your suitors,' Julain said.

Glorian bit the inside of her cheek. Helisent caught the look on her face. 'Why don't I fetch us some crispels?' she offered. 'The kitchen made a fresh batch today.'

She left before Glorian could stop her. For once, her belly was in too much of a twist for crispels.

'Jules,' she said, 'do you remember somebody called Wulfert Glenn?'

'Wulf?' Julain said, distracted. 'Yes, of course. You played together as children, we all did.' She slowed. 'Wait. Was that him, at the high table – the handsome cupbearer?'

'Yes. I'd forgotten him.' Glorian glanced at her. 'A housecarl is a curious playmate for a princess.'

'You two were so close. I remember being a little jealous,' Julain admitted. 'When Wulf came to court, no one else could hold your attention, Glorian. You would spend hours with him.'

A strange thing to forget. Glorian gazed at her cards, lost in a soft and sun-drenched memory of running.

****

The Royal Sanctuary at Drouthwick Castle was small, like many in the north of Inys, where the old ways had held strongest before the Saint founded Ascalun. Inside, Glorian fidgeted beside her mother while a sanctarian read from the story of the Saint and the Damsel.

'*And the knight said:*

'*Come, ye wretched, poor, and weary, come behold the wonders I have wrought. Hear the song of victory I bring from red and barren sands. I was born among you. I lived among you. I was among you when the earth roared, and when smoke eclipsed the sun. Then to the dusts of Lasia I rode, and there I slew the Beast of the Mountain. There I won the heart of Cleolind.'*

Her mind drifted back to Wulfert Glenn. Now she stood in the gloom of the sanctuary, she thought she could trace the strand of remembrance. Gilt thread woven through shadow.

'Behold, my dread sword Ascalun, forged of the night that gave me name. Behold, a scale of reddest iron, carved from the breast of the great fiend.

'And the people heard, and, believing in him, gave unto him their love and allegiance.'

Queen Sabran clasped her hands. Her eyes were closed, her lips moving with the reading.

'When her time came, Queen Cleolind bore unto him a daughter, Sabran, she who would rule long and rightwise. But her birth was Cleolind's doom, and as he blessed their only child, the Saint called to his anguished people:

'I tell you, to honour her, my line shall be a line of queens; my realm, a queendom mighty to behold; for she was my strength, the root of my heart, and her memory will live until the end of time itself. I tell you, our house shall be an endless river, a chain long as eternity. I tell you it will hold the wyrm at bay for ever more.'

Glorian looked down at the blue veins of her hand, branching under her skin.

'We call upon the Saint, who sits in Halgalant, to bless his descendants.' The sanctarian closed her book. 'May he bless our good Queen Sabran. May he bless her mother, Marian, Lady of the Inysh. And may he bless our princess, Glorian, whose womb will spring the next fruit of the vine.' Glorian shifted her weight. 'They are the river, the chain, the promise.'

'The river, the chain, the promise,' the congregation echoed. 'May he bless the Queendom of Inys.'

'Go,' the sanctarian called, 'and live in virtue.'

Queen Sabran made the sign of the sword. She was first to leave, flanked by her ladies.

At dusk, Glorian rejoined her in the royal solar, the Dearn Chamber. It was one of the few rooms in the castle with glass in its windows, thick forest glass with a green tinge. Her mother sat in the glow of a fire, with the Great Seal of Inys on the table in front of her.

'Glorian,' she said.

'Good evening, Mother.'

Beside her was Lord Robart Eller, the Duke of Generosity, as well-presented as always. 'Princess,' he greeted Glorian. 'How good to see you. Forgive me, but I had a matter of some import to examine with Her Grace. Our discussion went on longer than we expected.'

'It's quite all right, Lord Robart. The gold brooch you sent for my commendation is splendid,' Glorian said, remembering her manners. 'I have not seen one quite like it before.'

'Believe it or not, it was dug up from a field, likely buried there by Hróthi raiders,' Lord Robart said, raising her curiosity. 'Apparently its treasures originate from Fellsgerd. I thought the brooch would make a fine gift for the Princess of Hróth, so I asked a goldsmith to restore it to its former glory. I am glad you liked it.'

'Thank you.'

'Here, Robart.' Queen Sabran handed him the document. 'I will see you on the morrow.'

'Your Grace.'

He bowed to them both and made himself scarce, leaving Glorian alone with her mother, who was already writing again.

'Sit with me, please, Glorian.'

Glorian took the chair at the other end of the table.

'Your father tells me you found your suitors unimpressive,' Queen Sabran said. 'Is that so?'

'I did not take a ... special liking to any of them.'

'I hear Magnaust Vatten caused you particular affront.' She did not look up from her letter. 'You will agree, however, that no one can be judged by such a short-lived meeting.'

They grow too proud in Brygstad. Glorian lifted her chin. *He should have paid you more respect.*

'I took the measure of his person, Mother,' she said. 'He struck me as selfish and unkind.'

'Your father struck me as a cruel brute when he first came to Inys, wearing a crown of shattered bone.'

Queen Sabran dripped red wax on the letter and pressed her seal into it. She slid it closer to the fire to help it dry.

'Since the Vatten are Hróthi, they are your father's subjects,' she said, steepling her fingers on the table. 'Officially, they are only his stewards, governing Mentendon on his behalf.'

'Yes.'

'But you must have wondered why Heryon Vattenvarg knelt to your father in the first place. The man had already seized a realm of his own, after all. He could have defied his rightful king.'

'He could not stand against the Chainmail of Virtudom,' Glorian said. 'No one could.'

'No. But to ensure a lasting peace between Hróth and Mentendon, it was agreed that your cousin, Einlek Óthling, would be betrothed to Brenna Vatten, Heryon's only daughter.'

The fire was too hot.

'Your father did not just come here for your commendation. He also brought the sad tidings that Brenna is dead,' Queen Sabran informed her. 'She was to marry Einlek in the spring.'

'May the Saint receive her in Halgalant.'

'By his mercy.' Queen Sabran made the sign of the sword. 'Heryon has two other children – Magnaust, the firstborn, and Haynrick, who is only two. Since Einlek needs an heir of the body, he cannot wed Magnaust, who could not provide him with one.'

Glorian came to the miserable realisation: 'You want me to marry Magnaust.'

'I would sooner wed you to an Yscal – it has been too long since we showed our oldest friends our favour. But Heryon Vattenvarg is a proud man who grows prickly with age. With the Carmenti speaking against monarchy, we can risk no internal tension among the faithful. Your betrothal will appease Heryon and keep the Chainmail of Virtudom strong.'

A long silence. Glorian thought of Magnaust Vatten – that sneering face, a voice soaked in contempt.

'Why give me the impression of choice?' she heard herself ask. 'Why not just tell me it would be him?'

'Glorian, you are not a child any longer. I will not have you sulking over this,' Queen Sabran said coolly. 'Magnaust will one day be Steward of Mentendon. You will not have to spend a great deal of time with him, if he displeases you. All you require of him is a child.'

'Perhaps I don't *want* a child. Or a stupid companion,' Glorian burst out. 'Perhaps I never have.'

A terrible hush followed. Glorian thought she might faint. Her deepest secret – the secret she had kept for years – and there it was, out in the open, like the bone from her arm.

'Tell me, daughter,' Queen Sabran said, deadly soft, 'did you listen to the sanctarian today?'

Glorian trembled. She had just committed an unforgivable blasphemy. 'Yes,' she whispered.

Her ribs tightened like laces. What if her guards had heard, and spread the word that the heir scorned her calling?

'We have one bounden duty. To continue the bloodline of the Saint, and thus shield the world from the Nameless One. It is the only thing in which we Berethnets have no choice,' Queen Sabran said. 'A trifling sacrifice, in exchange for the privileges our crowns grant us.'

A thousand retorts screamed in Glorian. She wrestled them down. 'When am I to wed?'

'As soon as legally possible, when you are seventeen.'

Glorian stared at her mother, eyes filling.

'Our recent ancestors almost ruined this realm,' Queen Sabran said quietly. 'You and I cannot make a single misstep, Glorian. All eyes are upon us, waiting for proof that we are the same – that the Carmenti have it right, that you and I are not the holy shield. So we do not break. We do not falter. We do our Saint-given duty without complaint.' Pause. 'One day, you will sit across a table from your own daughter and tell her who she will wed for the realm, and you will remember this.'

'No. I will never be like you,' Glorian said, voice cracking. 'I have done pretending to be!'

Queen Sabran made no attempt to stop her as she threw the door open and rushed past her startled guards. At the end of the corridor, she almost crashed into her father.

'Glorian.' He caught her by the shoulders, stooped to look her in the face. 'Glorian, what is it?'

She took one look at his expression – so concerned, so tender – and burst into hot tears of dismay. Before he could ask again, she slipped his hold and fled, sobs wrenching her chest.

II

South

Esbar was sipping palm wine, as she often did before she slept, when Tunuva reached her room.

Jeda twitched awake. Esbar gave her a stroke along the muzzle, smiling at Tunuva. 'You look radiant,' she said. 'If this one hadn't had a nightmare, I would help you sate the—'

'I need you to stay calm.'

At once, Esbar turned to stone. 'What has she done now?'

'Esbar.'

'I promise that I will *try* to stay calm.'

It would have to do. Tunuva sat beside her. 'You recall when Siyu and Yeleni were lost?' she said. 'Yeleni and her ichneumon fell into the Minara. Siyu and Lalhar went after them, the current forced them downriver—'

'That was almost a year ago. Why speak of this?'

'Because of what they failed to tell us.' Tunuva spoke under her breath. 'They were all injured and exhausted, so they set up camp, and Siyu hunted for them. She went back to the river to fish, not realising how far east they had been washed. And she was *seen*.'

Esbar sat up. A trace of anger was already flickering, banked behind her eyes.

'A boy, about her age, trying to mend a makeshift raft,' Tunuva said. 'Siyu knew she was bound to kill him on sight, but mercy stayed her hand; so did curiosity. She helped and befriended this outsider, Anyso. He is from Carmentum.'

'Carmentum.' Esbar stared at her. 'What on earth was he doing in the Lasian Basin?'

'His family came to Dimabu to care for an elderly relative. Anyso wants to be an explorer. He was following the river, hoping to map the Basin.' Tunuva drew her shawl around her shoulders. 'Siyu has been meeting him in secret ever since. Esbar ... she is with child.'

Esbar answered these tidings with absolute silence. Tunuva waited for her to shape a reply.

'How long?' she said at last.

'She's missed her bleeding twice.'

'Did she imagine she could hide it?'

Tunuva looked away for a moment.

'Ez,' she said, with difficulty, 'Siyu climbed the tree because she wanted to do it once before she left. The pregnancy was unintentional, but when she guessed, she decided to flee with Anyso. They were meant to leave today, to go to Hróth. That was why her confinement distressed her.'

Esbar was good at concealing her feelings, but a shadow of pain crossed her face. 'She meant to abandon the Priory – her family, her duty,' she said, 'for an outsider?'

'To protect him. She wanted to ask for help, but she knew Denag would tell the Prioress.'

'As I now must.'

'No.' Tunuva gripped her hand. 'Ez, Saghul has finally agreed to send her to Nzene. If she learns of this, she will stop it. We don't know how else Siyu might be punished.'

'Because no one else has ever risked our secrecy like this,' Esbar bit out. 'Your love for her blinds you, Tuva. It always has. This is more than a mistake, more than desecration. Siyu has let herself be seen and known by an outsider. She has endangered our existence, our way of life, the *tree*. Five centuries this place has been a sanctuary, and now—'

'Saghul has treated her like a child, and she no longer is. She must have felt crushed here—'

'Enough.' Esbar wrenched free and strode to her balcony. 'I can't hear you excuse her folly again.'

'She swears she never told him about the Priory.'

'Even if that is true, this outsider must realise she is not living wild in the woods. She has well-made clothes, fine weapons, an *ichneumon*. If he has breathed a word to anyone in Dimabu, they will grow suspicious and seek us out, and if they find us, they will want the power of the tree for themselves. Our hope against the Nameless One will be lost.'

'Ez, please. There might be another way.'

'What?'

'Siyu deserves a choice in this,' Tunuva said quietly. 'Let me offer it to her.'

Esbar caught her gaze. Denag had always kept a supply of the sweet desert herb that brought on a miscarriage.

'There would be no proof of her encounters with the outsider.'

Tunuva kept her silence. For a long time, Esbar did the same, staring into the distance.

'If I am to conceal this from the Prioress,' she said, 'I have a condition.'

'Name it.'

'The outsider must still die. Only then will the Priory be safe.'

Tunuva thought of how Siyu had looked when she spoke of Anyso. The tenderness and joy in her smile.

'It will break her heart,' Tunuva said, a knot in her throat. 'And she will know it was us.'

'I will tell her it was me, and that I acted alone. In the end, she will see that it had to be done.' Esbar touched her cheek. 'I know you love her. I understand why you want to protect her from every pain she could suffer. But nothing comes above our calling.'

You cannot allow any love to overpower your love of her.

'I will go to Siyu,' Tunuva said.

'If she declines your offer, I will need to inform Saghul. You must forgive me for it, Tuva.'

'I already have.'

****

Siyu was not in her room. Tunuva went deeper into the Priory, to the men's quarters, her mind preoccupied. She would need to retrieve and prepare the herbs without Denag noticing, and Denag kept close watch on her supplies, counting them to the last seed and leaf.

Imsurin had dozed off on a daybed, a book on his chest. Tunuva gave him a gentle shake.

'Imin,' she said. He grunted. 'Imin, where is Siyu?'

He knuckled his eyes. 'She may have wanted to bathe,' he said, voice thick with sleep. 'I said she could use the spring, while this sickness has her in its grasp.'

'Thank you.'

The hot spring lay in the lowest cavern. A mighty root carved through the ceiling and one wall, cracks forming webs where it had broken in and out. Tunuva lit her flame. Its gleam flickered off the droplets, the steam, but there were no wet footprints. In fact, there was no sign of Siyu at all.

As Tunuva turned to leave, the water bubbled. She looked back at it, disquiet rising in her. As she watched, its whole surface began to roil and simmer, the steam clotting.

She retreated from the cavern. By the time she reached the top of the stair, her ribs felt crushed, like fingers bunched into a fist. When black eyes glinted from the gloom, she stopped.

'Nin.' She knelt before her ichneumon. 'Honeysweet, have you seen Lalhar?'

'She is not here. Farna is not here,' Ninuru said. 'They left with Siyu and Yeleni.'

Tunuva tensed, her flame guttering.

'Ninuru,' she said, 'where have they gone?'

Her ichneumon gazed at her. 'Eastward.'

12

East

Before the emperor reached the High Temple of Kwiriki, its inhabitants aired out the finest bedding, scrubbed every wall and floor, shovelled a path through the snow, and prepared the Inner Hall. No one knew how long he meant to stay, or why he had come without notice.

'Dumai. Kanifa.' The Grand Empress joined them on the sky platform. 'Are we ready?'

'Yes, Grand Empress,' Kanifa said. 'His Majesty should be on the stair.'

The Grand Empress grasped her walking staff, her expression hard to read. She had rarely seen her son since she had relinquished her throne to him, when he was only a child.

The hot spring had calmed, but the snowmelt around it served as a warning, as did its cloudy water. One of the younger godsingers was cooking eggs in it, humming a work song.

'It last boiled centuries ago. There are records,' the Grand Empress said, seeing what Dumai was looking at. 'Watch over your mother. Her burns are deep. Do not leave her side today.'

'Yes, Grand Empress.'

'Kanifa, see to it that the imperial entourage is fed and settled. His Majesty and I have much to discuss.' She breathed mist. 'Let us see what has called my son to the mountain.'

Unora lay in her room. Her feet and calves gleamed red, the skin weeping. She had drunk a flask of wine for the pain, sending her into a drowse. Dumai used the opportunity to daub salve on the scalds.

'Dumai.'

Slender, callused fingers brushed her wrist. Unora looked up at her with dull eyes.

'I did … something foolish,' she breathed. 'Before you were born.'

'Mother, don't speak,' Dumai said, distracted. 'Be still.'

Unora had already drifted back to sleep. Dumai wrapped her legs in fresh dressings.

The pillow had knotted her hair. Dumai found the box where she kept her possessions, looking for a comb. She sifted through oils and herbs and toothpicks, paper for her monthly bleeding.

The first comb she found gave her pause. It was pure gold, adorned with a real scallop and rare orange pearls. This was not for untangling hair, but adorning it. A gift from a wealthy climber, perhaps, though Unora never kept such things, preferring to leave them at the summit. Strange that she had held on to this. Dumai tucked it back into the corner of the box.

The Emperor of Seiiki arrived at sunset with a small escort. From the window, in the dimness, Dumai could not see much of him. He was neither short nor tall, fat nor slender. The Grand Empress greeted him, and they walked into the temple.

Dumai slept beside her mother again. When she stirred, it was dark, save for the tray of dying embers and a lantern in the doorway. The floorboards strained with a new weight.

'Unora.'

Through threads of her own hair, Dumai watched her mother wake, her face damp with sweat.

'He is here,' the voice muttered. 'Jorodu has found you.'

Above the temple, a sorrower let out its strange cry, like a child mustering its breath for a wail, *hic-hic-hic.*

'Manai,' Unora whispered, 'does he know?'

She was trembling so hard that Dumai felt it through the bedding.

'Yes,' the Grand Empress said. 'He knows.'

Hic-hic-hic.

'The saltwalker.' Unora sat up, shuddering. 'There's still time. Kanifa can lead her down the mountain. They can take the salt roads to the coast—'

'Unora, there are guards. They are on the stairs, along the pass. Jorodu knew you might try to run.'

Dumai continued to feign sleep, but her entire body was rigid, her arms prickling.

'I will go to him,' Unora said faintly. 'My legs—'

'I will help you, as far as mine will permit.'

There came a rustle and a creaking. Dumai waited, then shadowed her mother and the Grand Empress.

It must be deep in the night. Each time the lantern rounded a corner, she waited for the glow to disappear before she followed. Each time Unora stopped for breath, Dumai stopped, too, her heart loud as a bell.

At last, the Grand Empress led Unora across the snow, through the main entrance to the Inner Hall. Two guards flanked its front entrance. Dumai pressed herself against a doorway to avoid their gaze.

Kanifa can lead her down the mountain. They can take the salt roads to the coast...

Her mother wanted her to flee. That was all she could think, through the dryness in her mouth, the fog of dread. Perhaps she and Kanifa could lower themselves down the mountainside and use the eastern slopes to get away...

In ordinary circumstances, her mother would never have advocated for such a dangerous risk. Where could they even go from there, two children of the sacred mountain?

Curiosity pulled her gaze back to the Inner Hall. If she was to run from the life she loved, she had to know why.

There was a secret way to see and hear into that room. Kanifa had found it by accident when he was twenty. By chance, he had knocked a shelf, and a staircase had swung down from the ceiling, leading up to a crawlspace. Likely the templefolk of the past had used it to spy on visitors, so they could stay abreast of what was happening at court.

Dumai lowered the staircase and climbed. Without a sound, she opened the tiny panel into the Inner Hall. There was so little light, all she could make out were two shadows.

'... shared everything. For the first time, I knew what it was to be understood. To be seen.'

The Emperor of Seiiki had a quiet and measured voice. Dumai shifted closer to the spyhole.

'For so long, I wondered where you had come from. Sipwo always thought you were a spirit,' he said, 'but seeing you now, in your sunset years, I believe I understand. You are his lost daughter – Saguresi, my first River Lord. Is that why you came to court, to find him?'

'I wanted him to teach me how to irrigate the fields. If I had known who you were, I would have asked you to tell me where he had been sent.' Unora paused. 'Is he still alive?'

'No. He died in exile.'

The silence was a living thing, a thing that ached.

'Then I ask you another favour, Jorodu,' Unora said. 'Leave this place. Let our winter be a happy memory. A dream.'

Dumai frowned. Her mother should not be calling the emperor by his personal name.

'Yes. A dream,' he said, his tone almost resigned. 'I am told you called her Dumai.'

At the sound of her own name, a hook caught in her throat.

'Dumai,' he said again. 'A poet's word for a fleeting dream, a dream that ends too soon. It is a fitting name for a woman of the imperial house. Clearly you wanted her to have that droplet of her heritage – and yet, for twenty-seven years, you concealed her from me.'

'Of course I did.'

'You could have stayed. Both of you.'

'What life was there at court for me?' Unora asked bitterly. (*You never went to court*, Dumai thought in desperation. *You came from the sea to the mountain, you told me. You carried me all the way in your womb.*) 'What place for an exile's daughter and her child?'

'The highest place.' Pain trimmed his voice. 'I would have taken you as my principal empress.'

'They would never have let you. In any case, I left for Dumai. Neither of us would ever have been safe.'

'Did they threaten you?'

Dumai was starting to feel lightheaded. Their words had already painted a picture, but it could not be right, it could not be the truth.

It is a fitting name for a woman of the imperial house . . .

'The man who came here, disguised as a saltwalker, is called Epabo,' Emperor Jorodu said. 'He is one of the very few people I trust. He was not looking for you, though he did search for many years at my bidding. On this occasion, he was following an agent of the River Lord.'

'The young woman, Nikeya?'

'Yes. We believe Clan Kuposa is trying to spy on my mother,' he said. 'Lady Nikeya returned to court not long after Epabo. Did she see you, Unora?'

'Not my face. I was veiled.'

'Could she have seen Dumai?'

Unora was silent.

'It is too dangerous for her to stay here now,' the emperor said. 'There is only one place for—'

'Dumai.'

A soft voice from behind her. Dumai flinched in surprise, heart thudding.

'Grand Empress,' she whispered, staring at the drawn face in the shadows. 'How did—'

'Child, I've been in this temple longer than you've lived. I know its every secret,' came the gentle reply, 'and I'm not yet so old that I can't climb a ladder.' Her hand was cupped around her lamp, keeping its light from escaping. 'His Majesty planned to summon you tomorrow ... but I suppose now is as good a time as any. Don't you?'

Dumai swallowed.

The Grand Empress led her to the interior doors like a woman going to her death. Dumai followed her into the magnificent gloom of the Inner Hall, which was dominated by a colossal statue of the great Kwiriki. Snow Maiden stood barefoot and serene on his back. Gilding and engraved mirrors reflected the lambent glow of the oil lamps.

Unora rose. As their eyes met, Dumai realised she had never seen her mother look so afraid. Not even on the night of the snowstorm, the night they had almost lost their lives.

'Your Majesty,' the Grand Empress said, with a sigh of defeat, 'I have brought someone to see you.'

As Unora closed her eyes, tears escaped them. Behind her, a figure stood before a gilded screen.

'Come forward.' This time, the voice sounded cautious. 'Please. Come into the light.'

It took Dumai too long to remember how to move her legs. She forced her feet to step forward, folded to her knees, and lowered her forehead to the floor, just as she did at prayer.

'Rise.'

Keeping her eyes downcast, she did. After a moment, a finger tipped her chin up. Dumai lifted her gaze – and when she saw the face before hers, her every bone and sinew turned cold.

She was staring into her own eyes. At her own features, reflected as if in a dull mirror.

'Daughter,' the Emperor of Seiiki said heavily. 'I have waited a long time to meet you.'

13

South

'Siyu is gone.'

No sooner had Esbar opened her arms than Tunuva had rushed into them. 'Tuva, peace. It's all right.' Esbar clasped her face between strong hands. 'Who knows?'

'Only me and Nin.'

'Good. I will inform Saghul – I have no choice now – and if she agrees, then you and I are going to get Siyu back. We are not going to lose her.' Her voice was firm and calm. 'Do you believe me?'

Tunuva let herself be held, trying to keep from shaking. 'Yes,' she breathed. 'Yes, I believe you.'

Esbar kissed her and marched away.

Tunuva sank on to the bed. The ichneumons chose a side each and nuzzled close, sharing their warmth, the way they would comfort one of their pups.

Tuva, they haven't come back.

The present slipped from her grasp. Memories welled of the worst day of her life, the day she lost them, too strong to bank: the honey and blood, the body, the forest. Ninuru lying down in the rain with her, refusing to leave unless she got up. Esbar trying to console her as she sobbed in the night, her own belly swelling with the seed that would bloom into Siyu.

It wasn't your fault. You couldn't have done anything...

'Tuva.'

She jolted back to see Esbar, unloading fabrics from her chest. 'I explained the situation to Saghul. We ride now,' she told Tunuva, 'across the Ersyr. If they've gone farther, we'll need horses.'

'Horses are slow,' Ninuru said. 'And stupid.'

'Stupid,' Jeda echoed.

'I know, sweet ones, but the dull-witted Westerners would stare at you. There are no ichneumons north of the Harmur Pass – or, indeed, mages.' Esbar stripped off her drape and tossed it into the corner of the room. 'Did Siyu say which port they meant to leave from?'

'Sadyrr,' Tunuva said. Her tongue caught on the Northern word. 'Do you know the way?'

'Of course not.' Esbar swung on a tunic. 'But I know someone who does.'

Tunuva made for her sunroom and went through her clothes, taking out all she needed to impersonate a salt trader. There was no time to slide into the past. Each moment took Siyu further away.

She drew on undershorts and breeches, girded a white tunic, and found a coat suited for travel, lined with sheepskin for the desert nights. Even a mage would feel those in winter. She tucked the breeches into her riding boots and donned an Ersyri capara, to keep sand off her face. She packed cloths and moss, fresh chewsticks and bedding, saddle flasks, and collected her favoured weapon, a folding spear of her own design.

With Ninuru at her side, she continued towards the passage that led out through the roots of the fig tree. Esbar was already at its entrance, accompanied by a saddled Jeda.

'I have enough food for us all,' she said. 'I also have our guide.'

A broad-shouldered woman stepped from the gloom, leading a grizzled ichneumon. Her grey hair was drawn up in an Ersyri court style.

'Apaya,' Tunuva said, surprised.

'Tuva.'

Apaya du Eadaz uq-Nāra gave her a swift kiss on the cheek. She resembled Esbar in her curved nose and dark, piercing eyes, which she outlined with black paint. Even in her seventies, she remained tall and strong.

'How good to see you,' she said. 'Mother's blessings.'

'And on you. I thought you were in Jrhanyam.'

'I came to eat of the tree and make my usual report to the Prioress. Now I hear two of our sisters have fled.'

'We will find them.' Esbar climbed into her saddle. 'I will not let Siyu bring any more shame on the line of Siyāti.'

'Good.' Apaya crossed her sinewy arms. 'I will lead you to the Harmur Pass. With any luck, we will catch up to our sisters before they can reach Mentendon. If not, you're on your own. I will not set foot in Virtudom.'

No one could blame her for that. Tunuva secured the saddle and swung herself into it.

'First, we ride for Yikala.' Apaya mounted her ichneumon. 'You both know your way that far.'

14

East

'How much of it was a lie?'

The voice came from her mouth, but now it belonged to a stranger – Noziken pa Dumai, Princess of Seiiki, firstborn child of Emperor Jorodu, descendant of Snow Maiden.

She sat with her mother and the Grand Empress. They were screened away in her quarters, where lamps flickered, casting long shadows.

'I will ask a simpler question,' Dumai said to Unora, who had not answered. 'Where are you really from?'

Unora looked drained.

'Afa Province,' she said. 'My mother died when I was only a year old, of an affliction caused by thirst. Her death inspired my father to change things. He left me with a relative, walked all the way to the capital, and passed the examination to become a scholar, starting work at court. After four years, his request to serve as Governor of Afa was granted.'

'A man of no standing, raised to such a post?'

'The nobles don't want to be sent to the dust provinces,' the Grand Empress explained. 'You should have heard them whimper in horror when I packed them off to places like Afa.' She drank a little wine. 'Usually, I would never have appointed a man of common birth, but Saguresi was passionate and clever, and I thought it might shame the nobles who lived in fear of shouldering the same responsibility he sought. I gave him a chance, and he went straight back, this time with the power of a governor.'

Unora nodded. 'My father understood the land. He knew which crops to plant and when, and had ideas for irrigation,' she said. 'The governor before him had been lazy and corrupt, wanting to serve her time in Afa and rush back to court. She would take all our crops from us, and only give back what she saw fit. But my father cared. He cared for us.'

She paused for a moment, lowering her gaze.

'When I was eight, Emperor Jorodu, newly enthroned, made my father River Lord of Seiiki,' she went on. Dumai blinked. 'He moved me to his new mansion in Antuma. He was the kindest man in the world, but his promotion caused indignation among the clans.'

The Grand Empress snorted. 'To put it mildly. The most important position outside the imperial family, held by a man who had once been a farmworker. Even I would never have dared go so far,' she said. 'For centuries, the River Lord had always been from Clan Kuposa, but my son favoured talent over blood. The Kuposa did not like this.'

Dumai watched her. 'Surely everyone is meant to support the emperor in his choices.'

'I will come to that. For now, all you need to know is that they got rid of your grandfather. They claimed that no one of his standing could have brought water to Afa, and accused him of waking a dragon to do it.' She sighed. 'My son was too young to soundly question their evidence. To save Saguresi from execution, he agreed to banish him to Muysima.'

'I was thrown into the street that night,' Unora said. 'One of our servants found me and took me back to Afa.' Her face had turned to ceramic, brittle even as it held itself in a tight cast. 'Life in the interior can be … very hard. Without my father, things slid back to the way they had been.'

Dumai had always had food and water aplenty. It pained her to think of her mother like this.

'One year, a sickness killed everyone in my village but me,' Unora said. 'I walked to the pool of the dragon Pajati and asked for a way out. The next morning, an imperial messenger passed. When she came to pay her respects to Pajati, she found me collapsed there.'

'Did you wake Pajati?'

Unora remained as blank as fresh paper. 'No. I only prayed.'

Dumai nodded, reassured. Her mother would never be so reckless, not even when she was young.

'Butterflies are messengers of Kwiriki – symbols of the power the gods once had to change their shapes,' Unora said. 'Kanifa may have told you that in some provinces, people believe they can take the form of women. The messenger assumed I was a butterfly spirit, and took me to court.'

'And you met the emperor. My father,' Dumai said. 'Was he already wed to the empress?'

'Yes. I was her attendant.' Her voice was colourless. 'I had no idea who he was. When I realised, I knew it would be too dangerous to stay ... because I was pregnant, and my child would be an heir to Seiiki. I left at once, to spare you that fate. I brought you here.'

'You never saved your father,' Dumai murmured. 'You left before you could. To save me.'

'Yes.' Unora looked at her. 'I thought I would never love anyone as much as my father. But the moment I learned you existed—' Dumai set her jaw to stop it quaking. 'I gave birth to you in this very room, and ever since, I have tried to give you a happy life. But I had to keep you hidden from anyone who came from court. Now you understand why.'

Because Dumai so strongly resembled the emperor. Her features were soft in comparison, and she was almost a head taller, but it was as if two gifted artists had painted the same person, from their wide-set eyes to their rounded chins. They even had a tiny matching freckle on their left cheekbones. It was unnerving.

'I should have risked the sea. I should have taken you to Sepul,' Unora said bitterly, 'but I wanted to be near your father, fool that I was. Love bound me to this mountain. And now—'

She pressed a sleeve to her mouth.

'Rest,' the Grand Empress told her. 'I must speak with my grand-daughter alone, in any case.'

Unora quit the room. Dumai slowly looked back at the Grand Empress, the woman who had guided her for years, who was also her paternal grandmother. For the first time, Dumai looked hard at that face, searching for her own. The likeness was not as startling.

'When did you know?'

'Unora told me when she felt her first pains.' The Grand Empress looked towards the window, her mouth pinching. 'And all these years, I helped her hide you from my son.'

'Why?'

'The same reason she fled, Dumai. For fear that you would come to harm.'

Outside, dawn spread like red dye through water.

'More than two centuries ago, there was an uprising against our house,' the Grand Empress said. 'While the gods slept, a young man took advantage of their absence, calling himself the Meadow King. His revolt went on for several months, until his trusted swordmaker betrayed and killed him.

'The traitor was named Sasofima. She would have been a person of no consequence, if not for her extraordinary talent for metalworking. The House of Noziken rewarded her loyalty by giving her a clan name – Kuposa. Granting her this was a grave mistake.'

Dumai listened.

'Sasofima was charged with casting the bells across Seiiki. They were modelled after the Queen Bell, to wake the gods if there was ever another threat like the Meadow King. Since then, her descendants have only grown in wealth and ambition. Most rulers in the last two hundred years have been little more than figureheads, dominated by Kuposa regents.'

The revelation settled in Dumai like snow, turning her colder than she had felt in years.

'My cousin was empress before me. They moulded her from birth, keeping her weak and unassertive,' the Grand Empress said. 'Only when she died in the childbed – a day her son did not survive, either – was I called to the Rainbow Throne. Now the Kuposa had a problem. Up until that point, they had paid me no mind, so I had no loyalty to them. I was not only old and shrewd enough to resist their influence, but I already had a son of my own, by one of their rivals from Clan Mithara. I had a strong will ... until I conveniently sickened, forcing me to abdicate. I recovered, but I had given up my throne to be Supreme Officiant. I could not go back.

'They had removed me while my son was still a child. Jorodu tried his best to empower their rivals – but as your mother's story demonstrates, they always found ways to outflank him. He was too young to play the game. That was deliberate. He was forced to rely on them.

'Understand that they are patient, Dumai. Patient and careful. They are never so crude as to kill their rivals, but they will use every other means to uphold their power, often by eclipsing ours. My son eventually learned this, when he found himself married to Kuposa pa Sipwo.

'Twenty years ago, Empress Sipwo gave birth to a long-awaited Crown Prince. Seven years ago, she bore twins, a boy and a girl. Three years ago, both princes died in an outbreak of barnacle pox. This leaves her last remaining child as the presumed heir to Seiiki.'

Dumai finally spoke. 'Who?'

'Your sister, Noziken pa Suzumai.'

A younger sister. Two brothers, dead before she could meet them.

'Suzumai is sweet, obedient, and meek. Another doll to be propped on the throne,' the Grand Empress said curtly. 'Your father has known for years that the Kuposa would find a way to make him disappear before Suzumai comes of age. He had almost lost hope.'

Even as the sun rose, the awful truth was dawning on Dumai.

'But then he found me,' she said, throat dry as ashes.

'He found you. You see, Dumai, you owe no allegiance to the Kuposa. That gives you power.'

Dumai stared at her.

'The woman who came to the temple was a spy,' the Grand Empress said. 'I presume you met.'

'Yes. She must have seen the emperor in my face, as the saltwalker did.'

'You are fortunate that your father's agent reached Antuma Palace before she did.' She took Dumai by the chin and lifted it, as the emperor had. 'They know what you represent, as does His Majesty.'

'Tell me what he wants.'

'You were always clever, Dumai. You already know why your father risked coming here. If you do not take the Rainbow Throne, our house will lose its authority, and the people of Seiiki will be for ever deprived of their pathway to the gods. This, I cannot allow.'

'I have only ever dreamed of being Maiden Officiant.'

'I know. I wanted to spare you this battle. I tried, Dumai, for a long time, because I hated it myself – but when the gods return, they must find our house strong, and see that we have cared for Seiiki in their absence. Under Kuposa influence, we are fragile. We must resist.'

The realisation was swift and crushing as a snowslide.

'I have no choice in this,' Dumai whispered. 'I must leave all I know.'

'Yes.'

'I'm not ready.' It was hard to breathe. 'I know nothing of court, of politics—'

'That is where our plan comes in,' the Grand Empress said, a sparkle in her eye. 'The plan I have made with your father, that you made possible.'

'What is this plan?'

'When you take the throne, your father will continue to hold authority, under the guise of helping you. He will rule from somewhere far out of their reach – a shadow court – and speak through you. You will not be alone.' Her grandmother took her hands. 'This is how you will serve the gods, granddaughter. This is what the great Kwiriki has been calling you to do.'

Dumai shivered in the clothes of a ghost, as numb as if she had bathed in the ice pool.

'Kanifa.' Her stomach clenched. 'Did he know?'

'No, child. He never knew.'

That was something. She rose on trembling knees and bent into a bow.

She turned and left the warm gloom of the home she had loved all her life. She lurched outside, into the light of sunrise, and stumbled through the snow until she saw him on the sky platform, as he was on so many days, waiting for her. Before he could so much as frown, she flung herself into his arms and wept.

15

West

Langarth lay some way south of Drouthwick Castle – too far to go ahorse, given how little time Wulf could spare. Instead, he parted with a fistful of hacksilver and climbed aboard a riverboat.

The sun floated like a yolk in skimmed milk. As he glided a hand through the cool water, he thought of Glorian Berethnet.

The Saint's Marvel was real. The princess did resemble her mother, with her green eyes and long black hair, though hers had a forelock, parted down the middle. Glorian was also broader in the beam, generous where the queen was slim. Still, the likeness between the two was uncanny – both as pale as candles, exactly the same height.

Sly of the king to not remind Wulf they had met. How had he forgotten those long summers at Glowan Castle?

Of course, as soon as he had seen her, it had started to come back. He remembered now, as the boat slid under a fortified bridge – remembered her splashing him in the fountain, her peals of laughter. How they had run through the flower maze from different ends, trying to beat each other to the middle. They had been the same height then.

The bare, stern peaks of the Fells gradually shallowed into the greener hills of the Lakes. A brisk wind crimped the river. It was late in the day by the time the barge slid into Hallow Lake, where the two upper branches of the Lithsom joined before flowing to the sea.

On its east shore stood the old lake port of Marcott-on-Hallow. Voices clamoured, smallpipes played, and a crier roared from the market boss, almost drowned out by the clatter of carts piled with trout and roach and greased ropes of lamprey. Wulf shielded his eyes against the glister of the lake, so deep and blue it was almost black, though lower than it had been in years past.

The sun was beaten bloody by the time he found an inn. The room was cramped, but at least the straw was free of lice. He rose at cockcrow to hire a horse and rode from the town.

A bier road threaded across the misted peaks of the province, joining the settlements to the sanctuaries, so the recent dead might be taken for burial. By noon, the long thread of trampled grass had led him to Witherling Water. Beyond that lake, a wall of primeval forest stretched from east to west, from shore to shore, all the way across Inys.

The haithwood.

The sight of that place sent a chill through most northerners, for it was said a witch had lived there since the days before the Saint. It sent a deeper chill through Wulf. The haithwood was more than an old tale to him.

His rouncey clobbered down to the road, towards the moated estate in the distance, with its tiled roof and stone walls and tall brick chimneys. He dismounted at the gate and walked the horse to the stables, where the Mentish groom was brushing a stallion.

'Well met, Rik,' Wulf called.

Riksard turned, the frown on his face clearing after a moment. 'Master Wulf?'

'Aye. How are you?'

'Very well.' Riksard wiped his brow on his wrist and grinned. Like many Ments, he had ruddy hair. 'I hardly recognised you. Welcome home. Were we expecting a visit?'

'No. Is anyone here?'

'I think the mistress is in the rose garden.'

The rose garden was near the front of the estate. Wulf found his older sister reading on the swinging chair, wrapped in a mantle, snug as an acorn in its cup. He leaned on the gate.

'Mouse,' he said.

Mara surfaced from her book. 'Wulf,' she said in amazement, closing it. 'Is that really you?'

'Unless my twin has wandered from the woods.'

With a laugh, Mara came to him, and Wulf bundled her into his arms. She flung hers around his neck, wrapping him in the scent of the crushed lavender she kept in her pockets.

'I can't believe it,' she said into his cloak. 'Why didn't you write to tell us?'

'There was no time,' Wulf said, chin on her shoulder. The embrace took him straight back to when she would sit him at her side and tell him stories in the evenings, her warmth making him feel cushioned and safe. 'And I can't stay more than a night or two.'

'Oh, longer, surely.'

'I wish I could. Is everyone here?'

'Pa and Roland are resolving a dispute up in Strenley, but they should be back before supper. Father is poring over taxes.' Mara drew away and framed his face, her hazel eyes shining. 'Oh, Wulf, look at you. I never thought you'd grow as tall as Roland.'

'I'm sure I was this tall last time you saw me.'

'You were a boy last time I saw you.'

Mara looked the same as he remembered, though her hair had grown almost to her waist, strands of it wispy against her plump cheeks. He could hardly believe it had been three years.

'Sorry to interrupt your reading,' Wulf said. 'That looked a cosy spot.'

'I forgive you.' Mara retrieved her tome and took his arm. 'Come. Father will be overjoyed.'

Langarth had stood for centuries. A former priory, it had sixty rooms, all built around a courtyard that housed a damson tree. As the gloom enfolded him, Wulf drew its familiar smells into his chest: oak and dried herbs, the meadowsweet the servants used to scent the halls.

'How have you fared?' he asked his sister, patting the pale, beringed hand at his elbow. 'Since your last letter.'

'Much the same. Helping Father with the estate, courtesy visits about the province, helping at the almshouse now and then. There's little else to do for a middle child of noble birth, except to make a gainful marriage – which, as you know, has never appealed to me.'

'You ought to find some pursuit you enjoy. Roland has none of our freedoms.'

'Do you propose I become a brave Northern warrior, too?' she asked him lightly. 'Unless I can count or scribe away the king's enemies, I fear I wouldn't be much use to him.'

'Go to court. The queen must have room for a well-reared lady in her household,' Wulf said. 'If not, the Royal Chancery or the Exchequer would have you. You shouldn't hide your talents, Mara.'

'Not court. Too many ways to disgrace oneself.' Mara added, 'I did think of offering my services to Lady Marian. You know Queen Sabran granted her lands in the Lakes.' He nodded. 'I went to see her in the summer. She was not at all what I expected.'

'What did you expect?'

'A nervous halfwit, from what I'd heard of her reign. She did strike me as too gentle to make a strong queen, but as a private person, I rather liked her. She was gracious and attentive, and had a certain dry humour. Her companion is dead now, as are most of her ladies. I wondered if she might find a secretary useful. Befrith Castle is close enough to Langarth.'

'Have you told Father this idea?'

'Not yet. I'll ask him once you've returned to Hróth.' Mara pressed his arm. 'Today, I only want to hear about you.'

Lord Edrick, Baron Glenn of Langarth, was hunched over a parchment in the larger of his two studies. His seat faced a bay window of leaded forest glass, adorned with the crest of his barony: a proud alder tree growing in a steep vale, encircled by sedge.

'Father.' Mara bent to kiss his head. 'We have a visitor.'

'Visitor.' His voice was weary. 'Saint, I must have forgotten. I promised I'd call at Bowen Hoath.'

'This guest won't mind.'

Wulf breathed in to steady himself. With a crinkled brow, Lord Edrick turned in his seat.

He looked older. Of course he did. His hair was silver now, trimmed at the shoulders, and more lines scored his olive skin. Otherwise, he was still hale and lean.

'Wulfert?' He stood up, his grey eyes wide as thimbles. 'Surely this can't be my son.'

Wulf bowed with a broad smile. 'Father.'

Lord Edrick strode to him. Warmth flooded Wulf as his father crushed him to his chest.

'By the Saint. King Bardholt's sent us a grown man.' Lord Edrick held Wulf by the shoulders, taking him in. 'Ah, Roland will be furious. You remember how proud he was of being taller than you both.'

'Aye, I remember him threatening to hammer me into the ground like a tent pole,' Wulf said drily.

'From the look of you, you could threaten worse. Now, tell me, how long can you stay?'

'Only a few days, Father, forgive me. His Grace will sail for Hróth before the week is out.'

'Then we must make the most of it, before you disappear again and come back with your first grey hairs.' Lord Edrick wrapped one arm around Wulf and the other around Mara, drawing them close. 'I really must visit one of the tenants – but let's walk there together, shall we, the three of us? You need some good Inysh air in your chest, Wulfert.'

****

The tenant was an old knight who lived near a grouse moor, three miles from Langarth. Wulf took in the sights of autumn in the Lakes, a province aglow with tawny leaves and coppered light.

As they walked, he described the splendour of Hróth. The emerald ice that sparkled in its farthest reaches. The glowing curtains that marbled the sky. The nightless summers, and the waterfalls that froze to scrunched linen, staying that way for most of the year.

'It sounds like a dream world.' Mara skirted a puddle. 'I can see why you seldom come back to Inys.'

'Inys has its own beauty,' Wulf said. 'Not so strange or sweeping, perhaps, but richer. There's a bonny softness to it.' He breathed in the smell of sodden grass. 'I've missed autumn. I miss spring, too – the scents, the colours. One can grow tired of smelling snow.'

'Snow has a smell?'

'We have a word for it. *Skethra* – a scent that washes the air clean.'

'And you're still close to the other housecarls?' Lord Edrick asked. 'They treat you kindly?'

Wulf paused before he said, 'Aye, Father.'

Almost true. One particular housecarl despised him, but that would only worry his family.

'You have a Hróthi accent now, you know,' Mara remarked. Her cheeks were rosy with cold. 'I could hear it coming like the tide last you were here. Now it's set deep as the ice.'

131

Wulf chuckled and shook his head. 'Most Hróthi know me for an offcomer as soon as I open my mouth.'

'Och, you're no offcomer there. You've been striding on that snow since you were nine.'

'We're very proud of you, Wulf,' Lord Edrick told him. 'Whether you're here or in Hróth.'

'Thank you, Father.'

Lord Edrick was not long with his tenant. It was still late in the afternoon by the time they returned to the estate, shivering and caked with mud. By then, the housekeeper had prepared Wulf's old room. He touched the mark scratched into the doorframe, left by a former occupant of Langarth – a tiny circle, lines streaming from the top.

He, Mara and Roland had puzzled over it for years. They had found other scratchings by the hearths, the windows, the doors. Though they were clearly heathen, Lord Edrick had never had them removed. *They are part of Langarth as much as we are*, he had told them, *and erasing the past won't make us saints, children.*

Wulf only meant to lie down, to remember how it felt to sleep close to his family, but he fell into a doze and dreamed his childhood dream, the one that took him deep into the woods. He was searching for someone, though he knew not who, and no matter how long and hard he looked, or how loud he shouted, no one answered. He ran and ran, weeping with fear, until the trees widened into a clearing, where the ground smelled of blood. He could hear bees humming somewhere close – always there, never seen.

'Wulf?'

He snapped awake, still hearing them. Mara was sitting on the edge of the bed.

'Supper is ready.' His sister touched his shoulder. 'Were you dreaming?'

'No.' He rubbed his eyes. 'Are Pa and Roland back?'

'Close.' She had changed into a gown of olive wool, which brought out the green in her eyes. 'What troubles you?'

Even when they were bairns, she had always known. 'Nothing,' he said. 'I'll come down.'

They walked to the Great Hall. Wulf had always loved its understated beauty. He and Mara sat at the table, which was piled with food he had craved since his last visit: dock pudding and sausage, a stew of yearling lamb, damsons from the courtyard tree, flat pastry cakes, and apple pie served with white cheese from Rathdun Sanctuary. The servants were pouring elderberry wine when two men trudged through the arched doorway.

Lord Mansell Shore was the only southerner in the family, born near the coast of the Fens. He was stout as a kettle, with one dark eye and one grey. A horseshoe moustache grew from his brown face, grizzled where his receding curls were still black, for the most part.

Seeing Wulf, he stopped. 'Son?'

With a grin, Wulf said, 'Pa.'

Lord Mansell let out a rich laugh and opened his arms. Wulf stepped into them, smiling so much his cheeks ached. In the doorway, Roland laid down his gloves.

'The cub returns,' he said, and clapped Wulf on the back. 'Good to see you, Wulfy.'

'And you, Rollo.'

Roland now looked the part of heir apparent to the barony. He was broad in the shoulder and chest, nonchalantly handsome. The chestnut hair he shared with Mara was from their mother, Lady Rosa Glenn. She and her companion had been killed by thieves when Roland was four, and Mara just two – an act of violence that had shaken the queendom.

Lord Edrick had adopted his niece and nephew, who had grown up seeing him as their father. He had married Lord Mansell, and Wulf had made them a family of five, all gathered into Langarth.

'This is a welcome surprise.' Lord Mansell removed his cloak. 'What brings you home, Wulf?'

'Lady Glorian's commendation.'

'Ah, of course.'

'We hear some republicans haunted the feast,' Roland said to Wulf. 'What did you make of the heathen Carmenti?'

'Braw clothes, jewels, a grand retinue. Elected monarchs, to my eye.'

'And yet, the people can decide. Quite the distinction,' Lord Edrick said. As they all took their seats, he looked kindly at his companion. 'Any luck resolving your dispute, love?'

'If only. It will drag on for centuries at this rate.' Rolling his eyes, Lord Mansell sank into his chair and motioned to one of the servants, who filled his cup. 'Sir Armund Crottle. I've never seen one man so fixated on anything as he is on that Saint-forsaken path.'

'Aren't you delighted that this is your future?' Mara asked Roland, who arched an eyebrow and reached for a dish.

'We all must serve the Saint,' Lord Edrick told her. 'Your brother will make a fine baron in time.' He smiled from the head of the table. 'Look at this. All of us together again.'

'Indeed. The full valley.' Roland raised his cup. 'To our Wulf.'

They drank. As the candles burned down, Wulf settled into his seat and listened to Lord Mansell recount his dispute, realising how sorely he had missed their company, their voices.

'We heard strange tidings from the Marshes.' Lord Mansell finished his mouthful of buttered pease. 'You know they have a hot pool down there, the Ferndale Stews. According to our dear friend Sir Armund, the water boiled. Five people were bathing at the time.'

'How dreadful,' Mara said. 'Did they live?'

'One did. The rest died.'

'Something similar happened in Hróth,' Wulf recalled. 'The mudpots close to Mount Dómuth. They steam all year, but before we left, Bardholt heard they started spitting and bubbling like cauldrons, all at once.'

'Saint. I hope no one was in them.'

Wulf shook his head. 'We know to stay away. The mud always burns like vice.'

'Our little brother. Always a step from death, and so calm in his admission of it,' Roland observed. 'What could have caused the Inysh pool to turn?'

Lord Mansell grunted. 'An earthquake or eruption somewhere in the world, perhaps.' He drained his cup. 'Unless it's some omen of Mentish resentment, of course.'

'Soft, Pa,' Mara said in an undertone. 'Rik could hear.'

'Oh, Saint, let him. The Vatten brought them salvation, and all they can do is sulk.' Lord Mansell poured them all more wine. 'But let's not talk of politics. Wulf, tell us all about your adventures in the North.'

'Aye. I want to hear about the legendary Regny of Askrdal,' Roland said. 'Is it true she once shot a man in the eye when he questioned her skill with a bow?'

'Nah.' Wulf sipped his wine. 'She did, however, give him a solid kick in the pestle, to prove she could hit a small target.'

****

Later, in the middle of the night, he lay sleepless, listening.

When he was young, he had sometimes heard a clicking in the dark of Langarth. Every summer, it would come. Roland had told him he heard the sound, too, and that he knew what made it.

The Lady of the Woods, tapping the windows, trying to reach the children in the house.

No one knew who she was, except that she had walked the isle when it was still known as Inysca. The haithwood was her ancient lair. She saw through the eyes of its birds and beasts, watching for those who neglected their prayers, for they renounced the protection of Halgalant. She would stuff their mouths with clag and drag them deep into the trees.

Tick-tick. Tick-tick.

It was only when Wulf had wet the bed that Lord Edrick sat him on his knee and explained that there were deathwatch beetles in the rafters, so named because all summer long they beat their armoured heads on the wood, driving back the silence in the hours of vigil. They were still doing it now, in autumn.

Wulf turned over, one hand fisted over his ear. He was seven years old and the witch was aprowl, coming to drag him to his doom. The mist on the window was her mildewed breath. All he could hear was her fingernails, thick with dry blood and the loam of the wood.

Tick-tick. Tick-tick.

Wulf forced his eyes open, the hair on his arms prickling. He was not a bairn any longer, and he would not lie in a cold sweat and wait. He would look his old fear in the face.

The candle at his bedside wore a shroud of wax. With a sheet over his shoulders, he lit a fresh one and carried it along the corridor, to a window that gave on to the haithwood.

By the light of the full moon, he beheld them – thrawn and tongue-less, ancient as the isle itself. Thousands, myriad thousands of trees, their trunks hollowed by age: hazel and hornbeam, alder and medlar, wicker elm and rowan and yew, birch and beech and brittle willow, blackthorn and spindle and steadfast oak – but no hawthorns, not for centuries. The Saint had ordered them destroyed to end the old ways of the Inyscans, who had once praised hawthorns as their gods, and worshipped with violence and vice.

Wulf held the candle tight. Its glow haunted his countenance, so the glass reflected it, and his features were cast over the trees, giving them eyes. He looked at the haithwood, and the haithwood looked back. Blind and all-seeing. Soulless and eternal and alive.

And he could have sworn he could hear the witch calling: *Come back to me, Child of the Woods. Come home.*

16

East

Mount Ipyeda was as silent as the moon. Dumai sat on a roof of the temple, watching the stars.

Kanifa had sat beside her on hundreds of clear nights like this. More than once, she had drifted off and woken to find his fur over her, and him at her side, warm and steady.

He had come to the mountain when she was ten. Seventeen years of friendship, seeing each other almost every day. She dared not dwell on what would happen when they parted.

The solitude was too much to stand. She ducked back through the window and let her feet carry her as they would, until she found herself outside a familiar door. When she slid it aside, Unora looked up, eyes bloodshot.

'Dumai.' She dried her face. 'You should be sleeping.'

'I want to make this final night last.'

Unora watched her kneel on the floor. 'Can you ever forgive me?'

'There is nothing to forgive. It did hurt me that you lied, but everything you ever did was to protect me. Even by calling me your kite, you taught me never to look down.'

'That very advice has left you defenceless.' Unora shook her head. 'I should have taught you about court. Now he sends you to the wolves with no claws of your own.'

'You had no claws, either. You were a woman, not a wolf.'

Unora managed a weak smile.

'You know, the first year of your life, I barely slept,' she said. 'I was always so afraid, in the early days. That you would freeze here. That you weren't taking enough milk. I used to keep your cradle right beside me, so I could hear you breathe. You were the hinge of my world, and everything in that world was threatening to wrench you away.'

Dumai reached for her hands. They were always cold, as if her mother was part of the mountain.

'One night, the Grand Empress told me she would look after you so I could rest. I wept in dread all night,' Unora said, her voice soft. 'In the morning, your grandmother placed you back into my arms, and you smiled at me. After that, I slept easier. I learned to let you run and play. But in the end, I let the world come for you.' She closed her eyes. 'I'm so sorry, Dumai.'

'Mount Ipyeda taught me to survive. I have loved my life here. You gave me that life, Mama,' Dumai said, with resolve. 'But if I must go, why not come with me?'

Unora took her by the cheeks. 'They would find a way to use me against you and your father. I must stay with your grandmother, to beg the great Kwiriki to protect my child.' She touched their foreheads together. 'Please, my kite, be careful. Please fly back to me.'

****

She woke before dawn to a hand on her hair. Her mother was beside her, dressed for the day.

'It's time.'

Unora spoke in a low, rough voice, deep shadows under her eyes. Dumai stared at the ceiling before she stood.

She dressed in warm and simple clothes, the way she always had. By the glow of a lantern, she followed her mother down the steps to where a snow palanquin awaited her, with a mountain ox to pull it and six villagers to lift it when necessary. A second palanquin sat in front of it, locked and ready.

'Granddaughter,' the Grand Empress said, a stern cast to her features. 'You will be taken to the home of my late consort's niece, Lady Taporo. I trust her. Once you are prepared, word of a royal procession will be salted through the city, and you will be carried to the palace.'

The palace that had shone in the distance all her life. Dumai wondered how big it truly was.

'The River Lord, Kuposa pa Fotaja, is presently away. He was your father's regent,' the Grand Empress went on. 'As the head of Clan Kuposa, he will be your most formidable adversary – a man as charming as he is sharp and ambitious. Beware of him.'

Feeling like a soldier receiving orders, Dumai made herself nod.

'You have allies. Not as many as *they* have, but you are not alone,' the Grand Empress said, nodding to the other palanquin. 'Osipa will be among your personal attendants.'

'She'll be in danger.'

'My old friend has never cared for this mountain. Great as the risks are, she assures me she would sooner die with her feet on the ground. One other person has offered their services,' she added. 'His Majesty has agreed that Kanifa will join the palace guard. He will arrive at court in the spring, so the Kuposa will not realise that he is from your temple.'

Dumai looked between them. 'No,' she said. 'He can't. The Kuposa agent saw him here.'

'Do you suppose she would remember his face?' the Grand Empress said, eyebrows raised. 'Perhaps, or perhaps not. Either way, he will protect you from the shadows.'

'Kanifa,' Dumai said, 'may I speak with you alone?'

After a long moment, her grandmother inclined her head. Dumai walked a short distance from the others, Kanifa following her.

He had left the mountain only once, to visit the Bone Walk of Isunka – a shrine built inside the horned skull of a dragon. Paving stones had been laid all the way through its ribs, which drew a constant fog. It was a wonder of Seiiki, a remnant of the gods.

Dumai had waited for him to return, expecting him to be happy. Instead, he had been footsore and unstrung, troubled by what he had seen on the ground. He was as rooted to the mountain as the mountain to the earth.

When they were out of earshot, she faced him. 'Kan,' she said, 'you were not made for court.'

'And you were?' he said, arms folded. 'Osipa is known there. I am not. As a guard, I can be everywhere. They'll train me in the way of the spear, so I can protect you.'

'A godsinger shouldn't fight.'

'A godsinger shouldn't rule, either.' He reached into his padded coat. 'Remember our promise, Mai.'

He pressed something into her hand. A strand of their rope – the rope that had always kept them together.

'Together, then.' Dumai sighed in defeat. 'Let us hope we have a soft landing.'

Kanifa held her close. 'I'll see you soon,' he said. 'Princess Dumai.'

'You're not going to bow when you see me next, are you?'

'I must. But I don't mind.'

Unora waited beside the snow palanquin. She drew Dumai into a firm embrace.

'When I was at court,' she whispered in her ear, 'I would dance every morning, even in the snow. That was how your father first saw me.' Dumai pressed her face into her shoulder. 'Every morning, when I greet the sunrise, I will turn my eyes towards Antuma Palace.'

'And I will look towards Mount Ipyeda. Every day, until I see you again.'

They clung to each other. Dumai felt her mother trembling and held her tighter. Her chest hurt.

When Unora stepped back, Kanifa was there to steady her. So was the Grand Empress. Dumai allowed herself one more look at the third peak – the distant glint on the summit, a gold memorial to her dreams – and climbed into the darkness of the palanquin.

As soon as her boots left the snow, Dumai of Ipyeda was gone.

****

Throughout the journey down the mountain, Noziken pa Dumai woke in fits and starts. She dreamed of a white dragon, a woman trapped in her own bones, the parched earth splintering. It might have been hours or days before the door opened, and she was being helped on to the ground.

The ground.

For the first time in her life, no snow was underfoot. Instead, there was a path, leading to a house with a green roof, flanked by season trees in red leaf for autumn.

Mount Ipyeda stood godlike above.

She had never seen the mountain she had lived on all her life. Not in its full splendour. Now she took it in, speechless with reverence – its three white peaks, for the claws of a dragon.

'Princess?' a curious voice said. Dumai looked down to see a grey-haired woman, round as a pear, who stared at her in disbelief. 'Ah, Manai was right. You look just like His Majesty.'

Dumai tried not to lose her nerve. 'Are you Lady Taporo?'

'Yes. Forgive my surprise, Princess Dumai.' The woman bowed. 'I am Mithara pa Taporo, your ... now, let's see. Cousin once removed, I believe, through your grandfather. Welcome to my home.' She straightened, then smiled. 'Can that be you, Osipa?'

'Taporo.' Osipa limped to Dumai, leaning on her cane, and eyed the woman. 'I see you got old, too.'

Lady Taporo laughed. 'Certainly older. Welcome back to Antuma, my friend,' she said warmly. 'From what little I know of mountains, the two of you may be unwell for a time. You will grow used to the ground here, and I'll prepare you both for life at court.'

'I remember it well enough,' Osipa groused. 'What is it they used to say? *Court is a place where fortunes flower like spring, and fall like autumn leaves.*'

'I'm afraid it has only grown more treacherous since your departure.' Lady Taporo beckoned. 'Please, come in, and warm yourselves. We should keep you out of sight. Let us not warn the River Lord you are coming.'

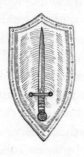

17

West

Seen at sunrise, the Lakes was finest of the six provinces of Inys. Witherling Water was calm as sheathed iron, save for the herons in its shallows, prodding about for early fish.

That was north. To the south, night clung to the haithwood. A woodpecker hammered at one of the trees, making it braver than most humans. Few would knock on that particular door.

'Wulf.'

Mara was walking towards him. 'You didn't need to get up,' Wulf said, touched. 'We've said our goodbyes.'

'Someone had to see you off,' she said. 'You look tired. Bad dreams?' He returned to preparing his horse with a shrug, smoothing a few creases from the saddle blanket. 'Wulf, I've been telling you for years, it's a foolish story. There's never been a witch.'

'In Hróth, they say the oldest stories have the deepest roots.'

'And this one is rooted in fear of dark places. There is no curse on that forest. Or on you.' As he lifted the saddle on, she leaned against the stoop. 'Why the frown?'

'I always frown.'

'Aye, but you're frowning more than usual. You'll be grey before you're twenty if you don't stop brooding.'

Wulf let something unlatch inside him, hard as he tried to hold it shut. Mara had always given him shrewd counsel.

'I defied the Knight of Fellowship,' he said. 'Regny. In the summer.'

'King Bardholt found out,' Mara guessed. He nodded. 'A woman of her rank must marry high.'

'I don't want to marry her. She doesn't want to marry me. We were just curious. Foolish.' Wulf took off his gloves to manage the buckles. 'Bardholt forgave me this time, but sometimes I'm afraid I'm not strong enough to walk this path. Not worthy of it.'

'Wulf, you must end this eternal quest to be *worthy*. We've never needed to do anything to make Father or Pa proud.'

'You know my situation is different.'

'No. You are as much their child as I am,' Mara said, quiet and firm. 'You've chosen a hard path, and there's a reason there are six virtues. If it weren't hard to follow them all at once, we'd all be saints, now, wouldn't we?'

She tapped the patron brooch that pinned his cloak, wrought like a sheaf of wheat. Their father had secured royal permission for him to wear silver, like the rest of the family.

'Your patron is the Knight of Generosity,' she reminded him. 'Be generous to yourself. If your gravest vice is to seek comfort in cold places, the Saint will forgive you. As will the king.'

'I hope so. Put in a good word for me if you reach Halgalant first?'

'I have sins of my own.' Mara kissed his cheek. 'Don't wait so long to visit again. And when you come back with your bright spurs and girdle, don't you expect anyone to call you Sir Wulfert.'

With a smile, he mounted. 'Sir Wulf will suffice.'

Mara laughed and waved him off. As he rode, she disappeared into the mist, and so did the drear wood behind.

****

Sunlight slanted through the windows of the Dearn Chamber. Seated closest to the fire, Adela steered a spoonful of stewed pear into her mouth. 'How are you feeling?' Glorian asked her.

Her pallor was a shock against her auburn hair, and her cheek was swollen. 'Thankful,' she lisped. 'The Saint stretched out his divine hand to stop my tooth from aching.'

Helisent blew on her pottage. 'Mastress Bourn stretched out their pincers, more like.'

With what looked to be great difficulty, Adela swallowed both the pear and her retort. 'I have some news,' Julain said, tucking back her hair. 'It seems I may soon be betrothed.'

Glorian stopped eating. 'To whom?'

'Lord Osbert Combe.'

'That would make you Duchess of Courtesy by marriage, at least after his mother dies,' Helisent mused. 'Would you have to change patrons?'

'No,' Glorian said. 'Julain is the descendant of Dame Lorain Crest. Justice will always be her patron.' Speaking of betrothal soured her stomach. 'When will you meet him, Jules?'

'He rides to court tomorrow.' Julain ran the end of her dark plait between her hands. 'I know I've no obligation to wed, but I've had moths in my belly ever since Mama told me.'

'Crush them. Nobody could not love you.' Glorian speared a rasher of bacon with unnecessary force. 'And I'm certain your mother wouldn't force you to marry anyone you *hated*.'

She pretended not to see their worried glances. Happily, Sir Bramel chose that moment to interrupt.

'Highness,' he said, 'King Bardholt invites you to join him in the orchard. May I escort you?'

'You may,' she said, standing.

The sky was so blue it made her eyes water. Her guards led her to the low wall of the apple orchard, where her father was waiting beside a hulking Yscali warhorse.

'Daughter,' he said in Hróthi, 'come for a ride. It's a fine morning.'

Glorian hesitated, touching her cast. 'Mastress Bourn told me I must wear this for at least three more weeks. And Mother said—'

'I know what Mother said, which is why I told the grooms to bring one of these.' He patted the saddle, and she saw its pillion. 'Come. We'll ride as we did when you were a child.'

Glorian grinned. Mindful of her arm, her father put her in the pillion, then mounted the destrier himself. 'I have you,' he told her, and spurred it.

The castle grounds went on for ever, stretching past Blair Lake to the queenswood, where her parents would often hunt among the windbitten oaks and snow pines. As she held on to his waist, Glorian pictured her father storming across Hróth, wielding his bearded axe.

Six housecarls rode after him at a distance. Regny of Askrdal was among them, proud on her bay stallion.

The destrier galloped over fallen leaves, startling a flock of geese. After a time, King Bardholt slowed to a canter, and his retainers fell away. He rode on until the trees parted, and Glorian gazed up at the breathtaking crags of Sorway Fell. Her father had carried her all the way through the queenswood, to the slopes of the largest mountain in Inys.

A waterfall churned a deep rock pool, clear and green as forest glass. Shading her eyes, Glorian could see more cascades – steps of a stream that ran from somewhere in the mountains.

'The Twiring Pools,' her father announced. 'A well-kept secret of this province. Few dare trespass in the queenswood.' He dismounted and lifted Glorian down. 'Is your arm healing?'

'Yes. It was just an accident,' Glorian said. 'I wish I could keep riding, Father.'

Bardholt tied the destrier to a tree. 'I'll speak with Her Grace.' He placed a hand between her shoulders. 'Sit with me.'

They found two suitable boulders. Bardholt took off his riding boots and footwraps and sat with his legs in the water. Glorian kilted up her skirts before she did the same.

'Your mother showed these pools to me the summer before you were born. A long, burning summer.' Bardholt squinted up at the peak with a smile. 'We cooled ourselves here every day for weeks.'

'Mother swam here, in this wild pool?' Glorian said, delighted by the notion. 'Was she ... only in her shift?'

For some reason, that widened his smile. 'Of course, dróterning. She certainly wore her shift.' He grew serious. 'After you left the Dearn Chamber the other night, I spoke with her.'

Glorian hunched over. 'She told you about our quarrel. What I said to her.'

'She did,' Bardholt confirmed, 'but I want to hear it from your own tongue, Glorian.'

For the first time in over a year, Glorian scrutinised his face in daylight, at close quarters. The skin under his eyes had pleated, the lines that etched his brow were deeper, and tiny silver needles frosted his golden beard and hair. She hated those signs of age.

'I told her I didn't want to marry.' She could barely force the words out. 'Or have a child.'

'Did you say it in anger, or were you honest?'

'Both.'

She braced for him to rebuke her, though he never had. Instead, her father rested his elbows on his thighs and clasped his enormous hands. His gold love-knot ring shone on his left forefinger.

'Somewhere in these mountains is the birthplace of the River Lithsom, the longest in Inys,' he said. 'It starts as a trickle, flows down this valley, and carves a path to the Ashen Sea. A never-ending line that helps to keep this land alive. In centuries, it has never run dry.'

The water that comforted the people, running from the Saint. His unending vine. Glorian had heard enough from the sanctarian to know this tune. 'Yes, Father,' she murmured.

'No. I want truth,' King Bardholt said, his gaze relentless. 'Tell me what you fear.' She looked away. 'Every warrior should know fear. Without it, courage is an empty boast. Folly by another name.'

His patron brooch was a gold shield. Like hers, except his shield was round, and hers curved down to a sharp point.

'I'm not a warrior,' Glorian said. Her throat ached. 'I want to be, Father. I want to be like you.' The cast of his jaw softened. 'But a warrior possesses her own body. Inys has mine.'

At this, his jaw clamped again. For a terrible moment, her laughing, passionate father looked weary.

'That is the hardest part. Knowing that you embody a realm,' he said. 'That your eyes are its vigilance; your stomach, its strength; your heart, its shield; your flesh, its future. Even I find it a burden, and I never had to grow an heir within myself. Your mother and aunt did that, and for all my victories in Hróth, I could not help them in those battles.'

Only the water broke the silence. Glorian wished she could shake the shadows from him.

'Glorian,' he said at last, 'do you think your mother is a warrior?'

'No,' Glorian said, confused. 'She doesn't fight.'

'Yes, she does. Every day, she fights to keep Inys safe and strong,' he told her. 'When I was on the battlefield, I had to make hard choices, choices that meant life or death. Your mother does the same. The only difference is her battlefields are council chambers, her weapons are letters and treaties, and her armour is Virtudom itself.' He looked up at the mountain. 'Sometimes, there is more than one choice. More than one way the river could flow; more than one way to win the day. Sometimes there is only one.'

The implication was clear. Still, since he was in the mind to talk, Glorian plucked up her mettle.

'There are others, Father,' she said. 'Not for me. The House of Berethnet is the chain upon the Nameless One – but you could have founded a republic, like the Carmenti.'

'I could have,' he conceded. 'Sometimes I even wish I could agree with them. But a monarch has councillors, Glorian. Who do the people have to guide and temper them?'

'Each other,' Glorian offered. 'Books and scholars. Like the Decreer told you.'

'What if they make the wrong choice regardless? What if the books are filled with errors, or the scholars are dishonest – or the people choose not to listen to truth? Who is responsible for the realm?' he asked her. 'No one, in a republic. No single person can be held accountable. But a monarch takes responsibility. And a monarch of Virtudom answers to the Saint.'

Glorian dropped her gaze. Even though there was truth in it, her belly felt unsettled.

'I chose to make myself a king,' her father said. 'You never chose to be born into the holy bloodline.' He stroked a hand over her hair. 'Duty is hard, Glorian. You are still only fifteen – but no great battle was ever easy. And yours is the greatest battle of all.'

'Mother thinks I will lose it. She thinks I'm weak, like my grandmother.'

'That isn't true. I know she can be stern with you, but you are the most precious person in her world.'

'A necklace is precious,' Glorian said, her voice thin and brittle. 'You do not love a necklace. You only show it off and keep it safe.'

'When you hold your own daughter, you will know how much your mother loves you.' A breeze chilled the valley, and he wrapped some of his cloak around her. Glorian nestled close. 'Magnaust Vatten will treat you with respect. He is my subject,' he said into her hair. 'If he ever offends you again, I shall take my axe, sail back to Inys, and bury it in his thick skull.'

That made her laugh. 'I don't think you can do that now, Papa,' she said. He pulled a face. 'A king must keep the peace.'

He kissed her forehead. 'What peace can there be if my own daughter is unhappy?'

Glorian wiped a sudden surge of tears on her sleeve. 'I'm not just afraid we won't like each other,' she said. 'I'm frightened of losing myself.' She sniffed. 'I sound silly.'

'Then we must both be silly,' he said solemnly, 'because I felt the same fear before I married your mother. The fear that in knitting my flesh to hers, I would have to sacrifice some . . . secret place inside me.'

'Did you?'

'Some of it,' he confessed, 'but because I loved her, I let her inside, and found it was good to have company there.' He smoothed her tears away with his thumb. 'Perhaps that will happen with Magnaust Vatten. Perhaps not. If he is a fool, you don't ever have to let him into that secret place – and if he isn't, you won't find it so hard.'

Glorian swallowed the gravel in her throat.

'I will marry Magnaust Vatten,' she said, even as unhappiness overwhelmed her. 'As long as I can send him back to Mentendon once we have an heir.'

It occurred to her that she had no notion of what she was agreeing to. She still had no idea how a child was made.

'I will send the ship for him myself,' King Bardholt agreed. 'Until then, I have a gift for you. For your commendation, and for the battles ahead.'

He reached behind him and passed her a bundle of wrappings. Glorian undid the cords that secured it, revealing a beautiful sword. When she held it into the sunlight, the blade gleamed. Even finer was its bone handle, inlaid with three large gemstones, the pale green of her eyes.

'Ice emeralds,' she breathed.

They glistened like the sky lights. Ice emerald was mined at the very north of the known world.

'The steel was quenched in the Roaring Sea,' her father said. 'The ivory is from my throne.' He handed her its scabbard. 'Now you will always have a piece of Hróth to keep you safe.'

'Did you carve the handle?'

'I did.' He leaned down a little, looking her in the eyes. 'You are Princess of Hróth, Glorian Hraustr Berethnet. Your cousin will rule with *your* blessing. You will never reign in the North, but you will always be Glorian Óthling, child of its first king. Never forget it.'

Glorian took in his strong face, realising she might not see it again for months. He had not silenced her fear – no one could – but at least he had armed her, inside and out. She set the sword aside and flung her arms around his neck.

'Come back soon,' she said, muffled.

He wrapped her into a tight embrace. 'When the midnight sun bloods the ice, I will sail the whaleway again,' he told her. 'Until then, daughter, I bid you mind my heart. I leave half of it in your keeping.'

****

Later, she waited outside the gatehouse as his entourage prepared to make for Werstuth. The sword was a comforting weight at her side.

'Lady Glorian.'

A familiar retainer was leading a stallion from the courtyard. He wore a green cloak over his mail, embroidered with the crest of the House of Hraustr. 'Master Glenn,' Glorian said. He saluted her with a fist to his chest. 'I see you made it back in time. Is your family keeping well?'

'Very.' His dark curls were tousled. 'It was good to see them.'

'I'm afraid I don't recall if you have siblings.'

'Aye, I do. Mara is the middle child, and Roland the eldest. He's the heir to Langarth.'

'I envy you.' Glorian watched a Hróthi banner rise among the horses. 'I always thought it might be nice to have a sibling.' She beckoned her guards to follow her. 'Do let me see you off.'

'Surely the princess is too busy to escort a humble retainer.'

'The princess still has a broken arm, and has nought to do but twiddle her remaining thumb.'

'In that case, I'd be glad of the company,' he said. With her guards behind them, they walked towards the gathering of horses and retainers, Master Glenn leading his stallion. 'You say you'd like a sibling. I hear no Berethnet has ever had more than one child.'

'Not according to the records. Always one. Always a princess. Always identical to the others.'

'What would happen if a Berethnet had a prince, or more children?'

'Nothing, I suppose. The child – or children – would still have the sacred blood of the Saint.'

'But it hasn't happened.'

'Not so far. My ancestor always maintained that his line would be a line of queens.' She looked at him with interest. 'You are the first person who has ever asked me a question like that. Perhaps you ought to have been a sanctarian, Master Glenn. You think most deeply.'

'Kind of you, but protecting your father was always my calling.' He glanced at her. 'Is there to be a battle, Highness?'

'Pardon?'

'You seem to have gained a sword since we last met.'

'A gift from my father,' she said proudly, grasping the hilt.

'Very fine. I see that's his boneworking.' He raised his thick eyebrows. 'Can you use it?'

Glorian bridled. 'Of course.'

'I meant no offence, Lady. It only seems to me that rulers have scant use for weapons.'

'You say that, serving my father?' She raised an eyebrow back. 'I am the daughter of Bardholt Hraustr, who won his throne by blood and iron. I assure you, Master Glenn, I am no stranger to blades.'

'His Grace has never needed a weapon since his coronation, except in sport. This is an age of peace.'

'I find it best to be prepared for all eventualities. There may be a time when I find myself without my guards, and then what would I do?'

'For a start, I'd cut the guards loose, Highness. But I take your point.'

Glorian smiled. Before she knew it, she said, 'Perhaps we could cross blades when you return. See how an armed princess fares against a sworn retainer.'

'It would be my honour.'

The wind changed, and Glorian caught the scents of leather and smoke from him. 'What will you do when you return to Hróth?' she asked. 'Where will you go next with my father?'

'A progress in the Barrowmark, I believe, then back to Bithandun to weather the long winter in comfort,' he said. 'Do you visit Hróth often, Highness?'

'Not since I was twelve. I miss it.'

'You are its rightful heir. Sole issue of its king,' he said. 'Pardon my ignorance, but I never understood why your cousin is óthling over you. May a queen not rule two realms?'

Glorian brushed her hair behind her ear. He had no idea it was a tender spot. 'My mother says not,' she said. 'I could be queen regnant of one realm, and queen consort of another, as she is – but Her Grace believes I must choose Inys over Hróth, regardless of my claim.'

She had fallen in love with the eversnow the first time she set foot there. Her mother knew it well.

'I'm sorry,' Master Glenn said. 'That you can't see it more.'

'Thank you.' As they reached the entourage, a birch horn blew. 'I wish you a good voyage,' Glorian said, facing him. He bowed low to her. 'Keep my father safe, won't you?'

'I'll try, Highness.' He cleared his throat. 'Forgive me. I never did learn courtly manners. But since we were friends as children, would it be improper to ask if you would call me Wulf?'

'Yes,' Glorian said lightly, making him swallow. 'But I think the Knight of Courtesy might permit it if you called me Glorian.' He relaxed. 'Farewell, then, Wulf.'

'Farewell, Your—' He tried again: 'Glorian.'

Glorian watched him ride to join her father, watched the procession thunder away. As she returned to the courtyard, she stopped, swaying. She felt too heavy and too light.

And then all at once she was on the ground, and the taste of metal was flooding her mouth.

18

South

A leap mouse skipped and bounded through the sand, keeping up with the ichneumons as they wove between boulders and weathered spires. As Ninuru slowed, Tunuva watched the mouse hop out of sight over a dune, twirling its tail.

Now they were on a plain south of the Spindles, which the Ersyris called the Grove of Stone. Heat heaved from the sand, making the mountains ripple in the distance. Tunuva drained the last drops from her waterskin.

She could hold a boiled pot for longer than most, soak in a hotter bath – but too much warmth could be troublesome, in the burning days after eating the fruit.

They had picked up on the ichneumons' trail as soon as they left the Priory, following a blackwater prong of the River Minara. Throughout the journey, Ninuru and Jeda had maintained they could smell both missing ichneumons, despite there only being one set of tracks in the forest. Tunuva had reservations, but all she could do was trust in their noses.

'Why did Yeleni go with them?' Esbar said testily. 'Is she in love with this boy, too?'

Tunuva shook her head. 'You know she worships Siyu. It was never wise to pair them.'

'No,' Apaya agreed. 'Siyu needed an older girl as her hunting partner. I told Saghul so when she was seven.'

She stopped her grizzled ichneumon on an outcrop, where the ground dropped away into a deep canyon. Dark water sparkled far below.

'The Last Well. Smaller than it once was.' She was unruffled by the heat, though melted black paint marbled her cheekbones. 'The Desert of the Unquiet Dream begins here.'

Ninuru panted. 'Soon, honeysweet,' Tunuva told her. Her fur was matted with sweat. 'A little farther.'

All that lay ahead was hazy gold to the horizon. There was no longer any sign of the runaways. That was to be expected, now they were out of the Lasian Basin and into the desert, where the sands were always shifting.

Underground water had climbed to the surface and pooled, forming a lake. A herd of red deer lapped at its edge. Scenting the ichneumons, they fled in a cloud of dust. In her excitement, Jeda gave chase before Esbar had quite dismounted, throwing her into the sand.

'I fed you, ingrate. From my own hand,' she shouted after Jeda. Tunuva snorted with laughter before she could stop herself. 'By the Mother, how she's not tired—' Esbar unknotted her wrap and used it to mop her face. 'Then again, I won't refuse a bite of fresh meat.'

Tunuva slid from her saddle. 'I would like to herd all sheep into a ship and shove them out to sea,' she said, drunk on the heat, 'to be sure I never have to eat dried mutton again.'

'I support this plot.'

'If I may season this conversation with sense,' Apaya said curtly, 'watch for snappers. They come for the deer.' She stayed astride. 'I shall see if any Nuram tribes are close.'

Sending a sour look after her birthmother, Esbar took off her clothes. 'You heard her.' She blew out her cheeks and waded up to her hips in the lake. 'Is the fever still on you?'

Tunuva shook out her hair. 'More than ever.'

'Come, then. It's cool.'

Rushes slithered underfoot, giving the lake its rich darkness. When the water enfolded Tunuva, she sighed in relief and turned on to her back. Esbar came to float at her side.

'We're not going to catch her before the Harmur Pass,' Tunuva said. 'We will have to go into Mentendon.'

Siyu with a noose around her neck. Siyu kneeling by a block, hands tied behind her back.

'Tuva.' Esbar touched her hand. 'Siyu has no magic yet. No one will mark her for a witch.'

'Let us hope not.'

They beat the sand from their garments, washed them, and spread them in the sun to dry. Esbar wrapped her lower body with cloths, wadding moss between the layers, while Tunuva built a cookfire. The men had steamed plenty of curd root for their journey, swathing each batch in plantain leaf so it would keep for days. They opened a parcel each and ate.

Jeda soon returned, sheepish, and dropped a bloody shank beside Esbar. Once they had padded their bellies, Esbar dozed off in the shade while the ichneumons drank their fill. By afternoon, only Tunuva was awake, pushing back the shadows on the edges of her mind.

Siyu had been foolish and selfish. And yet, seeing Esbar stir in her sleep, Tunuva felt the same tenderness she always did, and wondered if Siyu felt that sweet ache when she looked at Anyso. It was a heady thing, to be young and in love for the very first time.

She and Esbar had been fortunate. More fortunate than many in the realms beyond the Priory. Trying to love in those realms must be like planting a seed among thorns – thorns of rank, of marriage, of the need for heirs. How many great loves had been strangled before they could grow, or withered away at the first sign of hardship?

Yes, she and Esbar had been lucky. Siyu had not.

It was sunset by the time Apaya returned. 'No sign of the tribes,' she told Tunuva. 'A pity.'

Tunuva nodded. 'Jeda made a kill,' she offered. Apaya sat beside her and took a cut of venison from the spit. 'How is the Queen of Queens?'

'Cheerful and rich. She likes to surround herself with ... eccentrics.'

'Including you?'

When Apaya eyed her, Tunuva hid a smile.

'Including me,' Apaya conceded. 'Court is never quiet. Last year, Daraniya offered her patronage to three identical sisters who learned mechanics in Bardant. Great inventors, apparently. A year ago, she hired an alchemist from Rumelabar, who delights her with his lofty claims that one day, he will turn all the sand in her deserts to gold.'

'Is she religious?'

'Nominally. One of her grandsons fosters an interest in the Six Virtues, and is smitten with a princess of Yscalin,' Apaya said, with distaste.

Yscalin had a rich shared history with the South, but the adoption of the Six Virtues under Isalarico the Second had caused bitter divides. Since then, Yscalin had often sought to convert its neighbours, by marriage or by threats of force, depending on who was in power.

'She also entertains followers of this mysterious seer, the one they call Raucāta,' Apaya went on. 'Three of her marcher wardens are among them, as is one of her brothers.'

Tunuva was intrigued. The writings of Raucāta, who had foretold the flaming destruction of Gulthaga, had been in the Ersyr for centuries. It was only now that her teachings had dedicated believers, though most Ersyris still followed the ancient Faith of Dwyn.

'Yes, court is a busy place. Noisy.' Apaya opened her saddle flask. 'Still, Daraniya is a good queen, and I take pride in guarding her. Many of our sisters have protected fools.'

'I hoped Siyu could protect someone.'

'There is your error.' Apaya looked her in the eye. 'I've always liked you, Tuva. Esbar is strongest at your side – but when it comes to Siyu uq-Nāra, you are ruled by an old grief.'

Tunuva held her gaze. 'It does not feel old to me.'

'I know.' Apaya glanced towards Esbar. 'I know what it is to carry a child within oneself. To feel a life quickening. Had it happened to Esbar, it would have fallen hard on me.'

It. Even Apaya – Apaya, who had survived three miscarriages before she bore Esbar, who stayed close to the point as the neck of an arrow – could not quite speak of *it*.

'In the Ersyr, they wall their traitors up in stone and let them die of thirst. In Inys, they pull them apart with horses,' she said. 'You know Siyu will face no such punishment, Tunuva.'

Execution was forbidden in the Priory. No Prioress would ever think of killing her own daughters.

'We are about to enter the Desert of the Unquiet Dream,' Apaya said. 'Do you know how it received its name?'

Everyone did. The men had passed down many stories from the ancient South.

'The Melancholy King,' Tunuva said at length. 'He fell madly in love with the Butterfly Queen. When she died, he sank into such unhappiness that none could shake him free of it.'

Tuva, please. Speak to me. Let me in.

'His realm crumbled. His advisors despaired. Then, one night, a bearded star passed, and the king emerged to watch. For the first time in years, he saw beauty, and wept.'

The sun on her face, and wine on her tongue. Breathing the air without wanting to die.

'Then he looked down,' Tunuva said softly, 'and there was the Butterfly Queen outside his palace, beckoning him to join her. And even though he knew she was dead, he followed her out of the city, all the way to this desert, desperate to hold his love one last time. He had no water. No shoes. All the while, he told himself: *I am only dreaming. Only dreaming.*'

'And was he dreaming?'

'No. The desert tricked his eyes. He died there, and the sand took his bones. Had he looked harder, he would have seen the truth. Love blinded him.'

'The oldest story in the Ersyr,' Apaya said, 'and the wisest in the world.' She lay down to sleep. 'Think on it, Tunuva.'

****

For days, they kept close to the Spindles, until they reached the Harmur Pass. Flanked by cliffs, the way threaded between the Smoking Ridge and the Gulf of Edin, forming a corridor to Mentendon. Two lofty watchtowers guarded the pass, a pair of great bronze doors between them. Last those doors had closed, it had been to deter the Vatten from encroaching on the Ersyr.

The mountains of the Smoking Ridge had a more sinister cast than their southerly cousins. Like a scar on the land, they carved Mentendon from Yscalin, forming a wall thousands of feet high. Theirs was a dreadful beauty, holding equal measures of menace and allure.

'I go no farther.' Apaya tossed Esbar a pouch. 'For the tolls. Ersyri coins for the way there, Mentish coins for the way home.'

Tunuva took out a coin. One face showed the wheel of Clan Vatten, the other the crude portrait of a man – Bardholt Hraustr, King of Hróth, holding a sword. The very sword the Mother had used to vanquish the Nameless One, its image stolen to peddle the lie they told in Virtudom.

'Follow the salt road north along the Smoking Ridge. It will lead you to Sadyrr,' Apaya said. 'Be wary – Daraniya has received reports of small earthshakes and steaming vents.' Tunuva thought of the hot spring. 'Esbar, write soon. Tell me what becomes of Siyu.'

Esbar pocketed the pouch. 'Of course.'

Tunuva turned to her ichneumon, hefting the saddlebags across her chest. 'You should not go,' Ninuru said to her. 'There is a new smell on the wind.'

'Is it horse?' Tunuva stroked her ears. 'I'm afraid I'll be covered in that when I return.'

'No. It smells like the tree,' Ninuru said. 'Like the beneath.'

'No time for long farewells. A queen is without her protector.' Apaya spoke in clipped tones. 'Jeda, Ninuru – follow the scent of kingsrose, and you'll find water. Wait for your sisters there.'

Ninuru butted Tunuva with her nose and stalked away. Jeda licked Esbar and followed.

'Ready?' Esbar asked. Tunuva shook her head and trudged towards the Harmur Pass.

They walked through the sand to the watchtower, where an Ersyri soldier took their toll. In return for another handful of coin, he let them choose a horse each for the journey.

It had been years since Tunuva had gone anywhere on horseback. It took time to adjust to the saddle, the slowness. They rode with travellers from all walks of life: merchants, explorers, mirrorfolk of the Faith of Dwyn. Others were heading south, perhaps seeking warmer climes.

By evening, they had reached a waystop, where the eastern cliffs parted for a beach. A camp had formed on its white sands. Beyond the tents, the Gulf of Edin sparkled in the crimson light of sunset, crisscrossed by tiny fishing boats and cutters with bright sails. While Esbar sought their supper, Tunuva approached a Mentish water merchant.

'Do you speak Ersyri?' she asked. The merchant nodded. 'I'm looking for two young women, about seventeen, and a man, a little older. The women may have worn green cloaks.'

'Have they run away from home?' the merchant asked, sympathetic. 'Many young people take the Harmur Pass, hungry for more of the world. They will make their own way back.'

'Have you seen them?'

'Possibly. I've no memory for faces, but yesterday I sold to a girl in a green cloak, with a small gold fastening, like a flower. She had an Ersyri hunting sword – I remember thinking her a little young for such a blade. But there was just one woman. No man with her.'

Tunuva handed over the saddle flasks, overpaying for the water. Esbar met her on the beach with bread and bowls of lentil stew. 'One of the girls was here yesterday,' Tunuva told her. 'A green cloak with a gold fastening, and a sword. We should keep riding.'

Esbar passed her a loaf. 'They separated, then?'

'So it seems.'

Once they had eaten, they cantered out of the camp, into the silent dark. For a mile, shards of baked clay strewed the path, where travellers had tossed away their bowls.

At dawn, they reached the doors on the other side of the Harmur Pass, which were smaller, made of wood. 'Welcome to Virtudom,' a guard said in thick Ersyri as they approached. He wore the Vatten crest. 'May the Saint guide your way.'

'And yours as well,' Tunuva said, also in Ersyri.

Esbar just lifted her chin. When they were through, they beheld Mentendon.

In all her life, Tunuva had only been this far north once before. Thin brown grass flanked the dusty path that stretched out from the doors. To the west, the Smoking Ridge continued.

'Virtudom.' Esbar narrowed her eyes. 'We are lawbreakers and heathens now, Tuva.'

'Then let us leave as soon as we can.' Tunuva tightened her grip on the reins. 'I have no wish to be in any place where the people worship the Deceiver.'

'Agreed. Even if some were given no choice.' Esbar sighed. 'To the salt road, then. If I hear even one person insult the Mother, I will not be held responsible for my actions.'

19

West

The salt road cleaved to the Smoking Ridge. They rode for as long as they could by night, the air chilling as they moved farther north. By day, they slept among dark boulders or oak groves, out of sight.

Without their ichneumons to track the scent, they relied on reason. The salt road was the fastest way to Sadyrr, the way that Siyu would most likely have come. On the fourth day, they stopped for supplies and a hot meal at Svartal, where the Ments mined a rare black salt.

Mentendon had once been a mosaic of cultures and beliefs, even when its own ancient religion had been widespread. Before the Midwinter Flood, every faith in the world had earned followers here. The Six Virtues had been present for at least a century, especially in the west, where Yscali influence was strongest – but now the law enshrined their supremacy. Any other form of worship was severely punished.

In the past, the wine den at Svartal must have welcomed orchardists, mountain singers, mirrorfolk. Now there was one drunk sanctarian. Esbar eyed him over her cup of apple wine.

'Stop staring,' Tunuva muttered.

'Why?' Esbar said under her breath. 'What do I have to fear from his dead knight?'

'Do you want to spend time on a pyre?'

'I could always use a warding. It might be fun,' Esbar mused, 'watching him squawk as I refuse to burn.' Tunuva went to pay. 'What?'

They made camp in the foothills. Through a crack between two boulders, Tunuva watched a train of carts head north at sunrise, laden with lumber. Three riders in leather and mail, their hair oiled in a Hróthi style, barked orders at the Ments.

'Those must be salt warriors,' Tunuva said. 'Can they be taking all that wood for Hróth?'

Esbar grunted. 'Iron pine. I hear they cut all theirs down.' She turned over, bundling her cloak under her head. 'Get some rest, Tuva.'

Tunuva lay down beside her. 'What if Siyu doesn't want to come back?'

'She is coming back whether she likes it or not.'

'The Priory is not a cage.' Tunuva looked at her. 'Is it?'

'If it was, you and I would not be in this place,' Esbar said, her voice short with exhaustion. 'We are the Mother's secret. That means protecting our sisters even from themselves.'

'What if Siyu no longer wants to be a secret?'

'Perhaps none of us can do or be exactly as we please in life.' Esbar breathed out through her nose. 'If she were older, I might listen. She doesn't know what she's choosing.'

As she spoke, the ground trembled. Esbar snapped upright, wide awake. Tunuva watched the mountains. 'Perhaps we should move on,' she said. The rocks were hotter. 'Can you last?'

Even though Esbar looked weary, she nodded. They climbed back into their saddles.

Now they rode almost without stopping. It rained for the first time: cold, hard rain. Tunuva tilted back her head and relished the feel of it on her skin.

At last, on the cusp of a burnished sunset, hulking forms rose from a plain east of the road. Here the grouts of a crushed dome, and a line of pillars, all shortened like candles; there a crumbling archway, high and stern, or the face of a god whose name was forgotten. Tunuva stopped her mount to behold the Buried City.

Gulthaga. Once it had been a shining cauldron of knowledge and trade – a city of secrets, marvels and horrors, which might one day have grown into a cruel and thirsty empire. Now it lay in piles of stone, waiting for time to reduce it to dust, and then to memory.

At the same time, Tunuva and Esbar looked up in silence. Above were the terrible slopes of the Dreadmount. Eleven thousand feet of rock, armoured in black glass from the only day it was known to have erupted – the day it birthed the Nameless One.

Where the ancient Yscals had worshipped all mountains, the Ments had only feared this one. They had seen it as the lair of an earthbound god, the Smith of the World, enemy of the Smith of the Heavens. They had brought offerings to its slopes to appease him, sacrificed people to his boiling springs – though Tunuva suspected the second part was an untruth, peddled by the Vatten to justify their forced conversion of the Ments.

In fifty years, she had never seen anything that disturbed her more than the Dreadmount. Each sister came to behold it after her kindling, to remember what the Mother had defeated, and to understand the monumental heights of her courage. She had faced the vile spawn of this mountain alone.

Proof of its violence scattered the ruins – bones by the thousand, left where the heat had baked them centuries before. Crops would usually be grown in the rich soil around fire mountains, vineyards raised to make fine wines, but no one dared sow here. After all, it was arrogance that had doomed the Gulthaganians. They had taunted the mountain with their glorious city, and the Dreadmount had answered, smothering its splendour.

Tunuva looked past the tragic remains, towards a shape on the stump of a pillar. With Esbar behind, she spurred the horse off the salt road, down the incline to the skeleton of Gulthaga. As she drew close, the shape resolved into a girl, wrapped in a green cloak, staring at the mountain.

'Yeleni Janudin,' Esbar seethed. 'You've led us on a merry chase. Get down from there.'

'Esbar. Tuva.' Yeleni climbed off the column, face slick with tears. 'You came. I hoped it would be you.'

Tunuva called out, 'Is Siyu here, too?'

'No.'

'You little fool.' Esbar was already off her horse. 'You are very fortunate that I am not yet Prioress. Were it up to me—'

'Forgive me, sister, please.' Yeleni buckled, heaving with sobs. 'Siyu said I could go with them to Hróth. I wanted to see the sky lights, just once! She told me to ride all the way to Sadyrr, but then I saw the Dreadmount.'

She covered her eyes with one hand. 'I should never have forsaken the Mother. Not even to see the lights. Please, sisters, take me home.'

'You may not have one any longer,' Esbar bit out.

The girl looked terrified. 'Calm, child.' Tunuva spoke as gently as she could. 'Where is Siyu?'

Yeleni wiped her cheeks. 'They never came this way. She and Anyso told me to leave first, to lead you away. So they could wait a few days and then ride to Kumenga.'

'Then they are not going to Sadyrr.' A bitter realisation. 'Esbar, we have lost the—'

The ground shunted, so hard Yeleni lost her footing.

Dust hissed around them. The Dreadmount gave a long, hostile rumble, a sound that ground into the marrow, and smoke curled from its slopes. A flock of birds took off from the ruins. Tunuva caught her horse by the reins and held on as it huffed out a nervous snort.

A dead stillness followed. All Tunuva could hear was breath: hers, not hers. And her blood – she could have sworn that she could feel it, the hot melt of it through her veins.

She could have sworn her blood was simmering.

It happened faster than she had thought possible: the shattering, the crack of rock, the furnace that bellowed from beneath the skin of Edin. In her dreams, it had never taken a moment for the world to break, as it had five centuries before. It had always taken hours.

But in the time it took her to draw breath, stillness was turmoil. Silence was din. The ground heaved underfoot, and at last, lava came exploding from the mountain – an eruption so destructive in its force, so catastrophic, that Tunuva doubted her own eyes. Foul fumes came rushing forth with it; branches of lightning flashed. The few clouds overhead were torn away, as suddenly as if a god had snatched them to opposite sides of the sky.

The horses screamed and reared. Fighting to restrain her mount, Tunuva smelled brimstone. The stench ignited the magic within her. Her fingers burst unbidden into flame, a red flame she had never seen. Before she could absorb the shock, she had reduced the reins to char, and the horse broke loose with a squeal, eyes rolling.

Esbar had lost her horse, too, though she seemed not to care. She was gazing at the Dreadmount, her eyes reflecting chaos, holding fire. The sight unlocked Tunuva.

'Ez,' she said, 'we have to move. Esbar!'

'It's like us.' Esbar was rooted in place. 'Do you sense it, Tuva?'

Tunuva sensed it.

Siden. The same magic that lit the tree, that comforted and strength-ened her. There was nothing that felt the way siden did, and yet that was what she felt now from the Dreadmount, the cradle of evil. She fought a fearsome urge to walk towards the eruption – to dive into that sea of fire, drink it down like wine. She felt strong enough to do anything.

There was no time to wonder. Hot rocks and embers glittered in the sky, small as coins at this distance, and rained on to the slopes. They flickered out, only for more to fall. The slopes themselves were moving, shifting.

Another rumble shook the Dreadmount. Rubble came thundering down its sides; small chips were clattering on the ruins. Yeleni cried out as one of them nicked her cheek. Straining with the effort, Tunuva smothered the strange fire, seized Yeleni by the wrist, and thrust her into a gutted house. Not a moment too late, for a deep *boom* came next. The air scorched, more fire ignited in her palms, and she was thrown backwards, into the remnant of a column.

That shock could have killed her. If not for what they were, she knew they would already be dead. Waves of hot wind seared her eyes dry. Far away, her horse crumpled.

'Tuva!'

She stared past Esbar, at the river of flame that stemmed from the mountain, iron smelted in the forge. Bright firefalls seeped down the slopes.

'Yeleni,' she managed, 'quickly!'

The girl ran towards her. Tunuva grabbed her hand, and the three of them struck out across the plain.

Ash and rock pattered everywhere, cutting their skin. Above, day became darkest night.

Mages were swift, but the flow of molten fire was faster. This time, it would not consume Gulthaga. Instead, it was streaming down another side of the mountain, towards their way back to the Harmur Pass. Tunuva moved as she never had, pulling Yeleni behind her, wrapping herself and the girl in a warding. Overhead, a black pillar twisted towards the sky, bloated with lightning – billows climbing billows, wide as a city, already several miles high, so thick it looked solid, yet soft as a cushion.

Sooner or later, that ash plume would collapse.

'Tuva,' Esbar called, hoarse. 'The ichneumons!'

When Tunuva saw, a laugh of relief broke from her throat. Ninuru was racing towards them, a flash in the dark, Jeda a shadow behind. Without questioning their good fortune, Tunuva bundled Yeleni into the saddle and leapt on in front of her. Esbar dived for Jeda.

The Dreadmount was enraged. As the ichneumons' paws scuffed over the plain, slabs of burning rock crashed down around them. The ground rippled and broke apart. Yeleni tightened her arms around Tunuva.

A shove of her hind legs, and Ninuru flew across a steaming crack. Tunuva turned in the saddle to see a fireball hurling towards Jeda.

'Ez, behind you!'

Esbar threw up her palm. Siden flared and deflected the fire, leaving a trail of embers sparkling in her wake.

'Nin, hurry,' Tunuva urged her ichneumon. 'Hurry—'

Ninuru barked. Each leap and stride took her farther than the last. Tunuva looked up at the streams of fire, close now, nearing a scarp of rock, almost on top of them. She closed her smarting eyes and clung to Ninuru, committing herself to the arms of the Mother.

Lava poured over the scarp. Not a moment too late, Jeda and Ninuru flew out of its path. It washed down the steep wall of rock and bubbled across the plain in a livid river, steaming and marbled with black. Heat swept over Tunuva. She went limp as the tension slid from her muscles.

It was some time before the ichneumons stopped running. By then, they were back on the high stretch of the salt road, and ash thickened the reeking air. The only light was their own flames.

'Ninuru, stop,' Tunuva could hardly speak. 'Wait.'

She did, and Tunuva stepped down. 'Tuva, we need to go,' Esbar said, face lit by her fire.

Covered in a fine coating of ash, Tunuva gazed towards the Dreadmount. Glowing streams bled down its slopes. The black smoke had risen so high and wide, she could no longer see where it ended and the sky began. Stabs of lightning lit the gnarled knots and swells in it.

Again, a silence, pregnant with something unspeakable.

A tremor whispered beneath her boots, up her spine, back through her blood.

Then came a terrible sound, the like of which she had never heard, and hoped never to hear again. Not the crack of the eruption, or the sinister rumble that had been the herald. This sound was the grating of earth on earth, the ring of metal, the roar of a fire as it swallowed a house – a bellow of consuming rage that echoed across Mentendon.

As Tunuva Melim watched, five dark shapes emerged from the mountain and disappeared into the night. Five dark shapes with ten dark wings, flocked by dark moths that all screamed the same scream, old as the world.

****

In Drouthwick Castle, Glorian Berethnet woke from a strange dream. At her side, Lady Florell Glade cooled her forehead, which had been too cold a moment before.

'Glorian?'

As Florell stroked her hair, Glorian opened her eyes.

'It's risen,' she whispered.

After, she would not remember saying it at all.

20

North

The sunset had turned the snow to spun honey. Alone with his bow in the gathering dark, Wulf stood beneath the pines and took aim at an elk in the clearing. King Bardholt meant to have a feast to celebrate their return to Bithandun. Fresh venison would please him.

The elk sniffed the air. Wulf slowly released his breath.

And then he felt something he should never have felt. Not in that Northern forest on a frozen lake, the world all cast in grey and white. Heat, welling up from under the snow. Pleasure and pain, fear, and some deep recognition – all of it boiled together in his heart.

His knees gave way. The arrow went thudding into a pine. As the elk fled, Wulf dropped his bow to grip his chest, as if he could stop it from burning. He fell like a sack of stones.

21

East

Her court attire was twice as heavy as it looked, each of the six garments dyed a pale shade of the rainbow. All were interleaved with thin layers of white.

The servants had brushed pearl dust across her cheeks and brow. Nothing else. The world needed to see her face. Since her hair remained too short to shape, they had trimmed and combed it smooth. The crown on top put a strain on her neck – a delicate concoction of seashells and pearls.

Her cart was open to the world, cowries hanging from its roof. Lady Taporo had explained how important it was that the people knew she existed before she entered Antuma Palace. She would not be able to disappear if everyone knew she was there.

Lady Taporo had nursed her through her arrival. For days, she had been so unwell that she had not even tried to rise, listening to her cousin from within the safe nest of her bedding. She still had a dry cough, and her skull felt too small for what was inside it.

She must hide the earth sickness at court. Not for one moment could she appear weak.

Several guards had accompanied her through the city gate. Now they continued along the Avenue of the Dawn, where fifty thousand people had gathered to see the lost Princess of Seiiki.

Drums beat out her approach. Fascinated faces jostled for a look at hers. For the first time in days, she was glad she could no longer see Mount Ipyeda, though its presence was like a cold wind at her back. She could not look towards it. Only ahead.

Yet how could she help but think of her mother, who had lived here as a child? Unora had slept in one of these mansions, played under the willow trees that leaned over the cart.

The rooftops of Antuma had been painted every colour imaginable; from above, the city was one great rainbow. As for the palace, it was larger than Dumai had ever imagined. When she reached it, she would meet her sister, Princess Suzumai, the child she would eventually usurp.

Treading with care, Emperor Jorodu meant to confirm Dumai as his heir only after three years. During those years, she would need to prove herself worthy of the throne, so the Kuposa could raise no objection. She would receive a rigorous education in politics and law.

You will have to learn to be an empress, Lady Taporo had told her, *in a very short amount of time. It will not be easy.*

The cart rolled, the drums thundered, and at last, the people of Antuma fell away, unable to follow her any farther. Dumai shut her eyes, her skin clammy.

Great Kwiriki, please, let me not disgrace myself.

The clay wall of the palace loomed. So did its western gate. Over it, rooftops sloped towards the ground, silver glistening in their gables. Dumai kept her eyes closed as her cart went across the moat.

At last, they stopped. Courtiers and officials waited in a grand court-yard, their hair moulded into seashells, servants hovering close. In unison, they bowed.

Her father stood in robes like hers. His crown was a tower of coral and cowries, fronted with two silver dragons, a fist-sized dancing pearl between them. Dumai went to her knees in front of the steps, on the mat that had been laid there.

'Daughter,' her father said, loud and clear. 'Welcome to Antuma Palace. Your new home.'

'Thank you, Your Majesty.'

He came to her and helped her stand. Dumai looked up at him, so tired she thought she might sink through the ground.

'I have you.' He tucked her hand into the crook of his arm. 'Lift your face. Let them see.'

His kindness was a comfort. She did as he asked as he led her up the steps, into the largest building she had ever beheld, with ornate gables and a roof thatched with water reed.

Inside was a smoky gloom. Wooden dragons wound around stone pillars, wide as she was tall. The walls were darkly painted scenes from history and legend – some she knew, and some that she had yet to know. Silver and gold leaf glinted from blades and cresting waves and scales. There was Snow Maiden, Kwiriki curled at her breast, keeping to a small form while he healed.

Water dripped from decorative spouts and flowed through channels in the floor. Sunlight reflected off its surface, making the pillars ripple, and poured in through a sky window.

Beneath it stood the Rainbow Throne.

Dumai knew its story by heart. When dragons had first come to Seiiki, its people had feared the giant creatures and driven them away – but one woman had seen their beauty, and mourned their loss. She would walk on the cliffs of Uramyesi and sing her sorrow to the sea. The story called her Snow Maiden, for she would walk even in the harsh winter.

One day, she had found a wounded bird and carried it to her modest home. Unbeknownst to her, the bird was Kwiriki, foremost and greatest of all dragons. She had mended his broken wing. Once he had the strength to turn back into a dragon, he had given her one of his horns, to thank her. She had proven that humans could be wise and gentle. Their friendship had begun the mutual respect between dragonkind and the Seiikinese.

The Rainbow Throne bore witness to it – a gift to the first Queen of Seiiki. Its spiralled back almost reached the ceiling, curving like a ladle into a smooth seat. Every colour danced in that pillar of dragonbone, and mist drifted around it. Dumai looked at it in silence.

This was the throne she had to win.

Two people stood to the left of it. One was a woman, about the same age as Unora. 'Daughter,' Emperor Jorodu said, 'I present Her Majesty, Sipwo, Empress of Seiiki.'

Dumai locked eyes with Kuposa pa Sipwo. Her hair was spoked to resemble a spider conch. It must have taken her attendants half the day to shape it, and caused her no small degree of pain.

'Princess Dumai.' Her voice gave nothing away. 'It is my pleasure to be your stepmother.'

169

'And my honour to meet you, Your Majesty.'

Empress Sipwo continued to study her face. 'My younger daughter,' Emperor Jorodu said. 'Noziken pa Suzumai, Princess of Seiiki.' He offered a smile to the child. 'Suzu, finally – this is your sister, Dumai. She has come all the way from Mount Ipyeda.'

Suzumai stepped away from her mother. She was pale, like Sipwo, and small for her age, swamped by her long black hair. Downturned eyes peeked shyly at Dumai. A bundle of scarring had almost closed the left one, from the barnacle pox that had killed her brothers.

'Welcome, big sister.' She held out a box. 'For you.'

Dumai freed her hands from her sleeves to take it. Inside was a hairpiece, carved into the golden fish of the House of Noziken. 'How beautiful.' She closed it and smiled. 'I'm very happy to meet you, little sister.'

Suzumai smiled back. Her two front teeth had yet to grow in. 'I never had a sister.'

Empress Sipwo clenched her jaw and beckoned Suzumai into her arms. She nodded to a servant, who blew two long notes through a conch.

Courtiers filed into the hall and bowed before the imperial family. Dumai searched for the silver bell, finding it on the robes of the first man she saw, and the next. There were other crests, but not half as many.

'Before you stands a princess of the rainbow line,' Emperor Jorodu told them. 'Noziken pa Dumai, my eldest.'

A breeze of whispers crossed the hall.

'Since she was a child, my daughter has been a godsinger at the High Temple of Kwiriki. Now she comes to live at my side.' Murmurs. 'Though she was not raised here at court, she is closer to the gods than any of us, having praised them every day on Mount Ipyeda.'

He stopped when two more people entered. They strode between the two columns of courtiers.

Like the emperor, the man stood at middling height and build, but such was the confidence of his gait that he seemed to take up far more space than he occupied in body – a moon casting light a long way from itself. Dumai had never seen a person look so enormously content. His grey beard was braided into a fishtail, and his travelling clothes were sumptuous, broidered with silver thread. She guessed he was around seventy, still spry.

'River Lord,' Emperor Jorodu said, his tone cool. 'You were not expected until later in the season.'

'I came at once when I heard, Your Majesty. A new pearl for our court,' the bearded man exclaimed. 'I could hardly believe it. Can this be the mysterious Princess Dumai?'

'As you see.'

Never taking his gaze off Dumai, the newcomer brandished a wide smile and bowed.

'Your Highness,' he said, 'welcome. Welcome to Antuma. I am the River Lord of Seiiki, and granduncle to your sister, Princess Suzumai. How very like your father you look.'

And so the duel began.

'My lord,' Dumai said. 'I understand you were my father's regent.' He inclined his head. 'I trust your time away was restful, cut short though it was.'

'It was, Princess, and I thank you for asking. There is nowhere quite so beautiful or calming as the temple at Fidumi,' he remarked, 'or at least, not that I have personally set foot in. My daughter assures me that Mount Ipyeda is the most impressive place she has ever visited.'

Dumai finally noticed the woman beside him. It was her – the Kuposa climber. Nikeya.

Lady Nikeya, of Clan Kuposa.

She was his *daughter*.

'One must ask why you would ever leave such sacred precincts,' the River Lord continued. Dumai tore her gaze back to him. 'Perhaps a life of worship was not to your taste after all?'

'I have served the great Kwiriki for a long time,' Dumai said, 'and continue to serve him now. I dreamed he called me to the palace, and the very next day, His Majesty came.' She allowed her smile to widen. 'It is, of course, understandable that a man of your worldly experience should grow restless in a temple. Religious devotion is a difficult commitment.'

'As is devotion to the people. I trust you do not feel ill-suited to your position, Princess,' the River Lord said, 'having spent so little time on the ground. I am considered by some to be a gifted poet; I have worked at my craft since I was a boy. What a waste it would be if I were to throw away that skill so late in life, and to instead become a crude musician.'

Talking to this man was already like fighting a windstorm.

'A lute must have several strings to make a song.' Dumai spoke calmly. 'I think it never too late to learn.'

'We can only hope the ways of our palace will merit the same attention as the sacred rites. On that subject, you must tell us all how you came to be on the mountain in the first place! Such a precious thing, a firstborn child – how could she be unknown to us?' the River Lord asked the entire hall. 'Who was it that hid your splendour, Princess?'

'My mother is the Maiden Officiant of the High Temple of Kwiriki.'

'Ah, yes. My daughter had the pleasure of meeting her. May I present Lady Nikeya?'

The spy bowed. 'Unora,' she said warmly as she straightened. 'How good to see you again.'

The River Lord laughed from his chest. 'Daughter,' he said, the picture of amused surprise, 'what can you be saying? This is Princess Dumai.'

Lady Nikeya opened her mouth in mock astonishment. Dumai tried not to grit her teeth.

'Father. Forgive me,' Lady Nikeya said demurely. 'Only … when I met Princess Dumai on Mount Ipyeda, I thought she told me her name was Unora. Perhaps I misheard.'

Dumai glanced at her father, who had not uttered a word during this exchange.

'How unusual,' the River Lord said. 'You must indeed have misheard. After all, there is no reason the princess should have tried to hide her true name. Is there?'

'My daughter has had a long journey,' Emperor Jorodu broke in, 'and is too tired for questions, River Lord. There will be many opportunities to speak with her in future.'

'Of course, Your Majesty. Forgive your servant his enthusiasm.' With that faultless smile, the River Lord bowed low. 'Please, Princess, rest. And welcome, once again, to Antuma Palace.'

Without waiting for a dismissal, he strode away. Lady Nikeya smirked at Dumai, who looked back with as much dislike as she could muster with her eyes alone, before following her father.

****

Dumai had been assigned twelve attendants, including Osipa. Fortunately, Lady Nikeya was not among them, but from what Taporo had told her, at least half of them reported to the River Lord. Dressed in the same evening blue as the roof, they followed Dumai into the Rain Pavilion – a section of the enclosed Inner Palace, where the imperial family resided.

'Kwiriki's tears, why is it so cold in here?' Osipa asked the nearest woman, who was tall and wore a tart expression. 'Do you mean for the princess to freeze in her sleep?'

'It is autumn,' the woman pointed out, her tone as frigid as the wind. 'Autumn is cold.'

'Swords are sharp, yet we take steps to prevent them cutting us,' came the brusque reply. 'It was warmer than this on the highest mountain in the province. Stop pouting and make yourself useful, if that concept is familiar to you. Bring in another two braziers.'

With a stiff nod, the woman motioned to three of the other attendants, who left.

The building held a bedchamber and a withdrawing room, enclosed by a single corridor. Dumai walked along it. The windows had hinged shutters, pushed wide open, so only fine screens swayed in the breeze. When she reached for one, the women were ahead of her.

'Allow me, Princess Dumai.'

The screen was rolled up and tied in place.

'The Floating Gardens,' said the attendant beside her. She looked no more than fifteen. 'Are they not lovely?'

The north side stood in still greenish water, which spread as far as the eye could see, reflecting every cloud like a mirror. Low islands arched from it, joined by bridges, each island holding beauty: a stone lantern, a statue, an ornate pavilion. Dumai looked west, and there was Mount Ipyeda. Just as she had hoped, she could see it.

'They say the great Kwiriki himself made these gardens,' one of the ladies remarked. 'It was once a deep lake, but he drank enough of its water that thirty islands appeared.'

'The Crown Prince would swim every day,' the young girl said. Her cheeks were pink. 'He was very clever. We are sorry for your loss, Princess. That you never met your brothers.'

'Thank you.' Dumai stepped back. 'I wish to be alone with Lady Osipa. Please, do as you wish today.'

The chilly woman said, 'The Rain Pavilion is where we live, Princess. We are here to—'

'Do you have floss in your ears?' Osipa snapped at her. The younger attendants jumped. 'Princess Dumai has given you an order. It is not your place to question her. Fetch some wood for the braziers, air the bedding, stand idle. Whatever you do, do not do it here.'

'And when should we return?' the woman asked coolly.

'When you are summoned.' As soon as they were gone, Osipa said, 'Come into the antechamber, Dumai.'

Inside it, Dumai looked about. Osipa used a hook on a short pole to lower its screens.

'We will not often be able to speak here,' she said. 'They will always be close.' She faced Dumai. 'The gift from your sister. Where is it?'

Dumai handed the box over. Osipa looked at the headpiece inside it, her fingers stiff on the latch. 'I will drop it into a well,' she muttered. 'An identical replacement will be made.'

'Why?'

'Because I trust no one here.' Osipa slipped it into her robes. 'The River Lord is likely to use Suzumai against you. Armour your heart. She is the greatest threat to your throne.'

'Her throne. Which I am going to take.'

'Did you not listen to your cousin?' Osipa said impatiently. 'This is how the Kuposa work. If the throne passes to a child, it is theirs.' Her eyes were hard. 'This palace is now a battlefield. Emperor Jorodu and the River Lord are the generals. You and Suzumai are their weapons.'

'I am no man's weapon,' Dumai said, nettled.

'Then work harder. Be your own general.'

She lowered herself onerously to the mats. Dumai helped her. 'There is something I never asked Lady Taporo,' Dumai said, kneeling at her side. 'Who rules after me, if not Suzumai?'

Osipa glanced towards the blinds, just thin enough to see through. 'Ideally,' she said, 'you would have your own child. Take a consort as far away as possible from Kuposa influence.'

'And if I don't, or can't?'

'Then we shall find a minor Noziken to put on the throne.'

'Who?' Dumai said, despairing. 'How many are left with the blood of the rainbow?'

'Very few. You do have distant cousins still living,' Osipa added, 'though I can't imagine they have half a stomach between them, or they would already have come to support your father. Still, they could be an option . . . if a better one does not present itself.'

Dumai had never even considered the possibility of having a child.

'I want to go home,' she said.

Osipa snorted in disgust. 'And give up the fight?' she said. 'I think not. Kwiriki himself enthroned your line, Noziken pa Dumai. Do you mean to stop serving him now?'

A long time passed. Outside, birds chirruped in the Floating Gardens.

'No,' Dumai said. 'Not now, or ever.'

22

South

'Five, you say.'

Shadows wavered on the wall. In the dimness, Tunuva and Esbar stood before the Prioress.

'Yes,' Tunuva said. 'And many smaller ones. All winged.'

'The Mother never wrote of this,' Saghul muttered. 'We expected the Nameless One to return, not new beasts to emerge.' She drew a deep breath. 'Do you think one of them was him?'

'We can't know,' Esbar said. 'It was too dark.'

Tunuva was still covered in ash. The smell of fire and shattered earth was difficult to shake.

'Prioress,' she said, 'when the Dreadmount erupted, Esbar and I made a third kind of fire, a red fire.' She let the flame gutter in her hand again. 'Feel the heat of it.'

'We sensed siden,' Esbar said. 'More than we've ever felt from the tree. It was ... in the air, in the ground uncontrolled. As if the Womb of Fire were bleeding.'

Saghul grasped the arms of her chair.

'The Mother said his fire was as red as his scales,' she said. 'We will learn more, but for now, Tunuva, put it out. Let us not meddle with a power we do not yet understand.'

With a glance at Esbar, Tunuva obeyed.

176

'Did the Mother ever speak of seeing our magic in him?' Esbar pressed.

'I will have the archive searched.' Saghul tightened her grip on the chair. 'The battle we have expected for five centuries may now be imminent. Esbar, go to the initiates and tell them what has happened. Double training hours. The men should make as many arrows as they can.'

'They will begin cutting wood from tomorrow.'

'Good. Tunuva, while Esbar assists me here, I would like you to oversee ranging. We must find evidence of where these creatures have gone, their numbers … and what they mean to do.'

Tunuva said, 'Do you mean to inform Daraniya and Kediko, since we are bound to protect their lands?'

'Kediko has always been difficult. He needs to be approached with care. I will send word to Gashan,' Saghul said, 'but she may be too busy to notice my letter, *worldly* as she now is.' Esbar shook her head. 'You must visit Nzene before you return, Tunuva, to reinforce my words. You have the patience to convince both Gashan and Kediko.'

'I am honoured by your trust, and will do what I can.' Tunuva paused. 'Siyu and Anyso—'

'Intercepted on the western boundary of the Basin.' Saghul reached for her cup. 'Siyu has decided to keep the child. Since I have already informed Gashan of her posting, I will honour it' – Tunuva breathed out – 'but first, she will spend her pregnancy here, without her sisters' company, so she has time to understand how gravely she endangered them. Yeleni will be confined to her room until I decree otherwise.'

Tunuva nodded. It was a harsh punishment, but it could have been far worse. 'And … Anyso?'

Saghul swilled her wine.

'We shall see, Tunuva Melim,' she said. 'We shall see.'

23

East

Dumai allowed her new attendants to enfold her in a sleeping robe and comb her hair. They shut her into her boxlike bed, where she lay sleepless, listening to their snores and fidgets.

On Mount Ipyeda, she had trusted everyone. Here, she could only trust Osipa, at least until Kanifa arrived. Osipa was meant to sleep alongside the other handmaidens, but Dumai had ordered her bedding to be placed in the antechamber, where she coughed in her sleep.

Dumai coughed, too. The earth sickness refused to let them go.

Deep in the night, Dumai suddenly tasted steel, as if she had bitten her tongue. She crawled to her chamber box and retched over it, sweating ice. *Something is wrong.* She knew it like she knew the paths her veins took through her wrists. *The world is changed . . .*

The tremors were still racking her when Osipa came. 'Dumai.' A bony hand touched her back. 'A messenger is outside. His Majesty wants you to come to the East Courtyard.'

Dumai wiped her mouth.

Osipa lit an oil lamp for her. In the gloom, Dumai fastened her robe, feeling weak and strange, and draped a mantle over it. Her attendants were still asleep in the corridor. She padded outside, to where moths clung to the lanterns, and followed the messenger.

Emperor Jorodu waited for her in the starry dark. Dumai was surprised to find him with only one attendant, carrying a lantern.

'You were the saltwalker,' Dumai said softly.

'I was.' The attendant bent into a bow. 'Epabo of Ginura. Good to see you in your rightful place, Princess Dumai.'

'Epabo is my loyal servant. He goes where I cannot,' Emperor Jorodu said. 'Dumai, forgive me for disturbing you. You must be very tired ... but even the Kuposa sleep.'

'I could not.' Dumai drew her mantle close. 'You wished to see me, Father?'

'Not only to see you. To show you.'

****

There was a discreet way out of the palace. Two ox-drawn carts waited beyond. Enclosed in hers, Dumai could not see where they were going. By the time she stepped back down, the clouds had moved, so the full moon shone bright as the sun on fresh snow.

'Nirai's Hills,' her father said. 'This area is forbidden to all but the imperial family, and those they choose to invite.'

The peaks formed a boundary of the Rayonti Basin. They concealed a grove of sundrops, with leaves that stayed gold all year long. In turn, those trees encircled a lake that lay quiet and still as black stone, its shore seamed by a milky glow. According to Unora, that was a sign of a sleeping dragon in the water.

'Dumai,' Emperor Jorodu said, walking towards it, 'I did not sleep once at the temple, such was my remorse.' The corners of his lips turned down, matching his long moustache. 'I loved your mother. I would have left you on the mountain in peace, were you not my only way to fight. If our family loses power, Seiiki will have no affinity with the gods.'

'I understand, Father.'

'Do you?'

'Of course,' Dumai said. 'Snow Maiden earned their trust and respect. We cannot lose it.'

They walked down the incline after Epabo, who carried the lantern towards the lake.

'Our family were dragonriders once. In the centuries after Snow Maiden, we ruled the sky and sea and land,' Emperor Jorodu said. 'But

179

then our dragons grew distant and mournful. One by one, they chose to enter the Long Slumber … and we lost our ability to ride. But they can still fly, if they choose. They have simply chosen to conserve their strength.'

'Why did their strength wane?'

'If a godsinger does not know the answer to that question, surely no one living does.'

An old boardwalk led into the lake, to the small island at its heart.

'The gods are benign,' Emperor Jorodu said as they crossed, 'but they are not of our world. They prefer not to involve themselves in the politics and conflicts of humankind. Even if they were awake, they could not help us counter a threat like the Kuposa. That is why I needed you.'

'Why have you brought me to this lake?'

'I brought the elder of your two brothers first. In the Empire of the Twelve Lakes, the Imperial Dragon chose a worthy heir from the House of Lakseng, when she was still awake. Here, the firstborn usually succeeds their parent, but I think the Lacustrine had it right. After all, we are made of water, and there is no better judge of water than a god.'

Dumai stopped when she saw what waited on the island. A large bell, cast in bronze.

'Father,' she said, 'it's forbidden.'

'Not for us. In fact, there is a way for us to wake them all, if Seiiki ever had great need. You lived beneath it your whole life.'

'The Queen Bell.'

'Yes. If the Queen Bell rings, there are people across Seiiki who will strike all the others.' Her father laid a hand on the bronze. 'It has been centuries since a dragon was born in Seiiki. The last one to hatch – Furtia Stormcaller – chose to withdraw into this lake.'

'Did you wake this dragon when you brought the Crown Prince here?'

'Yes. I wanted to see what she made of him.'

'What did she say?'

'That his light was faded. I assume that she could sense the sickness that would kill him. Now I would like to see what Furtia Stormcaller makes of the child I found on the mountain.'

He nodded to Epabo, who struck the bell. Its call was clean and richly deep; the night seemed to resound with it.

The lake bubbled. Dumai watched, certain she was in a dream.

First came the pale shine of the crest, spreading through the water; next, the giant horns, the wild eyes and the snout. A shimmering river of black scales followed, and then the mane, like thundercloud. Dumai slid to her knees. She heard her own blood in her ears, her shuddering breaths that verged on laughter. Her father came to kneel at her side.

'Son of the Rainbow,' Furtia Stormcaller said, cold and sonorous. 'How long has it been?'

Dumai tried to catch her breath, tears soaking her face. The dragon sounded like the bell.

'Eighteen seasons, great Furtia.' Emperor Jorodu signed with both hands as he spoke, for dragons heard on land as humans did in water. 'I trust your sleep has been peaceful.'

'Do you wake me now to hold the fire at bay?'

Emperor Jorodu faltered. 'I see no fire tonight, great one,' he said. 'Am I blind to it?'

'It rises from the restless deep, beneath the broken mantle.' Furtia Stormcaller regarded him. 'Why have you come?'

'I seek wisdom, if you would grant it. Since we last spoke, my two sons have been taken from this fleeting life. I believed I was left with but one young daughter. I was wrong.'

Earth child, do you hear me?

Dumai slowly looked up. This time, the voice was in her head, which suddenly ached. Furtia gazed back at her. Though her crest had dimmed, her eyes remained luminous.

Yes...

'Great one, I have learned that I have another child, my firstborn,' Emperor Jorodu said. 'This is Noziken pa Dumai, Princess of Seiiki, and I wish to know if she is a worthy heir to the Rainbow Throne.'

Dumai shook all over as the dragon lowered her enormous head.

'This one's light, I can see clearly,' Furtia Stormcaller concluded. 'This one holds a woken star.'

II

As the Gods Slept

CE 510

The earth was not suspended in the air exactly balanced by her heavy weight.

– Ovid, *Metamorphoses*

24

North

In the gloom of the hall, fires huffed and laughter chimed. The tables were laden: smoked lamb and roasted goat and fish, plums wallowed in pine syrup, shadow grouse stuffed with prunes, dark bread steamed in the ground. King Bardholt sat at the high table with the Chieftain of Solnótt.

On the benches, Wulf was crushed between Vell and Sauma, listening to a group of grizzled elders from the Barrowmark. They worked in some of the more interesting trades the North had to offer. One was a fur trapper who hunted with the Hüran, another combed peat bogs for iron (but had twice found a preserved corpse), and a third had made a small fortune from the bile of black whales, which could, apparently, be turned into a spice.

Wulf could not remember a night with better storytelling. He was warm and heavy, the way he always felt on the cusp of drunkenness. Vell lolled against him, well past that cusp. Across the table, Thrit wept with laughter at a joke Eydag had cracked.

As a child, Wulf had dreamed of Hróthi halls. The roaring fires after an adventure in the snow; the tales and feasting, the joyous songs. With his friends around him, food in his belly, and the haithwood far away, he could cushion the ache for his family in Inys.

His family in Hróth was his lith. A division of household troops (of which Bardholt had many), they numbered seven: Regny, Eydag, Karlsten, Vell, Sauma, Thrit and Wulf.

'Fortunate that they're all laughing.'

Wulf glanced to his left, at Sauma, who watched the hall from beneath her fringe of tight black curls. She was the finest archer of them all, the middle daughter of a chieftain.

'Why?' he asked her.

She sipped from a goblet of boiled water. Summer freckles dappled her brown skin.

'They could be raging at Bardholt, demanding answers about the Dreadmount,' she said. 'After all, he converted Hróth for a queen whose divinity could yet prove false.'

Ever since the eruption, the air had been tight, though Bardholt had gone out of his way to slacken it. 'It isn't false,' Wulf said. 'I've not seen the Nameless One yet.'

'Yet,' Sauma echoed.

Eydag choked on her wine, and they both looked at her. 'Witchbane?' she snorted out. The old man at her side looked unamused. 'You must be joking. What sort of heathen name—'

'I did slay a witch.'

'This should be good.' Eydag lowered her cup and grinned, showing the chip in her front tooth, earned during a drunken tussle with Regny. 'Tell us, then. What sort of witch?'

'A witch is a witch. An evildoer, thirsting for the old ways. Some are snowseers who refused to follow the Saint. They turned to the ice spirits, fell to their will,' the greybeard said, unfazed by the mockery. 'I tracked this one to the Iron Grove, out near the Nárekengap. I saw her turn into a crow and eat the heart from her own mate. I crept into that grove while she slept, and I buried my axe in her heart. That was the last of her.'

Across the table, Thrit was flushed, hair stuck to the dew on his brow. 'You did this alone?' he asked the man, in a tone of false wonderment. 'Crept up and killed a sleeping woman?'

'That's what I do, now I'm too old for chasing whales. I'm the first witchfinder in the North.'

'How valiant.' Thrit raised his horn. 'And convenient, that we have only your word for this.'

'Not all of us have bards to sing of our deeds, boy.'

'They could use you in the West. Plenty of witches in Inys,' Karlsten ground out. His eyes were bloodshot. 'Tell our new friends, Wulfert. Wasn't the Witch of Inysca your mother?'

Wulf felt Sauma tense. 'Karl,' Thrit warned in an undertone, 'I'd shut the fuck up if I were you.'

'No. Tell them!' Karlsten pounded his fist on the table, rattling the cups. 'Tell them how the baron found you at the edge of the haithwood, with a wolf at your side and—'

'Fuck you, Karl.'

A fleeting silence fell as the Northerners looked at Wulf, who had locked gazes with Karlsten. Somewhere beneath the haze of drink, awareness burned in those small blue eyes.

'I need to piss,' Wulf said, holding on to his composure by a thread.

'Wulf,' Eydag started, but he had already stood and forged a path between the crowded benches. He marched until the walls fell away and he was out in the sharp, pungent air.

Though it was close to midnight, the sun was too shy to kiss the horizon. Dour light tawned the snow, which stopped at a field of steaming mudpots, spread before grim Mount Dómuth. Wulf walked through the drowsy settlement of Solnótt, past a small wool market and a blacksmith sweating at her forge. His heart matched the ringing strokes of her hammer. He strode off the wooden paths, on to the cracked yellow earth of the field, and sat as close as he dared to a mudpot, eyes burning.

There were no secrets in a lith, but he should have kept his mouth shut, the night Eydag had urged them all to share their stories, to bind them together. Before then, Karlsten had been a good friend. They had met at Fellsgerd as boys and survived the brutal training together, fast as brothers. Then Wulf had told the tale of his past.

Karlsten despised even the faintest whiff of the old ways. Verthing Bloodblade had sacrificed his grandparents to the ice spirits to win a victory. To him, Wulf now reeked of the same heresy and slaughter.

I am Wulfert Glenn. I am the son of Lord Edrick Glenn and Lord Mansell Shore. I am the brother of Roland and Mara. He repeated the words to himself. *I am a man of Virtudom. I have a place in Halgalant.*

When he could no longer feel his heartbeat, Wulf sleeved the tears away and took the letter from his tunic. He had saved it for a night like this, when he needed to remember he was loved.

*Wulf, I trust you are keeping well in your dream world. I imagine you
sitting in the snow, having stolen a moment to yourself to read this letter.
I shall be succinct, but first, permit me some poesy.*

*Sometimes, in the mornings, I walk about and see the webs the spiders
weave across the eaves and fences. They work so hard to build those lovely
bowers, and yet they remain brittle. Home feels that way now.*

*Father has grave concerns about the harvest. We have had fair climes
for a very long time, even the winters never too cold – yet all through
the spring, the sun shed a dark light, as if it wore a cowl. I envy you the
midnight sun, though doubtless you have suffered a far harder spring
than we have. I pray the warmth of summer clears the air, if we see
summer at all.*

Wulf glanced at the sun. Dust scumbled its face, lowering its light. It
was thinner, at least, than the thick grey murk that had hung in the air
throughout winter and spring.

*Until then, I am grateful that Father has always been prudent – our
granaries, at least, are full. Saint willing, no one in this province will go
hungry come winter.*

*On the merrier side of things, I feel a sense of purpose at last. Not long
after you left Inys, I began work for Lady Marian, who was most amenable
to my offer to be her secretary. She gives me a good salary and board at Befrith. She is the soul of kindness, ever careful of her servants' comfort, and
can even, on occasion, be full of mirth. My bedchamber is fit for a duchess!*

With a weak smile, he turned the page over. He pictured Mara in a
shaded room in the castle, writing beside a window, the larks chirping
outside.

*She has already begun to confide in me. Saint knows, she has been lonely
in her winter days. At present, she is afraid for the family she never sees –
Queen Sabran will not brook her at court. Marian knows her presence
there will do more harm than good, but at a time like this, with all of
us unsettled by the Dreadmount, she longs to be with her daughter and
granddaughter.*

*There have been no rebellions, thank the Saint. Not everyone believes
the Dreadmount erupted, since Queen Sabran never confirmed the ru-*

mours. The criers have said nothing. There are only whispers – which I suppose have the potential to be far more dangerous. What has it been like in Hróth?

Father and Pa and Rollo send their love. Saint keep you, Wulfert Glenn. Write to me soon.

He scrolled the letter and tucked it away. More than ever, he missed her. He missed his family. Small wonder the former Queen of Inys feared for hers.

Wulf knew more than most. He had poured the wine on the night King Bardholt received an envoy from Clan Vatten, who told him of a harrowing scream that had rung out on the night of the eruption. The work of fear-stricken imaginations, perhaps, or the grating of the broken earth – and yet that scream had seeded whispers of the Nameless One.

The sky remained silent, if grim. On the ground, there had been strange occurrences. Disappearances: sheep, cattle. Sounds from places high and low. Bardholt had burned every report, stone-faced. If people believed that anything had emerged from the Dreadmount, it threatened his consort and his religion, the cornerstones of his young kingdom.

Wulf breathed in the strong smell from the mudpot. The midnight sun ensnared him like a moth in amber. No matter how long he stared at it, this sky would not blacken again until autumn.

Less than a year ago, these mudpots had boiled and smoked like cauldrons, the day the Dreadmount burst. The day he had fainted into the snow. Thrit had found him lying there, icy cold and feverish by turns, while animals shrieked in the forest, birds flocking north and west.

'Funny place to piss.'

Wulf glanced up. Thrit had appeared by the mudpot, arms folded.

'Don't get me wrong. We've all wanted to,' he said gravely, 'but it does seem unwise.'

'I didn't try.'

'Good.' He eyed the midnight sun. 'I never liked this time of year.'

'Why not?'

'I always hated not being able to see the stars clearly.' Thrit came to sit beside Wulf, giving him room. 'In my grandparents' country, they believe stars are the eyes of gods.'

This conversation was now heresy. 'What sort of gods do they hold dear?'

'They were called dragons,' Thrit said. 'Many Easterners believe they rule the sky and waters, but they've slept for centuries, driven away by some tragic event.' A wistful look came into his eyes. 'I'd like to see that place one day. To know more of my ancestry.'

Wulf understood that. 'You'd go there, then,' he said, 'if you could go anywhere?'

'I'd pay a fortune to see the Empire of the Twelve Lakes. One day, when I'm rich and foolhardy enough to risk my neck on the Ships' Bane, I will. Where would you go?' Thrit asked. 'Far away from Karlsten, I take it.' Wulf chewed the inside of his cheek. 'Don't let him shame you, Wulf. We know your heart. His is small and hard with fear.'

'Doesn't matter.' Wulf stared at the shrouded sun. 'People have feared me since I was a child.'

'And no amount of brooding will persuade me to join them.'

Wulf met his gaze. Thrit often found something to laugh at, but for once, his dark eyes were sincere.

'I hope you two aren't planning to swim in there.'

The new voice made them start. Regny had arrived, a fur mantle over her tunic and mail. 'No need,' Thrit said with an easy smile. 'Steam is good for the skin. Aren't we glowing?'

'Beautiful.' Regny planted herself between them, one knee tucked under her chin. 'I heard what Karlsten did,' she said to Wulf. 'Tomorrow, at dawn, he will bear a burning coal.'

Wulf shook his head. 'It won't change what he said.'

'He made an oath to keep your secrets. A loose tongue cannot go unanswered.' She glanced from him to Thrit. 'I assume you both came out here to get away from him.'

'Karlsten boils the blood. As might this mudpot, should we fall in it,' Thrit added, 'but at least we'll die in better company.' He tossed a stone into the hot grey slurry. 'And I don't think I can bear another tall story from Witchbane.'

'If feasting bores you, I have something to stir your interest.'

'A lonely chieftain with a chiselled jaw?'

'That describes me.'

'Oh. Yes, so it does. A lonely chieftain, chiselled of jaw, who also happens to be a man?'

190

'If I had one of those, I wouldn't share.' Regny took a wineskin from her surcoat and drank, passing it to him when she was done. 'A messenger arrived this morning, bringing word of a sickness in Ófandauth. His Majesty commands us to ride ahead and judge whether it's safe for him to visit. If there *is* sickness, he wants us to ensure the safety of the Issýn.'

The Issýn had once been the most respected of snowseers. She had helped sway Hróth to the Six Virtues, later becoming a sanctarian. Bardholt still visited her village sometimes.

'All of us?' Wulf asked.

'We'll bring Sauma,' Regny said, 'but Karlsten will stay here. I've had my fill of him for a few days.' She took out her blade and whetstone. 'It will be nothing. Just sun folly.'

When Wulf snared her gaze, she looked away. He knew when Regny was unsure.

****

They slept on the floor of the feasting hall with most of the royal household. Every crack and opening was caulked to block the sunlight.

Close to dawn, Wulf woke to Sauma shaking him. With a stiff nod, he knuckled his eyes and groped for his fur boots.

The sky was a freshly scraped hide, raw and stretched. Outside the hall, the lith waited around a pit fire, Vell red-eyed and pasty. Though Wulf ignored Karlsten staring death at him, he was glad when Regny emerged.

'Hair of the hound?' he muttered to Vell, passing him a wineskin. Vell took it with a grunt.

Regny carried a pair of tongs. She used them to lift an ember from the fire, holding it up to all of them.

It was said that the Saint had held on to his sword throughout his duel with the Nameless One, even when its fiery breath had seared Ascalun to a glow. Bardholt liked that detail of the story – an illustration of courage and fortitude. Most red-hot swords would destroy the flesh, but sinners in Hróth could always atone by holding a burning coal for a time.

'Karlsten of Vargoy,' Regny said, 'you swore to your lith that you'd keep their secrets. Yesterday, you broke that oath. You betrayed the virtue of fellowship, which bound the Saint and his Holy Retinue.' She held the coal towards him, the light catching in her pupils. 'Ask the Knight of Fellowship for mercy. Show that you are willing to suffer for your vice.'

Karlsten sniffed in contempt. He plucked off his left glove and looked Wulf in the eye before he slowly turned his palm up. Regny opened the tongs, dropping the coal into his grasp.

Eydag winced and looked away. Karlsten bared his teeth, pain cording his throat and filling his eyes, but made no sound. Wulf forced himself to hold his gaze; Karlsten stared back hatefully. He held on for too long before he flung the coal aside, face drenched in sweat.

'My suffering is but a shadow of the Saint's,' he bit out. 'I will work each day to make my soul worthy of Halgalant.'

'I will ensure it, as your chieftain. Go for healing, and think twice before you flap your tongue again,' Regny said, her face as cold as the snow. 'Next time, I'll put the coal in your mouth.'

****

Later that day, as they rode north, snow fell in threads from a leaden sky. The Hróthi bred small, burly horses for travel, footsure on the rock and ice of the Barrowmark – the northernmost and easternmost domain in Hróth, where the eversnow was dense and hard, the ground black with old ashfall.

In its scattered farmsteads and villages, the people eked out a modest living by ice fishing and hunting in the murkwoods, as well as trading with the Hüran. They had almost no light in winter.

This was where the Issýn had chosen to retire when the snowseers had been deprived of their formal place in society. Some had become sanctarians or healers, while others had gone into exile. Virtudom had no mercy on women who conversed with spirits.

The Issýn had still helped persuade the Hróthi to accept the Six Virtues. That was why Bardholt always returned to her, to ensure her comfort and seek her guidance. A shadow of his younger, heathen self clung on, buried alive by his love of the Saint.

The land rolled bleak and rocky, pitted by the deep cauldrons of ice that surrounded the lynchpin of the region, the table mountain called Undir. Beyond it stretched a frozen plain, the Nárekengap, where all maps ended in the North. Many explorers had tried to cross it, as had some erstwhile snowseers, searching for a fabled valley where the ice had thawed.

Far into that endless plain, an ice tower loomed from the crags, billowing steam into the sky, the only guidepost in the endless white. How many corpses lay beyond it, no one knew.

Wulf chewed on strips of salted lamb and spoke as little as he could. His thoughts kept straying to that story of a witch in the Iron Grove – the witch who turned into a crow.

At Langarth, no one spoke of the Witch of Inysca within earshot of Lord Edrick. The last person to dare had been Roland, aged fourteen, too confident for his own good: *Father, I heard the cook say Wulf must be the witch's bairn, since we found him in the wood. Is that true?*

Their fathers had always been soft on them all, but Roland had been mucking out the stables for a month. *Wulf is your brother. He has naught to do with a witch*, Lord Edrick had told him sternly. *You will never speak of her again. Not to him or anyone. Do you hear me, Roland Glenn?*

Roland had agreed. Still, Wulf had learned enough by then. Their first cook had often whispered of the Lady of the Woods, before Lord Edrick had sent her away, and Roland had always passed on the stories. One was that the witch could turn herself into a bird.

Close to midday, Regny led them into a gorge, where a river purled over fragments of basalt. Their steeds galloped along its bank until Wulf tasted spray. When they turned a corner, he saw the horsetail waterfall that cut like a white knife.

'We're close,' Sauma said.

'Is that a sanctarian?' Thrit shielded his eyes. 'Saint, that's all we need. An unsolicited bout of prayer.'

Wulf followed his line of sight. A figure was coming down the steep dust path beyond the river, green robe crusted with snow, waving one arm. 'Stop.' As the man stumbled closer, Wulf made out a weak and broken voice: 'Please, friends. No farther. Turn back!'

Regny rode straight through the river to meet him. 'Sanctarian,' she said imperiously, 'I am Regny of Askrdal, bone of Skiri Longstride. We come here on the king's orders.'

'Go no farther,' the sanctarian said, wild-eyed. 'Go back, young chieftain, I beg you. Tell His Grace to cease his journey north. He should ride as far from the Barrowmark as he can.'

'Calm yourself.' Thrit knitted his brows. 'What's the trouble, friend?'

'A curse. A curse on Ófandauth. I would have sent a message to the king myself, but I no longer know who is afflicted, and who not. I have sat here in the canyon for a week, to warn those who would come too close. I can't go back. I would sooner starve than—' He made the sign of the sword, his hand trembling. 'No soul should enter Halgalant that way.'

'These people look to you for guidance, Saintsman,' Regny sneered. 'And you cower down here?'

'I am a sanctarian, not a warrior or a physician.'

Wulf drew up beside Regny. 'Sanctarian,' he said, 'where is the former snowseer, the Issýn?'

'Locked into her home. So is anyone with sense.'

Regny tacked her gaze to the path. 'We must see the village for ourselves,' she said, 'so I may describe this sickness to King Bardholt.'

'If you insist, then I beg you, touch no one. It starts with a redness in the fingers.'

Sauma narrowed her eyes. 'And how does it end?'

The sanctarian shook his head and collapsed on to a rock, clutching his face. Regny rode past him without a backward glance.

'I don't like this,' Sauma said, catching up to her. 'We should turn back.'

'And what shall we tell the king?' Regny said flatly. 'That we came here to understand the sickness and still have no sense of what it is? How will this help him, Sauma?'

Wulf knew the sharpness in her voice. She was nervous. 'Regny,' he broke in, 'you are the Chieftain of Askrdal. Let us go.'

Regny stopped her horse. 'When I rule Askrdal, do you suppose I will send others into danger in my stead?'

'Well,' Thrit said mildly, 'that is the way of this ranked world of ours. The common people sow, the high folk reap. You could question the sense of it, and the morality, but—'

'I am no craven, Thrit of Isborg.' She dealt them each a withering look. 'Stay if you choose.'

She spurred her silver horse up the path.

'She'll seriously injure anyone who stays behind. Hot coal, tender places,' Thrit stated. 'Yes?' Wulf gave a weary nod and rode after their leader.

The village at the end of the world was a sixfold ring of small rubble-work shelters, huddled around a sanctuary that had received all the care the rest had been denied. Places like these were grim and hardy. On the black plains and the eversnow, it was difficult for seed to thrive, forcing those who lived here to rely on milk, butter and meat.

That made it all the stranger that no livestock could be found. As Wulf dismounted, he caught a distinct scent of rot. All seemed forsaken. Their horses were skittish, huffing and snorting.

Regny led them towards the stacked roofs of the sanctuary. She was too well-trained to show disquiet, but Wulf saw it in the set of her shoulders, the tightness of her back. Every window had been shuttered. No woodsmoke rose through the roof openings.

The sanctuary doors had been chained together. Thrit unsheathed a blade and used the hilt to knock. 'Anyone in there?'

Only the wind replied. With slow resolve, Regny drew both her axes. 'Wait.' Wulf caught one by the haft. 'This was sealed from the outside.'

'If we don't look, someone else will have to. And whatever this sickness may be, we must get the Issýn away from it.' She looked from his face to the axe, which he released. 'Search the south of the village with Sauma. Find the Issýn. Thrit, with me.'

They parted.

Sauma nocked an arrow, while Wulf kept a hand on his sword as they padded through the snow. 'The animals might be grazing nearby,' Sauma murmured. Her dark eyes flitted between houses. 'Near a steamhole, perhaps. Grass would grow there.'

'I don't see any fires, either.'

Each time they rapped on a door, there was no answer or movement within. They stopped in unison when a hinge creaked somewhere in the village. Trading a glance, they waited, listening.

After a short time, they kept moving, finally reaching the thread of river that bounded the south of the village. Wulf approached the edge and looked down over the waterfall.

The gorge was deserted. Where the sanctarian had sat, there was only a long slide of blood.

'Sauma,' he said.

She joined him. When she saw, she drew a sharp breath through her nose.

'Wolves,' she said, releasing it in a fog. 'Or a bear. More and more they're swimming off the sea ice in the summers.' Her fingers tightened on her bow. 'If Ófandauth has a vicious bear as well as sickness, I might truly believe it's cursed.'

'I want to see what happened. Cover me.'

Sauma considered him. 'We need to find the Issýn.'

'Aye.' Wulf glanced at her. 'And then we need to get her away from here alive. And uneaten.'

Before she could talk him out of it – not that she would have tried – he went to retrieve his horse. Leading it by the reins, he returned to the path, cleats hooking into rock and ice, and faced the white cascade once more.

Once he had hobbled his mount, he glanced up to see Sauma, bow at the ready. She gave him a nod. He drew his sword and a deep breath before he stepped through the waterfall.

Daylight flickered into a cave. Smaller than most he had seen in Hróth, it was packed with tufted slabs of rock, walls like broken teeth. Wulf waded from the river, found his footing, and judged his surroundings. His cloak dripped, drowned by the roar in the cavern.

Trepidation was unfurling like a banner in his gut. He listened for any hint of life before he took another step, the *clink* of his cleats a little too loud. A thick, sharp scent burned his throat, clenching his chest.

The sanctarian was gone. As Wulf ventured deeper into the cave, the cold giving way to dry warmth, he watched for blood. Twice he came close to twisting his ankle. Turning a corner, he found himself in a small cavern. Glistening fangs of basalt jutted from above and below, so he had the sudden impression of standing on the lip of some direful mouth.

At first, he thought they were boulders – except boulders were rarely so alike in shape. They clustered together, dark and pitted. As if in a dream, he walked towards them, his nape slippery, sweat leaking down his cheek. The nearest came up to his breastbone. Following that strange instinct, he took off one of his gloves and placed his bare hand on its surface.

The stone was coarse enough to break his skin, as hot as if it had been set over a stove. As his fingers shook, an outpouring of sensations coursed in him, a great churning rush: affinity, desire, fear, and above all, a revulsion he could never have imagined. Whatever he was touching, it was not meant to exist. It was *wrong*.

A moment later, it cracked.

Wulf jerked back. Hairlines appeared in the rock, simmering red, and wisps of steam curled from inside.

He searched the ringing hollows of his mind. This cave must be joined in some way to Mount Dómuth, an extension of the fire mountain. As he watched the cracks smoulder, he smelled brimstone and foulness – and something else, something that sickened him.

'Wulf!'

The voice snapped him out of his trance. He retreated from the smoking rock and emerged with a shudder into the daylight, the torrent of icy water shocking him back to himself.

Sauma was there, astride her horse, with Regny and Thrit and a gaunt woman in furs, her hair and skin both pale as mist.

'Wulf,' Thrit said. 'What did you find?'

He tried to answer. Somehow, he needed to explain what he had seen and smelled and felt in that darkness. 'Follow me,' Regny commanded. The Issýn held on to her waist. 'Back to Solnótt.'

From somewhere above came a horrible cry, startling the horses. Soaked to his skin, Wulf swung himself up to the saddle, and the five of them rode like a flood down the gorge, away from Ófandauth.

25

South

Nzene was a city encircled by mountains. Walking its marble streets, one could almost feel cupped by a pair of giant hands, with the red Godsblades spearing like fingers above, casting the seven districts into shadow when the sun rolled low.

Tunuva stood on a shaded rooftop overlooking Abaso Place, one of the many pleasure gardens in the city. The River Lase flowed under it, feeding the wells and public baths. Merchants sold fruit ices, incense and flowers, while people cooled off in the famous bronze fountain of Abaso, the high divinity of water, enemy and lover of Washtu.

She had expected to see worry in their faces. The Lasians knew the threat of the Dreadmount in a way few others did – yet the inhabitants of Nzene appeared carefree, savouring their summer. That must have something to do with their ruler, Kediko Onjenyu. The Prioress had written to him of the danger, but he might not have seen fit to act.

Gashan Janudin had been his protector for twenty years. Tunuva meant to speak to her first.

She tucked a spring of hair behind her ear. Several Southern rulers of the past had gifted fine houses to the Priory, which Saghul called the *orangeries*. Esbar liked this one best – she relished the soaring clamour of the Lasian capital, the rush and roil of life – while Tunuva craved the isolated estate in Rumelabar, with its desert outlooks, vast library and quiet sweetlemon groves.

She glanced towards the sun with narrowed eyes. A dry fog hung across it, dulling its rays, as it had for months – softer by the day, but not yet gone. Lasia had a hazy season every year, when the easterlies blew dust off the Burlah, but never for so long. Never so dark.

'Lady.'

Tunuva looked down to see a young woman. Her black tunic was unsleeved for summer, her tan overskirt belted at the waist and stitched with Selinyi patterning. That livery, along with the gold in her braided hair, marked her as having come from the palace.

'May you rest in the shade of a flowering tree,' she called, a common greeting at noon. 'The High Ruler is ready to receive you.'

Tunuva nodded and went downstairs, leaving Hidat sharpening her axes on a balcony. They had long since learned that Kediko Onjenyu disliked feeling outnumbered.

Even though the sun was cooler with its mask of dust, the ground burned hot as a fresh loaf. Grateful for the thick heels of her sandals, Tunuva walked through familiar streets covered by trelliswork, where grapevines and pink flowers twined, offering pools of shade. Though she listened as she passed merchants and mapmakers, she heard no talk of the Dreadmount.

Soon they were on the broad white steps of the Palace of the Great Onjenyu. Flanked by orchards and cedar groves, it was built on a steep red promontory, twin windcatchers forming its highest points. Terraces were carved all the way up that mount, each a sacred garden for one of the high divinities of Lasia, who were enshrined in tall statues. Its walls cascaded with bright sprays of sunbreath, their perfume sweet as peaches.

Tunuva was led to the top of the promontory, home of the magnificent Upper Palace. The messenger walked her to an interior courtyard with an open roof, where two palms leaned over a fountain.

'Tunuva.'

At the sound of that voice, Tunuva turned with a smile. It dropped as Gashan Janudin approached, head shorn, in a fitted mantle that bared one elegant shoulder.

Twelve years had changed her. Her arms, once muscled, were soft and polished, loaded with gold bracelets to match her necklace. Gold lined her eyelids, too, bright against her smooth black skin, catching the sunlight that seeped in through the opening in the ceiling.

'How good to see you,' she said. 'It's been a long time.'

'Sister,' Tunuva said, once she had recovered.

By thirty, Gashan had been the finest warrior in the Priory. Had Saghul not sent her to guard the head of the House of Onjenyu – an immense honour – she might have been munguna, but Esbar had ultimately been chosen, and Gashan had made peace with her posting.

Four years later, Esbar had paid her a visit and returned in a foul mood. She reported that Gashan, rather than remaining detached from politics, had embraced the comforts and opportunities of court, climbing high enough that Kediko had raised her to the Royal Council. Tunuva had never seen Saghul as angry as when she had received that news.

All those years of instruction wasted. We are not servants or paid flatterers. Kediko insults us, and she conspires in it.

In private, Tunuva had wondered if they had all been too quick to judge. Gashan was trying to mould herself to life away from home, to keep her head above water – but now she saw how her sister was dressed, Tunuva knew she had drunk far too much of the sun wine.

Red might be the fashion here, but among their family, it was only for the Prioress.

'I expected Siyu uq-Nāra.' Gashan spoke clipped Lasian, the Libir dialect. 'Is she with you?'

Tunuva regarded her. *She does not call me her sister.* 'Siyu wishes to study for her position here for a little longer, to be sure she is a credit to Princess Jenyedi,' she replied, keeping to their mother tongue, Selinyi. 'The Prioress hopes she will join you by midwinter.'

'We wouldn't want her before she is ready.' Gashan motioned her through an archway. 'His Majesty awaits you. He is a busy man, Tunuva. I trust this won't take long.'

Gashan had come here to protect the High Ruler. Now, it seemed, she was more concerned with protecting his time.

'I will attempt to be concise,' Tunuva said. As they started to walk, she resolved to keep trying, shifting to Lasian. 'I hope you've been keeping well, sister. It's been so long since you last returned to give a report.'

'I write to the Prioress every season, but my duties prohibit me from travelling too far from court.'

Tunuva steeled herself. She had never relished confrontation.

'I wonder why you would accept a place on the Royal Council,' she said carefully. 'Your first duty is to the Mother.'

'I serve her by defending her family. That includes protecting their financial interests,' Gashan said briskly. 'We were fortunate that the dust came just after the last harvest, but this one will certainly be poor. Feeding a city demands a great deal of my time.'

Tunuva gave up and looked ahead, wishing Hidat had come.

Siyu had tried to escape from the Priory. Now Gashan had turned her back on its customs. The eruption should have drawn them all together. Instead, Tunuva's family was straining at the seams, and she had no idea how to bind it together.

Gashan led her across black and white tiles. Doors stood open, welcoming scents from the sacred garden: lemon, apricot, sweet redstalk. Tunuva waited for her sister to ask about the Priory.

'Tell me,' she said, when Gashan was unforthcoming, 'is Kediko ready to defend Nzene?'

'From what, precisely?'

'The Dreadmount has erupted, Gashan,' Tunuva said, her disquiet growing. 'Esbar and I saw something emerge that night. I thought the Prioress had sent word.'

'Yes, she wrote in the winter. Nothing has happened since.' Gashan kept walking. 'His Majesty has no wish to sow fear among the people.'

'Is he preparing in private?'

'No. He believes the Nameless One is just a story, told to frighten children. Sometimes I have thought the same.'

'A story.' Tunuva shook her head. 'Sister, that is sacrilege.'

'Asking sensible questions is sacrilege?' Gashan said drily. 'Perhaps in a closed world.'

'This is madness. If the Nameless One never came to Lasia, how would the Priory exist?'

Gashan lifted a shoulder. 'Siyāti claimed that Cleolind was Crown Princess of Lasia; others say that she was not the child Selinu favoured to succeed him. If she was *not* to be his heir, then does it not make sense that she would find something else to rule?'

Tunuva tried to steady her composure. Gashan spoke as if it were the only conclusion. 'Your words are a grave insult to the Mother,' she said quietly. 'They also dishonour the Lasians who died when the beast attacked Yikala. That you could imagine it was a lie—'

'I never said that. I am simply pointing out that stories can be embellished. As to what you saw in Mentendon: it was dark, and I imagine there was a great deal of smoke.' Gashan nodded to another courtier. 'Esbar always did have a fervent imagination.'

Esbar would have had a quick retort. Tunuva only had sorrow, clenched like a hand around her throat. When they reached the uppermost floor of the palace, two guards stood aside.

'His Majesty has many cares, sister,' Gashan told Tunuva. 'I trust you will not increase his burden.'

From her tone, Tunuva might have been there to beg favours of the man. She was beginning to see why even the long ride back to the Priory had not been enough to calm Esbar. 'I am here only to protect the High Ruler,' she said. 'You and I are on the same side, Gashan.'

'Of course.' A brief smile. 'Goodbye, then, Tunuva.'

She left. Tunuva stepped past the armoured women, back into the light of the benighted sun.

Usually it would be hotter up high. Instead, the terrace felt pleasantly cool, away from the baked ground. Tunuva admired the city from above before she found the High Ruler of Lasia.

Kediko Onjenyu was in his late forties. Seated beneath a canopy, he wore a barkcloth mantle, and was halfway through a roasted quail. Two servants fanned him, a third stood guard with a flywhisk, and one more held a bowl of oak-smoked salt.

'High Ruler,' Tunuva said. 'The Prioress sends her respects.'

He gave her a brief look. His drooping eyelids might have made him appear bored, had his highset brows not lent him an air of constant surprise. In that way, his face whittled at the nerves, since one could never be quite sure if he was pleased or disappointed.

'A sister of the Priory,' he observed in Selinyi. 'My treasurer said you would be coming.' His skin was the brown of aged bronze. 'I don't recall your face.'

'Tunuva Melim. I visited when you were still a prince,' Tunuva said, pressing down her instinctive reply: *She is not yours.* 'To deliver a token of friendship to your late mother.'

'Do you bear tokens of friendship this time?'

'In the form of a message. I come in place of our munguna, Esbar uq-Nāra.'

'I know who Esbar is.' (*Too well* was the implication.) 'Is she too busy to visit?'

'Esbar has many responsibilities at the Priory.'

'I have many responsibilities here, yet I make time to receive you.' After a long moment, Kediko nodded to the daybed on the other side of the table. 'Join me. Share in the bounty of Nzene.'

'You are most gracious.'

Tunuva sat on the daybed. Another servant drizzled a spoonful of date syrup into a cup for her, then filled it to the brim with a dark gold beer. As she took in the spread of food, her gaze settled on a mound of oranges – the small, bitter sort from the groves of Yscalin.

Kediko was watching her. Smoothing her expression, she reached past the oranges and took a black plum, leaving a pomegranate untouched. That was royal fruit, sacred to the House of Onjenyu. Even if he meant to mock her with his sour oranges, she would respect his customs.

'It's been nearly two years since a sister of the Priory last honoured me with a visit.' Kediko peeled a leg from the quail. 'Have you come here to reprimand or school me?'

'Neither.' Tunuva looked him in the face. 'You will know that the Dreadmount erupted some months ago.'

'No. I had no idea.' He turned the leg. 'My messengers must have forgotten to mention it. Without you, I would be quite ignorant.'

'That was not my insinuation,' Tunuva said evenly. Kediko grunted and took another bite. 'Our Prioress wrote to Gashan in the autumn, to warn her that something had emerged from the mountain.'

'Gashan has many duties as a member of my Royal Council, especially with the threat to our harvest.'

Tunuva swirled the cup of ice beer, stirring up the date syrup, which softened its tartness. 'Gashan is a sister of the Priory,' she said. 'Her first allegiance is to the Prioress.'

'If you insist on sending your ... warriors to my court, I will not have them standing idle in the corridors. I already have bodyguards.' Kediko indicated the armoured women at the entrance. 'Gashan was not required in that role. I decided to give her another.'

'With respect, sire,' Tunuva said, lining her voice with stone, 'that was not your place.'

'Whose place can it be but mine, since she is in my home?' Kediko motioned to a servant, who took the quail away. 'One of my ambassadors was in western Mentendon, the night the Dreadmount opened. They saw the eruption and the smoke, but nothing more.'

Most mages had farseeing eyes, but Tunuva sensed he would not like to hear that. 'We are not yet sure what arose from inside. What we do know is that they had wings.'

She had expected to watch understanding dawn on him. Instead, Kediko considered her, unreadable, and reclined into his seat.

'Why are you here?'

'Esbar wishes to reassure herself that you are prepared to defend Lasia.'

'I see. You imply that I require a stranger – a stranger with no experience of ruling – to remind me to protect my country.' His smile returned. 'By rights, I ought to be insulted. Instead, I will thank you for your concern and assure you that Lasia is ready for anything.'

'The Prioress can send more sisters if you need support.'

'A benevolent offer, but one of your sisters already cost me a small fortune in clothes and food before she became my treasurer. I understand the Priory now wishes to place another of its warriors here, to watch over my daughter.'

'For now, perhaps we could keep to the subject of your defences. I see none in Nzene.'

'And I see no evidence of wyrms. Why would they hide for so long?' he asked her. 'I will not terrify my people by surrounding their cities with war engines, based on smoke and rumour. Instead, I will wait for this fruit to ripen, and we will see what comes of it. Now, what else do you want?'

'I must press this, sire. I *saw* a flock,' Tunuva said firmly. 'If you make no attempt to ready your—'

'I have a large and well-trained army. Besides,' he said, 'I thought *you* were duty-bound to defend the South. Why are you so concerned about our defences when I have you?'

'Sire, we will fight to the last woman for Lasia, but the Priory will not be enough to—'

'What else?'

Tunuva considered his blank expression, seeing that she was arguing in vain. No matter how forcefully she told him what she had witnessed, Kediko did not want to believe her.

'Out of respect for our age-old alliance,' she said, 'I ask your permission to search the Godsblades.'

Kediko bathed his hands in a dish of water. 'To those who still follow the faith of the mountains, the Godsblades are sacred precincts. No one has set foot on them for centuries.'

'Our rangers have been following reports of disappearances in mountainous regions and those with hot springs. The Priory can make sure no danger lurks above your city.'

A fifth servant stepped out to lay a platter before Kediko. A platter that housed a raw honeycomb, puddled in its own sweetness. He picked up the golden skewer that held it.

'Have you ever considered that the Priory is an outdated institution?'

She needed to speak, but now he was biting into the comb, and the honey was dripping from his fingers, and she was in the clearing, she could see it, the spill of it, the blood in it.

'Centuries ago, it was agreed that the Priory of the Orange Tree would never be subject to Lasian rule. In exchange, you offered protection from the Nameless One,' Kediko said. 'I no longer require protection. In fact, I am starting to see the Priory in quite a different light to my ancestors. I am starting to see a dangerous sect that refuses to acknowledge the rule of law, or pay the tolls and taxes that sustain the Domain of Lasia. Not only that, but you place trained killers in my palace – killers who do not see me as their ruler.'

He set his teeth into the honeycomb again. Tunuva was conscious of every molten chew, every swallow.

'Cleolind could have had a child while she was in the Basin. You could be nurturing a usurper among your ranks,' he said. 'Your Prioress might even be conspiring to overthrow me. For all intents and purposes, the Priory is a separatist army on my doorstep. I consider that a cause for concern.'

'In centuries, we have never moved against you.' Tunuva finally woke her tongue. 'The bloodline of the Mother is as precious to us as her memory. We only want you – and Lasia – to be safe.'

'I'm sure.' He rinsed off the honey. 'Search the mountains. Then return to the Lasian Basin and tell Saghul Yedanya that my daughter will not require an armed handmaiden.'

Tunuva slowly absorbed the full force of the blow.

'High Ruler,' she said hoarsely, 'Siyu uq-Nāra is a devoted initiate, who has prepared for this posting for years. It is a great honour, in the Priory. And the princess must—'

'I have spoken. Do give my regards to your Prioress,' Kediko said. 'Farewell, Tunuva.'

He took another thick bite from the comb.

Tunuva let herself be led back downstairs, her senses dulled by denial. She had come here to strengthen a relationship, only for it to crumble in her grasp. Esbar should have been the one to visit after all.

She stopped when she heard a familiar voice. Gashan was in the garden, talking to an orchardist. With the bitter taste of defeat in her craw, Tunuva swept towards her, ignoring the guards' protests.

'You have not served him well.'

Gashan turned. Seeing the guards, she stopped them with a gesture and dismissed the orchardist.

'I remind you that this is a court, sister,' she said under her breath, steering her into the shade of a tree. 'Try not to behave as Esbar did, or you will not be welcome here.'

'It seems none of us are. He wants to break the agreement, Gashan. By allowing him to stop believing in the Nameless One, letting him think we are conspiring against him—'

'I have done nothing.'

'Yes. You have done nothing,' Tunuva said in frustration. Gashan pressed her lips together. 'However your beliefs have changed, I saw wings rising from the Dreadmount. Kediko is in danger. Make him believe it, Gashan, or all of Lasia will suffer.'

'Is that a threat?'

'How can you ask me that?' Tunuva lit her flame. 'You carry this, too. Does the orange tree mean nothing to you any longer?'

Gashan looked at the fire, and for a moment, something yielded in her eyes. 'It did. Once,' she said in soft Selinyi. 'But I will not be its prisoner again, Tuva. From what I hear, neither will Siyu.'

'Did you warn him against her?' When Gashan held her silence, Tunuva said quietly, 'Upon my return to the Lasian Basin, I will tell the Prioress that you have seen fit to forsake your duties. Farewell, sister.'

26

East

Of all the things Dumai had expected to find hostile on the ground, summer had never been among them. On the mountain, summer meant wind and fog, but no end to the cold. Cold was comfort. It was home.

Here, summer was heat. Thick, endless heat. When she drew the silk from her skin in the evenings, it was like peeling fruit. She clung to everything she touched, a moth in an elaborate web.

Most courtiers needed the suncaller to wake them in the mornings – especially now, with the fog in the sky – but Dumai was still her own rooster. On the Day of the Golden Catch, she woke to damp bedding and sodden hair. It was already too long for her taste, but Osipa had told her to let it grow, so her handmaidens could work it into more impressive styles.

She lay on her side, naked and shivering. A shadowy figure had haunted her dream, as had the dragon in the lake.

Careful not to disturb Osipa, she dressed and padded from the antechamber, towards the Floating Gardens. Drawing the door aside, she climbed with ease over the balustrade, startling a water shrew, and waded to the closest island, trying not to think of what her tutors would say if they could see their studious princess now, barefoot in the mud.

The moon was afloat in the grey, threadbare dark. She made her way across the bridges, to the seventeenth island, where an old willow slouched among hollyhock.

Kanifa waited under its branches. After a season at court, he already seemed larger. They had both been strong on the mountain, hardened by their climbs – but while he had gained muscle since the descent, training in spear and sword, Dumai was losing hers by the day.

'Are you ready for the rite?' he asked.

'I'm afraid I'll faint from the heat. Were you not the one who said I was cut from snow?'

'I have yet to see you melt. Though this warmth is harder than I expected.'

'My learnèd tutors agree – a rare thing – that it points to the eruption of a fire mountain.'

Curiosity sharpened his gaze. 'Where?'

'That is where they disagree. One believes the mountain is far to the north,' Dumai said, 'while the other is certain it lies across the Abyss. I think they enjoy the arguing.'

There had been a groundshake after her meeting with Furtia Stormcaller. It had struck the western coast of Seiiki, causing a harbour wave that had broken hard on Sunset Bay.

'I will keep a close watch on the River Lord today,' Kanifa said. 'I'm told I have a gift for archery.'

'With eyes like yours, of course you do – but keep them fixed on his servants. He will never strike me openly.'

No, Kuposa pa Fotaja was a blade wrapped in many rich layers of cloth. Dumai had never met a man who wielded courtesy and charm like he did. He had sent her invitations to join him for walks in the gardens, for parties and horse races, for archery contests and music performances. It had been all Osipa could do to invent excuses. After, he would always send Dumai a beautiful gift and a poem to grieve the loss of her company.

She could not bend in the face of this wind, no matter how fragrant its scent. If the plan was to work, she needed to starve him of opportunities to undermine her.

'It's his daughter who worries me,' Kanifa admitted. 'She's back at court.'

'Do you know where she went this time?'

'No. From what I've heard, she sometimes leaves to keep an eye on his estates. I imagine she also collects information.'

'There is no information she can gather on me.' Dumai placed a hand on his chest. 'Knowing I have you nearby has made this so much easier to bear.'

'There is nowhere in the world I would rather be than here,' he told her. 'With you.'

Wading birds chirped in the rushes. They both turned to behold Mount Ipyeda. As dawn gilded the horizon, Dumai gazed at the third peak and knew that her mother was looking straight back.

****

She was abed and wide awake by the time the suncaller arrived with his bell, to rouse everyone for a ceremony day. He started with her handmaidens, and they soon came for her. They combed oil through her hair and dabbed her eyelids with dew, chattering as they worked.

'I saw her crossing the pine grove this morning,' Juri told the others. She was the youngest handmaiden, always cheerful, often blushing. 'She cut such an elegant figure.'

'She was visiting Lady Imwo.'

A snort of disbelief. 'Imwo is too serious for her.'

'Ah, Puryeda, everyone is serious when they're widowed. Do you not remember her before?'

Dumai pretended not to listen. Osipa had told her that every morsel of gossip she heard at court could be key to her success.

Kuposa pa Yapara, the tallest and proudest of the handmaidens, was silent throughout. More than once, she yanked too hard with the comb, making Dumai grit her jaw.

Osipa spotted it. 'Lady Yapara,' she said, 'fetch the princess her cloak. I will finish her hair.'

Lady Yapara did as she was ordered without protest. She had finally learned not to spar with Osipa, who now took over, tucking in the last strands of hair with her stiff, knotted fingers.

Emperor Jorodu awaited Dumai in the sitting room of his private residence, the Water Pavilion. It overlooked a walled and flooded garden, which reflected the weave of blues and reds in the sky.

'Dumai,' he said, with a smile that touched his weary eyes. 'Join me, please. You may leave us,' he added to his guards.

They withdrew, taking their collared spears with them. Dumai knelt beside the table and removed her cloak. She still tried to eat as she had on the mountain, but it was difficult in the palace, where sea salt even seasoned fowl and greens.

'It's good to see you,' the emperor said. A black kitten slunk up to him, and he scratched between its ears, making it mew. 'I trust that you are still comfortable, and treated kindly.'

'Yes, Father. Thank you.'

'Truly?'

Dumai took a pair of eating sticks from their rest. She had never used such things in the temple.

'Empress Sipwo does not often acknowledge me,' she said, 'and not all of my handmaidens are inclined towards friendship.' She chose a slice of grilled pheasant. 'Suzu is always sweet and kind.'

'And that makes what you are here to do all the harder.'

'Yes.'

He served her a cup of barley water.

'This garden is not just a pleasant retreat. It is the old hatchery,' he told her. 'The first dragons came from the sky, but they spent so long in the sea that they started to lay eggs, like fish. A rare and wondrous thing. They would leave their clutches here, entrusting them to human care, and we would raise them from birth, watching them grow.'

'Where are they now?'

'When the gods withdrew from our world, they took their eggs. None had hatched for a long time by then.' He tasted his own drink. 'I asked your tutors to set you an examination. They tell me you answered every question with precision and clarity. Your success is a testament to your dedication, Dumai, and I thank you for it. I know you have had little rest since your arrival.'

That was true. In all the time she had spent in the palace, she had not slept more than a few hours each night. There was so much to learn: land and taxes and estates, the distribution of authority, which gods had gone to sleep in each of the twelve provinces.

Still, holding it all in her head had been easy. She had a good memory, and her mother and the Grand Empress had filled her with knowledge. In hindsight, Dumai should have guessed that something was amiss – no godsinger needed to both write and speak in Lacustrine and Sepuli. They must have both feared she would one day be found.

In all her lessons, she had heard almost nothing of the ordinary people of Seiiki, and what their lives were like. That troubled her. Her mother had once been one of those people.

What she *had* come to understand was how cleverly the Kuposa had consolidated power. They held every important position at court. She also sensed their hand in the absence of the other Noziken, who lived in isolation on remote estates, separated from each other, apparently for their protection. Osipa was right. Not many remained.

'I am happy to have pleased you,' Dumai said to her father.

'Are you?' he asked. 'Happy?'

Dumai drank. 'Yes,' she said. 'Standing before the great Furtia convinced me that this is my path.' She put the cup down. 'I had long dreamed that the gods would call.'

'So you are as much a dreamer as your name implies.' He smiled. 'Tell me something, Dumai. Did you have a happy childhood?'

'The happiest anyone could ask for.'

'Who did you think your father was?'

'A net weaver from the coastal village of Apampi. Mother told me he died in a storm.'

'How afraid she must have been.' His gaze strayed back to the garden. 'I have many regrets, Dumai. One is that I wasted years without knowing my daughter. The other is losing your mother.'

He always looked so tired. His eyes were set in shadow, and beneath his layers, he was thinner.

'Father, why do the Kuposa act as they do?' Dumai said, to distract him from the subject. Speaking of her mother seemed to pain him deeply, even now. 'Why not use their wealth and power to seize the throne, instead of controlling us through regencies and kinship?'

'I wish I knew. I can only think that they fear to usurp us outright, because we have the gods' friendship.'

She nodded slowly.

'In the past, the Day of the Golden Catch would be celebrated by the sea,' he continued. 'Then it was deemed too dangerous for the ruling family of Seiiki to travel so far from the Rayonti Basin. For all I have tried, I have not been able to override that old rule.'

Two lines were carved on either side of his mouth, which was soft and wide, like hers.

211

'When we did go to the sea,' he said, 'the dragons would rise from the depths to greet us, recalling the day they first came to our island. Without them, the Day of the Golden Catch is always a reminder of our loss. Our vulnerability.'

'You are not alone in this fight now, Father. We will grow strong,' Dumai said. 'Together.'

Emperor Jorodu pressed her hand. Dumai realised how similar hers looked now: nails polished, the calluses scrubbed off her palms. Only her three missing fingertips betrayed her past.

'How did it happen?' her father asked.

'An accident.' Dumai drew back. 'Kanifa is worried about the River Lord's daughter.'

'Lady Nikeya. It is true she is sharp as a splinter, and artful. Some call her the Lady of Faces,' the emperor said grimly, 'but Epabo has the insight of age. He is a match for her.'

Dumai hoped he was right.

'The River Lord traditionally hosts a celebration after the Day of the Golden Catch, during which I announce the new appointments. The Night Banquet,' Emperor Jorodu said. 'This year, you will attend.'

'Is that wise?'

'On this occasion, I believe so. He is not easily refused,' he said, 'as you are no doubt aware.' Dumai grimaced. 'There is a poetry competition, among other festivities. We will make it your party, daughter.'

****

There was only one salt lake in Seiiki. In centuries past, there had been none, so the only way to harvest salt had been to dry it from the sea. For most of the island, that was still the case.

While he still lived, Kwiriki had longed for a place to rest when he flew from coast to coast. One summer day, he had descended to Lake Jasiro and immersed himself, using his divine power to transform it to an inland sea.

To reach it, the court took a rocky pass through Nirai's Hills. Dumai fanned herself in her cart.

Empress Sipwo rode in front with Suzumai. Dumai smiled when her sister waved at her. Suzumai had wanted to be with her – she always wanted to be with her – but the empress had not allowed it. She had never been cruel to Dumai, but clearly wanted no affinity with her.

The River Lord also had the privilege of riding in a cart, unlike most of the court. It was grander than any Dumai had seen. She avoided his gaze with steely resolve.

The journey took them well past midday. By the time the procession emerged, the sun was sinking – still duller than usual, sickly yellow, the shape of it too clear.

Dumai sat up at the sight of Lake Jasiro. It stretched into the distance, bounded by mountains on one side and white sand on the other.

Tens of thousands of people had gathered around it. These were the people Kwiriki had charged Snow Maiden to protect – people like the young Unora, who worked the fields to keep Seiiki fed, whose taxes kept the capital in luxury. In the absence of the gods, they looked to the House of Noziken for guidance. Dumai meant to be worthy of that. This might not be the path she had sought, but here she was, rattling along it.

And she had seen a dragon now. The denial of one lifelong wish had, at least, granted the other.

When the procession trundled to a halt, Epabo was there to help Dumai from her cart. She glanced towards the guards and spied Kanifa, armed with his bow and three-pointed spear.

Emperor Jorodu and Empress Sipwo waded into the lake to perform their ablutions. Dumai took her sister by the hand, and they went into the shallows, Suzumai staying close enough to bump her hip. A crown of white pearls sat on her long hair.

'Dumai,' she said, 'I'm sleepy. And hungry.'

'I know, Suzu. We must be very brave now, and bear our discomfort, for the gods.'

'But I always nap in the afternoon.' Suzumai rubbed her scarred eye. 'When I'm empress, I'm going to make sure everything happens in the morning. And that there's lots to eat.'

Dumai forced herself to keep smiling.

Their handmaidens began to tip water over them both. Dumai closed her eyes, savouring the taste, the sting. When she opened them, she found herself looking at a face she knew.

'Princess,' Lady Nikeya said softly.

Bitterness was not something that Dumai had often felt in her life. Nothing had given her cause on Mount Ipyeda – but faced with this woman, it surged into her, making her stomach rise. 'Why are you here?' she said, dangerously quiet. 'You are no handmaiden.'

Nikeya knelt to fill a ladle. When she rose, she poured a stream of sun-warmed water over Dumai, making her shiver. It seeped past her collar, down to her navel.

'I have sometimes assisted my cousin, the empress,' Nikeya said. 'My beloved father thought you might appreciate an experienced hand, since this is your first water ceremony.'

An absurd remark to make to a godsinger. Dumai would have told her so, had Yapara not chosen that precise moment to upend an entire basin over her head. By the time she had dashed the soaked hair from her eyes, Nikeya had glided away, still with a coy smile on her lips.

'Your Highness,' Yapara said in her bored drawl, 'you may wish to return to shore.'

Dumai realised Suzumai had already joined her parents. She strode back towards the sand, feeling less cleansed than irked.

Nikeya had some gall, to show her face. If not for her, Epabo would never have been on the mountain, and would never have told the emperor about Dumai. Her old life would be intact.

The ceremony began with the burning of salt in kilns on the shore, led by godsingers from the White Temple of Ginura. Dumai watched them, aching for her old home.

When dragons had first observed humans on the beaches of Seiiki, they had brought them a gift of golden fish as a token of goodwill. The fearful islanders had driven them away, but each year, to commemorate the golden catch, the noble clans sent a lifelike sculpture of a fish to be cast into Lake Jasiro. Each had a name and wish engraved on its scales. Later, the people around the lake would make offerings of wood or paper.

Emperor Jorodu was first on the bridge that led into the middle of the lake. His attendants followed him to the storm haven at its end, laid the heavy baskets of fish within his reach, and retreated with bows. One by one, he made the offerings, including the gold imperial carp.

Empress Sipwo handled the many silver fish from Clan Kuposa. Suzumai stood in the storm haven next. With help from one of her nurses, she hefted a bream into the depths.

Dumai was last. She would take charge of the offerings from the provincial governors. She passed her father, stepmother and sister, hair dripping.

The walk to the storm haven went on for ever. Her handmaidens followed her with the baskets. Once they had stepped away, she took hold of the first sculpture, a catfish from Ginura Province. It hit the water with a splash, and she watched it sink into the darkness.

The surface shattered. With a gasp, Dumai threw up a hand to shield herself as Lake Jasiro erupted into white spray, and the mighty head of a dragon reared above her, glittering.

Uproar encircled the lake. People cried out in amazement, falling to their knees. Several kites came loose. Soaked to her skin again, Dumai stared up at the god in the water.

Furtia Stormcaller was far larger than she had looked at night. She towered above the storm haven, rivulets streaming down her armoured throat and lustrous grey mane. Her first roar was a storm through trees, rushing waves and rain on stone.

Those that remained standing prostrated themselves. For them, it was the first time a dragon had appeared for three hundred years, a wonder their ancestors had thought impossible.

Furtia looked down at Dumai. *Earth child.* Those cool tones in her head again. *Come with me.*

Dumai blinked, her bare feet rooted. When she did nothing, Furtia came closer and huffed, so Dumai could smell the brine on her breath.

And she understood what the dragon wanted.

With a hundred thousand eyes on her, she reached out with trembling fingers. A living dragon, slippery as a fish, real and alive beneath her palm. There was kinship in that touch, and strength. Furtia nudged back with her snout.

Come.

She made a sound like distant thunder, and Dumai took another step. She closed her eyes, feeling a pull, a likeness, a *want*.

The black scales were too slick to hold without slipping. Finding she was unafraid, she sank her hands into the waterfall of manehair. Her fingers closed in the heavy, oily mass, which smelled of steel and seaweed.

Even though court had drained her strength, she still had enough to hold her own weight. She climbed until she could hook a leg across the dragon. She looked towards her father, and she saw the change in him, the hope. She had one brief, dizzying impression of the blue above, the stunned faces below, before the dragon surged into the sky.

The wind howled, drowning out all sound. Dumai clung to Furtia, face already windburnt, and laughed as the sky welcomed her like an old friend. She had nothing to fear from it.

Furtia Stormcaller rose towards the sun, and Noziken pa Dumai was flying, just as she had always dreamed.

****

Evening painted over the last strokes of dusk. Furtia passed wisps of cloud, silvering them with the light that filled her crown.

Dumai breathed in the cleanness of the air. Her robe clung to her skin, but she relished the cold, even as her nose ran.

It was a long time before something interrupted the dark. Molten lava, pouring out from the land, exploding into thick billows of steam. That was her very first glimpse of the sea – but she could hardly make it out, let alone treasure the moment. She gazed at the firefall until her eyes hurt.

Long before Kwiriki came, Seiiki had often been restless, shuddering and shedding fumes. Once dragons had settled on the island, it had quietened, and now it was only steam it breathed, from the hot springs – but as the gods slept, this mountain had woken.

Furtia spooled her huge body into a cave, where the air was stifling and dry. Too warm. Dumai slid down, bending her knees when she hit the ground. She turned to face the dragon.

'Great one, ask what you will of me.'

Even as she spoke, her insides wound tight, making her feel unwell. Something was very wrong in this place.

I have brought you here to show you chaos . . .

Dumai concentrated. She tried to speak with her mind, though it gave her a headache. *Where is this?*

A tunnel from the deep beneath. Furtia moved farther into the dark, and Dumai followed, keeping a hand on her scales. *There.*

In the cavern ahead, molten rock flowed with a sizzling hiss. It took several long moments to see the nine rocks silhouetted by it – almost as tall as she was, webbed with glowing cracks.

'What are these?'

That terrible, leaking wrongness grew worse, and the strength went from her legs. Though it was sweltering in the lava cavern, she trembled with cold in her sodden robe.

There is a balance in the world, and it has been unsettled. The fire beneath grows too hot, too fast. The star has not returned to cool it. Furtia flickered her tongue. *I have sensed more across the sea…*

'Where?' Dumai asked her. 'Where across the sea?'

The closest lie north of this isle.

Much lay north of Seiiki, but the first land one would find that way was the Queendom of Sepul.

Furtia approached a boulder and breathed cloud over it. *These will break open erelong. I threw down the creature that sired them. It was alone and lost. We were fortunate.* The light and smoke waned from the cracks. *Others are laid. Many more.* She turned her gaze on Dumai. *Ride across the sea with me, so we might know how many will open…*

Dumai looked at the rocks. 'What will come from inside these?'

Chaos and destruction.

The boulders were still aglow within, simmering. Dumai returned to her knees before Furtia.

'Great one, I am not sure I can leave,' she said. The dragon watched her hands as she signed. 'The imperial house is threatened from within, by the ambitious Clan Kuposa. If I abandon my father, he may lose the throne the great Kwiriki bestowed on our family.'

Thrones and houses do not matter. Your disputes do not matter. If the fire rises, all will burn. Furtia lowered her face, unleashing her cold breath on Dumai. *Your ancestor made us a promise. A solemn vow between sea dragon and earth child, struck in the eye of a storm, that they would protect one another, always.* A flash of white teeth. *Do you mean to break it?*

Dumai looked up at her, her heart beating like hailstones. She was a princess, but she was also a godsinger – and here was a god, singing back to her, finally.

'Never,' she said. 'Your will is mine.'

27

North

King Bardholt had been with the Issýn for hours. In the false dark of the hall, Wulf tried in vain to sleep. Beside him, Thrit was awake, arms folded behind his head, a muscle rolling in his jaw.

There were no daymarks indoors, but Wulf guessed it was midnight by the time the Issýn emerged. Her hands were tucked into her sleeves, her face shadowed by a hood. Most of the former snowseers had darkened their hair after the conversion, but hers still gleamed white.

'They were in there for some time,' Thrit said under his breath. 'What do you think they said?'

Wulf stared at the covered smokehole in the ceiling. 'When the Nameless One flew to Lasia, he visited a plague upon it. A plague so vile even the Saint could never speak of what he saw.'

'His Grace will try to keep this quiet.' Thrit turned on to his side, so they faced one another. 'By the Saint, he must do something. What if the sickness goes farther?'

They were close. By the weak light of the nearest candle, Wulf took Thrit in – the hollow where his collarbone met his throat, the dark stubble that lined his jaw and upper lip. Wulf had the sudden instinct to run his thumb across it, feel how sharp or soft it was.

'Thrit,' he said, 'if I tell you something, will you keep it to yourself?'

'Of course. Do I look like Karlsten?'

218

'I found something behind the waterfall.'

'What?' Thrit asked him, shifting on to his elbow. Wulf shook his head. 'Wulf, you can tell m—'

He winced when Sauma kicked him. 'Saint's ribs, you two,' she muttered. 'Stop *whispering*.'

Thrit shot Wulf a sheepish look. When Sauma returned her head to the floor, so did they. Wulf lay awake for the rest of the night, thinking of the fire in the rock.

****

At daybreak, they set out from Solnótt, beginning the long journey back to the capital. The Issýn stayed close to King Bardholt, on a fine white horse the chieftain had gifted her. She wore the green wools of a sanctarian, with catskin gloves that reached her elbows.

'Are the people of Solnótt coming with us?' Wulf asked Regny.

Regny glanced at him. 'There is no evidence that the sickness has gone beyond Ófandauth. His Grace has ordered the Chieftain of Solnótt to burn that village to the ground.'

'Half its people had abandoned it by the time we got there. If any of them had the sickness—'

'Wulf,' she said, 'if I were you, I would not speak of Ófandauth again.'

She rode ahead. Sending a troubled look north, Wulf spurred his mount after hers.

For days, the royal party followed the amber road that led out of the Barrowmark, making for the River Dreyri. Far behind them, smoke needled into the sky.

They camped beneath the stars, reminding Wulf of his training in the forests of Fellsgerd. When he was not on guard duty, he sat with his lith beside a fire, and there was drink and song and merriment, as there always was around the King of Hróth. At night, in their cramped tent, he was too aware of the softer warmth of Thrit beside him. He had never taken such close notice of his friend before, and had no idea why he was doing it now.

After a long ride through wind and light snow, the party came to an inland port, where three Mentish cogs awaited them, all fitted with striped sails, teal and white. Though the Hróthi prided themselves on their shipbuilding, King Bardholt had accepted when the Vatten had sent him twenty of these stolen vessels, survivors of the Midwinter Flood.

That evening, Wulf approached the cabin. Eydag stood guard with Karlsten, whose golden hair was braided behind his left ear.

'I need to see the king,' Wulf said. Eydag nodded and went in, leaving Wulf alone with Karlsten.

Wind came wuthering into the sail.

'Does it hurt?' Wulf said, after a silence.

'Save your pity, Wulf.' Karlsten kept his hand closed. 'I imagine you're familiar with the smell of burning.'

'Why?' Wulf said, torn between irritation and amusement. 'You really think I was raised at the foot of a cauldron, the reek of vile potions hot in my nostrils?' Karlsten offered a mirthless smile. 'I hate to disappoint, Karl, but strewing herbs were the first scents I knew. And I take no joy in your pain, though it seems you take plenty in mine.'

Karlsten folded his burly arms. 'None.'

'They say a man speaks the truth in his cups. Say it again now. You believe the witch of legend was the one who left me at the edge of the haithwood. For what purpose?'

'I don't claim to know the ways of witches.'

'There are none. The haithwood is just that – trees and memory. There are no witches.'

'I see a witch now.'

Wulf followed his gaze to where a shelter had been raised for the Issýn. She was still wearing her gloves, and sat hunched and alone, dark crescents beneath her eyes.

'Ah, hush your twining, Karl,' Wulf sighed. 'She converted before you were even born. You're imagining vice everywhere.'

'The Saint made a new kingdom in Inys because the old was too twisted to save. The old world is all round us, Wulf,' Karlsten said. 'Stealing out of dark places, waiting for us to let it in.'

Eydag returned before Wulf could think of a retort. 'Go on, then,' she said, holding the door open. Her scalp had grown a dark stubble. 'Friendly game of foxes when you're finished?'

Wulf cocked an eyebrow. 'Will you spend it thinking of as many wolf jokes as possible?'

'Always,' Eydag said gravely. 'But I promise they'll be my most inventive wolf jokes yet.'

Wulf smiled. 'Well,' he said, 'if you promise.'

Karlsten turned his face away. Wulf stepped past him, and Eydag closed the door in his wake.

In the cramped excuse for a cabin, the King of Hróth was scratching out a message, a groove between his brows. Not born into nobility, he had been illiterate before he was crowned, and still had considerable difficulty writing. If he was using his own hand rather than summoning a scribe, he must want to keep this letter a secret.

'Wulf.' He tossed the quill aside with relish. 'Eydag said you wished to speak to me.'

'Sire.' Wulf weighed his words. 'While I was in Ófandauth, I saw something.'

'Go on.'

Bardholt listened as Wulf explained the disappearance of the sanctarian, the blood by the river, and the simmering clutch of boulders. None of it seemed to perturb him.

'Undir is an old fire mount,' he concluded, when Wulf had finished. 'It might not have stirred for many years, but its presence causes disturbances in the surrounding areas, even as far away as the mudpots at Dómuth. Strange, but natural. As for the blood – grey wolves, no doubt.'

The darkness had sheared his face gaunt. For most of the journey, he had not laughed once within earshot of Wulf, though he drank as much as ever.

'Sire,' Wulf said, 'when I touched the rock with my bare hand, it cracked. It reminded me of—'

He almost said it, but his courage abandoned him. It would sound like madness. 'What?' Bardholt said, his voice unusually soft. 'What do you think you saw?'

'Nothing, sire. It was a foolish thought.'

Bardholt picked up the goblet at his side and took a long drink.

'You need not think of Ófandauth any longer,' he said. 'It was a fever, nothing more. It has been burned away.'

'My king, forgive me, but most of the villagers had fled. Some say illness is spread by touch. Should messengers not be sent out to find them, stop them travelling any farther?'

'No one left. The villagers locked themselves into their homes. The Issýn assured me of this.' Bardholt retrieved his quill. 'Thank you for telling me what you saw. I must ask you not to share it with anyone else. One day you will be a knight, and a knight must always be discreet, as courtesy demands.'

Wulf knew when he was receiving an order, even if it was couched in religious wisdom.

'When we reach Eldyng, I entrust you to send this message to Inys,' Bardholt continued. 'It is of the utmost importance, and must reach Queen Sabran as soon as possible.'

'It will be done,' Wulf said. With the distinct impression that he had just been asked to choke one virtue to save the other, he turned away, stopping when he heard a commotion outside.

Bardholt looked up as a muffled screech came from the deck. 'Drunken clots,' he muttered. 'See to it that they disperse, Wulf, or I shall challenge them each to a duel.'

'Sire.'

Wulf opened the door, expecting to find a brawl. At first, that was what he thought he was seeing. The light of the boxed fires revealed a crush of people at the other end of the deck. Glimpsing a flash of white, Wulf tensed, a cold tug in his gut.

The Issýn screamed like she was being sawn in half. As she wrenched free of the crowd, Wulf glimpsed her arms, bare where she had pulled open the fastenings on her sleeves. From fingertip to elbow, her skin was scarlet, as if she had slathered it with paint.

It starts with a redness in the fingers.

The sickness. It had followed them.

Another terrible shriek from the Issýn. Every jerk of her body seemed like a cruel mockery of dance. 'Help me,' she moaned. 'Oh, gods, save me. It burns, I'm burning—'

'Help her,' came a cry, but no one knew how.

The Issýn slipped and crumpled, pounding her fist on the deck. With impossible strength, she reared on her knees and tore her herigald apart. Eydag gasped. Eyes wild, spittle on her chin, the Issýn writhed out of the roughspun, so she was only in a shift – and still she kept going, clawing at the linen and the skin beneath it, drawing blood from her throat.

'Put it out,' she sobbed at them all, agony in every crease of her face. 'Spirits, put it out!'

'Put what out?' Vell shouted at her.

'It's burning, all of it—' She clenched her hair. 'Can't you see, can't you *see* I'm on fire?'

Her plea came from the seat of her, animal and all too human. Each scream went through Wulf in a sickening shudder as the Issýn ripped bloody white hanks from her scalp and shredded her face with her nails. She crawled across the deck, foaming at the mouth.

Eydag and Karlsten drew their swords and closed ranks. 'In the name of the king,' Karlsten barked, 'come no closer.' His lips were skinned back, eyes wide. 'Stay where you are!'

'Sire. My king. Good king!' She was choking in agony. 'Help me, kill me—'

'Restrain her,' someone called.

Karlsten moved to block her way. 'No, Karl, don't,' Thrit shouted. 'Don't touch her!'

The Issýn made a grab for Karlsten. He ducked away from her, and instead she swung her fist and caught Eydag, who lurched away with a cry.

'What in the Saint's name is this uproar?' King Bardholt bellowed, emerging from his cabin. The Issýn saw her saviour. She lunged for him, and all that was left between them was Wulf. Before he could think, he caught her by the wrist and drove his sword through her middle.

The world stopped. Her face was a whisper from his, and he could smell her sweat, the rot of brimstone on her teeth. He saw shock, a flash of pure terror, and then, at last, a smile. She brushed his cheek with her thumb, almost tender, before she collapsed.

Silence fell like a heavy snow over the ship. Hunched against the mast, Eydag gingerly felt along her jaw. Vell knelt at her side and checked her face with a gloved hand.

'Back, Vell,' the king barked. Vell recoiled. 'Eydag, did she touch you?' Eydag nodded fearfully. 'Karlsten?'

'No,' Karlsten said, teeth gritted. 'The Issýn never took her gloves off. She knew she had the sickness when she came on board.'

Wulf stared at the blade of his sword, glazed with blood. His empty hand – the right hand – was shaking. He looked past both, through the blur, at the woman he had slain.

'Captain,' King Bardholt said, 'signal the other ships to stop.' His nostrils flared with every breath. 'Those of you the Issýn touched will remain here, sealed in the cabin, until we reach Eldyng. You too, Vell. We don't know how it spreads.' He looked at the body of his old friend, his face twisted in bitter regret. 'The rest of you, push the body into the river. Use the oars. Do not lay even a finger on her.'

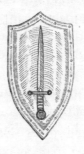

28

West

Late summer had always been bittersweet for Glorian. On the one hand, there was the Feast of Courage, which she loved – six days of jousts, boar hunts and wrestling – and the days were never more beautiful, especially at Glowan Castle. Wildflowers nodded and swung in the grounds, and the air smelled of the honeysuckle that frothed around the windows.

On the other, the end of summer was when her father always left. This year, he had not come at all.

She sat on the marble fountain with Julain, an ache in the base of her skull. Since the spring, she had often seen a distant figure in her sleep, standing in mist and shadow. It never moved or spoke. Those dreams always left her cold, as if she had slept on a bed of snow.

Between her troubled nights, the days lazed. The heat was hard to explain, since the sun gave so little. Coated in murk, it shone a dirty red on some days, edge sharp as a blade.

Her sixteenth had been a modest affair. No ambassadors from foreign lands, no dances or republicans, and no desire for marriage or a child.

Yet another year had passed, and still her betrothal troubled her. Sometimes she wanted to shake herself for it, and wished she were like a swan or a wolf, possessed of an instinct to partner for life. The Knight of Fellowship decreed that all souls should be bound in wedlock. Many people found happiness in it, yet she could not shed her disquiet.

How much easier things would be, if she could want as others did.

She glanced at her ladies: Helisent working on her epic poem in the shade of a walnut tree, and Adela with her back to its trunk, eating the last cherries of the season. Helisent would occasionally write verses for girls at court, tucking them unsigned into a pocket or under a door, but she never took the courtship further. Adela had no interest in anyone.

Julain, on the other hand, had always wanted a companion, and she had a choice in it. Her older brother was heir to her duchy, and he already had a child, leaving her to do as she pleased.

'What troubles you?' she asked Glorian.

'Nothing.' When Julain gave her a look, she sighed. 'It may be a matter for the sanctarian.'

'Why, have you committed some great sin?'

'Many, no doubt.'

They stopped when Sylda Yelarigas approached, draped in a gown of white silk – a sharp contrast to her copper skin and black hair, which rippled over her shoulders. 'Lady Glorian, good morning,' she said in Yscali. 'I wondered if I might speak with Lady Helisent.'

'Of course,' Glorian replied in the same language. 'If she agrees.'

Helisent stood and tucked her parchment into her girdle. She walked to join the Yscal, who linked her arm. 'How is Lord Osbert?' Glorian asked Julain, watching them leave.

'He writes often, and expressively.'

'Could you marry him?'

'It's still early. Mama says we won't be wed until I'm at least twenty.' Julain spoke gently: 'Glorian, most people don't marry at seventeen. You know it's all right, to not want it yet.'

And what if I never do?

Glorian was spared from answering when two of the Dukes Spiritual strode along the path: Lord Robart Eller, and towering Lord Damud Stillwater, Duke of Courage and Master of the Treasury. Seeing Glorian, they lowered their heads respectfully and moved on.

'They look worried,' Glorian said, toying with her necklace.

'There was a meeting of the Virtues Council. Mama says there's been a drought. Some brooks and rivers have run dry – the Lennow, the Brath. There are reports that people have crossed the Limber dryshod in some places, and boats have run aground. Coupled with the expectation of a poor harvest, the coming year may be harder than usual.'

Glorian frowned. She had not realised Inys, with its steady rains, could ever want for water.

Something had changed since the eruption of the Dreadmount. The sinister cast over the sun was an ill omen. The last time the mountain had spilled fire, it had also birthed the Nameless One.

'Your Highness.' A messenger had appeared. 'Queen Sabran requests your presence.'

With a fresh sense of foreboding, Glorian splashed the sweat from her face and tidied her hair. Her mother had a habit of always summoning her when she was dishevelled.

Queen Sabran was in her withdrawing room, where Liuma was lacing her gown. The Mistress of the Robes smiled when Glorian came in. Liuma had always been sterner than Florell, but the years had softened her a little.

'Glorian,' Queen Sabran said. 'I trust you have had a productive day with your tutors.'

'Yes, Mother. I undertook religious studies and learned more complex phrasing in Yscali.'

'Good. Your pronunciation needs refinement,' her mother stated. 'Janasta ruz zunga, fáurasta ruz herza.'

To know many tongues is to rule many hearts. Glorian mustered her confidence. 'Atha meisto áuda,' she said, making sure to articulate each word with precision, 'sa háuzas tu andugi gala háurasta.'

'A perfect sentence.' Liuma nodded her approval. 'Very good, Your Highness.'

'Yes. Come,' Queen Sabran said. 'I have news for you.'

Glorian sat opposite her mother at a table, and Liuma set two exquisite goblets before them, blown from ruby glass and caged in ironwork. 'How beautiful,' Glorian said, wondering.

'Gifts from the Carmenti. They have been scrupulously cleansed.'

It took a moment to understand. Poison had never even crossed her mind.

Liuma poured them both a dark cherry wine before retreating. Glorian sat up straight, the better to mirror Queen Sabran. After sixteen years, it was still a strange thing, to look at her mother and see her own features. *Lips as red as roses, as sacred blood on snow*, the rhyme went. *Eyes as green as willow leaves, and hair black as a crow.*

'First, I have news I imagine will please you,' Queen Sabran said. 'We have decided to annul your betrothal to Lord Magnaust Vatten. Instead, he will wed Idrega Vetalda, Princess of Yscalin.'

Glorian was careful not to smile, even as a sunbeam of relief shone through her.

'As you decree, Mother,' she said. 'I wish them every happiness.'

Arching an eyebrow, Queen Sabran lifted her goblet to her lips. The wine deepened their redness.

'The eruption of the Dreadmount threatens the stability of Virtudom,' she said. 'We could no longer wait until you are seventeen to strengthen our ties to the Vatten. Fortunately, Idrega is willing and of age. She will marry Lord Magnaust on the Feast of High Winter.'

'In such a dark time?'

'It is wise to give the people joy when the world offers them gloom and lack. As the Knight of Fellowship reminds us, it is in the darkest times that companionship is needed most. What else does the Feast of High Winter represent?'

'A new year.'

'Yes. A fair time for a new alliance.'

Glorian had a distant memory of Idrega, courteous and sweet. A strange fit with the scornful Magnaust.

'Your father and I will attend the ceremony, which will take place in Vattengard,' continued Queen Sabran. 'The newlyweds will then go on progress in Mentendon.'

Before Glorian could stop it, hope leapt in her. 'Mother, it's been so long since I last visited Hróth. May I go, too?'

'No,' her mother said at once. Seeing Glorian wilt, she sat back, her shoulders lowering. 'The heir and the sovereign cannot both be away from Inys, Glorian. You must stay.'

Glorian dulled as quickly as she had brightened. To distract herself, she drank some wine.

'All of this does not relieve you of your own duty to wed,' Queen Sabran reminded her. 'Princess Idrega has done us a great service. Our Yscali friends will need rewarding.'

And Glorian was the reward.

'Yes, Mother,' was all she said.

Queen Sabran looked at her, and then through the window, at the fields beyond the castle. 'I asked your father to marry me here,' she said. 'On the shore of Lyfrith Lake.'

'Truly?'

Glorian could not recognise this picture of her mother, cavorting in pools and proposing to strange heathen men. It had been years since Glorian had even heard her laugh.

'Yes.' Her gaze was distant, but soft, her lips tilted. 'I was afraid that day. Afraid to take such a great risk on a stranger, a man I knew had blood on his hands – but I did, to save Inys from the rot that had almost consumed it. The rot of decadence, envy, indecision. We must never let it creep back, Glorian.' She took one more small drink from her goblet. 'I will hear petitions this afternoon. I trust you will pay close attention to your studies.'

'Mother,' Glorian said, 'I am sixteen now. If I am to be alone in Inys, I should know more about ruling. May I join you?'

'What other lesson do you have today?'

'Music.' Glorian cleared her throat. 'I am to … refine my singing.'

They both knew her voice was as clear as marshwater. 'I see.' When Queen Sabran spoke again, her tone was lighter than usual. 'Perhaps we can dispense with singing for one day.'

****

Glowan Castle was a summer home. The timber-framed throne room lacked the daunting magnificence of its counterpart in Ascalun, but still had a dignified beauty – the walls painted white, the floors strewn with rushes. Its doors had been thrown open to the breeze.

Seventy petitioners stood in a crowd, waiting to speak to Queen Sabran. Her throne was polished walnut, set beneath a red canopy, before a banner bearing the True Sword.

For the first time, Glorian perched beside her mother on a faldstool. Once more, she sat with her shoulders back and hands in her lap, just as her manners tutor had instructed.

The Inysh came to their queen when they had found no satisfaction in their provinces. Most of their grievances were dull, complicated, or both – minor heresies by their neighbours, disputes over burial rights and land boundaries, the occasional plea for a royal pardon – and the heat made it hard to concentrate. Still, Glorian tried. When she wore the crown, it would be her duty to listen to her people, and to try to make things right for them.

'Lord Mansell,' Queen Sabran said when a man in his fifties approached. 'Welcome. How fares your companion?'

The man bowed. 'Your Grace. Highness,' he added to Glorian. 'Lord Edrick is very well.'

'And your children?'

A queen was always courteous, despite the demands on her time. 'Roland continues to learn the ways of the barony from Edrick,' Lord Mansell said. 'Mara has begun work for your own mother at Befrith Castle. She says Lady Marian treats her most kindly.'

It was the first Glorian had heard of her grandmother in a long time.

'I am pleased to hear it,' Queen Sabran said. 'And your younger son, Wulfert. He stands among my consort's retainers.'

'Indeed.' Lord Mansell smiled, his eyes twinkling. 'Wulf is very proud to serve King Bardholt, and we are very proud of him.' He sighed. 'Your Grace, forgive me. This is a dreary matter, to be sure, and yet it drags on. I would be grateful for your intervention.'

'I shall render what assistance I may.'

Lord Mansell began a story of a neglected path and a six-year dispute over who was legally bound to maintain it. Though Glorian tried to listen, trying to set her mind on it was like nailing whey to a wall. By the time she willed herself to concentrate again, Lord Mansell had retreated.

'Lord Ordan Beck,' the steward announced. 'Dowager Earl of Goldenbirch.'

The Dowager Earl approached on a plastered foot and a crutch, wearing the black and harvest gold that appeared in his heraldry. He was tall, like his daughter, his hair grey over a broad forehead.

'Your Grace, Highness. The Leas is honoured by your presence,' he said in his rolling northern accent, 'and I am, as ever, honoured to keep it in your name.'

'You have not petitioned me for many years, my lord. Since you have come with an injury, it must be a pressing matter,' Queen Sabran observed. 'Pray, unburden yourself.'

'My queen, I do have a story both urgent and strange. With me I bring Lady Annes Haster, companion to Sir Landon Croft. If it please you, she will tell it with her own tongue.'

'As you wish.'

An ashen woman stepped forward. 'Your Grace, forgive me. I hardly know where to begin.'

Queen Sabran inclined her head. The woman wrung her thick fingers.

'Our estate is close to the haithwood. All through the spring and summer, our livestock has been disappearing – the lambs stolen as soon as they were born, others taken in the night.'

Glorian was wide awake now.

'Given the Dowager Earl had broken his ankle,' Lady Annes said, 'he asked my companion to lead a lawful hunt in the haithwood, to try to kill whichever creature was responsible.'

She stopped, her shoulders rising. 'Take your time, Lady Annes,' Queen Sabran said.

'Thank you, Your Grace. I beg your pardon.' She dried her cheeks. 'Some way into the haithwood, Sir Landon found what he thought was a wolf den. Inside, among bones and blood, they found eleven boulders, about so high.' Her hand hovered by her fourth rib. 'He said they were hot as a cooked pot to the touch, with a reek like a boiling stew. Three of the rocks had split open, and within they were thick with … black honeycomb.'

'Honeycomb,' Queen Sabran repeated.

'I believe he spoke poetically, Your Grace,' Lord Ordan explained. 'Likely some pory rock.'

Glorian glanced sidelong at her mother.

'Sir Landon decided to retreat, and to return with axes to break another of the rocks open. He returned for supper and left again at dawn,' Lady Annes said. 'He never came back.'

Queen Sabran narrowed her eyes.

'Your Grace.' Lord Ordan took over. 'The southern reaches of the haithwood are my responsibility up to the Wickerwath. It's forbidden to stray from the bridleway without the approval and guidance of my foresters. Sir Landon and his party did not seek this before returning. Since they are now in contempt of royal forest law, I must ask your leave to carry out a search for them, no matter how deep into the trees it may take us.'

'I grant it, and commend you to the Duchess of Justice. We shall have a full inquest.'

'Thank you, Your Grace,' Lady Annes whispered.

'I will report my findings as soon as possible,' Lord Ordan said. 'Good day, my queen. My princess.'

They retreated, and the next petitioner approached the throne, a slender man with short brown hair.

'Your Grace.' He had pointed features, sharp blue eyes. 'Blessings on you, and on your daughter.'

Queen Sabran looked to her steward, who seemed at a loss. The petitioner took out a blade, a dull knife with a wooden handle. 'Mother,' Glorian cried, but it was not the queen that he ran toward.

It was *her*.

A weight collided with her side, thrusting her off the faldstool. She looked back to see her mother shove the man hard in the chest with her bare hands. He lashed out with the knife, just missing her bloodless face. As the Royal Guard wrestled him away, she threw herself beside Glorian and flung both arms around her, shielding her with her own body.

The man stabbed the young guard who held him, driving the blade straight into their throat, above their mail. He rounded on Glorian and her mother, the knife slick with blood.

'Liars,' he hissed. His hand was shaking. 'You never held him at bay. You never—'

A sliver of dark iron burst through his chest. Red sprayed the rushes. Glorian screamed as he fell to the floor, revealing Sir Bramel Stathworth, who slowly lowered his crossbow.

Glorian stared at the dying man, tears leaking down her cheeks. Queen Sabran gripped the back of her head, holding her so tight that Glorian could feel her trembling.

29

South

Autumn had come at last. Just as the ash cleared from the sun, the heat would start to wane – or so Tunuva hoped. The damp warmth of the forest had thickened in the months she had been gone.

Hidat rode ahead. Tunuva followed her to the fig tree, and they walked to the end of the tunnel, where Denag waited to greet them. The healer was past eighty, her hair white as cloud.

'Welcome home.' She kissed them both on the cheek. 'Tunuva, the Prioress wishes to see you.'

'Of course.' Tunuva rolled her tense shoulder. 'I will bathe first, if I may.'

'Not in the spring. It still boils now and then.'

Tunuva exchanged a weary look with Hidat. She would have relished a hot soak. 'How is Siyu?'

'She and the child are in good health. I expect labour to begin any day.'

The Prioress had decreed that no one was to speak to Siyu until she gave birth. Only Denag, who had overseen childbearing for decades, was the exception to that rule. Siyu also had Lalhar, since the ichneumon would languish without her.

She had always loved to talk and spar and dance with her sisters. Now she was denied their company and comfort in a time when she most needed it.

'I'm sure Saghul will let you see her once, discreetly,' Hidat said as they walked away. 'Will you ask to be with her when the time comes?'

'She may not want anyone there,' Tunuva said.

She tried not to remember how Siyu had looked the last time she saw her. Her cold, distant stare. The defiant set to her jaw.

'From what I know of birth,' Hidat said, 'I think she will, Tuva.'

They passed the scullery, where the men were baking onion bread, and ducked through the door to the thousand steps, there to behold the orange tree. Tunuva stroked Ninuru between the ears, finally home.

In the valley, Tunuva and Hidat waded into a pool beneath the lower roots, where they washed off the red sand and sweat and scraped mud from their calves. The men brought them long brushes, and they used them to clean the ichneumons.

Ninuru became a pup again as soon as she smelled water. Tunuva was soaked and laughing by the time both ichneumons were scrubbed. Hidat ushered them into the sun to dry, while Tunuva made her way back up the steps, her hands and limbs stiff from riding so far.

At least something had come from the months of ranging. She had a great deal to report to Saghul.

When she reached her sunroom, she was tempted to lie down and rest. Someone had taken care to welcome her: wine and a block of date cake on the table, incense in the burner, clean bedding and clothes.

She found Esbar in the open gallery that led to the Bridal Chamber. Her drape bared her to the base of her spine, and her hair had been cut to sit on her shoulders, thick and shining.

'Hello, lover,' Tunuva whispered.

Esbar turned. Tunuva noted the shadows under her eyes, the wilt to their lids. 'Hello, lover,' she said, smiling.

Tunuva drew her into a deep embrace. Esbar wrapped both arms around her neck, her warm cheek cradled by its curve, ribs sinking as she surrendered her breath. Too relieved for words, Tunuva held her by the waist, and Esbar walked her to the wall and kissed her.

'I was starting to think you would never return.' Esbar touched their noses together. 'By the Mother, Tuva, you were gone a long time.'

'Saghul asked me to go a long way.' Tunuva twined her fingers on her nape. 'Were you waiting for me?'

'Denag said you were back. I wanted a moment with you,' Esbar said. 'Saghul insisted on seeing you as soon as you were ready.' Her face hardened. 'We have a guest.'

'The Priory does not receive guests.'

'This may be a first. A woman arrived here a few days ago, claiming to be from … Inysca.'

Tunuva paused. 'Inys.'

'So she says. I may as well let her explain, else you will hear it twice.'

Tunuva followed her through the Bridal Chamber. Saghul and her guest were dining on the balcony, cooled by spray from the waterfall. As Tunuva and Esbar approached, the newcomer rose.

She stood as tall as Tunuva, and wore a sleeveless dress that fell to the floor, cut of blue and cream brocade and girded with a leather belt. It offered no connexions to a family or trade, though the Ersyri cloth looked costly. She was pale in a way few Southerners were, with an uptilted nose, amber eyes, and golden hair that rippled past a slender waist.

Tunuva stopped. As their eyes met, she felt a faint pull towards the woman. At the same time, inexplicable nausea wound through her, as if she had drunk cream to the point of sickness.

A strange thing to feel when faced with a complete stranger. Tunuva shook herself.

'Is that you, Esbar?' Saghul called over the rush of the falls.

'Yes. I have Tuva.'

'Tunuva Melim.' She raised her cup in greeting. 'Welcome home.'

'Thank you, Prioress.' Tunuva found her voice. 'I see we have a visitor.'

'Indeed. This is Canthe.'

Canthe. A name with no clear origin or associations. She gave Tunuva a brief smile.

'A pleasure to meet you, Tunuva,' she said. 'The Prioress has told me a great deal about you.'

Her voice was deep and soft. 'Sit with us,' Saghul said to Tunuva. 'An intriguing tale awaits.'

Tunuva took a seat on the opposite side of the table to Canthe, who returned to hers. It was hard to guess her age. Time had not yet left its marks – no droop to her unlined skin, no grey in her hair – but her bearing was that of a woman settled in her bones.

'The Prioress tells me you are the tomb keeper,' Canthe said. 'The guardian of Cleolind.'

Her Lasian was precise, with an accent both subtle and impossible to place. She spoke it in a manner that struck Tunuva as antiquated, the way orchardists and elders sometimes did.

'Yes,' Tunuva said. 'You know of the Mother?'

'Of course.'

'Canthe is a fellow mage,' Saghul said, chewing a morsel of fish. 'It seems there were once two other siden trees – a hawthorn in the West, and a mulberry in the East. The hawthorn tree grew on an Inysh island. Both, alas, are dead.'

Tunuva stared. 'Dead?'

'Yes,' Canthe said quietly. 'I protected the hawthorn for a long time, but I was its only caretaker. In the end, I failed it.'

'Ask your questions, Tunuva.' Saghul dabbed her mouth with linen. 'Canthe knows that we do not usually receive outsiders here. She is happy to sate your curiosity.'

Tunuva looked back at the newcomer, who nodded.

'I would like to know how the hawthorn died,' Tunuva said. 'Fire does not harm the orange tree; nor can it be pulled up from the roots – they go into the world's own womb.'

Canthe lowered her gaze.

'Once,' she said, 'the hawthorn was sacred to my people, the Inyscans. Then they came to fear it, and me, its guardian, in turn. They drove me away, and when I returned, it was dead. I know not how.'

'Inyscans,' Tunuva repeated. 'Inys has not gone by that name in centuries.'

'No.' Seeing her face, Canthe explained, 'As far as I can tell, I have not aged since I first ate of my hawthorn. It seems it bestowed a long life upon me.'

Esbar, unusually, had not said a word. She observed their guest with an impenetrable expression.

'If you grew up in Inys,' Tunuva said, 'then do you worship Galian the Deceiver?'

'I do not. My home was the isle of Nurtha, where the old way, the worship of nature, clings on. Galian tried to destroy it, but failed. I am one of the few who curses his name.'

'Oh, not few, by any means. We all curse his name here,' Saghul said, with alacrity.

Tunuva said, 'How did you find the Priory?'

'When the Dreadmount poured its fire, I sensed another wellspring of siden. I had sought a living tree for years, to no avail,' Canthe said. 'I followed my feeling here, to the orange tree. Imagine my joy when I found an entire society – a family – devoted to its protection.'

'Canthe wishes to join our ranks, to help us protect the orange tree,' Saghul said. 'As of now, accepting an outsider would violate the laws of our ancestors, but some laws can be reconsidered and questioned. I would be interested in your opinion, Tunuva.'

Saghul had always been forthright. Canthe cleared her throat, a small crease in her forehead. A gold ring shone on her left forefinger, showing two hands, twined at the bezel above her base knuckle.

'Perhaps you would excuse us, Canthe,' Tunuva said gently.

Canthe glanced at her. 'Of course,' she said. 'Thank you. I wait at your pleasure, Prioress.'

She walked back inside.

'The two of you and Denag are as near as I will ever stray to a Royal Council. Help me judge the matter of Canthe,' Saghul said. 'Tunuva, since you have sent her away, I will get straight to the pith of it. Do we silence this woman, or embrace her as a sister?'

'Before I share my opinion,' Tunuva said, 'I might ask what you have decided to do with Anyso.'

'As of now, nothing.'

He was still alone, then, locked on the postulants' floor. Tunuva could not imagine his misery. 'He's still alive?'

'For the time being, since Denag has requested that I put no further strain on Siyu.'

'Saghul, he has already been with us for too long. His family must be desperate.'

'No doubt, but they are no longer looking. I sent two of your sisters to Dimabu to make sure. His parents have given up. Thanks to the rumours of danger we've seeded, they were told not to search for him in the Basin. They returned to Carmentum a few weeks ago.'

All they would ever know was that the forest had taken their son. Tunuva pressed on: 'Surely we can't accept Canthe without also accepting Anyso.'

'One is a former mage, while the other brings nothing but risk to our ranks. The difference is stark, Tunuva.'

'Tuva,' Esbar said, 'the boy is lovesick, and was not raised with our perspective on family. He would not be content here.' Her jaw rustled. 'Siyu should never have let herself be seen.'

'I will deliver his fate at the right time,' Saghul said, 'but this discussion pertains to Canthe.'

'Fine. I vote we silence her,' Esbar said curtly. 'Siyāti forbade all outsiders from the Priory, clearly with good reason. We should heed her, and learn from this disaster with Anyso.'

'Siyāti did not know that there were other mages. She may have made an exception for them.'

As Saghul spoke, Tunuva looked at her face. The whites of her eyes held a distinct sallowness.

'Siyāti is dead,' Esbar said, 'so we cannot ask.' Saghul tutted. 'If Canthe has lived as long as she claims, her knowledge of siden may outweigh ours. She could use that against us.'

'Not without the fruit. I would not make her an initiate until she earns our trust.'

'I trust my instincts, Saghul. I mislike the way I feel in her presence.'

Despite the heat, bumps speckled her arms. Tunuva had rarely seen her so perturbed. 'Perhaps a mark of her long life,' Saghul said, 'if we believe in that.' Esbar snorted.

'The thought of an outsider joining our ranks unsettles me, too,' Tunuva told her, 'but the knowledge you mention may help us. Besides, she would not be safe in Inys. Where else is there for her?'

Esbar sighed in exasperation. 'Tuva, that is not our concern. We are here to defend the tree.'

'After what I have seen, I believe it would be foolish to turn a potential warrior away from it. Perhaps my report will have a bearing on your verdict, Prioress.'

'First, I want to know what happened when you saw Kediko,' Saghul said. 'You did visit Nzene?'

'Yes.'

Tunuva related the meeting. When they heard what Gashan had been wearing, both Esbar and Saghul huffed in disgust.

'Foolish vanity,' Saghul muttered. 'I knew there was a reason I never made her munguna.'

'Yes. Because I was better,' Esbar purred.

'And still no less arrogant,' Saghul said sharply.

'Oh, come. Gashan and I both earned just a touch of arrogance, wouldn't you say?'

'No Prioress was ever cursed with such a prideful choice of successors,' Saghul griped. She reached for her cup, her mouth a thin line. 'So be it. If she and Kediko do not want Siyu, they will not have her.'

'Princess Jenyedi needs a protector,' Tunuva said quietly. 'She is the heir to the Mother's land.'

'We can only ever offer our protection,' Saghul reminded her. 'Kediko would not be the first to refuse, but those who do all come to regret it.' Her fingers interlocked on the table. 'You truly believe Gashan has renounced the Mother, Tunuva?'

'Not wholly, but she is losing her faith.'

'Then she may pose a threat to us. Kediko clearly begins to see this society as his enemy.'

'Gashan is still our sister, lost though she is.'

'I agree with Tuva. Besides, Kediko is not inclined towards war,' Esbar said. 'In his heart, he fears our magic. Let Gashan count his coins in her red cloth, if she desires. In the meantime, perhaps you should send another sister to Lasia, as a palace messenger or servant – one of the younger girls, someone Gashan doesn't know, to keep watch on the situation.'

'Oh, very well. Doubtless she'll annoy Kediko sooner or later, and will come to us weeping,' Saghul muttered. 'Now for your report, Tunuva.'

'Hidat and I went first to Jrhanyam,' Tunuva said. 'There had been several disappearances across the Ersyr – livestock, for the most part, but people as well, mostly in regions near fire mountains or hot springs, like the Vale of Yaud. We visited a number of places. Agārin, Efsi, the Great Falls of Dwyn. In each, we found ... stones, boulders, tucked into caves. They were large and dark, all touched by siden. Neither of us dared get close. We sensed our magic might disturb them.'

'A strange thing, Tunuva Melim, to fear a pile of stone. Be plain. What is it you suspect?'

'That something dwells inside.'

Esbar lifted an eyebrow. 'You think these rocks might ... hatch?'

Tunuva nodded. 'I would like to return to the nearest clutch with more sisters,' she said. 'Those rocks reeked of the Dreadmount. If they stir, we will need many blades.'

Saghul tucked her lips in, thinking.

'For now, Canthe will stay,' she said. 'Tunuva, write me an account of what you saw in each region, then return to your usual duties while I decide who can be spared. You may not visit Siyu,' she added. 'She is using this time to reflect on her actions. I trust I make myself clear.'

'Yes, Prioress, but may I be with her during the birth?'

'You may.'

Saghul coughed as soon as she said it – a dry and hacking wrench from her chest. 'Saghul.' Esbar stood. 'Come out of the sun.' She glanced at Tunuva. 'I'll join you later.'

'Yes, Tunuva Melim. Rest,' Saghul said between coughs. 'Don't get old. It's tiresome.'

Esbar escorted her indoors. Tunuva stood in the spray for a time, hands on the balustrade, gazing at the orange tree.

****

In her sunroom, she cleaned her teeth with a chewstick and used a salve of rosewater to quench her skin after the desert. Months on the road had made her more grateful than ever for the small comforts of home.

Ninuru curled up by the hearth. Tunuva knelt beside her, and was brushing the last grains of sand from her fur when it started to hurt to keep her eyes open. Her knees were bruised from so long in the saddle, her sitbones aching. She lay on the tawny silks of her bed.

You, she thought before she drifted off, *are not quite as young as you were, Tunuva Melim.*

For a while, her dreams were too murky to grasp, filled with a black storm of wings. At last, they resolved into a welcome sight: Esbar, smiling beside her. Tunuva smiled back.

And then Esbar wrapped both hands around her throat, and crushed it.

****

She woke to a bleary shimmer of oil lamps. A familiar hand came to rest on her arm.

'Tuva, are you awake?'

'Esbar.' She rubbed her eyes. 'Is it morning?'

'No, the night is young. I thought you might want supper.' Esbar stroked her hair. 'Are you all right?'

There was a platter on the bed, laden with cold meat, saffron rice, and flatbreads. Tunuva breathed out, her hand ghosting to her throat. She had never had a dream like that.

'Yes.' She sat up, grimacing. 'I was more wayworn than I thought.'

'Are you in pain?'

'Nothing I won't survive.' Tunuva kneaded the tender spot in her shoulder. 'I would relish a fight soon. If I lie down for too long, I fear I may lock up and never rise again.'

Esbar chuckled. 'You would make a fine sculpture.'

Tunuva let her take over, sighing her assent. She almost dozed off again while Esbar worked on the burl, then smoothed her palms over the rest of her back.

'Do you know where Canthe is staying?' Tunuva asked her.

'The spare room near the scullery. I still don't like this situation.'

'You will have to make peace with it, if Saghul accepts her.' Tunuva winced as Esbar crunched a knot. 'Strange to think there are other mages. Do you suppose the Mother knew?'

'I wondered the same.' Esbar gentled her touch. 'Perhaps that was why she left us. To find the other trees.'

By the time she was finished, Tunuva could rotate her dominant arm with a little more ease. Esbar sprawled at her side.

'Siyu,' Tunuva said. 'How is she, in her mind?'

'Imin tells me she prays, and sings to her belly.' Esbar shook her head. 'Siyu has been a careless fool, but I do pity her. I would have found it very hard to grow her without our sisters' company. Let us hope she learns from this, and that it placates Saghul.'

'Saghul is not well, is she?'

'Denag fears not.' She took off her earrings. 'She is old, Tuva. Older than most of us live.'

Before Tunuva could reply, her breath caught in her throat. She tried to swallow the lump there.

'Tuva.' Esbar stopped. 'What is it?'

'I feel a great change in our lives. Siyu, Gashan, Saghul – our family is coming undone.'

'No. Don't say that, my love.' Esbar cupped her cheek. 'Listen to me. This family will always be here. I will always be here. I have loved you for thirty years, and my flame will light the tree beside yours. I am always with you, Tuva Melim.'

Tunuva held that promise close.

'Siyu will be fine,' Esbar said. 'When the child quickened, Saghul allowed her to eat of the tree, so it would know them both. She is warm, Tuva.' She placed a soft kiss on her forehead. 'You're home. Sleep.'

Esbar was right. It would all be fine. Surely nothing else could break their family apart.

Tunuva turned towards her, laying her head on her shoulder. Esbar leaned across her to blow out the oil lamp. They slept there, in the gloom of the Priory – limb to limb, heart to heart.

30

East

White Peak Hall was grand as a palace, situated in the outskirts of Antuma. Like so many things in the capital, it belonged to the River Lord. It was here that the yearly Night Banquet was held.

It took place under the open sky, on the banks of a stream that wound through the grounds. In a storm haven overlooking the water, Dumai sat with the rest of the imperial family.

As she ate, she watched the moon. Furtia had said she would return when it was full. The dragon wanted to take her north, to seek more of the sinister rocks they had seen in Mount Izaripwi.

The fire beneath grows too hot, too fast. The star has not returned to cool it. Dumai had gone over those words again and again, and they still confounded her. *I have sensed more across the sea.*

What the rocks were, why they troubled Furtia – she had no solid answers to these questions. According to accounts from before the Long Slumber, dragons had always been hard to understand. They were divine creatures, and humans often failed to grasp their meaning.

Dumai had told her father everything she had seen. He had encouraged her to go with Furtia. In the meantime, he would continue to lay his plans for a shadow court and comb his private archive for anything that might help cultivate her bond with the dragon.

Of course, before she could fly anywhere, she had to get through the Night Banquet.

'My uncle has outdone himself this year,' Empress Sipwo said. 'How charming it all looks.'

Dumai had to concede that it did. Courtiers talked and laughed beneath the gnarled willows that lined the stream, which were all decked in golden leaves. Some of the guests played a game with painted shells, while others sipped from cups of sea-aged wine. Miniature wooden boats floated down the stream, each carrying a tiny lamp.

'Indeed,' Emperor Jorodu said. 'Then again, autumn is already so beautiful. The River Lord could only enhance it.'

Empress Sipwo looked down at the fish collar in front of her. 'It is a delightful season,' she said. 'Though you always did prefer winter.'

'Not for some time.' His smile was thin. 'No. Autumn appeals tonight.'

The season of change, when fortunes rose or fell. Today, the court would shed its leaves.

The River Lord had spared no expense. The best musicians and dancers had been summoned from across Seiiki, as had the great clans. With every hour that passed, the merriment grew louder.

Dumai should have felt less stifled than usual. The air had a bite for the first time in months, and soon she would be free of court, but the smoking rocks lurked at the edge of her mind.

Others are laid. Many more. All will burn . . .

'I understand you used to live here with your siblings, Empress Sipwo,' Dumai said, to distract herself. 'It must have been wonderful to grow up in such a beautiful place.'

'It was. My uncle raised us all,' Empress Sipwo said. 'Every spring, my sister and I would sit by this stream and wait for blue blossoms, from the welkinwood grove where its waters rise. We thought the number of blossoms was the number of years until the gods woke.'

'Now I have a sister, too,' Suzumai said, nestling against Dumai. 'She woke up Furtia.'

'No, Suzu. No one has that power.' Dumai touched her under the chin. 'Eat your food.'

Kanifa was deep in conversation with his captain. As Dumai watched the scene, she knew she was being watched in turn. Ever since her arrival at court, she had been a curiosity, but now her strangeness had climbed to new heights. She was the first dragonrider in centuries.

Footsteps hooked her from her thoughts. The River Lord had entered the storm haven.

'Your Majesties. Your Highnesses.' He bowed. 'I trust you are all enjoying the evening.'

Dumai took note of his fine garments, embellished all over with silver bells. As always, his beard tapered into a fishtail.

'Yes, River Lord. Everything is perfect,' Emperor Jorodu said. His eyes were bloodshot, hand tight around a silver cup. 'I wonder if I could afford such extravagance myself.'

'A splendid party, Uncle.' Empress Sipwo smiled, sealing the cut before it could sting. 'Your hospitality is unrivalled.'

'Ah, the night has only just begun. I thought I would bring your next course,' the River Lord added, beckoning a servant. 'A prize from the hunt. I was grieved that you could not attend, Princess Dumai.'

Dumai hoped her smile was sufficiently apologetic. If there was one thing she never meant to do in her life, it was come within a hundred leagues of Kuposa pa Fotaja while he had a bow and quiver in his grasp.

Princess, how the loss of your company pains me, he would sigh as she bled to death. *I shall commemorate this moment with a poem.*

'Your dedication to your schooling is commendable,' he said in a warm tone, 'as is your pure love for my grandniece. It comforts me to know that when Suzumai is empress, she will have her loyal big sister at her side. A sister who studies hard to support her.'

'Dumai is the best sister in the world,' Suzumai told him with a gap-toothed smile.

'So she is, Suzumai. See how tirelessly she educates herself, so you will one day have a reliable advisor?' the River Lord said spryly. 'Why, when you are empress, you will never have to lift a finger.'

Dumai had to break his gaze. She drew her little sister close and kissed her soft hair.

He had guessed what she meant to do to Suzumai, and he was going to make every gain hurt. Even as she tried to put roots down at court, he planted weeds around her, to strangle her before she bloomed.

The servant set an iron pot on the table. 'Your kill, Sipwo?' Emperor Jorodu said, eyeing the stew of mushroom and wild boar. 'You always did know how to aim for the heart.'

Dumai had lost count of the cups of wine he had drunk. Empress Sipwo finished her salmon.

'No,' she said. 'These days, the heart eludes my eye.'

Emperor Jorodu looked at his consort, his expression flickering.

'While you enjoy the prize,' the River Lord said, after a polite silence, 'I wondered if Princess Dumai would care to join us by the water. A game is about to begin, and everyone is eager to see if their princess is as accomplished at poetry as she is at every other art.'

Dumai rose. 'As always, River Lord, you are too kind. I would be happy to join you.'

'Wonderful.'

She followed him down the steps. 'I am glad to have caught you alone, Princess Dumai,' the River Lord said as they walked along the edge of the stream. 'I trust you are finding court comfortable.'

'Thank you. I am settled.'

'No doubt, with a god at your beck and call. Did you learn the art of taming dragons as a godsinger?'

At this, Dumai stopped.

'My lord, a god cannot be tamed,' she said quietly. 'I am of the House of Noziken. My ancestor saved the great Kwiriki. They were bound by salt and blood, by milk and brine. It is that affinity, and that alone, that called the great Furtia to my side.'

The words swelled from the depths of her. The River Lord looked her up and down, fresh interest in his gaze.

'Of course,' he said, his smile brief. 'Let us hope she will remain there, Princess Dumai. Dragons, after all, are of the sea. And the sea holds loyalty to no one.'

He walked on. Dumai shadowed him, wishing she could wrest the final word for once.

Her handmaidens were beside the stream. Dumai knelt among them, and a table was brought to her, set with an inkstone and stick, a fine brush, a dish of water, and fresh paper.

'The rules are simple,' the River Lord told her. 'These little boats have borne food all night. Now they will carry poems.' He pointed them out. 'On the other side of the bridge, someone has been chosen to write to you. The challenge is to work out their identity. You will receive three poems, and send two in return. Once you have your clues, you can try to find your opponent.'

Dumai nodded. 'Will you be playing, my lord?'

'Alas, since I fashioned the game, I can only watch.' He bowed. 'Best of luck, Princess.'

When he had gone, a servant brought a dish of cooked milk. 'Is this not the most wonderful party?' Juri sighed happily, taking a slice of it. 'Such a pity Lady Osipa was too tired.'

Yapara snorted her disagreement. Dumai still wished Osipa had been in the mood to attend.

The general chatter loudened as the boats came back down the stream, each carrying a scroll. Dumai watched until she saw one with her name painted on it.

'That one,' she said to Juri, who lifted it from the water, soaking her sleeves. Taking the scroll from its prow, Dumai read the poem.

To whom shall I tell it, this news that delights me?
A secret unspoken shines brighter than silver –
revealed it will tarnish, and yet the heart whispers.

With a reluctant smile, Dumai ground her block of ink and dipped her brush. It had been a long time since she had indulged in poetry. She wrote:

A whispering heart seeks an ear in seclusion.
Tell me, why forge the silver and not let it gleam?
Clouds drawn by the wind never tarnished the moonlight.

She rolled and secured the poem, then placed it into the boat, which Juri sent into the dark with the others. Servants must be waiting to carry them all back to the start.

Across the stream, a young noble made a drunken lunge and crashed headfirst into the water, raising gusts of laughter. Kanifa waded to his rescue, hauling him out just in time to avoid the second procession of boats. Dumai opened the next poem with quick fingers.

How versatile silver is – bell, blade or moonbeam.
Come, share in its shine. I hear tell that the guard by
the water might freeze it, coming from the mountain.

She read the words again. *The guard by the water.*

Kanifa. Heart stumbling, she leaned out over the stream, searching the gloom. It had to be her.

Lady Nikeya.

She did remember Kanifa.

Clan Kuposa might not be able to move against a princess without arousing suspicion, but they could hurt a guard. Dumai reached for her brush again, smoothed the paper, and tried to steady her hand as she wrote.

I hear tell of a lady of many faces.
Has she many hearts, too, that I must entreat now
to give up her share in this hoard of bright silver?

Wisdom told her not to send it. It would betray her fear. She should wear a new face of her own – pretend she had no idea what it meant – but Nikeya seemed far too sharp to deceive.

Before she could stop herself, Dumai passed the poem to Juri. She could not take her eyes off Kanifa, who wrinkled his brow in question. When the boat returned, she almost knocked Juri into the water in her haste to grab it.

The heart takes its time to decide on its wishes.
Remember that knowledge shines brighter than silver;
it may take more earth yet to silence my whisper.

'Your time is up,' the River Lord declared at last. 'If you believe you have identified your partner, come, speak to them! If your instinct is right, they will give you a gift.'

Almost tripping on the hem of her robe, Dumai got straight to her feet and marched towards the bridge, past the delighted guests, who were drifting upstream to seek their partners.

'In the meantime' – the River Lord was a disembodied voice in the dark – 'we will watch a performance by the shining Lord Kordia, and my own beloved daughter, Lady Nikeya.'

Dumai stopped. A head rose from among the guests, and a shadow moved towards the nearest braziers.

Lady Nikeya wore white over grey, evoking snow on stone. Pearls frosted her hair. When a bearded young man joined her, garbed in shades of blue, they bowed to one another.

A reed flute pierced the silence first, drums pounding to meet it. Dumai recognised the opening of 'Snow and Sea' – an ancient composition, celebrating the romance between Snow Maiden and her consort, Dancing Prince, who Kwiriki had breathed to life. Their son had been born with the sea in his veins, for ever salting their bloodline.

The dance was slow, building to the faster cadences. From the first, Nikeya brought a liveliness to it – in the birdlike tilts of her head, her deft hand movements. Lady of Faces indeed.

Captivating though it was, Dumai saw the arrogance of this performance. Nikeya dared to play the first dragonrider, the first Queen of Seiiki. As the thought came, Nikeya cut a glance in her direction.

That was when Dumai knew she was no spirit. She only smiled with one side of her mouth.

Dumai closed her eyes. She was duelling with scraps of paper and whispers, and a woman who seemed to embody them both. How could she leave her father alone at court now?

You must, she thought. *The gods are calling.*

At last, the musicians stopped, and Nikeya and Lord Kordia went to their knees, heads bowed to the emperor, who stood and faced them all. It was time for the appointments.

Osipa had told Dumai all about this. For months, minor officials had been scampering through Antuma Palace, imploring those of higher rank to speak well of them to the emperor – or the empress, who some considered to be the more powerful. The majority would be disappointed. Clan Kuposa had an iron hold on the most important positions.

'Thank you,' Emperor Jorodu said. The wine had fettled his voice, so the words rolled into one another. 'River Lord, your daughter has many talents. How proud you must be.'

'Exceptionally, Your Majesty,' the River Lord said, eyes reflecting the firelight. 'Nikeya is the pearl of my world.'

'As my daughters are the pearls of mine. And the first of my appointments tonight – the most important – pertains to my eldest child, Princess Dumai.'

Hushed voices filled the night. Dumai watched her father, her heart kicking in her throat.

'It has become apparent,' he said, 'that Princess Dumai is remarkable. She is the first to fly with a god since before the Long Slumber. Now we have a dragonrider, we can renew our bonds with the world, removing the need for dangerous voyages. When the moon is full, she will go to the Queendom of Sepul with Furtia Stormcaller, to form a new alliance with the House of Kozol.'

More intrigued murmurs. Dumai released her breath. He was announcing her departure, nothing more. That was the story they had agreed to tell the court.

And then he said the words that changed everything:

'When she returns, she will be Crown Princess of Seiiki.'

Now Dumai stared at him, cold to her bones. So did everyone else.

Father, what are you doing?

'I am fortunate to have found this perfect daughter – praised by her tutors, beloved of gods. There could be no better successor,' Emperor Jorodu said. 'Princess Suzumai, as the younger child, will be her loyal helper in all things. Once I have abdicated in her favour, I know Empress Dumai will reign over a new age of prosperity and peace.'

The River Lord wore a carven smile, while Empress Sipwo had turned even paler. Suzumai looked at her mother, confused. As every eye fixed on her, Dumai had the sudden and unsettling sense of being naked.

'Now,' Emperor Jorodu said, with the barest hint of satisfaction, 'the remaining appointments.'

31

South

The War Hall was the largest chamber in the Priory, its ceiling a triumph of Ersyri mirrorwork. One side was open to the elements – a steep drop to the forest, guarded by nine columns. Detailed carvings adorned them, showing the lives and deeds of the nine handmaidens of Cleolind.

At the top of each column was a corbel, sculpted into the bust of a handmaiden. For those who had borne children, all women of their line were named beneath, etched in Selinyi. Tunuva read the lower ones as she limbered up. Five centuries of sister lines.

After her kindling, she had etched her own name into the second column, below many other Melim women, all branching down from their ancestor, Narha. It was said only she could comfort the Mother when she dreamed of the Nameless One.

Tunuva wished Narha could comfort her, too – that her forebear could lean down from that column and brush away her nightmares. In the last one, Esbar had stabbed her in the heart, and she had woken in a sweat, convinced it was blood.

She had not told Esbar.

Across the hall, Esbar was taking her time at the rack. When she nodded to an Ersyri sword, the armourer removed its silver-mounted scabbard, wiped its blade with an oiled cloth, and handed it to her. As she held the sword aloft to inspect it, Tunuva recalled the cold twist of the knife in her dream.

She shook herself. 'Are you ready,' she called, 'or examining yourself in the ceiling?'

'Why?' Esbar sauntered to the middle of the hall. 'Do you suppose I'd like what I see?'

'Unquestionably.'

Many of their sisters had gathered to watch. Yeleni stood in a far corner, away from the others. She had seen out the long confinement imposed on her for abetting Siyu.

'You flatter me, lover,' Esbar said, drawing her back to the matter at hand. She tilted the sword, resting the flat of its blade on her scarred forearm. 'But tread softly.' They circled one another. 'Fill me with too much confidence, and I fear you may come to regret it.'

'Confidence is a danger, true.' Tunuva spun her spear. 'Arrogance, however, I can tip to my advantage.'

Lips leaning into a smile, Esbar lunged.

Since they were children, they had mastered every Southern weapon, as well as some Yscali blades. What they trained to fight was not human, but the Mother had vanquished the Nameless One with an Inyscan sword, Ascalun. Even monsters were not impervious to steel.

Esbar slashed and stabbed, thews bunching in her upper arms. She was always most vigorous at the start of a duel, wearing her opponent down as quickly as she could. Tunuva knew better than to rise to it. She blocked with ease.

'Letting me lead, I see.' Esbar flicked back a grey strand of hair. 'Am I to take this as an early submission?'

'Ah, you know I like to warm the blood before a dance.'

Not long after their first kiss, they had faced each other in this chamber. Esbar always fought to win, and win she had. She had sent the healer away and tended Tunuva herself.

Nothing comes above the Mother, she had said, soft and resolute. *If we do this, we cannot let it call us from our duty. We are warriors, Tunuva.*

From that day forth, Tunuva had fought as hard against Esbar as she did against any other sister. In thirty years, she had never flinched.

Esbar kept hammering her across the chamber. She was an army in one woman, her sword catching the sunlight and splintering it between the mirrors. Its edge came within a fingertip of Tunuva; she flung up her spear just in time to deflect it.

They spun away from each other. Esbar pounced again. Tunuva swivelled the spear around her waist, over her shoulders, parrying each cut. Though Esbar was relentless, Tunuva had nurtured the patience to endure the onslaught, and for all Esbar tried to break her defence, it held.

Tunuva had never cared for the hunt, but fighting – that was something wondrous. Feeling her body surge and twist, marvelling at the power in it, at the way her eye spoke to her mind and her limbs. And of course, the force of nature that was Esbar.

The curved sword flashed towards her again. As she knocked it away, Tunuva recalled the first time she had seen Esbar fight, with Gashan, who was almost two years older. They had fought with pride and rancour, which had shown in their discordant blows, their shouts and gritted teeth – but when Tunuva fought Esbar, it was always courtship.

Esbar was finally slowing. As soon as she saw the glint of sweat, Tunuva drove the spear at her. Hissing out an exhilarated breath, Esbar sliced up and down, both hands on the hilt, barely keeping the spear from her face. She unlocked a store of strength and briefly won back the upper hand, only for Tunuva to feint and clip her jaw with the blunt end of the spear. Esbar grinned. The mark would bloom and fade before morning.

Tunuva whirled her weapon, drawing sounds of appreciation from their sisters. She had always favoured the graceful Kumengan spear. Tightening her grip, she ran forward, planted its end on the floor, and used it to pitch her weight towards Esbar, kicking her square in the chest. Esbar had barely fallen when she wheeled herself back to her feet.

Tunuva charged towards her and swung for her calves. Esbar jumped to elude the blow and struck down with all her might, pinning the spear. Mustering her strength, Tunuva broke the lock. In the same movement, she brought the spear all the way around her waist, thrusting its head back towards Esbar.

Esbar rallied once more. Tunuva glimpsed an opportunity and cracked her across the hand, forcing her to drop her sword. A moment later, Esbar was on her back, and Tunuva was astride her, pointing the spear at her throat. Esbar laughed, chest heaving.

'Sometimes I forget how good you are,' she said.

'Hm.' Tunuva kissed her. 'And then I remind you.'

She rose and held out a hand. Esbar took it, letting Tunuva pull her up. While their sisters applauded, Esbar passed her sword to the armourer, let down her hair, and glanced towards the witnesses.

'Canthe,' she called. 'Good of you to join us.' She clenched and unclenched her hand. 'Care for a spar?'

Heads turned. The newcomer was standing beside Yeleni, draped in ivory silks that left her arms bare.

'A kind invitation, Esbar, but I am no warrior.' Canthe inclined her head. 'I prefer never to fight.'

'If you are to become a sister, you must.' Esbar accepted a cup from one of the men. 'I think we would all be curious to see the gifts of an Inysh mage.'

'I fear it would be a one-sided battle.' Canthe glanced at the arched entrance. 'Besides, I think you are needed.'

Bare feet clapped along the corridor outside. One of the young postulants came rushing through the doorway.

'Tunuva, Esbar,' she said, breathless. 'It's Siyu.'

Murmurs filled the chamber. Tunuva looked to Esbar, who breathed in through her nose, expressionless. 'Go,' she said. 'Be with her, Tuva. I'll follow once I've told Saghul.'

Tunuva needed no further encouragement. She tossed her spear to the armourer and strode after the girl.

****

She heard the sounds before she reached the birthing chamber. Sounds brought on by an opened body – movement beyond knowledge, beyond thought. Ancient and unspoken urge. (*Clench, hold, push.*) Then the smells: sweat and herbs. Something like clay. Scent of wet earth taking form. Though she placed one foot before the other, each step pulled her back in time.

The chamber was more like a cave than the rest of the Priory, dimmed to calm the mind. Passage from one womb to another – that was how she had seen it then, in the first clouded hour of holding him close.

After the clearing, in her dreams, she remembered this room not as womb, but as tomb, as comb. No honey in a womb. No bees. She had brought him from the darkness to his end.

Siyu was huddled over her belly. When Tunuva stepped inside, she looked up, face tearstained.

'Tuva.'

'Hello, sunray.' Tunuva went to her. 'I missed you.'

'I missed you, too.' Her voice shook. 'It hurts.'

It will never stop, Tunuva thought, unbidden. *It will never stop hurting. All of your days, you will never know peace.* She drew Siyu as close as she could, and Siyu buried her face in her shoulder.

Every feature of the birthing chamber lived in perfect detail in her memory. Little had changed in almost two decades. There were the candles, the jars of oil, the fresh linen, basins of hot and cool water. On the hearth, the bronze statue of Gedali, high divinity of doorways and birth, delivering their child, Gedani, who held a pomegranate flower in each fist.

When Tunuva had laboured here, she had felt her sisters' love around her like a cloak. They had all gathered in support, to hearten and pray for her. Her birthmother had been dead by then: Liru Melim, who had given her life saving the Ersyri royals from a surprise attack.

So Esbar had been on both sides of Tunuva – breathing with her, soothing her. She had been there when Tunuva leaked water, through each wrenching pain, through the tearing. All of them had, all through the night. It had been the hardest birth in years.

This night, the room was empty but for Denag, purging her hands in fig wine.

'Denag,' Tunuva said, 'is it time?'

'Yes. She has opened enough.' Denag rinsed and dried her hands. 'Is Esbar coming?'

'I don't want anyone else,' Siyu said roughly. 'Just Tuva.'

Tunuva shook her head at Denag. 'Don't be afraid,' she murmured to Siyu. 'Denag has delivered many children. Including you.' She tucked her damp hair behind her ear. 'Are you ready?'

Siyu set a wide-eyed gaze on the birthing bricks. After a long moment, she nodded.

Tunuva led her to the stacks and helped her step on to them. 'Bend your knees. Denag will be there to take the child,' she said, 'and I'll be here to hold you. You're going to be fine, Siyu.'

Denag knelt before the bricks with her wrap of instruments, hidden from Siyu. Those would only be used if something went awry, or Siyu needed more assistance. She shook out the mantle she would use to catch the child, chanting a familiar prayer to Gedali.

First to birth, opener of ways, guardian of life, make this one strong. Protect her, protect the one who is coming. You whose womb's blood woke the fields, whose broken waters raised the rivers, whose milk nourishes the land...

'We're ready when you are,' Tunuva said gently to Siyu. 'You can start to push now.'

'I don't know how.'

'Breathe with me, slowly. Listen to your body leading you. It knows the way.' Tunuva guided her trembling hand to her belly. 'It feels a little like your bleeding pains, doesn't it?'

Just once more, Tuva. Push.

Siyu could hardly speak. 'Worse,' she managed. 'Much worse.' A groan ripped out of her. 'Tuva, I can't, I want it to stop.'

'It will stop. Bear down,' Tunuva said in calming tones. 'You will feel what to do.'

Siyu blew in and out. When she pushed, a cry tore from her throat, knifing into Tunuva. *I am with you.* Esbar bracing her shoulders, stiffening each time she sobbed. *We all are.*

'That's it, Siyu,' Tunuva said, keeping hold of her. 'Very good. You're being so brave. Push again, now.' Siyu shook her head, tears dripping from her chin. 'Siyu, you can do this.'

'I can't.'

'You must,' Denag told her. 'The child must come. You can see your sisters after this, Siyu.'

Siyu heaved with tears. Tunuva moved behind her and grasped her hands, helping her carry her own weight.

As Tunuva held on, and the candles burned low, she was not only herself. She was beside Esbar on the day she had Siyu, and she was in love all over again. She was weeping in relief, and Denag was bringing her child, and it was a boy, a sweet boy for the Mother.

Sweat dampened her skin. Siyu pushed again with a long raw sound, and Tunuva felt each sob and shudder deep in her own body, softly echoed. A ghost brushed tiny fingers over her face. A ghost fed at her breast. A ghost cried in the dark vaults of her memory.

She pressed her eyes shut, forcing that time back into its deep pit. Siyu needed her.

Over an hour passed. Siyu strained and panted, but for all she tried, the child would not come.

'Is it as it was with me?' Tunuva asked Denag, whose expression was grim. 'A footling?'

'No, but I suspect the face or brow is coming first. Apaya was born that way.'

'Then it will be all right.' Tunuva watched her. 'Denag?'

Denag placed a reassuring hand on Siyu. 'I need to see if the child is facing the backbone or the belly,' she muttered to Tunuva, who leaned closer to hear. 'Usually, I would prefer the backbone, but if I am right, that would make things … significantly more difficult. Either way, I will do my best to move the child into a better position.'

'No more,' Siyu gasped out. 'I can't.'

She pulled away and almost crawled towards the hearth. 'Siyu,' Tunuva said, following, 'it's all right.'

'So tired.' Siyu slumped against the wall, glazed in sweat. 'Gedali, have mercy. Make it stop.'

'Gedali is with you. They hear.' Tunuva knelt beside her. 'Tell me what you're feeling.'

She saw the depth of fright behind those eyes. Siyu was a warrior, but for all her cuts and bruises, she had never had to weather this kind of pain. She had no idea what to do with it.

'Siyu,' Tunuva said, smudging a tear from her cheek, 'Denag needs to reach the child.' Siyu shook her head. 'I'm right here. I'm with you, Siyu. Don't try to bear the pain alone.'

'I have to.' Her voice cracked. 'I see now. What I did. The Mother is punishing me.'

'No, sunray.'

Tunuva moved her drenched curls from her face and used a cloth to blot her sweat, barely restraining her own fear. Not once had she allowed herself to think they might lose Siyu, but childbirth always came with risk, even with a guide as capable as Denag.

'The blend of relief,' Tunuva said to her. 'Please, Denag.'

Denag reached for a box. 'Siyu, I have something that will make you less aware for a short time. It's harmless, and you can push again after. Would you like to take it?'

'Yes,' Siyu rasped.

When she was young, Denag had discovered that the milk of a rare flower, mixed with certain herbs, could blunt the senses. As soon as

Siyu had drunk it, she softened and sank against Tunuva, letting Denag reach inside. Denag frowned in concentration.

'Good. Face first, as I thought,' she said, 'but turned towards the belly. A great mercy.' She released a breath. 'Come, little one. No need to confront the world so brashly.'

Siyu murmured in discomfort. Finally, Denag withdrew, just as Siyu started to break from the haze.

'Tuva,' Denag said, 'turn her on to her side.'

Tunuva did. Whatever Denag had done, it had worked – Siyu pushed twice more, and at last, the child was out. 'It's over,' Tunuva told her. Siyu wept in relief. 'You did so well.'

A little cry rose. Tunuva helped Siyu walk to the daybed, where Denag brought the baby. 'Here she is, Siyu. A new warrior,' she said. 'The Mother is very proud of you.'

Siyu blinked at the newborn on her chest with bewildered curiosity. It was hard to tell who looked more dazed. 'Thank you, Tuva,' she whispered. 'And you, Denag. Thank you.'

Tunuva smiled, her mouth tight at the corners. *Here he is, Tuva. Here he is.*

The close air clotted in her throat. 'Denag,' she said, 'I will come back. Take care of them.'

Denag did answer, but Tunuva only heard a faint roar, like the inside of a shell. She faltered into the corridor, smelling fresh bread and flowers instead of birth. Her head was heavy as an anvil.

'Tuva.'

She looked up. Esbar was striding towards her with Lalhar, followed by the rest of their family, waiting to welcome Siyu back into the fold. The banded ichneumon sniffed the air.

'Tuva.' Esbar embraced her. 'I'm sorry.'

'Why didn't you come?' Tunuva said, weary.

'Saghul collapsed.' Esbar drew back. 'Is Siyu all right?'

'Yes.' So tired she could hardly think, Tunuva touched her cheek, smearing it with a little blood. 'Go to her, Ez.'

Tunuva moved past her, stroking Lalhar as she went. The ichneumon licked her elbow.

As soon as she was out of sight, she broke into a run. She stumbled up flight after flight of steps, towards her own sunroom and its open doors.

On her balcony, she fell to her knees, unleashing the scream that had risen and writhed in her, all those hours in the birthing chamber. For the first time in years, she let the pain break free and flood her.

She would not drown in grief again. Instead, she swam in it, bathed in it. She drank it like a bitter wine, until only a sliver of her soul was left to gasp for breath. She could see him again: his soft head, his eyelids, his perfect fingers curling around hers, his first smile. With a cry, she pressed both hands to her face, lost in the agony of remembrance.

I'm sorry.

'Tunuva?'

Eyes overflowing, she looked back. Canthe, the unexpected guest, came to sit at her side.

'Canthe, you can't be here,' she said, the words strangled.

'I'm sorry. I saw you run past, and ... it seemed wrong to leave you.' Canthe watched her, aching sorrow in her eyes. 'I'm so sorry, Tunuva. It is the most painful thing. To lose a child.'

Tunuva stared at her. 'How?' she whispered. 'How could you possibly know?'

Canthe hesitated, then said, 'I just know.'

Tunuva tried to speak, to no avail. There was nothing to say. Canthe wrapped an arm around her, and Tunuva wept bitterly into her shoulder, as if she had known this strange outsider all her life.

32

East

Dusk had fallen early in the Rain Pavilion, fastened as it was against the wind. In the warmth of her antechamber, Dumai wrote to her mother with news of her journey, careful with her words. She had no doubt the River Lord read all her correspondence.

Beyond the screens, her handmaidens huddled around a brazier, reading to one another from *Recollections of the North* – the writings of a Sepuli explorer who had sailed away from the East, beyond the unfathomed Abyss. Even Yapara had mustered the interest to listen to the tales, filled as they were with snow bears and singing ice.

The moon would soon be full. Furtia was coming, and when she arrived, Dumai meant to put everything at this court to the back of her mind. Her principal duty, both as a godsinger and a princess, was to serve dragonkind. She would help for as long as Furtia needed her.

Whatever the dark rocks were, she sensed they were far more dangerous than the Kuposa.

The fire beneath grows too hot, too fast . . .

She pressed the ache in her forehead. For several days, she had dreamed of a faceless figure, and woken with it etched on her eyelids. It must be related, somehow, to her task.

'Dumai.'

Osipa joined her on the mats. 'Are the handmaidens still outside?' Dumai asked her.

'Lady Imwo is on the porch. I believe she is trustworthy, but let us keep our voices low. As for the rest,' Osipa said, 'I asked them to fetch me a good handful of fickleberries.'

'What are fickleberries?'

'Figments of my imagination. They'll be gone for a while.'

Dumai smiled. 'I'm worried about going,' she said. 'Surely it will leave my father vulnerable.'

'You have no choice. A god has called – but you can still help your family, even while you tend to other matters. You must visit the Sepuli queen, after all, to explain why you have come. I doubt she would take kindly to a foreign princess barging into her skies on a dragon.'

Emperor Jorodu had said as much to Dumai. *There have been no official visits to Sepul in some time, and the sight of a woken dragon is likely to cause a disturbance. Go first to Mozom Alph, to reassure Queen Arkoro of your purpose. You should warn her that a threat lurks in her land.*

'Make her a friend, if you can,' Osipa said. 'The more allies and supporters you have beyond these shores, the less influence the Kuposa will hold, and the stronger you will be.'

'I will try.'

Lady Imwo came in from the porch. She was a quiet and gentle musician of Clan Eraposi.

'Your Highness,' she said, 'forgive the disturbance, but the River Lord's daughter has asked for an audience.'

Dumai exchanged a long glance with Osipa.

'Don't,' Osipa warned.

'I should see what she wants.'

'Under no circumstances will I leave you alone with that woman, after those poems of hers.'

'Please, Osipa.'

Osipa pursed her lips. Then she said, 'I will tell your guards to stay close.'

She left, and Dumai returned to her letter. This time, she would keep a level head.

At last, the screen moved aside, and she caught the scents of woodfall and apricot. Curious fragrances to blend – the precious and the commonplace, the sea and the orchard.

'What is it, Lady Nikeya?' Dumai kept writing. 'If you intend to make a threat, make it quickly. I have no time to waste today.'

'Princess, I would never threaten you. It's only poetry,' Nikeya said. 'May I sit?'

'No.'

'Then I will get straight to the point. Your friend from the mountain. Did you truly think I wouldn't remember a handsome face in a new uniform?'

Dumai finally glanced up.

Nikeya was closer than she had thought, standing with her hands folded in front of her. She wore a hunting jacket – crimson silk embroidered with silver, a dark tunic peeking through the neat slashes below her shoulders. It was a bold choice for court, where red was rarely seen or worn. The wind had dishevelled her hair and painted her cheekbones with a flush.

At all their other meetings, she had been pristine. Now a wildness clung to her.

'The River Lord has taken note of him, too. He is a fine archer,' she said lightly. 'In fact, my father thinks to promote him. Perhaps some time on the northern coast to defend Seiiki from outlaws … though that would have its dangers. I hear the pirates are vicious.'

Dumai returned to writing.

'And Lady Osipa. A fixture of court,' Nikeya said, with a heavy sigh. 'My father has always admired her tenacity. It would be such a loss if she were ever to take ill.'

'You said the heart takes its time to decide,' Dumai said coolly. 'Am I to assume that yours has a wish?'

'You are to ride to Sepul.' Her smile widened. (*Great Kwiriki*, Dumai thought, *their cheeks will crack from smiling, all these courtiers.*) 'My wish is simple, Princess Dumai. Take me with you.'

'So you can smother me in my sleep?'

'I assure you, I mean you no harm. Even if I did, I am sure the great Furtia would protect you,' Nikeya said. 'No, Your Highness. I simply wish to know you better than I do. After all, you are to be Empress of Seiiki, and no one will be closer to you than Clan Kuposa.'

'That is not as comforting a thought as you clearly believe. Besides, Furtia may not wish to take you.'

'I say you could persuade her.'

Dumai leaned back from her table, considering her next move. 'A dragon can fly higher than a mountain stands,' she said. 'Tell me, did you have a headache during your stay at the temple?'

'A little.'

'At best, that is what mountain sickness will give you. At worst, your eyes will bleed.' Dumai raised her brows. 'Courtier, dancer, spy – there seems to be no end to your faces. Still, I wonder if you have the stomach for this flight.'

If Nikeya was unnerved, she gave no sign of it.

'You flatter me, Princess,' she said, with that crooked smile, 'but I have only this one face. I can't help that it serves me well.' She bowed. 'Thank you for warning me of the risks. I'll come ready to travel.'

She retreated. Dumai looked down and found that she had smeared ink across the letter.

Osipa returned before the scent of apricot had gone. 'Osipa,' Dumai said, 'I need you to ask Kanifa to meet me in the Water Pavilion. Then I need you to pack your belongings.'

'Am I going on a journey, too?'

'Yes, back to Mount Ipyeda.'

'Why?'

'Lady Nikeya has threatened you and Kanifa.'

Osipa snorted. 'Kind of you to show concern, Dumai, but I will not be going anywhere.'

'I can't leave you to—'

'I have met a thousand simpering courtiers like her,' Osipa said, with disdain. 'You forget, I was closest of all to your grandmother. Her rivals and flatterers all wanted to seduce, coerce or banish me, but I endured. The waves may pound the rocks, but they do not give way. Remember that, Dumai. Remember who you are. Let their threats wash over you.'

'You have the thin protection of your clan and reputation, at least. Kanifa has no one.'

'He has you, and he'll never leave you. I can't tell if he's in love with you or the most loyal friend in the world – perhaps both – but his life is twined with yours. It has always been so.'

'Then only I might persuade him.'

'Perhaps. Good luck with him,' Osipa said. 'You will have none with me, Dumai.'

****

The Floating Gardens were too risky now. No doubt Nikeya had seen them meet there. Instead, Dumai waited for her friend in the old hatchery, which her father had allowed her to use.

'Dumai.' Kanifa joined her. 'Osipa asked me to meet you here.'

'I need you to leave.' Dumai turned to him. 'Lady Nikeya remembered you from the temple. She wants to come with me to Sepul, and if I refuse, I fear her father will harm you and Osipa.'

Kanifa thought for a time, his thick brows knitted.

'Then take me with you,' he said. 'Let it be two against one. Three, if we count the great Furtia.'

'That would only keep you safe for so long.' Her voice softened. 'Please, Kan. Go back.'

'I assume you made the same request to Osipa, and she refused.'

'Yes.'

'Then I don't know why you thought I would accept.'

'Osipa is as stubborn as an ox. I thought you had more sense.'

'Not as much as you might think,' Kanifa said, with a faint smile, 'else I might have stopped loving you long ago.'

Dumai stared at him, unable to speak. Not once in two decades of knowing him had she suspected that he felt this way.

'Kan,' she managed.

'It's all right.' There was an old sorrow in those dark eyes, but no bitterness. 'I've known for years, Mai.'

'I'm sorry.'

'I'm not. Being your friend is enough. You have made my life richer in so many ways, and I would never seek to change it.' Kanifa pressed her hand to his chest. 'Answer me one thing. If you say *yes* in truth, I promise I'll leave for the mountain tonight.' Dumai waited. 'If I were in your position – if we found out that I was a lost Prince of Seiiki, that I was the one the gods had awaited – would you leave me friendless in this court?'

She tried to lie to him. With all her heart, she tried. 'No,' she finally said. 'Of course not.'

'Then take me with you, and we'll hold each other up. Always together. You promised me, Dumai.'

'We were children.'

263

'It was still a promise.'

She dropped her head in defeat. 'All right. If the great Furtia agrees,' she sighed. 'At least you will be safe for now, away from court. We can decide on our next move when we return.'

'Don't be afraid for Osipa. Nothing fazes her.'

'I know.' She looked up at him with a reluctant smile. 'Are you ready to ride a dragon?'

****

That night, the moon shone brighter than it had in weeks. Her father waited for her in the North Courtyard, along with the most important officials, the Council of State. She carried his Privy Seal in her pack, to show that she travelled with his authority. He took her to one side.

'I await your safe return,' he said, his voice low. 'By then, I hope your grandmother and I will have established a safe place for the shadow court, and loyalists to fill it.'

'I wish you well. Be careful, Father.'

'I have survived this long. I am glad Kanifa is going with you.'

'So is Lady Nikeya.'

'Lady Nikeya.' A pair of lines appeared in his forehead. 'Daughter, have you lost your senses?'

'I will explain when I return. She forced my hand,' Dumai said under her breath, 'but with us, she is outnumbered, and isolated from the others. Let me use this opportunity to spy on her.'

Emperor Jorodu narrowed his dark eyes.

'Perhaps it is time we played them at their game,' he said, just as quiet. 'I trust your judgement, but do not let your guard down. She is their sharpest weapon.' He beckoned Epabo. 'I have a gift for you.'

Epabo came forward with a box. Inside lay a pair of fine gauntlets. Dumai pulled them up to her elbows. They were thick yet supple, and the right one had been sewn to fit her.

'Thank you, Father,' she said, touched.

'They were meant to be yours,' he said. 'Do not neglect to stop in Mozom Alph. Furtia may not understand the reason, but we must pay heed to diplomacy. I know you will find a way to explain. Let us reach out to the world before we are swallowed from within.'

'Yes, Father.'

They both glanced towards the River Lord. He was deep in conversation with Nikeya, who had dressed as if for a jaunt in the snow, in pleated trousers and a smart hunting coat.

'She can't be serious,' Dumai muttered as Kanifa came to her side. Like her, he wore his warm layers from the mountain, down to the deerskin boots. 'She'll freeze like that.'

'Courtiers can, on occasion, be foolish.'

'You astonish me. Do you have furs to spare?'

'Yes.' The corner of his mouth twitched. 'Shall we let her suffer just a little first?'

'I think we must.'

A familiar sound distracted them both. Every head turned as Furtia Stormcaller glided towards the palace, salted with white sparks, a dragon cut from night. When she landed, her moonlit eyes found Dumai.

It is time.

Dumai locked eyes with her father. He gave her a tiny nod, his expression hard to read. She walked towards the dragon and placed a gloved hand on her scales.

'Great Furtia,' she said, 'I am ready to leave.' In her mind, she added, *I would bring two riders with me.*

Who are these earth children?

One is my friend and protector, who would lay down his life for mine. Dumai beckoned Kanifa, who stepped forward and bowed low. Furtia sniffed him. *The other is no friend to me, but I must try to learn her secrets, so I might choke the threat.*

So be it.

Nikeya came forward with a complacent smile, which disappeared when Furtia snapped at her.

My father asks that we begin in the city of Mozom Alph, so we might see its queen, and ask her permission to search for the rocks. Dumai stroked her black scales, hiding a smile of her own. *It would be easier to ride if I could use a saddle. Would you permit it, great one?*

In answer, Furtia lowered the mighty coils of her body until they touched the ground.

The saddle had been recovered from a storehouse, thick with dust. Now the lacquered leather had been oiled back to glory, the gilt and steel restored. It took fifteen guards to fasten it in place. Dumai climbed to it, finding it spacious, with hollows for her feet. Kanifa shinned up

265

next. When he lost his grip, Furtia caught him with her tail, lifting him to sit behind Dumai.

'Use those.' Dumai pointed out the straps. 'Do you have the rope?'

'Always.'

He knotted them together, as he had on the mountain. A lifeline between their waists.

Nikeya approached. Grasping part of the saddle, she scrambled towards it, arms trembling. Suddenly Furtia shook herself, and Nikeya fell hard on her backside, drawing gasps. The River Lord kept smiling, but his mouth looked strained.

'Try again, Lady Nikeya,' Dumai called. 'I'm sure the great Furtia will hold still this time.'

Nikeya looked up with a glint in her eye. *You win*, it seemed to say. With a hearty laugh, she brushed herself off. 'I hope so, Princess,' she said. 'Perhaps you could ask her to take pity on me?'

Polite chuckles followed. When Nikeya tried again, Furtia permitted her to retain her dignity, and she tucked herself just in front of the cantle.

'No straps for a third rider,' she observed. 'It appears I'll have to hold on to you, godsinger.'

Kanifa clamped his jaw. Smiling, she curled an arm around his waist and nestled close.

Dumai took hold of the horn. She looked down at her father once more, and she saw, then, how small and vulnerable he looked, alone among the bells. *Great Kwiriki, please let this be the right choice.*

Furtia raised her head, her crest like a round mirror on her brow, reflecting the moonlight. The courtiers made room with exclamations of pure wonder. As the dragon took off, Dumai watched the lanterns of the city fall away, down and down into the dark, until they disappeared.

33

North

Eydag had been awake for hours. Glazed hazel eyes stared into a place that only she could see. Her sleeves were rolled to the elbow, showing her broad hands – once white with pink knuckles, now red all the way through. Her breath crackled. Wulf watched from his corner, waiting for the change.

Every day, someone opened the door to throw in waterskins and clapbread. Never at the same time. Never predictable.

They kept to their own areas, drawing unseen lines. There was no way to refresh the air, but they could at least try not to breathe on each other.

Eydag had eaten less and less as the days passed, like the two others the Issýn had touched before Wulf slew her. For a time, they had been well, even as the red stole past their knuckles.

Wulf swallowed, a heavy thickness in his craw. He looked down at the backs of his own hands, ribbed with scars from sparring. No red. Not since he had scrubbed off the blood.

There is no curse on that forest, Mara had told him. *Or on you.* And yet he had killed, and he was untouched, while Eydag – good, tender Eydag – wasted away before his eyes. He had not often been to sanctuary, but he knew the words of the Knight of Justice.

Evil doth know itself.

'Wulf,' Eydag said, 'it's coming.' Her chest heaved. 'I need you to kill me. Please.'

'I can't.'

'Please.'

Whenever he missed Inys, Eydag was the one who gathered him into a bone-cracking embrace. It was her laugh that kept them all in good spirits on the hardest, coldest days. Beside her, the two men groaned. Vell shook his head wildly and pounded the door.

'It's happening,' he shouted. 'Sire!'

'Vell,' Eydag cried. 'Wulf.' The plea was in every crease of her face. 'Please. I don't want to hurt anyone.'

Jaw clenched to stop it trembling, Wulf took her by the hand – skin to skin – and squeezed her fingers tight. 'The oath we made. Remember?' he said hoarsely. 'None go to death alone.'

Her hot fingers wrapped around his. 'Do you remember the first time we sailed?' she croaked. 'I showed you how to use a sunstone.' She reached under her collar and held it out to him, the clear stone on a cord. 'Keep it. Use it, Wulf. You'll find the truth in the end.'

Wulf took the stone and passed the cord over his head. 'Eydag.' He had no words to express what her kindness had meant to him. 'The Saint will welcome you with open arms.'

'Thank you.' Her lips were cracked. 'Wulf, remember. You are loved.'

So are you, he wanted to say, but his throat locked.

Vell was watching them, his expression tortured. He had always been closest to Eydag. Now he was powerless to comfort her.

Across the cabin, the two men bellowed, one after the other. Eyes rolling, foaming at the mouth, they began to pound and claw at the floor, just as the Issýn had. One tore at his shirt. As she stared at them in terror, Eydag seized up. Wulf held her hand tighter.

His patron was the Knight of Generosity. On his twelfth birthday, he had sworn to honour his virtue above all others, to repay the generosity his father had shown by taking him in. Letting a friend die in agony would not be doing that.

'Eydag.' Vell had tears in his eyes. 'Fuck this—' He threw his shoulder against the door. 'Damn you, soulless cowards! Let her see the light. Give her air, a fucking physician!'

She was beyond physicians. Her body writhed, red spume bubbling on her lips. When she let out a ghastly scream, Vell broke. He drew his sax and drove it straight into her heart.

'I'm sorry,' he sobbed. 'Eydag, I'm sorry.'

She tried to speak. Her fingers twitched, and then she slipped away without a sound. Wulf stared at her body, tears on his cheeks, before he unsheathed his own blade and threw it to the burning men.

Not long after, the cabin fell silent.

****

When sunlight blazed in, Wulf hardly noticed. He had been gazing dully at the bloodstain for so long, he had almost succeeded in forgetting Eydag lay beside him. Her hand was rigid around his, the fire in her skin quenched.

'Wulf.'

Slowly, he looked up, numb to the wind that rushed inside. *Skethra.* He breathed it in. *The scent that washes the air clean.*

Regny stepped into the cabin, one hand on her axe. She took in the bodies, the blood, with the same cool expression she always showed the world. When she saw her oldest friend, it faltered.

'Eydag,' she said, almost too softly to hear. Collecting herself, she drew the sign of the sword. 'Hear, O Saint, the knock upon your door, for a guest has come to the Great Table.'

In Inysh, the prayer was a plea. In Hróthi, it had the ring of a command.

'You're alive,' Regny observed.

'Of course he's alive,' Karlsten said, disgusted. 'Did you need more proof that he's unnatural?'

'Be quiet, Karl.'

Karlsten glared at Wulf with loathing, then knelt and wrapped an arm around Vell, who was splashed with his own vomit. Regny came to Wulf, swung off her cloak, and draped him in it.

'Come,' she said. 'The king is waiting.' She saw then that he was still clutching Eydag. 'Wulf, she's gone. Let go.'

'You shouldn't touch me.'

'Don't be a fool. You're not afflicted.' She looked him in the eyes. 'Stand.'

Some fundamental part of him still knew to obey her. He pried off the cold fingers – the hand of an ice spirit – and tried not to see that waxen face, the eyes he had brushed shut. He forced himself up on stiff legs. Regny guided him from the bloody room.

They emerged into crisp air, fog in their breath. The *hark-hark* of gulls made Wulf recoil against his will. He blinked hard against the whiteness of the sun, the mist that spread its light, to see an inlet cradled by low and weathered cliffs. Vessels from many shores crossed its waters, from magnificent Hróthi longships and galleys to tiny fishing boats – even an ornate Ersyri cutter, with elegant yellow sails and a curved prow.

As if in a dream, he turned his head. Sprawling beneath the milky sky were tens of thousands of wooden dwellings, a drunken horde jostling towards a hillfort. The Iron Mountains towered behind it, and atop stood Bithandun, the Silver Hall, seat of the House of Hraustr.

All that time – days, weeks – they had been anchored just off Eldyng.

The daylight burned like grit on his eyes. He followed Regny into a rowboat. Vell huddled inside, wrapped in a blanket, drinking from a wineskin.

Regny and Karlsten sculled them all to shore, where traders and seafarers milled, unaware of the threat that lurked in their harbour. As the rowboat shunted him closer to the city, Wulf caught strains of Yscali, Mentish and Inysh among the dialects of Hróthi. A woman was fishing in the shallows, trousers rolled up to the knee.

Karlsten stopped rowing and climbed out with Regny. Once the boat was shored, they led Wulf and Vell to a horse-drawn cart. Vell kept a tight hold on the wineskin. 'Get in,' Regny ordered them, taking the reins from the ostler. 'You're both too weak for the climb.'

Wulf knew it was because they looked and smelled appalling. They could hardly ride up to the fortress in this state.

In silence, he sat beside Vell. As the cart lumbered through Eldyng, he watched its people go about their lives: carpenters, whalers, blacksmiths, shipwrights, leatherworkers, Hüran merchants selling pelts and horses. For the first time, he noticed how closely all these people lived and worked together.

A bairn plunged muddy hands into a washtub. A strong-armed man dashed the sweat from his brow, drew a shirt from the same water, and spread it on a rack to dry. The water trickled on to the ground. A hound lapped at it, then padded across the street, to the flesh stall, and licked a slab of mutton. The butcher chased it off, and the hound loped away.

Someone would buy that meat before the day was out.

'I won't ask if you're all right,' Vell said.

He drank again from the wineskin and offered it. Wulf shook his head. 'What you did was noble,' he said hoarsely. 'You honoured the Knight of Courage.'

'I didn't only do it for Eydag.' Vell stared towards the sea. 'If your place in Halgalant was forfeit, you needed somebody to join you in the fire.'

Usually, Wulf would have smiled. Instead, he watched the innocent people of the city, and his insides swashed. None of these people knew his sins.

For murder, the price was death.

'Vell, only I saw you kill Eydag. Let me take the blame,' Wulf muttered. 'I've already killed the Issýn.'

'I'm not letting you do that.' Vell looked at him, eyes puffy. 'Why did your hands not stain?'

'I don't know.'

'You must be Saint-touched.'

At this, Wulf managed a bleak chuckle. Karlsten threw him a suspicious glance from his saddle.

The cart rolled past the enormous wicker sculptures of the Holy Retinue, which each held a bowl of whale oil, on fire. After the Knight of Courage, they were on the path that led up the hill. Sauma and Thrit waited for them outside the feasting hall.

'Eydag?' Thrit murmured.

Regny shook her head. She escorted Wulf and Vell through the doors.

Bithandun was the grandest stronghold in Hróth. King Bardholt had wanted it to stand here, facing the sea that led to Inys. His former enemies had built and adorned it – part of the heavy toll they paid for not choosing his side. Some said not a tree remained where Verthing Bloodblade had once lived; they had all been felled to build Bardholt his city.

Inside, the hall was darkly golden, the floor strewn with fresh rushes. Inysh applewood flamed in a cavernous hearth, releasing fragrant smoke, and Yscali tapestries hung on the walls.

The King of Hróth sat at its north end. His throne was a dread presence, made from the polished skull of a trolval – rarest and greatest of toothed whales, the swallower of ships.

'Wulfert, Vell,' he said. 'Eydag is dead?'

'Aye,' Wulf rasped. 'So are the others.'

'She was a fine warrior. Among the best in my household,' King Bardholt said, rubbing his brow. 'And I can't bury her.' He grasped one arm of his throne. 'At midnight, the ship burns.'

'Sire,' Vell said weakly, 'please. How will she reach the Great Table?'

'I am a king of Virtudom, and a bonesmith. I will entreat the Saint to let her in.' King Bardholt looked to Regny. 'See to it.' She exited with Karlsten and Sauma. 'Vell, since you seem unafflicted, see a healer. Thrit, stay with him. None of you are to speak of what you saw.'

The rest of the lith withdrew from the hall, leaving Wulf before the throne. He kept his head down.

It would be easy to hate this man for what he had done. His liege had locked him in the dark to watch his friend die, sent no healers, and put Vell at risk – yet Wulf could not blame him for it. Bardholt Hraustr always made the necessary choices, no matter how brutal.

'Vell,' the king finally said, 'I can understand. He touched Eydag with gloves. Putting him in the cabin was a precaution. But you, Wulf – I cannot imagine how you are still alive.'

'I wish I knew, sire.'

The rustlings of the fire were all that cracked the silence.

'I knew the rumours when I took you into my household,' King Bardholt said. 'Lord Edrick told me, fearing I might hear them from a crueller tongue. I never believed. Heathen folly has no place in Virtudom. Still, another king might want you gone.'

Wulf closed his eyes.

'But I am not another king. I am a warrior for the Saint. Whatever this sickness may be, he held out his shield to spare you,' King Bardholt concluded. 'I will not spit at him.' A long pause. 'Don't think I've forgotten that when the Issýn touched you, it was because you placed yourself in front of me. I might have joined Eydag if not for your courage.'

'I swore an oath.'

'You did. And you kept it.' Bardholt ground his jaw, an old habit. 'Someone tried to kill my daughter. Tomorrow, we sail for Inys, where we will remain until the royal wedding.'

'Is Her Highness well?'

'Of course. Glorian knows no fear.'

That might have been true once. After all, nothing had ever broken into her safe court, until now.

'You see why I had to keep you on the ship. I would not carry this Saint-forsaken plague to Inys,' King Bardholt said, resting his chin on his knuckles. 'Get some rest, Wulf. We leave at dawn.'

Wulf rose stiffly and bowed. He felt like an old man, weighted by loss.

Out he stepped, into the cold world. A world without Eydag to soften its edges. Grief milked the strength from his bones. He needed to walk to the sanctuary, to pray for mercy from the Knight of Justice. He needed to sleep. Simple needs. Yet his feet were riveted.

He gazed at the rooftops of Eldyng, the dark ship in the harbour, and heard the deathwatch beetles.

Tick-tick. Tick-tick.

'Wulf.'

A gentle voice pulled him back to himself. Heavy-eyed, he looked at Thrit, who grasped his shoulder. Without a hesitation, he wrapped a strong arm around Wulf and said, 'It's all right.'

His warmth released something in Wulf. He gave a great shudder before he held Thrit back and wept.

34

South

Now Siyu had seen out her sentence, Saghul had restored her freedoms and granted her the use of a sunroom. Their family united to help and cheer her. Between feeds, the men would take the newborn so she could sleep and mend from the delivery. Her crime was forgiven, if not forgotten.

Just as peace returned to their home, Tunuva had to leave. Soon she and Hidat would ride to the Vale of Yaud, one of the places where they had found the strange rocks, to investigate. This time, they would go with enough force to slay anything that emerged.

Before she left, she decided to pay Siyu a visit, remembering the exhaustion and soreness after childbirth. Even sitting had been hard, and her ankles had swollen to twice their usual girth – so when she glanced into the sunroom, she made sure to be quiet, in case Siyu was sleeping.

She sat awake on her daybed, feeding the child. Cloth wrapped her beneath the mound of her belly, padded with moss to soak up the long bleed. Seeing Tunuva, she smiled.

'I hoped you'd come.'

'I know the feeds can be dull alone.' Tunuva kissed her forehead, relieved to find it cool. 'How are you?'

'Tired. I don't know why, when I sleep so often.'

'Because your body has spent months forming a future warrior. Now it works day and night to nourish her, and to heal.' Tunuva studied her face. 'Tell me truthfully. Are you in any pain?'

'I feel bruised.' Siyu shifted the baby. 'Tuva, I don't think I'm doing this right. Today she seems happy, but yesterday she screamed so much I thought I must be hurting her.'

'No, no. Some newborns just don't take to the breast. Imin can enrich longhorn milk to help. You lived on that after the first month,' Tunuva told her. 'Esbar tried to feed you until then, but she found it so exhausting and painful, she had to stop. It can be very hard.'

'But I thrived?'

'Yes. You were perfect.' Tunuva sat beside her. 'Siyu, I know the Prioress has been too unwell to anoint the child, but have you thought of a name?'

'Lukiri du Siyu uq-Nāra.'

An old Selinyi name, meaning *orchard child*. Tunuva had not heard it in some time.

'Beautiful,' she said. 'It suits her.'

'When will the Prioress be able to anoint her?'

'Soon, I hope.'

Once Lukiri had stopped, Siyu dabbed her mouth with a cloth. 'Would you like to hold her?' she asked Tunuva. 'Denag explained how to help her bring up wind, but I never can.'

Tunuva started to speak. *Yes*, a voice said in her head. *Of course.*

'You don't have to, Tuva,' Siyu said quietly.

'No.' Tunuva made herself smile again. 'Let me show you.'

Siyu smiled back and passed her the child. Tunuva held Lukiri under the arms, and the tiny girl curled up her legs, sleepy and drunk with milk.

'Hello, little sunray.'

Lukiri blinked. Tunuva sat the child on her thigh, tilted her forward, and cupped a hand under her chin.

'Oh,' Siyu breathed. Lukiri waved her fists, frowning. 'I've been putting her over my shoulder.'

'That suits some babies.' Tunuva made sure she had a firm hold on Lukiri before she started to pat and rub her back. 'Others prefer this way.'

'Tuva ... Imin held me after I was born. He told me so. May Anyso not hold Lukiri?'

'Imin was an anointed member of the Priory.'

'So might Anyso be,' Siyu said, appeal in her eyes. 'Tuva, he could lead a happy life among the men. He's so gentle and patient. His family are bakers, so he can make bread and cakes, and he helped raise his two sisters. I'm sure he could learn to sew and garden.'

'He also loves you.'

'Esbar loves you.'

'Our situation is different. Anyso wants to marry you and take you to his family. You must see the danger in that.'

Siyu was silent for a time. 'I could make him understand, if I could talk to him,' she said, shaken. 'It's awful to keep him here like a prisoner, Tuva. He didn't do anything wrong.'

'I know.' Tunuva gave her a regretful look. 'This is why we try to stay hidden, sunray.'

'I should never have gone to the river. I should never have been seen,' Siyu said in a disquieted whisper. 'Tuva ... if he can't stay and he can't leave, what will happen to him?'

'That is for the Prioress to decide, when she feels stronger.'

Lukiri broke the silence with a burp and spat up milk, startling herself. Siyu managed a snort of laughter.

'There.' Tunuva turned Lukiri and used a fresh cloth to wipe her mouth and chin. 'Shall I take her to the men?'

'Yes, please.' Siyu set her head on the bolster. 'Will you ask Imin about the milk?'

'I will.'

Tunuva hitched Lukiri up to her shoulder. Her movement woke Lalhar, who twitched her nose and climbed on to the daybed to curl up with Siyu. Tunuva left them both to sleep.

Lukiri yawned in her arms, smelling of roses and milk. Tunuva gave her scalp a gentle kiss as she descended. The pang came, as it always did, but it was softer than she had feared.

She knew exactly how Saghul would want to remove the difficulty of Anyso. Siyu was supposed to have killed him. He had known too much as soon as he saw a girl in the depths of the Lasian Basin. If there was another way, Tunuva had failed to think of it.

'Explain to me how this happened, Alanu. Explain it as if I am one of the children.'

Imsurin was holding a grey cloak, glaring at one of the older boys. 'Brother, we were low on clothing soap,' Alanu was saying, his tone earnest, 'so I thought I would try—'

'You must forgive my ignorance, Alanu. I was under the foolish impression that *you* had something to do with maintaining our supplies. Are we usually graced by a soap divinity?'

'I hate to interrupt,' Tunuva said. They both turned. 'This child will need changing soon.'

'Alanu will be pleased to oblige,' Imsurin said curtly. Alanu dipped his head to Tunuva, leaving with a sigh. 'Is she fed, Tuva?'

'A full belly.' Tunuva handed the baby to him. 'Siyu has named her Lukiri.'

'Lukiri is a fine name.' Imsurin turned his grandchild towards him with practised ease. 'Denag says Siyu is well in body and mind.'

'I think she is. She may wish to use longhorn milk.'

'I will prepare some,' he said. Lukiri hiccupped. 'Do you know if the Prioress is any better?'

'There has been no change, as far as I know. Esbar will keep you abreast of her condition.'

Imsurin nodded, his brow knitting into deeper lines. 'I wish you well on your travels, Tunuva,' he said. 'May the Mother watch over you.'

'And you, Imin.'

Tunuva made her way back up the stairs. In the scullery, the older men were hard at work cooking the midday meal, filling the corridors with the smells of milk-rubbed bread and lamb stew.

'Hello, Tunuva.'

She stopped at the sound of that full-toned voice. Canthe stood at the end of the corridor.

Tunuva almost turned away. Canthe had been so kind when she wept, embracing her without question or judgement. Showing such vulnerability to a stranger had left her feeling naked and shaken.

'Canthe. Are you all right?' Tunuva said, with reserve. 'This floor is for the men and children.'

'A mark of my predicament. I'm afraid I keep getting lost,' Canthe admitted. 'There are so many rooms.'

Tunuva softened. 'No one has shown you the Priory?'

'No.'

That would not do. 'Then I will,' Tunuva said. 'Come. We can share a loaf of hot bread.'

****

They visited almost every room. Tunuva took Canthe into the War Hall, the armoury – the walls glinted with hundreds of weapons – and the refectory, which rang with general disorder as the men tried to feed the children. They glanced into the Fire Chamber, where Hidat was leading the younger initiates in a practice session, lighting candles and oil lamps with magic.

'Above us are the sunrooms,' Tunuva said as they wandered along a corridor. 'Those are for titled sisters – presently myself, Esbar and the Prioress. Those who are pregnant and nursing may also use those rooms.'

'How lovely.' Canthe smiled, looking touched. 'Siyu is using one now, then?'

'Yes.'

'You seem very fond of her.' When Tunuva gave a small nod, Canthe said, 'I understand Esbar is her birthmother. She must be like a daughter to you, in some ways.'

'A sister. We are all daughters of the Mother.'

'Of course.'

They went to the next floor, where a fountain trickled and miniature trees grew in stone urns.

'This is where the initiates live,' Tunuva told Canthe. 'They rise from the lowest rank – the postulants – by proving themselves to the Prioress. When she deems it suitable, an initiate will eat of the tree for the first time and receive her white cloak. We call this a kindling.'

'How old are they when this happens?'

'Usually around sixteen.'

'Goodness.' Canthe laughed. 'If the Prioress lets me stay, I shall be a latecomer indeed.'

Tunuva wondered exactly how old this woman was. 'Once they have the sacred flame,' she said, 'the initiates are sent to uphold the stability and safety of the South. We are bound to protect the ruling families of Lasia and the Ersyr. Only they know of our existence.'

'But your highest duty is to ensure the Nameless One never returns. Where is it you think he is now?'

278

'One of the great mysteries. The Mother vanquished him with the sword Ascalun, but to where, no one knows. Most of us suspect that he crawled back into the Dreadmount.'

'Which has now erupted.' Canthe glanced at her. 'Do you suppose he has returned?'

Tunuva recalled the flock of dark wings, the tang of siden on the wind.

'Let me show you more,' she said.

It was quiet in the dim rooms below. The men kept the children outside for most of the day.

'Each child learns to read and write in Selinyi,' Tunuva said as they crossed the playroom. 'At the age of five, the path splits, with the girls becoming postulants. They begin their training as warriors and guardians of the Southern courts, and bond with an ichneumon pup. The boys stay with the men, who teach them needlepoint, cooking, husbandry – everything to do with maintaining the Priory. They also prepare to support us in battle.'

'Like squires to knights,' Canthe said, nodding. 'Is it possible to change paths?'

'In certain circumstances.' Tunuva picked up a woven doll and returned it to the chest of toys. 'One of my brothers was raised as a warrior, but later, he knew he belonged with the men.'

In his early twenties, Balag had often stayed up very late, studying the arts he had not been taught as a child. Whenever she had woken with an unquiet dream, Tunuva had known her beloved guardian would be awake, poring over books and scrolls.

'And if one were like Gedali, neither man nor woman?' Canthe said. 'Is there a middle way?'

'It would be easier to choose one or the other. Both require so much knowledge and instruction, it would be hard to commit by halves, though it may have been attempted.'

They walked down the corridor, heading for the steps. Canthe slowed. 'What lies that way?'

Tunuva stopped. 'The burial chamber,' she said. 'Where the Mother rests.'

'Princess Cleolind. How did she die?'

'That is another of the great mysteries. The Mother departed suddenly one night, leaving no word as to her purpose. Some time later, her body arrived here.' Tunuva paused. 'You must never try to enter the burial chamber. It is the most sacred place in the Priory. Only the titled are permitted.'

'I understand.'

Canthe followed her, dealing the chamber door a final look. Tunuva slid open a lattice.

'Farther down are the archives, where we keep most of our records and artefacts,' she said. 'Some way beneath those is the hot spring. But much of the work goes on outside.'

She took Canthe back through the higher corridors, out on to the thousand steps. When Canthe saw the orange tree, she reached for her own breastbone, as if to take her heart in hand.

'It never stops being magnificent, does it?'

Tunuva smiled. 'Never.'

Upon reaching the valley floor, they meandered across it, the grass cool underfoot.

'We buy supplies, if necessary,' Tunuva said, 'but we prefer to be self-reliant, so we are beholden to no one. We sisters forge our own weapons; the men make our clothes and food. They raise crops to the south of the Priory: rice, millet, curd root and so on. We have a vine-yard and a winepress.' Canthe stopped to slide off her sandals. 'Some vegetables and groundnuts are grown here in the valley, but most fruit is collected from the forest.'

'Such bounty. I remember how well plants took to the earth around my hawthorn – the warmth and softness in it,' Canthe said fondly. 'Nurtha had more life than all Inysca.'

'Nurtha is its own island?'

'Yes. It lies just east of Inys.'

Tunuva showed her where the livestock and chickens were kept, and where the ichneumons reared their pups. In the creamery, Balag poured them cups of buttermilk, which they sipped as they visited the herb gardens, the icehouse, the earth cellar, the kiln and forge.

'How do you keep all this a secret?' Canthe asked. 'Surely people have tried to chart the Basin.'

Her eyes held curiosity and sorrow. After all, she had failed to protect her own tree.

'Our ancestors planted rumours of fearful creatures in the forest,' Tunuva explained. 'We also lay wardings around our farms, so we have

280

time to prepare, should anyone come – but the forest is too large and dense for more than a few to have made it this far.'

'I see.' Cream lingered on her upper lip, which was fuller than the lower. 'I came through it to reach the Priory, but I imagine you know its most beautiful places. Do you have time to show me?'

Tunuva glanced at the sun. It was on its way down, but she had already prepared for her journey.

'Very well.' She whistled. 'Nin!'

Ninuru was lazing in the shade of the orange tree. Hearing Tunuva, she perked up and padded towards them. 'This one smells of iron,' she said, gaze fixed on Canthe. 'And night.'

'This is Canthe. She wants to see the Basin.' Tunuva scratched her between the ears. 'Shall we go for a run?'

'Yes.'

Tunuva climbed on to her back and offered a hand to Canthe. 'Truly?' the visitor said with a laugh.

'Truly. Nin won't bite.'

Canthe accepted her hand, climbing on. Tunuva felt that odd sense of queasiness again. She kneed Ninuru east, and her ichneumon loped along the river, out through the neck of the Vale of Blood.

Ninuru was in high spirits, and ran hard. Every so often, Tunuva would stop her to show Canthe a wonder of the Lasian Basin. They waded through the flooded caves behind a waterfall, startled clouds of red butterflies from a bower, swam in a limpid pool.

'What bird is that?' Canthe asked as Tunuva mounted again. 'I have never heard anything quite like it.'

Tunuva looked up. An elegant bird cocked its head at them.

'A honeyguide,' she said softly.

'It seems as if it wants us to follow,' Canthe said, charmed.

'She does.' Tunuva lowered her gaze. 'Honeyguides know where the bees dwell. When they call that way, it means they want to show you.' The bird chirruped. 'The men smoke the bees and open the hive. They take the honey, while the birds take the wax and the young bees.'

'Ought we not to help her, then?'

'I brought no axe.' Tunuva trilled to the bird with the tip of her tongue, and it took off from the branch to hunt elsewhere. 'Come, Nin – let's show Canthe more of the river, shall we?'

Ninuru took them to where the Upper Minara roared into a deep gorge. Tunuva dismounted at the top and gave Canthe a hand down.

This sight was among her favourites. Spray misted the air, and beyond the cascading waterfall, thousands of treetops spread all the way to the horizon. She sat with Canthe on a rock that elbowed into the water, while Ninuru waited for fish, paw raised.

'We should return soon,' Tunuva said. 'I leave at dawn.'

'For the Vale of Yaud?' Canthe said. Tunuva nodded. 'I hope you find nothing to fear.' She beheld the forest. 'Perhaps, when you return, the Prioress will have decided my fate.'

'Yes.' Tunuva tamped down her pride and said, 'Thank you for your kindness, after Siyu gave birth.'

'No thanks are necessary.'

The waterfall thundered.

'It was here. In the forest.' Tunuva heard herself speak as if from a distance. 'Where my birthson died.'

Later, she might ask herself why she had laid the unvarnished truth before a stranger. For now, she found she wanted to – had wanted to since that night, since the birth – and did not question it.

'Tunuva, I'm so sorry.' Canthe drew her knee up to her chest. 'How old was he?'

'As long in the world as he was in my womb,' Tunuva murmured. 'Just starting to walk.'

Balag holding his tiny hands, helping him take unsteady steps. He waddled to her again, fell headlong into her arms, and she swung him up and showered him with kisses, making him laugh from his belly. She had loved that sound. In her dreams, she still heard it.

'I never expected to love him so much. In the Priory, we are not supposed to cleave too close to our own flesh. We all belong to the Mother,' she said. 'Yet as soon as he was born, he had my heart.'

Now it was as if Canthe was no longer there. She was telling herself the story once more.

'His birthfather was best at finding honey. The birds would perch on his finger. That was why I chose him. His gentleness. I wanted our child to be gentle, too, even if I bore a warrior.'

Canthe watched her. 'Were you not with Esbar then?'

'Yes, I was. Childbearing here is a gift to the Mother, and we both wanted to help strengthen the Priory. Saghul gave me three choices. I chose Meren. We were close friends.'

She could see him in the sunroom, waiting for her. He had made her chuckle to set her at ease. For as long as she could remember, it had been women she desired, but Meren had done his best to make her comfortable on those nights. When she had told him she was pregnant, he had grinned as if his face would crack, tears of joy in his brown eyes.

'Can you ever choose someone from the outside?'

'Rarely, if someone wants a child and there are no suitable matches. They will go into the world, have a discreet entanglement, and return pregnant. But it is not the preferred way.'

It took Tunuva a moment to carry on. Now she had thought of Meren, the wound was raw again.

'One morning, Meren went out for honey, taking our birthson with him,' she said. 'When they didn't come back, I went looking for them. Meren could often get distracted.'

Every word was a root, pulled from the deep hollow where she had crushed her grief.

'His body was in a clearing. The smell of blood, the honey—' She gazed at the horizon, trying not to see it. 'Our birthson was gone. I ran blindly into the forest to find him, but as night came, so did a terrible storm, so heavy the Minara burst its banks. I could not even raise my flame without it flickering out. For the first time in my life, I lost my bearings in the Basin.'

Ninuru nuzzled her. She was there again, in the flooding hollow, wet fur at her side, water gushing on them both.

Go. Leave me, Nin. Waiting to die there, wanting it. *Leave me…*

I will die with you. You fed me.

'Nin came after me. She saved me,' she said, stroking the ichneumon. 'When Esbar realised we were gone, she mustered the others. By the time they reached the clearing, the spoor had been washed away, but it must have been a wildcat. No trace of my child was found.' She closed her eyes. 'And all I have been able to imagine, all these years, is the pain he felt before the end. Whether he heard me calling. How his sweet laughter must have turned to screams, and then to nothing.'

Her own voice cracked away. It was only when she tasted salt that she realised tears had run down her face . . .

'I'm certain that he knew how much you loved him,' Canthe said quietly. 'What was his name?'

Tunuva swallowed. It had been so long since she had let it pass her lips.

'Only if you want, Tuva.' Cool fingertips found her wrist, raising chills all the way along her arm. 'Only if it helps you.'

It was a strange place to touch someone, the wrist. The skin that knew the patterns of the heart. 'His name,' Tunuva whispered. His face filled her sight. 'I named him—'

'Tuva?'

She turned to see a familiar black ichneumon. Esbar was astride, grasping the hilt of her sword.

Canthe took back her hand. 'Esbar,' Tunuva said. 'Nin and I were just showing Canthe the forest.'

Esbar released her sword, casting her gaze towards the outsider. 'So I see.' Jeda growled. 'I wanted to speak to you. Have you shown our guest enough?'

Tunuva frowned a little at her expression. For the first time in thirty years, she did not quite understand it.

'Yes,' she said. 'Let's go home.'

****

All the way to the Priory, Tunuva could not displace the tension from her shoulders. She watched Esbar, hoping to catch her eye, but she never looked back. Her jaw was set like a brick to mortar.

Canthe held on to Tunuva, not speaking. Long strands of her hair blew about them both.

They reached the entrance in the old fig at sunset. While Esbar strode up the steps, Jeda stalking in her wake, Canthe stopped Tunuva. 'I hope I didn't upset anything,' she said, looking troubled. 'I'm sorry, Tunuva, if so.'

'Everything is fine.' Tunuva spoke with more confidence than she felt. 'Duty calls.'

'I understand. Thank you for trusting me with your story. If you ever wish to talk – about your son, or anything else – I am here, for as long as the Prioress permits me to remain. I know I'm not a sister, but perhaps we could be friends.'

'Yes. Goodnight, Canthe.'

'Goodnight.'

They parted ways. Tunuva sent Ninuru to the river and carried on to her sunroom, where Esbar was waiting on the bed they shared so often, hands clasped between her knees.

Tunuva stood in the doorway. 'It's been a long time since we had anything to fear from the Basin,' she said, a question in her tone.

'It is not the forest I fear.'

'Canthe.' Tunuva sat beside her. 'Ez, have you no faith that I can protect myself, after all these years?'

'Tuva,' Esbar said, iron in her gaze, 'we have no idea who this woman is or what she can do. Until we know more, none of us should be alone with her. Why risk it?'

'Because I feel for her. Imagine it, Esbar – the loss of the tree.'

There was a fleeting quiet between them.

'You think she might understand your loss,' Esbar finally said. 'Perhaps better than I do.'

Though she tried to mask it, Tunuva saw that she was shaken. 'Ez,' she said, moving to clasp her by the hands, 'no, my love. I didn't mean that. Only that Canthe has suffered a terrible hurt. You know – you saw, when Nin brought me back to you – that to be alone with so much sadness is a dangerous thing. Please, let us at least give her a chance.'

Esbar searched her face. Tunuva could almost see her terrified eyes, that night in the rain.

'If it comforts you, Tuva,' she said. 'I only ever want you to be happy.'

She rose. 'Sleep here,' Tunuva said, standing with her. 'I may not see you for weeks.'

'Saghul needs me. She can no longer hold down food, or move without help,' Esbar said shortly. 'Denag and I will take it in turns to care for her – one in the day, one through the night.'

'Ez, you never told me this,' Tunuva said softly. Esbar nodded once. 'Has Denag learned what ails her?'

'She thinks it is a … malicious growth, somewhere in her belly. Apparently such things can root and spread for many years, only for death to strike within a few weeks of the first warning.'

'Is there a cure?'

'No.'

Regret took hold of Tunuva. She had been so preoccupied with Siyu that she had missed this weight on Esbar: the shadows under her eyes, the careworn slope to her shoulders.

As Esbar turned to leave, Tunuva caught her hand. 'Esbar,' she said, 'if anything happens while I am gone, you are ready. You have been ready since the day Saghul chose you.'

Esbar softened. 'Come back soon,' she said, placing a gentle kiss on her lips. 'In one piece, if you please.'

The door shut behind her. Tunuva sank on to the bed, heavy with so many layers of grief.

As if sensing her troubled heart, Ninuru slunk in and lay at her side, where Esbar usually would. Calmed by her warmth, Tunuva drifted to sleep and dreamed again of Esbar, this time drowning her in honey.

****

Deep in the night, she woke, expecting to find herself soaked in sweat – a common occurrence in recent years. Instead, her skin was dry. Beside her, Ninuru looked up, ears pricked.

Tunuva touched her flank. 'Nin?'

Ninuru sniffed the air. 'It smells of the black mountain,' she said. 'The hidden fire.'

Now Tunuva sensed it, too. She followed Ninuru to her balcony. As she watched, a swathe of the stars went out, then returned. It was too dark for anyone but a mage to see the shadow that had just descended.

Without pausing to think, she made for the corridor, Ninuru hard on her heels.

The smell of vomit clung to the Bridal Chamber. Saghul was asleep. By the light of her own flame, Tunuva found Esbar on a mat on the floor, her head resting on a bolster.

'Esbar.' Tunuva shook her, and she stirred. 'I'm sorry, my love.'

'Tuva?'

'There's something in the valley. Nin says it smells of the Dreadmount.'

Esbar sat up and grasped the sword under the bed. 'I need to fetch Denag,' she said. 'Gather a small group.'

Tunuva moved through the Priory, choosing those she trusted most to be discreet. Hidat first, then Izi Tamuten – she tended the ichneumons – and Imsurin, who she found drip-feeding Lukiri with a spouted urn.

'Imin,' Tunuva said, keeping her voice low. 'Come with me.'

He passed the baby to one of the other men. Tunuva sent Balag to keep watch on Saghul.

They headed down to the valley, their flames opening a way through the dark. With no light of his own, Imsurin went in the middle. Tunuva kept hold of his shoulder to steady him.

'The tree,' Hidat murmured.

Tunuva looked down at it. The fruit was burning in the dark, so its boughs appeared to be covered with embers.

At the bottom, she followed her senses over the grass. They let their flames drift overhead, to cast a wider light. When she saw the shape at the base of the tree, Tunuva stopped.

'Hidat,' she said. 'It's just like the rocks we saw.'

'Yes.' Hidat nocked an arrow. 'How did it come to be here?'

'Something brought it to the tree.'

Ninuru huffed through her nose. 'It almost looks like pitchstone,' Izi said, kneeling close to it. 'How strange.'

Esbar drew her sword. 'Let's see what lies within.'

'Be careful, Esbar,' Imsurin warned. 'I don't like the way it feels.'

Tunuva raised her spear. Esbar circled the boulder, searching for a weakness. Finding none, she swung the sword above her head and sliced down, only for it to glance off the surface with a distinct *clang*, sparking in all directions. She tried stabbing and sawing it, to no avail.

'Let me try,' Tunuva said.

Esbar stood aside. Slowly, Tunuva pushed up her sleeve, moved her hand towards the searing rock, and did exactly what she had dared not in the Vale of Yaud.

She laid her naked hand upon it.

Above, every fruit gave a rutilant flare. Beneath her fingers, the rock broke apart, starting right beneath her palm. Hot steam scalded through the seams, followed by the selfsame light and stench that had come from the Dreadmount.

'Tuva, get back,' Izi urged her, retreating. Tunuva could not. She was looking at a broken mirror, at death and life, at things she understood and failed to understand.

Esbar pulled her away. Tunuva stared at her own smarting hand, finding it pitted with tiny, reddened holes. A mark like a honeycomb. In all her life, no heat had ever wounded her.

Cracks pronged through the boulder. It heaved and lurched, rocking from side to side, and its surface rippled, as if it were loosening. Imsurin held up his saddle axe.

One side of the rock swelled, and a sharpness punctured it. Even with the eyes of a mage, Tunuva could not understand what she was seeing. Two horns, like polished iron. A cloven hoof, and then another, shattering the dense shell that enclosed them. Nostrils snorting out black smoke, and two embers above, set deep where its eyes should be.

Most of her mind still clawed for reason. Surely it was a great ox, or a beast of that sort. But when the front part of its body had arched free, steaming and marbled with molten lava, no hind legs followed. Instead, there was a thick scaled tail.

'What in the name of the Mother is this?' Esbar breathed.

Its hooves scraped furrows into the earth. When it opened its mouth, dark metal teeth glinted in the firelight, and it let out an excruciated scream.

'I don't know.' Hidat aimed her arrow. 'I want it dead.'

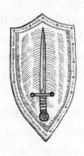

35

West

Who are you?

The figure had no face, and stood in a grey mist. *A dreamer,* it said, in a voice like pure water. An impossible voice, without pitch or inflection, or any trait at all. *I suppose you are, too.*

Is this your dream or mine?

They stood on either side of a stream. Outside of its glassy trickling, all was deathly silent.

And are we really dreaming?

Her voice echoed, identical to the other.

I remember falling asleep. The figure held a loosely human shape, and did not move. *How strange. In all the dreams I have had, I have never crossed paths with anyone else. Either I am lonelier than I thought, and now I am imagining a friend, or you are a messenger from the gods.*

There are no gods.

Of course there are. An expectant stillness. *Very well. You are a dreamer, and so am I, and this is both my dream and yours. What could have brought us to each other?*

I don't know. Where are you in this world?

I am on an island.

I am on an island, too.

****

The dream broke, and Glorian woke in her bed with a shudder. Beside her, Helisent sat up.

'Did you have a nightmare?'

It was a moment before Glorian could reply. Her tongue seemed sewn to her teeth. 'I think so.'

Helisent touched her shoulder. 'You're frozen,' she murmured. 'It's almost morning. I'll have a bath prepared.'

'Thank you.'

She went to the windows to check they were latched. Once she had stoked the fire and left, Glorian turned over, trying to recall the dream. The taste of silver filled her mouth.

Her ladies bathed her, driving the chill from her skin. After, she dismissed Helisent and Adela, letting Julain stay only to comb and dry her hair.

'Shall we go to the queenswood today, since you have no lessons?' Julain asked her. 'A long walk is always a tonic in winter.'

'It looks as if it will rain.'

'You love the rain.'

'I have a headache.' Glorian grasped her own arms. 'Let's just stay here and play cards.'

'It isn't good to be so cooped up, Glorian. Why don't we look for oak galls again?'

Glorian wondered how many people who wanted her dead were lurking in those trees.

'Perhaps when the sun is out,' she said.

Julain sighed. 'As you wish.'

While her ladies sweetened her bedchamber, Glorian broke her fast in the Dearn Chamber, with her guards so close she could almost smell the steel in their scabbards. Her world, once closed and soft as a rosebud, had sprung thorns.

Her mother had joined her at first. As always, she had said little. Queen Sabran did not indulge fear or accept weakness. But she had sat with Glorian as she worked, for a time.

In the hours after the attack, no one could have come between them. Queen Sabran had marched Glorian to the royal apartments, tucked her into her own bed, and watched over her all night, stroking her hair whenever she woke. Glorian had slept fitfully – yet also never felt so safe, comforted by her own mother, swaddled in her love at last.

Queen Sabran had not touched her since. She had been colder than ever, as if that night of gentleness had turned her to pure stone.

Today she was in the Council Chamber. There had been more reports of livestock disappearing. Something was afoot in the world, and Inys was starting to sense it. King Bardholt had not made his usual summer visit, and all Glorian had wanted was to see him. Still, he would be with her soon. He never usually left Hróth during the darker months, when his own people needed him most. It had to be because of the attempt on her life.

The man with the dull knife had come from the mining town of Crawham. She had watched him die on the rushes. The next morning, her mother had ordered the court to move to Drouthwick Castle, where Glorian had hidden in her rooms with her ladies and her fear. She flinched at the faintest sound, expecting to see that wan, embittered face.

He had wanted to kill her because he thought the Nameless One was free, and her bloodline had no claim to Inys.

All because of the Dreadmount.

She looked out of the misted window. The morning was as grim and leaden as her mood, as mornings often were in the Fells.

The door creaked open, making her stiffen. 'Highness,' Dame Erda said, 'King Bardholt's party has passed Worhurst. They should be here before long.'

'Thank you.'

The knight left, and Glorian was alone again. Alone was the safest choice.

****

It was past midday when her father arrived at Drouthwick. As the procession of riders passed beneath her window, Glorian saw Wulf among them. He glanced up, and their gazes met.

In that glimpse of him, she saw the shadows under his dark eyes. He saluted her, dipping his head, and rode on.

King Bardholt liked to bathe when he arrived at court. While Glorian waited for him, she played cards with her ladies, but her mind was elsewhere, and they let her win at least twice. By the time her father summoned her, her candle clock was halfway burned.

He awaited her in the Witting Room, where documents and manuscripts were stored. King Bardholt hated reading, but he liked the quiet and coolness of that part of the castle.

Two of his retainers flanked the door. One was stern and pale, with a scar across his cheekbone – Karlsten, that was his name – while the other had tousled black hair, a trim beard, and dark olive skin. He offered her a smile.

'Good day,' Glorian said in Hróthi. 'I don't think we've met.'

'Thrit of Isborg, Highness. An honour.' He raised a fist to his heart. 'Joy for your hall.'

'Fire for your hearth.'

Inside, her father was sitting with his elbows on his knees, stroking his beard, as he always did when he was deep in thought. He rose when she entered the room.

'Glorian.'

'Papa,' she whispered.

The sight of him made her eyes well. Even without his mail and furs, her father was a solid wall no blade could ever pass. As soon as the doors closed behind her, she rushed to him, and he scooped her into his arms.

'Dróterning,' he murmured. 'Are you all right?' She tried to speak, and instead began to cry. 'Come, my warrior. All is well.' He drew her on to his knee, as if she were still a child. 'Weep all you need. It's good for the heart. I cried the first time someone tried to kill me.'

'Truly?'

'And the second. And the third.'

Glorian huddled against his chest, tears flowing down her face. Her father sang in his deep, slow voice, holding her tight. Whenever she had asked him not to leave Inys without her, he had calmed her with this old lullaby, which would have chilled the Saint himself.

'Papa,' she said, drying her eyes, 'why did you not come to visit in the summer?'

'There were matters that needed attention in Hróth. But I am here now.' King Bardholt looked her in the face. 'The miner is dead. He cannot hurt you now, Glorian.'

'But there must be others like him, who hate us,' Glorian stammered. 'I know how to fight – you made sure I knew – but I was so scared, Papa. I couldn't even move.'

'That has happened to me, too. To freeze is an instinct shared by all living things. Think of how a deer stills when it scents a threat. There is no shame in it, Glorian, but you can conquer it.'

'What if someone comes to hurt me again before I do?'

'Then the Royal Guard will stop them again. Sir Bramel has been rewarded for his courage.'

'Good.' She tucked her head under his chin. 'Was it in the war, when it first happened to you?'

'No. In Bringard,' he said softly, 'when I was fourteen. One of the villagers came for your aunt.' He smoothed her hair. 'I was tall and strong, even then, but he was stronger. He beat us both to the floor. My mother returned from hunting just in time, and shot him dead.'

He had never told her this awful tale.

'That was why we fled to Askrdal,' he said. 'Skiri Longstride sheltered us. She was kind.'

Glorian wished she could have met more of his family. Though their craft was useful, the Hróthi had once feared boneworkers, believing they brought death wherever they walked. Their situation had worsened when his sister had been born with a white streak of hair. In that cruel time, it had been seen as proof that she was cursed by the ice spirits.

'Mother saved me. Like yours saved you,' Glorian said. 'She pushed the man away.'

'I heard. Did I not tell you she was a warrior?'

Glorian nodded.

'The day it happened … Mother was so tender with me,' she said. 'But now she speaks to me even less warmly. I never talk or laugh with her as I do with you, Papa.' Her eyes brimmed again. 'Did I shame her?'

'No. Never,' he said, low and resolute. 'You could never shame either of us, Glorian.'

'Then why does she not love me as you do?'

'She does. Just as much. But some of us run hot, and some run cold. Queen Sabran is the latter sort, and I am the former,' he said. 'It is what makes our partnership so strong.'

Glorian looked at her hands.

'Have you been outside since it happened?' King Bardholt asked. She shook her head. 'Don't let fear command you. If I had hidden every time someone tried to hurt me, I would have walled myself up and never come out.'

'I won't hide.' Glorian tried to sound brave. 'Could we ride together in the queenswood?'

'Of course.'

'How long will you stay?'

'Until the marriage of Lord Magnaust and Princess Idrega. Your mother and I will depart from Werstuth.' He kissed the top of her head. 'I must speak with the Virtues Council. Go to sanctuary and pray to the Knight of Courage. Let your patron fill you with his fortitude.'

'Yes, Papa.'

As she stood, he took her hand.

'I would have slain the man myself, as I slew Verthing Bloodblade,' he said quietly. 'If he has a supporter left in Inys, they will die the way that wretch did. I swear this to you, daughter.'

Glorian believed him. Northerners never broke an oath.

****

Outside, Helisent was waiting to walk her back to her guards. 'Helly,' Glorian said, once they had rounded a corner, 'do you still remember how to find the secret room – the spyhole?'

'You don't mean to use it.'

'I want to know why Father missed his summer visit to Inys. He said there were pressing matters in Hróth – I think it must be something of great import.'

'Why not ask Master Glenn?' Helisent said stiffly. 'Jules says you rekindled your acquaintance with him.'

'If two brief conversations count.' Glorian said, amused. 'And why, Helly, does the possibility make you look as if you've swallowed a sour plum?'

Helisent stopped to frown at her. 'Glorian … you do *know* about Wulf, don't you?'

'What about him?'

Before they could go on, a door opened. Helisent swept Glorian behind a curtain, and they held their breath as King Bardholt strode past with the two retainers, speaking Hróthi.

'Go on, Helly,' Glorian said, once they were gone. 'What do you want to say of Wulf?'

Helisent glanced out of the window. 'Father told me the story,' she said. 'Some years ago, a boy was found at the northern boundary of the haithwood. A child who was said to bear marks of a witching.'

'Witching.' Glorian tried not to laugh. 'Helly, I know there are certain tales in the north, and I like some of them, but—'

'This tells of a woman of old Inysca, who lives deep in the haithwood, waiting to torment those who renounce the Saint,' Helisent whispered. 'She's real, Glorian. I'm sure of it.'

'Who?'

'The Witch of Inysca. The Lady of the Woods. She who twists the trees.' Her voice shook. 'Wulf came from in there. Baron Glenn took him in that night, and gave him name.'

'That was very kind of Lord Edrick. He is a man of generous heart.' Glorian folded her arms. 'To me, this sounds quite simple. Wulf was a foundling, given a loving home. Any talk of witchery is nonsense.'

'You might think so,' Helisent said, folding her arms right back, 'but I believe the haithwood is an unhallowed place, forsaken by the Saint. Father has been its keeper to the south for decades, and he has seen too much for me to trust those woods.'

'That doesn't mean you can't trust Wulf. It's hardly his fault that he was abandoned there.'

'I never said it was. I'm just asking you to be careful around him,' Helisent said softly. 'I know you like him, but to some, Wulfert Glenn is a reminder of the old world. We don't know what might have seen him in there. What might still be watching him.'

'Helly, none of this helps me find out why my father did not visit Inys in the summer.'

Helisent considered for a time. Glorian could see her mind at work behind those dark eyes.

'Ask for a period of seclusion in the Royal Sanctuary tonight. To ... reflect on your future as queen, or something. That will give you time.' Helisent paused. 'Glorian, some things in the shadows are put there for a reason. Are you sure you want to do this?'

'If I am to be queen, I must learn to find the truth myself. I must be braver. In all things.' Glorian drew herself up. 'Mother retires after eventide. I will need to be at the spyhole by then.' She grimaced. 'Let's not tell Jules. She'll only worry.'

They looked at one another. 'Or Adela,' they agreed in unison.

****

After the evening meal, she and Helisent changed and walked to the Royal Sanctuary. Sir Bramel and Dame Erda closed the doors behind them, leaving Glorian to her supposed reflection.

'Take this.' Helisent took a fire pouch from under her cloak. 'Do you know how to use it?'

'Of course.' When Helisent canted an eyebrow, Glorian sighed. 'I am aware I lack certain practical skills as a royal, but do you truly think a princess of the North can't light a fire?'

'I sometimes forget you've a claim to two thrones.' Helisent presented her with a set of iron pincers. 'For the nails.'

They had worn cloaks of different colours, which they now traded. Helisent drew up her hood and knelt in prayer, while Glorian slipped through the sanctarians' door.

Helisent had discovered the secret when she was fifteen. Since she had a sharp eye for detail, her father had asked her to find some coroners' rolls in the castle archives. During the search, she had come across an old plan of Drouthwick and noticed two windows she had never seen from the outside, adjacent to the room that was now the royal bedchamber. Combing the castle, she had found a dusty nook, bricked up at one end.

The stonemasons must have grown lazy and not filled it in all the way. Content that no one was using it to spy on Queen Sabran – there was no sign of disturbance, save mouse droppings – Helisent had burned the plan and told Glorian. Now it was theirs.

The entrance lay in a passage behind a rusty iron grate. Glorian knelt beside it and used the pincers to pluck out its nails, revealing an opening. She slid through the gap.

In the dark, she unpacked the firesteel and flint. When she had a candle lit, she pulled the grate back into place, a thread of fearful excitement winding through her. In sixteen years, she had never eluded her guards.

The steps were cramped. Helisent thought the Malkin Queen must have used them to bring lovers to her bed, but the tyrant had paraded her adultery. More likely all of this was just unwanted space, sealed up to strengthen the castle. Glorian had never dared to visit it before.

Her slippers made little sound. She curled her hand around her candle, her shadow wavering. When she heard voices, she blew it out and crawled until she saw a faint light.

A fracture in the brickwork let her see straight into the Great Chamber. Her mother was sitting on her bed in a flowing ivory shift.

'—never dare resist the Vatten. They have milk in their blood and feathers in the lining of their bellies.'

'Now Heryon is appeased, I agree,' her mother said. 'But we have other things to fear.' She watched her consort pace the room. 'You say this sickness came from Ófandauth.'

'My retainers found it almost deserted.' King Bardholt sounded grim. 'The Issýn caught it, Sabran. She is dead.'

'By the Saint. She was the peacekeeper. Who knows?'

'Only those who boarded the ships we took to Eldyng.'

'What measures have you taken to stop word spreading farther?' Queen Sabran rose. 'Bardholt, we are already walking on sand. First an emboldened republic, then the Dreadmount—'

'It is ended. Everywhere it tainted is now ash, along with the remains of the dead. I have riders waiting to inform me if it rears its head again.' He grasped the shelf over the hearth. 'One of my retainers survived it. Have Forthard examine him.'

'You brought this retainer here?'

'He is not afflicted.'

'Any trace of it in Inys will feed the doubts the Dreadmount kindled. Glorian is already a target.'

'Yes. I spoke to her.' He sighed. 'Ranna, you must show her more gentleness, more affection. You are her mother, the woman on whom she models herself. She barely knows you love her.'

Queen Sabran raised her chin. 'You say I am too hard?' she said. 'I say our daughter is too soft.' Glorian flinched. 'A sword cannot be shaped without fire and force. You and I were both raised in a furnace, Bardholt. What does Glorian know of true hardship?'

'Are we to be the furnace, then?' King Bardholt said, his voice tight with anger. 'Her parents?'

'I must be the hammer, since you, ironically, refuse. She is sixteen and afraid to leave the castle. She spurns our highest duty. The Malkin Queen would have done the same, had she not feared an end to her rule.'

'Do not compare our daughter to that—'

'I must, because Inys always will.' She walked to his side. 'In the eyes of the law, Glorian may have a child of her own when she turns seventeen. A year later, she will be old enough to rule this queendom without a regent. If she were called to fulfil either of those duties now, today, are you confident she would be strong enough?'

'Ranna, you are not even fifty. For the love of the Saint, permit her the childhood neither of us had.'

'Easy for you to say. If you wanted, you could make as many bastards as you wished.' She held a hand to her middle. 'Glorian is my one and only successor. She must be strong – she must be perfect – because I will not bear another child. Saint knows, we have tried enough.'

Glorian blinked hard, as if she could wake up somewhere else. She was caught in the numbness after a fall, when the bone had been snapped, but the pain had not come.

'Sabran.' King Bardholt spoke quietly. 'I would never. You are my own heart's root.'

Queen Sabran released a long breath. 'I know. I'm sorry, Bard.' She sank back on to the bed. 'I cannot pamper or coddle Glorian. Already she is too like my mother. I kept Marian away, all these years – but Glorian has her blood, too.'

Marian the Less, weakest of the three worst queens of Inys. Glorian wanted to shrivel into nothing.

No Berethnet queen had ever conceived more than once, but her parents had always hoped, all those years. They had wanted more than her.

'Stop this.' Her father sat beside her mother. 'Glorian is not Marian. How could she be, when she is us?' He laid a hand on her thigh. 'Sweetheart. Are the shadows on you?'

'Don't fuss, Bardholt. It is not my head that gives me care,' she said in an undertone. 'It is the past.'

'Damn the past,' he said, his voice low and rough. 'We are the future, and together we have changed the world. There is nothing that we cannot do. That we cannot take.'

Queen Sabran interlaced their fingers, looking him in the eyes.

'This night,' she said, 'I bid you take what is already yours. And let me take what is already mine.'

She lifted his hand to her lips. King Bardholt waited, watching her caress his knuckles, before he leaned down and kissed her.

Glorian knew she should leave. This was private. She had to get back to Helisent before the guards realised.

Yet something kept her where she was. Curiosity, perhaps – about how it was between companions. *You'll find out when you're wed*, Florell had said when she asked. *No need until then, sweeting.*

Why should she only know then, and not before?

How would she ready herself?

So she watched as her parents undressed – not gently, but like they had slept in the sun and needed to cool down. *Leave*, a voice in her head urged, but Glorian was rooted, face burning in shock. All she could see were naked limbs, the sweep of hair on skin as her parents embraced on the bed. Not with courtesy or temperance. Something else had taken hold.

When they both started to breathe hard, it startled Glorian back to her senses. She scrambled down the steps and out through the opening, shoved the grate into place, and fumbled the nails in, palms sweating. Desperately, she gathered her borrowed tools and hurried along the passages, wishing she could scour what she had just seen from her mind.

'Who goes there?'

Without thinking, she turned, and a housecarl stepped from the courtyard, carrying a torch.

'Glorian.' Wulf peered under her hood, his brow puckered. 'What are you doing out here alone?'

'I told you. I can look after myself,' Glorian said thickly. 'My father said that if he hid away every time someone tried to kill him, he would have walled himself up and died long ago.'

Wulf found a smile. 'That's true.' His expression softened. 'Let me take you to your rooms, at least.'

'I can make my own way,' she said, recoiling from his solid presence. 'I'm fine, Wulf. Just leave me alone.'

36

South

The creature lay in an old storeroom, where they could keep it out of sight. Blood as dark as tar had seeped into the patterns on the stone table, drying like black inlay. Tunuva took in every detail.

From its head alone, she might have thought it was a bullock – except for its burning eyes, gone cold in death, and its horns, each stretched longer than an arm. Izi Tamuten had sawn one off for study, and concluded that it was bone sheathed in iron. The same metal had strengthened its teeth and hooves, and the teeth had formed keen points, like the horns. Its swollen body, including the hind legs, had tapered into a serpentine tail.

This creature had the taint of the Dreadmount.

It had been in torment when it died. Even though it had hatched like a newborn, instinct told Tunuva that it had once led a different, peaceful life.

She touched the brittle hairs of its neck, not flinching when they cut her fingers. Those hairs had turned to brassy glass, each sharp as a needle, some of them matted with black drops. The stench of the corpse was already unbearable, as if a fumarole had opened in the room.

Hidat had put an arrow in its eye and another where she thought its heart might be. Both arrows had caught fire. Screaming and thrashing, it had pulled itself towards them and hissed with a cloven tongue. Only when Esbar had severed its head did it finally cease to move.

Izi had found its heart, in the end, and scooped it from its body. Left in a balance scale, it was oily black, streaked with red, like the rock of the Dreadmount.

Tunuva could not be alone with the thing any longer. She made her way to the top of the Priory. The indents remained on her palm and fingers, the healing slower than usual.

Esbar worked in her sunroom, shearing a nib into a hollow reed, a lamp beside her. Her seal lay in reach, along with a thin stack of letters. Those would be reports from their sisters across the South. Tunuva sat on the arm of her chair and kissed her head.

'I'm writing to Apaya,' Esbar told her. 'Queen Daraniya must know what we encountered.'

'What will you say it was?'

Esbar shook her head. 'Now I see why the world calls him the Nameless One,' she muttered. 'What name could be put to such a beast?' Their whispers made the candles on the table flicker. 'How many of those rocks did you say you and Hidat counted, Tuva?'

'Almost fifty in the Vale of Yaud alone. At least twenty more in Efsi; the same for Agārin.'

'By the Mother.' Esbar dipped the reed in ink. 'At least you can remain here, now we know what lies within the rocks. The question is, are they only in the South, or beyond?'

'It was not so hard to kill.'

'Neither is a spindle wasp – but kick a nest of them, and you are not long for the world.'

'We are prepared,' Tunuva said, with more certainty than she felt. 'We can open them by touch, as I did. Slay them before they can do any harm.'

Esbar pressed the furrows between her eyebrows. 'Do they follow the Nameless One?' she said. 'Is it hatred or hunger that drives them?' She tapped the letter with the dry end of her reed. 'Tuva, tell me. Can you still call the red flame, the flame from the Dreadmount?'

'Saghul told us not to.'

'Try.'

Tunuva opened her hand. Without the fumes from the mountain, this would require concentration.

She cleared her mind, as she did when she stretched her body after a fight. Eyes closed, she pictured tapping a tree, to where siden ran like sap in her blood, waiting to be ignited.

For the first time in her life, she kept tapping. She threaded into herself, peeling off layers of bark, hammering past the heartwood, farther. Sensing resistance, she breathed in and pushed, broaching some locked cask of her siden – and there it was, a resin thick and rich with power, deep in her pith. She willed it down her arm, watching her veins swell with it, and took it in hand, where the scarlet flame roared at last, almost too hot to bear.

'It's much harder to sustain,' she said. 'I think I will burn through it quickly.'

'I called it yesterday. It drained me.' Esbar watched, the light haunting each line of her face. 'We are like the Dreadmount. Like the Nameless One.'

Tunuva smothered the flame. 'We always knew our magic came from the same cradle.'

'Perhaps now we must ask why,' Esbar said. The dark hair on her arms had risen. 'Why does the Womb of Fire birth ruin and chaos, even as it lights our tree, which offers only life and protection?'

'I don't know, but I know the Mother. She gave us this gift. Not her enemy.' Tunuva framed her cheeks. 'Esbar, you are holding too much shadow. Keep the faith, my love.'

Esbar nodded, linking their fingers. 'Forgive me. It weighs on me, to see Saghul so unwell,' she said. 'I can't convince her to eat.'

'Let me take care of her tonight. You need to sleep.'

Footsteps came down the corridor. They both looked up to see Hidat in the doorway.

'It's done,' she said, her voice as tired as her gaze. 'Esbar, will you tell the Prioress?'

Esbar rubbed the corner of her eye. 'Tell her what?'

'Surely she told you about the Carmenti boy.'

Tunuva could feel her heart through her whole body, down to her fingertips. 'Anyso,' she said. 'What about him?'

'The Prioress is bedbound.' Esbar stood. 'She spoke with you?'

'She came to me in the armoury. She did seem frail, but—' Hidat was beginning to look troubled. 'The Prioress told me she had made a final decision about Anyso of Carmentum: that he had to die, to protect the Priory. She said there was no other choice.'

Tunuva stared at her, her chest tightening. Esbar said slowly, 'When was this?'

'Not more than an hour ago.'

'I was *with* her an hour ago, Hidat. I was with her from dawn until dusk—'

'Hush. Siyu will hear.' Tunuva shut the door. 'By the Mother, Hidat. Is he really dead?'

'Tuva, I promise you, the Prioress gave me the order.' Hidat spoke with the utmost conviction. 'She asked me to do it at once, and tell no one.'

'Either you are telling the truth, and I am the liar,' Esbar bit out, 'or the other way around, else we have both lost our minds. Saghul was in bed until dusk. Denag took over then.' She sank back into her seat. 'This will break Siyu.'

Tunuva swallowed. 'Hidat, how did you do it?'

'Poison. It was painless. He is in the same room,' Hidat said. 'I swear on the Mother, I only did as the Prioress asked.' She lowered her head. 'If I did wrong, sisters, I beg your forgiveness.'

'Put ice around his body.' Esbar gave the order in a hollow voice. 'Lock his door and bring me the key.'

Once Hidat had gone, silence bowered the room.

'Saghul can't even sit up without my arms around her,' Esbar forced out. 'How could she have reached the armoury?'

Tunuva grasped her elbow. 'Ez,' she said, 'we both knew what Saghul would decide. Perhaps she found a final surge of strength to go to Hidat, thinking you or I would not be able to face it.'

'It still would not explain how she left without me seeing. I have been weary, but I know I never fell asleep.'

'Denag could have. Perhaps this happened after she took over,' Tunuva said gently. 'Hidat did not give us a precise time, and the line between dusk and night is not clean.'

'I feel mad.' Esbar kneaded her forehead. 'But it's done.'

'How long can we keep it from Siyu?'

Esbar looked as if all the light had gone out of her. 'He escaped into the forest,' she said at last, 'and we have no idea what became of him. We'll tell her after Saghul passes.'

Such a disappearance was believable. After all, it had happened before.

'She trusts us. She loves us,' Tunuva said in a whisper. 'How can we deceive her?'

'To protect her. The truth stays between the two of us, Hidat, and Imsurin.'

Tunuva breathed in, arms drawn over her heart, fingers pressed into her shoulders. She imagined the terrible weight of that secret; the way its sharp edges would chisel at her. She imagined having to lie to Siyu every day for the rest of her life.

And then she imagined losing her for good, and one moment with that thought was too long.

'I will speak to Denag,' she finally said. 'You should rest, Esbar.'

Esbar let out a low, dark laugh, a sound Tunuva had never heard her make. 'I will try.'

Tunuva padded into the Bridal Chamber, where she found Saghul in a light drowse, eyes restless beneath their lids. Finding Denag asleep in a chair, Tunuva woke her with a touch and sent her to her own bed. They could speak in the morning.

She sat beside Saghul, whose ichneumon was still awake at the foot of her bed. His fur had long since turned grey, but he would stay with his little sister until the end.

'Saghul,' Tunuva said softly. 'It's Tunuva. Can you hear me?'

A tiny nod.

'Anyso is dead. The outsider. Did you ask Hidat to do this?'

With clear difficulty, Saghul reached for her, lips moving. Tunuva leaned close, but even with the sharp hearing of a mage, she could make out no more than a faint sough of breath. She took Saghul by the hand, which felt too fragile to have ever held a blade.

'I'm here, old friend.'

Saghul looked towards her voice with a deep weariness, yellow in the whites of her eyes. Tunuva stroked her head until she dozed back off.

****

Tunuva stayed in that chair all night, praying for the woman who had led them for so long. At dawn, when Esbar came, she went to where Anyso lay, finding a silent Hidat watching over him.

Anyso was on his bed. The poison had stained his lips, but otherwise he could have been asleep. Tunuva sat beside him and brushed his loose curls away from his brow.

Forgive us. She closed her damp eyes. *Forgive us.*

37
East

Ashort way beyond the city of Mozom Alph, a waterfall tumbled into a sheltered gorge. Above its plunge pool, Dumai dashed along a bridge, soaked from her last swim. Wind rushed in her ears as she jumped off the edge and plummeted again, slicing into deep water.

When she was a child, she had splashed in the hot spring, but it was too small for swimming. Now Kanifa could teach her what he had learned off the mountain.

The pool was as cold as the one on Mount Ipyeda. Enfolded in it, Dumai opened her eyes, letting herself float.

Far below, ghostly fish swam over a darkness. During the Long Slumber, most Sepuli dragons had settled on riverbeds, or near waterfalls – they preferred fresh, running water – but a pair of human divers had disturbed the sleeper in this pool, startling him elsewhere. Furtia slept in these abandoned depths now, regaining her strength after her flight.

Dumai surfaced with a waft of white breath. Nearby, Kanifa sat on a flat rock, eating a pear.

'I hope Queen Arkoro will see us soon.' Dumai joined him and wrapped herself in a mantle, and he passed her a flask of hot barley tea. 'While we wait for her, this threat could be growing.'

'Give her time. Our arrival was sudden,' Kanifa said. 'Furtia alone must have surprised them.'

'Dragons have little concern for diplomacy. I may not be able to keep her here much longer.'

As if woken by their voices, Furtia spoke from her new lair: *We must begin the search, earth child.*

The queen has still not called me. Suddenly the tea tasted of iron. *Soon, great one. You have my word.*

I told you. Your crowns and thrones do not matter.

A few more days, I beg you.

Dumai was sure the water bubbled as Furtia growled in irritation.

'At least Lady Nikeya has not been too troublesome,' she said, to distract herself.

'So far.' Kanifa glanced towards the temple, high above. 'She should have recovered by now.'

'Flying was clearly not one of her many talents.'

Her withdrawal did concern Dumai. She had seen climbers die from mountain sickness.

'You warned her of the danger,' Kanifa said, reading her face. 'Don't forget who she is, or what she's doing here. The Royal Guard took my weapons. You must stay vigilant.'

She held up her cropped fingers. 'If a mountain failed to get rid of me, no courtier will.'

Kanifa smiled. 'I believe you.' He nudged her. 'You should go up to get warm.'

'What about you?'

'I'll sit a little longer.'

Dumai nodded. She turned to start the long climb back, leaving him to watch two otters capering in the water.

****

It was sunset by the time she reached the temple, which stood between the middle and lower shelves of the waterfall. Twelve members of the Royal Guard observed her crossing the stepstones to its entrance.

She wondered what they thought of her. Centuries since the last Seiikinese delegation, and now here she was, in all her strangeness – an islander only just learning to swim, a princess who dressed in no finery. *I know*, she wanted to tell them. *I know I make no sense.*

Furtia had brought them here under cover of darkness, guided by signal fires. Until they were summoned to the palace, the pool was the farthest her riders were permitted to go.

Dumai walked through the temple. After its dragon had fled, it had been dedicated to one of the Queens of Spring. Those who honoured her wore pink on white, and their rites were unfamiliar, but it comforted Dumai, to be in a place of worship. It also made her miss her mother.

Oil lamps burned in the bathhouse. She undressed, face tingling with cold, relishing the ache in her muscles. Already she felt more like her old self. She and Kanifa still had the mountain in their blood – neither of them had sickened on dragonback. Furtia had let them drink water from her scales, flying low enough that they could all stay conscious.

Dumai knew not to take that concern for granted. *The sea holds loyalty to no one*, the River Lord had warned, and it was true. A dragon could only be a friend as much as wind or water could.

She was still resolved to help this one. At the same time, she could not risk insulting the Queen of Sepul by not telling her why she was here, or seeking her permission to begin a search.

There had to be a middle way between deference and diplomacy. Surely a godsinger princess could find it.

The sunken bath was empty. A dish stood at each corner, filled with fine black salt for polishing the skin. Dumai rinsed herself before sitting on the side, drawing one leg up to reach her foot.

'Princess.'

The voice made her start. Nikeya stood in the doorway, hair loose, wearing an unlined robe.

You must stay vigilant, Kanifa had said, and here Dumai was, alone and defenceless.

'Lady Nikeya.' This time, she would keep her composure. 'You arise.'

'You were right about the headaches, but my eyes never bled,' Nikeya said. Her cheeks and nose were still a little sunburnt from the flight. 'I must be stronger than you feared.'

'Not enough, apparently, to keep yourself from vomiting on a god.'

Mercifully, Furtia had appeared not to notice.

'Oh, come, Princess. Crowing over your subjects' faults does not become a future ruler.' Nikeya slid the door shut behind her. 'Why not commend my accomplishments instead?'

It must be possible to fluster this woman. Like her father, she seemed unflappable.

'Thank you for your advice,' Dumai said. 'What is it, precisely, you believe I should commend?'

'My survival, surely. None but the Noziken are known to have ridden a dragon and lived.'

'Kanifa did the same. He does not expect praise, like a child.' Dumai worked salt up her arms, mindful of her own sunburn. 'I assume you came here to bathe.'

'Of course. Why else should I come to a bathhouse?'

Nikeya shouldered out of her robe. As she came to lounge on the other side of the bath, bare as her ambition, Dumai made a failed attempt to shrink her body behind her knee, lowering her waist.

'Now we're alone, we could talk, like we did at the temple,' Nikeya said lightly. 'You were friendlier then. That stuffy court brings out the worst in us all, but we are far away from it. Let us get to know each other.'

'I know you are here to spy on me for your family. I know you have threatened people I love.' Dumai kept scrubbing. 'Is there anything I missed?'

Nikeya gazed at her, hands on either side of her hips. Her hair was thick and long.

'Well,' she said, 'I have my secrets, as we all do, but let me see. I was born on the outskirts of Nanta. My father and I are from a large clan, but I am his only surviving child. My mother died when I was seventeen. I am a poor swimmer, a fine dancer, an excellent archer. I hate the cold. I love spring. It was my childhood dream to sail across the Sundance Sea.' She slid into the water. 'Most importantly, I care about the people of Seiiki.'

'Then perhaps you should press your father to spend less of his time entertaining, and more on helping those in the dust provinces. I hear that he prefers to exile anyone who tries.'

That seemed to catch her interest. 'What do you care for the dust provinces?'

'My mother was born in one. Of course I care.'

'Then why not ask Furtia to send rain?'

'One dragon could not end this drought alone.'

'But you believe my father can?' Nikeya smiled. 'You must think very highly of his talents, Princess.'

308

'Furtia is not yet at her full strength,' Dumai reminded her. 'And she is not mine to command.'

'Neither is my father mine.'

Nikeya sank up to her collarbone, all her dark hair fanning around her. Against her will, Dumai imagined winding her fingers through it.

She washed away both the salt and the thought, rising to fetch her robe. 'No bath after all?' Nikeya said, resting her folded arms on the side. 'I can always close my eyes.'

'I'm tired.'

'Then let me comb your hair before you sleep. I'm told I have the touch for it.'

'I am twenty-eight. I can comb my own hair, Lady Nikeya.'

'You might think so, sweet princess – but remember, I met you before you had attendants. You couldn't style it for this court if your life depended on it. I hope you're not planning to try.'

Her laugh was soft as a feather, sending a shiver through Dumai. 'Do you never tire of your intrigues?' Dumai said, fastening the robe too hard. 'Truly. Do the Kuposa never stop?'

'A bell that stops can only rust.'

'Your father's words?'

'Mine. Am I not my own woman, and a poet?' Nikeya emerged from the bath and walked towards her. 'I'm not your enemy. Not unless you give me reason.'

'That sounds like a threat.'

'Does it?'

Dumai kept her gaze on those lively eyes, which held the light from the oil lamps.

'Let's agree to be friends,' Nikeya said, softer. 'I think we both want the best for Seiiki.'

Before Dumai could reply, Nikeya reached for her, making her flinch. Nikeya smiled a little more.

'You would think I was a wolf.' With surprising care, she drew a thread of damp hair between her fingers, teasing out a pine needle. 'Are you certain you don't want me to comb this, Princess?'

Dumai could feel her own breath betraying her. A warm drift in her darkest waters.

Daughter, have you lost your senses?

'I will manage,' she said, starting to draw away. 'Wait. You said I couldn't style it for this court.'

'Oh, yes – a messenger came at noon.' Nikeya smiled. 'Queen Arkoro will see us tomorrow morning.'

Dumai stared at her in exasperation. 'Did you not think to tell me that earlier?'

'I must have been distracted.' Nikeya returned to the bath. 'I'll see you in the morning, Princess.'

****

In the guest quarters, Dumai lay on her bedding. As she tried to sleep, she remembered her strange dream – the figure who had spoken with her.

On the mountain, the Grand Empress had started teaching her to control her dreams. The dreamer had to fall asleep, but also stay aware.

Dumai turned on to her back, heels and hands planted on the floor. As sleep drew her in, she concentrated on those anchor points, trying to float instead of sinking deep under the waves.

Are you there?

There was the stream, winding like silver thread through cloth. *I'm here*, the messenger answered. Dumai glimpsed movement in the dark. *I suppose we can't say where we are.*

This realm is like a bubble, floating between the mortal and celestial worlds. A bubble that serves as a bridge. Perhaps if our discussion strays too close to our real lives, it breaks, and we fall back to wakefulness.

This sounds a very fragile bridge. I'm not sure I would pay the toll…

Dumai smiled. *We can keep testing its strength.* Her lips shaped the words in Seiikinese, but that was not the language in her dream. This was a language she had never learned. *I still wonder where in this wide world you are. If you feel the same disturbances, the same strangeness.*

What do you mean?

You must have seen. The earth quaked, and groundwater boiled, and the sun hid its light for almost a year.

If you don't know why that happened, you must be very far away. It was a fire mountain that caused all of it. The other presence faded, then strengthened again. *I feel our rickety bridge straining. Let's not speak of such things. How is it we can meet in dreams?*

I would say the gods allowed it, but you claimed not to have gods. Who is it that you praise, that rules you?

A warrior. Dumai sensed a sudden reserve, shot with curiosity. *You spoke of magic. Are you ... a sorcerer?*

Only a dreamer. Feeling herself sink too deep, she reached for her bedding and grasped it until her hand ached. *This bridge must have formed for a reason.*

Perhaps we're just here to comfort each other. Even if this is a trick – or if I'm only talking to myself – it's nice to be less alone in the dark. Silence. *I don't know what to call you. Could you tell me your name?*

I think it will separate us again.

Let's try. We can find our way back to one another.

Dumai is my name. And yours?

I am—

At once, the connexion unravelled, and Dumai fell headlong from the dream, so cold her teeth chattered. She huddled closer to the stove, wishing she could speak to the Grand Empress. Her grandmother might know how to make sense of this.

It took mental strength to sustain that dream, and her body was drained from swimming. This time, she let herself descend into a heavy slumber.

Halfway through the night, she stirred, thinking of a smile that curved like a blade. Her hand slid to the ache between her thighs. In the loose, warm hold of sleep, she imagined that it was someone else touching her.

Have you lost your senses?

She sat up with a sharp intake of breath, heart dancing in her chest. This time, the voice in her head was her own: *Are you so hungry for touch that you would crave it from a hunter?*

****

She stole to the bathhouse before dawn to wash, dressing in the garments that had been sent from the palace – a white tunic under a pale blue jacket, trousers of soft yellow silk that sat high on her waist. (The flight had creased her own clothes beyond saving.) She combed her hair, smoothing it several times, frowning uncertainly. She looked down and saw two drops of blood on the floor.

A breath of pure relief escaped her. That was why she had yearned in the dark. She often felt soft ripples of desire on her first day.

It was nothing to do with Kuposa pa Nikeya.

One of the worshippers brought her bloodleaf. *No more.* Dumai rolled it into a stopper. *No more.*

She faced her reflection. Her father had told her not to take a crown to Sepul – only a modest headpiece and his Privy Seal. She tucked it into a sleeveless overcoat, fastened with a silver belt. Queen Arkoro had been generous to send clothes appropriate for a princess.

Kanifa took her to the palanquin at the top of the waterfall, where Nikeya waited on a horse, dressed in a fine pink coat. 'I don't recall inviting you, Lady Nikeya,' Dumai said irritably.

'Good morning to you, too, Princess.' Some of her hair was unbound, while the rest was rolled and braided over her scalp. 'Queen Arkoro has summoned all three dragonriders.'

'Why?'

'I have no idea, but let's consider it a blessing. I understand you aren't yet fluent in Sepuli,' Nikeya said. 'Fortunately, I am. I can serve as your interpreter.'

'Queen Arkoro will have her own.'

'Surely you need one as well, to ensure you don't blunder Seiiki into a political disaster. You may have learned to swim, Princess, but a fish in a pond does not know the sea.'

'This fish is weary of your unsolicited advice,' Dumai informed her, and climbed into the palanquin.

The journey was rocky at first. Once they had descended from the low mountains, Dumai was carried through the east gate of the city. Tucked into the palanquin, she watched through a tiny slot.

If anyone had told her that a city could shimmer like gold, she would have thought it a myth from the ground. Mozom Alph had long been celebrated for its artistry, but to behold its splendour – buildings so intricately worked, down to each tile on their roofs – was enough to render the heart still. It was a harbour on the Bay of Kamorthi, where stonemasons, goldsmiths and artists flocked, ornamenting all they touched.

Marble arches opened into sculpture gardens. White apricot and snowbell trees lined the streets. A monumental starwatch, designed by a Sepuli princess, marked the ancient cradle of the city.

The palanquin joined the carts, horses and crowds, bound for the cliff way that led to the palace. They crossed a channel of the River Yewuyta and passed a coastal market beside the Sundance Sea. In the distance, she glimpsed the Bay Legion, anchored in deeper waters – a navy of sailboats and ironclad spearships, for defence, exploration and commerce.

Through its wide fishnet of trade routes, like the Snow Road, the Queendom of Sepul reached all the way across the Abyss. One could buy from half the known world in this market. A handful of Seiikinese traders had risked the dangerous voyage, selling out of rowboats: amber and gold, woodwork, dark lacquerware inlaid with pearl mantle.

Dumai drank it all in. As the palanquin stopped for a procession of city guards on horseback, a group of seafarers caught her eye. Their clothes were cut in no style she recognised. One showed a silver bowl to a Sepuli woman, who nodded, reaching for her purse.

'Who do you think they are?' Dumai asked Kanifa, who rode beside her palanquin.

He looked. 'I'd say they're from over the Abyss.'

'Southerners,' Nikeya confirmed. 'An Ersyri prince sailed here long ago and married a Princess of Summer. Some Sepuli have since converted to his religion of light and mirrors.'

Dumai said, 'Queen Arkoro permits this?'

'Our gods have not been seen in centuries, Princess. People need something to believe in.'

One of the seafarers wore a medallion around her neck. It caught the sun as she laughed.

Mozom had been the original capital of Sepul, until a queen had borne four identical daughters. She had divided the peninsula between them, naming each territory for a season, and Mozom had become the Spring City.

Now the four had merged back into one, with a single Queen of Sepul, who resided in the Old Palace. White as bone, with layered roofs, it sprawled across a high cliff on the east side of the bay, commanding a view of both city and coast. Its main bridge crossed the River Yewuyta where it met the sea, forming a thousand-foot waterfall.

The building must have been adorned over centuries, every flying eave and pillar beautifully carved, the roof beams whittled into spines and decked with curving ribs. A gold sculpture of a Sepuli dragon defended its entrance, with a flowing beard and four long claws.

Dumai climbed from the palanquin, still marvelling at the palace, finding no end of intricacies. The spines and ribs must hearken back to the founding story of the Queendom of Sepul, which spoke of a dragon who had lost a bone during a transformation. The bone had turned into a small girl, who had spent twenty years following her creator, trying hundreds of tricks to catch her attention. When the dragon finally noticed her, they had claimed Sepul together, and since then, women had always ruled the peninsula, in deference to Queen Harkanar.

Three court ladies met them at the entrance, which was flanked by what Dumai soon realised were dragons' horns.

'Princess Dumai,' the middle woman said in Sepuli, offering a small bow. 'Welcome – welcome to the Golden City. Queen Arkoro awaits you in the Summer Garden.'

'I look forward to meeting her.'

The woman hesitated.

'The sea wind is so strong today. I've had to tidy my hair several times,' she said with a nervous laugh, gesturing at it. Her coif was sturdy and perfect, strung with loops of river pearls. 'Would you care to have yours combed, Princess, before you see Her Majesty?'

Nikeya covered her laugh with a cough. Dumai crushed a childish urge to step on her foot.

The palace was even more beautiful inside. Designs representing the seasons – autumn leaves, flowers, persimmon, evergreens – paid tribute to the Age of Four Queens. White dragons curled around the pillars. A stream of the Yewuyta purled along the corridors. Dumai allowed a servant to style her hair and reposition her gold headpiece, shaped like a leaping fish.

They followed the woman into a walled garden, where season trees were in yellow leaf.

'How?' Dumai said in surprise. 'It's winter.'

'Heated floors. They trick the trees,' the woman said, with pride. 'Kindly wait here,' she added to Kanifa and Nikeya. 'The Queen of Sepul will greet the Crown Princess of Seiiki.'

They lingered under a tree. Dumai continued along the warm path, where flowering shrubs spiced the air.

Queen Arkoro sat in a curtained pavilion, her ivory and black layers secured with a belt of gold openwork, circling a slim waist. Pearls frosted her crown, which had tall branches, like antlers. Her face was shaped like an ash leaf, wide cheekbones tapering into a pointed chin.

A strong-featured man was beside her, wearing a look of polite curiosity. From his shorter crown, he was her consort – brown of skin where she was pale, muscular where she was slight, gold drops in his earlobes. His trim moustache just touched the corners of his mouth.

'Princess Dumai,' she said in a soft voice. 'Please accept my apologies for not receiving you for so long. It has been necessary for me to spend many hours with my Council of Nobles.'

Dumai bowed. 'Your Majesty, I was content to wait at your pleasure – I know my arrival was unexpected. I pray the spirit in the bone is strong.'

'So it remains, and always will.' Queen Arkoro inclined her head. 'This is my consort, King Padar of Kawontay.' She placed a delicate hand on his. 'You speak Sepuli, then.'

'Not especially well, Your Majesty. Forgive me.'

'I do not know your language, either. How is your Lacustrine?'

'I write Lacustrine better than I speak it, but I should manage.'

'Lacustrine it shall be.'

Dumai nodded. She would not need Nikeya.

King Padar gave her a fleeting smile. 'Please, Your Highness, sit.' Dumai did. 'We are intrigued to meet you. Perhaps you would care for refreshment. Kelp tea is a speciality of Mozom Alph.'

'You are kind.'

A servant brought a dish of pressed sweets, shaped like shells, and served a pale tea, salting it for King Padar.

'I know you may wish to see proof that I am who I claim,' Dumai said. 'My father would have written to you in advance, but there was no time.'

'I received the letter you gave to my Royal Guard. Emperor Jorodu was clearly reluctant to explain your purpose here – for fear of interception, I assume – but he empowers you to speak on his behalf,' Queen Arkoro said. 'He also said you would carry his Privy Seal.'

Dumai presented it to her. The queen looked at it for some time, turning it with slender fingers.

'Thank you.' She handed it back. 'Perhaps you don't know, but we are distantly related.'

'I had no idea, Your Majesty.'

'Your paternal grandfather was a member of Clan Mithara. That line was founded by a Sepuli prince, who voyaged long ago to Seiiki. You are welcome here.'

'Thank you. I know there have been no official visits for several generations.'

'I do admit surprise at your arrival. We have traded, of course, but the House of Noziken has seemed content to keep to itself, by and large. When letters have come, they have been from an official named Kuposa pa Fotaja, the River Lord.'

'This River Lord must be a trusted counsellor,' King Padar remarked, with an arch of eyebrow that belied his words. 'We understand one of the riders who accompanied you here is also a Kuposa.'

Dumai glanced through the fine curtains at Nikeya, who was attempting to talk to Kanifa.

'Yes.' Dumai cleared her throat. 'I am certain that my father would have sent a delegation sooner, but without our dragons, it has been difficult to cross the Sundance Sea.'

Her palms grew slick. She had been briefly educated as a princess, not an ambassador.

'That has been true on our side, too,' Queen Arkoro said. 'But now your gods have woken.'

'So far, only one. Furtia Stormcaller. May I ask if they are rousing here?'

'Three emerged from waterfalls in the autumn,' King Padar said. 'Others, disturbed by divers and fishers, have chosen not to return to their slumber. Something has changed.'

'I may be able to find out what. Furtia has given us a dire warning,' Dumai said. 'I have come here to share it with you, Your Majesty – and to act on it, with your permission.'

Queen Arkoro narrowed her eyes a little. 'Then this warning affects Sepul?'

'I fear so.'

Dumai told them everything, from her first meeting with Furtia to the sinister black rocks.

'Furtia says she has sensed them here, too, and wishes to know their number,' she finished. The two royals had been silent throughout. 'She believes they will bring chaos and destruction.'

'The gods are said to speak in riddles, but that seems clear enough.' Queen Arkoro exchanged a look with her consort. 'Does the Stormcaller know where these rocks might be?'

'She did not specify, but those I saw in Seiiki were inside a fire mountain.'

It was a fire mountain that caused all of it, the voice in her dream had told her.

'There is one here that still erupts – Mount Yeltalay,' King Padar said. 'It lies to the east, in the Broken Valley.' He stroked his chin. 'The gods that woke this year spoke of a risen fire, too.'

'This mountain,' Dumai said. 'Has it stirred recently?'

'Last year. Not long after, the sun darkened, and since then all the seasons have been strange, even outside the palace. In some regions, the crops will not ripen. There have been rumours of a significant eruption across the Abyss,' he added. 'Perhaps all this is connected.'

I am coming to you, earth child. We must leave, Furtia said, startling Dumai. *It must be now.*

Queen Arkoro looked concerned. 'Are you well, Princess?'

'Yes,' Dumai said, lightheaded. 'Forgive me.' Her skin was cold. 'If these rocks can unnerve a god, I fear it bodes ill for us all, Your Majesty. I ask your leave to fly to the Broken Valley.'

'Even the Queen of Sepul cannot command a dragon. Furtia Stormcaller must go where she pleases,' came the reply. 'I think you have an affinity with her.'

Dumai slowly nodded. Queen Arkoro used her thumb to turn a gold ring on her finger.

'The Broken Valley steams and rattles. Foulness spits from the earth beneath it,' she continued. 'After the last groundshake, my grandmother forbade anyone from setting foot there.'

'I am willing to face danger.'

'So I see.' Queen Arkoro met her gaze. 'Your arrival here may cast diplomatic ripples, Princess Dumai. The last time a Seiikinese royal landed on our shores, she came with a ferocious thirst for power. Your visit may also raise questions within the House of Lakseng.'

'I understand. This is too sudden. If you wish, I will remain at the temple while Furtia searches.'

'I will not disrespect your bond by separating you.' She took a breath. 'You have my permission to go to the Broken Valley – but I will send two of our Sepuli dragons with you.'

She stopped. Nikeya had come to the pavilion.

'Princess,' she said, 'Furtia Stormcaller is outside the palace.'

Queen Arkoro considered Nikeya, her amber eyes difficult to read. 'You must be Lady Nikeya,' King Padar said as a servant poured him more kelp tea. 'Welcome to Mozom Alph.'

'Thank you, honoured king. I have long dreamed of seeing the Golden City.' Nikeya spoke in fluent Sepuli. 'Great queen, forgive my intrusion. Furtia Stormcaller is at your gates.'

Queen Arkoro raised her fine eyebrows. 'Mozom Alph must be astir,' King Padar said, sipping his tea.

'I believe it may be in uproar.'

'No dragon has flown here by daylight in centuries,' Queen Arkoro said, 'but they had to know at some point that their gods begin to wake.' She rose, her sleeves brushing the floor. 'Princess Dumai, time is clearly short. King Padar will escort you to the Broken Valley.'

'Thank you.' Dumai bowed to her. 'I am grateful for your hospitality, Your Majesty.'

To her surprise, Queen Arkoro came to her and took her by the arms. 'I would have a friend in Seiiki. Let us not be strangers again,' she said gently. 'Return here soon, so we might forge a long friendship between our houses. Farewell for now, bone of my bone.'

38

West

Dark iron came singing towards Wulf. He deflected it with his sword and swerved away as Regny hefted her shield at him. Her axe followed and caught his sleeve. They fought at the threshold of the queenswood, within sight of the castle, as snow drifted around them.

The day before, he had received a letter from his father, wishing him a safe voyage to Vattengard. He longed to visit Langarth, but there was no time. Soon the ships would leave.

Regny slammed the rim of her shield into his ribs, hard enough to bash the breath from him. 'Wake up.' Her cheeks held a flush from the cold. 'The Ments will not wait for you to blink the sleep from your eyes.'

'Do the Ments hit as hard as you?' he asked, winded.

'Does the sheep bite as deep as a bear?' She pointed her axe. 'They have not the teeth for it.'

Grimacing, he straightened, and they clashed across the clearing, trampling their own footprints. Regny always fought to win. Wulf could best her with a sword, but she swung an axe like it was part of her arm.

She thrived in these winter days. With paint under her eyes and snow in her hair, she was what he had always imagined an ice spirit to look like.

They had been training harder than ever. While Virtudom had been at peace for a long time, Bardholt had never fully trusted Heryon

Vattenvarg, and there had always been a chance that the Mentish nobles would finally mount a revolt against Hróthi rule. Both would be at the wedding.

Regny charged him with her shield. He hooked his boot behind her calf. She pitched into him, and they crashed into the snow, Regny with a blinding curse. Wulf wheezed his first laugh in days.

'You're learning.' Regny got her legs free. 'Did I not tell you the cold kills courtesy?'

'Aye.' He held his ribs. 'The world isn't as soft as the Saint teaches.'

'No.' She leaned over him, her damp hair tickling his cheek. 'But we are Hróthi. We are not soft.'

They were close enough for their breaths to smoke into one cloud. Remembering himself, Wulf shifted back and hitched up his gloves. Regny sat back in the snow.

'Do I have fleas?' she asked. 'Rotten teeth?'

He frowned at her. 'What?'

'Every time I come near, you recoil.' Her gaze was relentless. 'What the fuck is wrong with you?'

Wulf looked away. 'I can't know for sure.' He clasped his hands. 'I won't risk you, Regny.'

'You're a fool,' she said, low and cold. 'Do you mean to never touch anyone again – to fear your own body for the rest of your life?'

'If it means I never have to see anyone die like Eydag.' Resentment boiled in him. 'She was your friend. Do you even mourn her? What the fuck,' he said, 'is wrong with *you*, Regny?'

'Eydag is gone. I wept for her. But she is feasting in Halgalant now, at the Great Table.'

'Stop it. Stop pretending.'

'Screaming and beating my fists will not bring her back. Neither will your rage.'

Before Wulf could utter another word, she took his face in her bare hands and kissed him.

It was not a gentle kiss. Then again, Regny of Askrdal had only softened once that he recalled, the first time they had slept together, when neither of them had known what they were doing. She had been tender with him that night, and let him be tender to her in return.

Now she was full of hard resolve, as she was in all things. She tasted sharp and sweet, like lingonberry, and her hair smelled of fresh bread and snow. It swept him back to Eldyng, to that night she had kissed him under the sun, taking him by surprise, as she so often did.

Before he could stop himself, he wrapped an arm around her shoulder and reached under her loose hair, grasping her nape. She stroked from the small of his back, around his hips to the clasp of his belt, the heavy lilt of breath making him rise for her. Her thumb skimmed his jaw, and she nipped his bottom lip, drawing blood.

Regny was forbidden. Until this moment, Wulf had not thought he still wanted her. Anyone could find them here, report them to the king again, but now she was kneeling across his waist, and his lips were parting hers. The kiss deepened until he thought it would devour him.

She reached for his wrist, and he let her, expecting to be shown the way. Instead, she worked off his thick glove, clasping his fingers tight in hers before she led his hand into her shirt. He huffed as the warmth of her filled his palm, and at last, he found the will to break the kiss.

'Regny,' he said hoarsely, 'we agreed.'

'I know.' She gripped his chin. 'Let this serve as a reminder that I fear nothing. Not blood, not war, not a fucking plague – and not sullen boys who don't know how to love themselves.'

Wulf sank against her with a nod of defeat. Regny kissed him once more, then stood and brushed off her surcoat, leaving him sprawled in the snow.

'I'm going to hunt,' she said. 'See the physician, then return here to keep training. Thrit is leaving today.'

'Leaving,' Wulf said, still in a stupor. She eyed his straining trousers, and he cleared his throat. 'Why?'

'Ask him. I'm not his milk nurse.' Regny picked up her axe. 'Go. Forthard expects you.'

She strode away, towards her horse. Wulf let his head fall back into the snow and closed his eyes, his heart thrumping.

With the taste of steel and lingonberry on his lips, he walked alone to the castle infirmary and knocked on its studded door. A towhead in her fifties appeared, wearing an ivory kirtle over long black sleeves, and a leather belt with pouches and several loops for tools.

'Doctor Forthard,' Wulf said in an undertone. 'The king asked me to see you.'

Her expression changed. 'Master Glenn.' She stood aside. 'Thank you for coming.' He stepped into the light of a roaring fire. 'This is my new assistant, Mastress Bourn.'

The assistant in question was tall and slim, high of cheek, with skin of a cool light brown and thick hair that fell in black waves to their shoulders. 'Good day, Master Glenn,' they said. 'Please, make yourself comfortable.' Pause. 'Did you have a mishap?'

'Pardon?'

'Your lip.'

Wulf dabbed it, finding it swollen. 'Ah, nothing,' he said. 'I was riding. A low branch.'

Their deep grey eyes twinkled. 'I see.'

While the two physicians donned thick gloves, Wulf laid his weapons on the floor and hefted off his mail and wools. Once he was down to his undershorts, Forthard had him sit on a covered bench.

'King Bardholt has told us about the sickness, in confidence,' she said. 'An afflicted person touched you. Is that right?'

'Yes.'

'What had you eaten and drunk beforehand?'

Wulf raided his memory. 'Salted herring with garlic. A bite of black bread. I think that's it,' he said. 'I'd not much appetite that day.'

'Garlic is known for its curative properties,' Bourn mused. 'Yet I suppose your fellow retainers ate the same, and all three perished.' Wulf bobbed a stiff nod. 'May they rest well.'

'Tell us everything you saw,' Forthard said. 'Everything that happened on the ship.' By the time he finished, her frown had deepened considerably. 'It may be that the Saint protected you. It may be that there is another reason.'

'If so, we could use the knowledge to help others,' Bourn said.

'Yes. May I draw some of your blood, Master Glenn?'

Wulf held out an arm. 'Anything to stop this sickness.'

'Thank you.'

Forthard used a sharp little tool to draw blood from his elbow, then examined his eyes and took a scraping from his tongue. After, she had him spit into one jar and pass water in another. While Bourn cleaned the cut, Forthard consulted a chart depicting a rainbow of flasks. (Wulf wondered what poor bastard had ever pissed lilac.) Once they had everything, Bourn started to rinse their tools with vinegar.

'Thank you, Master Glenn,' they said. 'You may go. Take care not to ride into any more branches.'

'Aye, I'll try.'

By the time Wulf was back outside, the sun had risen, and the smell of baking wastel filled the corridors. He glanced up at the tower where Glorian bided, seeing no face at the window.

In the clearing, Thrit was sparring with Karlsten while Sauma sat on a trunk, roasting a skinned rabbit over a fire. Despite the cold, both fighters were shirtless. Unusually for a housecarl, Karlsten wielded a northern Inysh greatsword, showing off the strength in his arms.

Thrit favoured the bearded axe, like the king, but his limber build lent itself to skin fighting as well. He swung into a hard kick, and Karlsten crashed to the ground.

'Damn you to the fire.' He grasped his chest with a chuckle. 'What the fuck was that?'

'The unexpected, Karl. Expect it.' Thrit flipped his axe to his other hand. 'The Ments might surprise you, too.'

'I doubt it.' Karlsten spotted Wulf, and his face hardened. 'Still alive, Wulf?'

Thrit sighed. 'Saint's tooth, Karl.'

'Eydag was my sister. She's dead, and he isn't,' Karlsten sneered. 'Care to explain it, Thrit?'

'Enough, Karlsten. Only the Saint chooses who will live and who will die,' Sauma said. 'You should respect his judgement.' She rose and drew her sword. 'I'll fight. Watch the fire, will you, Wulf?'

Wulf took her place on the log. Thrit came to sit beside him, hair scraped into a knot. Sweat gleamed on his river-gold skin, the clean lines of his chest and waist.

'Ignore him,' he said.

'I've been ignoring him for years.' Wulf turned the spit. 'Regny says you're leaving.'

'Aye, to fetch my mother and grandparents to Eldyng. Sauma and Karl are coming with me.' Thrit wiped his face with his shirt. 'Bardholt gave me leave, as they live close to the Barrowmark. I want them far away from this sickness.' Sauma parried as Karlsten slashed his sword at her. 'If the Saint is good, I'll be able to see the end of the wedding.'

'I wish I could lend you whatever shield the Saint gave me.'

'I'll be fine. Nonetheless, I appreciate your concern.' Thrit took out his wineskin. 'What did the physicians say?'

'Not much. They made me piss into a flask.'

Thrit snorted. As he opened the wineskin, he raised his eyebrows. 'She's up early.'

Wulf followed his line of sight to see four people approaching from the castle, led by none other than the Crown Princess of Inys.

Glorian walked into the clearing, dressed in a heavy green cloak. 'Good morning. Forgive me for disturbing you,' she said in Hróthi. They all knelt. 'I heard fighting and wondered if we were being raided.'

'No, Highness – far more serious. We're preparing for a wedding.' Thrit winked. 'Dangerous affairs.'

Glorian laughed. 'Indeed. Easier to escape a battle.' She motioned for them to stand. 'Speaking of which, Master Glenn promised me a spar when we last spoke. Would now suit?'

Wulf regarded her. From her tone, he might never have found her alone and shaken in the dark, but her eyes told a different story, as did the tiny crease between her brows.

'Highness,' Sauma said, hesitant, 'we should not raise our blades to the bone of the Saint.'

'I think it may be forbidden,' Thrit mused.

'I unforbid it.' Glorian never took her eyes off Wulf. 'Will you oblige me, Master Glenn?'

After a moment, he nodded. 'Highness.'

Thrit offered him a sword, which he took. As he walked towards Glorian, he glanced at her ladies. Two were unfamiliar, but the third he did remember, from their childhood – a young woman of short stature, just shy of four feet, with an olive complexion and thick dark hair.

'I believe you know Julain,' Glorian said. 'May I introduce Adeliza and Lady Helisent?'

Wulf inclined his head. Adeliza looked away, a blush climbing into her apple cheeks.

'It's been a long time, my lady,' he said to Julain Crest, who smiled. 'I heard of your betrothal to Lord Osbert Combe – my brother, Roland, speaks highly of him. I wish you joy.'

'Thank you. It's good to see you, Wulf,' Julain said warmly. 'Are the Barons Glenn well?'

'I fear you'd know better than I do. I haven't had time to visit.'

'Oh, what a shame.'

Lady Helisent was looking knives at him. He took her in – eyes and skin of a deep brown, hair that sprang in tiny curls around a slender face – and suddenly remembered her. The Dowager Earl of Goldenbirch had once brought his daughter on a visit to Langarth.

Her family had guarded the south of the haithwood since the days of the Saint. If anyone knew his past, she did.

Glorian took off her cloak. Beneath, she wore a white linen shirt and breeches tucked into fur boots. As Sauma handed her a steel buckler, Helisent passed Wulf, stopping to grip his elbow.

'Give her so much as a scratch,' she said under her breath, 'and you'll regret it, witchling.'

She let go of him and followed the other two. He clenched his jaw. *So much for Saint-touched.*

Glorian walked with him into the middle of the clearing. Wulf dredged up a smile. 'Go easy on me,' he said, so only she could hear.

This close, he saw how tired she looked, but she returned his smile. 'I will endeavour to be gentle.' She drew the fine blade her father had given her. 'You have my word.'

She used her left hand, like him. Wulf nodded, and the spar began.

It was clear from the first strike that she was far better than Wulf had imagined. Though her blows lacked heft, they were precise, her form and footwork sure.

She moved far more like a Hróthi housecarl than an Inysh knight. Small wonder. Bardholt would only have trusted one of his own warriors to instruct his daughter in swordplay.

Unlike a housecarl, a princess could not devote every day of her life to the blade. She had not faced years of ruthless training in the wilds of Fellsgerd – so Wulf did see it coming when her sword clipped his mail, the first time. The shine in her eyes made it worthwhile.

'Mind you don't nick his throat, Highness,' Karlsten said flatly. 'What a shame that would be.'

Glorian glanced at him. 'Your care for your lithsman is admirable,' she said. 'I'll be sure not to damage him.'

Karlsten just folded his arms. Glorian gave her sword a very Inysh twirl, the flourish of a knight – Thrit laughed in surprise – before she thrust at Wulf again, and their steel clashed, bright and sharp.

Sparring with her was an unexpected joy. When she fought, she was the girl who had raced with him through the plum orchards, wild and free and full of mirth. The second time she hit him, with the buckler, it did catch him off his guard, a steel punch to the shoulder.

Glorian grinned. Wulf smiled and fought back a little harder, giving her a challenge. She rose to it. He forgot everyone but her, and their dance.

At last, he let her tap his thigh with the blade, and the others broke into applause Wulf knew was sincere. Glorian breathed in white gusts. 'Thank you,' she said, high colour in her cheeks. 'It's been some time since Mother let me fight.'

'I assume Her Grace isn't to know about this.'

'Not unless you'd like to spend a few days in the dungeon,' Glorian said lightly. 'Fear not. She won't hear it from me.' She stepped back. 'Good day, Master Glenn.'

'Highness.'

Sauma took the buckler from her. Glorian sheathed her sword and walked away, her ladies following. 'What was that about?' Thrit wondered aloud.

'I believe I know.'

They looked back. Regny had emerged from the woods, another rabbit slung over her shoulder. She joined them in the clearing and watched Glorian return to the castle.

'After sixteen years,' she said, 'we are seeing Glorian Óthling take her first steps as a queen.'

****

As the royal wedding approached, Glorian could taste midwinter the way others smelled it – the fresh, crisp taste of skethra, the air washing itself clean. She hoped it would flush the dust from the sun.

Time was running out. As soon as the Feast of High Winter came, it would be the year she turned seventeen, and every day would take her closer to her own inevitable marriage. She would wear a small gold shackle and find herself sharing a bed with a stranger.

The thought tightened her ribs as she sat in her Yscali lesson, trying to listen. She had stayed up for most of the night, not sure whether she wanted to risk another chilling dream.

In sixteen years, she had never had the same dream more than once. Not until this figure had appeared. She could ask a sanctarian if they were visions from the Saint, but Helisent had sown a seed.

Inys had been built on strangeness and wild things. Surely they must steal through the foundations, like weeds between cobblestones.

She shook herself. Helisent might hold to the old northern tales, but a princess could not.

Wulf and his lith trained in the queenswood every day, starting at dawn. She could see them from her window. At noon, he would always go to Blair Lake, and today she meant to join him. Her father had given her the confidence to wander the grounds again.

'I need a walk,' she told Adela, once her lesson ended. 'I won't be long.'

'Oh, Glorian, it's so cold today.'

'I like the cold.' Glorian drew up her hood. 'It's all right. You stay indoors and keep warm.'

Adela was only too pleased to obey. With her guards a short distance away, Glorian left the castle walls.

Wulf stood alone at the lakeside. Seeing a figure, her guards' stances changed. 'Peace,' Glorian said. The wind teased a few strands of hair from her circlet. 'It's only Master Glenn.'

He was flicking stones across the lake. They made a silvery, juddering din as they skittered over brittle ice. Hearing her footsteps, he turned, one hand snapping to his sax.

'Glorian,' he said, letting go of it at once.

'Are you so eager for another fight, Wulf?'

'Forgive me. I didn't realise you walked here.'

'Well, now you know, you must leave,' she said, keeping a perfectly straight face. 'I require at least a league around my royal person at all times.' He blinked. 'I'm only teasing, Wulf.'

'Ah. Sorry.' He rewarded her with a rare smile. 'Thrit's always telling me I'm too serious.'

Glorian smiled back. 'Father loves to skim stones,' she said. 'He told me the Hróthi used to live in terror of the frozen lakes, believing cruel spirits lurked under the ice. Of course, they're far less frightened now.'

'Aye. On dark and chilly mornings, the king likes nothing better than to sweat in the stovehouse, then have us break a hole in the ice so he can swim. Bravest of all of us, as always.'

'I miss the stovehouses.'

'You should build one here.' Wulf flipped the stone. 'Do you know why the lakes were feared, in particular?'

'Tell me.'

His gaze went distant.

'In winter, when the ice thickens and cracks, it makes … the most terrible sound,' he said. 'It's like being underwater, hearing your own heart and blood. The roar when you hold a cup to your ear.' His throat shifted. 'I think it's the song of the womb. A sound we know before we breathe, before words come to us. Some find it beautiful, but I see why the Hróthi used to fear it. I suppose it's why they started to imagine spirits in the first place. When the ice splits over and over, it sounds like a fist knocking on a door, asking to be let free.'

Glorian looked across the lake, huddling deeper into her cloak.

'To calm the spirits, the Hróthi would sing back to the ice,' Wulf said. 'Herders still use those lullabies to get their animals back from the pastures – just without the words.'

For the first time, Glorian wondered about the lullaby her father sang for her.

The wind skirled around them. 'A turn?' Wulf offered the stone. 'See if your throw is as strong as your swordplay.'

'You're flattering me.' Glorian took it. 'A fight with me is never fair.'

'True, but you move well. Better than—'

He stopped himself. 'Better than you expected?' Glorian finished, grinning. 'I did tell you I could fight.'

'You did.'

She drew back her arm and hurled the stone. It made a fine clangour on the ice, then a sound like a chirping bird. Their smiles widened. There was something joyous in that clatter.

'There. No spirits.' Glorian looked up at him. 'Wulf, I want to apologise for how I spoke to you, that evening.'

'You seemed upset. Are you all right?'

She wished she could tell him the truth. The temptation to open her heart to him – her fears, her resentment, everything – was almost too much to resist.

'I am. Shall we walk by the trees?' she asked him. 'The queenswood is lovely in winter.'

They trudged through the deep snow beside the oaks and pines, followed at a distance by her guards. 'I understand you won't be at the wedding,' Wulf said.

'The heir must be in Inys if the queen is not. It's for the best,' Glorian said, with false conviction. 'I was supposed to marry Lord Magnaust, you see, until Princess Idrega stepped in.'

'Really?'

'Yes.' When he frowned, she said, 'Is it so funny to imagine me with a companion?'

'No, not at all. I just didn't know royals married so early.'

'We don't, usually. My grandmother was in her thirties. It's only in times of need, when an heir becomes more important.'

'Ah.' Wulf glanced at her. 'Sixteen is very young to know if you love someone.'

'Love has no part in it for us.'

'Your parents love each other. King Bardholt never stops talking about Queen Sabran.'

'Yes, that's true. They were fortunate.'

They stopped when a man emerged from the woods, making her body stiffen, her heart hammer. Wulf reached for both his axe and her, as if to draw her behind him.

'It's all right,' Glorian said, relaxing. 'It's only Lord Robart.'

The Lord Chancellor came towards them. Snow crusted his hair and shoulders. 'Lady Glorian.' He bowed, his cheeks ruddy from the chill. 'And Master Glenn, I believe.'

He spoke with a similar burr to Wulf, though it came less from the throat than the tongue. 'Good morrow, Lord Robart,' Glorian said. Wulf released her. 'I trust you are having a pleasant day.'

She had not often spoken to the councillors individually, but Lord Robart had always been kind to her. 'Very much. My apologies for startling you,' he said. 'I like to take short turns among the trees. They clear my mind.' His smile was brief. 'Forgive me, but I was just on my way to a meeting of the Virtues Council. I shan't keep you.'

He walked on. 'Have you met Lord Robart before, then?' Glorian asked Wulf. 'He recognised you.'

'Aye. He's my father's liege.' Wulf looked troubled. 'That's the second council meeting today.'

'I think we both know why.' Glorian glanced after Lord Robart, then said: 'Wulf, I must ask. Is there a sickness in Hróth?' He tensed. 'My father has ordered you not to speak of it.'

'Don't ask me to break my oath to him, Glorian.'

'I never would.'

They walked in silence for a time, a silence Glorian filled with imaginings. If her father had sworn his retainers to secrecy, the sickness must be unlike anything Hróth had seen before. She glanced at Wulf, who looked troubled.

'Helisent told me about your past,' she said. 'About the haithwood.' A muscle started in his cheek. 'I have seen nothing but gentleness and courtesy from you, Wulf. I want you to know I'm not scared of you. When I am queen, no one will show you disfavour.'

His eyes met hers, dark and wary. 'Do you not fear the ways of heathens, Highness?'

'Why should I think you a heathen?' she asked. 'I see a patron brooch. I see a virtuous man, a good man.'

Some of the heaviness lifted from his features. 'You're kind,' he said. 'Glorian, forgive me – it's time for me to guard your father.' He stopped and turned to face her. 'I suppose we won't meet again before I sail for Vattengard.'

'No.' She made herself smile. 'Enjoy the wedding, Wulf. May the winds carry you well.'

'Your Highness.'

He pressed his fist to his chest and walked away, the braided hem of his cloak gathering snow. Glorian continued along the path, her boots crunching through deeper, untouched drifts.

He was gone. The chance to unburden her soul had slipped like thaw between her fingers.

She walked until her legs ached, out to the old marcher oak on the western edge of the queenswood, where snow dusted a scattering of withered leaves. Among them, she spotted an oak gall, one that must have fallen late. Intrigued, she used one of her bone needles to work it open, hoping for a bumblebee.

What lay coiled within was a brandling worm.

It was curled around the dead white grub that had been forming in the gall. As Glorian stared at it, it unwound from the corpse and slunk over her knuckles. Sickness filled her, as it had once before. She breathed out in rushes. The thing emerged, hungry and blind.

Her knees hit the ground, and then her palms. She was aware of her guards running to her, calling out, before she fainted into the snow.

39

East

It took most of the day to reach the Broken Valley. Furtia flew after King Padar, who rode one of a pair of dragons, both with scales like polished iron. He carried a staff of pure dragonbone, which attracted wisps of cloud and marked him as a member of the House of Kozol.

They followed the coast for a time. Only when Dumai could see the eastern end of the peninsula, where it met the Empire of the Twelve Lakes, did the three dragons turn inland, cloaking themselves in cloud.

'Aren't you glad you came with us, Lady Nikeya?' Dumai called over the wind.

Nikeya coughed hard before replying. Her nose was pink where she had staunched a bleed.

'Delighted, Princess,' she said with a weak laugh, shuddering in her bearskin. 'Flight is so refreshing.'

Dumai managed to refrain from needling her again. For once, she looked too pitiful.

In the cloud, it was hard to see their own hands, let alone the queendom far below. Only when they soared over a pine forest did the dragons shake the clouds off, leaving their riders cold and soaked. Dumai shuttered her eyes against the low bronze sun.

I sense the risen fire.

As Dumai leaned out to touch her scales, Kanifa tightened his hold on their rope. *I feel nothing, great one.*

You are not a dragon, earth child.

I do see something. Strands of damp hair snapped at her face. *That must be the place we seek.*

Mount Yeltalay shouldered up from a great swathe of cloud, flanked by hills and shallow mountains. The dragons landed before they could enter it. As they exchanged rumbles, Dumai slid from the saddle and held a sleeve to her nose. The rotten smell was terrible – the stench that had clung to her clothing for hours after she had seen the boulders in Seiiki.

'Here,' Furtia hissed aloud.

'Here,' the Sepuli dragons agreed in unison.

King Padar dismounted with caution, the bone staff in a holder on his belt. He had exchanged his crown for a gilded helmet, bearing the crest of the House of Kozol. After judging the damage to his drenched overcoat, he led them to a tall stone gateway, etched with Sepuli and Lacustrine characters that warned of death and poison. They could just see the tip of the mountain from this low viewpoint, wearing a tattered hood of snow.

'There should be guards here.' His gaze darted, and his hand went to his dagger. 'Be mindful, Princess Dumai. There are pools of mud and water that will boil skin from bone.'

Nikeya coughed, still ashen. 'How exciting.'

Kanifa drew his sword. Dumai wished she had her own, not knowing what she would use it against. The dragons parted around the gateway, floating a short way off the ground.

Every tree they passed was dead. Steam fumed from simmering caul-drons and bloody cracks in the slopes, forming the thick white roof that Dumai had mistaken for cloud. Sculptures were hewn throughout the valley, seeming to sweat in the warmth, the rock holding a stain like rust. The dragons flinched irritably from the steam, keeping their heads down while trying not to touch the valley. Dumai reached up to place a hand on Furtia.

It's only steam, she said. *No water can harm you, great one.*

Water turned by tainted fire.

They trod with care into the soupy foothills of Mount Yeltalay. Houses rotted on tall stilts, while towers had crumbled into heaps of stone, thick with yellow moss.

A rickety boardwalk greeted them, winding through the mist, into the ruins of a settlement. King Padar tested it underfoot before he put his weight on it. Dumai followed him.

'This was an outpost,' he said. 'People lived here for decades, to broaden their knowledge of the world – alchemists, metalsmiths, skywatchers.' He frowned at a large bronze urn, dulled by mud. 'That is a Lacustrine instrument, for measuring the tremors in the ground. They must have left in a hurry, to have abandoned an object of such value.'

Dumai eyed it. 'What drew them to this place?'

'They saw the earth was open here and came to hear its deep secrets.'

'And smell them.' Kanifa watched the steam rise. 'I'm not sure I could stand these fumes.'

'Listening to the earth sounds like Northern oddness,' Nikeya said hoarsely. 'I hear they have conversations with ice.'

'They did once,' King Padar agreed. 'Now they praise a warrior.'

'You seem half a warrior yourself, good king, traipsing through dangerous valleys with strangers.'

'I had another life before I wore a crown.' He glanced back at Dumai. 'Much like you, Princess.'

They kept going, walking in the dragons' shadows. Behind the base of a fallen tower, Dumai spotted a cave. Clearing the trailing moss from its mouth, she saw a faded mural of a peak brimming with fire, and people reaching for the stars.

A yelp pulled her attention away. Nikeya had put her boot straight through the ground. She lurched away from the scalding pool beneath, losing her footing.

'Nikeya,' Dumai said, starting towards her.

'I'm fine.' Nikeya caught her breath. 'Stay there.'

Kanifa stretched out a hand for hers. Nikeya grasped it and let him drag her away from the pool.

'Come to the boardwalk,' King Padar said, beckoning. 'The Broken Valley is fragile. If you had slipped into that pool, there would have been nothing left to send back to Seiiki.'

Dumai gave Nikeya her flask before she followed him. For once, the Lady of Faces was silent. Her hands shook as she drank.

The sun had gone down, making the fog much harder to cross. Furtia raised her head, and her crest shone like a clear full moon; the Sepuli dragons did the same.

King Padar stopped where the boardwalk did. When Dumai saw the reason it had buckled, she took a careful step forward, so she could see over the edge, to where the earth had yawned wide. Furtia bared her teeth, eyes wildening.

Too many.

Dumai stared into the rift. Inside, pitted boulders were clustered together, leaking molten lava through their cracks, rattling. Not one small clutch this time, but hundreds. King Padar knelt beside her, the glow catching in his eyes.

What are they?

Twistings of fire and earth. Furtia hissed. *They cannot be calmed now. The sky will burn . . .*

Something broke through the nearest rock, cracking its dark crust.

'Princess Dumai,' King Padar said, his voice calm, 'go with the Stormcaller back to Seiiki, to warn them. I must fly to Her Majesty.' He looked at her sidelong. 'I fear we are too late to stop whatever is about to happen.'

'Yes.' Dumai became distantly aware that she was trembling. 'Good luck, King Padar.'

'And to you.'

A tail with a ridge of spines curled through the rock. As she turned, King Padar caught her sleeve. 'There's a Lacustrine alchemist – Kiprun of Brakwa,' he said. 'Kiprun will know how.'

A thrum and rumble made them both look up, Dumai with a heartbeat like a swallowed bird. She knew to fear any unexpected sound from a mountain. At once, she was back at the temple, watching a snowslide rip down the first peak, praying it would miss the village.

Rocks clattered down the slopes, jolting her back to the present. At first, she thought Mount Yeltalay would erupt – until something moved in the steam, a vast and hulking shape her mind refused to understand. Reeking black smoke threaded through the greyness.

Suddenly she was staring into eyes like two great braziers, disembodied by the murk. Dread bound her limbs. She was no longer aware of anything but herself and the beast.

This is the sire. From beneath the mantle. Furtia roared at it. *Too strong to fight alone.*

One of the Sepuli dragons came for the king. He lunged for the saddle rope and was gone. Kanifa spaded Dumai to her feet, and they stumbled towards Furtia, pulling Nikeya with them.

Behind them, the creature threw its jaws open. The boardwalk started to burn, and every boulder cracked, turning the valley to a furnace, as if the very bedrock of the world had broken.

40

West

They thought she had sheepsbane at first, from the blood-drinking ticks that lurked in the Fells. Then it was the throttle – except she had no soreness in her throat, no cough. Sometimes she was hot, and sometimes she was terribly cold. Doctor Forthard settled on winter gripe.

Time became shapeless and strange. Her ladies were barred from her chamber. Thanks to the spyhole, she knew why.

At last, she woke to see her father on the edge of her bed, dressed for a ride, cooling her brow with a damp cloth. The ruddy glow from the fire cast half of his face in shadow.

'Father,' she said, 'you shouldn't.'

'I had winter gripe as a child. It doesn't come back.'

'What if it isn't winter gripe?'

In firelight, his eyes were more amber than hazel, like those of a hawk. 'What else could it be?'

Glorian judged his expression. He would sooner hear a lie than talk to her about the sickness.

'I don't know,' she said.

'Then let us trust in the physician.'

He dabbed her cheeks. After a time, he returned the cloth to the ice basin, and a servant took it away.

'Glorian,' he said, 'do you know what day it is?' She shook her head, setting off a dull throb in her temples. 'The *Conviction* leaves today. Your mother and I set out at sunrise for the royal wedding. The Virtues Council stands ready to keep the queendom strong, as it has whenever your mother has visited Hróth. You need not fear.'

'I'll be all right, Father.'

'I never doubted it.' He stroked her hair. 'Time always passes too quickly while I'm here, doesn't it?'

Sadness hooded his eyes. She wanted so much to prove she was brave, but the fever had left her weak as a mayfly.

'I wish we could always be together, Papa,' she whispered. 'All of us.' He leaned closer to hear. 'That you never had to leave again.'

'I wish the same.' His callused hands clasped one of hers. 'I make you this promise. One day, when you give your throne to your own daughter, when your mother and I have white hair and wrinkles, we shall all live in Hróth together. Every winter, we will watch the sky lights, and every summer, we will dance and laugh under the midnight sun.'

'Truly?'

'My solemn oath.'

Glorian nodded, tears prickling. 'I'd like that,' she said. 'I'd like that more than anything.'

'Then let it be our dream.' His smile creased his eyes. 'For now, I will see you in the summer, dróterning.'

Mustering her strength, Glorian shifted on to her elbows. Her father drew her into his arms, and she burrowed into his embrace, the fur of his collar tickling her cheek.

'I love you, Papa.'

'And I you.' He planted a kiss on the top of her head. 'Look after my heart. Rest, Glorian. Be strong.'

He released her back into the pillows and left. Unexpectedly, Queen Sabran took his place.

'Glorian, are you awake?'

She tried to prop herself back up. 'Yes, Mother.'

Queen Sabran came to stand a short way from the bed. 'I came to bid you farewell.' Her gold crown shone in the firelight. 'I trust you are feeling better.'

'Yes, thank you.'

'Good.' Queen Sabran looked down at her gloved hands. 'Glorian, this is the first time I will be leaving you for so long. The Virtues Council has Inysh affairs under control, but should you need me, you may write. Give your letter to Lord Robart.'

'I'll be fine, Mother. You've left me here many times before.'

'Times have changed.'

She sat on the chest at the end of the bed and gazed into the flames.

'I know I have been unfeeling to you. All your life,' she said. Glorian listened. 'It is because I care, not because I do not. No one taught me how to be a mother, or a queen. I have only tried to armour you. The crown does not show mercy. It is cruel. You must have iron in your bones, as the Hróthi say, to stop yourself buckling under its weight.'

The fire crackled.

'I am cold, too. Cold to my blood,' Queen Sabran said, low enough that Glorian only just heard. 'I felt the same cold after the Dreadmount opened, though I took pains to conceal it. I have had dreams that seem as real as if I were awake. I have heard a voice in the night.'

'So have I,' Glorian whispered.

'What do you see, when you hear the voice?'

'I think I remember … a shape, like a person.'

'It will speak to you. You will not always understand.'

'Who is it, Mother?'

For the first time, Glorian thought she glimpsed a flicker of disquiet in those green eyes.

'I believe it is the Saint,' her mother said, 'but he speaks to us in mysterious ways. For me, the figure was a woman, who I believe was my higher self, the part of me that will rise to Halgalant. Sometimes there was just a voice. It allowed me to converse with the divine. Through those dreams, the Saint consoled and guided me, reminding me I was never alone.'

'You don't still have them?'

'I learned how to control when they come. When I return from Vattengard, I will teach you, as best I can. In the meantime, you must speak of these dreams to no one, Glorian. Some, in their ignorance, would see them as proof of witchcraft or madness.'

A smart knock interrupted them. 'Your Grace,' a muffled voice said, 'it's time to leave.'

Queen Sabran stood. 'Be well,' she said. 'Florell will stay here to help you.'

'Are you sure, Mother?' Glorian said, surprised. 'Florell is your closest friend.'

'I have Nyrun and Liuma. Florell knows you best. I trust her with you.' Her face was back to pale stone. 'Farewell, daughter. May the Saint, in his kindness, keep you safe.'

Glorian tried to find the words she wanted to express. *I will make you proud. I am afraid. I love you, even if I do not think you love me half as much. I will never treat my daughter the way you have treated me.*

'Goodbye, Mother,' was all she did say. 'I bid you a safe voyage. Please send my good wishes to Lord Magnaust and Princess Idrega.'

'I will.'

Queen Sabran turned away. Glorian found a deep well of courage and said, 'I will be a good queen.'

Her mother stopped.

'You think me weak,' Glorian said, willing her voice not to quake. 'You always have – but I know whose bone and blood I am. I am the chosen of the Saint, the fruit of his unending vine, the iron of the eversnow. I am the daughter of Sabran the Ambitious and the Hammer of the North, and I will rule this realm without fear. My reign will be remembered for centuries to come.' She let the words soak through the silence, then said, 'I am enough.'

For a very long time, Queen Sabran said nothing. Her expression was impossible to read.

'Belief is only the first step,' she said, very softly. 'Start forging your armour, Glorian. You will need it.'

After she left, Glorian rose for the first time in days, and went to the window. The last she saw of her parents was two figures riding into the mist.

****

The *Conviction*, white from prow to stern, its planks like so many stacked ribs. The most impressive longship in the Inysh fleet, a wedding gift from a king to his queen. It carved its way through the grey waters of the Ashen Sea, flying the ensigns of Inys and Hróth.

Unlike most Hróthi ships, the *Conviction* had a deckhouse at its stern. Inside, Sabran Berethnet curled deeper into the furs on the bed, the cold gathering on her like frost on grass.

Bardholt returned from his walk on the deck, snow in his hair. Sabran watched him undress. Decades after his last battle, he still had the build of a warrior. Naked, he lay beside her and slipped a hand beneath the furs, finding her thigh. He was always warm as a coal.

'Has the chill not passed, sweetheart?'

'It will.'

Sabran tucked her head under his chin, tracing the old scars on his chest, which was still firm and muscular. He ran his fingers through her hair with the tenderness he reserved for his family.

Bardholt had bared his whole self to her. She knew every one of his sins from the war, the evils committed against him, the nightmares that drenched him in sweat. In return, she had told him about her leaden days, the days when she felt desolate without obvious cause.

Yet she had never found the mettle to tell him of the chilling dreams, the ones that had afflicted her for years, until they frightened her enough that she had locked the door. She had thought Bardholt a heathen once, all while she had nights when she was colder than an ice spirit, hearing voices in her head.

'Is the fog still thick?' she asked him in Hróthi.

'Heavier than ever.' He wrapped an arm around her. 'Fear not. We've left in good time.'

It would still take more than a week to reach Vattengard. Bardholt had described it as a bleak fortress, leering at the Ments from across the Ashen Sea. Decades after seizing a realm for his family, Heryon Vattenvarg hungered for more. Magnaust was a proud fool – a Vetalda princess was too good for him – but Idrega was three years his senior, and clever, like her grandmother. If anyone could keep the Vatten in line, she could.

Now more than ever, the Chainmail of Virtudom had to hold strong. Clan Vatten had to remain loyal, and the Ments had to remain quiet. Rozaria Vetalda knew this, too. She had offered up the relative she thought would strengthen the links best, and Sabran had offered hers in return.

She had yet to tell Bardholt. He wanted Glorian to marry a Hróthi – he trusted his friends from the war and their heirs – but the Yscals had stood with Inys for centuries. Glorian would marry Therico, Magnaust would marry Idrega, and Virtudom would be safe.

She would tell him in Vattengard. He would be crestfallen, but she would make him see things her way, as she always did.

Bardholt was falling asleep beside her. His gold love-knot ring was polished, as always. 'I told Glorian she could write,' she said, making him stir. 'If she needed my counsel.'

'I am sure she took heart in that.'

'Not just heart. Courage,' Sabran said, very softly. 'She told me she would rule without fear. That she was enough. She faced me, as I once faced the Malkin Queen when she dared underestimate my will. I saw my own eyes staring back.'

'I told you. When Glorian is crowned, Inys will be in good hands.' He caressed the underside of her breast. 'And we can be together. No sea need ever stand between us.'

She imagined having him at her side every day, in her bed every night. Living as other companions did. 'That dream is a long way ahead of us,' she said, turning to look him in the eyes. 'You and I may have silvers in our hair, but we cannot yet abandon our thrones.'

'No. We fought too hard for them.' He traced along her jaw. 'And for each other.'

He lowered his lips to hers. She skimmed her fingertips through his beard, his mane of golden hair. Even now, so many years after their wedding night, his touch made her ache. When she took him inside her, he breathed her name like a prayer, as he always did.

After, he lay with one arm folded behind his head and the other around her waist, his damp brow furrowed in thought. 'What troubles you?' Sabran asked him, watching his face.

Bardholt stroked a hand up her back. 'Glorian.' There was doubt in his voice. 'Forthard says she has winter gripe, but I have seen that many times. Twice now she has had these turns.'

Sabran closed her eyes. This was not another golden opportunity to tell him, but a tarnished one, years too late.

Instead, she could use it to smooth an old splinter.

'The Royal Guard told me something,' she said. 'Before she collapsed, Wulfert Glenn had just left her side.'

'What of it?'

'He was with her the first time, too.' She sat up to look him in the face. 'Bard, I know you see yourself in him. I understand why you wanted them to be playmates – it gave him safety and legitimacy, to be seen as a friend of the princess. But though we scorn the old ways, we both know their hold on our lands. The Dreadmount has not ceased its smoking. After the attempt on Glorian, I fear what could happen if anyone learned of her closeness with the Child of the Woods.'

'What has this to do with her sickness?'

'Some northerners say fainting is a sign that a person has been near a witch.'

'They called me witch, too. Heathen and accursed,' he reminded her. 'Even my own people, once. You saw through all that baseless fear, but you now ask me to hold it for Wulf?'

'You must do as you will in your own household. But he and Glorian are not children now, and times have changed. This friendship you encouraged is dangerous for them both.'

'What is it you propose?'

'Send him away until the smoke clears. Have a sanctarian vouch for his virtue.'

'And if he fails their tests?' he said, quiet and bitter. 'His father asked me to watch over him. How can I make him stand trial, as I did, when his only offence in this world was to be born?'

Sabran brushed his cheek, the one with the deep scar. 'Think on it,' she said. 'That's all.'

Bardholt watched her reach for her comb. A smile pulled at the corner of his mouth as she worked out the tangles in her hair, something Florell would usually do.

'What?' Sabran said, eyeing him over her shoulder. 'What is it?'

'I never thought, when I was young and foolish, that you could grow more beautiful.' His gaze pierced her. 'Before I take my seat at the Great Table, I could give you Yikala, as I gave you the North.'

She stopped.

'Yikala,' she said. 'How could you?'

'It was the Saint's dream, to convert the South,' Bardholt said. 'Let Kediko Onjenyu give up his old gods at last. Let him join the Chainmail of Virtudom. Let them all. I am the Hammer of the North, and you are Sabran the Ambitious. There is nothing we cannot do.'

Sabran saw the oath written into his eyes. Without answering, she kept combing her hair.

An hour later, he was sound asleep, the years stripped from his face. Sabran lay awake, wanting the other intimacy, the one she never dared reveal. It was the love of the divine, mysterious and terrible. For the first time in years, she opened the door, sinking below that first threshold of sleep.

Are you there?

Yes, said the voice that was not a voice. *I was sleeping.* A shiver that tasted of caution. *It has been some time since you last called, old friend.*

It is fear that draws me back. For my daughter.

The silence returned, and she thought the shadow had refused her overture.

Daughters, the voice said. *From the moment when they stirred in our wombs, they possessed us. We made them, knowing they would leave us, but their flesh was ours, at first, and we can never let them go.*

Sabran was certain of it now. The woman was her – but not in her body, the body she could feel, the body that had grown a child and borne her through the world. This was the divine self, the part of her that was also the Saint.

I see now that you were never a curse. She opened her eyes a little, watching how the waking dream silvered her breath. *You were always my friend, and I miss your counsel.*

As I miss yours. She sensed grief from the other side. *I wish we could meet, and embrace, as sisters. I wish I had some certainty that this was not a dream.*

A dream is no less true than any other thing.

Sabran dressed in a red gown. When she looked back, Bardholt was still asleep, his hand open on his chest – her proud Northern king, still hungry to exalt the Saint.

When they reached Vattengard, she would pray for guidance.

Swathed in a cloak, she stepped outside and walked towards the prow. Her subjects cleared a path for her. She caught sight of Wulfert Glenn, who dipped his head respectfully.

Small wonder Glorian was drawn to him. He, too, was caught between two realms.

The fog hung dark, with no trace of the sun behind it. Sabran stood tall at the head of the ship, as she had the day of her coronation. She watched steam waft from the black waters.

For a moment, she was that Sabran again, dressed in green for a new age. The crowd, the crowd was calling her name – calling to her, their Queen of Inys. That day she had laughed for the first time in years. She was young and alive and the world was before her.

A wind blew from the south. Her body stilled, and she faced it, her hair curling about her throat.

****

The fog was like smoke, except it was freezing. Rain would fall soon, and on a birling, there was no escape. Wulf shook his wet hair out of his eyes as he pieced a halyard back together. Beside him, Vell mixed hemp into tar, making caulk. He shivered in his furs, his pale cheeks raw.

'Can't hope it will be much warmer in Vattengard,' he said. 'Winter is no time for a wedding, whatever the Saint says.'

'Aye.' Wulf put the halyard down to blow into his hands. 'I feel for Princess Idrega. A grim time to wed, but especially to wed a sneering upstart like Magnaust Vatten.'

He let his gaze drift to the greyness above. It felt as if the clouds had come to join them on the ship. His hand went to the sunstone under his tunic, the one Eydag had given him.

'Would you ever wed?' Vell asked him.

Against his will, Wulf glanced towards Regny, who was watching the sea with folded arms.

'I don't think I'm fated for it,' Wulf said. 'You?'

'I could die merry either way. What I want is to serve King Bardholt until his death, and then see out the rest of my days in the South, where it's warm. If anyone wants to share that with me – friend or lover – well, that would be a fine thing. But I could go just as well alone.'

'I always thought you were rooted to Hróth,' Wulf said with a chuckle. 'Where in the South?'

'Kumenga, in Lasia. A port on the Halassa Sea. I met a merchant from there once. She told me Kumengan wine is like sundrops. Ever since, I've imagined what the sun must taste like.'

'Sounds a good way to live. I might join you.'

They both lowered their heads when the queen emerged from her cabin. Dressed in rich red, she stood out like a bent nail among the crew. She cut Wulf an unreadable look as she passed.

When she reached the prow, strands of her black hair pulled free. Wulf wondered when the Inysh had first realised their queens were always born with the same face. How they had avoided suspicion on that isle, which feared the shadow of its past, and a witch. Perhaps because the Berethnets had wealth and high walls and a legend behind them.

Wulf had nothing. No legend, no past, no explanations. Only a vague dream of bees.

'Vell. Wulf.'

They looked up. King Bardholt had appeared, draped in his bear pelt. 'Sire,' they both said.

'Wulf, I need to speak to you.'

Vell shot him a curious glance. Wulf rose and walked beside the king across the deck.

'How are you?' Bardholt asked him.

'Glad to be back on the waves, Your Grace.'

'Good.' His smile was tight. 'Wulf, I need you to do something for me after this wedding. I need you to return to Inys and spend a few weeks with the sanctarians at Rathdun.'

'Sire?'

Bardholt stopped and faced him. His expression drifted between resolve and deep sorrow, and his throat worked. 'My daughter has experienced some fainting turns,' he finally said. 'I understand that on both occasions, she was in your company just before she collapsed.'

'Is Lady Glorian all right?'

'She is, but the coincidence is unfortunate. It has stoked some of the old misgivings about you.' Bardholt took him by the shoulder. 'I swore I would protect you, give you a place of honour at my side. But to silence these backbiters once and for all, I think it best we ask the sanctarians to confirm that you carry no curse.'

Wulf stared at him as the words sank in. 'Do you mean I'm to ... leave your household?'

'No, no. You'll only be there for a time, Wulf. You are my retainer, sworn to me for life.'

He tried to steady his breathing. 'What if the sanctarians say I am a witch?'

'They will not.' Bardholt tightened his grasp. 'Have no fear. I know the Saint is with you.'

He looked as if he might say more. Instead, he strode away, leaving Wulf with his heart ramming at his chest.

All the training he had done, all those years. His fathers' love for him. Their sacrifices to give him a good life. His dreams of knighthood. All of it would slip away when he set foot in Rathdun Sanctuary.

He grasped the mast to keep standing. Roland had told him what those witchfinders did – the questions that were always traps, ordeals meant to force out any trace of witchery. Through brimming eyes, Wulf watched King Bardholt join Queen Sabran.

That was when he heard it. A slow and cadenced beat, like oars striking in unison at water.

Every head on the ship turned. Bardholt placed a hand on the side. 'Archers,' he called. Along with half the seafarers, Regny nocked an arrow. 'Steady.'

'Sire, what comes?' a voice said.

'Let us see.' Bardholt narrowed his eyes. 'It has been a long time since I last heard drums.'

Not drums, Wulf thought at first, but Bardholt would know better. After all, he had been to war.

It could be the Ments. Perhaps even the Vatten. The wedding might have been their chance to lure Bardholt to the sea, where they were strong. Perhaps they were tired of being his stewards, and even an Yscali princess could not temper their ambition. With those possibilities loud in his head, Wulf looked into the fog, one hand on his sax.

What emerged from that fog was no enemy ship. It came not from the water, but the sky.

A dark bird of prey, soaring on the wind. *A sea hawk*, Wulf thought distantly – except its wings were wider than the ship was long. They sheared the waves. In those first moments of seeing it, as his mind grasped for a touchstone and his senses slowed to a trickle, he recalled tapestries, sanctuary windows, prayer books, and the monster that haunted their borders.

Its eyes were firepits, each slashed with a pupil as black as its scales. Eyes both empty and ferociously alive. The beast loomed above the *Conviction*, held aloft by those dread wings.

And Wulf remembered he was flesh. He was skin papered on sinew, wrapped around bone, sprouting nails and teeth and hair, and all of it could be consumed.

The wyrm – for wyrm it was – did not utter a word. Instead, it opened its mouth wide, showing rows of teeth (*Saint, save us, save us*), and from its abyss of a throat, light rose.

Bardholt did not baulk. Neither did the Queen of Inys. It could have been courage; it could have been the numbness of fear, a fright that stole the voice and bound the limbs.

They never cried for mercy. Nor did they try to fight or flee. Instead, with their last breaths of life, the king and queen reached for each other. Wulf saw Bardholt move in front of Sabran, as if he had even a faint hope of saving her – saw the stark flash of his face, her long hair streaming in the wind – before the fire devoured them both.

It did not stop at the prow. Though Wulf had no time to escape the red death, some instinct made him lunge for the mast, the only protection. He shouted as his cloak went up. Scarlet flame roared across the deck, sparks blistering his knuckles and nape, strokes of searing metal on his skin.

The top of the mast crumbled away, and scraps of sail came loose, on fire.

All was red. All was white, all was black. The screams of the dying shredded the air. Everywhere, they were burning, and he could smell the bubbling melt of them, fat and copper, a choked sweetness. Through the glare, he glimpsed a tail as thick as a tree, ending with terrible iron spikes. That was the last of the creature he saw before the fog enshrouded it.

The Nameless One. He had returned at last, come to take his vengeance.

Wulf ripped off his cloak, but everything he touched set him alight again. His gloves held flame. His footprints. Tears streamed down his cheeks. He had never seen fire like this.

He dropped to the deck. With sleeved hands, he scrubbed, crazed by pain, at his eyes, more tears blurring them. Bodies, writhing as they ruckled out their final sounds, others already husks. He found Vell, but that was not Vell, that *thing* was not Vell—

He could hear Regny now, her cries of agony. She thrashed in a lake of spilled tar, snarled in her own blazing furs. Breathing in hot ash, he crawled to her, clenching his teeth.

The wind changed, and the day fell dark, so all that lit the ship was the fire. The creature must be wheeling around, coming to finish its work. Embers fell like a shower of molten glass. Everything they touched burst into flame. Wulf pulled himself forward, even as they landed all over him.

Howls rose from the blackening fog. The other ships. Almost blind from the smoke, Wulf gathered Regny, hands slick with tar. He brought her to his chest, coughing, and burned with her, a wicker man.

Death by fire or death by water. Twenty seemed too young to ask. He thought of staying on the deck, to feel his death to the last throe before he never felt again. Then he stood.

Only witches died by fire. Let his last day, his last choice, be the truth.

41

East

It was not the return she had expected. When her boots touched the snow of Mount Ipyeda for the first time in over a year, she ran straight for the bell tower. Below, the sorrowers called from their nests.

She knew what to do.

She knew how to protect Seiiki.

Only the moon shone, but she would have known her way in complete darkness. She stopped before the giant bell, and there was the inscription on its waist, the one she now began to understand:

TO HOLD THE RISEN FIRE AT BAY

UNTIL THE NIGHT DESCENDS

Dumai wrapped a rope around each hand and hauled back the striker, the great log she and Kanifa had oiled and cleaned for years, straining with all her might. She flung her weight the other way, hurling the beam towards ancient iron.

The Queen Bell rang out.

She let go of the ropes. The sound rolled low and deep, through her every bone, booming into the black night.

Little by little, it tapered away. Dumai slumped into the snow, listening to the quiet beneath the roar.

Perhaps no one would answer. It was winter, and the dead of night, and no one had ever heard the bell calling. No one who still drew breath.

Somewhere below, a second bell clanged. After another period of silence, a third answered – farther away, but loud enough to be heard above the wind.

The music pealed across the city, and with each strike and toll came another, far away. Dumai rallied. She used every drop of strength in her body to draw back the hammer and swing it again – over and over, until her arms were shaking and her knees gave way.

The summoning filled the Seiikinese night. It rippled out from the Rayonti Basin, west to Sidupi and north to Ginura, east to Isunka and all the way south, to the stormy hook of Ampiki.

And at last – at long last – the gods woke from their slumber. From deep in the rivers and down in the lakes; from the harbours, the old mangrove forests, they rose. Each and every star appeared to splinter into thousands more, the dark sky dazzling with dragons.

**

And somewhere, a woman awoke with a cry as the figure in her dream flaked to pieces and blew away like ash, and with it, the long thread between them, leaving her alone.

III

Age of Fire

CE 511

Wulf is on īege, ic on ōþerre.
Fæst is þæt ēglond, fenne biworpen ...
Ungelīce is ūs.
– Anonymous, Wulf and Eadwacer

42

South

Tunuva gazed at nothing as Hidat parted her damp hair. Oil lamps flickered, staving off the starless dark.

By dawn, the Mother would have a new representative. Tunuva had worried over this night, knowing she might not be able to conceal her sorrow. Grief made every hour a climb, but she had to bear the weight, for Esbar.

Saghul Yedanya had died quietly, her body shrunken and yellowed. As tomb keeper, it fell to Tunuva to conduct the funeral rites. It was a duty she had carried out rarely, but when she did, it was a balm, to lead their family in honouring the dead.

At dawn on the same day, she and Esbar had washed their old friend, praying to the divinities of passage and death. At sunset, they had laid Saghul to rest at the foot of the tree, letting the roots take back her fire, while their sisters and brothers sang a lament. Her ichneumon had curled up on the mound and died later that night, and they had buried him beside her. Tunuva had planted sabra on both graves, watering the seeds with resin wine.

Saghul would live on, in the fruit of the tree. Her flame would continue to guide all her daughters.

When Hidat had finished, she brought Tunuva a mirror. She looked at the intricate braiding along her scalp, then met her own gaze. There were crescents beneath her eyes.

'Thank you, Hidat.'

It was the first time she had spoken in hours. Hidat placed a hand on her shoulder. 'You can make it through this, Tuva.'

'We all must.' Tunuva set the mirror down. 'For Ez.'

'You and she were always closest to Saghul, save Denag.'

'I'm not sure now. Decades of friendship, and Saghul could still take me by surprise.'

There was no answer. Hidat turned away and adjusted the gold cuffs in her own hair.

Siyu waited in the corridor, the green cloak of a postulant draped over her shoulders. Though she had eaten the fruit while she was pregnant, she had yet to be formally initiated. Her hair curled down her back, adorned with a headdress of carnelian and leafen gold.

'Oh, Tuva,' she said, embracing her. 'You're so beautiful. I wish I were as elegant as you.'

'You always are, sunray.' Tunuva forced a smile. 'Are you ready?'

'Yes.' Siyu grasped her hands, eyes bright. 'I'm so happy for Esbar. She was born for the red cloak.'

Siyu looked just as happy as she claimed to be. She had no idea that Anyso was gone. Tunuva wished she knew where his family lived, so she could get word of his death to them.

'You look so much like her today,' Tunuva told her. 'Will you help me support her in this duty?'

'Of course I will.'

The initiates had unanimously confirmed Esbar as Prioress, including those who were posted elsewhere. Gashan had sent a short endorsement. In five centuries, a munguna had only been rejected twice – one because she had neglected her ichneumon, and once because a Prioress had nominated her own birthdaughter. Esbar had earned the right to rule.

Hidat emerged in her white cloak, bearing a wooden chest inlaid with gold. 'For you, tomb keeper,' she said, and held it out.

Tunuva accepted it. It was lighter than it looked, but what it contained would lie heavy on Esbar.

The three of them walked through the Priory, joining the procession down the stepway to the Vale of Blood. Tunuva spotted Canthe and gave her a small nod.

Saghul had engraved a tablet with her final wishes, including her desire for Canthe to join the Priory. It would be up to Esbar to decide whether to honour that request. Tunuva knew she would. She had loved and respected Saghul too much to do otherwise.

The ceremony always took place at night, beneath the fruits that smouldered with the flames of their departed sisters. Tunuva had been only twelve when Saghul was invested, but she remembered the wonder of it, watching a woman transformed to a Prioress.

The warriors stood on one side and the men on the other, leaving a path for Esbar. Siyu went to stand with Yeleni, while Tunuva joined Denag and Apaya – both in initiate white – at the base of the tree. She smelled ichneumon musk and blossom and fruit.

When Esbar appeared on the steps, silence fell. The men and the postulants raised their lamps, and the kindled initiates held up their own flames. Many eyes reflected the wavering light.

Esbar had renewed her magic at dawn – a fire divinity, bright from the forge. She wore a Selinyi wedding garment, made of netting, with nothing beneath. Her face was a carving, but she brushed hands with everyone she passed.

She knelt before the tree. As the eldest, it was Denag who first laid a hand on her head.

'Esbar du Apaya uq-Nāra,' she said, 'you have served the Mother faithfully and without question. Now you come before the orange tree, as many sisters have before. You kneel beneath its branches, as the Mother did. This family now asks you to represent her as Prioress, to lead and unite us in defiance of the Nameless One. Will you accept our call to arms?'

'I will,' Esbar said.

Denag brought the necklace Saghul had last worn, which held a precious cabochon of amber from the tree. Esbar lowered her head to receive it. Apaya came forward next, with the sap.

'Esbar du Apaya uq-Nāra,' she said, 'I attest that you are the fruit of my womb, blood of Siyāti du Verda uq-Nāra. Are you ready to be a mother to all children of the Priory?'

'I am.'

Apaya anointed her. Though her face was not the sort to soften, her pride was clear tonight.

Tunuva was the last to move. She handed one of her keys to Jontu Yedanya, who knelt before the chest and unlocked it. With the utmost care, Tunuva took out the most precious of the relics.

It had a smell to it – an ancient and disturbing scent, like meat left in the sun, like iron and time. Crisp with age, it was dried almost to the stiffness of bark. It was only by caring for it meticulously that past tomb keepers had kept it from becoming too rigid to wear.

'Esbar du Apaya uq-Nāra,' Tunuva said, 'this is the death cloak of the Mother, soaked in the blood of the Nameless One.' She draped it around Esbar. 'Do you accept its weight, and all that comes with it?'

'I do.'

In the final step of the investment, Denag presented Esbar with the iron spear named Mulsub. Gold and silver banded its haft, and its head was polished darkness, kept clean and trenchant for thousands of years.

Esbar took the weapon. When she rose, she faced the rest of their family.

'I am Esbar du Apaya uq-Nāra, Prioress of the Orange Tree. I pledge myself anew to the Mother,' she said. 'With humility, I stand in her place. With pride, I guard the orange tree. With love, I look upon you all, and offer myself to you, as parent, sister, guardian, and spearhead.'

'May she keep your blade sharp and your heart full of fire,' the Priory answered, 'and may your name strike terror into that which must remain unnamed.'

****

Tunuva woke in an unfamiliar bed. Her hand strayed across it, finding the sheets damp and furrowed.

Outside, a waterfall roared. She drank in the patterned ceiling of the Bridal Chamber, the last sight Saghul must have seen. Esbar had not wanted this bed – to her, it was a bier – but Tunuva had counselled her to begin as she meant to go on, or her new room would haunt her.

And so Esbar had consummated her sacred marriage to the tree by sleeping here, on a deathbed smoked with the scent of roses. It could only have been Imsurin who arranged that small comfort. He knew Esbar held to the Ersyri belief that the rose kept unquiet dreams at bay, and had made sure their room was full of that scent when they made Siyu.

Tunuva had still held her close all night. Even roses had no power over waking fear.

The celebrations had gone on into the early hours. Sun wine lingered on her tongue. Siyu had danced and laughed the night away, overjoyed by it all. Esbar meant to wait a few more days to break the news about Anyso. Siyu would be devastated, but left with the hope that he could be alive.

If she ever learned the truth, her happiness would rot away.

Sunlight dappled the floor. Beyond the latticed window, Esbar stood naked on the balcony, as she always did when she had a night sweat.

Tunuva stepped out to join her. She was staring at the horizon, hair glistening with spray. At dusk, her eyes seemed almost black – but now, at first light, they were a deep amber.

'Prioress,' she said. 'It feels like a dream.'

'Did the roses work?'

'I think it was your presence, more than roses.' She was still wearing the necklace. 'Hidat will be munguna. She has much to learn of leadership, but she is strong and temperate.'

'She will learn from you.'

Esbar nodded. 'I have taken up the mantle just as the world moves against us,' she said. 'When Saghul chose me, I was confident I was meant to wear the cloak, but I was young and brash.'

Tunuva knew better than to touch her when she was in a sweat, but moved as close as she could. 'Doubt and fear are natural,' she said. 'You have inherited a sacred duty to us all – but we are here to support you, in turn. No sister of the Priory stands alone.'

Esbar took her hand and kissed it.

'Prioress.' They both turned. Apaya stepped on to the balcony, a robe over her arm. 'My bird just brought a letter from Daraniya. She has received an urgent message from the harbourmistress in Padāviya. A serious malady has arrived there from Mentendon.'

Drawing on the robe, Esbar said, 'Malady?'

'Reports are confused, but it has a violent nature, turning the arms red and causing terrible pain. Her Majesty has closed the port, as well as the Southern side of the Harmur Pass.'

'What in the Mother's name is happening?' Esbar muttered. 'Has the world gone mad?'

And with his breath and the wind of his wings came a plague that poisoned all before him. The people sickened. Their blood ran hot, so hot they screamed and brawled and perished in the streets.

'The burning plague,' Tunuva murmured. 'The curse the Nameless One breathed into Yikala.'

'I had the same thought,' Apaya said. 'We should be safe. I doubt a sickness from beneath could take root in our blood.'

'But what of the men, the children?'

'We will consult the archives. Siyāti or Soshen may have left us some knowledge – Siyāti was a perfumer, and they shared an interest in healing and alchemy. Clearly this plague came and dwindled once before. If there is a cure or shield, they might have known it.'

'We should see this sickness for ourselves,' Esbar said. 'To be sure it is what we think.'

'Yes. Perhaps you could send Siyu,' Apaya said. 'If you still mean for her to go out in the world.'

Tunuva glanced at Esbar, who sank into thought, twisting the gold ring she had received when Saghul chose her as munguna. It was mounted with a sunstone flower.

'I must address the Priory,' she said. 'Apaya, gather them all in the War Hall.'

She strode back into the shade. Tunuva looked to Apaya, who raised her thin eyebrows. 'Stay close to her, Tunuva,' she said quietly. 'The Priory is her rudder, but you will be her sail.'

****

By midmorning, they were all assembled. Esbar stood before the nine pillars.

'Some time ago, a creature was born here, fire in its eyes, reeking of the Dreadmount,' she said. 'There will be others of its like. Our time has come, brothers and sisters. We must fulfil our purpose, and defend the South.'

They were all silent, listening.

'A small number of you will ride out tomorrow with Apaya uq-Nāra, to learn more of the threats we face. The rest of you will remain here to protect the tree, and await any calls for succour from our Southern allies,' Esbar said. 'Every postulant and initiate will train from dawn until sunset. Every man will make arrows as part of his work. Sisters, be sure to practise your wardings. Remember you are not invulnerable to flame.'

Tunuva watched with rising pride.

'Yesterday, you saw me invested with the cloak of Cleolind, dyed with the blood of the Nameless One. Today, I give you a chance to share in this glory. These creatures born of earthly rock are likely offspring – offspring of the wyrms that flocked from the Dreadmount. Should any initiate slay a wyrm, she will have earned the right to stain her white cloak with its blood. Those with blooded cloaks will be known as Red Damsels.'

She almost spat that Inysh word, the name they had forced on the Mother.

'Galian the Deceiver came to Lasia to found a priory – a house for a religion he invented, with himself as its overlord. Cleolind told him she would found a priory of a different sort, and so she did,' Esbar said, to grimly satisfied chuckles. 'He also came here for a bride. A damsel. So I shall make you *damsels* of a different sort – damsels who would make him tremble. Damsels soaked in blood. A third rank. A new rank for a new age.'

The War Hall rang with cries of agreement.

'After five centuries of waiting, we are the generation who will not only exalt the Mother, but do as she did,' Esbar declared. 'Ready yourselves. From today, we are at war.'

Tunuva walked with her as they all disbanded, clasping her hand. She stopped when she sensed a chill of magic. Canthe was waiting by the entrance.

'Canthe,' Tunuva said.

'Tunuva.' Canthe inclined her head. 'Prioress, I did not want to disturb you last night, but it moved me to see such respect for the tree, and to watch its new protector rise. I am so grateful I was there to see it,' she said, with a relieved smile. 'And that I have a home again.'

Esbar frowned. 'What do you mean?'

'The late Prioress told me I could remain here as a postulant.'

'Saghul entrusted her last wishes only to myself and Denag. When did she tell you this?'

'Esbar.' Apaya approached them, looking irritated. 'I couldn't find Siyu. Where is she?'

'She is in the Lasian Basin,' Canthe said.

Instinct curled in Tunuva. 'Siyu is not supposed to be out there,' Esbar said, frown deepening. 'When was this, Canthe?'

'I saw her leave this morning.' Canthe looked between them all. 'She was with her ichneumon and her baby, dressed for riding, so I assumed—'

Esbar and Tunuva were already rushing away. Instinct curdled into unease. *Please*, Tunuva prayed as they ran up the stairs. *Please, Mother, let her only be hunting…*

When they reached the sunroom, they found her green cloak, carefully folded, and a note. Esbar opened it, letting Tunuva read with her.

I know what you all did. I found Anyso in the icehouse. I pray you never have to see anyone you love that way.

I have taken Lukiri and Lalhar, but no one else. Yeleni knew nothing this time.

I will not raise my child where her father was murdered. I will take Lukiri somewhere where I know we'll both be safe and loved. Do not try to find me, or I will tell the whole world of the Priory.

'He was never in the icehouse. Hidat and Imin buried him.' Esbar shook her head. 'I respect the divinities, but never have I blamed them for our worldly affairs. Now here I sit, wondering if Old Malag plays with us.'

'Someone must go after Siyu. She has never even been beyond the Basin, let alone—'

'No,' Esbar cut in. 'No, last time I could justify it, but as Prioress, I cannot send anyone chasing after my own birthdaughter when we need every sister ready to fight.' She put the note down, looking tired. 'Let her rage burn itself out.'

'Esbar, she has an ichneumon. Lalhar will attract hunters as soon as they leave the Basin.'

'Then she will come back sooner.'

'If I follow her, will you stop me?'

Esbar looked at her. 'You don't know where she's going.'

'Nin can still catch her scent – and I think I do know, Ez. She'll go to Anyso's family in Carmentum,' Tunuva said. 'You can't follow her, but I can. Let me bring her home.'

Esbar turned to face the hearth. 'I have told you my ruling, Tuva,' she said. 'If you go, you do not go with my blessing.'

Tunuva considered. When she spoke again, she felt herself split down the middle.

'So be it,' she said, and walked away.

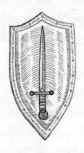

43

West

A fistful of snow shattered against Glorian. Breathless with laughter, she scooped powder into her gloved hands.

She savoured the burn in her skin. It was rare for snow to settle for long, even in the Fells. Now the Saint had sent a flurry from on high. He, too, was celebrating the new year.

The Feast of High Winter had come and gone. The Virtues Council had arranged the usual celebrations, but Glorian had noticed that less food than usual was served. After the feast itself, she and her ladies had built a snow knight, skated on the frozen lake, and foraged for hazelnuts and sloes in the queenswood.

All of it stifled her longing for Hróth. One day, she would always wake to sparkling frost. She would drink sap from the birches and dive into icy water every morning.

For now, she would enjoy the last stretch of her favourite season. Even Adela had given in to the joy of the fight, laughing as if she would burst, hair lank and bronze with meltwater. She flung a snowball at Helisent, only to run straight into Glorian. They fell with a shriek.

'Highness,' Sir Bramel called.

'I'm fine,' Glorian said, and meant it.

She collapsed into a heap with her ladies, damp and smiling. As she lay there, the cold seeped into her.

She had not dreamed in recent days. After what her mother had revealed, it was both a comfort and a burden. Queen Sabran thought the dreams were from the Saint, but she had seemed afraid of them.

What did it mean when the Saint stopped speaking?

'We ought to go inside,' Julain said. 'Before we freeze.' She sat up. 'Oh, look.'

Glorian followed her gaze to a black stallion, galloping towards the castle. 'She rides as if the Nameless One were behind her,' Helisent observed. 'What can be the hurry?'

The gates were heaved open, and swallowed the rider.

They stayed out until noon. When they returned indoors, they huddled around the fire in the Dearn Chamber. A servant brought white cheese and figs and mulled cranberry wine, and all afternoon they played checkers and straw heap, warming their bones.

'I wonder what Princess Idrega will wear,' Julain mused. 'Red, for the pear of the Vetalda?'

'Yellow,' Adela said, with certainty. 'It is the colour Yscals associate with fellowship. Mama wore it to her wedding.'

'That will make a cheerful sight in Vattengard.' Helisent slid a painted stick from the pile. 'It sounds a fearfully stern place. Then again, Lord Magnaust sounds a fearfully stern man.'

Just then, a knock came at the door. When the guards opened it, Florell stepped inside.

Glorian had never seen the First Lady of the Great Chamber look anything other than perfect, down to the last curl and fastening. Not so today. Her curls sat awry beneath their net, and her eyes were bloodshot.

'Your Highness,' she said. 'Ladies, please excuse us. I must speak to the princess alone.'

They left, and the guards closed the door. 'Are you quite well today, Florell?' Glorian asked her.

'I wanted to tell you myself. Before the Virtues Council summons you. I think your lady mother would have wanted that.'

'The Virtues Council?'

Florell went to her knees in front of Glorian and took her by the hands. Glorian blinked.

'Glorian,' Florell said, 'I have … news, sweeting. I can think of no kind way to give it.' A long silence. 'Your parents' ship never arrived in Hróth.'

'Were they blown off-course?' Glorian asked, surprised. Cruel winds were known to ride the Ashen Sea in winter, but her father only hired the best captains, weathered old sea hounds who relished a storm. 'Heryon Vattenvarg will be terribly insulted.'

Florell lowered her head. When she looked up, Glorian saw that her eyes were full and shining.

'Earlier today,' Florell said, 'another rider came from Queens' Lynn. For several days, fishers have been seeing fragments of wrecked ships in the Ashen Sea. Among them they found numerous white pieces, and a figurehead. They could not have come from any vessel but the *Conviction*.'

'But ... there was no storm. There have been no storms since the *Conviction* left.'

'The pieces were blackened. By fire.'

At this, Glorian let out a huff of laughter. 'That's absurd. They would have fled the ship—'

'Glorian,' Florell said, with effort, 'we are in the depths of winter. Even in summer, the Ashen Sea is perishing.' A tear seeped down her cheek. 'Queen Sabran and King Bardholt—'

'No.' Glorian stood. 'No. There were seven ships in the royal entourage. Pray, was no rowboat on the *Conviction*, Florell? Would none of the other captains have taken them on board?'

'None of the ships docked.'

'That isn't *possible*. You expect me to believe that a single fire destroyed seven vessels?'

'We don't yet know what happened.' Florell could hardly get the words out. 'It may have been an attack, Glorian. The Ments—'

'We must send ships and divers to comb the Ashen Sea. Pay them, give them what you wish, but make them find my parents.' Her heart was trying to break her ribs. 'My father is the Hammer of the North. My mother is Sabran the Ambitious. They ended the War of Twelve Shields, the Century of Discontent. The Saint would not let them die at sea!'

Florell kept shaking her head. 'Even the Saint could not have—'

'They are not gone. You'll see. My father *is* alive. He would never have let my mother die. He promised. He promised me we would live in Hróth.' Tears bathed her cheeks. 'Papa—'

Something was foaming up inside her. All sense of control crumbled. She had a sudden urge to rip and strike, run and scream, fling open the doors and run until her legs gave in – anything to be out of this room, to not have heard these tidings. Anything on earth.

Before she could, Florell pulled her close, and the sound that escaped her throat was so awful, she could not think it hers. It stemmed from some place deep within, the seat of her very self.

'It's not true,' she heaved out. 'Florell, say it's not.'

Florell only held the back of her head. Glorian clung to her, the warm blue anchor in the wrathful sea.

****

She lay in bed, not caring how she got there. Florell kept watch beside the fire. Now and again, Glorian would see her weeping into her hands, so hard she made no sound.

The doors were closed against the world. It did not stop Glorian from hearing Adela scream in anguish. Her mother had been on the *Conviction*, too. So had hundreds of others, including one of Julain's brothers. Every noble family had sent at least one member to the wedding.

And Wulf. Her old friend must be among the many dead, beside her father to the last.

Outside, in the gloom of dusk, the snow thickened. Florell roused herself enough to send for wine, while Glorian tried to think. How was it possible that seven ships could have burst into flame on the water, and been torn apart with the force of a storm?

What sort of fire could leap between decks, across leagues of sea?

When the idea stared Glorian in the face, she said, 'Florell, may I have some?'

When the goblet came, she drank, long thick gulps that burned her chest, and listed back into the bolsters. She remembered the worm, curled around the dead thing in the gall.

Wyrm. It was her own voice she heard as she drifted into a fitful sleep. *Only a wyrm breathes so much fire.*

****

News of the seven shipwrecks would fracture the West and the North. For as long as possible, it was to remain a secret, guarded by the Dukes

Spiritual. They let Glorian lie in bed for two days. In the end, she did weep, until her eyelids puffed and her throat ached.

At last, Florell opened the drapes around her bed. Glorian lay still as a cool hand found her hair.

'The Dukes Spiritual have requested your presence.'

Glorian stared at the canopy. 'It is him, Florell. The Nameless One.'

'You must not say or think such things.'

'How else would you explain all those ships burning on the sea?' Before Florell could answer, she rose, so heavy she thought her bones had turned to lead. 'I will speak to them.'

It took her a long time to dress. Since the truth was to remain hidden, she could not wear the grey of mourning. Instead, her gown was deep blue, trimmed with bear fur, appropriate for winter. Florell helped her with the fastenings, and laced her hair into a virtue braid.

Rumours must be spreading through Inys. Soon, people would thread the strands together.

The Dukes Spiritual waited in the Cloven Chamber. It housed a large tapestry that had once depicted the Saint beside the Damsel, which had been cut in half, removing Queen Cleolind. The Saint had destroyed every depiction of his bride after her death, such was his pain at losing her – every statue and painting, even written accounts.

When Glorian entered, the Dukes Spiritual stood as one. These were the most powerful members of the larger Virtues Council. All were descended from the Holy Retinue, the six trusted friends and retainers of the Saint, and each was the guardian of a virtue.

Lord Robart Eller, the Duke of Generosity, stood at the head of the table. Sunwise, she took the rest in: Lord Damud Stillwater, Lady Brangain Crest, Lady Gladwin Fynch, Lade Edith Combe, and Lord Randroth Withy. The latter two had been called to replace relatives – an aunt and a nephew, respectively – who had been aboard the ships.

'Lady Glorian.' Lord Robart was a picture of poise in his green doublet. 'Thank you for joining us.'

Glorian took the chair opposite him. A moment later, they all sat, too.

'As you have been told, there is evidence that the wedding fleet, including the *Conviction*, met a violent end on its way to Vattengard. What precisely happened, none can say.'

'I bid you find out,' Glorian said hoarsely. 'Lady Gladwin, you are Warden of the Twelve Ports and Keeper of the Sea. You must send out a search party.'

She had never spoken by herself to the whole council. The youngest, Lade Edith, was ten years her senior, and the rest far older. If they were to take her seriously, she had to maintain her self-possession.

Lady Gladwin was a tiny, spruce woman in her early seventies, all angles. Years at sea had weathered her brown face. 'Highness,' she said, 'from what I know of ships – which is no small amount – there is no chance the *Conviction* survived. I have had fire towers lit to guide any survivors, but given the dire cold of that sea, I fear none will appear.'

'My father is a Northerner. He could bear it,' Glorian whispered. 'If not, then we must recover as many bodies as we can.' Her voice shook a little. 'To send them safely to Halgalant.'

'Yes, Highness.'

'Now we must consider our next steps,' Lady Brangain said, her voice dull. 'The law states that if the Queen of Inys is absent without discernible reason, she must be assumed dead or incapable. After a grace period of twelve days, the heir must inherit the throne. Since the first evidence that Queen Sabran is missing was seen three days ago, nine remain.'

Nine days. No time at all.

'At sixteen, you are not of age to rule. This invites the possibility of pretenders to the throne.'

'I am the heir to Inys,' Glorian said. 'There is only ever one.'

Lady Brangain looked too tired to answer. Her own heir – her son – had been lost on the waves.

'Sadly, that has not always stopped pretenders,' Lord Damud said. 'Let us not forget the saga of Jillian the Merrow.' Lady Gladwin snorted into her cup. 'We may also see contenders who make no claim to Berethnet blood. Once the queendom knows the truth—'

He stopped himself. There was a foreboding silence before Glorian said, 'You think it was the Nameless One. That people will question the divinity of the House of Berethnet.'

Lord Damud paused a moment too long before saying, 'Of course not, Highness. But others may.'

'It would be wise to crush all talk of fire,' Lady Brangain said. 'We have instructed officials in the coastal settlements to destroy any evidence they see.'

Glorian touched the ring her father had given her. 'Since I am not of age to rule, who will?'

'Lord Robart is the ceremonial head of the Virtues Council,' Lade Edith said. Their walnut hair grazed the high white collar of their tunic. 'You will be crowned, but until you turn eighteen, he will serve as Lord Protector of Inys.'

Glorian looked at Lord Robart, and he at her.

He had a solemn face – strongly boned, not gaunt. Smooth hair was combed back from his brow, swept a little to the left, the same pewter as his beard. They held tongues of the auburn that must once have set his head aflame.

She thought he must have greyed before his time. He was only a little older than her father. His skin reminded her of tallow, making him look somedeal unwell, but he was fit and stalwart, his blue eyes wick as running water.

'My lord,' Glorian said, 'I would be honoured to have you as my regent – but surely my grandmother, as a Berethnet, should be offered the position of Lady Protector.'

'I do not think Queen Sabran would like that idea, Highness,' Lord Robart said quietly. 'Do you?'

Glorian was silent.

'Lady Marian will be escorted to a stronger castle within the next few days,' Lord Robart said, clasping his fingers. 'I have resolved to move the court to the capital before we announce your parents' deaths. Ascalun will be easiest to defend in case of unrest. We'll travel by ship – a risk, of course, but safer than having you out in the open countryside.'

Out of sight, Glorian fisted her hands in her skirts. She would be in the sea that had taken her parents. 'Do you agree, Lady Gladwin?'

'Highness, I mislike it profoundly, but, on balance, yes. I believe sea travel is the smaller risk.'

'I charge all of you to instruct the court,' Lord Robart said. 'We ride tonight, to Werstuth.'

44

East

Snow fell without a sound over Antuma Palace. Far above its rooftops, the sky rippled with dragons.

Dumai watched a pair from the bell tower. Three centuries after they
had entered their sleep, two gods were circling the capital – one the
slippery green of wrack, one grey as young ice. Lichen and moss still
crusted their scales, from slumbering in the damp for so long.

From this distance, they might have been kites. She could hear them,
like a roar of far-off waves.

Chaos, they are chaos, ruin…

… called us, calls to us…

Dumai gripped the balustrade. As the dragons swirled towards her,
eyes misty, her temples ached.

For salt, the star, born with the star…

She pressed her eyes shut. It was as if her skull was another bell, and
the gods were speaking into it, resonant voices overlapping. Her nails
sank into rotting wood. Slowly, the voices faded as the dragons turned
their attention elsewhere, leaving her with a chill.

It had been weeks since she had rung the Queen Bell, not stopping
to seek guidance or permission from the Grand Empress. Now the sky
was full of dragons – and only dragons. No winged beasts. Nothing had
attacked Seiiki.

As the sky darkened, Kanifa came to join her. Though he wore an overcoat, his brown face was raw from the cold.

'They don't seem angry,' he said, reading her face. 'If the great Furtia can sense the fire, so can they.'

'Osipa, a woman of seventy, is almost always furious when woken without good reason.' Dumai folded her arms. 'What of divine creatures that have lived for time untold?'

'Rain can't be angry. Neither can they.' A sharp wind ruffled his hair. 'His Majesty asked me to find you. Will you come?' With a last glance at the dragons, Dumai followed him inside.

Not long after the bells had woken every dragon in Seiiki, three of their elders had come to the palace. Dumai had recognised the largest as Tukupa the Silver, kin to Kwiriki, whose mane was like poured moonlight. Emperor Jorodu had met with them alone in Nirai's Hills, where Tukupa had last been seen. Queen Nirai herself had once been her rider.

Emperor Jorodu had found the remnants of her diary in his private archive. Some were yellowed and blackened, uneven at the edges, as if they had been collected from a fire. Dumai had still taken them to read.

How I wish I understood this tether to the gods – a thread between the mortal and divine, the upper heavens and the earth, Queen Nirai had written. *I wake holding a restless star; I dream of rain, and voices flow through me like water. This is indeed a world of strange wonders.*

Dumai found her father in the Water Pavilion, wrapped in more layers than most courtiers. Snowflakes blew in from the porch, and two cups of clear wine steamed in front of him.

Two cups. He had company – a guest with a small frame, wearing a grey veil. Dumai stopped.

'Mother?'

Unora turned. 'My kite.'

Dumai could hear her smile. They had seen one another at the temple, the night she had sounded the bell, but not since.

'What is this about?' she said, smiling in return. 'Why have you come?'

'Your father summoned me here, to conduct the formal rites to welcome the gods back,' Unora said, beckoning her. 'Now they are awake, we godsingers must serve them in all places.'

Dumai knelt beside her, and Unora grasped her hand. She smelled of the temple, like woodfall and ginger.

'We have much to discuss,' Emperor Jorodu said. 'Dumai, I met Tukupa the Silver. She spoke of this risen fire.' Shadow murked the skin below his eyes. 'What you saw in Sepul is surely a consequence. What we must find out is how much danger is to come.'

'The fire stems from beneath the earth, caused by some … imbalance. Furtia has not explained any further,' Dumai said. 'Father, have you heard anything from Queen Arkoro?'

'No.'

The silence lingered for some time. Dumai prayed King Padar had reached Mozom Alph.

'I searched the temple repository for any explanation of what you saw in the Broken Valley,' Unora said. 'I found nothing about creatures hatching from rock, but I did uncover a curious record, entitled *Tales for Winter Nights*. The godsinger who wrote it would ask climbers to share the most interesting story they knew, and record it for posterity.

'One told a famous legend from across the Abyss. Centuries ago, a winged creature emerged from a fire mountain in the West. In the short time it lived, it brought ruin and sickness to a land called Lasia, where the people knew it as the Nameless One. At some point, the creature was vanquished, though no one knows where it went.' Unora placed an engraved scroll container on the table. 'The godsinger tried to capture its image.'

Dumai opened it and unfurled the paper inside. Alongside rows of characters, a creature had been painted.

'This is what the Westerners fear. A wyrm – a serpent of the earth.' Unora watched her. 'Is it like what you saw?'

Flames spilled between its pointed teeth. Its wings evoked a bat, but the rest of it was more like a serpent or lizard, including its forked tongue.

'It wasn't red,' Dumai said. 'Its scales were tawny, like raw amber – but yes. They could be siblings.' She rolled the page. 'If this tale is from over the Abyss, should we not send an envoy there to find out how this Nameless One was routed?'

'I fear to risk it,' her father said. 'From what Epabo has heard on his travels, the Northern king is a conqueror who kills those who do not follow his faith. We should not tangle with him.'

'That aside, there is evidence that dragons will not cross the Abyss,' Unora said, 'and no ship that set out has ever returned. The waves are too high and rough. It would be a doomed excursion, Dumai.'

'We have knowledge aplenty in the East. Let us find it. Dumai, you say King Padar spoke of an alchemist – Kiprun of Brakwa,' Emperor Jorodu said. 'I know of her. She serves the Munificent Empress.'

'What is it that alchemists do?'

'Many of them seek immortality,' he said, his expression thoughtful, 'specifically by refining metals into tonics. They know the secrets of the earth better than miners. Alchemy has long been outlawed here, but there are many Lacustrine who study the golden art. I believe you should do as King Padar counselled, and fly to the Empire of the Twelve Lakes to consult with Mistress Kiprun. See if she knows anything about these rocks and what they mean.'

'You brought me here to bolster your rule,' Dumai said quietly. 'How can I leave again?'

'Because I trust you to protect this island. Because you have a bond with Furtia, and that should not be denied.' He held her gaze. 'And because you rang the Queen Bell.'

Dumai looked between her parents.

'I have the right to call,' she said. 'You told me this, Father.'

'Your blood protects you from punishment. Not from misguided opinions.' He sighed. 'People here have not seen what you saw in Sepul. It appears that you woke the gods for no reason.'

'You explained it to the Council of State.'

'They advised me not to tell the court, to avoid sowing panic. Unfortunately, this means that rumours have flourished. Epabo has heard them – rumours that you dream and have visions by day, or that you crave immense power, and that is why you struck the Queen Bell.'

'You think the River Lord is responsible for these rumours?'

'Yes.'

'But his daughter knows the truth. She was at my side in the Broken Valley.'

'You took the Kuposa woman with you.' Unora stared at her. 'Dumai, why?'

'She gave me little choice. I wanted to learn more of her ambitions.'

'Now you will learn,' Emperor Jorodu said grimly. 'She has done nothing to counter these rumours.'

'But she *saw* the creature, the rocks. She should be supporting my actions, robustly.'

'Lady Nikeya knows this court like a spider knows its web. She might understand the danger, but she also knows that your story of a winged monster sounds unbelievable. Better to keep her silence and let the whispers spread. The suspicion will eat away at your standing at court, and lay the groundwork for a regent to be forced on you.'

'But if the wyrm comes here, how will the River Lord explain her silence?'

'He might deny she ever saw anything. He might say *she* deceived him. It depends on how much he values her.' Emperor Jorodu pressed his lips into a seam. 'This is another reason I think it best you leave again. Without your presence, the rumours will have nothing to stick to. Another flight will also show you still have the gods' favour.'

'I don't want you to leave, my kite, but we are running out of time,' Unora said. 'Sooner or later, these creatures will find Seiiki.'

'Furtia has agreed to carry you. I will do all I can to prepare our people.'

'Father, we should persuade the gods to return the streams and lakes to the dust provinces,' Dumai said, 'or no one will be strong enough to fight this threat. The fog on the sun must already have hurt the harvest.'

Unora looked at the emperor.

'I will try, Dumai,' he said. 'Our dragons may be too weary to summon enough rain – remember, they slept because they were weakened – but I will speak again to Tukupa the Silver. Either way, we will survive what comes. Water must always quench fire in the end.'

'Your Majesty.'

A servant had appeared in the doorway.

'I come from the River Lord,' she said. 'He wished to welcome Lady Unora with a gift.'

Unora tensed. Once the guards had stood aside, two more servants entered the room and set a stand on the table. On that stand was a sorrower, propped upright by the arrow through its throat.

'Empress Sipwo was hunting with her uncle earlier today, and saw one of these foul birds that sing a deadly song,' the servant said. 'She killed it, to spare all mothers who wish to protect their beloved children. Alas, she cannot kill every sorrower in the forest.'

The arrowhead was silver. Dumai gazed into eyes like drops of ink, slick and still and dead.

'Please thank my consort for the gift,' her father said in a soft voice. 'The Maiden Officiant and I are grateful.'

As soon as the servants and guards retreated, Unora stroked the dead bird, tracing the scars on its breast.

'I see this is a threat,' she said, 'but not its meaning.'

'A sorrower feeds her young with her own blood,' Dumai said, feeling a little unwell. 'Surely the River Lord is warning you to leave court, Mother. Not to bleed too much for me.'

'Perhaps. Or perhaps it is more direct.' Emperor Jorodu considered the bird, an odd look on his face. 'There is a belief that a sorrower's song can cause a stillbirth or a miscarriage. Even if they will never admit to it, we know the Kuposa tried to kill Dumai before she was born. Fotaja wishes you to know that he still has the power to finish that work, if you do not dissuade Dumai from her path.'

Unora withdrew her hand from the bird.

'Go, my kite,' she said, her voice strange. 'Get out of this fishnet. Fly, and find the alchemist.'

****

Dumai marched along the covered walkways, her anger like a boiling spring. She strode through several pleasure gardens and a thick pine grove, and then she was outside Belfry House, a palace unto itself, where the most important members of Clan Kuposa stayed at court.

'I want to see Lady Nikeya,' she said sharply to its guards, just as her own caught up. 'At once.'

'Lady Nikeya has retired, Princess—'

'I don't care.'

Dumai brushed straight past them. The guards managed to overtake her, showing her to the right door, which she yanked open without ceremony. Nikeya was sprawled on her bedding in a crimson robe, a table on the floor beside her.

'Your Highness,' she said, unfazed. 'What a delight to see you in my bedchamber. How may I serve?'

'Your father and cousin just sent my mother a dead sorrower.'

'That is too many relatives for such a small number of words. My head aches.' Nikeya set her brush down on its silver rest. 'I have cousins all over Seiiki. Which one do you mean?'

'Empress Sipwo,' Dumai bit out. 'Is this another threat, Lady of Faces?'

'No, Princess. Just a game.'

'I am not here to play games.'

'You have no choice in that,' Nikeya said, 'because I am always playing. I know no other way.' She rose in one smooth movement. 'As I told you in Sepul, I do not command my father.'

'You seem content to let him slander me for striking the Queen Bell.'

'He has done no such thing.'

'I may appear naïve to you, but I am not a fool.'

'Yes, you are, or you would not have bolted to my room like a terrified horse.' She passed Dumai to close the door. 'I told my father what we saw. How he acts on this is his decision.'

'The court is awash with rumour that I am mad. I have not heard you defending my sanity.'

'Surely you don't need a simple poet to defend you, Princess. You have the love of the gods.' Nikeya raised her eyebrows. 'On that subject, have you asked them to give the people water?'

'They will.'

Nikeya looked hard at her face, unusually serious. In this light, her eyes were cooler, darker.

'I hope so,' she said.

She was close enough for Dumai to smell the perfume in her hair, and to see the piercings in her earlobes – uncommon in Seiiki. A tiny gold willow leaf hung on each side.

'Did you get those from Mozom Alph?' Dumai said, before she could think better of asking.

Nikeya reached for one. 'No,' she said, the shine returning to her eyes. 'A gift from a friend.'

'A family friend?'

'I'm flattered that you take an interest in my private life.'

'It's *in* my interest to know who you whisper to, and who whispers to you in return.'

'Ah, so many people. So many good friends. But only one or two I take into my confidence.'

Nikeya turned away. Dumai watched her choose a comb from a small box and sit with it beside the window.

There was an old tale of a woman of Ampiki. Poor and starving, she had been trying to catch fish when a storm destroyed her boat. Most

374

would rest easy in that grave, but not her. She had not been ready. She had walked from the sea as a water ghost, her skin for ever cold.

On calm nights, she could be found wading in the shallows, searching for the fishhook she had dropped in the moment of drowning. A passerby might be tempted to help. She was alone and in need. But if they caught her attention – if they met her eyes, deep as the Abyss – they had already sealed their fate.

Because then she would ask for her fishhook. She would ask four times, her whisper like waves on the shore. If the traveller could not find it for her, they would wake in the night with her drenched hair around their neck, and drown in the water that poured from her kiss.

'I am going to the City of the Thousand Flowers to seek the Lacustrine court alchemist,' Dumai said, in the hardest tone she could muster. 'Are you coming, Lady Nikeya?'

'I'm touched you'd invite me, Princess.'

'I imagine I have no choice. I am simply depriving you of the pleasure of coercing me.'

Nikeya shook her head with that lopsided smile of hers. It was so quiet in the room that Dumai heard each graze of the comb, the long slow rasp from root to end.

'What we saw in Sepul is more important than silver bells or golden fish,' Nikeya said. 'It threatens us all. We must unite in the face of those things, now the gods have returned. All my father wants is for us all to be closer. I want that, too, for my own reasons.'

'What reasons might those be?'

'Perhaps I'll tell you in the Empire of the Twelve Lakes.' She returned the comb to its box, then looked sidelong at Dumai. 'Perhaps we could go alone this time.'

If you meet her gaze, she is already too close.

'Kanifa,' Dumai said, 'is coming. You will have to make peace with his presence, Lady Nikeya.'

Never forget how dangerous she is.

Before Nikeya could speak, or move closer, Dumai turned and left, striding back into the snow.

She made her way to the Rain Pavilion, where Juri brought her sleeping robe and brushed the snowflakes from her hair. With each stroke, Dumai found her thoughts drifting back to Nikeya. She imagined the comb in different hands, a breath against her ear, lips soft as a flower on her jaw.

At first, she tried to crush those imaginings. They tasted of loneliness, a weak will. She could not think of Nikeya that way – never, not as long as she lived.

Later, in her bedchamber, she changed her mind. She let Nikeya fill the darkness in her room, and the dream seemed as real as any real thing. Nikeya on her bedding, warm and soft.

There was no harm in that. No harm in a dream. It might keep her from saying, *Yes, I'll find your fishhook, yes.*

45

South

Winter rains blew over Lasia. Far from the Priory, Tunuva and Ninuru wended their way southeast along the forest road, which threaded between steep green hills, past fields and orchards and farmsteads. Over two centuries, many Lasians had drifted towards the coast or to the capital, where summer droughts were easier to bear, but many had remained in the interior, sustained by water from the White-Haired Mountains, which had once worn heavy crowns of snow.

To keep Ninuru safe, they moved only by night and kept away from settlements. When the road filled with travellers, they found shelter, and Tunuva would sleep, dreaming of Esbar.

Esbar turning her back on Siyu, leaving her to weep and plead. Esbar holding out the poisoned cup to Anyso. Each time, Tunuva woke as cold as stone, wanting to shake herself.

These dreams were branches of her disquiet. She and Esbar had not had such a sharp disagreement in years. For the first time in three decades, they had chosen separate paths.

The weather troubled her as well. Tunuva had never seen snow this far south, but for several days, it flickered down. The sky still held a sour darkness, the sun a blind white eye in the murk.

Before long, they joined the saffron road. The leafy thickets and lush valleys soon gave way to redder land. Each autumn, this region would turn purple as the safflowers bloomed, scenting the air with honey and hay. Now they were just green tussocks, stripped of their precious threads.

Tunuva rode hard. By morning, they reached Suttu's Highway, a wide road that ran from Nzene to the far south of Lasia. They rested in a tree, returning when the stars were out.

Ninuru had not gone a league before she stopped and sniffed the air. She ran down a slope and through a palm grove, to the cracked shore of a lake Tunuva knew, which had dried to a puddle of murky water. Here they found ichneumon moult, the remains of a fire, and two soiled clouts. Siyu must not have risked time to wash them for Lukiri.

Tunuva tamped down a surge of misgiving. Siyu had no idea how to look after a baby beyond feeding, and Lukiri had not taken well to the breast.

Mother, I beg you, let me find them.

Ninuru went straight back to the road. All the while, Tunuva watched the sky, waiting for the sweep of wings.

The dressed stone of Suttu's Highway made the rest of the ride easy. The day the rains cleared, Tunuva looked up, damp and fatigued, to see the flash of sunlight on the River Gedunyu. Bujato – the end of this road – sprawled on its northern shore. A few miles downriver, the waters split for the last time and flowed in two long branches to the sea.

Tunuva shielded her eyes. On the other side of the river stood the ochreous cliffs that flanked the Valley of the Joyful Few. After that, all that remained was the Republic of Carmentum, built beside the endless white salts of the Eria, where the known world became unknown.

'Are they here?' she asked her ichneumon.

Ninuru snuffled at the ground. 'They were,' she concluded. 'Their scent is still strong.'

For once, they would have to risk entering a settlement by day. The Valley of the Joyful Few would be too dangerous to traverse by night, even for a mage and an ichneumon.

Bujato was a small and busy fishing town, built in a Taano style. The houses were of sun-dried brick, painted white, their roofs thatched with water reed. Ninuru received no end of fascinated looks. When a brave girl approached to pat her, she endured it. All Tunuva could see was five-year-old Siyu, meeting the blind pup that would be hers for the first time.

Ninuru stalked away to lap from the shallows, pursued by excited children. Keeping an eye on her, Tunuva walked to the riverfront market. She doubted anyone here would harm Ninuru – ichneumons had once been sacred to the Taano – but they still needed to move on quickly.

The harvest might have been poor, but here on the river, fish was plentiful, sold fresh from the water. Tunuva bought as many provisions as she could carry, as well as fresh cloths. She recognised the tightness in her belly. Once she had found a house of easement and swathed herself from thigh to hip, she followed the fragrance of sweet redstalk to a sacred garden, silent and calm, where hardy blooms grew in abundance.

An orchardist knelt beneath a peach tree. It must have come from the Ersyr, which traded with the East. If Siyu had any faith left, she would have prayed before she set out for Carmentum.

Close to the garden wall, Tunuva removed her dusty boots and washed her face in the fountain. As she crossed the grass, the orchardist turned. He wore barkcloth, red against crinkled black skin, and a circlet of copper leaves.

'Rich and unspoiled the fruit of the vine,' Tunuva said in Lasian.

'Strong and unbroken the roots,' came the age-old reply. 'How may I help you, traveller?'

'I'm trying to find a relative. Have any young women come to this place with a child?'

'Many,' the orchardist said. 'This is the only river crossing for hundreds of leagues. But not all had an ichneumon.' He looked in admiration at Ninuru, who had propped her head on the garden wall. 'I saw a wild one as a child, in the Uluma Mountains. Beautiful.'

'She is.' Tunuva stepped forward. 'When was this woman here?'

'Yesterday evening. I understand she was gone before dawn.'

Siyu must have stopped to eat and rest. She could only have stolen the money from Balag, who took care of the coffers. He would be surly for weeks. 'Did she seem well?' Tunuva asked, afraid of the answer. 'Did the child?'

'She seemed tired and weak. The child was unsettled.' As Tunuva made to leave, the orchardist said, 'Wait, traveller.' He picked a peach from the branches and held it out to her. 'Take the divinities' strength with you.'

'Thank you.'

She took a small bite as she returned to Ninuru. Its flesh was sweet, its skin soft as a kiss.

The River Gedunyu could be a fickle friend. Most people took the hourly barge to avoid its needlers and traitorous currents. Tunuva could not afford to wait for the next crossing. She secured herself to Ninuru, who sniffed the water and stepped into the shallows. Ichneumons were strong swimmers, but Tunuva still eyed the river with caution. It was deeper and colder than usual in winter.

'Tunuva!'

Ninuru looked back with a woof. Tunuva turned to see Canthe of Nurtha appear from the crowds on the riverfront, barefoot and wrapped in a linen dress. She ran down the steps to the sand.

'Malag's guiles—' Tunuva turned in the saddle to face her. 'Canthe, how did you get here?'

'Denag and Hidat were worried that you had gone alone. I offered to go after you.' Canthe waded in. 'They allowed me to take an unclaimed ichneumon. I've sent him back.'

'Did you ask Esbar for permission?'

'The Prioress seemed preoccupied.' Canthe gave her an arch look. 'Since I have no rank yet, I assumed I could still come and go.'

'Assumption breeds error. The Priory is a secret,' Tunuva said, exasperated. 'Outsiders are never permitted to leave the valley alone. You may have just scotched your chance to join us.'

'But I am no longer alone.' Canthe reached Ninuru, submerged almost to her waist. 'Tunuva, please. Except for the late Prioress, only you have welcomed me. I want to repay your kindness.' She grasped the saddle. 'I know Carmentum. Let me guide you.'

'You don't even know why I came.'

'I can guess,' Canthe said, softer. 'Siyu has run away, hasn't she?' Tunuva averted her gaze. 'Carmentum swallows those who go through its gate blind. You can't take Ninuru.'

In her determination to stop Siyu, Tunuva had barely thought of how she would find one family in a city of thousands, without her ichneumon to catch the scent. Defeated, she said, 'Ride with me.'

Canthe climbed straight into the saddle and wrapped an arm around her, holding the cantle with her free hand. Tunuva felt the curve of her hip through the soaked linen. Ninuru sniffed the river once more. She dived out of the shallows and swam, nose just above the water. A crowd of people cheered. Tunuva grasped her fur, feet cramping on the loops of rope, and hoped she had made the right choice.

****

A beach hemmed the other side. While Ninuru shook herself dry, Tunuva craned her neck to see the tawny cliffs, which cast the whole beach into shadow.

Ninuru flew through the canyon at first, following the footpath that marked the safest way for travellers. After a time, Tunuva kneed her ichneumon off it, down a long slope, to where the walls were sheer and close. They would need to sleep where no one from Bujato could find them, somewhere too high for even the best climbers to reach.

The light was fading. Once she was deep in the labyrinth of red gorges and ravines, Ninuru climbed back into the sunlight, almost to the top of a cliff. She bounded with ease between ledges and prowled into a cave. Tunuva got down and offered Canthe a mantle.

'Thank you.' Canthe wrapped herself in it. 'It's been a long time since I last saw the Valley of the Joyful Few.'

'It's as far south as I've ever come.' Tunuva opened a saddlebag and unwrapped a steak of roasted snake for Ninuru, who wolfed it down and licked her chops. 'I wanted to learn the way through the valley, but I never had the urge to see Carmentum, so I turned back.'

'When was this?'

'Oh, long ago. I was barely thirty.'

'Carmentum was less splendid then. This Decreer has gone to great lengths to enliven her republic.'

Tunuva took out her gourds. 'I only brought enough food for one. We'll have to live leanly from here.'

'You keep your supplies, Tuva. I can manage.'

'Do you live on air and wishes, Canthe?'

Canthe chuckled. 'As I told you, my hawthorn granted me long life. I like to eat, for comfort and warmth, but I can manage on water.'

Finding it could be a trial in the valley. Negotiating her way between two rock faces, Tunuva pulled herself on to an overhang and searched out a shallow pool of rainwater, where she filled the gourds.

Now the sun was a deep bronze, the canyon had turned cold. Returning to the cave, she handed Canthe a full gourd and tended to Ninuru, checking her teeth and footpads.

Halfway through having the sand groomed from her fur, Ninuru dozed off, purring. Canthe drank and said, 'Why did Siyu leave?'

Tunuva slowed her brushing. Esbar had told her not to speak of it, but that had been to keep the truth from Siyu. Now there was no real harm in telling Canthe.

She related the story down to its fine details, except for the fact that Hidat had been the one to kill Anyso, which Siyu had never known. Canthe listened, no judgement in her expression.

'We must find Siyu,' she concluded. 'Do you know anything more about Anyso?'

'His family are bakers, and he has two sisters.'

'That will give us a start, though Carmentum does have many bakers.'

Tunuva nodded, glad to have this company. She cherished Ninuru, who had been at her side for most of her life, but ichneumons were not talkative by nature, usually keeping to the point.

'How do you know Carmentum?' she asked Canthe.

'I lived there for several years. There are few places I have not been. I even visited the East, long ago.'

'You must have great courage, to have gone so far. What is it like across the Abyss?'

'Like any place. Some things are different, and some the same.' Canthe leaned against the wall of the cave. 'Their gods are wyrms of the water. Most of the people are enthralled to them.'

'Wyrms.' Tunuva stopped. 'The Easterners ... worship them?'

'Not all, but most. Theirs breathe cold and storms instead of flame, and sometimes tolerate humans,' Canthe said, 'but they expect obedience, just like the Nameless One.' A low, tormented moan drifted in from outside and filled the cave, waking Ninuru. 'What a haunting sound. One would think the ice spirits of Hróth were here.'

'This valley is said to be cursed by one of the wind divinities, Imhul.' Tunuva noticed her rubbing her arms. 'You ate of a siden tree once. How much do you feel the cold?'

Canthe drew the mantle closer.

'Once a woman eats of a siden tree, she is for evermore a lamp, her blood a rich oil where others' is water,' she said. 'The oil is strong. We even pass it to our children – but without the fruit, we cannot keep ourselves afire. We burn out, and the shadows come.'

Even with the mantle, she shivered. Her hair was still a little damp.

'Come,' said Tunuva quietly. 'Sleep beside me, with Ninuru. We can all keep each other warm.'

The other woman nodded, relief and exhaustion mixed on her face. She crossed the cave and sat beside Tunuva, close enough for their thighs to touch, and they both rested against Ninuru, tucked under their mantles.

The wind blew out the fire.

46

West

Glorian gazed out at the Ashen Sea, eyes raw from lack of sleep. Her hair clung to her cheeks as the wind battered her cloak.

Every fire tower was lit to guide the *Shearwater*. Grey fret mantled the waves. To distract herself from what might lie unseen and hungry in that fog, she pictured her mother huddled in a rowboat, and her father warming her with his bearskin, fist raised to signal the ship.

'Glorian.' Julain touched her elbow. 'We're here.'

Summerport was named for the sandstone of its buildings, a rich honey yellow that warmed the heart after a crossing. It warmed hers, in that first moment of seeing it. They had survived a haunted sea.

Rain battered the red tiled roofs. People in the harbour went about their lives, not noticing who had just arrived. Lord Robart had chosen to borrow a modest ship from a merchant.

To avoid attention, the Dukes Spiritual separated to cross Summer-port. Lord Robart led Glorian through the cobbled streets, flanked by the Royal Guard. In the warmer months, Summerport came alive with pink sea thrift, and its doorways cascaded with coral roses – but in winter, in her sorrow, all Glorian could see was decay: the wet rot in the planks, the cracks and tiny holes where the salt wind had chewed on the buildings.

'Queen Sabran!'

A woman had opened her shutters to wave. All along the street, voices, hands and cheers rose at once, chatter erupting. 'Your Grace,' they called to her. 'Your Grace, welcome back!'

Glorian stopped. It was only thanks to the fog and her cloak that anyone could have made the mistake. She and her mother had shared the same features, but Glorian had a fuller shape, and her manners tutor had not yet managed to school a queenly posture into her.

Lord Robart gave her a small nod. Glorian raised a tentative hand, and the cheers became a roar of welcome.

Her hood kept her face concealed as the court rode northwest out of Summerport. The sea road was as thick with fog. Beside her, Lord Robart sat proud and wordless, a cliff of a man, gloved hands tight on the reins of his destrier. He cut a daunting figure at the best of times, but astride that warhorse, he was almost as tall as her father.

She resolved to make conversation. He was to rule in her name for over a year. 'Lord Robart,' she said, 'I understand there has been drought in Inys. Will this rain be a remedy?'

'I'm sure it will be of some help, Highness. Get the rivers flowing, at the very least,' Lord Robart said, 'but it may not resolve the drought altogether. It's been worsening for years.'

'Do you know the cause?'

'No. Only that the ground is thirstier than usual, despite the rain. Nature must have her secrets.'

'Indeed. Last year, I heard of strange happenings in the haithwood,' Glorian said. 'It borders your province, does it not?'

'Yes, though I leave its care to the Dowager Earl of Goldenbirch and the Barons Glenn.' He wore a sword at his side. 'Deep forests always invite strangeness, whether real or imagined.'

'In the spring, a knight found suspicious rocks there. Did he ever return with news?'

'Sir Landon Croft was never found. A tragic case of misadventure, in my view, Highness. He went looking for wolves, and likely found them. There are bears in the haithwood, too.'

'Do you think the bears' hunger is what started the rumours of a witch?'

'Possibly.' Lord Robart glanced at her. 'What do you know of the Lady of the Woods?'

'Very little, except that some believe in her.'

'Aye. When the world is awry, some find comfort in the old ways. It won't endanger your rule, Highness.'

It was dusk by the time they rode into Ascalun, capital of the Queendom of Inys. Its castle had pale sturdy walls, which loomed above a deep crook in the River Limber. Under the Malkin Queen, its water had reeked like a corpse. Now it was clear and frozen stiff.

In five centuries, there had been no wars or sieges here. Ascalun was unconquered.

Her mother had grown up in the castle. Glorian had been born there, like most Berethnet women. The bells had rung for days, and all had called her the Gift of Halgalant, for with her arrival all wounds had been healed. *I was meant to bring peace*, she thought. *Now I stand on the brink of war.*

Snow was banked on every street, dirty and trampled, torn by footprints. The procession rode through the wards of the capital, where torches lit the pending night. They had arrived at eventide, when most of the city would be at home or in the sanctuaries at prayer.

Still, a royal entry required ceremony, even when unexpected. Trumpets called out her approach. Glorian set her gaze on the castle and withdrew into the secret place inside her, where she could not hear or see.

The ride passed like a dream. Blazing torches, candles fretting in windows, rain against her face. People shouted out to her, still thinking she was her mother, returned from the North. Only when they were past the castle gates did she breathe painlessly again.

'Lady Florell, take Her Royal Highness to her old rooms in the Queens' Tower,' Lord Robart said. 'She must be very tired.'

****

The Queens' Tower – called the King's Tower for centuries, before the name became absurd – had been made to withstand both attack and invasion. Its sides were round and sanded, impossible to climb, not one foothold between its lower windows. Glorian followed Florell up hundreds of steps.

Her bedchamber was just as she remembered it. A fire crackled in the arched hearth, and a supper of game stew and hot wastel had been left on a table. Helisent removed her damp cloak for her.

'I wish to bathe,' Glorian said, as if from a distance. 'I have a chill.'

Florell nodded. 'Mariken,' she said to her Mentish servant, 'have hot baths prepared for everyone, if you would.'

'Yes, my lady.'

'I'm well, Florell,' Julain said, her voice quaking a little. 'I should stay with Glorian.'

'Julain.' Florell took her by the shoulders. 'You cannot watch over a princess – or a queen – if you don't have a care for yourself first. All of us are grieving and shaken.' She took the cloak from Helisent. 'Go, all of you, and rest this night. Mariken will bring your supper.'

Glorian sank on to the bed and took off her gloves. She was too tired to cry, or to undress, or do anything but stare at the nearest candle.

She wondered if her parents had been taken by the fire, or by the sea.

'Sweeting,' Florell said, 'may I speak frankly – as your mother's friend, and yours?'

'I do not expect deference from you of all people, Florell.'

'You should expect it from us all. In seven days, you will be Queen of Inys.'

Glorian managed a nod.

'The Lord Protector is a resolute man, of holy blood and iron will,' Florell said. 'He may yet prove dependable, but we must have a care in the months to come. Regencies can be a dangerous time.'

'How so?'

'A regent has the means to shut a young queen out of Inysh affairs. That would create a weak ruler, dependent and easy to manipulate. After the Century of Discontent, we can let no one think that of you, Glorian. Lord Robart must always treat you as a queen. He must empower and nurture you. If he will not, it is a different sort of control that he craves.'

'I'm sure that I can trust a man my mother held in such regard.'

'Yes. I only ask you to remain vigilant while he wields the authority of the Saint, which belongs, by right, to the House of Berethnet.' Florell sat beside her and took her by the hands. 'Glorian, you are only sixteen. None of this should happen to a child – but your people will look to you for strength and courage. They must come to love and respect *you*. Not another.'

'How do I persuade them to love me?' Glorian asked her. 'How did my mother?'

'You know how. You watched her for years,' Florell said. 'Queen Sabran was devoted to her duty. She was firm but fair, which meant she was respected, but not feared. Your situation is different. You will need a coronation, as soon as possible, to show yourself to the people. You will need an heir. You will need nobles who are loyal to you above your regent.'

Glorian bit her lip. If Florell had not been grasping her hands, they would have trembled.

'Do the Dukes Spiritual doubt me?' she said. 'Do they think it was the Nameless One that set the ships to light?'

For the first time, she noticed that Florell had aged. She saw the whorls of silver in her hair, tucked among the tow, and the lines that creased the skin around her eyes.

'After the Dreadmount, they may have private doubts,' Florell admitted. 'So will your people.'

'Do you, Florell?'

'Never. Your mother was my dearest friend. I watched her pull this queendom from the brink. Unless I see the Nameless One with my own eyes, I will *never* believe he has returned. The Saint made Inys a promise, and I have faith in him. I have faith in you.'

The fire quickened the shadows, so nothing quite lay still.

'I can make you look like a queen. Liuma taught me to do that,' Florell said. 'But you must show Inys who you are – the daughter of Sabran the Ambitious, the greatest queen in our history, and Bardholt Battlehold, whose name made the unfaithful quake.'

'What if I cannot?'

'Then you will show yourself to be a weak and ineffective queen, like your grandmother. Like the two queens before.'

She is too like my mother. Queen Sabran in her bedchamber, candlelit. *I kept Marian away, all these years – but Glorian has her blood, too.*

'I need to speak to Mariken,' Florell said. 'Rest. I won't be long.'

She left. Glorian worked off her own boots and sat in the silence of the bedchamber.

Show Inys who you are.

Some of her possessions were already here. In the smallest chest, she found the mirror her mother had given her. A younger, haunted portrait of Queen Sabran stared back.

Not her alone. No, this face was a legacy almost five centuries long, the chain, the endless vine. Nineteen queens with the same face all gazed out from the cold silver. Deep beneath, in her blood, was her father – never seen, but always present. All her life, she had defined herself by him, and by her mother. She had lived as, and in, their shadow.

Who was she without their light?

Who was Glorian Hraustr Berethnet?

****

The remainder of the twelve days passed slowly. In that time, Glorian did nothing of use. She walked in circles with her ladies. Little was said. Sometimes she gazed across at the White Tower, where the Dukes Spiritual met each day, and wondered what they spoke about.

She prayed: *Gracious and loving forebear, send me a sign. Teach me how to atone for my sin, for my unwillingness to give. Saint over us all, in your virtue, heed my prayer. Grant me your forgiveness. Lend me your candle in the dark. Make me your instrument, your servant, your vessel. Send me word from Halgalant.*

There was no answer. The woman from her dreams – her messenger – had gone silent.

She was abandoned after all.

****

On the eleventh day, Lord Robart summoned her. Before she left her bedchamber, Glorian looked once more in the mirror. She tucked a stray hair behind her ear and tried to harden her drawn face into a mask, like the one her mother had always worn.

A future queen must know how she appears to others.

She could not bring a sword to a council meeting. Instead, she had asked for a leather jack, which called armour to mind, to be fastened over her pleated gown. Tonight, she would be every inch a queen and warrior, the heir and weave of Queen Sabran and King Bardholt.

Candles glowed in gold holders, and the shutters were closed against the wind. When she entered, the councillors rose. 'Lady Glorian,' Lord Robart said. 'Good evening.'

Her heart clenched at the sight of him. He had told her she must not wear mourning dress until her parents' death was known – yet there he stood, in a surcoat of fine grey wool over a lighter tunic, a dark mantle across his shoulders. Even his belt and fastenings were silver, washed of colour. The others wore the same.

'You are in grey, Lord Robart,' Glorian said, stunned.

'As you see, Your Highness.' He paused. 'You didn't receive my message?'

'Is that not evident?'

Mortification stung her into the tart reply. Lord Robart inclined his head. 'My sincere apologies. I prayed last night and felt we should begin mourning today. I will reprimand the messenger.'

She had to regain her composure. Expressionless, she sat, and so did they.

Her gown was a rich, deep blue. Not bright, but among her grey councillors, she must look insolent.

There was no firewood in the hearth. The only warmth and light came from the candles. 'I hope you will forgive the cold,' Lord Robart said. 'I like to keep my mind sharp as I work.'

'It is of no consequence to me, Lord Robart.'

'Good. I have called you here to inform you that tomorrow, at noontide, the presumed deaths by drowning of Queen Sabran of Inys and King Bardholt of Hróth will be declared across Virtudom. Your own ascension to the throne will, of course, be proclaimed at the same time. In this way, the Queen's Peace should hold.'

'Have you searched the sea?' Glorian asked Lady Gladwin.

'Yes, Highness. I even sent divers to look for the wrecks, but little could be found.'

'Do we know what caused the fires?'

'I have made enquiries with the Steward of Mentendon. So far, there is no evidence that the wedding fleet came under attack. No weapon on this side of the Abyss could obliterate seven ships.'

'On *this* side?'

'Well, in theory, the Easterners could have one. We know so little of them, after all.'

'Why should the Easterners want to harm us?' Lade Edith said, frowning. 'I doubt they know Inys exists.'

'When I was a young man,' Lord Randroth croaked, 'I heard a rumour that a Southern prince survived crossing the Abyss. Years later, one of his servants returned, claiming the Easterners were enthralled to scaled creatures of the sky. I say it is a possibility.'

'We should consider the Ersyris, too,' Lady Brangain chimed in. 'They are said to dabble in alchemy.'

The Duchet of Courtesy looked unconvinced.

'I agree with Edith. I do not believe this has anything to do with the East, or the Ersyris. Neither of them has cause to attack us,' Lady Gladwin said. 'The Ments are the most likely. The murder of King Bardholt would send a message against the Vatten occupation. They could have harnessed the fire of the Dreadmount – they have lived in its shadow long enough.'

'Initially, I suspected Vattenvarg. We know his strength on the sea,' Lord Damud said, 'but he makes no move to claim the Hróthi throne, which would seem to be his only motivation. I think the man too old and comfortable for war. He has no obvious grievances.'

Glorian said, 'Then the Vatten stand with us?'

'It would seem so, Highness. If this *was* a Mentish plot, they will find and punish the perpetrators.'

'Whoever is responsible, we now have no choice but to announce your parents' deaths.' Lord Robart clasped his hands on the table. 'The Steward of Mentendon has already informed Einlek Óthling. He is loath to be crowned, but understands the need for it.'

Little wonder Einlek was hesitant. He must fear his uncle would march in to reclaim the throne.

'Your Highness, as I'm sure your parents told you, you must formally renounce your claim to Hróth – the strongest of anyone alive – and declare the line of succession vested in Einlek Óthling and his descendants,' Lord Robart continued. 'This is necessary, to secure the House of Hraustr.'

He beckoned a servant, who brought the document to Glorian. She silently read the words before her.

I, Glorian the Queen of Inys, the third of that name, descendant of King Galian the Saint and divine flesh of the House of Berethnet, the Chain upon the Nameless One, do here declare and affirm that I am the sole heir of the body of King Bardholt of Hróth, the first of that name, begotten on his lawful companion, Queen Sabran of Inys, the sixth of that name.

In this the five hundredth and eleventh year of the Common Era, I do freely relinquish my birthright to the Kingdom of Hróth, preferring my first cousin, Einlek Óthling, son of Ólrun Hraustr of Bringard, and those heirs of his body lawfully begotten, to hold that realm in perpetuity . . .

Since she was a child, she had known the day would come when she must abandon her dream of ruling Hróth. It deepened the dark pit of grief, but Einlek had already bled for his country, and her father had loved and trusted him. He would be a good king.

A quill was brought, and an inkhorn, filled with the blood of an oak gall. Glorian thought of the brandling worm again.

She dipped the quill. Some instinct made her touch her face, to assure herself she was still in the same skin, before she formed the signature she had learned on her twelfth birthday.

Glorian Quene of Inys

'Einlek Óthling will not be crowned until he receives it, Highness,' Lady Brangain said. 'He awaits your blessing.'

'After the announcement, mourning will begin in Inys,' Lade Edith said, breaking a silence. 'Usually, this would last six months. Since we have lost both our queen and her consort, twice as long would seem appropriate.'

'We also think it proper to hold a symbolic entombment, six days after the announcement,' Lord Damud said. 'Your mother's tomb stands ready at the Sanctuary of Queens. We propose that some of her possessions be placed inside, as well as the tooth held at Rathdun Sanctuary.'

Every queen gave a tooth to the ancient sanctuary in the north, in case her body should ever be lost. They were sacred relics, for even in death, a royal body was the realm. It had to be preserved, protected, laid to rest with due respect.

Glorian closed her eyes. Against her will, she pictured her mother on fire, her hair blazing away, skin melting like candlewax.

'Yes. We must see my parents through the gates of Halgalant,' she said, her voice straining. 'I would also like the ceremony to acknowledge my lord father. One of his pelts, and his tooth, should be placed in the tomb. I believe he also provided one to Rathdun Sanctuary.'

392

'His Grace pulled it out himself,' Lord Randroth confirmed. 'It will be brought to Ascalun.'

'Very well.' Glorian twined her fingers in her lap. 'Has a day been set for my coronation?'

'It will be in good time, Highness,' said Lord Robart.

'It is a matter of propriety,' Lade Edith explained, before Glorian could ask. 'The disappearance of the sovereign without proof of her death is unprecedented in Inysh history. Your mother cannot be declared officially dead without evidence. Before then, a coronation may not be considered appropriate, or in good taste – unless there were to be a witness. A survivor who could confirm or deny that Queen Sabran was deceased.'

'We must be realistic, Edith. No one could have survived that sea,' Lord Robart said. 'There will be no witnesses.'

Lady Brangain looked away. Across from her, Lord Damud clasped his hands against his forehead.

'If no witness comes forward, I recommend we wait at least until after the year of mourning,' Lade Edith concluded. 'By then, the people will have accepted you as queen, Highness.'

Glorian could not think of anything else to say. Pushing any harder for a coronation would make her seem heartless.

They cannot see the Malkin Queen.

'So be it,' she said. 'A witness. Or a year. Has there been any word of the sickness that appeared in Hróth?'

Lord Robart raised his eyebrows. 'Who told you of that, Highness?'

Glorian met his gaze without answering. 'Unfortunately, it has spread,' Lord Damud answered. 'Einlek Óthling has closed the ports. So far, there have been no outbreaks here, thank the Saint.'

Lord Randroth made the sign of the sword. 'Perhaps we should close our ports, too,' Glorian said. 'As a precaution.'

'We will keep a close watch on the situation.' Lord Robart looked her in the eye. 'If we might turn to a more urgent domestic matter, Highness.'

'What is that, my lord?'

'It is wise that you conceive an heir as soon as possible.'

Deep inside Glorian, something fragile snapped at last. 'Why, Lord Robart?' she heard herself ask. 'I am but sixteen. Shall I be dead before long?'

Breaths were drawn across the table.

'Highness,' Lade Edith said, their voice hushed. 'I beg you, never speak of your own death.'

Glorian lifted her chin.

'Lady Glorian,' Lord Robart said, 'this is your highest duty. It is the best way to keep Inys safe.'

'Usually, we could wait longer.' Lady Brangain looked at her, sorrow in her dark eyes. 'But we face so many threats. The Dreadmount, your parents' disappearance, the Carmenti, this sickness, the attempt on your life, possibly the Ments. Without an heir, we are vulnerable.'

Glorian tightened her grip on her own hands. She and her grandmother were the only living Berethnets, and her grandmother had been weak and disliked. Lord Robart was right.

She did need an heir, to strengthen the house.

'Your mother arranged a match before her disappearance,' Lord Randroth ground out. 'Your consort will be Prince Therico of the House of Vetalda. He is thirdborn of the Donmato.'

'Prince Therico is your age,' Lady Brangain told her, 'and very kind, according to Queen Rozaria. You met him once in Kárkaro, though I believe His Highness was rather shy of you.'

'Theo,' Glorian said. It could have been worse. 'Yes, I remember. He had a smoky kitten that followed him everywhere.'

'Yes, Your Highness.'

'Most importantly, he will never be King of Yscalin. That duty will fall to his elder brother,' Lord Robart said. 'Prince Therico is free to live at your side. He has already been summoned to Ascalun.'

Glorian tried to restrain the shudder that built in her gut at those words. It burst its thin restraints and went skittering along her arms, raising the fine hairs beneath her sleeves.

They saw her body as another document to sign.

'You would be wise to set your mind to motherhood now, and to not exert yourself before your marriage,' Lord Robart said, tidying his papers. 'The entire Virtues Council is here to guard the queendom for you. Leave everything to us, Lady Glorian.'

47

North

Throughout the cruel winters of Hróth, the light died at midday. With its cloak of sea mist fallen, the high cliff known as Hólrhorn could be seen for leagues off the western coast, though few ships ever sailed nearby. Only gulls and rock crabs moved, and even they were quiet.

Below was a black beach, miles long. The waves pared thick snow from its sand and withdrew with a roar, leaving a lace of foam. The coast they washed became a mirror in their wake, reflecting the grim cliffs, the birds, and a bank of grey cloud, all tarnished with copper.

Rock stacks towered from the spindrift. Most called them the Six Virtues of the Sea, but those who still cleaved to the past, who lullabied the frozen lakes, knew them by a far older name.

Thousands of years they had stood guard.

Now they watched the dead appear.

For days, only the rocks witnessed the corpses washing in, charred and broken, released from the sea. Only they saw the entangled pair – one in the holdfast of the other – come ashore to rest at last.

The red sun took its leave. When darkness fell, it fell entire.

So it was until the sky lights woke. Colours sketched the sky, flowed tall and bright, and billowed like sails through clear water, ghosting in shades of blue and green. They picked out the remains on the long beach and reflected in the eyes of a young woman with brown hair. Like the other corpses, she was burnt, the skin and flesh torched from her arms – though her face remained whole, white as ice. Whether it was the water or the fire that had killed her, no one could have told.

Beside her lay the last survivor.

A strong wave rolled in and broke across his back. He coughed seawater, his nose stinging. When he peeled his eyes open and saw the lights, he knew this was not Halgalant.

His fingers were swollen and blistered. The sea had almost wrung him of all strength, but he found the will for one last crawl, to gather the dead woman close and drag her up the beach.

Each inch opened his salt sores. Each one unlocked the agony the bitter cold had kept at bay, drawing raw, tearless groans. When he had gone as far as he could, he collapsed beside her, the woman who had never feared him. With cracked lips, he kissed her brow. He had fought hard to get her home, and it was done. Her bones were safe.

He had only one regret – that he had never known why. Why he had been left alone in the wood.

By dawn, the lights had disappeared, and the seafarer was still alive. He thought of walking back into the sea, letting it take him under this time. Better that than face the fact that he had failed his king. In the songs, nothing was sadder than a knight without a liege.

But his liege had never knighted him, and there were two others who needed his sword. In the North, a wise man who had lived through a war; in the West, a young queen with the snow in her blood. He had to live, to tell them both what all the world needed to know.

The Nameless One could not return, but something else had come.

****

Two days later, a family of Bálva herders pulled their rowboat to the beach, fleeing the plague that had reached their small camp. By the dim light of dawn, they came upon the four hundred and thirteen bodies, burned or drowned or frozen to death – and one man who still breathed.

He saw them from a distance, through eyes scorched dry by salt. Regny lay damp and cold at his side. He had failed to save her from the fire, but she would save him, one more time. He reached for the horn around her neck and set it to his bleeding lips.

The sound was so low and faint, it only pricked one pair of ears. An elkhound came running and barked, licking his face.

'Hampa, no. Here, boy.' Footsteps slapped through the sand, then stopped. 'Fa, someone's alive!'

Twelve others came running up the sand. He had a few moments to realise his survival was now in others' hands – he could lie down and sleep, he could let go – before a thick pelt and a fur hat were bundled on to him, and he was gulping water from a birchen flask, swallowing so fast it made him choke.

When they tried to take Regny, he grasped her to him, his voice cracking on his sound of protest.

'Leave him, by the Saint's bones,' an elderly man said in Hróthi. 'He's grief-stricken.' He crouched in front of the survivor, dark eyes nailed on to his. 'Boy, what in the holy name has happened here?'

Wulfert Glenn mustered the words.

'Tell Einlek Óthling,' he rasped. 'Tell him. The king ... is dead.'

48

South

Two monumental statues guarded the southern gate of the Valley of the Joyful Few. Suttu the Dreamer, with the spear she dipped in starlight – Mulsub, the spear Esbar now possessed – and the other, Jeda the Merciful, a beloved queen of the former Taano State.

From the valley, it took three more days of riding before they reached the ridge that marked the end of Lasia. Now and then, they passed the ruin of a bone tower or pillar. Hunks of basalt littered the dunes for a time.

Mages held more warmth than most, and in such dry and stagnant heat, even small movements were draining. They rested in what little shade could be found at midday, only riding when dusk fell. At length, they reached the Erian Pass, the quickest way to Carmentum. Hundreds of dwellings were carved into its inner walls, caves stacked around and over each other, joined by rope bridges that climbed up as far as Tunuva could see.

The passage opened on to a dusty cliff on the other side of the ridge, where thick-bodied milk trees stood with branches fanned out to embrace the sky. In the far distance, through the rippling haze across the land, Tunuva could just about see a city.

'Nin,' she said, 'can you still smell them?'

Ninuru waited for a flurry of wind. 'Lalhar.' Her nostrils flared. 'She was here.'

Tunuva nodded. Her instinct had been right.

The sun was a gold platter. As it started its long descent, Canthe directed them towards the Halassa Sea. It sparkled to the west, unbroken all the way to the horizon. No one had ever crossed it and returned.

They found an opening in rock, where two faceless statues showed the way to a cracked set of steps, leading to an underground cavern. Daylight shone through a wide break above and danced in a clear pool of water, a rare desert spring. Ninuru bent her head to drink.

'Ninuru should be safe here,' Canthe said. 'There are ghost adders to eat.' Ninuru licked her chops. 'Tuva, you will need to leave your sword. The Carmenti do not carry weapons.' Tunuva took it off. 'Given its design, you could risk the spear, but keep it out of sight.'

'Very well.'

Canthe knelt beside the water and splashed the dust from her neck, while Tunuva stroked her ichneumon. 'Ninuru,' she said, 'I need you to stay here until I come back for you.'

Ninuru stopped lapping the water and gazed at her. 'Ichneumons do not leave little sisters.'

'You can't come with us into the city, honeysweet.'

'They have no weapons.'

'Some of them will, even if it's in secret.' Tunuva held her face. 'We won't be apart for long, I promise. Do you trust me?' Ninuru blew through her nose. Tunuva placed a kiss on it. 'Good. Get some rest, and I'll be back in no time with Siyu and Lukiri.'

****

Now they were on foot, Canthe piled up her long hair, so her nape was bare to the sun. She seemed not to sweat, which confounded Tunuva. Even in winter, this region was hot as a kiln.

They walked through groves of olive and desert apricot, towards the high city wall. 'Do you know the story of Carmentum?' Canthe asked, stopping at a well.

'I do.'

Canthe worked the crank while Tunuva took out her gourds. Never had she been so parched.

'Yikala was not the same after the Nameless One. Many had lost their loved ones,' she said. 'After the Onjenyu compensated those families for their losses, a large group of Yikalese left. They went as far south as they could and started building a new settlement.'

The bucket sank into water, and Canthe began to pull it back up. She was stronger than she looked.

'An ancient ruin gave them a foundation,' Tunuva said. 'Years later, the survivors of Gulthaga heard of the city and joined the Yikalese, to help them build Carmentum. Soon many others had flocked there. The Onjenyu eventually gave the city independence from Lasia.'

'And here it stands,' Canthe said, reaching for the bucket. 'A city at the edge of the world, flourishing as port and haven and young republic. The first on this side of the Abyss.'

'Are there any republics in the East?'

'Perhaps beyond the great mountains, in regions we have yet to map.'

Tunuva shook her head. 'It never fails to surprise me that so few see the folly and insult of monarchy.'

'Tradition is steady, and change is a risk. The Carmenti were brave, to choose the latter.'

They both filled their gourds with clean water before continuing. Tunuva drank long and deep.

'I'm surprised you've never come this far south, Tuva,' Canthe remarked. 'Were you not curious about the only republic in the known world – a place with no crowns, like the Priory?'

'I heard enough of it to sate my curiosity. It's a hard journey to make without reason.'

'Now you have all the reason in the world.' Canthe stopped to pick two apricots. 'We do great and terrible things for our daughters.'

Tunuva took the fruit she offered.

By the time they drew close to the city, the sun hung low, a pomegranate on the branch of the sky.

Carmentum hooked around an isolated outcrop, the Lonely Hill, which rose from the desert like the shoulder of some buried god, windcatchers spearing up around it. Canthe paid a small toll to enter on foot, and then they were surrounded by people. Most of the dwellings were whitewashed, partly dug into the ground, with a shade tree.

Beneath a salt oak, a crier read out news ('Good electorate, the Master of Beasts reminds you to join him for a show like no other, three silvers a seat, tomorrow at noon'), watched by a crowd of Carmenti. Tunuva searched the nearest faces, hoping against hope for Siyu.

'We should find an inn,' Canthe said.

Reluctantly, Tunuva nodded. Siyu would run no farther, and the search could take days.

They reached a paved street at least half a mile wide, cast into shadow by sandstone arches, which swept over it like giants' ribs. People there were parting for a woman in a purple cloak. Her tight curls were bound up beneath a circlet, dripping pearls across a lined brown forehead.

'That must be the Decreer,' Tunuva said.

'Yes – Numun, on her tour. Each day, she visits a district to see the people and hear their concerns.'

Beside her walked a redhead in cream silks, the neckline arrowing to her waist, soft and shapely where Numun was formed like a knife. Freckles dusted her pale face and shoulders.

'Ebanth Lievelyn,' Canthe said with a smile. 'An interesting woman. She was a courtesan in the Mentish capital until the Vatten outlawed her profession, in keeping with the Six Virtues. I'm sure you know that Numun also has another consort, Mezdat Taumāgam.'

'Yes, that caused quite a stir in the Priory. Mezdat infuriated Queen Daraniya by renouncing her titles to become a republican. She still has a protector, but the sister here must be discreet.'

'Should we pay her a visit?'

'I had better not interfere with her work.'

Tunuva watched the two women pass. No one bowed, but the people made gestures of respect.

Canthe led her onward, to a row of carriages. While she arranged payment, Tunuva climbed inside and let her eyelids sink.

Carmentum went on and on. By the time the carriage reached the southern face of the hill, it was dusk, and the dry chill of a desert night had already set in. At the foot of the rock, Tunuva followed Canthe to a narrow set of steps, tiredness like an anchor on her. Once they had reached the inn, she was ready to sleep for as long as the Nameless One.

Inside, it was cool and candlelit, silk curtains swaying in the gentle breeze. Canthe spoke in lilting Lasian to the innkeeper, who guided her towards yet more steps.

The room he unlocked was like a cave, with two beds and a hearth. Tunuva went to its small balcony. Carmentum spilled out before her, disappearing back around the Lonely Hill. Nothing could be seen beyond the city wall, so thick was the moonless dark.

'I'll fetch us some food,' Canthe said. 'There should be oil and water for bathing.'

'Thank you.'

Far below, lamps glinted and music soared, shot with chimes of laughter. Tunuva drank it all in, senses pricked. Lalhar would be the key to her search. No one would remember one young woman and a baby, but they would notice an ichneumon.

She had to find them all quickly.

The cold made her shiver. She withdrew and fastened the door before shucking her clothes. Beside a drain shaped like olive leaves, she found linen, water, and a jar of oil, and knelt to cleanse her skin.

She was still patting herself dry when Canthe returned, carrying a platter and a jug.

'Forgive me,' she said, turning away. 'I should have knocked.'

Tunuva raised a smile. 'No need. I'm too old to be shy of my body.'

Canthe smiled back, putting the meal down.

'I wish mine were as strong,' she said. 'I have forged weapons, but I cannot wield them.'

'You can work a forge?'

'Oh, yes.'

'We could use that skill. And even if you never master a sword, you could make a fine archer.'

'I'd like that. I always thought archers so graceful.'

As Tunuva reached for the jug, she glanced up, just as Canthe took off the last of her clothes. She was slim and soft all over.

Tunuva poured the wine. For the first time in years, she wondered what a stranger had thought of her body. Though it had changed over the decades, it was as sturdy as ever, sinewed by a lifetime of training, even if it sometimes craved more rest than it once had. She studied her callused hands, the dark freckles that fanned across her neckline.

She had never fully lost the thickness in her belly. It was her last reminder that her body had once held another.

Canthe drew on a robe. As she turned, Tunuva glimpsed a welter of faint scars below her navel, certainly made by a blade. They were the only marks on her. She belted the silk over them and joined Tunuva at the table, wet hair combed to one side of her neck.

'We should set out at sunrise to search. Most people here sleep at noon,' she said, reaching for a cup of wine. 'Does Siyu have any talents she might use to earn coin?'

Tunuva considered asking her about the scars, then decided against it.

'Hunting, of course. She plays the flute,' she said, 'but perhaps not well enough to make a living from it. Her mind wanders too quickly to pursue a single interest.'

'Can she use a spear?'

'Very well. I taught her.'

'Good. We can search for her in the harbour. They always need spear-fishers.' Canthe reached for one of the forks on the table. 'First, though, let us eat our fill.'

The food was rich with flavour. Flatbread dipped in olive oil, white beans stewed with chopped almonds and fiery salt-cured sausage, cheese and dates, served with a dry red wine.

'The key you wear,' Canthe said, taking a sip from her goblet. 'What does it open?'

Tunuva touched it. The floral key rested between the hollow of her throat and her breastbone. 'I don't know,' she admitted. 'Saghul entrusted it to me, as tomb keeper.'

'But never revealed its purpose?'

'No. She would have told Esbar.' Tunuva tore off a piece of bread. 'May I ask the significance of your ring?'

Canthe looked at it, then worked it from her finger and placed it on the table between them. 'I was married once.' She sat back, crossing one pale leg over the other. 'A long time ago.'

Tunuva picked it up. A joint ring, made of two open circles, locked together at the bezel. The two hands – one on the end of each circle – were clasped as if in friendship. Their fingers held the ring together, and lines had been etched across the inner band.

'Morgish. A spell for eternal love,' Canthe said. 'Something I believed in then.'

'Fine artistry.' Tunuva handed it back. 'Who did you marry?'

'Someone who has been dead for a long time.' Canthe returned the ring to her finger with a tiny smile. 'When I first saw you with Esbar, I envied you – the ease of your intimacy, your laughter. No one has held me close in years. I fear I am too cold to touch.'

'You will find warmth and comfort with us.' Tunuva paused. 'Canthe, earlier, you mentioned that ... we do great and terrible things for our daughters.'

Canthe turned the ring.

'Yes.' She moved a hand over her middle. 'I still think – sometimes, when the solitude lies heaviest – that I feel my newborn girl in my arms. I wake with such a strong belief that when I realise her absence, I mourn all over again.'

Tunuva could only manage a stiff nod. There were too many words in her throat, thick with dust – things she had longed to say in the past, swallowed halfway down and trapped.

'I wish I could tell you the pain leaves. The loss of a child is not such a rare thing,' Canthe said, 'but it is the most unnatural.' She put the goblet down. 'I see the strength of your love for Siyu. Perhaps that was why I came after you. You deserve an easier life, Tunuva – you, who have remained so kind, despite the cruel hand you were dealt.'

Tunuva reached across the table, covering her hand. Canthe turned quite still.

'Canthe,' Tunuva said, 'your pain is not my pain, but I know its shape. I am sorry for it.'

Their fingers interwound.

'I am so sorry for yours.' Canthe forced a smile. 'Please, Tunuva, sleep. You look tired.'

She went to the balcony. Tunuva drained her own cup of wine, then lay down on the bed, her thoughts soaked in him for the first time in months.

Outside, in the dark, the sea washed the Carmenti shore.

49

South

For a time, Tunuva slept as if she lay beneath the waves. When she opened her eyes, Esbar lounged beside her in the bed, stroking her hair. Her smile was a sunrise. Tunuva reached for her with a sigh of relief. Esbar had come after her, because she loved her, and she loved Siyu.

As their lips met, Tunuva tensed. Somewhere, bees were humming. They swarmed from Esbar, from her throat, deep into Tunuva. She woke with a gasp, chest heaving, cold all over.

'Tuva?'

Canthe raised her head. The fire had almost died, leaving the shadows to swallow the room.

'It's all right,' Tunuva said. 'Just a dream.'

She sat up and drew her bare knees to her chest. 'Do you want to share it?' Canthe asked, turning on to her side.

Tunuva let her cheekbone rest against the wall. Speaking of it felt like betraying Esbar, but she wanted it out of her head, in the light. 'I have been having nightmares about Esbar.'

'What happens in these nightmares?'

'She hurts me.' Tunuva kneaded her forehead. 'I don't know why I would imagine such things. She has given me no cause to fear or mistrust her. It ... troubles me.'

'I knew a snowseer once. A wise woman of Hróth,' Canthe said. 'She told me dreams are the truths we bury.'

'Ez would never harm me.'

'Not intentionally. But she has to put duty first.'

'Our love for the Mother comes above all.'

'Some loves must come very close.' Canthe knelt by the fire and slid wood from the alcove beneath. 'I know the sisters of the Priory believe no one should cleave too close to their own flesh. That must have been hard to remember, when you lost your son to the Lasian Basin.'

Tunuva closed her eyes. She felt the cold mud of the hollow again, the rain on her skin. The smell of clay. *Leave me*, she had whispered, while Ninuru lay down beside her. *Let me die.*

Ichneumons do not let little sisters die.

'You must have learned a great deal about siden,' Tunuva said, wanting to change the subject. 'Do you know why the Womb of Fire made a beast like the Nameless One, yet also lights the orange tree?'

Canthe sat back.

'Siden trees – and mages – are the only natural outlet for the magic in the Womb of Fire. We let it wick away enough to stop itself burning too hot,' she said. 'The Nameless One was a miscreation. An affront to nature, made when that magic rose too quickly.'

'Then we are not like him, we mages.'

'No. We take only what siden is offered.' Canthe drew her fingers through her damp waves of hair. 'Tunuva, what will you do if Siyu doesn't want to return to the Priory?'

Tunuva looked away. 'She is still a child,' she murmured. 'I can't leave her alone in the world.'

'We will find her,' Canthe said. 'I promise.'

Tunuva wished she could believe it. Canthe made it sound like truth.

****

At dawn, she woke to find Canthe already dressed in leather sandals and a gown of sunset silk, combing her hair. 'Good morning, Tuva,' she said. 'I have new garments for you, so we might blend in.'

'Thank you.' Tunuva rolled the stiffness from her shoulders. 'You went to the merchants so early?'

'After you fell asleep. There is a night market here.'

'Do you speak Carmenti?'

'Yes, but most people here speak the Taano dialect of Lasian.'

Tunuva dressed in a tunic of pleated linen, with light trousers beneath, and tied on her armguards. Instead of taking the sandals, she pulled her dusty boots back on, and her riding coat, to hide her spear. Finally, she picked up a length of what she thought, at first, was soft brown wool – except that when she held it to the light, it turned to spun gold in her hands.

'Sea wool.' Canthe set her comb aside. 'I thought it would suit you.'

'Canthe, I can't accept this. Sea wool costs—'

'It's cheaper on the coast, and I've saved coin. What point is there in wealth if one can never share it?' Canthe asked. 'You've been kind to me, Tuva. Kinder than anyone has been in a long time.' She smiled a little. 'You know, in my day, it was an insult to refuse a gift.'

Tunuva relented with a smile of her own. 'Thank you.'

The wrap appeared delicate, yet as she drew it around her shoulders, she could feel how well it would warm her when night fell. She would give it to Siyu, when they found her. Siyu had always loved beautiful things.

'Before we leave, I want to show you something.' Canthe went to the balcony door. 'This inn is called the End of Edin. Do you know it's the most expensive in the city?'

Tunuva canted an eyebrow. The night had been comfortable and quiet, but she had seen far grander establishments across Carmentum. As if reading her mind, Canthe beckoned.

'Trust me.'

She kept her hand out. When Tunuva stepped on to the balcony to join her, all the breath left her chest.

Daybreak had cast a blush across the desert. From this high on the Lonely Hill, they could see over the city wall, to a sea devoid of water – a sea of purple wildflowers. They bloomed around a monumental arch of pale and weathered rock, which swept as wide as a small mountain.

Like a desert rose, it had been cut and windblown into being, a thousand feet in height or more. Beyond it, the land broadened into salt flats, pure white as far as the eye could see.

'Ungulus,' Tunuva breathed. 'And the Eria.' She held the balustrade. 'I never thought to see it.'

'I doubt that there is any grander sight in all the world.'

Tunuva stared at it until her eyes hurt. The endless salts the Joyful Few had somehow conquered. She could not imagine the fear Suttu the Dreamer must have felt, facing such a journey.

'Come,' Canthe said. 'Let's find Siyu.'

****

The air was still a chilly haze at this hour of the day. They descended the steps, into the morning bustle of the city, where people waited at the wells and a mirror temple was opening its doors. As she and Canthe walked north, Tunuva tried to catch a glimpse of every face, but soon found it impossible. Already there were thousands of Carmenti on the streets.

'We'll start with the bakers' guild,' Canthe told her over the din. 'It isn't far.'

It had a domed roof and two windcatchers. Tunuva waited outside, grateful Canthe had come. Every sister could track, but Tunuva had always been inclined towards introspection and stillness, calmest in forest and mountains. Cities overwhelmed her senses.

Esbar had never had that trouble. Apparently, neither did Canthe, who seemed perfectly comfortable. When she returned, she said, 'None of their bakers have a son named Anyso. Plenty of Carmenti bake without joining, but guild bakers sell from one street, which would have made things easier. We'll have to try there, and see if anyone happens to know of a family in the trade who lost a son. I'm certain that news would have spread.'

An inviting scent heralded the street. Here, bakers made every sort of bread, spading hot loaves from stone ovens and griddles while the Carmenti lined up to break their fast. Canthe spoke first to a muscular man, who shook his head at her description.

Tunuva tried not to give in to her fear that this was a lost cause. Carmentum had a population in the hundreds of thousands, and they were trying to pinpoint just one family. They had walked almost the whole length of the street before something made Canthe stop.

She spoke to a baker who wore an antique Libir necklace, her curls piled up and held in place with a wide band of cloth. The woman spoke to Canthe in Carmenti, her expression strained.

'I have their names,' Canthe said to Tunuva. 'His parents are called Meryet and Pabel, and they have a bakehouse in the stonecutters' district. It's across the Jungo, near the harbour.'

'You're certain it's them?'

'They have three children, including a son named Anyso, who disappeared in Lasia last year.'

'Take me there.'

The Jungo ran shallow and green, a braided river thirsting for the rains that seldom fell on this city. They took an arched white bridge and walked in the direction of the port. Canthe paused every so often to ask questions, and they were pointed to the bakehouse.

The right street was shaded by its own buildings. Outside the bakehouse, a girl with brown hair was hunched a bench, a familiar baby nestled into her embrace. Tunuva stopped, heart in her middle.

'Excuse us,' Canthe said in Lasian. The girl startled. 'Do you know a baker named Meryet, or Pabel?'

'Yes. I'm their daughter,' the girl said. 'Did they send you?'

Tunuva and Canthe exchanged a look.

'Hazen, is it?' Canthe said, sitting beside the girl, who answered with a small nod. 'We didn't come from your parents, but to ask after someone who may have approached your family for shelter. Her name is Siyu.'

Hazen peeked up at them with dark, bloodshot eyes. She looked about thirteen. 'Who are you to Siyu?'

'I'm her aunt,' Tunuva said. 'This is my friend.'

'She was staying with us.'

'We've been so worried about her,' Canthe said. 'May I ask why she came to you?'

'My brother, Anyso – he disappeared up north in Dimabu. We waited and looked for as long as we could, but we ran out of money. Siyu wanted to tell us what happened to him.'

'What did happen?'

Hazen swallowed. 'Our parents always warned him not to go into the Basin, but he wanted to explore. He got lost for weeks, and came out on the other side, in the village where Siyu lived,' she said. 'She helped him get better. All that time we thought he was dead, he was staying with her. He did try to get back to us, but a snake bit him on the way. A poison snake.'

409

Tunuva felt as if she were still in a nightmare. Never had the Priory been so entangled with outsiders.

'Siyu asked to stay with us. She said I was an aunt,' Hazen said, looking down at Lukiri. 'We gave her my brother's old bed.'

'Where is Siyu now?' Tunuva asked gently.

'We had nowhere for her ichneumon. Siyu found a place for it to sleep under the docks, but you can't keep that big a secret here. The Master of Beasts must have got word. He catches animals, makes them fight. When his hunters came, Siyu fought them with a spear, but there were so many. My parents tried to help. The hunters took them away.'

Tunuva tensed. 'Siyu, too?'

'I heard them say she'd go to the Liongarden. I don't know where they put my parents.'

'Hazen, did the hunters see you or your sister?' Tunuva asked. The girl shook her head, tears in her eyes. 'All right. Stay here. When we have Siyu and Lalhar, we'll come back and take you somewhere safe. Do you have any other family in the city?'

'Our uncle.' Hazen looked at her. 'How long will you be?'

'We'll come back as soon as we can.' Tunuva held out her arms. 'Let me take Lukiri.'

Hazen handed her the baby. Lukiri peered at Tunuva and smiled, reaching a hand for her face. 'Hello, little sunray.' Tunuva gave her a gentle kiss. 'It's all right. You're safe.'

****

'The Liongarden was a pastime of Gulthaga,' Canthe called as they crossed a market square. 'They would pitch warriors against wolves and bears and other beasts, either for glory or punishment. Inys and Yscalin had such places, too – I hear the Malkin Queen enjoyed a baiting.'

Tunuva followed, Lukiri tied to her with the shawl. 'The Carmenti tolerate a violent thief in their midst?'

'The Master of Beasts claims he buys legally, but the hunters are all in his pocket. I should have thought of it myself.' Canthe skirted a cart of dyed silks. 'You'll really go back for the girls?'

'Yes.'

Saghul would have counselled her against further involvement, but she could hardly abandon two children. Helping them was the least she could do, to make up for it all. She would find their parents or take them to their uncle, and that would be the end of it.

Please, let that be the end of it.

Her first sight of the Liongarden stopped her in her tracks, making Lukiri blink. Carved of liverish sandstone, at least a hundred feet tall, the hulk of a building stood out like a snapped bone among the small Carmenti houses, carved with bestial reliefs. This must be some attempt to resurrect the stonework of Gulthaga, along with its bloody traditions. Canthe led her away from the entrance, where people showed tokens to enter.

'We won't get through there. Each token is numbered.'

They followed the curve of the outer wall and stole down a set of steps to the undercroft. Tunuva lit the way, revealing a heavy door. Reaching into that deep place, she turned her flame red and curled her hand around the padlock. The iron melted to the floor, leaving her fingers unscathed.

She hefted the door open. Beyond stretched a barrel-vaulted chamber, where daylight shone through grates in the ceiling and beasts were locked in cells. An olyphant, staring out with sad, flyblown eyes. A desert lion. A grimy white bear, far too thin, with a cub.

At the end of the chamber, several cages were empty, the doors left open. Tunuva picked a tuft of brown moult from the last one.

'Lalhar.'

'The fight must have begun,' Canthe said. As if to confirm it, cheers went up somewhere above. 'We must hurry.'

'You're no fighter. Stay with Lukiri.'

Canthe nodded. Tunuva passed her both the baby and the shawl, then ran up a slope, back into the midday heat.

Inside the Liongarden, a great awning shaded tiers of stone benches, which held thousands of people. On the sand below, Lalhar swept her tail. Blood matted her fur, and her flesh was badly torn in several places, bite marks on her flank.

Three lean wildcats circled the ichneumon. A fourth lay dead, and the survivors all bore wounds, but they kept prowling, not seeming to mind a whit that Lalhar was larger by a head and shoulders. A familiar young woman stood with the ichneumon, spear in hand, poised to strike.

With her sharp hearing, Tunuva caught a bored voice, speaking Lasian with an accent: 'Time to give up, young tamer. Spirited though you are, you will not survive much longer against my cats.'

She could see him now: the sallow, bearded man seated on a balcony. A red cloak was draped over one shoulder, a shade darker than his hair, and his polished gold coronet was fashioned like a serpent eating its own tail. A servant held a small canopy over him.

Siyu was trembling. 'Not without my ichneumon.' Her voice shook. 'Let us go, and I will not kill you next.'

'My ichneumon. I paid its weight in gold,' the Master of Beasts said, silken. 'Can you pay me that much?'

Siyu spun her spear around herself before driving its tip towards him with a shout of defiance, and despite the fear, despite her frustration with Siyu, Tunuva felt a hot surge of pride.

It faded when one of the wildcats charged. Tunuva nocked an arrow, drew and loosed, movements her muscles knew by rote, and it thrashed to the ground, roaring in pain and fury.

Siyu whipped around. Claw marks striped her chest and arms, leaking blood, and her shoulder had been mangled.

'Tuva?' she cried.

Excited shouts. Tunuva ran forward, snapped her folding spear to its full length, and threw with all her might. It struck a second wildcat through the hind leg – a bad enough wound to lame it, not kill. She wrenched the spear free and rolled, just in time to stop the smallest of the three predators from tearing into her.

Reeking breath gusted on her face as the wildcat gnashed at her across the haft of the spear, and huge paws wrestled with her shoulders, claws ripping deep into her arms. Blood flecked its whiskers. On any other day, Tunuva would have admired the creature.

As it happened, she was having a bad day. She dropped her shoulder and threw the beast over her back, while Siyu fought the other. Cheers and applause came bursting from the spectators. The wildcat let out a deafening snarl.

'Peace, now, queen,' Tunuva said softly. 'Let us be friends.'

The wildcat bared long yellow teeth at her. She was thin from hunger, wounded and baited. Tunuva held her amber gaze, circled with white fur, and knew she would try again.

She hunched low, hackles raised, growling from deep in her throat. When she swiped with a massive paw, Tunuva thrust with the spear, warding her off.

'Enough,' she snapped at the Master of Beasts. 'Your hunters stole this ichneumon.'

'I will not accept slander, warrior. I purchased the beast in good faith. These people have gathered to watch it fight.' He drummed his long fingers on the arms of his seat. 'If neither of you can compensate me for what I paid for this rare beast, then—'

'I will pay.'

Tunuva turned. Canthe was walking across the blood and dust, skirts fanning in her wake, Lukiri still in her arms. Taking advantage of the distraction, Siyu edged closer to Tunuva.

The Master of Beasts elevated a pierced eyebrow. To him, Canthe must look like a Carmenti noblewoman, in her yellow sand-washed silks and fine jewellery. 'And who are you?'

'Someone who has what you seek,' Canthe said. The wildcats retreated from her, snarling. 'But my suspicion is that you do not need gold, Master of Beasts. You crave the riches and glory this sacred animal can bring you for months, and then you want her bone.'

'It is mine to do with as I please. Still, I will accept no stains on my reputation.' The Master of Beasts leaned out from his balcony. 'Let me make you an offer that satisfies us all.'

They never did find out what he was going to offer.

Tunuva heard them first – the screams. A hush fell on the stands. The wave of unrest built and rumbled like thunder, tens of thousands of terrified cries.

The Master of Beasts rose. Before him, the Liongarden was still, save the tense rustle of voices in the stands, sounding for all the world like bees.

Suddenly the canopy above was torn in two. Darkness blocked the sunlight – and then something landed on the sand, making the ground tremble. Tunuva Melim could only stare, for here was the thing she was born to destroy, dropped from the desert sky.

Time seemed to slow in that first moment, as she took in as much detail as she could. Her bones had known it was coming, but seeing it was another matter. It had the shape of the Nameless One, horned and with spines on its back – except that its hide was brindled, the scales like burnt wood, and its front limbs were one and the same as its wings.

A *wyrm*.

Its searing gaze went to the Master of Beasts, isolated on his balcony. He stood bloodless and stiff, the grey in his eyes almost swallowed by white. The creature reared on to its muscular legs and spread its wings wide.

When it roared, the wildcats joined it, backs arched, ears flattened. The Master of Beasts had no time for last words before its throat glowed like a coal, and fire came hurtling from its mouth.

Siyu gasped. So did the spectators – those who could. The blaze cooked the Master of Beasts like a steak before it swept across the stands, setting hair and clothes aflame. Now more wings sliced overhead, and the sky was twisting and writhing with monsters. Tunuva took Siyu by the hand and pulled her towards the underground chamber.

'Lalhar, Canthe,' she shouted, 'to me!'

The wounded ichneumon shadowed them, sporting a limp. 'Tuva, the girls,' Siyu cried. 'We have to get the girls—'

'I know.'

Tunuva towed her through the tunnel of animals, breaking cages open as she went. 'Go, now, king of beasts,' she urged the desert lion. 'No one brings you to your knees.'

Growling, the lion stood.

Siyu ran up the steps ahead of her. They emerged into beating sunlight and turmoil – Carmentum, stripped of order, harrowed by wyrms. Talons snatched at people and livestock, lifting them from the paving stones. Long tails smashed into houses. Red fire exploded across every street, feasting on both the quick and the dead, setting the trees aflame.

The Priory had never anticipated this. For five centuries, its warriors had waited for the Nameless One, knowing they stood ready to defeat him – one wyrm, never hundreds.

No story had warned of that.

The wildcats ran past, along with a pack of painted hounds, barking in a frenzy. Spear in hand, Tunuva followed Siyu. Instinct told her to stop and fight to the death, but this was not a battle she could win. Better that she survived, to warn Esbar.

She caught the waft of brimstone. Turning, she tightened her hands on the spear. A creature was lumbering up the next street.

It had clearly been a lioness once. Some nightmarish force had bloated it – stretched out the spine, the claws, the neck. Its head was set too high, swaying as a hooded serpent did before a strike. She remembered the ox, the tormented ox that had hatched in the Priory.

This beast fixed its soulless gaze on her, teeth skinned and smeared with gore. She ran straight towards the creature, slewing her body straight between its legs. Behind her, Siyu sliced at its flank, while Canthe hurried past its other side, protecting Lukiri.

They found the little street crumbled, and a winged beast dying on its shattered roofs, brought down with a harpoon. 'No,' Siyu cried. She dropped her spear. 'Dalla, Hazen—'

She started to grab desperately at the rubble. 'Siyu.' Tunuva restrained her. 'Siyu, it's too late.'

'I have to look!'

'Listen to me. They might have got out and gone to their uncle. I hope so. If not, they are dead.' Tunuva grasped her elbows. 'I have to leave now, to warn the Priory. Come with me.'

Siyu stared back at her, her eyes full. 'Did you kill him, Tuva?'

'No, sunray. Saghul ordered it. I'm sorry.' Tunuva looked her in the eyes. 'Please, Siyu. Don't run from who you are.'

Lukiri choked on the smoke and ash as she cried. Trembling, Siyu watched Canthe shush her.

'The Mother needs her warriors,' Tunuva told her. 'We are the only ones who might be able to stop this.'

'Esbar won't forgive me.'

'Esbar is Prioress. She must.'

'Siyu,' Canthe said, 'you have a home. The sort of home I have walked the world to find.' Lukiri clutched her dress, whimpering. 'Don't throw it away. Don't choose to live as I have.'

Siyu swallowed, her mouth tightening. A tear washed a line of dust from her cheek.

'I'll come.'

Tunuva nodded. She took Siyu by the hand again, and this time, Siyu gripped hers tight.

They wove through narrow alleys and emerged near the harbour, where all was uproar. Frantic people swamped the boats or thrashed into the shallows. As Canthe led the group along the beach, a surge of screaming made Tunuva stop. Through a smog of smoke and dust and ash, she saw another monstrous form, soaring from the Halassa Sea.

This time, she chose a barbed arrow. She held the draw until the beast was close enough for her to count the spines on its back. This had never been anything but a wyrm, she was sure – no trace of ox or lioness, nothing of the natural world. Only the face of the enemy.

She let fly.

Her arrow found its eye. Its wrawl of pain stiffened the hair on her arms. The press of bodies hardened as the Carmenti shoved and scrambled, crying out when the wyrm crashed into the waves.

'Tuva,' Canthe said, 'hurry. We're close.'

She led them back to the streets. Black smoke boiled from the buildings, so much of it that dusk mantled Carmentum. Long ago, its people had agreed to cast off the gold helm of monarchy. Now there was no rule but fear.

Camels were snorting in terror, horses pulling carriages in flames, bodies smoking where they fell. Keeping hold of Siyu, Tunuva imagined it all as a fever dream, and the city wall as the threshold between trance and truth.

Siyu took Lukiri as they fought towards the city gate. All around, voices, mad with dread, crowds of Carmenti. Tunuva tried to shut them out. Too many lives. Too many deaths. They were penned, choking the throat of Carmentum. Still limping, Lalhar barked to forge a path, and then they were out, back into the waste, no shelter from the open sky.

The war was here.

At last, after five hundred years, it had come.

They ran, Lalhar panting in distress, too weak to bear even one rider. 'Tuva,' Canthe shouted.

Tunuva spun, an arrow ready. When she saw, she lowered the bow, her arms turning to stone.

Whatever had appeared in the Liongarden, whatever was burning Carmentum – those were nothing in comparison to this.

This, *this* beast was the spit of the Nameless One. Four legs, wings that could throw a city into shadow, a tail as strong as a battering ram, and two horns, fearful to behold. Like the smaller creatures, it seemed hewn from the earth itself, its hide like ironstone. Its claws and the baleful spikes on its tail were metal, formed deep in the world.

In a single breath, the wyrm torched through a hundred fleeing Carmenti. The flames came as if from the Dreadmount, destroying all they touched. Tunuva drew on her siden and enfolded the others in a warding.

This plain was now a hunting ground.

The firestorm tore around her shield. Even wrapped in the fist of her magic, the heat almost brought her to her knees. She was deep in the heart of a sun, hearing Siyu gasp for breath. As soon as it stopped, they kept going, while the wyrm slowly wheeled back, too massive for swiftness.

When it saw them again, its eyes burned so hot Tunuva thought they would spark. In the face of its terrible breath, she crouched, so she needed less siden to cover herself.

They had to reach the cave where she had left Ninuru. It would keep them safe until the monster had its fill of violence.

In the third wave of red fire, Tunuva shook with the effort of holding up her warding. Siyu called a weak one with the remnant of her magic, but she was untaught. It thinned dangerously on one side as she tried to shield Lukiri on the other, her right arm blistering in the heat. Tunuva widened hers.

The wyrm covered the sun, then swooped low. Its shadow grew large before it landed in front of them, hard enough that the ground shuddered and Lalhar lost her footing. Tunuva nocked two long arrows and loosed them at its chest, where its heart must burn.

One arrow rang off its armour, while the other shattered. Forsaking the bow, Tunuva elongated her spear and pictured herself in the War Hall with Esbar. She slowed her breath. Calmed her soul.

Do not be afeared. The Mother's words filled her mind. *You are the very sun made flesh.*

Wide as three men, the tail came rushing towards her. She ducked it. Scorching wind howled in its wake, making her nape burn. Taking aim, she hurled the spear at the underside of its jaw, finding her mark. The wyrm roared in rage. It countered her with a furnace, and once again, Tunuva met it with all the power she could bring to bear.

By the time the smoke cleared, she was on the ground, drenched in sweat and shuddering. The creature bared rows of teeth, each longer than her arm. Blood seeped down the haft of the spear.

'Die.'

That voice was so deep – the breath of an earthquake – that it took her a moment to recognise the word, through the haze in her mind. *Ersyri, it speaks Ersyri.* Its eyes were empty yet aware, blind instinct with an edge of malice. Tunuva stared up and into them, drained. *How does it know a human tongue?*

Already she had burned through half her store of magic. In training, she had learned to recover, but never had she faced an enemy like this.

'Get up,' Siyu sobbed. 'Tuva, get up!'

The wyrm opened its cavernous maw. Tunuva lifted her hand for one more warding – she was sure that one more was all she had left – when a white streak of fur leapt upon the beast.

Ninuru.

She ripped at the wyrm, clamping her jaws on its wing. Her claws were fully out, hooked deep between its scales, as if they had been made to fit. The wyrm managed to shake her off, but Ninuru twisted straight back to her paws, bounding in front of Tunuva. Her hackles were up, her fangs bared to the root, and she made sounds Tunuva had never heard, deep snarls and chattering shrieks. She was no match for it in size, yet she squared up to the monster.

Once its head came low enough, Tunuva reached up and wrenched her spear free. Tarlike blood streamed from the wound, sizzling where it struck the ground.

Thick armour covered most of the wyrm, but when the Mother had fought the Nameless One, she had spotted a weak spot under his wing, where scale became limber flesh. Tunuva knew she had to strike it there, or in its eye. She found the strength to stand and face the beast.

It shifted its attention to her.

In that same moment, Lalhar sprang forward.

The wyrm caught her and crunched down, and Siyu screamed in anguish, as if its teeth had pierced her, too.

'Lalhar!'

The young ichneumon whined and fell limp, her ribs caving under the weight of that bite. Yowling in fury, Ninuru pounced again, clawing up the wyrm, tearing and biting the spines of its face, seized by primeval wrath. Lalhar slipped from its mouth and hit the ground.

'Lalhar!' Siyu fell with a cry on her ichneumon. 'Lalhar, no—'

'Siyu, move,' Tunuva barked.

Siyu turned, trying to protect Lalhar with her smaller body. The wyrm bore down on her, its teeth dripping blood, and cracked its jaws wide as a cave, to swallow her entire.

Canthe stepped between them.

Straight away, the wyrm looked from Siyu to her, nostrils flaring. Canthe betrayed no fear. She lifted her left hand, and a winter sun rose between her fingers. No, not a sun – a white orb of lightning, an exploding star. It was cold and blinding.

Nothing like fire.

Tunuva stared in disbelief as a redolence sharpened the air, metal and rain and bitter almonds, knifing forth with beams of light. As the glow became unbearable, the wyrm threw up a wing and screamed, and Tunuva buckled to the ground, her blood spurning the brutal power spilling out of Canthe.

It is not siden, was her last thought. *There is another magic...*

Her own siden recoiled into its deepest vaults. She heard Siyu collapse beside her, Lukiri screaming, and then Canthe erupted with light.

****

The smoke mounted, the ashes fell, and soon the sky turned red. The cries took half a day to wane. By nightfall, they had reached the south end of the Erian Pass – two mages on foot, one on the ichneumon, and the child in a sling, no longer weeping.

And Carmentum was just as it had been before the Yikalese had built it – a ruin at the end of the world, silent and alone.

50

East

Dumai woke to the deep chill of flight. She raised her head, the base of her neck sore in a way that was familiar now.

Dawn had broken like a cup of molten gold, limning tufts of cloud while leaving all the land in shadow. This was the Empire of the Twelve Lakes, the largest country in the East.

At present, this was a realm divided. The territories north of the River Daprang had been captured by a large Hüran tribe, the Bertak, while the rest still belonged to the ancient House of Lakseng. The Treaty of Shim had ended hostilities, with the Bertak ruling from the city of Hinitun, and an exchange of Lacustrine and Hüran heirs to ensure peace.

Dumai had no intention of involving herself in politics. She was here to speak to the alchemist Kiprun, to see if she knew what was tormenting the deep earth, and what had caused a wyrm to emerge. In the meantime, she willed her father to remain strong at court.

He managed without you for years, she told herself. *He can manage while you try to stop Seiiki burning.*

She glanced back at Nikeya, pale and shivering against Kanifa, still asleep. Dangerous as she was, she was still human. A small threat compared to the glistening beast in Sepul.

Furtia flew in silence. Red stained the snow below, which spread white and untouched as far as the eye could see. Though Dumai ached for her old life, she would not have missed this sight for anything – the world from dragonback.

It was almost midday by the time the southern capital appeared. In the summer, the Lakseng moved to the coast, but for now, the Munificent Empress ruled from the City of the Thousand Flowers.

A thousand thousands would have been closer, according to legend. In spring, blossoms flared on every street, on peach and apricot and plum trees, scenting the air like sweet pastry.

Dumai tried to absorb it, this city that went on and on. She had studied paintings and accounts before leaving Seiiki, but nothing could have prepared her for the width of the street called White Blossom Way, or the myriad districts that fanned out from it, separated by frozen canals.

She glimpsed the famous water-driven clock tower, the ironworks and quarries, the windpiercers and merchant ships on the River Shim. The Moonbow swept across its narrowest point – a great arched bridge without middle supports – and the Lakra Mountains rose in the distance.

As Furtia descended, Dumai could see the houses more clearly. Most were made of worked stone or rammed earth. *Good*, she thought. *Stone does not burn.*

People started to call out to the dragon. Furtia landed in front of Black Lake Palace, which was still under construction to the south – a city tucked within a city, its secrets hidden by high walls. Its many roofs were carved of petrified wood, and a celestial globe crowned its starwatch, which was said to be the tallest in the known world.

So far, it had taken eleven years to build, and no wonder. Golden crows flew on the ridge of each roof, a stone relief was carved above its doors – two dragons circling a full moon – and the doors themselves showed five constellations, large silver bosses marking the position of each star. Dumai recognised the Deathless Queen and the Doorway.

As she dismounted, those black doors were wound open to let a small procession through. From the stars on their robes, they were imperial officials, though some looked hastily dressed and heavy-eyed, as if they had just woken up. All stared in wonder at Furtia Stormcaller.

Kanifa helped a clammy Nikeya from the saddle. Unknotting their rope, Dumai turned to the Lacustrine, interlocking three fingers of each hand before her, thumbs tucked against her palms.

'The Crown Princess of Seiiki requests your hospitality,' she called. 'I am Noziken pa Dumai, daughter of Emperor Jorodu.' She wished she looked less unkempt after a flight. 'Please forgive my sudden arrival. I seek an urgent audience with the Munificent Empress.'

She used the court dialect of Lacustrine she had learned from her grandmother. A tall woman with thick grey hair came forward, her gaze shadowed with both interest and caution.

'Princess Dumai.' She returned the salute, using all but her thumbs, echoing the four claws of most Lacustrine dragons. 'Welcome to the Empire of the Twelve Lakes. I am the Minister of Ceremony. What a delight to have guests from Seiiki – its future empress, no less.'

'We had almost forgotten you,' a tiny wizened man said cheerfully. 'What have you been doing all these centuries?'

'Waiting for the gods to wake,' Dumai said, with a rueful smile. 'I regret that we have not been closer. The sea is never kind to ships – but I need no ship to reach you now. This is Furtia Stormcaller.'

Furtia puffed cloud through her nostrils, and the officials bowed again.

'And these are my travelling companions – my sworn guard, Kanifa of Ipyeda, and Lady Nikeya of Clan Kuposa,' Dumai said. 'My father would have sent word ahead, but there was no time.'

'No need to explain, Princess Dumai,' the Minister of Ceremony said. 'The King of Sepul told us of your coming.'

'I see.' Dumai released her breath. 'King Padar has already warned you of the threat, then.'

'Yes.' She beckoned them. 'Please, come out of the cold. Her Imperial Majesty – she who is bestarred and moonlit, rightful Empress of the Twelve Lakes – is pleased to welcome you into her palace. Alas, she is unable to receive you at this time. Consort Jekhen will see you as soon as possible. Until then, you must rest and refresh yourselves, after such a journey.'

Dumai nodded. The Munificent Empress was known to rely on her formidable consort.

'King Padar may have told you that I wish to consult the court alchemist,' Dumai said, following the Minister of Ceremony. 'Given the urgency of the situation, I wondered if Mistress Kiprun might be able to see me today.'

'The alchemist is now known as Master Kiprun. He has been away, but should return within a few days.'

'Very well.'

Beyond the constellated doors, a set of steps led to a courtyard so large it made even Furtia appear small. Dumai walked at her side. From what her father and tutors had told her, Black Lake Palace had been built to reflect the world of the gods – which they believed was in the sky – as perfectly as still water.

Servants in dark quilted coats dug footpaths, shovelling new snow into the river that coursed like blood between the buildings, the Inner Shim. Otherwise, the enormous space was deserted, save a giant statue of a Lacustrine dragon, a human bestriding its back. They held a lantern filled with a smokeless glow, which billowed slow and calm, like a white banner.

'The Lightbearer,' the Minister of Ceremony said as they walked under it. 'The first dragonrider, who founded the first great Lacustrine civilisation at Pagamin. The light is from the Imperial Dragon, reminding us that she is always present, even as she sleeps.' She motioned to the nearest guards. 'Furtia Stormcaller may stay in the Hidden Lake.'

Nodding, Dumai placed a hand on Furtia. *The guards will take you to water*, she told her. Furtia hummed her approval. *I will try to find the one who knows the secrets of the earth, so we can try to stop the fire from rising any more.*

No child of earth could ever stop it. Only fallen night can stop it.

Dumai frowned.

What do you mean, great one?

With a cantankerous snort of fog, Furtia drifted after the guards, leaving Dumai to stare after her.

****

The apartments they were offered had belonged to the last Seiikinese ambassador. Dumai could rest on dragonback, but as soon as she had tucked herself into a chamber bed, fresh from a hot bath, she stepped over the cusp of sleep, and found she wanted company.

Are you there?

A stirring. *Yes*, came the reply, as the figure smoked into being. *I thought you had gone.*

Dumai pressed her fingertips into the bed. *Between dreams and the waking realm, this place seems to float untethered. Hard to find and hold.*

Her other form walked to the stream. *This is an interstice, and we, two wandering stars.*

She knelt beside the water, seeing only shadow where her body ought to be.

Stop, the figure warned, just as their surroundings darkened. *I think that trying to cross will break it. Tell me why you speak to me.*

I know not what I am to you. Only that you and I are bound. Dumai stood. *Strange things are afoot, I fear. There are forces at work I do not understand – but we can meet here, to comfort each other. Perhaps that is the reason we were called to this place, to be sisters.*

I would like that. There was a long quiet, and she felt a heaviness on the other side. *I have lost the people I love most, the ones who guided me. Now I have no idea where to turn, except to you. Yours is the voice that steadies me.*

As yours steadies me. Dumai breathed in, eyes flickering beneath her lashes. The connexion was already waning. *You must be on your guard. Wherever you are in the world, I warn you: they are coming.*

What is coming?

A beast of the earth. A wyrm, Dumai told her. Their interstice quaked, and she focused once more, making her temples hurt. *Whatever I learn, I will tell you. Be careful, my sister, my mirror. Be ready.*

'Mai?'

Dumai lurched awake. Kanifa sat beside her, his face lit by an oil lamp.

'Kan.' She tasted salt. 'What is it?'

'Consort Jekhen has requested your presence at midnight. It seems the Lacustrine court wakes at dusk and sleeps at dawn.' He held up a tray. 'The messenger came with a meal.'

'Now we know why it was so quiet when we arrived.' Dumai rubbed the grit from her eyes. 'How long do I have?'

'Two hours. She sent new clothes for you, since the servants took yours to be cleaned.'

'I haven't worn most of them.'

'I did tell her.' As she drew the tray on to her lap, he said, 'Are you all right?'

She took the lid off a cup, letting out the scent of ginger. 'Kwiriki has been sending me strange dreams for some time.'

'What is it you see?'

424

'A figure in the dark. She says she is from an island.'

Kanifa considered, brows down. 'I don't claim to know much of dreams, but it sounds like she is your reflection. A way for you to clear your thoughts, by talking to yourself.'

'I thought the same. The person I need to become, mingled with the person I am. Yet she feels separate from me – as if she has her own spirit, not mine.' Dumai shook her head. 'Never mind. This alchemist is the most pressing matter. Will you bring Nikeya here?'

'Really?'

'She has her uses. A future empress should know her limits.' Dumai glanced at him. 'Call her once I've finished eating.'

By the light of the lamp, she finished the meal: steamed crab served in a hollow orange, chestnut cake and plums and sliced peaches, and a strange honey wine that gave her a headache. Her new garments were richest blue and trimmed with gold, the colours of the Seiikinese crest. Dumai put on the shirt and a darker skirt that came over her chest.

'You summoned me, Princess?'

She glanced over her shoulder. Lady Nikeya was in the doorway, looking better for a bath and sleep. 'I am granting your request,' Dumai informed her. 'You may comb my hair.'

'Kanifa has a fine set of hands. Should I be flattered that you asked for mine?'

'You were right in Sepul.' Dumai offered a comb. 'Do as you will.'

With a smile that could have been victorious or simply pleased, Nikeya took it. 'Sit, then.'

Dumai perched on a drum stool in front of a mirror. Nikeya stood behind her and tilted her head, holding her by the jaw.

From the first touch, her body answered. Each fingertip sowed a seed of sensation, budding into warmth, blossoming with shivers. Her hair was still damp from the bath, hopelessly tangled from days in the wind. She let her eyes close as cool fingers ghosted over it.

'I should trim it a little,' Nikeya said. 'My clan makes excellent shears.'

'If you suppose I will ever let you hold any blade near my throat, you will be waiting some time.'

'It pains me that you still believe I want to hurt you, Princess.'

'Prove me wrong.' Dumai watched her in the mirror. 'For now, tell me what you know of Consort Jekhen.'

Nikeya smoothed both hands over her scalp before parting her hair down the middle.

'Jekhen was an orphan. She came to the palace with only her wits, and charmed her way inside.' She spoke in soft and calming tones. 'One night, the Crown Princess overheard a chambermaid telling stories to the other servants. She hid behind a screen to listen.'

Dumai felt a little drowsy. The comb glided through her hair, sleaving it into layers.

'The Crown Princess was a sheltered girl. She had never been outside the palace; never heard such marvellous tales, let alone heard them told with such flair. They freed her mind from the stifling confines of duty. From then on, each time the chambermaid told one of her tales, the princess was listening behind a screen. That chambermaid was Jekhen.'

Deft fingers slid up her nape, warm and fleet, to loosen a knot in the place she always missed. It should have hurt. Instead, there was a sweet tension that built with every touch.

'One day, Jekhen caught the princess. Some say she always knew she was there.' A tug, and long nails on her scalp. 'She said there was no need to hide. Her Imperial Highness was welcome to listen ... or she could always tell her tales in her own chamber.'

Nikeya reached for the comb again. Dumai held still as it grazed to the blunt ends of her hair, catching her bare shoulder.

'I imagine Consort Jekhen takes unkindly to any acknowledgement of her roots, romantic though the story is.' Nikeya gave her a smile in the mirror. 'Let's keep it as our secret.'

'If it's a secret, how do you know it?'

'Our world floats on secrets, Princess. I make it my business to know as many as I can.'

After that, there was a hush. Footsteps passed outside, and birds sang, but all Dumai could hear was Nikeya: the rustle of her clothes, her breath. Each draw and glide of the comb raised a chill.

When it was done, Nikeya stroked her scalp once more, slow as falling asleep, before placing the gold headpiece.

'There.'

It took Dumai a moment to come back to herself. She had gone into a waking trance.

'Thank you,' she said. 'The coat, if you please.'

Nikeya held it out. Dumai eased her arms into the broad sleeves, and Nikeya planed the shoulders before she came around to knot the long ties at the waist.

Suddenly she folded. Dumai caught her by the elbows. 'Nikeya,' she said, softer. 'What is it?'

'I feel somewhat faint.'

'Is this one of your games?'

Nikeya laughed a little. 'Showing weakness would be a poor tactic.'

Dumai could see the bright scrap of bait, but swallowed it whole, fish that she was, as soon as Nikeya trembled against her. Now Dumai could see the darkness of her lips, from spending too long in the sky. She guided her straight to the bed, knowing her fear was justified when Nikeya failed to make a coy remark.

Nikeya curled into the quilts. Dumai checked her brow for sweat, her fingertips for the grey tint. She skimmed a thumb under her sleeve, finding her pulse a weak flicker.

'Breathe slowly,' Dumai said. 'It's mountain sickness.' She picked up the cup. 'Here. Ginger.'

'My mother used to fuss over me.' Nikeya took a tiny sip. 'Whenever I took fever.'

'I never asked who she was.'

'Nadama pa Tirfosi, the poet.'

'I know her work. A great talent.' Dumai nodded to her tunic. 'Did she give you that brooch?'

Nikeya often wore it, close to her heart. It was shaped like a mulberry fruit with delicate gold leaves. Each berry was a drop of blood amber, such a deep red it was almost black.

'No,' Nikeya said, touching it. 'This is an heirloom from my father.' She made a tired stab at a flirtatious smile. 'That's the second time you've enquired about my trinkets, Princess. I've heard people only start to notice such trifling details when they fall in love.'

Dumai moved away. 'You go too far.'

'I must, else I would never go anywhere.'

'I don't want you to go anywhere.' When her smile widened, Dumai added, flushing, 'I mean that you should stay here, in the apartments, while I speak to Consort Jekhen.'

'Very well. I will take a night in your bed instead, Princess.'

'Good for you. I will not be in it.'

427

****

Just before midnight, Dumai and Kanifa were sculled along the Inner Shim. Night had woken the palace, set it glittering with chatter and candles. Owls hooted from the willows that overhung the river, and fish with their own tiny lanterns chased after the boat.

All was calm, yet at any moment, something could swoop from the sky to shatter it.

The rowboat stopped at a bridge. On the other side, in the depths of the Black Lake Palace, courtiers had gathered on the roofed walkways around a pool, watching a water opera unfold. The performers sang and danced on floating platforms, dryshod and graceful, their footwork demanding perfect control.

It was easy to find Consort Jekhen, alone in a pavilion. She was a large woman in all ways, from her frame to her features to the height of her crown – a tower of delicate silver, gemstones and freshwater pearls, beaded along the band.

'The princess. Or is it the priestess?' she said, once Dumai had been presented. Her voice was slow and deep. 'Sit at my side, Noziken pa Dumai. I dislike needless formalities.'

'Thank you, Consort Jekhen.'

Kanifa stood back in the shadows. Once Dumai was settled, a servant offered her a cup.

'Ice wine, from beyond the Abyss.' Consort Jekhen drank some of her own. 'I realised I know almost as much of the people who made this wine as I do of the Seiikinese. A curious thought. We have puzzled over your island, gone silent for so long.'

'I understand the last ambassy was several centuries ago.'

'Before the gods slept. It has passed into myth for some Lacustrine – mysterious, faraway Seiiki. Utter dramatics, of course. Some Seiikinese ships and merchants have reached us here, and some of ours have gone to you. I am partial to your pearls, myself.' She wore a flake of silver leaf on either side of her mouth, so even the smallest of her smiles glinted. 'So you will be Empress of Seiiki. I know some of your story from King Padar.'

'He also spoke to Master Kiprun?'

'Indeed. Our reclusive alchemist is suddenly in great demand,' Consort Jekhen said drily. 'He's been in the Nhangto Mountains. King

428

Padar flew to see him, but you need not – I've summoned him to save us from the idiot who occupies his tower at present.'

'I may speak to Master Kiprun, then?'

'If you wish. King Padar vouched for your conduct. I would usually not permit strange princesses to poke about the palace, but one has already been foisted on me. Why not another?'

Dumai had no idea who she meant.

'Besides,' Consort Jekhen said, 'like me, and like King Padar, you were not reared for a throne – so I doubt you are here to spy on us, Princess Dumai, as I might otherwise suspect.'

'I am grateful for your trust.' Dumai watched one of the actors execute a perfect headstand, drawing applause. 'I didn't establish whether the Sepuli had a way to wake all their dragons.'

'You wonder if we do.' Consort Jekhen finished her wine. 'Except for a few loners, most of our gods obey the Imperial Dragon. For now, she remains asleep. The empress and I have been debating whether we should try to wake her, or hope she returns of her own accord, which is the popular school of belief. King Padar made a persuasive case for the former option – but you were daring, to rouse all your dragons at once.'

'I saw no other choice.'

'This creature must have frightened you.'

'It did,' Dumai said. 'I was raised on a mountain that ate at my strength, and even my flesh. There are few things I fear.' She showed her shortened fingers. 'But what I saw in Sepul – it terrified me, Consort Jekhen.'

Consort Jekhen took in her hand, then her face, her midnight gaze a little sharper.

'I hear you enjoy stories,' Dumai said, risking it. 'Do you know the tale of the Nameless One?'

'Loosely.'

'I think there is some truth in it.'

'Only one beast came, the first time. One,' Consort Jekhen reminded her, 'and it was soon defeated.'

'But this is not the first time. And we don't know how it was defeated.'

Consort Jekhen made a low sound in her throat, which Dumai took as a concession.

Just then, a tall white horse in feathered barding came galloping on to the bridge. The woman astride it had high cheekbones and brown skin, flushed from the cold. She dismounted and strode to the pavilion, removing her helm to show the braids looped under her ears.

'Irebül, I have a guest. From a trade partner we have not seen in centuries.' Consort Jekhen sighed. 'Must you always make such an entrance?'

'Swiftness was of the essence,' the newcomer said, with a sharp accent. Her leather boots were crusted with snow. 'I bring tidings from the North. The Munificent Empress will need to be roused.'

Dumai suddenly realised who this must be. The Hüran princess who had been exchanged for the Lacustrine heir.

'If I am to wake Her Majesty, I will have to explain *why* she must leave the comfort of her bed, despite the threat of sickness, and her ailment,' Consort Jekhen said icily. 'May I have the honour of an explanation?'

Princess Irebül huffed out in a thick fog. 'As you wish. You will all know soon,' she declared loudly, so everyone could hear. The opera stopped. 'The King of Hróth is dead!'

Dumai stiffened. All around her, murmurs broke out. 'King Bardholt,' Empress Jekhen said, eyebrows raised. 'Dead?'

'According to the North Hüran,' Princess Irebül returned, cool and steady. 'If the Hammer has fallen, there may be war.' She folded her arms. 'There is another matter. News closer to home. Someone joined me on my way back from Golümtan – one I did not expect.'

'That ludicrous bird?'

'No. Even better.' Princess Irebül smiled for the first time, glancing upward. 'Nayimathun of the Deep Snows.'

Cries of elation rose from the walkways. Dumai leaned out from the pavilion to see a dragon far larger than Furtia, claws dug into the wood of the rooftop, teeth gleaming white.

'Well, Princess Dumai,' Consort Jekhen said, unruffled. 'It seems the Empire of the Twelve Lakes may be about to follow your lead.'

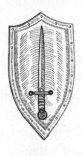

51

West

Glorian wore grey from her fur collar to her shoes. Even her necklace was hoary, made of silver and sheet pearl. She twisted the broad ring from her father as Florell dabbed rosemary oil behind her ears, making her smell of misery.

'It feels wrong that Lady Marian isn't here,' Florell said.

'Queen Sabran wouldn't have wanted her at the entombment.' Julain handed her a comb. 'Would she?'

'No, sweeting, but Queen Sabran is gone.' Florell stoppered the oil. 'I never wanted children of my own, but if I did, I could not bear the pain of not being allowed to show my grief.'

Even now, Glorian could hardly absorb those impossible words: *Queen Sabran is gone.*

Helisent set the cloak on her shoulders and pinned on the new patron brooch – the True Sword, which united the Six Virtues. Next came the mourning veil, crusted with grey pearls, and a pair of sheepskin gloves. Florell brought a silver circlet, forged for her mother to honour her as queen consort of Hróth, and used it to fix the veil in place.

'Do you want to see?'

Glorian almost shook her head, then remembered: *A queen must know how she appears to others.* When she nodded, Adela brought her the mirror.

There she stood: Glorian the Third, Queen of Inys. Twentieth monarch of the House of Berethnet. *Wherever you are in the world, I warn you: they are coming.* She could just see her own eyes. *Be careful, my sister, my mirror. Be ready.*

Her mother had said it was the Saint calling. At last, he had acknowledged her again, broken his long silence – but now he offered a warning. *Destruction.*

'Come,' Florell said. 'It's time.' Glorian let herself be led from her chambers.

The sky was black, studded with tiny cloves of star. It was customary to hold entombments just before dawn, so the dead could follow the sun as it climbed to the heavenly court.

Outside, in the Royal Garden, the Virtues Council waited – not just the six Dukes Spiritual, but most of the Earls Provincial and Knights Bachelor, as well as other noble members of the court. All wore grey veils or mourning caps or wimples. Lord Robart was at the front.

'The queen is gone,' he said, unreadable. 'Long live the queen.'

They all bowed. Among them stood Lord Edrick Glenn and Lord Mansell Shore – Wulf's fathers, wearing the alder tree. Grief seemed to have unsouled them both, miring their eyes in shadow.

Glorian walked with her guards down the river stair, into the candle-lit royal barge, its usual red canopy replaced with a grey one. Lord Robart sat beside her.

Ascalun was deathly quiet. As the barge slid through the deep waters of the Limber, Glorian saw scores of people on both sides, faces lit by the torches that smoked along the riverfront. Not all wore grey, but most had found appropriately dull clothing and covered their heads. They held candles in silence. The air smelled like tallow, rosemary and pitch.

Sabran had been the queen who guided them from darkness. Now they would see her home.

The Sanctuary of Queens stood on Rose Island. Here the narrow River Lyttel split before it met the Limber, carving an eyot from the ward. For centuries, this tiny isle in the city had been the resting place of queens and consorts, with its own detail of defenders – the Rose Guard – to ensure no harm came to the bones, protecting the dead's places in Halgalant.

When the barge docked, Lord Robart offered Glorian a hand. They walked through the ancient garden of the sanctuary, where fruit trees and rosemary grew. Sleet had frozen on two apples not long before they rotted to the ground, leaving ice ghosts on the stalks.

Lord Robart wore the gold signet ring of his ancestor, the Knight of Generosity, engraved with a sheaf of wheat and flanked by emeralds. 'The entombment must be witnessed,' he said. 'Three hundred people from the city will be allowed inside.'

'Is that wise, after what happened at Drouthwick?'

'I chose them all myself, Your Grace.'

He spoke as if that settled the matter. Glorian kept her lips still, even as her brow tightened.

They reached the tall wooden doors to the sanctuary, and a guard knocked thrice on the wicketway – a smaller entrance, built into the larger. When it opened, a young man looked out, draped in a grey herigaut with tucked sleeves, belted at the waist.

'Your Grace. Lord Protector,' he said. 'Welcome. I assist the Arch Sanctarian.'

'Good evening.' Lord Robart eyed the windows. 'I trust you are ready.'

'Almost, my lord. Let me take you to the warming house.'

'Your pardon, Lord Robart,' Florell said, 'but perhaps Her Grace could have a little time alone, to pray.'

Lord Robart seemed to consider. 'Very well,' he concluded. 'You've a candle clock inside?'

'Yes, my lord,' the assistant said.

'Down to the nail, then.'

He strode away, towards the other Dukes Spiritual. 'Please, Queen Glorian,' the young sanctarian said. 'Come in.'

He held the wicketway open. Glorian stepped inside with him, and he closed and locked it behind them.

Candlelight unnerved the cold stillness. The dark was so thick that she could only just make out the baldachin, let alone the high ceiling. Along the edge of the room were pairs of creamy marble tombs, spaced at like distance in a great circle, each surrounded by candles, each with a rose in an urn beside it. The effigies' feet pointed towards the boss.

'I will return soon,' the assistant told her. 'The Damsel's balm for your losses, Your Grace.'

'Thank you.'

433

When his footsteps had receded, Glorian listened to her own breath. This was where her skeleton would rest. She stood in her own mausoleum.

The candle clock was set into the wall, the wax seeping towards the next nail. She walked between the tombs, starting with a recent ancestor, Jillian the Third. By all accounts she had been a sour, unhappy person, and had died by murder just a year after her coronation.

To her left was the only tyrant, the Malkin Queen. Glorian tried not to imagine those stone eyelids cracking open. She moved on, touching each cool face. Carnelian the Peaceweaver was missing her nose and part of her intricate plait, thanks to a botched attempt to loot her tomb. When Glorian reached her own namesake, she stayed for a long time.

Glorian Hartbane did not smile in death. Her hair was cut in line with her chin, and she grasped her magnificent bow.

Her companion reposed beside her. Isalarico the Benevolent, who had brought Yscalin into Virtudom. He had forsworn the old gods for her love, just as King Bardholt had for Queen Sabran.

Another effigy wore a wimple, and another, a gown that covered her to the chin. Yet every face, every queen was the same, all the way back to Sabran the First, daughter of the Damsel and the Saint. Always the same chins, the same high cheekbones, the same lips.

Queen Cleolind was not among them. She had been laid to rest in a plain tomb in the Sanctuary of the Sacred Damsel.

The next tomb waited to receive her grandmother. The one beside it already held her consort, the late Lord Alfrick Withy. Glorian laid a hand on his chest – the grandfather she could hardly remember. A few more steps, and she stood before the last two effigies, the newest.

She was still for a long time. At last, she stroked the nearest tomb, limned by candles.

'I miss you, Papa.'

Soon he would be at the Great Table. The Saint would have saved him a place of honour – but for now, in the hour before he ascended, his spirit must be somewhere close. He must hear.

'I will find the truth.' Her voice strained. 'I will give you cold justice, Papa, I swear it.'

Her mother lay beside him, hands clasped in prayer.

'Mother, forgive me. I wish our last words had been warmer.' She traced a marble strand of hair. 'I miss you, too, and love you. Even if you never let me tell you so.'

A draught made the candles flicker. When she straightened, she looked at them all, the Queens of Inys. *I pray you all, do not abandon me. I am Glorian the Third. Shine a light upon my reign.*

In silence, she stayed with her parents' tombs. At last, the nail slipped from the wax and clattered into a small dish.

By the time the wax had reached the next nail, the witnesses had filled in the circular aisle between the tombs and the raised boss, where the Arch Sanctarian oversaw the rites. Glorian stood between Lord Robart and Julain as they sang for the souls of the dead.

A feast upon a table, a wonder to behold,
the apple trees, the river green, the court where none grow old.
A place of true magnificence, away from war and hate,
our eyes shall see in Halgalant, beyond those joyful gates.

Forget us not in happiness, ye good departed souls,
ye feasters in the merry hall, who dance in fields of gold.
Though our hearts ache for your welcome, for now we can but wait
to meet again in Halgalant, beyond those joyful gates.

'We gather beneath Halgalant to lay our good Queen Sabran to rest for the last time.' The Arch Sanctarian broke a long hush. 'Sabran Berethnet, the sixth of that name, who ruled over this queendom for close to twenty years. She was our sunlight. Our saviour.'

Weeping. Lady Abra Marchyn, one of her mother's attendants. Florell drew her close and hushed her.

'Queen Sabran perished at sea on the *Conviction*,' the Arch Sanctarian continued. 'That ship was a gift from her devoted companion, Bardholt Hraustr – the first of that name, King of Hróth, victor in the War of Twelve Shields, who redeemed his country, and saved it from vice, by accepting the Saint. With their love, all wounds were healed. With their union, the Chainmail of Virtudom begot its third and strongest link.'

Glorian tried to keep her back straight. A numbness overtook her body, the same as in the early days of grief.

'They will be missed beyond reckoning,' the Arch Sanctarian said. 'Not only by their loyal subjects, but by their daughter, Queen Glorian, who now steps forth to guide and rule us.'

A novice approached with a wooden box. The Arch Sanctarian used a pair of pincers to draw a tooth from inside and hold it up.

'A tooth,' he said, 'from the mouth of Queen Sabran. Here is her salvation, the key by which she steps into Halgalant. Let it be placed inside her tomb, and let the tomb be sealed for ever.'

He returned it to the reliquary and locked it fast. The assistant carried it to the tomb, which the six Dukes Spiritual heaved open. Lady Brangain took the box and lowered it inside. Glorian wished she could have done it, but queens were forbidden to handle remains.

'A tooth from the mouth of King Bardholt. Here is his salvation, the key by which he steps into Halgalant.' The Arch Sanctarian held it up. 'Let it be placed inside his tomb, and let the tomb be sealed for ever.'

Tears washed her cheeks. As the repository was placed in the tomb, she tried to hold in a shudder.

This was not how it should have been. Her parents' bodies should have been carried through the streets in dignity and splendour, a thousand horses and knights riding with them. All that remained, all the proof that they had ever existed, were two brittle teeth.

Once the tombs were closed, the Arch Sanctarian read the needful prayers, wreaths of rosemary and queensflower were laid, and then it was the end, the honours done, and all the living left the dead.

First light stained the horizon. Glorian drew up her hood and crossed the bridge over the Lyttel. They would return to the castle on horseback, following the Strondway – the river path – so the sun would tail them as it rose. Seeing her up close, the people crowding the streets lowered their heads.

They will not hurt me. Glorian recited it to herself. *I am the unending vine.*

Lord Robart waited for her to climb into her saddle. As she bestrode her grey stallion and rode after him, her sorrow welled into her throat, and then so did her voice. It burst forth, rich and clear in a way it had never been in her lessons, and she sang with all her might in Hróthi.

Mourn, he is gone, the warrior bold – hallow the bones, hallow the bones!
See him above to the highest of halls – hammer the drums, muster the
*   horns!*
Witness the glory he leaves in his wake! Carve his name into the ashes,
*   the walls!*

Her regent looked over his shoulder at her. His expression was as calm as ever, his gaze pricked with something like curiosity.

Many of the Hróthi had settled in Ascalun. They echoed the third verse, their fists raised to the sky, stamping in time with the song. Glorian called out again:

Run, he is rising, the one who is gone – look to the sun, look to the sun!
Show him the way to the Saint's open door – bring forth the ship, lift
    him aboard!
Weep ye no more for the fallen exultant! Light every beacon to high
    Hólrhorn!

Rejoice, he is risen, the King of the North – loud did he roar, loud did
    he roar!
Open the gates to the heavenly court – lay out the feast, let the wine
    pour!
Shatter to dust all his enemies' war horns! Sing to the eaves of his glitter-
    ing fort!

A red sun edged over the horizon. Glorian felt alive and strong for the first time in days.

Then she felt something else.

Her horse snorted and huffed. Somehow she knew where to look, and so she saw it first.

It fell like a shadow over Ascalun, into the bloody light of dawn – black its hide, black its wings, dark the dread horns that speared from its skull. Smaller beasts flew with it, limber where the first was thick and unwieldy. From this distance, they could almost have been a flock of birds.

Glorian listed, at the mercy of her weak grip on the reins. Her ears clanged. If she had not known the Nameless One was red, she would have thought he was plummeting towards her.

A woman saw, and screamed, and then so did the crowd. People shoved and scattered before the wyrm – for wyrm it surely was, soaring down the Strondway, straight for Glorian. Her horse swung its head and reared, and before she knew it, she had slipped from the saddle.

This time, she took the blow on her shoulder. If anyone called to her, the roar smothered it, for now the mourners were a stampede in the thousands, fighting to escape. Glorian crawled until someone grasped her wrist and pulled her up – Helisent, shouting at her, but there was too much of a clamour to hear, terror breaking like a wave on the city.

They both fell when the wyrm landed, shunting the street underfoot. Every horse in the procession fled, strewing the Strondway with their riders. Glorian looked up, deep into the eyes of a monster.

Red fire burned in its skull, in its nostrils. Each tooth was longer than a sword, the fangs like bear spears. She could not move, not to breathe or blink; its gaze bound her to the spot, as if she were prey that was already dead. *Fire it was, purposely wrought – fire as makes a blade, for slaughter. Its eyes seethed with flame, not good nor evil*, the sanctarian read in her mind, *but also that which makes a wyrm, that is, its cunning, and its malice.*

Arrows splintered against its scales. Blades scraped at its flanks in vain. Dame Erda threw herself in front of Glorian, only to be swiped aside with force enough to break a wall.

'QUEEN OF INYS.'

The sky echoed that stentorian voice. It scraped all the strength from her bones and thundered over every roof, leaving her people cowering. Some screams cut off, while others loudened. Adela took one look at the wyrm and slumped to the ground in a faint.

Glorian felt her skirts dampen as the wyrm towered over her. She had to crane her neck to hold its gaze. Its roasting breath reminded her of standing too close to a bonfire – a heat that tightened her skin, leaving her face so dry and raw that blinking scratched her eyes. Helisent kept hold of her hand. Their fingers were locked together, their palms slick.

'For your empty tombs,' said the wyrm.

Glorian was trembling so hard her jaw rattled. Her mind was boiled and slippery. It took her a moment to realise the wyrm was not only speaking in a human tongue – it *spoke*, monstrous horror, it spoke – but in Hróthi. When something landed with a clatter in front of her, she covered her head with an unbidden cry, embraced by Helisent.

A charred pile of bones, two cracked skulls among them.

'They suffered, little queen,' the wyrm told her. 'Be sure.'

Helisent made a tiny sound. Glorian stared at a thighbone, part of a rib, the nearest skull. Still she could not move – not with her nerveless hands, the absence of feeling below her chin.

'The middle realm will be littered with bone.' A red tongue flickered at its teeth. 'All will be razed.'

To freeze is an instinct shared by all living things. Think of how a deer stills when it scents a threat. Glorian kept looking at the skull, into the hollows that had once held eyes. *You can conquer it . . .*

'The flesh queen does not speak.' A sound like moving rock. 'Does silence already descend?'

With what little control she still possessed, Glorian reached for the skull and touched it with her fingertips. It was the chip in its cheekbone that proved it.

Papa.

He was with her. Knowing it gave Glorian the courage to look up and unlock her throat. 'What grievance have you with Inys, wyrm?' Her voice came high and brittle. 'Who are you?'

She spoke in Inysh. Recognition sparked in its eyes.

'Who comes after the one before,' came its answer. 'I breathed flame into life, and made death flesh. I am the fire beneath, unleashed.' Its Hróthi was rumbling and harsh. 'I am Fýredel.'

This was the beast that had murdered her parents.

The Dreadmount had birthed destruction again.

Its eye fell on Lord Robart, who had managed to keep both his seat and composure, though his face had gone white, and his eyes wide. Seeing him spurred Glorian to rise. If she was to die, she would die as her father must have, when he faced this monster.

'I am Glorian.' For all she tried, she could not steel her voice, but she could raise it: 'Glorian Hraustr Berethnet, Queen of Inys and Princess of Hróth. My ancestor was Galian Berethnet, Saint over all Virtudom, he who vanquished the Nameless One.'

It bared more of its fangs.

'That which is unnamed was first,' it said. 'But I am named, flesh queen. Remember.' Its pupils thinned. 'The cold one on the ship. She was your kin.' Glorian looked at the other skull. 'She fell to my flame. So will this land. We will finish the scouring, for we are the teeth that harrow and turn. The mountain is the forge and smith, and we, its iron offspring – come to avenge the first, the forebear, he who sleeps beneath.'

Every warrior should know fear, Glorian Brightcry. Without it, courage is an empty boast.

'You confess,' Glorian said, 'that you slew the blood of the Saint.' Her voice kept breaking. 'Do you then declare war on Inys?'

Fýredel – the wyrm – let out a rattle. A score of complex scales and muscles shifted in its face.

'When your days grow long and hot,' he said, 'when the sun in the North never sets, we shall come.'

On both sides of the Strondway, those who had not fled were rooted to the spot, fixated on Glorian. She realised what they must be thinking. If she died childless, the eternal vine was at its end.

What she did next could define how they saw the House of Berethnet for centuries to come.

Start forging your armour, Glorian. You will need it.

She looked down once more at her parents' remains, the bones the wyrms had dumped here like a spoil of war. In her memory, her father laughed and drew her close. He would never laugh again. Never smile. Her mother would never tell her she loved her, or how to calm her dreams.

And where there had been fear, there was anger.

'If you— If you dare to turn your fire on Inys,' Glorian bit out, 'then I will do as my ancestor did to the Nameless One.' She forced herself to lift her chin in defiance. 'I will drive you back with sword and spear, with bow and lance!' Shaking, she heaved for air. 'I am the voice, the body of Inys. My stomach is its strength – my heart, its shield – and if you think I will submit to you because I am small and young, you are wrong.'

Sweat was running down her back. She had never been so afraid in her life.

'I am not afraid,' she said.

At this, the wyrm unfurled its wings to their full breadth. From tip to hooked tip, they were as wide as two longships facing each other. People scrambled out of their shadow.

'So be it, *Shieldheart.*' It steeped the word in mockery. 'Treasure your darkness, for the fire comes. Until then, a taste of our flame, to light your city through the winter. Heed my words.'

Its jaws yawned. Helisent wrapped both arms around Glorian, and Glorian held her back, eyes shut.

But Fýredel did not kill them. Instead, a wordless bellow came from its throat, loud as ten thousand war cries, and its underlings descended on the city. Fire leapt on the rooftops of Ascalun.

No...

Fýredel took wing. The downwind blew hundreds of people to their knees. With an anguished sob, Glorian tried to gather the bones, but then strong hands had gripped her arms, and she was hauled bodily off the Strondway. She tripped on a cobblestone, almost lost her footing, before Sir Bramel Stathworth caught her.

A skull slipped from her grasp. They kept pulling her on. 'No,' she cried. Sir Bramel scooped her clean into his arms without stopping, as if she were a child. 'Let me go. Papa—'

'Get her away. Take the Old Bridge,' Lord Robart roared from horseback. 'Archers, lancers – to me!'

Glorian hung like a broken puppet, head flopping. Her body had quelled the worst of the fear, but now it swept free, unhooking her joints. Horses screamed with their riders. Then a burning wind – a shattering – and black smoke, thick and searing hot, just as she breathed in.

52

North

Einlek Óthling sat on the skull of a whale, gaunt and pale enough to be part of it. A circlet rested above his brow, and he wore a pelt over chainmail, sword resting at his side. Though he shared the same thick hair as his uncle, it was short and brown, his prominent eyes the grey of steel.

He was fine of features, mild of voice – yet no one had dared cross him since he buckled on his iron arm, a replacement for the one he had personally severed, the night he and his younger uncle had been taken captive.

Einlek had been seven at the time. He had cut a hand off to escape a shackle, then run to safety, preventing Verthing Bloodblade from using him against Bardholt. Bloodblade had soon been defeated. If Bardholt had been the Hammer of the North, Einlek was the knife. That burnished limb was not the only reason people called him Ironside.

'You are certain.'

Wulf leaned on a padded crutch in the firelight. Even though he was bundled in thick furs and stood as close to the hearth as he could bear, he could still feel the killing cold of the sea.

'Certain,' he rasped.

Einlek pinched the bridge of his nose, which tilted up a little at the tip. Like his mother, he had a broad white streak in his hair, licking down on to his brow. Wulf waited in silence.

They had taken him to a healer first. His soles had been frostbitten, hands bloated with blisters, skin peeling and saltworn. For a time, he had not been able to speak. His lips had bled. His throat had scorched.

The healer had worked hard to save his life. Shivering and sleepless in the night, he had listened to her whispering forbidden songs, asking the ice spirits to stop tormenting him. She had slowly warmed his hands until the blisters receded, leaving black scabs on the back of his fingers. She had wicked the wetness from his skin and treated the salt wounds.

She could not treat the scars the wyrm had gouged across his mind.

'I didn't believe it,' Einlek said. 'Even as the corpses came ashore, I refused to believe. I still feared as soon as my arse touched this throne, he'd walk in and throttle me for daring to take his place before my time.' He blinked hard. 'Tell me what happened out there. Was it the Ments?'

Wulf tried to swallow past the dusty coal that burned in his craw. He had drunk his weight in fresh water on the journey, but days of gulping brine had scoured him dry.

'No,' he said. 'Something far older.'

'The Dreadmount.' Einlek placed his softer hand on the throne. 'No. It's not possible.'

'It wasn't the Nameless One. All stories say his hide was red. This one was black, but they must be kindred,' Wulf said. His throat was in agony. 'It came with … others. Offspring, thralls, Saint knows what. They razed the fleet with their breath. Every ship.'

'Wyrms.'

'Aye.'

Einlek tightened his grip. His gaze skitted about the hall, as if he counted unseen things.

'How are we to fight such an enemy?' he said. 'How can we defend against it?'

'There is nothing on earth or in Halgalant that could.'

'How, by the Saint's jaw, did you live?' Einlek demanded. 'I have swum in that sea, Wulf. I'm not too proud to admit that it beat the breath from me in midsummer. You were adrift in high winter, for days. A woman from the *Fortitude* was found on the wreckage, frozen to death. Yet here you stand.'

Flame on flesh, foul smoke and embers. The melted thing that had been Vell. Regny in his arms, on fire. He remembered all of this from the *Conviction*, branded deep into his mind.

By chance, he had been carrying a wineskin, fat with sweet water. It had kept him alive as the waves pushed him through the blackened fog, and underneath indifferent stars.

He had managed to drag himself on to a broken mast, and tie Regny to it. It had saved him from drowning or losing her – but how he had survived that cold, only the Saint could tell. There had been frost in his hair, barbing his eyelashes. After the first night of searing agony, he had lost all feeling in his skin, and slept without a hope of waking.

'I chose the sea,' he finally said. 'Better ice than fire. Thought I'd just ... slip away.' Einlek nodded. 'I don't know why I'm still breathing. The Saint would not let me into Halgalant.'

Einlek regarded him, looking torn between pity and disquiet. Wulf tasted salt in the corner of his mouth.

The family had let him keep holding on to Regny. Only when they reached Eldyng had they prised her from his arms. She waited in the sanctuary for burial in Askrdal.

Wulf said, 'Was I really the only one who lived?'

'It appears so. The rest were burned, drowned or frozen. I sent divers and ships to look.'

He closed his eyes.

'The Plague of Ófandauth is spreading,' Einlek said. 'The Nameless One brought a sickness from the Womb of Fire, a plague that beset the people of Yikala. It must have returned. Whatever attacked our king, we can be sure it serves our enemy. We will fight.'

'Nothing could defeat it, sire. No blade could have pierced its hide.'

'And no Hróthi dies a feather death,' Einlek said firmly. 'You were my uncle's retainer. Now he is dead, you may leave with honour – or you can swear to me. A son of Hróth deserves a hall.'

Wulf clenched his jaw, his eyes aching.

'If you accept, sail to Ascalun,' Einlek said. 'My cousin has relinquished her birthright to me, and for that, I owe her succour. You were on the *Conviction*. You can swear that Queen Sabran is dead, which will strengthen Glorian's legitimacy. You can help her, Wulf.'

'You want me to go back on the Ashen Sea.'

'Yes.'

'Sire, I don't know if I can.'

'Don't let that fear take root, or you'll never move again.' Einlek leaned forward, his knuckles blanching on the throne. 'Hear me. Glorian is only sixteen, and she is now the divine head of Virtudom. She must have iron in her bones, and I must make it clear to those who circle her that Hróth will defend its beloved princess. You and your lith can help me do that.'

Glorian could wield a sword. She was strong. But Wulf had seen her gentleness, her hunger for approval. The nobles would smell opportunity in a young queen, yet to find her voice.

'You can go home, tell your family you're alive. Lift their sorrow,' Einlek said. 'First, will you pledge to me, and to the Queen of Inys?'

Wulf took several moments to restrain a violent shudder – a shudder with deep, tangled roots, born of a feeling still unnamed. Keeping hold of the crutch, he bent to one knee.

'My king,' he whispered, 'as the Saint is my witness, I will.'

****

The ship did not look seaworthy; nothing in the harbour did. Grey waves crashed against weak hulls, and sails threatened to catch afire. Wulf hirpled towards a birling, the *Wave Steed*. The tastes of salt and bile swashed in his mouth.

A Hróthi fighter could not fear the sea. Yet his palms sweated, and his stomach clenched.

'Wulf?'

He looked up in a haze. Three people were waiting to board the *Wave Steed*, bundled in heavy furs. Karlsten, Thrit and Sauma – all that remained of his lith.

It was Thrit who had called out to him. When Sauma saw, she stared, her lips parting.

'Wulf,' she breathed.

Karlsten turned. His face ripened with anger, but Wulf was too weary to care. Before either of them could speak, Thrit stepped forward. His expression was guarded, and that hit Wulf like a thump to the chest. He could not bear Thrit, of all people, to fear him.

He stiffened when Thrit touched his cheek. Slowly, he looked into those warm, dark eyes.

445

'I had to be sure.' Thrit took his face between both hands. 'You came back.'

Wulf nodded, shivering. 'Vell and Regny,' Sauma said. 'Are they alive?'

'I tried.' Wulf spoke in a whisper. 'I tried.'

'Not enough.' Karlsten spat on the boards, making Thrit flinch. 'Bardholt, dead. Sabran, dead. Eydag and Vell and Regny, dead – and all they have in common is Wulfert fucking Glenn.' His nostrils flared. 'Our new king would have been wise to kill you. He'll be next.'

'One more word and it will be you, Karl, I swear it,' Thrit bit out.

'Are you head of the lith now?' Karlsten sneered. 'By whose command?'

'Enough. Both of you, shut up,' Sauma snapped. 'We have all pledged to Einlek Óthling, and to Glorian. We are all that remains. We cannot break.' She spoke between her teeth. 'You swore to the House of Hraustr again, Karl. You missed your chance to walk away from Wulf.'

'I swore before I knew.' Karlsten glowered at them both. 'Damn you. I'll not be near a witch.'

He marched back up the boards, towards the city. 'Karl,' Sauma shouted after him. 'Karlsten!'

'Leave him,' Wulf said. 'There are worse things than a broken oath.'

Thrit turned back to him. 'What happened?' he asked. 'Tell us, Wulf. What happened on the ship?'

Sauma was waiting, too. Wulf thought of telling them, but then the smell of melted fat and smoke greased his thrapple again. 'I can't. I will,' he said, 'but—' His eyes were seeping. 'I can't.'

Thrit nodded. 'Tell us whenever you're ready,' he said softly. 'For now, we have a ship to take.'

53

South

Tunuva watched a waxbill fly between the giant teaks of the Lasian Basin. Her clothes still reeked of smoke.

The wyrm and its followers had not yet come. The Nameless One had stayed for many days in Yikala – not just eating its people, but poisoning the land, making the world exactly like the Womb of Fire. The creatures would feast on the bones of Carmentum.

The Priory would be at the vanguard of the opposition. Tunuva had permitted a stop only for Siyu to feed Lukiri.

No one this far north would know about Carmentum yet. To still her nerves, Tunuva took the stopper from her gourd and gave Canthe a little water. She coughed as she drank, looking for all the world like a sick child. Her skin had greyed around the lips, and though Tunuva had wrapped her in all the layers they could spare, her body would not warm.

Whatever she had used against the wyrm had been the most powerful outpouring of magic Tunuva had ever felt, save the eruption of the Dreadmount. She had not been able to summon her flame or work a warding since – not while a steely tang drifted from Canthe.

Once Lukiri had taken enough milk, they climbed on to Ninuru. The ichneumon glanced back before she stalked into the undergrowth.

Tunuva kept one arm around Canthe and her free hand on the saddle. As rain sprinkled their shoulders, she ignited a tall flame, revealing slicks of water and branches folded into archways.

She had no idea what to expect when she saw Esbar. Her stomach formed a fishers' knot. By the time dusk hardened to the solid black of night, she felt as ill as she had in her pregnancy.

Ninuru could not see in full darkness, but her nose and ears led her. Tunuva let the flame go out and leaned against her withers. She must have drifted off, for suddenly there were smudges of stern grey sky between the trees, and Siyu was heavy against her back. When the sun once more swayed low on the horizon, the trees began to thin at last – and here was the old fig, and there its braided roots, and deep within, the door to home.

Siyu got down with Lukiri. Even on the ship they had sailed from Imulu, she had barely said a word.

'Ninuru,' Tunuva said, dismounting, 'you come with me to Esbar.'

'Lalhar.'

'Yes. We must tell her.' She held the furred face that had looked at her with utter loyalty since she was five. 'I will never let anything hurt you, honeysweet. You know that, don't you?'

'Yes.' Her eyes were steady, trusting. 'Little sisters do not let ichneumons die.'

Even after seeing Lalhar slaughtered, she believed it. Tunuva kissed her on the nose. 'You can eat and sleep all you want tomorrow, wyrms be damned. You were very brave.'

Ninuru wuffled her approval. Tunuva got Canthe from the saddle, pulling her arm around her neck.

She had never been so tired. The acrid stench and taste of wyrm was thick under her nails, between her teeth, in the roots of her hair. Somehow, she carried Canthe through the tunnel and up the steps, to where one of the young men was tending to an urn of roses.

'Sister,' he said, stunned.

'Sulzi. Will you take Canthe to her room and bring Denag to her, please?'

'What happened?'

'I'm not sure I know, but tell Denag it isn't poison.'

He marched away with Canthe in his arms. As Siyu caught up, silent and dragfooted, Imsurin came down the corridor. His hair had turned almost white since their departure.

'Siyu, give Lukiri to me,' he said, always calm. 'She needs to be dry and warm.'

Siyu did as he asked. Lukiri gave a fretful whimper before Imsurin supported the back of her head, cupping her body to his heart, and took her down the steps to the men's quarters.

'We must go to Esbar now. To tell her what happened,' Tunuva said to Siyu. 'Are you ready?'

'No, but I see no other choice.'

She was hollow-eyed. In a matter of days, she had lost the man she loved and the ichneumon she had raised for years, as well as the family that had taken her in. Tunuva wanted to comfort her, but it would have to wait. Better that she faced her punishment first.

And there would be a punishment. The loss of an ichneumon was an unspeakable thing.

The Bridal Chamber was dark, save two candles and a low-burning fire. It was rare for Esbar to light one in winter. Now she sat at her table with the flames at her back, studying a stone fragment.

Tunuva drank her in. She wanted to see her like this now, at rest, in the stillness, before her cruel tidings shattered the peace. Esbar looked up, and breathed out.

'Tuva,' she said.

'Hello, lover.'

Her face softened. It hardened again when Siyu stepped into the chamber.

'So,' she said, putting down the fragment, 'you have deigned to return to our ranks, Siyu.'

Siyu kept hold of her composure. 'Tuva found me in Carmentum and asked me to come back. She said the Priory needed all the help it could muster, and I saw that it was true.'

'You both smell of smoke. Why?'

'Because as we speak, Carmentum is burning,' Tunuva said. 'Burning with wyrmfire.'

Esbar rose from her seat. Tunuva watched an archive of emotions flit across her face.

'Tell me what happened,' she said. 'Tell me all of it.'

Tunuva did, from the beginning. She described the Prince of Beasts, the battle in the Liongarden.

'You brought that family to the hunters' attention,' Esbar said coolly to Siyu. 'Not only that, but you allowed your ichneumon to be captured for blood sport. Have you tended her wounds?'

Siyu shrank a little. 'On our way out of the city,' Tunuva said, 'a wyrm of unspeakable strength followed us. Ninuru and Lalhar fought it to protect us both. It overpowered Lalhar.'

Esbar stared at her birthdaughter. Jeda rose from her mat by the bed, ears pricked.

'Siyu,' Esbar forced out. 'Is Lalhar dead?'

'I'm sorry,' Siyu whispered. Her eyes shone with unshed tears. 'I didn't know there were people like that, who would hurt an ichneumon. I didn't know the wyrms would come.'

'You would have known,' Esbar erupted, 'if you had been with your family when I addressed them!' Siyu cringed from her anger. 'You would have known there were rocks hatching across the South, and that leaving without your sisters was dangerous. Perhaps then you would not have towed a baby or your poor ichneumon with you. Or perhaps you still would have.'

'No,' Siyu said, her voice shaking. 'Esbar, if I'd known, I would never have taken—'

'You used your ichneumon as a beast of burden, to indulge your absurd fantasy,' Esbar said hotly. 'Lalhar had no choice but to follow you. Her devotion to you was absolute, and you had a duty to treat her with the respect she deserved in return. You have disgraced the line of Siyāti. You endangered Lukiri, you may have killed Anyso's family—'

'You killed *him*,' Siyu screamed at her. Tunuva stiffened. 'Tuva says you didn't, but who hated him as much as you?'

'I didn't hate him, Siyu, I feared him,' Esbar shouted back. 'I feared what his presence here might bring, as did Saghul. There is a reason the Priory exercises the greatest caution around outsiders, and now you see it plain before you. Because of your folly, your ichneumon is dead, and you came very close to losing your birthdaughter.' Her nostrils flared. 'I did not lay a finger on your Anyso. Saghul ordered his execution.'

'And who carried it out?'

'Someone who had to clean up your mess. You should not have allowed Anyso to see you in the first place,' Esbar said, cheeks flushed. 'Your carelessness was what killed him.' Siyu choked back a sob. 'The sister who carried out the order – all she did was obey the Prioress.'

Siyu let out something like a laugh. 'So that is the way of things in the Priory. Blind submission?'

'No, not blind. Joyful, willing obedience, given by choice.'

'I wasn't allowed to choose,' Siyu said, with spite. 'Anyso chose to bake. I never chose to be a weapon.'

'Siyu,' Tunuva said, hurting for them both, 'please, sunray.'

There was a brief silence.

'I just wanted more choice,' Siyu said.

Esbar scoffed. 'Did you, indeed, Queen Siyu?'

'I thought our people had wasted centuries, all in fear of nothing.' Siyu made the admission with courage. 'But I choose the Priory now, Esbar. I understand why it matters.'

'Because you would not believe until you saw.'

'Is that so terrible?'

Esbar turned away and crossed her arms. 'Well,' she said, 'now you have seen. Now you know why the Priory has prepared for all those centuries. We had no idea when the time would come, and now it is here. All those sisters were waiting for this day. For this hour.'

Tunuva waited, wishing she could comfort either of them.

'I would not be so imprudent as to strip a trained warrior of her cloak. We need every sword,' Esbar said. 'But you will not have another pup until I deem you worthy once more. Until then, you can ride a horse or a camel. Perhaps you can take care of those.'

'I don't want another pup.' Siyu could barely speak. 'I want Lalhar.'

'Lalhar is dead.' Esbar placed a hand on her own ichneumon. 'Jeda, tell the others.'

'I'm sorry, Jeda. Tell them, please. I'm sorry.'

Jeda stalked from the room. Ninuru followed her in silence.

'I'm sorry to you as well, Prioress,' Siyu said thickly. 'For abandoning the Mother, and for endangering the orange tree. And you, Tuva. I put you and Ninuru in danger. I am grateful you helped me see reason.'

Tunuva managed a small nod. 'I forgive you, Siyu.'

She did not say, *I forgave you everything the moment I first saw your face. Nothing that you have ever done has me love you less.*

'Since Tuva accepts your apology, I will do the same. Now you must work to earn back my trust,' Esbar said. 'Am I to expect you to vanish in the night a third time, Siyu uq-Nāra?'

Siyu raised her chin. 'No, Prioress.' A tear dripped to the floor. 'I choose the Mother.'

'I pray she forgives you.'

Though her lip quaked, Siyu was dignified in dismissal. She lowered her head to Esbar before leaving. Tunuva waited until she was out of earshot before she closed the door.

'Don't you dare,' Esbar said, 'tell me I was too hard on her. Both you and Nin could have died.'

'You will hear no objection from me.'

'Good.'

Esbar stared into the hearth. She had always been most beautiful by firelight.

'You left,' she said, her voice strained. 'When your family most needed you, Tuva.'

'You know why. You gave Siyu my name, and with it, some part of my heart.' Tunuva stepped forward. 'I missed you, Esbar.'

Slowly, Esbar looked at her.

'And I missed you in this … haunted chamber.' She pinched the bridge of her nose. 'Carmentum was one city. We can defend others. I will send some of the men after our sisters, to warn them of the threat. Most of them will go to Daraniya, who can station them where she sees fit. I will have to send a messenger to Kediko.'

'Kediko will not refuse help when he knows what is coming.'

'After that hooded threat of his, I must be certain.' On her way to the door, Esbar stopped. 'Will you wait for me?'

'Always.'

Tunuva took the chair and examined what Esbar had left on the table – tablets and fragments of text from the archives, inked on to parchment or etched into clay. Since even a little damp could damage them, they were usually stored in cold and darkness. Understanding the remnants of their past could be a test of patience – Cleolind had often used both Selinyi and Old Yikalese in one sitting, the two scripts presented like oil and water.

Most of the pieces Esbar had found had been composed in archaic Ersyri by her ancestor, Siyāti uq-Nāra, the second Prioress. There were also scrolls of Pardic, a language brought across the salt plain with Selinyi.

'I've been trying to find a cure.'

Tunuva glanced up. Esbar had returned to the room.

452

'Siyāti had a theory,' she continued. 'That the Curse of Yikala – the first plague – was caused by siden.'

'What?'

'She believed it struck those whose first exposure came directly from a wyrm, rather than the orange tree. Instead of granting them its gifts, the magic caused anguish, like burning oil poured in the veins.'

'Did she know how to stop it?'

'Possibly. She believed the tree might be able to leach siden from a tormented body without turning the survivor into a mage, as the fruit does.' Esbar leaned over her shoulder a little. 'Look, here – she speaks of crushing and soaking its blossoms, the way she would have made rosewater. Clearly she discussed the idea with her sisters.'

Tunuva nodded slowly, reading. Esbar opened a scroll with care, revealing neat lines of Pardic.

'Soshen records this meeting and its aftermath,' she said. 'The cure failed when they made it by pounding and steeping the blossoms. She proposed they distil an essence with steam.'

'Because steam is water born from heat, and might return balance to the body.'

'Exactly.' Esbar pointed to one of the diagrams. 'This is a design for the instrument they made – the still, or limbec.'

'Do we have one?'

'Yes, but it's ancient and rusted. The men are making a new one of the same design. I think Siyāti and Soshen did have it right, else they would have noted their failure or destroyed these writings. I've charged Denag and Imin with patching their instructions together.'

'If it works, will you share the cure beyond the Priory?'

'Daraniya and Kediko should have it, but Soshen noted that the distillation takes some time, and many blossoms yield only a small amount of medicine. I do not see how we can share it widely. If anyone hears word of a tree that cures this plague, they will come for us.' Esbar sat on the arm of the chair. 'Did you see any sign of a sickness in Carmentum?'

'None. Its people have worse things to fear, if anyone is still alive.'

'Do you think you could sketch the creatures you saw?'

It had been a long time since Tunuva had drawn. In her twenties, she had helped decorate and restore the paintings on the walls and pillars, enjoying the attention to detail it required.

453

After the clearing, her love for it had disappeared. Certain shades of paint had reminded her.

'I could try,' she said.

Esbar took a splinter of wood from the fire and blew out the flame, leaving it charred, then rolled fresh parchment on the table. As Tunuva traced a thin black line, she saw the last picture she had drawn, of the dark happy eyes that had never stopped haunting her.

First, she breathed life into the wyrm on the sands, capturing its muscular legs, the way it held its weight on folded wings, the spikes at the end of its tail. Next she drew the serpent lioness. She lost herself in her work, calm for the first time in days, the act of recreation enwrapping her. All the while, she was aware of Esbar, warm at her side.

She blew dust from the drawings. 'This is the large wyrm,' she said, showing Esbar the first one. 'And that is what attacked the Liongarden – you see, it has two legs, not four, and it's smaller. Finally, a melding of serpent and lion. I suspect it hatched from one of the dark rocks.'

'How did you escape the large wyrm?'

'Canthe used magic against it.'

Esbar tensed. 'I thought Canthe had no magic. That her siden had burned out long ago.'

'It was not siden. Esbar, she has another power, like nothing I have ever seen or felt. She gave out cold white light, as if she had become a star. Every wyrm fled from it.'

'Where is she?'

'With the men. She was unconscious for most of the journey home, so I could not ask her more.'

Esbar returned the sketches to the table. 'Saghul told me to make her a postulant,' she said. 'I want to follow her wishes, but this casts the matter into doubt again, in my mind.'

'You said we need every sister,' Tunuva reminded her. 'After Carmentum, that is truer than ever.' When Esbar stood, so did she. 'Ez, I just watched a republic crumble in a day. Surely we can't squander a warrior who can wield such a force.'

'I think it far more foolish to trust her with the fruit, giving her twice as much power as she already has. Besides, if this magic has such a ruinous influence on wyrms, it may weaken us as well.' Esbar raised her eyebrows. 'Did you feel it, when she used that power?'

'Yes,' Tunuva admitted. 'My flame was very weak for the next hour.'

'Then you understand the risks I have to weigh. She may help us fight the wyrms, but at what cost?' Esbar said, her gaze flinty. 'What if she were to turn that power against us?'

'Why would she?' Tunuva asked her. 'Esbar, I understand your fear, but this is a fellow mage, with nothing in the world left to her name. She lost her tree, her family – everything she ever had. We are her chance to belong again. She has no reason to betray us.'

'Her family,' Esbar said. Tunuva nodded once. 'You must have grown close to her on the road.'

'I learned more about her,' Tunuva agreed. 'I know it's too soon to give her the fruit. I only think you should do as Saghul requested, and make her a postulant. She would still have to prove herself worthy of the tree – but give her a place here. Give her a chance.'

Esbar looked at the fire, her jaw working.

'Canthe may remain here as our guest,' she said at last, 'but I still trust my instincts, Tuva. Something tells me not to let her into our ranks. I mislike the way she appeared out of nowhere. I mislike what you tell me of this other magic. How can I make a sister of a woman I don't trust?'

'If not for her, I might not be standing here—'

'Perhaps you should not stand here, then, Tunuva Melim,' Esbar snapped. 'In fact, if you are so grateful to Canthe of Nurtha, why not go to her chamber instead?'

A terrible silence rang.

'Don't,' Tunuva said quietly, a hot stone in her throat. 'Don't ever speak that way, Esbar.'

Esbar looked shaken by her own words. 'I'm sorry, Tuva. I was—' She held herself tighter. 'No. I will not make excuses for it.'

'Explain it, then.' Tunuva went to her. 'Esbar, it's us.'

'I have not slept well.' Esbar braced a hand on the table. 'What is happening to us, Tuva?'

Tunuva could bear it no longer. She closed the space between them and kissed Esbar with as much resolve as she had on that first day in the desert, thirty years before. A lifetime. No time.

Esbar came to life in her arms. She kissed back with frustration and love, whispering her name. Breathing hard, they stripped each other, not waiting to reach the bed. Their hands trembled in a way they never had since they were young and hungry, clumsy with desperation.

455

Tunuva pressed Esbar to the wall. She pulled at the sash of her brocade robe, and Esbar wrestled with her tunic in return, opening it to her waist, pressing kisses to each breast. Tilting her head back, Tunuva savoured the feel of those lips on her burning skin. Her clothes were travelstained and she was clammy from the rain, but Esbar had never cared.

They knocked a platter to the floor and fell in a tangle to the bed. Tunuva mounted Esbar, so they faced one another, and looked her in the eyes. When they kissed, it was sure and deep, and the more she had, the more Tunuva wanted.

Esbar drew her nails all the way down her spine. Tunuva groaned at the flare of smarting pleasure, the fire-tipped arrow it sent to her depths. While Esbar nipped at her ear, her jaw, Tunuva grasped her hair in answer, needing to hold all of her, draw this woman close enough to knit the sinew of their souls. She wanted to make love, slow and tender, and she wanted to be seized in passion – two sacred wants, as pressing as thirst, as radiant as the fruit. Though war had come for them at last, there was still this. There would always be this.

She lowered Esbar to the bed and kissed the rippling scars on her hip. Esbar wrapped a leg around her. Their lips met, each kiss hot and urgent. Esbar sighed a soft 'yes' as Tunuva stroked a hand between her thighs, stowing her fingertips there, in the warmth of her.

She was sleek as a river. Tunuva found the sweet place where she most loved to be touched. Esbar arched her hips, and Tunuva slid deeper, their noses brushing as they closened.

'Are you trembling?'

'I fear so.' Esbar laughed a little. 'Feel my heart. Like the first time.' She took Tunuva by the hand not working in her, clasping it to her breast. 'Here, and all the way through me.'

Tunuva kissed the hollow of her throat. 'We have so many years, Esbar uq-Nāra,' she whispered. 'Let me remind you how slow I can be.'

Esbar took her by the nape. 'Don't leave me again,' she breathed. 'You steady me, lover.'

Tunuva shook her head, smiling. 'Who else but you would keep me in the sun?'

****

She slept deeply, without the dreams that had troubled her for months. Her body was sore and leaden from so long on foot and in the saddle, her mind weary from days without rest.

Only once, in the deep of the night, did she wake. Esbar, usually too hot, had turned cold as a corpse.

'Ez.'

Esbar made a quiet sound in her throat. Tunuva gathered the bedding around her shoulders and wrapped a tight embrace across her chest, giving her all the warmth she could spare.

When she woke again, the sky was overcast. Ninuru slept at the foot of the bed, while Esbar was gone. For a long while, Tunuva lay where she was, heavy and content, smelling roses on the pillow.

It would take more than one night to heal the wound of her departure, but even when she and Esbar fought, it was with love. They would survive. They always had, and always would.

Esbar had left her robe over the bedpost. Rubbing her eyes, Tunuva sat up and drew it on. The sleeves were a shade too short.

'Honeysweet,' she whispered. Ninuru cracked one eye open. 'Do you need anything?'

The ichneumon raised her head and gave Tunuva the same look she had often used when she was a pup, her black eyes shining, a sweet twitch in her nose. Tunuva chuckled.

'All right.' She scratched at the base of her left ear, making her purr. 'Since you were so brave.'

Ninuru licked her wrist, then laid her head on the floor and dropped straight back to sleep. Her body was flung out like a great fur rug, forcing Tunuva to step over her.

She found Esbar in the hot spring. 'There you are,' Tunuva said. 'I thought you might have left.'

'Not yet.' Esbar sank up to her neck. 'I have a chill. A reprieve from the wretched sweats, at least.'

Tunuva stepped into the water. It had been some time since it boiled, but they stayed close to the edge. She slid up to Esbar, who gathered her close and kissed her on the lips, soft as a whisper.

They helped each other wash. Esbar touched the shallow marks she had left, and Tunuva brushed her swollen lip.

'Tuva,' she said, 'I am afraid.'

'I am, too.' Tunuva pressed their brows together. 'Five hundred and eleven years. All those sisters who came before us, who lived and died without seeing the war they knew was coming – we must realise their destinies as well as ours. We must win against an evil that does not hear reason, and you must lead us.' Esbar nodded. 'But the Mother defeated the Nameless One. Now her cloak is yours. You were born to be her successor.'

Esbar linked their fingers. 'I ride tonight for the Ersyr, to tell Queen Daraniya what comes next. The men will leave sooner with supplies.'

What came next would be evacuating the most vulnerable people of the Ersyr to the mountains and caves, the mines and catacombs and quarries, and readying the rest for fire to rain down from on high. 'Nin needs to recover,' Tunuva said. 'We'll join you in a day or two.'

'Take three, if you need. She deserves a long sleep.'

They stayed in the water for some time, cleaving to this moment of peace, this last silence. At last, Tunuva said, 'I promised her some cream. I always told you they had cat in them.'

Esbar smiled, and for a moment, she was her old self. 'You know,' she said, 'I never thought I would be fortunate enough to confront our enemy with such a woman as you at my side.'

'We face the world together.' Tunuva kissed her, sealing the promise. 'Be safe, my love.'

****

She went to the scullery for the cream. Only two men were left in there – the rest were already leaving the Priory in regimented groups, clad in layers for the desert, carrying saddlebags of arrows, dry food, clothing and armour, among other provisions.

Once Ninuru had her cream, Tunuva descended to the men's quarters, where she found Imsurin in a riding coat, checking on the younger children. Lukiri was sound asleep in her cradle.

'Imin.' Tunuva joined him. 'I just wanted to wish you luck. I'll be two or three days behind you.'

'Thank you, Tuva.' Imsurin straightened. 'Esbar says the war is here at last. That it began in Carmentum.'

'I saw it with my own eyes.'

He nodded, looking wearier than ever. 'Terrible as our enemy is,' he said, 'I am honoured that I lived to help this generation of sisters, who will fight as the Mother did. We men will be there to support you, as our forefathers promised Siyāti uq-Nāra.' An Ersyri saddle axe hung from his belt, a weapon the men studied for defence. 'Are you ready, Tuva?'

'To embrace my destiny?' Tunuva said. 'Oh, yes. Part of me wishes the call had come when I was younger, with fewer aches, but I am also glad that we knew peace, for a time. That we lived in the Priory when it was a dreamers' garden, and not just a fortress.'

'Yes. A precious gift.'

They both looked down at Lukiri. Tunuva grasped his hand. He had fathered the child she loved. Siyu was Esbar, but she was also Imsurin. Her gentler side had come from him.

'Is Canthe here?' she asked him at last.

'Yes, in the room beside Siyu. The eldest men will remain here to take care of the children.' He pressed her hand tight. 'See you soon, Tuva. May the Mother watch over you.'

'And you, Imin.'

He walked out. Tunuva bent to kiss Lukiri on the cheek before she went to the right door.

Canthe lay in a small room, her bare shoulders protruding from the heavy mantles that had been tucked around her. Her bed had been pushed close to the hearth, and her eyes were closed, lashes flickering in her sleep. A hint of warmth had returned to her cheeks.

Tunuva was about to leave when Canthe murmured, 'Sabran.' She shifted, and her eyes opened. 'Oh. Is that you, Tuva?'

'Canthe.' Tunuva sat at her bedside. 'How are you feeling?'

'Weary.' She sat up a little, drawing the covers over her breasts. 'How long have I been asleep?'

'Since Carmentum. Do you remember what happened?'

'I think so. Most of it, in any case.' She glanced at her own hands. 'Is it cold in here?'

'Not especially.' Tunuva poured some straw wine into a cup and handed it to her. 'You just called out for Sabran in your sleep. I assume you didn't mean the Queen of Inys.'

'That name is older than the House of Berethnet.' Canthe gazed into the cup. 'Sabran was my daughter. I named her for the sabra flower that grows beside Ungulus.'

She sipped the wine. 'I named my birthson for the stars,' Tunuva said, before she had given her tongue leave to say it. 'They were bright as oil lamps, the night he was born.'

'In Inys, they say a night-born child is always grave.'

'Oh, no. He was so happy,' Tunuva said, a world away. 'Even as a newborn, he was always smiling.' She took the cup from Canthe. 'I must set out for the Ersyr soon. The war has begun.'

'It will not be a war, but a slaughter,' Canthe said. 'That creature resembled the Nameless One, and no arrow could pierce him. No sword but one could break his hide.'

'Ascalun.'

'It has had many names.'

'Do you know what became of it?'

'No one does. Whatever Galian Berethnet did with it, he took the secret to his tomb.' Canthe glanced at her. 'You want to know what I did to the wyrm.'

'Yes.'

Canthe looked away. 'I entrust this secret to you alone, Tunuva,' she finally said. 'I hope you will not fear my knowledge.'

'I am difficult to scare.'

'Siden is the magic of the deep earth, from the Womb of Fire. My other magic stems from above.'

'From ... the sky?'

'Yes. Our world is a pendulum, moving between two equal and opposite powers. The white light I summoned – I call it sterren, the obverse of siden. It is cold instead of hot, and flows like water. It waxes with the coming of a comet named the Long-Haired Star.'

Tunuva felt a shiver along her back. Nothing in the archives had ever spoken of this.

'That is why it hurt the wyrm,' she said. 'Why it weakened me, too.'

'Yes. I called forth the magic of starlight, as I could once call fire.'

'Could you do it again?'

'I doubt it. As you see, it drains me. My stores are dangerously low, and I have no way to replenish them. Only the comet can do that.' Canthe looked bleak. 'I'm so sorry, Tuva. I had only one good weapon to offer the Priory, and I have exhausted it.'

'Do not apologise. Fifty years of training, and I was unprepared for the strength of that wyrm. You saved us.' Tunuva covered her hand. 'I am leaving now for Jrhanyam, to support Queen Daraniya. Is there anything I can do for you, before I go?'

'No, but I think I may be able to help you. Our visit to the valley reminded me of something,' Canthe said. 'The spear Esbar possesses – did it really belong to Suttu the Dreamer?'

'As far as we know, yes. Cleolind took it from her father, Selinu. It was all she claimed of her birthright.'

'Suttu dipped her spear in starlight, according to myth. I wonder if she knew the secrets of sterren, as I do. A weapon infused with that magic could do grievous harm to a wyrm.'

Tunuva slowly nodded. 'It's worth a try. I will take it with me.'

'I hope it works.' Canthe hesitated. 'Did you tell Esbar what you saw me do?'

'Yes.'

'And she mistrusts it,' Canthe said. 'She fears me.' Tunuva said nothing. 'It's all right. It's natural that the Prioress should be wary when she has so many people to protect, and I can't regret showing that power, if it saved you. You are my friend, Tuva. My first in so long.'

'And you are mine. Esbar must be cautious, but I believe she will come to trust you, in time.' Tunuva got to her feet. 'If you feel strong enough to join us in the Ersyr, the men staying behind will point you to a horse.'

'I can't fight, Tuva. I would be no use.'

'You could help get people to safety, but it is your choice. For now, I will let you sleep.'

She had almost crossed the threshold when Canthe said, 'Tuva, there is something else you should know.'

'What is it?'

Canthe seemed to weigh her words, her eyes like two deep pools.

'Perhaps I should have told you sooner. It took me some time to put the pieces together,' she said. 'I didn't want to raise your hopes, Tuva. Now I feel I must.'

'I am listening.'

'Over the years, I have travelled far, but Inys always called me home sooner or later. Last time I returned, I bided in a northern province called the Lakes. There is a forest there, wild and dark and beautiful, that crosses the whole island, shore to shore. A place feared without cause. They call it the haithwood, and as the story went, a witch dwelled in it.'

461

Tunuva returned to her bedside and nodded for her to continue.

'Until a few years ago, I lived on a small piece of land near that wood, working as a healer,' Canthe said. 'The province was overseen by a nobleman named Edrick Glenn. He was always respectable and fair, never involved in scandal – so it did catch my attention when rumour swirled around his family.

'I first heard it at the market in Wulstow. It was common knowledge that Lord Edrick had adopted his sister's two children, but now he apparently had a third. The birth had never been announced. Most guessed this child was also adopted, and that was nothing unusual. The Inysh claim to value generosity, and what better way to show it than to take in a poor foundling?

'But within a few years, there was less generous talk in town, from a cook who had once worked for Lord Edrick. She was telling everyone who would listen that this boy – a foundling – had been abandoned in the haithwood, and that he had strange powers. He seemed not to feel the cold. He never sickened, cried often, and spoke a heathen tongue. People said the boy had the mark of a witching.' When Tunuva shook her head, Canthe said, 'An old superstition. A witch, or one cursed by a witch, bears a mark, which makes them easier to hunt.'

'Such as?'

'It could be a physical sign – a birthmark, a scar – or a suspicious power. As I said, some Inysh think a witch dwells in the haithwood. People had no real proof, so they traded in rumour. They wondered if this boy was hers, or marked by her, and shunned him. Lord Edrick did his best to protect him, but the mistrustful whispers followed.

'I visited the estate some time later, to discuss the forest law with Lord Edrick. It was a hot summer day, so he had the windows of his study flung open – and I chanced to see him, the Child of the Woods, playing with his brother and sister. He still had no idea what people said of him beyond those walls.

'As I spoke with Lord Edrick, we heard a cry. A queen bee had flown past the children. The child was sobbing in panic, hands over his ears. Lord Edrick said he must go to him; that he would not sleep that night. His younger son had always been so terribly afraid of bees.'

The smell of honey, welling with the memory of it. 'When was this?'

'Twelve years ago.'

As long in the world as he was in the womb. Tunuva could feel a vast thing cresting in her body, too big for her ribs to contain. 'Canthe,' she said, 'why have you told me this story?'

'Because the longer I've spent with you, the longer I've felt I'd seen you before. It's been twelve years, but finally, I remember where. The Child of the Woods did not look like Lord Edrick. His face did hold something of you.'

Tunuva felt all the careful stitches unravel, a stitch for every breath she had taken since that day. She pressed her fist low to her belly.

'What was his name?' Her voice came out in a raw scrape. 'The Child of the Woods.'

'Wulfert,' Canthe said. 'His name is Wulfert Glenn.'

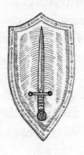

54

West

Last he had sailed towards Inys, the Hammer of the North had still ruled Hróth. Regny had been by his side, Eydag had drunk heather beer, and laughter had rung on the deck of the *Longstride*. Now, he could not shake that evil smell from the white ship, the taste of death under his tongue.

On the third day, a body drifted past the *Wave Steed*. Swollen and charred, it floated with its arms fanned out, reeking of rotten smoke. Sauma and Thrit watched in silence until the fog enveloped it. The captain – a mardy old raider – had the sign of the sword chalked on to the mast.

There was little talk during the voyage. Sometimes Wulf caught Sauma watching him and wondered what she was thinking. *You should be dead*, Karlsten whispered from his mind. He drank enough ale to muffle the voice, staying close to the mast and away from the waves.

On the sixth evening, he lay beneath the rain shelter that tented the middle of the ship. He was aware of every movement: the creak of rope and sail, the waves licking the sides.

Deep in the night, Thrit came into the shelter and nested in the pelts beside him. Wulf said, 'Did you find them, Thrit?'

Thrit looked at him, dark eyes reflecting the lantern.

'Your family.' Wulf could still not speak without pain. He had swallowed so much smoke and salt. 'Bardholt asked you to get them to Eldyng. Did you?'

'Aye. They're safe from the plague, for now.'

'It came from beneath. From the wyrms.' Wulf coughed from his chest. 'Just as the Saint told it.'

'The Curse of Yikala.' Thrit looked grim. 'The Saint defeated the Nameless One, but he had an enchanted sword. If magic ever existed, it's gone. It's been gone for centuries.'

'In the East, too?'

'I think so. The dragons – the gods – were supposed to have magic. A divine force that allowed them to turn into animals, or even humans, and gave them power over water.'

'What do they look like, these dragons?'

'Giant snakes with the scales of fish. They flew without wings, swimming like whales.' He took something from under his shirt. 'My grandfather gave me this when I saw him, to protect me.'

He passed Wulf the amulet, which was carved of pale stone. It showed a sinuous creature with a mane, coiled like a snake, four toes on each foot.

'Looks like a knucker. A wyrm of the water,' Wulf murmured. 'Always thought those were just a story.' He handed it back. 'You can't let anyone see you with that, Thrit.'

'You're not just anyone.' Thrit returned it to his neck. 'My grandparents aren't believers, really. They say the gods slept through war and drought, and they owe them no devotion.'

'They converted to the Six Virtues?'

'Of course. Bardholt demanded it. In truth, though, I think they believe only in what they see.' Thrit rested his head on a folded arm. 'I sent them to Skelsturm. I thought they'd be safer on an island when the plague moves south, which I suspect it will.'

Wulf looked up, to the canvas above. That canvas kept him safe, kept him concealed.

'I won't ask if you're all right,' Thrit said. 'I'll ask if there's anything I can do.'

'No.' Wulf swallowed, eyes watering from the pain. 'Karl is right. All of them died close to me.'

'Well, I'm not dead, as far as I can tell, and neither is Sauma. Neither is Karl, unfortunately – though I suspect he'd love to die in some revel of witching, just to prove his point.' Thrit paused. 'You don't have to ask, Wulf. I'll never fear you. Regny didn't. I don't.'

He reached into the space between them. Wulf breathed in the smell of his palm: tar and wood, the sweet oil he combed through his hair, the ring on his thumb. That thumb stroked Wulf from cheekbone to jaw.

'Get some sleep,' Thrit said. 'Saint knows what we'll face in Inys.'

Wulf resisted the urge to grasp his hand. He nodded and huddled into the pelt, knowing there would be no bees in his dreams. There had been no dreams at all since the wyrm came.

He woke to a roar in his ears, the sweep of icy air across the ship. Choking on fear, he drew his sax, waiting for fire to blind and devour him. His heart was a heavy fist on his breastbone.

Slowly, he felt the wind, the rain. The cover had been taken off. Over the twine of the sail and the creaking, he could just hear Sauma shouting to the captain. The fog had cleared enough for moonlight to cut through, and there, in the middle distance, were cliffs, skelped by the black and monstrous waves.

Inys.

'Wulf,' Sauma called as he got up, 'this will be a bad storm. We'll have to make land where we can.'

'Where are we?' he tried to say. She leaned close to hear. 'Where is this?'

'Not sure.' Her curls were painted to her forehead. 'We can take shelter, sail again when it passes.'

In another life, Wulf would have relished the ride to the coast. He would have savoured the spray on his face and the salt on his lips, laughed at the prospect of thunder. Now all he could do was hunker beside the mast, hoping on hope he could keep his last meal down.

By the time they were close enough to smell land, the wind howled and the Ashen Sea battered the ship. Sauma and Thrit sculled with the merchants while the captain worked the rudder and Wulf sat feckless in the hull, staring into the distance, his bandaged and mittened hands in his lap. Though his soles had healed enough for him to walk without the crutch, the others had refused to let him oar while his fingers were healing.

Soon they were lowping into the shallows to haul the ship ashore. Wulf disembarked and promptly vomited on to the sand. He wiped his mouth with a shaking wrist, sweat dripping from his hair.

'Look,' Thrit shouted over the wind. He pointed up the beach. 'Is that a cave?'

Wulf squinted through the rain, to where the cliff opened its mouth. 'Aye,' one of the leather traders agreed. 'It is.'

They slept around a fire inside, spreading their wet clothes and provisions on rocks. By morning, the storm had blown elsewhere, leaving tired daylight and a shimmer in its wake.

Sauma found Wulf on the beach, fastening his boots. 'We're ready to sail again,' she said.

'No.'

'What?'

'I'll get myself to Ascalun.' Wulf glanced at her. 'Sauma, I can't be on that sea again.'

She looked southward, down the long stretch of wet sand and shingle. 'I don't envy you, but if you insist,' she said, breathing out damp fog. 'Thrit can keep you company. I'll go with the traders and find somewhere to stay in the capital. Meet me there.'

'Thank you.'

'Regny would tell you to find your iron.' A sigh left her nose. 'I am not Regny.'

She trudged back towards the ship. Thrit emerged from the cave, his wicker pack slung over his shoulder.

The beach was a slick, fettled by rain and the tide. As light blanched the ominous clouds, Wulf watched the *Wave Steed* fight back on to the choppy waters. He and Thrit followed in its wake, moving south at a slow clip. Though he loved the snow, Thrit had never enjoyed the dank chill of Inys, and wore an expression of pained resolve, face scrunched up against the mizzle.

They walked without speaking, too weary to muster a word. When Wulf next looked up, the fog was at the coast again. Through it, he made out a dark hump in the water.

'I know where we are,' he called. 'This is the Fens.'

'How do you know?'

'That wee skerry. Yelden Head.' Wulf paused to cough. 'Marks the boundary between the Leas and the Fens. You can only reach it when the tide's out. My aunt mentioned it once.'

'Does she live nearby, this aunt?'

'A few miles off. Someone should be able to point us to her manor.'

'If we find anyone.' Thrit puffed out a grey smudge. 'She'll help us reach Ascalun?'

'Aye, I think so.'

'Good. I need a hot bath and some bland Inysh broth.' Thrit raked his wet hair from his face. 'Lead the way.'

They forged on, battered by the wind. Something made Wulf want to cleave to the sea, even if he had no wish to sail on it. They stopped to collect fresh water before continuing, watched by the black gulls that picked at the crabs and beached fish on the coast.

Wulf had met Baroness Shore several times, when she visited Langarth. From what he remembered, she was loud, rich, and had always treated him with kindness. She was a southerner, raised in the Fens, beyond the shadow of the haithwood – it would have been ghost lights and swamp hounds that had terrified her as a child, not a witch in the wood.

Their boots left deep wells in the sand. Wulf walked with his head stooped against the wind and his fists across his chest. Hours passed before Thrit touched his shoulder, and he looked up to see a Hróthi longship on the beach, listed to one side. The wind lashed at its tattered sail, which was split crossways into four, two panes of white and two of crimson.

Wulf knew that sail. Everyone did. Clan Vatten were virtuous now, but anyone with any sense still feared the blood and bone.

'Not like the sea wolves to run a ship aground,' Thrit said. Beneath his lambskin hood, his nose was pink. 'Caught in the storm?'

'Aye.'

Barrels jostled in the shallows. Wulf eyed the footprints that pocked the beach, weaving back and forth until they vanished beyond the cliffs. 'A drunken stride,' Thrit observed. 'Fools must not have seen the shore while they were in their cups.'

Wulf had a different notion. The callused skin of his palms itched. He climbed a tangle of salted netting, trying not to use his frostnipped hands, and pulled himself up the flank of the ship, grimacing at the ache in his arms, the broad soreness between his shoulders.

When he had an elbow over the gunwale, his blood stopped.

The longship had been carrying wool, which was still there, bundled in packs. Now it also held corpses – red to the elbow, tongues swollen and eyes rolled back, arms riven by deep and dirty gashes, blood under their broken nails. Even in death, their faces were contorted in agony.

'Thrit,' Wulf croaked, 'stay away.'

'What is it?' Thrit gripped the haft of his axe. 'Wulf, what's there?'

Wulf looked down at Thrit, watching his brow turn overcast.

'Saint,' Thrit whispered. 'It's here.'

****

Glorian stood at the window of her bedchamber in the Queens' Tower. The smell was in her hair, her bedding, everything she touched, and for all the heat, she could not stop trembling. She watched the dark reveal the flares of flame across the city.

Sir Bramel had got her away. She had woken in bed, coughing so hard she feared her ribs might break, Doctor Forthard at her side. She had coughed while the blaze mantled the river on both sides, watched fire leap between buildings and strike the Sanctuary of the Sacred Damsel. Twelve women had run inside to save her remains, only for the heat to drive them back. One had caught molten lead from the roof in her eye.

Queen Cleolind was safe. She was entombed in stone, and dead.

On the second day, Glorian had drifted into a feverish sleep, waking to a surge of screams as Rosarian's Bridge buckled, taking fifty people with it. In Hayharbour, a throng of boats had overturned as hundreds tried to board them, drowning many, for the River Limber ran swift and cold, especially at this time of year.

On the third day, the fire had reached the shipyards on the south bank, and then the ward of Mistlegate.

On the fourth day, Helisent made it to the castle. She had searched in vain for the mislaid skull, only to be swept up in the stampede across the city, unable to reach Queenside. Trapped by the fire, the smoke, and the crush in the streets – frightened people, abandoned carts, livestock running wild – she had finally reached the Limber. With the fire at her back, she had risked swimming between wards, clinging to the mooring rings, and had since been with Kell Bourn, pained by bloody feet, a chill, and a ferocious cough.

The skull was lost. All that remained of Bardholt Hraustr was the thighbone Glorian had been clutching – but Helisent was alive, and so were Adela and Julain. That was all that mattered.

By the sixth day, the blaze had spread farther, forcing many north across the Bridge of Supplications. It must have felt safe until a strong wind blew a sparkling cloud of embers across the river, illuminated garnets that ignited everything they touched.

After that, she lost count of day and night. The fire was a midnight sun, and this was the Womb of Fire. Florell tried to keep her abreast, though Glorian could chart the blaze from the play of light, the cries, the reek. *You were supposed to be their protection*, she reminded herself when she passed her window. *You were supposed to be their shield.*

The haze over the city – sallow by day, ruddy by night – had seeped into the castle. The fire in her own hearth seemed a profanity, and at last, she bid a servant bank it, afraid to do it herself. The boy fumbled as he worked, and when he looked at Glorian, she could not understand his expression. Once he was gone, she bolted the door.

His family must be out there, while she was in a stone fortress. Ascalun Castle stood far enough from the other buildings that even its gardens would likely be safe. Beyond its high walls, there was wood and wattle, thatch and hay and wool, a city made of tinder.

The Saint had never promised that nothing else would come. Only that the Nameless One would not return. The people of Inys had never prepared, because they thought their queens would shield them.

Mother, Father, please, I beseech you, help me. Saint, help me. Damsel, help me. I will give you anything. Glorian clasped her hands. *My sister, you were right. Send me a message—*

A knock startled her from prayer. 'Your Grace?'

Glorian groped for the latch, letting Florell in. 'What is happening?' she said, clutching her. 'Florell, tell me.'

'Ten wards are on fire, more threatened by the hour,' Florell said, eyes bloodshot. Glorian let go and turned away, a fist clenched to her heart. 'The droughts have left the thatch very dry. The blaze will keep spreading. No doubt the violence will spread with it. The people are turning on each other, blaming friend and enemy alike for the wyrms' coming.'

'What is to be done?'

'Lady Gladwin believes the buildings closest to the fire should be pulled down to break its path. Lord Robart has agreed to her proposal, and will compensate the owners from his own coffers. They are riding to overtake the southern edge of the fire now.'

'You told me to assert myself,' Glorian said. 'Instead, Lord Robart will be the one to end the violence my bold words began. I should be riding at his side.'

'Glorian, no. You are the heir.' Florell gripped her shoulders. 'You did all you could. You defied this Fýredel, just as your father would have. Lord Robart is right – you must stay safe and hidden.'

'I could be no more hidden if he shut me in a wooden box and dropped me into the sea.'

'It is far too dangerous for you to step into that fire. We must put our trust in the Saint.'

'Why has he not stopped this?' Glorian said, her voice breaking. 'Why has he done nothing?'

'Only you can know that. You are his successor.'

'If you were his successor, what would you think?'

Florell looked out at the city. 'A test,' she said. 'I would think it was a test of faith.'

'Perhaps it is a warning.' Glorian pulled away and paced her bedchamber. 'We shamed him in the Century of Discontent. Perhaps even Mother was not enough to save us from his wrath.'

'Your mother was good enough to make up for all three of her predecessors and more. She was *the* great queen of your bloodline,' Florell said fiercely. 'His heir, his embodiment. You have her heart and spine, Glorian. I saw that when you stood and faced the wyrm.'

'I taunted him, and he answered.'

'If you had bowed, you would have spat at your ancestor. He did not kneel before the Nameless One.'

Glorian had wondered. She could have pleaded for her people to be spared; she could have asked the beast for mercy.

'Prince Therico,' she said. 'Is he on his way to Inys?'

'He was. But now, the danger—'

'Get him here. Florell, I cannot go out there for one reason, and one only. It is because I do not have a child. If I did, you would all let me ride in the city.'

'Glorian—'

'You will tell the Lord Protector to get Prince Therico here, by hook or by crook. Let it be done.'

Florell closed her eyes for a moment. 'I will express your wishes to Lord Robart,' she said. 'Your Grace.'

Once she had gone, Glorian sank to the floor beside her cold hearth, clutching a bolster from her bed. She was a small child again, needing warmth and heaviness for comfort.

471

I will wed. I will do all you command. I will marry Prince Therico or whoever else is put before me. I will bear the fruit, I will be the unending vine, and then I will fight to the bitter end. Glorian pressed her eyes shut, reaching for that inbetween, where a stream flowed like tears. *Let it end. Please, let it end. Saint, messenger, sister, help me. Send me rain.*

****

It must have been hours later that she woke on the floor, her cheek pressed to the flagstone, to a rumble that made her fear the walls had crumbled. She reached her window just in time to see a flash of lightning as the sky opened like a hand from the heavens.

Then it came: the unmistakable, merciful smell of rain.

I hear.

55

East

Dumai woke with a gasp. Her skin was drenched, as if she had been hauled from the sea and thrown to her bedding, wet from the depths. It took her a moment to remember where she was.

Her heart rolled like a wave. She sat up and rested her brow on her knees, sweat dripping from her hair.

First light came through the window screens. Here she woke at the wrong time, to silence and stillness at dawn. Each morning she would pace the walkways, trying to tire herself to sleep before midday. She might drift off in the hour before sunset, only for the music and chatter of the Lacustrine court to keep her up all night.

For a long time, she had not heard from the figure in her dreams. She was too tired and unsettled to sink into that middle place. Yet suddenly a voice had come. *Let it end*, it had called. *Help me. Send me rain.*

Somehow, Dumai had known that she could. She had woken to a thunderclap, smelled rain, yet heard none on the roof. *You have sent me so many signs. Help me understand*, she willed the great Kwiriki. *Tell me who this woman is, and what she wants.*

She found Kanifa on a swing in the courtyard, drinking from a steaming cup. 'You should try this,' he said, slowing the swing for her.

Dumai sat beside him and took it. The drink was red and a little bitter, but warming. 'Is Nikeya asleep?' she said, drawing her pelt close.

473

'As far as I can tell.'

'Once again, the Lady of Faces adjusts to everywhere but the sky.' She passed back his cup. 'Have you heard from the alchemist?'

'No. The Night Council must be considering what happened to this Northern king.'

'Surely that doesn't concern Master Kiprun.'

'It may. What if the King of Hróth was slain by the same creature we saw?' Kanifa asked. 'What if there are more of these creatures as far away as that?'

'If more come, we must all be doomed.' Dumai looked at her friend. 'How long should we wait for him, do you think?'

'As long as it takes. We can afford some patience, Mai,' he said, seeing her face. 'You woke the gods to protect Seiiki. The Night Council will be debating whether to do the same here.'

Why Nayimathun of the Deep Snows was awake, no one had explained. She was an ancient Lacustrine dragon of the north, enshrined in legend as a wanderer with a strange and playful nature.

The homeless and lost prayed to Nayimathun. She was beloved of tricksters and thieves, orphans and travellers. Even the Hüran, who had brought their own gods from over the mountains, respected the Green Sister, since their people, too, had once been rootless.

They were picking at a meal when a servant loped into the courtyard, a little out of breath. 'Princess Dumai,' she said, 'I bring word from Master Kiprun. He is ready to receive you – now, if you wish.'

Dumai stood. 'Thank you.'

Black Lake Palace was a box of many secrets. Even though she and Kanifa had explored its many courtyards and gardens, its layout remained as bewildering by day as by night. Open paths interleaved its main buildings, with walls high enough that only the sky could be seen overhead. It was hard to map a path without a vantage point or guide.

The servant approached one of the colossal archways that divided these inbetween paths, and they climbed the stepway hewn into it. This brought them to the gate tower, which formed the base of the starwatch, a masterwork of black marble. High above, the celestial globe caught the light of sunrise as it turned, powered by a waterwheel.

Inside, they climbed hundreds more steps, sweet and fusty smells filling their noses. At last, the servant stopped outside a doorway. 'This is the chamber of life,' she said. 'Please, enter.'

Candles fanned the dark to its corners. A stone bench took up one side of the room, lit by open stoves. Their light danced across a cabinet of glazed earthenware pots, each labelled in Lacustrine.

A small figure in crimson stood before the bench, sleeves rolled to the elbow, muttering. Dumai cleared her throat.

'Master Kiprun?'

The alchemist whipped around. He wore round amber panes over his eyes, clipped to his nose, huge and misty with steam. 'I did ask for duck feathers,' he said, in a tone of sincere annoyance.

Dumai could only blink. His cheeks were flushed, threads of hair were stuck to his forehead, and he brandished a grey feather.

'You brought me goose feathers. Goose,' he barked, making her jump. 'You do know the difference between a duck and a goose, don't you? One quacks and the other honks, not to mention the neck. The neck alone—'

'Master Kiprun,' Kanifa interjected, 'this is Noziken pa Dumai, Crown Princess of Seiiki.'

The alchemist sleeved the fog from his eyeglasses.

'Ah. Yes.' He interlocked his fingers. Each bore a ring of a different metal: gold, silver, iron, copper. 'Princess Dumai. I am Master Kiprun, who shines – well, flickers, really – for the Munificent Empress. And you?' he said to Kanifa. 'Who are you, the Prince of Seiiki?'

'No.' Kanifa cleared his throat. 'I'm just a guard, a friend to Princess Dumai. Not a noble.'

'Is it not noble to be a guard?' Master Kiprun wafted a brown hand, webbed with scars from deep burns, like his arms. 'No matter. I never understand these things. Yes, your message caught my interest, Princess Dumai of the Faraway Isle. You don't look much like a princess,' he said, cocking his head. 'Aren't you supposed to wear a crown, or something?'

Dumai reunited with her tongue. 'Well,' she said, indicating her headpiece, 'this is—'

'Madam, that is a fish.'

After a moment, Dumai decided not to kick against the current. 'It is a fish,' she agreed, taking a step towards him. 'My fish and I flew here to seek your help, Master Kiprun.'

'Yes, I did fear as much. Last time, it was a king who disturbed my work. He found me in the mountains, just to annoy me.' The alchemist snorted. 'Once, it was the poor who sought my services, asking me to turn grass to gold. They were, at least, polite, if wildly optimistic. Now I am summoned hither and thither, disturbed by everyone from Golümtan to Ginura.'

He inspected the vessel, sniffed its contents, and promptly threw the contents over his shoulder, into a cauldron of slurry. Dumai exchanged a nonplussed glance with Kanifa.

'The silence was an invitation for you to explain yourself, Princess,' Master Kiprun said, distracted. 'Time is long, but also short.'

'Of course.' Dumai followed him. 'King Padar must have told you what we saw in the Broken Valley.'

'You're not going to ask the same questions he did, are you?' Master Kiprun groused. 'I can't abide repeating myself.'

'May I show you something instead?'

Master Kiprun pursed his lips and removed his sooty eyeglasses, showing a freckled nose and lines around his eyes, which aged him by a decade. He wiped his hands on a cloth before taking what Dumai offered.

'These are quite old,' he observed, unrolling the pages Unora had found. 'Ah, yes, the Nameless One. I heard the story from a chambermaid, a descendant of Ersyri traders. She said it was a tale to frighten children.'

'Clearly it is not,' Dumai said impatiently. 'We saw a wyrm just like this one. King Padar must have described it to you. I want to know where they come from, and why this is happening.'

'No, you don't.'

'I assure you—'

'You don't want to know why they've come, Princess Dumai. I imagine such complexities would bore or baffle you,' Master Kiprun cut in. 'You want to know how to defeat them.'

'Yes.'

'According to the tale, the first creature emerged from a fire mountain. No fire mountain can be sealed. Even if it could, it would be as much use now as closing a cage weeks after the bird has flown.' He handed back the pages. 'As I told the King of Sepul, there is little to be done, except to hope that dragonkind can defend us.'

'There must be another way. A human vanquished the Nameless One.'

'Yes, with a magic sword, apparently. Do you have one?'

'No, but—'

'I deal in truth, Princess, not magic.'

476

'What if *magic* is just a word for power beyond our understanding, like the gods possess?' Dumai pressed. 'I have no sword, but I have clues, Master Kiprun. I put my trust in you to decipher them. You have studied the layers and contents of the earth. Help me understand what I saw, and what Furtia Stormcaller has told me.'

Master Kiprun scratched his shaven head. 'The black dragon?'

'She converses with me.'

'How?'

'In my mind. She says there is a balance in the world, a balance that has been unsettled; that the fire beneath has grown too hot, too fast – and the star has not returned to cool it.'

Until this point, the alchemist had only appeared to tolerate her presence. Now he stared at her.

'The star,' he said, grasping her sleeve. 'Wait. The dragon said a *star* has not returned?'

Dumai nodded. 'She says that only *fallen night* can stop what is to come.' He clamped a hand over his mouth and let it slide to his smooth chin, gaze fixed on nothing. 'What is it, Master Kiprun?'

'The night skies.' A sharp laugh. 'I should have thought of it. Stay exactly there, both of you.'

He bounded from the room and up another flight of steps, leaving Dumai to clutch her pages. Nikeya chose that moment to step into the chamber of life, examining the instruments with interest.

'Princess,' she said, when Dumai dealt her a withering look. 'I see you met the alchemist.'

'I see you followed.' Dumai tucked the pages away. 'How long have you been there?'

'Not long. I would hate to miss the rest of such a fascinating conversation.'

'And I would hate for the River Lord to miss even a moment of my private meetings.'

Before Nikeya could reply, Master Kiprun barged past her with an armful of scrolls. A moment later, he turned and raised a finger, narrowing his eyes. 'You were not here before.'

'I was not.' Nikeya smiled. 'Please, do go about your work, learnèd alchemist. Ignore me.'

'Gladly,' he said, and deposited the scrolls on a bench. 'Princess Dumai, you have the rare privilege of having prodded my mind. What you say made me remember something.'

'What is it, Master Kiprun?'

'This is a world of many contrasts. Night and day. Fire and water. Sky and earth – that is, what is above, and what beneath. Beneath is rock and molten fire. We alchemists have always known the power that burns underfoot. Metals and precious stones are formed there, in the furnace of the world.' He flashed his rings to demonstrate. 'We try to imitate the process in alchemy. We cook the metals on smaller fires, hoping to alter them – turn iron into gold, and so on – or to understand their nature, such as why stone lasts longer than flesh.'

'What has this to do with what Furtia said?'

'Alchemists study the earth. Astronomers look to the sky. Since each of them takes a lifetime to master, only a rare few have tried to wed the arts of gold and silver.' He unrolled a large sheet of parchment. 'I read this theory a long time ago. The theory of the weighing scales.'

He moved aside to let them all see the drawing – a set, indeed, of weighing scales, like those for measuring herbs – and indicated its two bowls, both engraved with a word.

'Two sides,' he explained, 'in perfect balance. *Above* rules the bowl of cold, water and night. *Below* rules fire and warmth and day. At any given time, we are in one of these two ages. For example, in a time ruled by the celestial forces, the days might be colder, and water might flow in abundance. The basic principle is that all the world is tuned to this duality. As one of the two waxes, the other wanes – an eternal balance. I have also seen it illustrated as a wheel or a sandglass, by those with interest in the notion.'

'It's said the first dragons came from the stars,' Dumai said, catching on. 'From above.'

'Indeed, and now is not their time. That's why they have been asleep. It stands to reason that something must originate from *beneath*, too – equal but opposite in nature. Something from the fire mountains, perhaps.'

'But fire mountains often erupt – or used to, before the gods settled our lands,' Kanifa pointed out. 'Usually they bring no dangerous creatures with them.'

'No,' Master Kiprun agreed, his nose inching closer to the chart. 'I have wondered if eruptions keep the fire in check, like steam when a pot boils. But if something has thrown off the balance, and there is too much fire . . . perhaps the overspill collects in this Dreadmount.'

Dumai said, 'Do you know where it is?'

'Over the Abyss, the sea even our best ships can't quite conquer yet. But things far away can still affect us. A leaf could fall in Brakwa and cause a groundshake in Jarhat.'

'Could it?'

'Probably. I find most things I say do turn out to be true.'

Nikeya came towards them, her expression thoughtful. She stood beside Dumai to consider the chart.

'What could have caused this great unbalancing of the forces, do you think, Master Kiprun?' Her hair slipped off her shoulder as she looked. 'It must have been a notable event, to set the world awry.'

Her usual arch tone was gone.

'No idea. It stands to reason that we are in an Age of Fire,' Master Kiprun said, 'but one where the fire burns too strong. The ground has been dry, racked with drought, the rivers low. Even the ice in the North has been melting. Whether that extremity is the cause or the result—'

He tapered off into mutterings, too low and swift to decipher. 'If these wyrms are indeed born of an imbalance,' Dumai said slowly, 'does it mean they possess no motive, no reason?'

'I suspect not. They might have a small degree of intelligence, but not enough to overcome their nature.'

'Which is … evil?'

'No, no. A wildfire destroys blindly, but would you call it evil?'

'But dragons are good,' Kanifa said, a statement and a question at once.

'Again, no. Consort Jekhen would execute me on the spot for saying so, but it is simplistic, to describe a dragon as *good*. They are in harmony with nature. Is that the same as goodness?'

Dumai watched the alchemist, waiting for his verdict. Master Kiprun stared down at the chart.

'An Age of Fire would be ended by something from above.' He slapped his hands flat on the table. 'An *astronomer*. I never thought I'd say this, but we need one.'

'Wait.' Nikeya was looking towards the window. 'Do you hear that?'

They fell silent. On the wall below, guards were shouting to each other, the wind snatching away their words. Dumai walked to the window to see columns of smoke, black and growing.

Without even drawing breath, she was gone from the chamber, down the stairs and through the doors, out on to the wall. In the city, screams were rising, even as the smoke billowed higher. 'That smell.' Kanifa was already at her side. 'Just the same as in Sepul.'

'Stay inside with Nikeya,' Dumai told him. 'These walls are stone. You should be safe.'

'Dumai, where are you going?' Nikeya called after her, but Dumai was already running.

****

The Hidden Lake was in the middle of the palace. Dumai rushed through the woken court, following the Inner Shim, until she reached a marble terrace overlooking a stretch of deep blue water. Furtia and Nayimathun were both in the lake, looking towards the city.

Nayimathun was larger, older. She could have swallowed Furtia whole and still had room to spare. At a less urgent moment, Dumai would have stopped to admire her scales, like frosted grass, and her mane, a sharp contrast, bronze spun into silk. Her horns were long and white.

Dumai pulled off her shoes and plunged into the shallows, wading towards them both. 'Furtia,' she shouted.

The dragon jerked her head towards her. *Earth child.* She flared her nostrils. *They have come.*

I know, great one. We must see what we face.

Only fallen night can stop it.

'But we might slow it.' Dumai signed as she spoke. 'Please. We must try to drive it away.'

Rattling in agreement, Furtia lowered her head, and Dumai climbed her neck like a ladder. No time for the saddle, or to fetch her riding boots, but her feet were surer now, used to the instability of dragonback – she could sense where to place them. Once she was secure, she gasped to find Nayimathun of the Deep Snows considering her from above.

Who are you, island child?

A new voice in her mind. Nayimathun moved her enormous head closer, and Dumai stretched out a hand to touch her snout.

'My name is Dumai,' she said clearly in Lacustrine. 'Noziken pa Dumai.'

I see the waters of your mind. Nayimathun smelled of green rivers and moss. *How is it that you carry the light?*

Before Dumai could answer, Furtia had lit her crest and swum into the sky, over the palace walls.

480

Furtia made for where the smoke was thickest. Dumai coughed until her throat scorched. It tasted rotten, scarring. Trusting the strength of her knees, she tore a strip off her tunic and plunged it into the manehair around her, letting it sop up thick brine. When it was drenched, she tied it over her nose and mouth.

The City of the Thousand Flowers was being set on fire.

Boats were striking out from the harbours. Below, a street of shops and houses had burst into flame, the fire a livid red, like feathering tongues of a sunset. Tens of thousands of people were running towards the River Shim, some with young children or goods in their arms.

Furtia growled. Droplets formed like gems on her armour, soaking Dumai to the bone. Her teeth chattered. She felt cold muscle shifting, smelled the sweetness of a storm, as the dragon swelled, soaking up the nearest wisps of cloud. Coasting low over the rooftops, she shook herself, drenching the streets, fires winking out in her wake.

Dumai looked up just in time to see a winged creature hurtling towards them. In the split second she had to absorb what she was seeing, she made three observations, as if from a great distance:

It is like what I saw in the valley, though smaller.

It has only two legs, not four.

It could be no less deadly if it can breathe fire.

When it came, the collision almost unseated her. Her shout was lost to an explosion of noise – Furtia roaring, claws scraping, the scream of the wind. The scent of storms was seared away, replaced by something hot and suffocating. Her head doubled in weight. Her stomach pulled against its root as Furtia rocked to the left. Through dark banners of her own hair, Dumai glimpsed teeth like iron blades, snapping shut with a sharp *clang*, before the beast was gone.

Great one, are you hurt?

Furtia shook herself off. *That is a lesser thing...*

Dumai was starting to regret her decision to ride with no saddle. Her hands ached from grasping manehair; her thighs cramped with the effort of staying put on a slippery hide. She glimpsed the winged creature twist through the air – singed brown scales, copper spines along its back – and throw its leathery wings open to swoop downward again.

Nayimathun rammed her brow into it. As it spun away, one wing clipped a temple, breaking three columns and trimming an eave. As soon as it swung around for another attack, the Lacustrine dragon bit down, crunching its wings, and flung its body into the river.

There.

Dumai looked back into the wind, and stopped breathing.

At first, she was sure it was the wyrm from the Broken Valley. Two horns and four legs, separate from its wings. Then she saw the way the light hit its scales – not with a glisten, like the sun on honey, but a clean, polished glow. From snout to tail, the creature was plated in gold bright enough to reflect the fires, gold stolen from the core of the world. It would have been magnificent if not for the complete absence of mercy in its eyes.

Its bulk was appalling. So was the din from below, as people started to see it. Dumai had never laid eyes on a living thing so large – its wings could have touched both banks of the river. Not even Nayimathun could match it, and Furtia, far younger, was spindly in contrast. Like all Seiikinese dragons, she was long and sleek, made for dives into the sea.

She flew towards the creature without a trace of fear. Dumai was frozen stiff. She could smell the beast, its wrongness, and the closer it came, the harder her heart pounded.

Its eyes were fixed on her.

'Great one, stop!' Her heels slipped as more briny water bubbled up beneath her. 'Furtia—'

Stop, it's too strong!

Furtia opened her jaws in a roar. Then a wave of hot air struck her, and so did a terrible iron horn, scraping along her side.

The white light in her crest hissed out.

The sound that followed was like nothing Dumai had ever heard – the screech of the wind, threatening to rip her eardrums. Furtia seemed to collapse on herself, and then she was in freefall, silver blood spraying from her side like rain.

The world reeled. Eyes streaming, teeth set, Dumai clung on. Furtia shuddered beneath her. Her crest flared back to life, and she whirled away from the approaching rooftops – but the upward pull was too hard and sudden, and Dumai lost her grip.

In years of climbing on the middle peak, she had never fallen any farther than it took to gasp. Not with Kanifa to catch her. This time, she had no rope around her waist.

She knew how to land: on her feet, knees loose, so she would break her legs and not her skull. There was no time for that.

Something clipped her shoulder. A blinding flare of pain, and then she landed, in a downy snowdrift at the base of the clock tower. It took the brunt of her fall, but pain burst in her shoulder and hip.

At first she was afraid to move, to see how badly hurt she was. People ran in all directions around her – some of them spilling out of the clock tower, others into it. She glimpsed merchants and soldiers, parents and children. Somewhere in the madness and black smoke, she heard dogs barking, screams and hooves.

Stay calm. Her mother spoke from her distant memory. *If you fall, always stay calm.*

Dumai curled her toes first. She could feel both legs. With care, she sat up, groaning at the throb in her shoulder. Her coat had been torn open where the corner of a roof had struck her. Blood was already drenching her sleeve.

A shadow overhead. The golden wyrm. It let out a reverberating call – a call meant to inspire fear – before red fire blazed from its maw, a wall of flame as wide as White Blossom Way.

Dumai warded her eyes from the heat. Coughing, she edged through the snowmelt, beneath a shroud of darkness. Furtia would never find her now, in the crush of people and horses rushing through these alleys. Her best chance was to get back to the palace.

She stayed low, afraid to breathe the rancid fumes. Her ribs flared with every movement. Splinting her side with one hand, she kept crawling, through wet footprints, soot and blood, until her fingers brushed a charred husk. *Do not look*, she told herself, quelling a retch. *Do not look.* She rose and stumbled out of the alley, into a street the wyrm had destroyed, where a building leaned and fell before her eyes, thickening the grey around her.

The hairs pricked on her nape. She looked to her right to see what she thought, at first, was a horse. Lightheaded, she wondered if it was in barding, and that was why it looked so strange – until a gust of wind thinned the embers and smoke.

It must once have been a stag. Now it was covered in scales. They armoured its head, its neck and flanks, everywhere but its hind legs, which were stretched, with a second knee, so it stood taller than it should. Blood leaked from open wounds where wings had broken through its flanks. Its teeth had sharpened and turned to metal, as had most of its antlers, bone needling from iron. A man lay dead behind it, his skull trodden beneath its hooves.

Dumai trembled. When its eyes found her, the sound it made was half whinny, half scream.

She forgot she was barefoot and wounded. The agony in her side disappeared, swallowed by the need to survive. Heaving for breath, she made for a low fence, scrambled under it, and rounded a sharp corner. She slipped on ice, twisting her ankle, slammed into a wall and kept going, not letting the hurt reach her.

In her years on the mountain, she had learned the dangers of the cold. In her time at court, she had learned the dangers of whispers and manipulation. Those paled in comparison to being a human among things reared by the deep unknown beneath the earth.

Another monstrosity lumbered across her path, almost twice her height, furred as well as scaled. The engorged bear stalked after a crowd, its eyes afire in its skull, huffing sparks through its nostrils. Dumai changed direction, only to see a terrible wolf. Its lower jaw was out of joint. When it barked at her, she hurtled down another street, soot burning in her throat.

This time, she had tripped over the wrong threshold – not into a dream world, but a nightmare.

Something pitched her to the ground. She rolled, protecting her head with both arms, until she crashed into the icy shallows of a canal. Soaked, she pulled herself on to the bridge above it, fear making her strong.

The canal returned her sense of direction. Following its course, she slid under a cart of ruined cloth, collided with another woman, and tripped on to White Blossom Way, where carts and shops were on fire as far as the eye could see. Dumai buckled, exhaustion overwhelming her body.

Island child.

Her head snapped up. Nayimathun was coming towards her. She mustered her strength and ran towards the dragon, the pain like a heated blade in her shoulder.

Nayimathun sailed low enough for her underside to skim the street. Other people were clinging to her scales, making grabs for the fronds of her tail. She caught Dumai and rose from the smoke, holding her with care between sharp claws.

Dumai fell limp as Nayimathun took her over the besieged city, finally laying her on the snow. Coughing uncontrollably, Dumai watched the green dragon shatter the ice on the Lake of Long Days.

When Nayimathun surfaced, she was not alone.

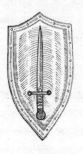

56

West

The downpour lasted three full days. As soon as it had smothered the last fire in Ascalun, Lord Robart had sent riders to the provinces. They reported that a flock of wyrms had destroyed countless fields and orchards in the Leas – the breadbasket of Inys – and left the pastures soaked in blood before they flew south, heading across the Saintsway to Yscalin.

Glorian watched her people jostle and shout beyond the castle gates. Another riot in as many days. All she wanted was to ride out and console them, but instead, she was confined to the Queens' Tower, stored like a cask of wine in a cellar, waiting for Prince Therico.

Florell came at noon. 'Your Grace,' she said, 'the Lord Protector requests your presence. A royal messenger has arrived.'

Glorian stood at once. 'From my betrothed?'

'I couldn't say.'

'He must get here soon,' Glorian said, more to herself than to Florell. She paced the bedchamber. 'I must be on the battlefield as soon as possible.'

'Glorian, your life will not be of any less value once you have borne a child. Would you leave your newborn an orphan?' Florell protested. 'Remember your temperance. You have Hróthi blood in you, but also Inysh. Not everything can be solved with a sword.'

I must believe it can, Glorian thought, *or I will lose my mind.*

Her ladies arrayed her in a tunic and skirts of middle grey. Julain braided her hair, while Adela and Helisent brushed her cloak and sleeves. Helisent still had a stubborn cough.

'Florell,' Glorian said, 'will you fetch me a padded coat?'

Florell slowed. 'For armour?'

'Yes.'

A sleeveless gambeson matching her measurements was brought, quilted dark wool with a high collar, iron sewn into its lining. It was heavier than Glorian had expected, but she found its weight a comfort. Florell fastened its buckles before she positioned her crown.

Still Glorian felt like an imposter playing at queens. Everything she wore was a trapping, with no meaningful power behind it.

Lord Robart waited at the bottom of the Queens' Tower, a sword at his side. 'Your Grace,' he said, taking in her choice of attire as he bowed. 'Thank you for joining me so quickly.'

'I would be obliged if I could join you more often, my lord, so I might stay abreast of what is happening in Inys.' Glorian walked with him into the garden. 'I am of little use in the Queens' Tower.'

She spoke with a resolve that took her by surprise. Since facing Fýredel, something had changed within her. Having looked evil in the eye, she had less fear of everything.

'Your Grace, you will be informed of all you need to know,' was his composed reply. 'Of course, you may leave the Queens' Tower as you wish, but it is the safest place for you. Let us not forget the attack at Glowan Castle.'

They passed a group of courtiers, who parted for them. They wore the same grey as the sky.

'As for your claim to be of little use there,' Lord Robart said, 'I must object to that assessment.' He walked past his own ancestor, the Knight of Generosity, who held a sheaf of wheat. 'You are remaining safe and well, in preparation for your greatest service to the queendom. Now more than ever, your people crave the comfort of knowing their queen has an heir.'

'On that subject, is this messenger from Prince Therico?'

'I know as much as you, Your Grace. I may not receive a royal messenger without the Queen of Inys.'

They walked into the throne room, enormous and carved of pale stone, made to evoke the entrance to Halgalant. Glorian took in the arch of its ceiling, its towering windows and polished floor.

'What is happening in the city?' she asked.

'We are dealing with the people's most pressing needs. Food will be brought from the Marshes and the Downs. Those without homes will have to rely on the sanctuaries until we can rebuild.'

Whenever that may be, Glorian thought. What point was there in rebuilding, when the wyrm had promised to return?

'You are the Duke of Generosity,' she said. 'What of the almshouses?'

She was breaking her mother's rule: *never ask questions*. Still, she saw no harm in it. She had no power. Knowledge might secure her some.

'Overwhelmed. I will ensure they receive as much relief as possible,' Lord Robart said as they neared the steps. 'While we consider our options.'

'What of our defences?'

'We have none, other than archers and warships. I have seen the state of the city, Your Grace. I am convinced there is no shield or weapon that could keep the wyrms from wreaking the same violence again.'

'I would have stood beside you on the streets.'

'Of course.'

Glorian wished she could read this man.

'What is your plan, Lord Robart?' she asked him. 'Even if we can't defeat Fýredel, the smaller wyrms might be beaten in the field. Surely we must set about calling the people to arms.'

Her frustration must have shown. Lord Robart stopped and turned to face her.

'Queen Glorian, I am not a man given to strong passions. I often think I should have been descended from the Knight of Temperance,' he said, a little drily. 'I have always preferred to scrutinise every situation from a distance, not allowing myself to give in to grief or fear. It allows me to think clearly, rationally – but do not mistake my dispassion for a lack of care. I care very much for this queendom, and I will do what is necessary to save it.'

Glorian nodded, placated. 'I understand.' They kept walking. 'My mother was not given to strong passions, either.'

'But you are. Just like your father,' Lord Robart said, with a rare smile. 'You are like him in many ways.'

'Thank you.'

'Your tribute to him after the entombment was marvellous.'

'It has long been tradition at funerals in Hróth. They call it *sithamál* – the last tale. It was the same before the Saint,' Glorian said, 'except they used to burn their dead.'

'They sang so the land itself would remember the departed,' Lord Robart said. She gave him a curious look. 'I have an interest, Your Grace. No matter how deep we bury the past, it always wells back up. I find it best to understand, rather than fear.'

At the top of the six narrowing steps, made steep for a dynasty of tall queens, Glorian stopped. Before her stood the high throne of the Queendom of Inys, cut from creamy Morgish marble, elegant in its simplicity. A faldstool had been placed beside it. Overhead soared a vinous canopy emblazoned with the True Sword, which towered above the throne.

Glorian turned and lowered herself into it. Even through the cushion beneath her, it was hard and cold.

'Your Grace.'

Lord Robart had come to stand over her. 'I'm afraid I must sit on the throne,' he said quietly. 'It signifies royal authority in Inys, which I presently hold.' He nodded to the faldstool. 'Forgive me.'

Her face burned. 'I understand.'

Lord Robart waited politely for her to move to the faldstool before he sat upon the throne, seeming to take no joy in it. He motioned to the stewards, who pulled the doors open again.

A woman strode into the throne room. Chestnut hair streamed to her waist. Her clothes were damp and dishevelled, her cheeks flushed.

'Come forward.' Lord Robart beckoned her. 'Who stands before the Queen of Inys?'

'Your Grace. Lord Protector.' She bowed to them both. 'My name is Mara Glenn. My father is Lord Edrick, Baron Glenn of Langarth.'

'Wulf's sister,' Glorian said, realising.

'Yes, Your Grace.'

'I'm very sorry.'

'Thank you.' Mara paused to cough into a gloved hand. 'Forgive me. The smoke.' It still formed a dark hood over the city. 'Your Grace, my deepest condolences. Queen Sabran was—'

'If you please, Mistress Glenn,' Lord Robart cut in. 'I was told you bear a royal message.'

'Aye, from Lady Marian Berethnet.' Mara gripped one hand in the other. 'Lord Robart, you sent my lady and her household to Cuthyll, but the wetness of the Fens is not good for her, and the castle is in disrepair, cold and leaking. I beg you to let her come here, to court. She is already heartbroken to have been refused attendance to her own daughter's entombment.'

Glorian looked aslant at her regent, who remained expressionless.

'With this threat facing Inys, Lady Marian wants to be with her only remaining family – Queen Glorian – so she might support and counsel her, and share the burden of her grief.' Mara looked to Glorian. 'Please, Your Grace, a drop of generosity. All she desires is to be at your side.'

Lord Robart sat back a little. 'Is Lord Edrick aware of your journey, Mistress Glenn?'

'No, my lord. I came from Cuthyll.'

'Then I can forgive your ignorance. Lord Edrick was alive during Queen Marian's reign,' Lord Robart reminded her, 'and would recollect how close Inys came to ruin in that time. I believe your own birthparents were killed. If she believes she can return simply because Queen Sabran is not here, I'm afraid she is mistaken.'

'Lady Marian means no disrespect, Lord Robart,' Mara said, her voice firming, 'but surely she can do no more harm as a private individual. She is old and unwell. If she could just have—'

'That will be all, Mistress Glenn. I have much to do to protect this queendom in the weeks to come.' He sat back. 'I will send a stonemason to seal the leaks at Cuthyll. Good day.'

Mara pressed her lips together. 'My lord,' she said. 'I shall pass on your message.'

She made to leave. Before she knew it, Glorian had called out, 'Mistress Glenn.' Mara turned back at once. 'Please send my lady grandmother my regards, and my condolences.'

'I will, Your Grace.' Mara gave her a relieved smile. 'Thank you.'

As she walked towards the doors, Lord Robart said, 'That may not have been well done, Your Grace.'

'May I not comfort my grandmother, who is my own flesh, and the blood of the Saint?' Glorian asked, frowning. 'Why have you sent her to a castle in disrepair, Lord Robart?'

'Cuthyll is a strong and remote fortress. Lady Marian is safest there. I only ask you not to give her false hope. We cannot allow her to return when Inys is so fragile.'

Suddenly the doors were thrown open again. A red-faced squire came running in, almost falling over his own boots, and Mara stood back in surprise.

'Queen Glorian,' the squire cried out. 'A survivor! From the *Conviction* – from the ships, the lost ships!'

Glorian stood at once. A long moment later, so did Lord Robart, though his face remained a picture of calm. 'I assume you have some way to prove this,' he said. 'What say you?'

'He was among them, my lord. I can attest to it,' the squire insisted. 'I remember him well.'

'Bring him inside. Quickly, boy, bring him.'

Outside, there was a great commotion before several figures entered the throne room, followed by a crowd of courtiers. With a cry, Mara flung herself on to a tall and windswept man. When she finally let go, Glorian saw his unshaven face. His hands were dressed in linen, he was damp and gaunt, and fatigue had nailed horseshoes under his eyes.

Yet there he was, alive.

'Wulf,' she whispered.

****

Wulf stepped towards the marble throne. He and Thrit had ridden hard from Caddow Hall, across the rotted causeway that snaked through the fog and black peat of the Fens, down to a smoking capital, chased by fear of the plague all the way.

'Lord Robart,' he said, 'I am Wulfert Glenn of Langarth, younger son of the Barons Glenn.'

'Two Glenns.' Lord Robart Eller regarded him. 'You were a retainer to King Bardholt.'

'Until his last breath. I come to you now, sent by Einlek King of Hróth, to tell you what I witnessed on the Ashen Sea, aboard the *Conviction*. And to bring you a dire warning.'

'I wonder at the likelihood of this, Master Glenn – if that is, indeed, who you are,' Lord Robart said, eyes narrowed. 'No one could survive the Ashen Sea in midwinter.'

'I beg your pardon, my lord, but I did.'

Even though the stewards had tried to shepherd people away, more were jostling to see. 'This *is* Wulfert Glenn, Lord Robart.' Glorian had found her voice. 'I can attest to that myself.' She stepped forward. 'Please, Wulf, tell us what you saw.'

'Your Grace, there is something I must do first.'

He was so saddlesore he feared he might fall on his backside, but he managed to kneel at the foot of the steps.

'Queen Glorian,' he said, 'I offer my sword and my axe to you, as I did to your lord father, and then to your cousin, Einlek King. Though I serve him now, I would also serve you, who share his blood – the blood of a man who was, for a decade, my liege and chieftain. I pledge, once again, to the House of Hraustr. I pledge to you. If you will have me.'

Glorian held out a hand, the one that bore a Hróthi ring.

'Yes,' she said. 'I bid you stand, Wulfert Glenn, as a knight-elect of the Queendom of Inys.'

'Your Grace.'

When he rose, Mara stayed close to him on one side, Thrit on the other. His sister gripped his arm, as if she were afraid to let him go.

'I will tell you what happened aboard the *Conviction*,' he said, loud as he could with his damaged throat. 'But first, I must tell you of another threat, a few miles south of Yelden Head. There is a plague, Your Grace – a sickness that began in the village of Ófandauth, and spreads in mighty strides through Hróth. It is here in Inys, somewhere in the Fens.'

Mutterings from the courtiers. Among them, Kell Bourn, the bone-setter, looked grim.

'I urge you to close your ports. Find where it has taken root and make sure it goes no farther here.' Wulf released a heavy breath. 'Now I will tell you. I will tell you everything I saw.'

****

Alone in her solar, Glorian wept bitterly and wrathfully, pulling at her hair. Wulf had spared no detail. He had told her that her parents had faced Fýredel with courage, at the end.

If they had done that, she could suffer a prince in her bed. She could give Inys an heir.

She could also now be formally crowned. Wulf had witnessed the death of the sovereign. He had come through fire and snow and swamp, from the brink of death itself, to warn her of what was to come.

A few lights guttered in the city. By the glow of her own candle, she broke open the letter from her cousin, sealed with the crest of the House of Hraustr. Einlek had given it to Wulf.

Cousin, I will keep my words concise, for time is short, and the fire is surely closing in. I wake each morning still loath to believe this has happened — that I should see the fall of a legendary king, and the rise of an evil so terrible, it far eclipses the war of my childhood.

My mother and I send our bitter condolences. I send my gratitude for the kingdom that was rightly yours. Above all else, I affirm, in the strongest terms, my loyalty to you, who now find yourself with a heavy burden, at so young an age. It is unfair, and it is cruel, but so are all tests from the Saint. He, too, was tried, and suffered, to vanquish evil from our world. Now you must stand in his place, at half the age he was when he faced the Nameless One. You must be the sword and shield.

I am not too much your senior, Glorian, but if you will permit me to offer you one piece of guidance, as one who found himself plunged into war at a tender age. On every battlefield, there are warriors and ravens — the warriors on the snow, the ravens waiting in the trees. Look to those closest to you, and decide which is which. Work out who will fight, and who will feast on your flesh. Who will stand beside you, and who will wait for you to fall. Knowing this may save your life.

She traced the dark wing where he had smudged the ink.

In the months or years to come, we must each look to our own shores, our own people. I am now head of a very young house, the successor of a king who brought a country to its knees, and for that reason, I must keep my eyes on the North. But be assured, cousin, that Hróth is with you always. Our sea realms will fight under the Saint's banner, to rise from the fire, brightened by it, stronger than before.

There may be no victory in this war. There are too many foes. I do not believe the Saint intends us to win. He seeks the absolute destruction of the world, to usher in the new. Our test is to survive, and to keep our realms together. And so, together, let us hold the Chainmail of Virtudom.

Remember, Glorian, that evil is earthly, and you are something else. All great rulers heed to counsel, but you are answerable only to the Saint, who lives within you, the voice of the divine. Look to him first, and to yourself.

Glorian committed the words to memory. She pressed a brief kiss to the letter, then put it in the fire.

For several days, she paced and waited – for Prince Therico, for other news. She tried to reach her mirror self, but the Saint was quiet again. Outside, her people cried for bread.

At last, after what seemed to be a short eternity, something changed. A hand shook her awake. 'Glorian.' Florell was at her bedside, holding a candle. 'The Virtues Council wishes to see you.'

Glorian sat up. The sun had only just risen. 'Why do they summon me so early?'

'I don't know.'

The Council Chamber held a chill, the fire young in the hearth. Glorian entered to find only three of the Dukes Spiritual waiting for her.

'Your Grace,' Lady Brangain said quietly. They all dipped their heads. 'Forgive us for disturbing you at this hour. We thought it right that you heard as soon as possible.'

'Where is the Lord Protector?' Glorian asked her.

'He rode out with Lord Damud and Lady Gladwin before dawn. They are on their way to instruct the earls and barons of the northern provinces, so they can muster your people to defend our queendom. He should be back before long.'

'What is it you need to tell me?'

'There is no easy way to say this,' Lade Edith said softly. 'Prince Therico of Yscalin is dead.'

The words woke her like a fall through ice. 'How?'

'As I believe you were informed, the wyrms flew south after their attack on the Leas. From what we understand, they fell upon the Yscali port of Tagrida and burned it almost to the ground. Prince Therico was aboard one of the ships docked there.'

It took Glorian a moment to digest the news. He had been just days away from Inys. 'May he find his place at the Great Table.' She caved into a chair. 'Sixteen is no age to die.'

'No, Your Grace.'

'What is to be done, then?' Glorian finally asked. 'You all agreed that I should have an heir as soon as possible.'

'There is a way to remedy the situation quickly,' Lord Randroth said, dabbing his nose. 'A proposal that Lord Robart wishes us to submit for your consideration.'

'Yes?'

'Your late mother made arrangements for you to wed Prince Therico, but the contract includes a clause. In the event of his death, the heir to Inys may wed another relative of Queen Rozaria of Yscalin – in the first or second degree, specifically – within the next month.'

'Usually the clause is included because one of the parties has some illness, or partakes in dangerous pursuits,' Lade Edith said.

'A sensible precaution. Prince Therico had a fragile constitution.' Lord Randroth set the document in question on the table. 'Two members of the House of Vetalda who fit the description were, tragically, killed with him. However, there is another, who is free to wed. If you were to accept him, it would mean we could proceed as planned. We would not have to seek other candidates or negotiate favourable terms, which will prove almost impossible in wartime. We would preserve our historic union with Queen Rozaria.'

'I thought all her other grandchildren married,' Glorian said.

'You had it right, Queen Glorian.' Lade Edith loosened their collar, looking a little faint. 'Forgive me. I truly do not believe we should consider this, but the Lord Protector—'

'—is in favour,' Lord Randroth finished. 'He knows the man well, and vouches for his conduct.'

Glorian nodded. 'Who is it?'

'Prince Guma Vetalda.'

Florell, who had been waiting outside the Council Chamber, now ventured into it. 'Prince Guma,' she echoed. 'Lord Randroth, you can't possibly be talking about the Duke of Kóvuga.'

'You are not permitted to enter the Council Chamber, Lady Florell.'

'Who is Prince Guma?' Glorian asked. 'Who is he to Queen Rozaria?'

Florell stared at the three councillors, then let out a high, queer laugh that unsettled Glorian.

'Prince Guma,' she said, 'is her twin brother.'

'Queen Rozaria is ... at least seventy years old.'

Lade Edith drained their entire goblet of wine. 'Seventy-four in a few weeks' time.'

In the hearth, the fire crackled and spat.

'What in the Saint's name is this madness?' Florell whispered.

'The Lord Protector stresses that it would be your choice, Queen Glorian,' Lady Brangain said, though her face was pinched. 'He told us we should be honest with you, and that he trusted you to take the wisest course of action.' She slid an envelope across the table. 'He left you a letter.'

It was sealed with green wax, the seal shaped like a crowned sheaf of wheat. When Glorian broke it, she found lines of neat handwriting.

Your Grace, I must leave to instruct the Earls Provincial, and so I write in haste. I trust you have been informed of the tragedy clause in your marriage contract.

Prince Guma is a good and canny man, who spent much of his youth defending Yscalin from free raiders and other threats. I have met him several times during my visits to the mainland and found him amiable, honourable and kind.

His castle sits in the Saurga Mountains, giving him command of the Ufarassus, the largest gold mine in the West. I am reliably informed this mine is nowhere close to playing out. I will be frank: after the Century of Discontent, our coffers are all but drained, thanks to mismanagement and greed. We are in no position for war, or for rebuilding after fire.

I would understand if you refused this match. I would not usually endorse a union between two people so disparate in age, but I have no fear for your safety or comfort with Prince Guma, whose virtue I trust. He would be an asset to Inys. It would be remiss of me, as regent, not to inform my sovereign that this option exists. The choice is yours.

Your servant,
Robart Eller, Duke of Generosity, Lord Protector of Inys

'Time is of the essence,' Lord Randroth said. 'Refuse this, and we could waste months on finding a suitable consort.'

'For the love of the Saint, he is old enough to be her grandsire! Just marry her to a lesser Yscali lord, a Hróthi chieftain,' Florell erupted. 'You are all lusting for gold, and it has overcome your—'

'Lady Florell, you are not a duchess,' he snapped. 'Queen Glorian is half Hróthi. Our bond with the North is already strong. Meanwhile, our last Yscali prince consort was shackled to the Malkin Queen, and died under mysterious circumstances. The Vetalda will not have forgotten. Nor we must we forget that they conciliated the Vatten for—'

'None of that, *none* of it, justifies this!'

495

Their voices were becoming distant, lost to a dull roar in her ears. Glorian gripped the table.

'And in exchange?'

They all stopped talking to stare at her. 'Glorian.' Florell came to her side. 'Nothing in the world is worth—'

'What will Inys receive in exchange?'

Lord Randroth shot Florell a galled look, and composed himself.

'Prince Guma will bring a far more significant dowry than Prince Therico – an enormous sum,' he said. 'The Yscals have strong trade connexions with the South, which could be priceless in the months ahead, for salt and so forth. Most importantly, he would bring a large company of trained soldiers, including archers.'

'Queen Sabran weeps in Halgalant.' Florell was choking with rage. 'As for King Bardholt, he would have killed you all with his bare hands if you had dared voice this in his presence.'

Lord Randroth rose in a fury. 'Lady Florell, you will hold your tongue, or you will quit this Council Chamber!'

'Stop,' Glorian said, silencing them. 'How soon can Prince Guma be here?'

The Duke of Fellowship returned to his seat, cheeks red. 'He could be here as soon as he secures a ship.'

'So be it. I will marry him,' Glorian said quietly. 'For his gold, and for my people.'

'Glorian, no,' Florell croaked. 'There are other ways.'

'I see none that unlock the wealth of the Ufarassus.'

Lade Edith seemed unable to look at her. 'If this is truly what you want, Your Grace,' they said, 'we will summon Prince Guma to Ascalun. Since he has already agreed to the match, he has given his assent for a marriage by proxy. You could be wed tomorrow.'

'Tomorrow, then. Let it be done.'

Florell covered her mouth. Glorian sleepwalked from the Council Chamber, sending her thoughts as far from her body as she could, imagining herself into that dream realm, with her secret self.

57

East

After centuries of slumber, the Imperial Dragon was awake. Together, she, Nayimathun and Furtia had been able to drive off the golden wyrm, which the Lacustrine royals had named Taugran – *splendid death*. Days later, soldiers were still on the streets, fighting off the creatures left in the capital. The sky was stained as if with iron, dirty red and black.

The smoke had sunk into the palace, where two rooftops were on fire, lit by the embers that blew across the city. Dumai limped after a servant, who wore cloth over his mouth. Her ankle was splinted, her left shoulder dark with bruising, the wound sewn. Beside her, Kanifa kept a hand on his sword, as if he expected something to break in at any moment.

Consort Jekhen received them on a roofed balcony, breaking her fast on porridge and fruit. Princess Irebül sat beside a burner, hair in a Lacustrine style, a gilded band across her brow.

'Princess Dumai,' Consort Jekhen said. Her eyes betrayed a lack of sleep, but otherwise she was pristine, down to the pearl set into each cheek. 'Do join us. Master Kiprun was just about to give us a short demonstration, which may enrich your interest in alchemy.'

'I would be glad to join you, Consort Jekhen.'

They looked down at a courtyard, where Master Kiprun was holding some manner of iron gourd, a long thread trailing from its mouth. He placed it on the paving stones and took a candle from his assistant.

'This is why I hired him,' Consort Jekhen said conspiratorially to Dumai. 'It makes his fits of temper worthwhile.'

Master Kiprun lit the thread. A bright tongue licked towards the pot. Together, he and his assistant backed away behind stone columns, and a line of guards raised their shields.

A shattering din burst from the gourd, a blinding eruption that shook the tiles on the roofs and rang every ear in the vicinity. Dumai shielded her eyes with one hand as heat rushed into them, and when she dared to look again, half the courtyard was scorched and broken.

'Kwiriki's breath,' Kanifa muttered.

Dumai wished she had breath of her own. Beside her, Nikeya stared in fascination.

'Black powder. Drawn from the deep earth, unlocked by the golden art. It makes all matter leap and tremble,' Master Kiprun explained. 'For years, I have built on other alchemists' work, chasing this substance they had created – a secret lost to us for centuries. In the Nhangto Mountains, I found the final ingredient and refined the recipe.' He came to stand on the ruins. 'I am certain it will help defeat these creatures from the West. The fire and heat may not harm them, but the force of the explosion should.'

'A significant discovery,' Consort Jekhen said. 'It pleases me when you prove useful, Kiprun.'

'May I have a higher salary?'

'Perhaps, if you can make enough of this, and if you manage not to be impertinent for a few days.'

Master Kiprun bowed in a sweep of crimson sleeves. Dumai took in the damage, heart punching in her throat. She smelled brimstone and char, and something like steel.

It smells of the wyrms.

'Do enlighten me, Princess Dumai,' Consort Jekhen said. 'When was the last time Seiiki went to war?'

'Centuries ago.'

'Hm. Until our recent truce with the East Hüran, we battled them for nearly a year.'

Princess Irebül surveyed the damage to the courtyard, seemingly unperturbed by the reminder.

'Fortunately, that means we are prepared,' Consort Jekhen went on, 'for now it seems we must fight again, for more than a city. For survival against something far stronger than humankind. Do introduce me to your fellow dragonriders.'

Ears still muffled from the blast, Dumai said, 'My sworn guard – Kanifa of Ipyeda – and Lady Nikeya, daughter of the River Lord of Seiiki.' They both saluted again.

Consort Jekhen gave Kanifa a passing glance, and Nikeya a longer one. 'You have an uncommon beauty,' she told the latter. 'I imagine that oils the wheels of existence for you.'

'You are too kind, Consort Jekhen.' Nikeya inclined her head. 'Your own beauty is the sun to mine, brightened by a sharp mind.'

'Oh, hark at you. Such pretty airs. You are a flower grown for court.' Consort Jekhen studied her. 'I am curious to know who this River Lord is.'

'My beloved father is a loyal councillor and servant to Emperor Jorodu,' Nikeya recited.

'It is an old position,' Dumai said. 'Its holder is bound to nurture the land and join its people, as rivers do.'

'Sounds to me like a role the emperor should hold. Instead, your dynasty compares itself to a rainbow – fragile, distant, fleeting. Rivers have more use than rainbows, Princess, and last significantly longer. Give Emperor Jorodu that message, from me.'

Dumai wanted to shrivel. Even this woman she barely knew could see how weak her family had become.

Nikeya said nothing more. Her polite smile had stiffened, but she kept it in place. She smiled the way a tamed bird sang. Princess Irebül swirled her drink in its cup, observing with open interest.

'Furtia Stormcaller.' Consort Jekhen broke the silence. 'I heard she was injured.'

'She has gone to the Sleepless Sea with Nayimathun to recover her strength,' Dumai said. 'Now the Imperial Dragon is awake, I wondered if she means to rouse the others.'

'Fortunately, yes, else I fear humankind would be ash in a week.' Somewhere in the palace, one of the burning towers crumbled, raising shouts of frustration. 'We still may be. She might wake her followers, but they entered the Long Slumber for a reason. Some may choose to return to it.'

'Do you know that reason?'

'I have only one clue. Before the Imperial Dragon slept, she said the sunset of the gods was near – but to look to the night for the dawn. Quite the riddle. On the subject of riddles, I hear you spoke with Master Kiprun before the attack.'

'Yes.'

'I have met with him, too. He seems to think the wyrms have something to do with things being altogether too dry in recent times. What say you, dragonrider – is he raving?'

'I don't claim any knowledge of his arts, but his words made sense to me.'

'How fortunate. I must not have the head for alchemy. Now he's insisting on speaking to an astronomer, despite initially refusing my invitation to court *because* of its large population of astronomers. I had to pay him twice their salary to convince him.' Consort Jekhen ate a slice of grapefruit. 'I sent our most talented from the Office of Ceremony. Kiprun threatened him with a broom and demanded a stargazer, not a sycophant. A less forgiving person might have banished him by now, but I grow soft with age.'

'What is to be done, then?'

'You may wonder why Princess Irebül is sitting over there. You see, Master Kiprun has agreed to see *one* astronomer . . . and she lives on the mighty peak named Brhazat.'

Kanifa made a sound of disbelief.

'Brhazat strikes the roof of the world,' he said in halting Lacustrine, when Consort Jekhen lifted her eyebrows. 'Consort, forgive me, but no one could live that high.'

'Apparently, this astronomer does. To save time, which is now a precious commodity, it would make sense for someone to carry Master Kiprun to her on dragonback.'

Dumai slowly frowned. 'You wish for me to go, Consort Jekhen?'

'You were raised from birth on a mountain. You might have a hope of surviving Brhazat. You could visit the astronomer and see what can be gleaned. Princess Irebül would ride ahead to advise the East Hüran of your coming.'

Dumai searched her instincts. It seemed unwise to be away from her father for any longer.

'If you need motivation,' Consort Jekhen said, 'I can provide it.'

She motioned with one hand. Four guards hauled a wheeled cart into the courtyard. Upon it was a huge crossbow, mounted with a lance of proportionate length, its iron head almost as long as an arm. From one side to the other, the crossbow was wider than two men were tall, with three limbs: two alongside one another, and a third at the rear, pointing in the opposite direction. Twin cranks were used to draw the lance into position.

'The bed crossbow. A war engine, designed to launch spears over a great distance,' Consort Jekhen said. 'I would be happy to give you one, so you might build your own.'

Dumai watched the soldiers rotate the platform it was fixed on, so the lance could be loosed at anything.

'And all you ask in return,' she said, 'is knowledge?'

'The most valuable asset in the world,' Consort Jekhen confirmed.

'It will be worth the journey, Princess. The astronomer I wish to see is the one who created the theory of the scales,' Master Kiprun said. 'She will have the answers we seek.' He reached up to pat the crossbow. 'I've decided I would like to see the stars from Brhazat.'

One of the soldiers slapped his hand away, glowering.

'Well, Daughter of the Rainbow,' Consort Jekhen said. 'Everyone is willing. All we need is a dragonrider. What say you?'

Dumai looked down at the crossbow for a long time. *Furtia,* she thought, feeling the dragon stir to attention, *if I asked you to carry me north, to help find a way to end this, would you go, once you are healed?*

The fire was strong, earth child.

The mountains lie north, Nayimathun of the Deep Snows interjected, making Dumai start. *She will recover in deep water. Then we will go north.*

A headache chipped at her temples. *You would honour us with your presence, too, great one?*

The sea dweller knows nothing of the land of many lakes . . .

'This city is clearly not safe any longer. The empress and I plan to move the court to Whinshan Ridge, where the mountains should keep us hidden,' Consort Jekhen continued, unaware of the conversation. 'Once you have seen the astronomer, you could send Master Kiprun and Princess Irebül back to us, and return to Seiiki yourself. I will let you share in the knowledge, Princess. All you have to do is bring it down the mountain for me.'

'What if it's meaningless?' Dumai asked her. 'What if this astronomer is mad or dead, or gives no useful aid?'

'Then you will at least have this weapon, as a token of my friendship, and I will be able to rule out the astronomer as an answer to this chaos. That would be reasonably useful.'

Dumai glanced at Kanifa, who was worrying at the inside of his cheek.

'Furtia needs time to recover first,' she said. 'She is not strong enough to fly such a long way.'

'Then wait. It will give Princess Irebül time to warn her people, so they won't shoot down the Stormcaller. They do not all revere dragons, as we do.' Consort Jekhen looked her in the eye. 'Fire wells from the earth, Princess. Shall we find out what will put it back?'

****

In the apartments, Dumai drank from a bowl of hot broth. Kanifa sat with her beside the hearth.

'Do we need siege weapons?' she asked him. 'Is it worth making such a perilous journey to obtain one, even if the astronomer gives us nothing of use?'

'Yes.' Nikeya was leaning against the wall. 'Trust me, Princess. We have nothing like that in Seiiki.'

'I hate to agree,' Kanifa said, 'but I agree. Mai, our dragons are awake, but they remain weak. We must support them. It's worth a try, to understand what might end this.'

'Seiiki should be safe, in the meantime,' Nikeya said. 'Thanks to you.'

'Be plain with me,' Dumai said to her. 'Does your father intend to usurp mine while I'm away?'

'Not as far as I know.'

'How reassuring.'

'Centuries we have watched over and served the House of Noziken. Perhaps we have overstepped our bounds, out of concern for Seiiki – but never have we speared the golden fish. You have the gods' favour, so we cannot overthrow you. Do you not understand by now how it works?'

Just as her father had thought. The Kuposa feared the gods would answer only to the House of Noziken.

Nikeya came to sit on her other side. 'You asked for honesty. As a Kuposa, I advise you to return to Antuma, where we can keep you safe.' Her smile was warm, the fire turning her eyes to dark honey. 'As a Nadama – as my mother's daughter – I tell you to go to the mountains.'

You will be the first empress to have started life as a godsinger. The first to ride a dragon in centuries. The first to leave Seiiki, Osipa had said. Dumai closed her eyes. *You are here to break the mould.*

'Find me a writing box,' she said. 'I must inform my parents I will not be home for some time yet.'

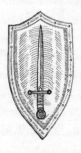

58

West

Wulf slept for days with his back to a hearth. After the wild gallop through the Fens, his body, brought twice to the cusp of death, had refused to take another step. As soon as his head hit the pillow, he fell into merciful, dreamless slumber, too heavy for nightmares to pierce.

As a child, he had dreamed of bees. He would wake thinking they were swarming his bed, stuck with honey to his fingers. At first, Lord Edrick had tried to reason with him, telling him bees only stung out of fear. *Bees work hard for us, Wulfert. If not for them, no crops would grow.*

Gradually, they had all understood that the fear was some remnant of the time before, of which Wulf had no memory. Not knowing what had caused it, all his parents had been able to do was strip every hive and skep from the grounds and tuck the honey out of sight.

He knew he would not dream of bees again now. For the rest of his life, his nightmares would be wyrms, and then the cold black water.

****

Mara woke him now and then to give him sips of broth. When he found he could keep his eyes open, the light between the shutters was copper, and his sister was putting wood on the fire.

'Mara, don't fuss,' he murmured. 'The servants will keep it burning.'

'Och, hush. I've not been able to fuss over you since you were wee.' She came to his bedside and touched his forehead. 'Well, you're beaten and burned, but you don't have marsh fever.'

He sat up, sore all over. 'Is Thrit all right?'

'Tired and cold, like you. Tends to happen when you ride through wetland in the night.' She checked the fresh linen on his hands. 'Doctor Forthard says your frostnip is healing well.'

Wulf took in his surroundings for the first time. He was tucked into a canopy bed in a chamber with pale walls. 'I missed Inys.' His voice was returning. 'I missed you. Didn't think I'd see either again.'

'I was with Marian when the news about the ships came, so I heard it first. I had to ride home and tell everyone. I've never seen Father like that. He just . . . sank into himself.'

'I suppose he'll be out mustering the people of the Lakes.'

'Aye, Lord Robart will likely have reached him by now. I asked him not to tell Father you're alive,' she added quietly. 'I'd like us to show him ourselves.'

Wulf nodded.

'Should Lord Robart be leaving the capital?' he asked. 'Surely the regent should stay with the queen.'

'He still has provincial duties. We must all adapt in the face of wyrms.' Mara patted his arm. 'Will you eat?'

'I could.'

The daylight left while she was gone. When she returned, she brought slices of fresh bread and nettle cheese, a goblet of mulled wine, and braised pheasant legs, weltered in a spiced red sauce. Wulf ate and drank slowly, chewing each mouthful as if it were his last.

On his way to the castle, he had seen the scarcity of food on the burned streets of Ascalun: people jostling at the remaining bakeries, quarrelling over the fish traps in the river. From snatches of their conversations, he was certain it was the wyrm from the sea that had led the attack on the city. A wyrm with a name.

'What were you doing in Ascalun?' Wulf asked his sister. 'Were you here during the fire?'

'No. I arrived when you did.' She lit the candles. 'I came because Lord Robart has sent Marian to Cuthyll. He clearly has his reasons, but—'

'Cuthyll.' Wulf almost dropped what he was eating. 'The Fens is where the plague is. Lady Marian can't stay there.'

A soft knock kept Mara from replying. She shook the taper out before she cracked the door open.

'Lady Helisent,' she said in surprise.

'Mara, I know it's been some time since we last spoke. May I come in?' a voice said, with a northern accent. 'I just heard you were at court, and I've been wanting to unburden myself.'

'Of course.'

Mara stood aside. Helisent Beck stepped into the chamber, dressed in a simple gown of grey wool with a mantle, looking as tired as Wulf felt. Noticing him, she said, 'I heard you were alive.'

Wulf stayed in the bed. 'Now you see.'

'Did you want to speak to me alone, Helisent?' Mara asked. 'We can go elsewhere.'

Helisent locked gazes with Wulf.

'No,' she said. 'You may as well both hear.' She sat beside the fire. 'Mara, when my mother died, you invited me to Langarth. I was adrift in grief, but you reached out, to talk me through the loss. Your kindness helped so much. I'm sorry to impose upon it now.'

'You could never impose, Helisent. We are both girls who lost mothers, and time cannot thaw such a bond.' Mara took the chair beside hers. 'Tell me, how can I help?'

'These are scattered thoughts. I'm not sure how they fit together.'

'Take your time.'

Helisent allowed herself a moment to begin.

'Queen Glorian was to marry Prince Therico of Yscalin. Several days ago, we learned he was killed by the wyrms. Glorian agreed to marry his granduncle instead. The Duke of Kóvuga is more than seventy years old.'

Mara traded a shaken look with Wulf.

'She's not even seventeen,' Wulf said hoarsely. 'Why would she ever agree to that?'

'To strengthen Inys. To honour the last contract her mother made. Because she thinks it's the best way to do her duty. I don't know.' Helisent rubbed her temple. 'She says Lord Robart gave her the choice whether to press ahead, that he didn't force the match – but he gave his tacit approval. Tell me, what sort of man would even entertain the thought?'

'Is it common among royals?'

'Saint, no. There are occasional differences in age, but never so great.' Helisent shivered. 'Here's the second part of the thought. I promise it has some relevance to the first.'

Wulf tried to soften his jaw. It was screwed tight enough that it was sending an ache through his teeth.

'There have always been unlawful visits to the haithwood,' Helisent said. 'Six years ago, my father saw a group of lamps going that way in the night. He saw it again the next year, around the Feast of Early Spring.'

Mara said, 'Heathens?'

'I'd say so. A sort of procession. Once my father was certain it was a yearly occurrence, he reported it to Lord Robart, who said the matter would be dealt with. No lamps came again for some time after that.

'I wrote to my father about Queen Glorian and Prince Guma. I received his reply this afternoon.' Helisent swallowed. 'Father said his foresters had come to him with a confession, just a few days ago. Even after he made his report to Lord Robart, he has always sent them into the haithwood on the eve of the Feast of Early Spring, to be certain it lay undisturbed. Last year, they decided to cross the boundary to the other side – your side – and saw the lamps again. The trespassers must have started entering from the Lakes.'

'Our fathers never noticed any such thing,' Wulf murmured. 'We never did, either.'

'They wouldn't have had to pass Langarth.' Helisent glanced at the door. 'Here is the root of my fear. The foresters told my father that Lord Robart himself was among them.'

A long silence descended.

'Be plain,' Wulf said.

'I fear that Lord Robart Eller is a heathen, and has been helping others follow the old ways.'

'You thought I was a heathen, too. Everyone does,' Wulf pointed out. 'Do you not think Queen Sabran would have noticed if her most trusted advisor was not a man of faith?'

'No,' Helisent said forcefully, 'because she chose him for the very qualities he could have used to cover that fact – his diligence, his cleverness, his patience. A regent who doesn't believe in the Saint would not recognise the authority of the House of Berethnet. That puts Glorian in even greater danger.'

'Why pressure her to have an heir, if he was trying to undermine her bloodline?'

'I don't know. I can smell a rotten scheme, but can't quite see it. What I know is that if Robart Eller is a heathen, he could use his authority as regent to weaken the Six Virtues. He could bring the old ways back out of the shadows. How the marriage fits into this, I'm not sure, but I have a feeling in my gut, and I've learned to listen to it. That's why I need help.'

'Your father,' Mara said. 'He didn't report Lord Robart?'

Helisent shook her head. 'He had no proof but the foresters' word, and didn't want to stir the pot. But now Lord Robart has the power of a king. Can we risk not looking into this?'

Wulf said nothing. He knew what it was to be feared based on nothing but whispers.

'I could be wrong. Perhaps the foresters were lying,' Helisent conceded. 'But what if I'm right?' She folded her hands in her lap. 'Father is away from home, taking stock of the damage to the Leas. I can't leave court. But you both could.'

'What is it you want us to do?' Mara asked.

'The Feast of Early Spring is nigh. If you caught him participating in a heathen rite, we'd have grounds to unseat him as regent.'

Wulf narrowed his eyes. 'And then what?'

'Lady Marian.' Helisent looked at Mara. 'A poor queen, to be sure, but could she take over?'

'Yes,' Mara said, with conviction. 'She has grown stronger in her winter years, and she loves Glorian.'

'Aye. I'm just asking you to establish the truth,' Helisent said, mostly to Wulf. 'It's too late to undo the marriage, but we can secure the queendom from within.'

Mara contemplated. 'I think Marian could manage without me for a few weeks. She still has loyal servants. Wulf, what do you think?'

'I'll go, if only to prove once and for all that there's nothing uncanny about that damned wood. Einlek asked me to ensure Glorian is safe in Inys.' Wulf breathed out through his nose. 'Could I see her, Helisent?'

'She should be on her way by now.' Helisent stood. 'Don't tell her about this, Wulf. I don't want her to mistrust her regent without cause. Just tell her you're going to see your family.'

'Wait—' Wulf coughed. 'What do you mean, she's on her way?'

'She asked me to arrange a meeting with you at midnight. I just decided to come early.'

When she was gone, Mara came back to his side. 'Wulf,' she said. 'Are you certain you can face the haithwood?'

'It's past time. Let me look it in the eye at last. See for myself that it's only a wood.'

Mara sighed. 'I'd better write to Marian, then. Can you ride in a day or two, do you think?' He nodded. 'We'll visit Langarth first. We can't move against Lord Robart without Father.'

'I agree,' Wulf said. 'I'll need you to find Sauma – my lith sister. She said she'd be staying in Ascalun. Tell her to go back to Einlek. Thrit and I will join her when we can.'

'I'll try.'

Without Mara, there was nothing but the crackle of the fire to break the silence. Wulf gazed at it for a moment too long, and saw the flames dancing on the *Conviction*.

At midnight, the door opened again, and the Queen of Inys entered his room, wearing a bedgown over her shift, and closed the door behind her. Her hair hung to her waist, wet from a bath.

'Your Grace.' With effort, Wulf rose from bed, holding on to the post for support. 'Glorian.'

'I never thought I'd see you again.' The firelight played over her as she came closer. 'I grieved you, Wulf.'

'The Saint doesn't want me just yet.'

'I wanted to thank you in private. After so much suffering, you still returned to help me.'

'Glorian,' Wulf said, low and soft, 'why have you agreed to marry Guma Vetalda?'

She was carefully expressionless. 'He brings a significant dowry to Inys, among other things.'

'Could he not marry your grandmother, then?' Wulf asked, frustrated. 'Could you not—'

'Remarriage is forbidden to queens, unless we are left childless widows. Besides, it was the Inysh heir my mother offered the Yscals. Inys might stand at the head of Virtudom, but we have a small army, no war engines, and poor finances. We are in no position to outlast a prolonged attack.' She turned away from him. 'And I need to have a daughter. I need it . . . to be done with, Wulf. This is the quickest way for me to get with child.'

'When are you supposed to be marrying him?'

'I have already married him by proxy. An Yscali courtier stood in his place, and I wore grey.' Glorian was vacant. 'He is on his way to Inys, or will be soon.'

'Saint's ribs. Does he know you're sixteen?'

'I'm not sure.'

'If he does, he's a monster.' He looked at her drawn face. 'You can't even know what you've agreed to.'

'I know perfectly well what happens in the bridechamber,' Glorian said curtly. 'But Fýredel swore to return here by summer – and Wulf, I must be with child before then.'

'Why not just wait until it's safer?'

'Because if I die without an heir, the Nameless One will be released as well. And I need the Virtues Council to stop looking at me as a womb – a jar, created to be filled. They will not let me fight alongside the people until I yield the fruit. It must be done, else I will not be free. I will not be able to choose my own fate. Can you imagine what that's like – to be seen only for the life you could make, not the life you already possess?'

'No. I'll never know how that feels.' Wulf came to stand in front of her. 'But I do know a thing or two about other people's expectations, and not always giving in to them.'

'It's not the same. I am a queen, a Berethnet. My body has never belonged to me, and it never will, until it pays this divine tax to Inys. Only then can I be a warrior queen.'

Wulf could hear no more. He grasped her by her hands, and he said, 'Lie with me.'

Her expression shifted. 'What?'

As soon as the offer had left his mouth, he had known he should take it back.

'Lie with me,' he said again, firmer. 'Let it be me. Make this one choice for yourself. You could try to get with child before the old prince even reaches Inys.'

'I can't.' Glorian stared at him. 'It would be adultery. You would be executed if we were discovered.'

'Aye. And the child would be a bastard – the daughter of an outcast, a nobody.'

'Wulf, you're not—'

'I am, Glorian. By the laws of this land, I was a foundling before Lord Edrick gave me his name,' Wulf reminded her. 'And I doubt I'm secretly a prince.' He looked her in the eyes. 'But if anyone found out, I wager they'd not care so much, in a time like this.'

'Prince Guma would have to know.'

'If he's a good man, he'll encourage it. If not, he'll at least look the other way, because he'll still be prince consort of Inys – a fine position for his winter years, and more than he'd deserve. All he has to do is say the marriage was consummated.'

Glorian studied him. 'You would truly risk your life for this, Wulf?'

'I would.'

'Why?'

Because seeing her so trapped, he could do nothing else. He could not leave his friend with no choice but the Prince of Yscalin.

And something in him had always called to something in her.

'You said love had no part in it. Ours might not be a romance for the ages,' Wulf said, 'but I care for you, Glorian. You were my first real friend, while I settled into Hróth. You made my circumstances easier to bear, and I'd like to return the favour, if you'll let me.' He touched her under the chin. 'I promised your cousin I'd keep you safe.'

'I sincerely doubt he meant this.'

'No.' He cracked a faint smile, which she returned. 'But I doubt he meant for you to lie with this Prince Guma, either. I doubt the Saint himself would expect you to endure that.'

He set his forehead to hers. She closed her eyes and reached up to hold him there, cool hands framing his face. It stirred a memory of summer.

I don't think I'll ever meet anyone I like more than you, Wulf. Let's always be friends, as long as we live.

The first oath he had ever sworn to anyone but her late father. In the rose garden, they had pricked their fingers on the same thorn and pressed them together, blood on blood.

'Let me think on it,' Glorian said under her breath.

'All right.' He drew away. 'I'm going to see my family. I'll return after the Feast of Early Spring. If you agree, I'll stay in Inys a bit longer, and we'll try. If not, I'll go back to King Einlek.'

Glorian nodded. 'Send my regards to your family – and my thanks, for all they must do in the days to come.'

'I will.'

'Before you go, I had a question. My mother,' Glorian said. 'What was she wearing when she died?'

The question caught him off his guard. He was back on the *Conviction*, in the grey fog. 'Red,' he said quietly. 'The finest red you can imagine, rich and bonny, like the Inyscan rose.'

'Thank you. May the Saint keep you, Wulf.'

'And you, Glorian Shieldheart.'

Glorian turned very still. 'That was what the wyrm called me.'

'Aye, I heard. I say it suits you.'

She looked back at him, and he saw Hróth awaken in her, iron and ice.

59

South

Jrhanyam, the Rose of the South, had stood for twelve centuries. It had risen from the sands of a great plain, unfolding petals of music and trade, nourished by ancient underground tunnels that drew water from the Spindles. Tunuva rode Ninuru east along its streets, past troops of soldiers in masked helmets, through an arched gate to the inner city.

Corpses strewed the ground – scorched or mangled, or both. Here and there, keyhole openings in the walls gave entry to the water tunnels. Some Ersyris were hurrying down those stepways with their children, while others fought on the surface with whatever they could find.

Tunuva breathed hard into her capara. Even through the cloth, she smelled the char and burning hair. If this attack lasted for more than a few weeks – if it went on for much longer than a year – then it would be the end of human life. Not even the Priory could stop it.

Canthe had been right. *It will not be a war, but a slaughter.*

The wyrms had hatched an army of beasts. On her way from Lasia, Tunuva had seen creatures that had once been cattle and deer, given new life. She had seen lesser wyrms gnawing at carcasses, soaring in flocks over city and sand. All at once, they were everywhere.

Yet what Canthe had told her was lodged at the front of her mind, and for all she tried, for all the turmoil around her, she could not shake it loose. Her breath came sharp and hot.

What if it's him?

She had mourned him. Twenty years she had lived with the scar, and now it was torn open, bleeding.

What if he lives?

Shoving the thought down, she kept riding, towards the hilltop fort of Jrhanyam. Ashes fell, dark snow on a desert city that had never seen it.

To her left, a wyrm shattered a windtower, which crumbled on to the houses below, throwing up a thick cloud of brick dust. Mounted soldiers charged through it, wielding lances, while the unarmed ran out of their way. Ninuru entered the colonnade of a market circle, where many people had taken shelter from the fire, some grievously wounded.

Screams and roars clashed together. Tunuva kneed Ninuru to the right. As they emerged, a boulder crashed down on the domed roof of a water cistern, cracking it like a skull.

Most Ersyri houses were built of stone or clay. For the most part, they had withstood the fire – but there was plenty more in the city to burn, and not enough water to hinder the spread. The blaze was making its own wind, devouring all it touched, hay and cloth and flesh.

What if he dies in the fires of this war, thinking that his mother abandoned him in the dark wood?

When Ninuru reached the gatehouse, Tunuva rolled from the saddle. The ichneumon grabbed a lesser wyrm that had swooped low, shaking it by its tail, while Tunuva strode for the path that led up the hill. Seeing her cloak, the guards stood back without question, their gilded armour clinking. She marched up the steps to the stronghold and through its cavernous halls, past balconies and fountain gardens. Servants were clustered at the windows.

By day, the throne room shimmered with silver and mirrorwork, its ceiling an exploding sun of symmetry. Now its floor was awash with blood, and a winged serpent, thick as a palm, was slumped beside a shattered window, head severed from its body. Darkness had spilled like pitch from both halves.

The throne itself was an impressive piece. Made of solid gold, its back swept into the feathered wings of a dove, an old emblem of the House of Taumāgam.

Queen Daraniya sat on it, face lit by the silver flame that hovered in the middle of the room. It was the gentlest fire a mage could cast – purposeless, but beautiful, a fire that burned only where it was bidden. Apaya uq-Nāra stood beside the queen, her white cloak wallowed in red.

'Your Majesty,' Tunuva said.

'Tunuva,' Queen Daraniya said. Her crown was the throne in miniature, white hair scrolling to her shoulders, and she wore a mirrored collar of the Faith of Dwyn. 'Thank you for coming.'

Despite her calm demeanour, her slim brown hands were tight on the throne. 'I am here in the name of the Mother,' Tunuva told her. 'I swear I will defend your walls.'

'I'd be grateful. Apaya tells me I should go to my ancestors' tombs, but that seems like tempting fate, doesn't it?'

Four young women, each with a fall of dark curls – her granddaughters – held each other close in the corner. Their protectors must be out in the city. Apaya stepped over the serpent and kissed Tunuva on the cheek.

'Tuva,' she said. 'I thought you weren't coming. Esbar said your ichneumon needed rest.'

'She's recovered. I had to come. How long has it been?'

'This is the fourth day.' Apaya looked gaunt. 'The Ersyri soldiers can't stand for much longer.'

'What needs to be done?' Tunuva strode back across the room with her. 'What *has* been done?'

'The soldiers who are too exhausted to fight are taking the wounded and vulnerable to the tombs and water tunnels. Esbar is leading our sisters, holding off the wingless beasts that can't surmount the walls. You'll find her to the east, outside the Dawn Gate.'

'Are there any great wyrms?'

'Just one. We suspect it's overseeing an attack on Isriq, too, flying between the two cities, keeping a distance. Until we deal it a blow or we all collapse in defeat, this siege will continue.'

'When does it come?'

'As the sky darkens. Did Siyu ride with you?'

'She'll be on her way soon, but she's on horseback.'

'Yes, Esbar told me about Lalhar – terrible. What about the Western woman?'

'Canthe is still too weak.'

As she spoke, a deafening crash came from above, shaking a curtain of dust from the ceiling. Apaya unsheathed her sword. 'Go to Esbar,' she said. 'Earn your red cloak, Tunuva Melim.'

'Use our catapults,' a woman in white robes urged. 'They will strike wyrms from the sky.'

With a nod, Tunuva turned on her heel and stepped back into the city, unfolding her spear. Time slowed as she wheeled to meet a beast and struck its head with all her might.

In the Priory, battle had always been a dance. War, she soon found, was something quite different. There was no joy in this brutality, no rush of exhilaration each time she landed a blow. There was only sweat and toil, which tired her faster than she had thought possible.

She buried her spearhead in one creature, wrenched it free in a clenching gush of blood, drove it hard and fast into the next. Her enemy was nameless, screaming; it spoke only the tongue of wrath. In the smear of it, she thought she saw a wyrm with half a human face.

The siden in her blood glowed bright, warming her thews. Still, she was graceless at first. The body she had drilled for decades was suddenly heavy and slow, as if she had drained a cup of wine. It took six gruelling kills before she began to understand why.

They had all been trained to fight, but never to contain their fear, for there had been no real threat in the splendour of the War Hall. Keeping fetters on it was draining.

Coated in ash, she hewed her way through the city. Her weapon was one with her arm. As she ran up a steep thread of steps, something landed in front of her. She blocked its tusks with the haft of her spear, catching herself on the step below, and before she could wrest free, Hidat leapt from above and sliced her blade down on its neck. The head rolled away.

'Tunuva.' Hidat caught her by the arm, pulling her to the top. 'Thank the Mother you're here.' Her eyes reflected the fires. 'Tuva, this is beyond us. How are we to defend the whole South?'

'As best we can.' Tunuva blotted her upper lip on her sleeve. 'I'm going to help Esbar.'

'I'll join you soon.'

Hidat returned to the rooftops. Tunuva ran on. She saw Yeleni protecting two children, Butnu defending an entrance to the water tunnels, the men darting out to salvage arrows from the corpses.

Ninuru caught up with her as she continued south, finally reaching the deep outer wall of the city. She climbed it, using loose bricks and chips as handholds, and touched down on the other side, close to one of the fortified gatehouses. A throng of creatures stormed towards the doorway of glazed brick, held at bay by twenty women of the Priory.

By the light of the torches on the gate, she saw Esbar in the thick of the fray. Her vambraces shone in the firelight as she sliced with precision, as she had in every duel, every day since her childhood. She cut the head off a howling stag and stabbed another in the heart.

She had cast off her cloak, the better to move without its weight. Her tunic was ripped at the shoulder. Nearby, Jeda clawed among the creatures, a shadow with gore on her teeth.

'Ez,' Tunuva shouted.

Esbar looked up, and Tunuva saw at once how tired she was, how long and hard the fight had been.

'Tuva.' A laugh of relief. 'I thought you might not make it.'

'Washtu was watching over me.'

They fought together, the sword and the spear. Each time a creature lunged for the gate, they rebuffed it. Each time anything clawed up the walls, the ichneumons pulled it down and killed it. Each time a lesser wyrm flew overhead, Tunuva used a warding to protect her sisters from the outbreak of fire, drawing on her fuller stores of magic.

They fought on and on as the sun disappeared, and the sky became a wash of red and grey on black. Archers rained arrows from the walls. Still there was no end to the onslaught. At last, they heard a familiar and chilling sound, which echoed across the whole of Jrhanyam.

'The great wyrm,' Esbar said. Her blade dripped. 'No arrow or spear has yet broken its hide.'

'The catapults. Shatter its bones,' Izi said, coughing. Her tunic was dark above the hip. 'That's our only chance.'

'Yes, go. Tell them to aim true.'

Slinging her bow across her back, Izi skirted the flock and made for the cliffs, where the catapults were being loaded. Tunuva whistled for Ninuru, who came loping back, bloody from muzzle to tail. 'Esbar,' she said, reaching into the loops of the saddle. 'Try this.'

Esbar caught what she tossed. The spear gleamed in her hands. 'Tuva, this is a relic,' she called over the din.

'No.' Tunuva grasped it with her. 'Suttu the Dreamer dipped Mulsub in starlight. I never understood what that meant before now. What if she used the same magic as Canthe?'

Esbar looked at it, her expression resolving. 'Hold the gate,' she ordered their sisters. 'I need higher ground.'

Tunuva ran towards the cliffs with her. Royal tombs were carved into their western face. In their wake, the gates cracked open to let out a flood of Ersyri soldiers, roaring as they made a last foray.

Those operating the catapults went up and down the cliffs on a wooden platform, pulled by chains. Esbar and Tunuva climbed on to it. Feeling their weight, someone above began to hoist them up, and as the platform swayed above the tombs, they saw the whole city, on fire from one end to the other. Below, their sisters grew smaller, beating away the horde at the gates.

'They're coming from the north,' Esbar said, watching.

Tunuva nodded. She looked down at her cloak, once white, and found it soaked in blood.

At the top, they stepped off the platform to find the city guard cranking down the arm of the largest catapult, Izi observing them. From here, starlight could be glimpsed through the smoke. 'Izi, get to the tombs to recover,' Esbar told her. 'You've fought enough.'

'I'm fine, Prioress—'

'That was an order.'

With a nod of defeat, Izi went to the platform, holding her side. Tunuva craned her neck to see the catapults, which stood as tall as old bone towers. A stab at her senses drew her gaze north.

'There,' she announced, seeing the shape in the distance. 'It's coming.'

'Release on my command,' Esbar called to the soldiers. 'Not a moment before or after.'

Tunuva crouched on the edge of the cliff. When the great wyrm came into the glow of the burning city, she said, 'It's the one that killed Lalhar. The one that led the slaughter in Carmentum.'

'Dedalugun,' Esbar said, as it moved closer and closer to the palace. 'That is what the Ersyris have called it.'

Begetter of ashes.

'It's too near the Royal Fort,' one of the soldiers warned. 'We have to release, or—'

'Wait.' Dedalugun lifted itself with a sweep of its wings, and Esbar bellowed, 'Now!'

The soldiers pulled on a rope, releasing the weight. It hurtled downward, and the long arm of the catapult swung up to hurl the boulder high over Jrhanyam. It tumbled over and over before it struck its mark full in the flank, hard enough to obliterate a building.

The soldiers roared in triumph. Dedalugun banked away from the Royal Fort with a sound that made the cliffs tremble. Below, the lesser wyrms and beasts echoed its cry.

'They're bonded,' Tunuva murmured. 'All of them. Dedalugun is the master, the sire.'

'Good.' Esbar grasped the spear. 'Let's hope they all die together.'

Dedalugun had seen the threat. Its eyes brightened like a pair of red suns.

'Move,' Tunuva shouted to the soldiers, who ran for their lives just as the wyrm breathed explosive fire over the catapults, engulfing them in a roar of light. Esbar chased after it, Tunuva hard on her heels, until it disappeared into the moonless dark beyond the city.

They stopped at the edge of the cliff. Esbar hefted Mulsub. 'Last chance to change our minds,' she said. 'Should we be throwing away one of our most treasured artefacts?'

'Ez, it's a weapon. It was made to be thrown.'

'I know.' Esbar gave it a forlorn look. 'It's just ... such a beautiful spear.'

'Honour it with a beautiful throw.'

Esbar pursed her lips. Her face hardened, and she drew the spear back, aiming into the desert.

Dedalugun returned from the shadow, wings spread wide as a storm, and opened its mouth, fire rising within. As Tunuva cast a warding over them both, Esbar hurled Mulsub, so it hit the creature in the breast, penetrating its thick armour.

Its scream was a thousand blades clashing, so loud and terrible it seemed to break the very substance of the air. Tunuva dived on Esbar, and they slammed to the ground just as Dedalugun swooped overhead, close enough that one of its scales nicked Tunuva. Roaring its fury, it flew back into the night, heading the same way it had come, northward.

They crawled to the edge to watch it leave. 'Well,' Esbar sighed, 'I enjoyed the few moments I held it.'

Below, Jrhanyam burned and smoked.

****

That final roar ended the siege. Everything stained by the Dreadmount retreated, leaving the survivors to emerge from the water tunnels, find their dead, and lie down to sleep wherever they could. Soon they would need to move elsewhere, to seek out food and sanctuary.

In one of the burial chambers, twelve warriors of the Priory recuperated from days of fighting. Most of the ichneumons had wounds from rancid claws and teeth. They picked at what little meat could be found while their sisters cleaned and closed their hurts, working by candlelight.

Tunuva dozed against a stone coffin with Esbar. Jeda and Ninuru slumbered on either side of them, already tended. After almost a week on her feet, Esbar slept like the long-dead king at their backs, her cloak spread over her knees, her head leaden against Tunuva.

She had proven herself a firm and fearless leader. Saghul had chosen well.

It was hard to tell when night became day, the smoke was so thick over the plain. At some point, Tunuva stirred to find Esbar gone, and Hidat crouched beside her.

'Something to eat, sister?'

'Thank you.' Tunuva took the flatbread and dried lamb. 'How much food is there in the city?'

'Not enough. The wyrms burned half the granaries and carried off most of the livestock. The people have had to use the cisterns meant for drinking water to put out the fires.'

'By the Mother.'

'The Royal Council wants to use the water tunnels to move the people towards the Spindles, where there's more shelter. Queen Daraniya will go to an old refuge castle there.' Hidat glanced at the entrance to the tomb. 'With luck, Dedalugun hasn't found the Wareda Valley, but when he does, I fear for the Ersyr. This is not a land that can bear much more heat.'

The Wareda Valley was its most fruitful region, a taper of rich green between the sands and the Gulf of Edin. 'I was only on the field one night. Is there anywhere I could be useful?'

'I think Ez is managing. You get a little more rest, Tuva.'

Tunuva nodded heavily. She would have sprung back from that fight when she was thirty, but her body craved sleep.

They had narrowly saved the city from destruction. Now Esbar would have to decide whether to send all her warriors to one settlement at a time, or spread them between several.

The ichneumons pressed close. She leaned against Ninuru, smelling blood and wet fur, and slipped back into a drowse.

Suddenly the sun was on her face, warm and amber. She looked down to see her child tucked into a sling at her breast, sound asleep. Love came flooding through the dams that had contained her grief, so unbearably strong she thought it would crush her. She dared not breathe as she stared at her baby, so small and perfect, still wrinkled from the womb.

Sleep, she willed him. *Sleep, my happy one, my love. Stay exactly as you are.*

Her hand drifted to cup his head. All it grasped was bloodstained cloth, swarming with bees.

She gasped in denial, and then she did wake, as cold as the coffin at her back. This time, it was Canthe beside her, ash in her hair.

'Tuva,' she said, looking shaken. 'Tuva, are you all right?'

Tunuva looked down at her empty arms and stained tunic, paralysed. She had not dreamed of him in so long. 'Canthe,' she said faintly. 'Just a dream.' A tear leaked down her cheek. 'When did you get here?'

'Just now. One of the men let me ride with him. He brought more food and supplies.' Canthe examined the cut on her arm, which had been slow to heal. 'Is this from a wyrm?'

'Yes. The same one from Carmentum.'

'It recovered faster than I hoped. Did you use the spear?'

'Esbar did.' Tunuva leaned away from the coffin, neck aching. 'Mulsub didn't slay the wyrm, but it did hurt it – enough to end the siege. You must have been right about Suttu the Dreamer.'

'I am relieved it worked.' Canthe came to sit beside her. 'I suspect Ascalun was another weapon touched by sterren, and that was how it vanquished the Nameless One.'

'Are there others?'

'Perhaps.' Canthe looked at her. 'Tunuva, I came to ask permission to return to the West. We know the wyrms are there. I could discover what they and the hatchlings are doing, and what is being done to stop them – but as an outsider, I would not be able to go alone. I wondered if you might come.'

Tunuva shook her head. 'Canthe, I can't leave my sisters now.'

'Even if it helps them?' Canthe said softly. 'If we were to visit Inys ... perhaps we could also find Wulfert Glenn.'

Tunuva met her gaze. Scouting beyond the South would help Esbar, but also give her a reason to go to the land of the Deceiver, to the dark wood and the boy who was discarded at its boundary. She could feel the weight of her child in her arms again, as she had in the dream.

An ache filled her throat and her chest and her stomach. The deep ache of loss, and the need to undo it.

'Tuva?'

Esbar had returned. She stopped at the mouth of the burial chamber, dusted with ash, hands bloody.

'Canthe,' she said. 'You came.'

'Prioress.' Canthe inclined her head. 'I'm sorry I arrived so late. I was weaker than I expected.'

'We could have used your magic. The same magic as must have been within Mulsub.' Esbar folded her arms. 'Dedalugun has flown off with it, so we can't repeat that approach – unless you know a way to put this mysterious power of yours into another weapon.'

'I wish I could, but I have nowhere near enough to do that. I do have another way I could be useful,' Canthe offered. 'In fact, I was just putting the idea to Tunuva.'

'Indeed?'

Tunuva wrung her hands and passed her fingers over their backs, restless. The cut in her side burned.

'Canthe,' she said, 'would you leave us a moment?'

When she opened her eyes, Canthe had done as she asked. She stood to face Esbar, who raised her eyebrows in question.

'Canthe wants to go back to the West,' Tunuva said. 'She could scout for us, take the measure of the situation beyond the South.' Esbar slowly nodded. 'She can't go alone, of course, as an outsider.'

'It's a good idea,' Esbar conceded. 'It would be helpful to know where the wyrms are concentrating their forces, and how many creatures hatched elsewhere, so we can anticipate their movements.' Her brow furrowed in thought. 'I could send one of the men with her.'

'I think it should be someone kindled.'

Esbar grunted in agreement. 'One of the postulants, then. Siyu, perhaps, since she has no ichneumon.'

'I could go.'

The silence fell hard, and lasted too long.

'You only just came back from Carmentum,' Esbar said, cool and guarded. 'Are you so eager to be away from us again, Tuva?'

Tunuva tried to keep hold of her composure. 'I can assess the situation. You need someone you trust.'

'Tuva, I've known you more than half a century. I can tell when you're keeping something from me.' Esbar stepped close enough to touch her. 'What did Canthe say to you?'

'She says—' Tunuva stopped, knowing it was useless. 'She says he might be alive, in Inys.'

'Who?'

'My birthson.'

Esbar turned as still as a sculpture. 'Tuva,' she said, 'how could that possibly be true?'

'A boy who came from the woods, with strange gifts and eyes like mine. A boy with a fear of bees. The years match.' Tunuva spoke in a strained whisper. 'Ez, I know it's impossible. But what if she's right?'

'Tunuva.' Esbar took her by the arms. 'My love, this is madness. Your sisters are here, I am here, and we need you now more than we ever have. You left us to go after Siyu, and now—'

'You gave her my name on the day she was born. You knew that would for ever bind her to me, making her my comfort for that loss. Now I hear it might not be a loss, but a theft.'

'No. Listen to me. I know you want to stop the pain. I *know* it never left you. I know how much you want this to be true – but how? How could the child have got all the way to Inys?'

'I don't know.'

'Because it makes no sense. Canthe should not have touched this wound.' Esbar grasped the back of her head. 'Tuva, please. You have come so far. Do not slide back into that pit. He is dead, my love. He's been dead for years. It was never your fault. Let him go.'

'I can't.' Her voice was quaking like an arm holding a heavy draw. 'I can't, Esbar. I never can.'

It was the first time she had ever confessed it. Those dams she had built – brick by brick, day by day, for more than eighteen years – now crumbled into dust. Grief washed her all the way back into that flooded hollow, and now there was only one way to climb back to herself. Canthe had stretched out a hand to offer it to her.

She could feel him in her arms, all his tiny fingers curled around just one of hers. He was warm and soft and sound asleep, and he was laughing, he was laughing in her dreams...

'Tuva.' Esbar looked disturbed now, afraid, realising she was serious. 'Even if, by some wild chance, this boy is your birthson, he will be like an outsider. Inys will have turned him into one who worships the Deceiver. What if he rejects you as a heathen, a witch?'

'So be it. I would know he lives. Canthe says they have treated him cruelly, that he always wept. You remember how happy he was with us.' Her cheeks were wet. 'I have tried. All these years, I have tried. You have, too, to comfort me. But a sister must not cleave to her own flesh. She must always be stone. It has been so hard, for so long, to be stone – to act as if the grief is gone, when I have only grown around the hole that day ripped through me.'

Esbar gazed back at her in pained silence, eyes filled with anger and pity, with love.

'We must have been betrayed,' Tunuva whispered. 'Don't you want to know who stole a child from us?'

'No, Tunuva. I want you to live in this moment, with me. You know I can't follow you this time.' Esbar tightened her hold. 'We were meant to face this war together, just as we took our first steps into the world. Don't leave me again. Please.'

Esbar had only ever beseeched her like this once, when Tunuva had sunk to the lowest point of her grief, into a night that had never ended. All she had wanted was for it to end.

Please, Tuva, fight. Esbar had knelt in front of her and gripped her face, tears in her eyes. *Fight your way back to me, my love, or I must go with you into the dark. I will not leave you in the dark...*

'I need this,' Tunuva said. Tears flowed down her cheeks. 'I'm sorry. I can't let him slip away.'

Esbar had never looked so empty, so bleak, as she did in that moment.

'I see that I can't stop you. Your heart is set on this, as mine is set on fighting for the Priory.' She turned away. 'Let the outsider lead you on a hopeless chase. I have warned you against it. When you realise it was all for nothing, and it shatters your heart again, I will be waiting here, with our family – to remind you what you had, and what you decided was not enough.'

60

West

The promise of spring was thawing the frost. In another, softer time, Wulf would have savoured being in Inys to see it. He would have watched the green return to the trees and bluebells freckle the haith-wood. He would have picked parsley and garlic with Mara while the birds threaded their nests. He might have joined his father for a lambing, as he had as a child.

Not this year. All was hushed in the Lakes, as if even the birds could sense the danger, which they likely could. So far, there seemed to be no sign of plague.

Summerport was closed by order of the Lord Protector. Not wanting to risk the causeway again, they had ridden first to Merroworth, where some ships were still permitted to fish and coast in Inysh waters, though not beyond. A karve had taken them past the Fens, to the port of Queens' Lynn. Now they approached the haithwood, and the manor at its threshold.

That forest had always struck trepidation into Wulf. Today, it filled him with burning resolve.

'Very quaint,' Thrit observed as the three of them reached Langarth. 'The chimneys are smoking, at least.'

'Doesn't mean Father is home.' Wulf dismounted. 'The servants keep the fires burning.'

'Must've been strenuous, roughing it with the Hróthi churls when you had *servants*, Lord Wulfert.'

'Ah, quit your jawing.'

'On that note, how do I address your father?' Thrit said with interest.

'He's Lord Edrick, or Baron Glenn,' Mara said. 'And Pa is Lord Mansell.'

'And your brother, the heir?'

'Roland. Master Roland, if you want to be courteous, but Rollo isn't one for airs or graces.'

'So he's not a lord, but Helisent Beck – the heir to Goldenbirch – is a lady. How so?'

'Lady Helisent is the only child of an earl. Our father is a baron, a lower rank. None of his children receive titles.'

Thrit nodded sagely. 'In Hróth it's much simpler. Chieftain or not.'

Finding no ostlers, they stabled the horses themselves. 'So,' Thrit said, 'we're here to tell your father that we want to spy on the most powerful man in Inys, to see if he's a heathen.'

Wulf gave his rouncey a pat. 'That's the essence of it.'

'Does it matter if the man honours a few of the old ways, if it doesn't distract him from his work?'

'I don't care overmuch about his private beliefs. Bardholt was a heathen once,' Wulf said. 'I do care about my oath to Einlek. If I'm to make sure Queen Glorian is safe before we leave, I need to be certain what sort of man her regent is.'

'Fine by me.' Thrit took off his fur hat and smoothed his hair. 'Better here than in that grim capital.'

'Aye,' Mara said. 'Things will go awry there before long, with so much in ruin.' They crossed the moat, and she used her key to unlock the main door. 'Father, Rollo, are you here?'

No one answered. They split up to search the lower rooms, meeting again in the Great Hall.

'Can't see a soul,' Wulf said, stumped.

'Sanny is here. Our cook,' Mara added to Thrit, who shook his head. 'She says Father is with the Countess of Deorn, but he should be back by tonight. Rollo and Pa are off calling the people to arms.' She rubbed her eyes. 'I'll see to it that there's enough supper. You two should get some rest. Show Thrit to a room, will you, Wulf?'

Wulf took Thrit through the cloisters and up the stairs, to the guest bedchamber he liked best, which protruded over the moat.

'So this is where you grew up,' Thrit said, looking about with interest. 'A fine place.' He set his pack and weapons down and rolled his shoulders. 'When you talked about the haithwood, I didn't think it was right on your doorstep.'

'I do sometimes wonder why Father kept me so close to it. Rathdun Sanctuary takes bairns now and then. He could have stuck me in the foundling wheel and had done with it.'

'Foundling wheel?'

'A hatch in a sanctuary, for abandoned bairns. Keeps them from dying of exposure before the sanctarian finds them.' Wulf loaded the hearth with firewood. 'Our parents never let us go beyond the treeline. Roland would, because he was the eldest, and liked to prove how fearless he was. When Father saw, he was so livid I thought he'd skelp Rollo.'

'There won't be anything in there, Wulf. Just like there was nothing in the frozen lakes of Hróth.'

'There are some things. Wolves and cave bears and such.' He took out his firesteel. 'That's how I got my name. When Father found me, there was a wolf close by. He scared her off, but later, he wondered if she was guarding me. He named me *wolf heart* in Old Inysh.'

He sparked the kindling. As soon as the flame appeared, he dropped the firesteel, seeing the fire on the ship, on her.

'Wulf?'

'I'm fine.' His brow dampened. 'Thank you, Thrit, for coming here.' He picked up his firesteel and stood, hooking the tool back on to his belt. 'You could have sailed with Sauma.'

'And miss a grand adventure in the woods?' Thrit snorted. 'No chance.' Wulf smiled a little. 'I have no plans to leave your side. You bury things, Wulf Glenn – you always have – but no matter how deep you bury what you saw on the *Conviction*, it will come back up. You shouldn't be alone when it does. Even Bardholt needed to talk about the war.'

'I know.' Wulf took a deep breath. 'I still can't believe he's gone.'

'Aye.' Thrit leaned against the bedpost, arms folded. 'How is Queen Glorian?'

Wulf watched the fire take hold of the wood. 'I said I'd lie with her.'

'What?'

'I said I would lie with her,' he said again, almost too softly to hear. 'That I'd help her get with child.'

Thrit huffed a disbelieving laugh. Wulf glanced at him, and the smile dropped off his lips.

'Wulf—' He rubbed the bridge of his nose. 'I know what happened with Regny.' Wulf tensed. 'You're less subtle than you think. You got away unreprimanded, but Glorian is the Queen of Inys, the blood of the Saint. You'd be executed. Wake your wits.'

'Inys needs to wake its wits. The Virtues Council is pressuring her to have an heir now.'

'A legitimate heir, presumably, begotten in wedlock.'

'Aye, and Lord Robart has married her off to a prince nearly sixty years her senior.'

Thrit stared at him. 'Saint.' He sat on his haunches. 'That's why you suspect Lord Robart.'

Wulf nodded stiffly. 'Einlek told me to see her safe, and I will.'

'Saint, Wulf, I don't think he meant to *swive* her.'

'It's not about that,' Wulf said quietly. Thrit raised an eyebrow. 'Aye, she's bonny. I'm not claiming it would be some great hardship. But me and her – it's not that way. We made a vow, as bairns, that we'd always be friends. What sort of friend would I be if I let some old man plough her?'

Thrit grimaced. 'A sound argument,' he said, 'but for the love of the Saint, Wulf, be careful. Adultery with her is high treason. Your head is far too handsome to be on a spike.'

'I will. She may not choose me, either way.'

'I think we both know that's a lie.' Thrit hitched up a smile. 'She'd be a fool not to.'

Wulf frowned as he looked into those dark eyes. Thrit cleared his throat and turned away.

'We should both get some rest,' he said. 'I'll see you this evening.'

'Aye.'

Standing in the corridor, Wulf was left to wonder if he had just missed something.

He thought of going to his own room to sleep off the long journey. Instead, he returned downstairs to find Mara tucked into the inglenook, as he had often found her in the past, with a tome in her lap.

It occurred to him that this might be his last visit to Langarth. When Fýredel returned with its flock, there would be no mercy, and no end to the destruction.

He sat beside his sister and wrapped her into his arms, planting a kiss on the crown of her head. 'What was that for?' she said, looking up at him.

'Nothing.'

Mara reached up to pat his cheek. 'I love you as well,' she said. 'I wanted to tell you – because I never have, and I bitterly regretted that fact when I thought you'd gone and died – that the day Father brought a bairn from those trees was the best day of my life.'

Wulf swallowed, heat in his eyes. Mara leaned into him and slept.

****

At first, he thought the row of hailstones on the shutters had woken him. Mara stirred at his side, eyes opening. They both stilled when they heard footsteps and voices in the entrance hall.

'Let me talk to him first,' Mara whispered. 'He'll go into a nervous shock if he sees you.'

She left to meet their father.

'Mara,' Lord Edrick said in surprise. 'I thought you'd be with Lady Marian. How long have you been here?'

'Not long. I'll explain later, I promise,' Mara said. Wulf slowly followed their voices. 'Father, I brought the most wonderful news, but I think you might want to sit down.'

Wulf could see Lord Edrick now. He looked even older, damp from the downpour. 'I can't imagine how there could be any.' After handing his cloak to a servant, he let Mara guide him to a settle. 'But it's a comfort to see you, hen. What brings you north?'

Mara glanced over her shoulder at Wulf. He stepped into the light. Lord Edrick saw him and sank back, his face turning pale.

'Mara,' he said hoarsely, groping for her hand. 'I see an apparition. Saint, it is from Halgalant.'

'No, Father. It's me,' Wulf said, worried he might be about to die of fright. 'I survived.'

Lord Edrick had frozen stiff. When he finally cracked his jaw to speak, he whispered, 'Is it truly you?' He got to his feet, almost wheezing.

'Wulfert. My son.' He seized him in a tight embrace, and Wulf gripped him back, trying not to weep yet again. After all the hardship, it was a relief he could never articulate, to be held tight by his father.

It took some time to soothe Lord Edrick. Mara and Wulf ushered him to the warmth of the Great Hall and got him a goblet of barley wine, to quell his trembling. Wulf sat at his side and told him everything.

'The Saint intervened,' Lord Edrick rasped, when he was finished. 'It's the only explanation. It's true you never seemed to feel the cold when you were young, but the Ashen Sea—' He drained his goblet. 'I'll have to call Roland and Mansell back.'

'Not yet.' Mara poured him some more wine. 'Father, Wulf and I need your help with something.'

'Anything.'

Between them, she and Wulf recounted their meeting with Lady Helisent Beck, and her fear about Lord Robart. Their father calmed as they spoke, clearly sifting the facts.

'Do you know,' he said thoughtfully, 'Lord Ordan did tell me of those lamps, all those years ago. I never saw a thing, so we both assumed the matter had been put to rest. Strange to hear otherwise from Helisent.' He drank. 'Our prince consort. Do you know his name?'

'Guma Vetalda.'

'The Hermit of Hart Grove?' he said, surprised. 'Saint, I didn't realise he was in his seventies. I've no idea why he would marry this late in life – he's rich and comfortable as it is, with those mines. Mind you, they do say he's wanted more power for decades. He was born a few breaths after his sister, else he would have been King of Yscalin.'

Wulf watched his father think. Lord Edrick had always had a weakness for mysteries.

'All this is pulling at some thread in my mind,' he murmured. 'I assumed Lord Robart had returned to Ascalun, having instructed us up here. If he's still at Parr Castle—' His brow pleated. 'I suppose there's no harm in the two of you keeping watch on the place, to see what he's doing, and whether he does go into the haithwood for the Feast of Early Spring.'

'We could follow him,' said Wulf. 'We might even catch him in the act.'

'To accuse him, you'd need an anointed witness. Someone from the Virtues Council.'

'Could we get one?'

'Perhaps.' Lord Edrick glanced at them both. 'I am glad the two of you came to me with this, rather than probing alone, but you know Lord Robart has a great deal more power than I do.'

At that moment, Thrit appeared in the doorway in fresh garb. Wulf beckoned him.

'Father,' he said, 'this is Thrit of Isborg.'

'Ah, the famous Thrit.' Lord Edrick addressed him warmly. 'Fire for your hearth.'

'Joy for your hall, my lord.' Thrit held a fist to his chest. 'It's good to finally meet you.'

'And you, son. Wulf has sung us your praises for years.'

Thrit glanced at Wulf with a smile, arching an eyebrow. 'Has he, indeed?'

'He has. I am so very sorry for your losses – the king and your lith. A cruel thing. But perhaps we can assist Queen Glorian, between us.' Lord Edrick rose, taking Mara by the arm. 'Join us for supper, Thrit. From what I heard on the road, there won't be good fare on our tables much longer.'

****

Glorian was ensconced in the Royal Chancery when the bonesetter came to see her. All day, she had been combing through old treasury records, trying to wrap her mind around them.

One of the palace mousers sniffed at her skirts, mewing. She picked it up and stroked it as she took a break. The sun had vanished, and the candles burned low in their holders.

She had never understood figures, but Helisent and Julain did. From what they could tell, Lord Robart had told the truth. Queen Sabran had been frugal, helping to fix the ruin of the Century of Discontent, but her marriage had been for peace, not riches. King Bardholt had brought no dowry. His family had been paupers when he took up arms for Skiri Longstride.

Glorian had known the situation must be grave, but this was worse than she had feared. Her ancestors had stabbed holes in the coffers and let the gold run out. There was evidence of past embezzlement, too, ignored or unnoticed by the three worst queens in Inysh history.

Prince Guma was the answer. He was said to be so rich that he ate off plates crusted with emeralds. Glorian glanced down at the ring on her finger, yellow gold from the Saurga Mountains.

She had told Wulf that she knew what happened in the bridechamber. True to a degree, but no one had ever brought her abreast of the fine details. In the end, Julain had given up on subtleties and asked her mother.

Now Glorian understood why Wulf had been so ready to prevent the consummation. She had thought for days on his offer, weighing the risks.

He was her friend, and she trusted him. The thought of doing that with him, the thing that sounded so embarrassing and intrusive – it made her feel shy, but not sick enough to crawl out of her skin. She thought she might endure it with him.

Adultery was the worst possible affront to the Knight of Fellowship. It would go against everything her mother had taught her – that she had to be perfect and virtuous, always.

The danger to Wulf troubled her. A queen might not be punished for an affair, but her lover could.

'Queen Glorian.'

She looked up. 'Yes, Sir Bramel?'

Her guard wore full armour. 'Mastress Bourn desires an audience.'

'Let them in.'

Almost at once, the bonesetter appeared, clutching what Glorian thought, at first, was a dead fox.

'Your Grace.' Usually composed, Bourn now quaked with restrained anger. 'Forgive me, but I have already gone to the Regency Council, and they will not listen to me.'

'I will help you if I can, Mastress Bourn.'

'Inys must take harder action against this sickness in the Fens. We are being too lax. I have just visited the launderers, and they were blowing white wine on to clothes by mouth.'

'Whatever for?'

'It's how wet furs are revived,' Florell said from the corner. 'Is there a problem, Mastress Bourn?'

'Yes, my lady, a grave one,' came the sharp reply. 'Sickness can be spread by bodily expulsions, whether breath or blood or the milk of the breast. Such practices must be stopped immediately.'

'Then how are furs to be refreshed after rain or snow?'

'Not with—' Bourn took a deep breath. 'Brush them, Lady Florell. Warm them by a fire.'

'You are a bonesetter, not a physician,' Florell said, defensive. 'What does Doctor Forthard say?'

'Forthard still deals in toothworms and toadstones, like most Inysh physicians. I do not.' Bourn put down the fur. 'Your Grace, I have learned from healers across the world, as far away as the East. Lord Robart made a fair start by closing the ports, but he is away, and the other Dukes Spiritual are not taking this matter seriously. The people must wear cloths over their mouths and noses.'

'Wait. You have been to the East?' Glorian shut the ledger she had been reading. 'Truly?'

Bourn hesitated. 'I was born there,' they finally said. 'My mother was Inysh, my father an Ersyri coppersmith. He wanted to sell in the East, so they sailed to join a small Southern enclave. I first saw Inys when I was sixteen, when my mother returned home.'

'Where in the East?'

'Mozom Alph, in the Queendom of Sepul.'

'I thought no ship could cross the Abyss,' Glorian breathed. 'How did your parents get so far?'

'There is just one sea lane – the Ships' Bane. One must cross the Northern Plain from west to east to reach the port. It's a long, hard journey, and most ships wreck on the Bane, but it is the only way to reach that continent. My mother was fortunate to survive it twice.'

Another queendom, far away. For the first time, Glorian wondered. 'Tell me, Mastress Bourn,' she said, 'do the Easterners know any arts that are beyond our ken in Inys?'

'I'm not sure what you mean, Your Grace. Forgive me.'

'Ascalun was an enchanted blade. There must be magic in the world. Did you see any in the East?'

Bourn glanced at her ladies, who looked uncertain. 'No, Your Grace. The Easterners are ordinary people, just like us,' they said. 'I saw no evidence of unearthly powers.'

'Do they have gods?'

'Most of the Sepuli worshipped gods of the sky and water, which were said to fly on the winds.'

'Could they speak in dreams?'

533

'Glorian, this is heresy,' Adela said nervously. 'You shouldn't—'

'Hush, Adela.'

'I don't know,' Bourn said. 'My mother raised me to follow the Six Virtues. I do know the Sepuli claimed the gods once lived among them, but had withdrawn into a deep sleep.' They held up the wet fur. 'Please, Your Grace. We need firmer measures. People must keep to their homes as much as possible, use vinegar or wine to wash their hands, and cover their mouths and noses with cloth.'

Florell frowned. 'For what possible reason?'

'Until we understand more about how this plague spreads, we must take all precautions, Lady Florell.'

'I can do nothing without my regent,' Glorian reminded the bonesetter. 'I have no authority here, Mastress Bourn. Lord Robart carries it with him. But I will try to convince the rest of the Regency Council.'

Bourn looked grim. With a bow, they retreated, leaving Glorian in the quiet with her ladies.

'What a peculiar person.' Florell shook her head in exasperation. 'Cloths over our mouths and noses – how are we to breathe?'

'Glorian, we should leave the capital.' Adela wrung her hands. 'Before the wyrm returns and the plague comes.'

'We can't,' Glorian reminded her. 'The Regency Council will not move without orders from Lord Robart.'

'So we stand about like mommets to wait for Fýredel?' Julain said, frustrated. 'The court needs the regent. Why isn't Lord Robart back by now?'

'He sent me a letter. He means to remain in his province until the Feast of Early Spring.'

Helisent slowly turned her head. 'Why?'

'To inspect the haithwood. He wants to take stock of how much timber could be cut for weapons.'

'But the barons could do that.'

'They are busy mustering the people, making sure they're armed for war.' Glorian looked at her friend in surprise. 'Saint, Helly, you look as if you've seen an ice spirit. Are you well?'

'Yes.' Helisent swallowed. 'Sorry, I've come over … a bit faint. May I be excused?'

'Of course.'

As she left, Glorian prayed her regent would return sooner, so she might hear his plan. She hoped he had one.

Her father had fought a war against his fellow Hróthi. She had seen some of his battle scars, heard his tales of human cruelty – but the enemy *had* been human. He had known that it was possible to win, matching strength with strength. Glorian had no such guarantee.

Papa, what would you do?

She looked up with a start when screams came from the city. The cat jumped off her lap, hissing. In moments, she was at the window, but found it too dark to see anything but torches. She threw the door open and stepped into the corridor.

'Sir Bramel?' she called. 'Sir Bramel!'

It took him a minute to come from his post. He was followed by his new partner, Dame Rose Suddow, whom Lord Robart had sent from his own household to replace Dame Erda Lindley.

'Your Grace,' Sir Bramel said, 'I just received word of creatures amassing outside the city. The gates have been barred, but it seems some of these fiends have wings.'

'Wyrms?'

'Something like them, to be sure.'

Fýredel had been lying. She should have known better than to trust a forked tongue. 'What is to be done?' Florell asked Sir Bramel. 'Did Lord Robart leave plans for a defence?'

'All I've been told is to protect Queen Glorian, and to keep her safe inside.'

If these creatures breathed the plague, Ascalun would soon fall. Before she knew it, Glorian had said, 'Bring me armour.'

'Your Grace?'

'I asked you to bring me armour, Sir Bramel.' When neither of them moved, Glorian squared up to them. 'I may not have been crowned, but I am Queen of Inys – and when I sit the throne, I will remember those who respected my position.'

Dame Rose glouted, while Sir Bramel only looked thoughtful. 'Very well,' he said. 'I'll send my squire to the armoury.'

'Send it to the Queens' Tower. You may take me there.'

Glorian watched him leave. Without another word, Dame Rose escorted her from the Royal Chancery.

Let them take her for a foolish child, wanting to play at war. She deserved that. The first time she had faced a wyrm, she had soiled her skirts. This time, she would go to battle astride a horse, with sword in hand. She would show her people that she loved them as much as her mother and father had. That she was not Glorian the Less.

Sir Bramel brought the armour to her bedchamber. 'Your mother never had mail made for you, but my squire found a coat that should fit.' He paused. 'You do mean to go out there, don't you?' Glorian was silent. 'Your Grace, I would counsel against it.'

'Because I have no heir?'

'Because you are the Queen of Inys.'

'I am also the daughter of Bardholt Battlebold. I will not shy from a fight,' Glorian said. 'I would need a company of knights, willing to disobey the Lord Protector.'

'That is treason.'

'I believe he is a reasonable man. He will understand, when I explain why I took this course of action.'

Sir Bramel glanced over his shoulder. 'We could take the postern gate, cross the river to Fiswich,' he said. 'His guards will try to stop us.'

'The Knight of Courage will reward you, Sir Bramel, as will the Saint in Halgalant.'

Fresh resolve hardened his gaze. He bowed low before he strode away.

When her ladies came, Florell looked first at the armour, then at Glorian. 'Glorian,' she said, 'what is this about?'

'I mean to ride. Lord Robart left orders,' Glorian said, 'but he is not here, and the enemy is.'

'Glorian, you can't,' Adela said, clutching her sleeve. 'You can't go into the streets.'

'Why should my people risk their lives for a craven queen?' Glorian asked her. 'Lord Robart rallied the city while it burned. This time, it must be me. I must show myself.'

'What if you're killed, or you catch the plague?' Adela said fearfully. 'Glorian, please, don't. You have no heir!'

'Until I do, I will not cower in a castle.' Her voice shook. 'I will give my people heart. I can do this one small thing, before—'

None of them had to obey. She could not yet command – only request. Julain stepped forward first and took her by the hand.

They removed her shift, and instead put on a fine wool tunic, trousers and a gambeson, lighter than the one she had worn in the throne room. After that came the sleeveless coat of mail. She had thought it would feel too heavy on her shoulders, but it made her feel stronger, to bear its weight. Florell covered her hair with a mail coif. Last came the circlet.

'Stay here, and pack your most precious belongings,' Glorian told her ladies. 'If the creatures have come, this sickness may already be in Ascalun.' She paused. 'Where is Helisent?'

'She went for a walk in the orchard,' Julain said. 'She was not feeling well.'

'Find her. We must leave with all haste.'

'Where?'

Glorian only considered for a few moments. 'Arondine,' she said. 'Father always said it was a good stronghold. It's far enough from the Fens, it has several walls and a river nearby, as well as the caves at Stathalstan Knott. We will take the people with us.'

'You mean for *everyone* to follow?'

'Arondine cannot house the population of Ascalun – but if each city, each cave, takes some of the people, we should be able to shelter them all. We have been blessed with a land that can hide us.'

She spoke with confidence, and found it gave her confidence in truth. Her father had told her of the tactics he had used in war. He had not completed her education, but he had laid the cornerstone.

Find your stronghold first.

'Ready the court to move,' she said. 'Tell the Regency Council my orders – and that they cannot stop me.' She picked up the sword her father had given her. 'All of us must be warriors now.'

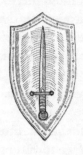

61

West

Parr Castle was a stern building, high and strong, made bleaker by the winter morn. A fortress on the water.

Just as Wulf watched the castle, so he, in turn, felt watched by it. It was a queer impression, given the building itself had so few eyes. One turret on the east side had no windows at all.

He shook himself. Stone and mortar could not have eyes. No, he was tired and bored, not to mention freezing his cleppets off, and it was making him imagine.

Thrit shifted in his sleep. Wulf covered him with another blanket, careful not to wake him.

Days they had hunkered down in here, in the skeleton of a sanctuary on a hill above Parr Castle. The ruin had sat untouched for decades, commanding a view of the lake and the two islands the fortress spanned. The banner of the Duke of Generosity still hung upon its walls – a sheaf of wheat on a green field – and from its highest turret flew the True Sword, the sign of royal authority. Together, they proclaimed that the Lord Protector was in residence.

The wind blew hard. Wulf coughed into a gloved hand. Inys might not be half as icy as Hróth in late winter, but their hideaway was damp and cold, and they dared not risk a fire.

As the sun rose, Mara returned from her scouting, coming on foot from the hills. Wulf stared when he saw who was with her. While Thrit slept on, he stood aside to let them in.

Lord Mansell folded him straight into his arms. 'Wulf,' he breathed. 'Saint, I can't believe it. You don't even look hurt.'

'I missed you, Pa.'

When Lord Mansell finally drew back, his eyes were stony with resolve.

'I came from Langarth,' he said to them both. 'Father brought me abreast of your doubts.' He set down a basket. 'Last night, a messenger arrived from Lady Helisent – she paid him for his haste. Queen Glorian had word that Lord Robart means to stay here until the Feast of Early Spring.'

'How does he explain that?' Wulf folded his arms. 'The regent should be with the queen.'

'He claims to be taking stock of the trees in the haithwood. To see how much timber Inys has for weapons.'

Wulf rubbed his stubbled jaw. 'By the Saint.'

'The Saint wants nothing to do with this, son.' Lord Mansell went to the window. 'We all have our orders in the north. There's no reason he can't return to Queen Glorian.'

'Has the plague reached this province?'

'In one village, at least. Its inhabitants have sealed themselves off, so Roland and I have been leaving supplies at its boundary stone.'

'They all mean to die there?'

'If needs must.' Lord Mansell nodded to the basket. 'I brought you some more food.'

Mara passed Wulf a loaf of seeded bread. For now, it could still be made in the province, but when the wyrms returned, once the mills stopped and the flour ran dry, there would certainly be famine. People were already hungry after the poor harvest.

'If Lord Robart does go into the haithwood on that night, we'll need a member of the Virtues Council to act as witness,' Lord Mansell continued. 'The Dowager Earl of Goldenbirch has agreed to speak on behalf of his foresters, but one of the Dukes Spiritual should help us investigate, someone of the same rank as Lord Robart. I must ride to Lady Gladwin.' He kissed Wulf on the cheek. 'Be careful, all of you. Don't be seen.'

When he was gone, Mara took out a pear. 'I had an idea,' she said. 'If Lord Robart does leave on the Feast of Early Spring, I was thinking I might stay behind and have a look through Parr Castle.'

'Sneak inside the home of the regent?' Wulf sat opposite her. 'Why would you do that?'

'To see what I can see.' She tossed him the pear. 'You did tell me to find a pursuit I enjoy.'

'Mara, I meant hawking, not housebreaking.'

'I know which one is more useful.'

****

On the eve of the Feast of Early Spring, Roland arrived on horse-back from Langarth, as finely dressed as if he were attending his own wedding, as usual. He had made a fair attempt to grow a beard.

'Wulfy,' he said as Wulf embraced him. 'Never thought I'd see your face again. How are you?'

'Always worse for seeing you.'

'Ass.' His brother patted his back. 'I'll kill you later. If Lord Robart catches us, he'll bring a hammer down hard on Father. What do we think he's doing in the deep, dark wood?'

'Not his job,' Thrit proposed.

Roland seemed to consider this. 'Fairly put, Northman.' He held out a hand. 'Roland.'

'Thrit.'

'Good to meet you at last. Father's half a day behind,' he added to Wulf and Mara. 'Pa will keep an eye on things at Langarth.' He slung down a sack of food. 'Whoever needs to sleep, do. I expected to be Baron Glenn, but perhaps night watcher was my calling all along.'

Lord Edrick arrived at dusk. He gathered his children close, and took Thrit by the shoulder.

'This is the moment of truth,' he told them. 'I've just heard word from Ascalun. A host of creatures gathered there – beasts that might well have the plague. Saint knows what they are. Apparently, Queen Glorian emerged and rallied the city.'

'Glorian fought?' Wulf said, surprised. 'How did she get out without his guards noticing?'

'I have no idea, but this does not reflect well on Lord Robart. He should sail back at once, but I see his banner is still flying.' Lord Edrick took a deep breath. 'I like the man. I don't want this to be true.'

'I think we are right, Father. We need to stop him tonight.'

'Aye. Thrit, Mara – you sleep. We may have a long night ahead. Roland, you take the first watch, if you will. I must speak to your brother.'

'I never stopped watching,' Roland said, staring out of the window.

'Good lad.'

Wulf followed his father. They trudged a short way down the hill, out of sight of Parr Castle.

'Wulfert.' Lord Edrick embraced him, and Wulf held him close. 'How are you, son?'

Wulf looked at him. 'I feel cold,' he said. 'I see it, sometimes. The white ship.'

'You might see that day for the rest of your life,' Lord Edrick said quietly. 'It will remain, and it will ache, but with every year, it will feel more a part of you.' He grasped Wulf by the nape. 'I have a task for you. Lady Gladwin is on her way here, to help us look into this matter. Should we follow the Lord Protector into the haithwood, I want you to wait at the boundary, ready to see her safe to her ship. A trapped animal will bite, and if the regent sees we have a witness of holy blood, he may try to remove the threat. You must shield her.'

'No. Father. I want to go into the wood.'

It was only when he said it that he knew it to be true. His stomach gave a soft wintle.

All his life, he had lived in fear of it. He had run from it to the eversnow. But the haithwood had gazed into him when he was a bairn. It was past time that he looked back.

'Wulf,' Lord Edrick said, 'as your father, I don't want the same.'

'Do you worry it will hurt my standing?' Wulf asked him, strained. 'It has. All my life. I have to see it for myself.'

He stopped, breathing hard. Suddenly his father looked tired, and desolate, and very old.

'Wulfert,' he said, 'you remember the scratchings in Langarth.' Wulf nodded. 'Those are called witch marks. Our ancestors carved them to ward away the Lady of the Woods.'

'You always said she was just a story.'

'I told myself that. All your life, I told myself you were abandoned, like so many children, because your parents couldn't feed you,' Lord Edrick said. 'But you came from that wood, and all these years, I have lived in fear that it might try to take you back. It's the reason I asked King Bardholt to accept you into his household. It broke my heart to send you to Hróth.

'The witch marks have been there for centuries. My grandmother had them rubbed down, thinking them ugly, but two days after I found you, I traced and deepened them again. I even cut marks of my own – beside your door, under your window, into your bedposts. Because a small part of me feared the witch was real, and that she did want you back.'

Wulf unfastened his throat. 'We never spoke about that night,' he said. 'Tell me what happened.'

Lord Edrick cast his gaze south. 'I woke in the black hour,' he said. 'One of my foresters was pounding at the door. They're tough, foresters – have to be, to face poachers and heathens, to walk for hours in the dark. But this man looked as if he had seen his own death. He told me there were voices and fires in the haithwood, and that the trees themselves were twisting.

'Mara was awake. She pleaded with me not to leave her, and since we had the foresters, I took her out with me. The first thing we saw was the glow in the sky – a white glimmer, stemming from deep in the trees.

'I couldn't hear any voices, at first. I thought the forester must have lost his wits to fear. Then Mara pulled my sleeve and told me she could hear a bairn. When I heard, I ran into the trees, following your cries, even as the foresters called after me to stop. They were afraid to follow.

'And there you were, beside an oak, a wee lad. There was the grey wolf, standing near. I told you this,' Lord Edrick said. Wulf nodded. 'I loosed an arrow, and she ran. When I picked you up, you kicked and sobbed, shouting in a language I've not heard before or since.'

'Do you remember what I said?'

'Not any more. I carried you out of those woods, and found you unhurt, save one small wound.'

'The wolf?'

'Aye, maybe. Just a nip. By morning, the haithwood was still and quiet, and so were you.'

Wulf tried and tried not to imagine. His father held his face.

'You,' he said, 'are not evil. Every night, I thank the Saint he brought you to this family. He saved you from the Ashen Sea. But it is possible that something dreadful had you in its grasp, Wulfert. Nothing magic – I don't believe in that. But heathens, I can well believe.'

'How do you explain the light?'

'Candlestick mushrooms, maybe. They're known to glow by night.'

'I want to see it,' Wulf forced out. 'Father, it's clung to me all these years. I might be able to remember the way.'

'You were no more than two when I found you. You won't remember.'

'I might. Let me see it's just trees. I need this,' Wulf told him. 'I need it.'

Lord Edrick searched his face. Wulf could see his fight behind his eyes, his instincts as a father pulling him in both directions. 'You stay at my side.' He used the voice he had used to warn them as children. 'Promise me, Wulfert. You go no more than a few steps from me.'

'Yes, Father.'

'Very well.' Lord Edrick kissed his brow. 'Go, now. Get some rest.'

Inside the ruin, Wulf lay close to Thrit, who was already asleep. For all he tried, his mind would not close itself off.

All his life, he had heard bees, bustling in his every dream. By dawn, he might know why, or he might not. Lord Robart might be counting trees. Lord Robart might yet kill them all.

Some time later, a hand shook him awake. 'Lady Gladwin is here,' Lord Edrick murmured. 'Will you watch, son?' With a nod, Wulf rubbed his eyes and took his place at the window.

In the thick of night, he could see nothing from Parr Castle but the torches that burned at its gates. Behind him, his father showed Lady Gladwin in, and they spoke in low voices.

'I have a ship waiting at Queens' Lynn,' Wulf heard the Duchess of Temperance say. 'In the unlikely event that your claims prove true, I will go to Queen Glorian. If nothing happens tonight, I will have no choice but to inform the Lord Protector of your accusation.'

'I understand.'

'Father,' Wulf hissed.

He had sharper eyes than most. Now he strained them, fighting the dark, to see a ruddy light in Parr Castle. With his father and the duchess beside him, Wulf watched it descend.

'He really is leaving,' his father breathed. Lady Gladwin came to join him. 'Quickly.'

Wulf roused the others. Together, they stole from the ruin and climbed ahorse. Lady Gladwin had brought a small detail of armed retainers. 'Mara, do as you will,' Lord Edrick told her, 'but—'

'I'll be careful,' she said. 'Saint go with you all.'

****

They could risk no light on the road. Still, the ground was dry, and before long, they had reached the shore of the lake. Twelve lamps had emerged from the castle.

'This is it,' Lord Edrick muttered. 'We must keep our distance.'

'And hope he has no hounds.' Lady Gladwin sounded disturbed. 'Saint's tooth, what is he doing?'

They rode in the wake of the lights. After a while, the water fell away, and they were riding over the slanted earth beside a hill, across slick grass that seemed to knot and welter underhoof.

The lights drifted upward as the riders struck the bier road. Wulf spurred his horse after them, and its hoofbeats fell in line with his heart. He thought of the ride along the causeway, worrying a hag might drag him into the peat. Here, at least, the ground was solid on all sides.

It must have been hours they followed the regent through the countryside, beneath the milky sash of stars the Inysh called Ascalun's Hew.

At last, the lamps stopped, and so did they. Ahead, the star belt disappeared into a wall of pure black, where the lights nodded closer to the ground. 'They're dismounting,' Roland said under his breath. 'If we lose those lamps—'

'We mustn't.' Lord Edrick glanced at the narrow moon. 'Roland, you stay with the horses.'

The lamps were already back on the move. Wulf urged his steed forward at a canter until they reached the boundary stone, where they hobbled their horses and lit three lanterns.

A rush of wind came from the east. The boughs creaked like old rafters, and the horses flicked their ears and snorted.

Wulf smelled it now, the louring wood. The old rot in its earth, the grave of animals and trees, all its life grown from decay. He looked up at the branches, drew a breath, and walked after his father.

In the distance, firelight winked between the trunks. Lord Edrick handed Wulf his lantern. 'Keep your hand in front of it, Wulf,' he murmured. 'We don't want them to see its light.'

Lady Gladwin held up a lantern of her own. Wulf glanced over his shoulder and found Roland already gone, as if the haithwood had sealed itself behind them. Above, the branches strangled the moon, leaving them with only their small flames to ward away the dark.

Such blackness. It was almost solid. The flames beyond floated in an abyss, like disembodied eyes.

There were yews and oaks so thick they could have fit whole families inside them. Some had bark scraped off. Birches rose and curved like ribs, dented with black, and reddish shoots sprawled everywhere, some with no apparent cradle. It was terrible and wild and quiet.

No, not just quiet, but silent, save their footsteps through the leaves. Not a dead silence, but a living one, as if the trees had simply held their peace. As if they, too, were listening.

The haithwood had only one path: the old bridleway that needled from north to south, connecting the Lakes to the Leas. This was deep and unmapped forest. An ancient beck – the Wickerwath – coursed somewhere in the dark, but there was no sound or sight of it.

It felt unnatural, this stillness.

At last, their lights caught on something with a dull shine. Wulf held his lantern up and saw a pair of iron jaws among the leaves, beside a blackthorn – a bear trap, not yet sprung. The tree was already in flower.

'Watch your step,' he muttered.

In hundreds of thousands of years, no one had tried to tame the haithwood, except to cull its wolves when they stole livestock. Its floor was a snarl of thick, gnarled roots and rotten logs, of thorny shrubs that threatened to unpick his cloak. Moss shrouded everything, so the drops of water from above made no sound. Several times they had to climb over fallen oaks, or crawl under a bough that had slumped over.

This was Inys as it had been before the Saint. Not even he had been able to break it. It was said that, long ago, a knight had tried to torch the haithwood, but the trees had absorbed the flames without burning, and water had come bubbling up to quench the embers on the ground.

It's just a wood. Wulf tried to concentrate on his boots. *Just a wood...*

Close by, a wolf gave a howl, and others answered.

'Oh, Saint.' One of the servants made the sign of the sword over himself. 'Saint, have mercy on us all.'

'Hold your tongue,' Lady Gladwin said testily, 'and perhaps he won't need to.'

The wolves kept calling, dire and doleful. Wulf felt the hairs on his nape stiffen – and out of nowhere, a memory landed, a feeling of being watched. He groped for a tree to steady himself, only for its bark to crumble in his grasp, and insects to swarm underneath. He backed away and stumbled into Thrit, who grasped his elbow.

Ahead, the lights kept moving.

As he followed, Wulf found that he was no longer surefooted. The memory – the sudden, overwhelming terror – had unhinged his balance. He slipped in mud, almost fell into a pool. The haithwood rantered itself around them, until it seemed as if every step broke a twig. Wulf bit the inside of his cheek when a sharp branch lashed his brow. All the while, the lights were still ahead.

A grey wolf padded out from the trees and stood in front of Lord Edrick, who stopped, raising his dirk.

Wulf had only ever seen wolves from a distance. Though it stood tall, it was too thin, bone in a sack of fur. Long fangs reflected the firelight, which kindled the pale gold of its eyes.

'Easy,' Lord Edrick said, keeping his voice down. 'There's just the one—'

'More,' Thrit cut in.

Others were prowling from the gloom. Wulf drew his sax as they appeared – eight in all, muzzles seamed into snarls. The largest of the pack flicked its tongue over its teeth.

One of the first things Eydag had taught Wulf was how to face the wolves of Hróth. *Always calm*, she had told him. *Always still*. He tightened his grip on his sax as the largest snapped at them.

These wolves were not the sort that would have left a child uneaten. The first one flew at Lord Edrick, who slammed his lantern down in front of it, making the ground burst afire.

The rest of the pack lunged. Before Wulf could move, one of them had torn into him, pain searing along his forearm. He lashed out with his sax, forcing it to retreat, and then ran to protect his father, who was on the ground. Pinned beneath a snarling beast, Thrit brought up the haft of his axe to protect his face, while half the servants made a stout attempt to defend Lady Gladwin. The others fled into the night.

'You fools, you'll be lost,' she barked after them.

Lord Edrick seized Wulf and pulled him close. 'Wulfert,' he said, panting, 'go after Lord Robart.' Blood soaked his collar. 'Hurry. We'll find you.'

Wulf snatched up a lantern and ran. He could draw the wolves off the others.

Branches grasped and pulled at him. The ground fell away, and he went rolling down a slope, roots and rocks thumping his back, to crash into a ditch. Somehow the lantern stayed alight. Dread pounded in his chest and slicked his nape. He reached out to grab a root.

The pack slewed in his wake. Back on his feet, he kept running, fear crushing his chest, as memories washed through him in cold waves. He was himself and not himself; he was in the wood and somewhere else.

In his dreams, he had always been searching for someone, and for the first time, he had an impression: kindness, a voice singing low, love that crushed the breath from him. Then another face, pale and terrified. The memories were far away, so far they no longer held a clear shape, and ran like water. But he knew he had been to this part of the wood before.

How had he escaped, the first time?

He was laughing and the sun was bright, and he tasted honey like a prayer on his lips.

Who are you?

He stopped, a stitch ripping into his side. His hand shook so hard the candle guttered in the lantern.

Light was glimmering through the trees. He stepped towards it, so entranced that all fear left his bones. Above him, a long mark was daubed on an oak, silver and faded, sending a sickly glow over the trunks. Even though its shape was strange, it was familiar.

He knew, then, to turn north. A few more paces, to another tree. As he approached, more marks flared to life on the trees, each one extending his path through the blackness.

At the end, there was light, both white and gold.

Wulf glanced over his shoulder. He had thought Lord Robart would have heard the commotion with the wolves, but the wood was so gathered and dense, there was no trace of anyone else.

It occurred to him that he might not find any of them again. There must be thousands of skeletons in these woods.

Keeping low, he moved into the undergrowth. He bent a branch aside, and it was suddenly there, the place he had sought – a clearing surrounded by hulking oaks and beeches. In front of them grew smaller trees, their branches heavy with white blossom.

Hawthorns. Growing them had been forbidden since the days of the Saint, who had ordered them all uprooted. Instinctively, Wulf knew this was the heart of the haithwood. Its very oldest part, its cradle.

Two layers of memory were purling over one another, both so distant as to be almost unreachable. The honeybees and the dark wood. Two faces and two voices. Cold and warm light.

He shook himself and kept watching. Lord Robart wore a green tunic, like a sanctarian, and the brown pelt of a cave bear over his broad shoulders. He, too, was crowned with flowers, though his circlet was also home to twigs and antlers and acorns. He stood before a yew that looked as old as Inys itself – twenty armspans wide, at least. Corpulent branches reached across the clearing, hung with hundreds of straw figures – some that looked coarsely human, others braided into wreaths or intricate loops and knots.

Below, the Lord Protector of Inys was intoning in a tongue Wulf knew. The realisation soured in him. Even if the song was nonsense to his ear, it was a salve to his heart.

He had heard it before.

Across the clearing, barefoot dancers circled among the blossom trees, moving widdershins to the beat of a drum, singing in the same language, their lanterns hung up on the lower branches of the oaks. Each wore a wreath of white blossoms and a mask of tree bark, crude holes cut for eyes.

Each time they passed the yew, they flicked a cup at it, wetting it with a darkness like blood. A figure in red walked among them to replenish their cups from a large cauldron.

'Ondoth,' Lord Robart bellowed to the tree, as if it could hear a word. 'Ondoth und astīgath!'

Wulf stole closer. As he did, the nearest oak illuminated its queer rune, and the dance came to a sudden end, the drums stopping dead.

'She walks.' One of the dancers broke it. 'Alderman, at last! The Hawthorn Mother walks again!'

Cries of joy and relief went up across the grove. The dancers embraced one another like family. Only Lord Robart did not join in. He considered his surroundings, his gaze sharpening.

'No,' he told his followers. 'It isn't who we hoped for, but one called by her, on the first of the spring.' As they hushed, he lifted his chin. 'You may as well come out, Master Glenn.'

Wulf stiffened.

Lord Robart waited. As Wulf slowly emerged, the markings gave a shimmer. Some of the dancers melted into the trees with gasps of fright, but most remained, still holding their bloody cups.

'The Child of the Woods,' came a reverent whisper.

'Aye. I always did wonder if you would come, Wulfert. If you would feel the call,' Lord Robart said, watching him approach. 'Sometimes I thought I should invite you myself.'

'You're in violation of Inysh law, Lord Robart,' Wulf said. 'It seems you are a heathen.'

'I presume you did not come here alone,' Lord Robart said. 'Better hope the others see our lights. The haithwood grows straight through the bones of those who lost their way. It opens only to those who know the path.' He smiled. 'She told me about you.'

Wulf swallowed. 'Who?'

The trees soughed, as if they shared a secret.

'No. There's no witch.' Fear had stripped his voice dry. 'Only heathens, who do evil in her name.'

'Evil?' Lord Robart glanced at the tree, the glister on its bark, and sighed. 'It's wine, Wulf. Blood of the vine, not the vein. Our ancestors made such offerings from the dawn of time.'

'Do you think *your* ancestor would hold with this?'

'Mine?'

'The Knight of Generosity.'

Lord Robart smiled, but his blue eyes remained bleak. 'Her name was Sethrid Eller, and she knew the old ways as well as I do.' He seemed to admire the brightest mark, the one closest to Wulf. 'You have seen better than anyone what happens when we neglect the earth.'

'What do you mean?'

'The wyrms. What do you expect, when we abandoned the trees, when we stopped the harvest rites to praise just one man and his lie?' Lord Robart asked. 'Small wonder the earth now cries for our notice. Small wonder its torment produced such a reckoning.' He took a step towards Wulf. 'Tell me, Child of the Woods. Do you really think some dancing worse than forcing queen after queen to bear fruit, all to uphold a story?'

'You are forcing Glorian.'

'Oh, no. I never would have forced her. I meant to mould her into a Queen of Inysca – one who honours the sacred truth of this isle. The truth her own father once knew.'

'With help from Prince Guma, I assume.'

'If you expect me to betray any other believer, you will be waiting a long time, Master Glenn.'

Lord Robart did not sound as Wulf had imagined heathens, cruel and arrogant. He sounded perfectly reasonable.

'How do the trees glow like this?' Wulf said, hoarse. 'What did you do to them?'

'Not me, Wulfert. It's you they see.' Lord Robart walked around him. 'I envy you. I had to draw her attention, but you – for a time, you were hers. You were meant to be her successor.'

'You think she's going to come now?' Wulf managed a weak chuckle. 'That she's brought me here?'

Lord Robart beheld the marks.

'For a moment, I did,' he admitted. 'I thought she had heard the summoning. Spring is her time, you see, when the hawthorns bloom – or did, when they still grew wild in Inysca. I managed to plant some here, after many years of searching for seeds. See how early they flower.' He motioned to the white petals. 'Each year I have tried to bring her back, but she never returns, for we drove her away. She would know what to do.'

Wulf grasped the hilt of his axe. 'Lady Gladwin is among those who came with me to the haithwood,' he said. 'Once she sees this, she'll be able to speak against you.'

'Not if you come with me, Master Glenn. I can tell you far more.' Lord Robart held his gaze. 'Will you embrace your rightful place as heir to the haithwood, or return to the deceiving Saint?'

A part of Wulf – a tiny kernel, buried deep – wanted to go with him. To understand.

But that was not a part of him he could ever allow to speak.

'You know the answer,' was all he said.

Lord Robart looked weary. 'Then I have no choice,' he said. 'I'm sorry, Wulf, but I can't let you leave to bear witness to this.'

'You mean to fight a housecarl.' Wulf stayed where he was. 'I'd counsel you against it, my lord.'

'Alone, I would certainly lose,' Lord Robart conceded, as the masked dancers closed in. 'But I am not alone.'

'Neither is he.'

Wulf turned at the firm voice, heart clobbering. There was Thrit, smothered in dirt and gore, both axes at the ready, and from behind him came Lady Gladwin and a bleeding Lord Edrick.

'Robart,' Lady Gladwin said in astonishment. 'What in the Saint's name is this?'

As one, the dancers bolted for the other side of the clearing, disappearing into the trees. 'Alderman, hurry,' one of them cried, but Lord Robart shook his head, waving them away.

'I have done nothing in the Saint's name. This was for the Lady of the Woods,' he said to Lady Gladwin, as self-possessed as ever. 'I have kept my faith a secret for too long. I have no shame, Gladwin. Your Saint has done nothing to stop the destruction. He is dead and gone.'

She beheld him with something like pity, this man in petals and dead bear, looking as if he had grown from the earth.

'I imagined many things,' she said, 'but not the ravings of a heathen. I'm disappointed in you, Robart. I thought you would be our noblest regent.'

'I have tried to be. Let me continue my work, Gladwin, in the shadows. It matters.'

'You know full well I can't.' She nodded to her remaining servants. 'Seize the Lord Protector.'

They moved towards Lord Robart, who held still as they bound his wrists, with no expression on his face.

'Heed what you saw tonight, Master Glenn. Continue my work,' he said. 'I know she hears the haithwood call.'

The grove was all too still around them, but the markings still shone. Eyes among the trees.

62

East

A *re you there?*
      She opened her eyes at once, finding herself before the stream.
Yes. Her eyes fluttered. *I'm here.*

Dumai. How strange that we can say your name, but not mine.

My name is a word for a dream, so it is a part of this realm. I wish I could know yours, and where you are.

I came to thank you for the storm. It was you who made the sky open, came the voice from the darkness. *I think I know where you are. I have tried to work it out for so long. I thought you were a messenger, an aspect of myself, and perhaps you are ... but I also think you might be on the other side of the dark sea.*

The walls of the dream trembled in warning. Dumai let her eyes close again, but she could still see her sister. *I believe this is real,* she said firmly. *I think we are destined to meet.*

I am not free to leave my lands. Dumai sensed her frustration. *I am not free in my own flesh.*

I am still free to leave mine. Dark seas I cannot cross, but snows I can.

Now it was uncertainty she felt. *Do you have wings?*

Not wings. I have the wind and rain itself to carry me. She clung to her pillow to keep herself aware. *You are free to speak here, with me, sister. There are times when I want to escape my flesh, too. Times when I am weakened by it.*

You have spoken of gods before. I thought you were divine, not flesh. And yet you seem to have a place in the world. I feel your presence in it, somehow, as keenly as I feel my own. Is this a dream, or is it not?

What is the world, Dumai asked her, *but a fleeting dream, from which we will all one day wake?*

I suppose I never thought of it that way. Dumai smiled a little at the feeling that blossomed: reassurance, understanding. *Your mind feels heavy,* the other woman told her. *Is that fear I feel?*

Perhaps not fear, but doubt. I am on a journey to find out why the earth trembles, but I have left those I love behind, and I am afraid for them. And when I do return to them, I am destined to wear a crown for which I fear I am too weak.

I envy you your long journey. I am soon to be sealed away, my body no longer my own. The shape in the darkness was fading. *The crown lies heavy on the head, and on the flesh as well. Take it if there is no other choice, but do not let it imprison you, sister. Keep wind in your sails. Do not condemn yourself to be as I am — tied to your own blood, and trapped.*

****

Dumai woke to sunlight on her tent, and Nikeya and Kanifa both gone. This time she was so cold that her right hand ached in remembrance, and the dream was already dissolving.

She groped for her writing box and wrote down the shreds of dream she remembered. The Grand Empress had taught her to always record them, if she could. There were dreams that spoke of the future. False dreams, woven from fear. This one was leaving her faster than she could pin it down.

I envy you your long journey. She wrote in clumsy brushstrokes, trying to figure the dream language into Seiikinese. *Keep wind in your sails …*

It was right that she went northward, to the mountains. Her dream had confirmed it.

'Mai.'

She looked up to see Kanifa. Noticing the brush, he said, 'The dreams again?'

'Yes.' Dumai returned to the paper, only to realise there was nothing left of the dream in her head. She cast the page aside in frustration. 'We must get to Brhazat. Furtia has stopped answering me.'

'It was a grave hurt she took from Taugran.'

'If something has happened to her, how will we ever get to that mountain?'

'We could reach its foothills on horseback, but it would take weeks,' Kanifa said. 'We may as well keep with the Lacustrine court, since Consort Jekhen is content for us to stay. We're moving in the right direction.' Dumai nodded. 'I found a spring, if you want a drink.'

She pulled on a coat, following him from her tent.

After the attack, around half of the Lacustrine court had departed the capital on the River Shim. The rest had gone to their homes to find shelter. Across the City of the Thousand Flowers, the harbours had shed fishing skiffs and paddle-wheel boats, mostly bound for Kenglim and Xothu. At least half of the storehouses and granaries had been destroyed in the fires, and there were whispers of a sickness that had spread from the golden wyrm, but thousands had elected to stay, perhaps expecting not to be attacked a second time.

The fleet had turned north at the Lake of Long Days and followed a deep tributary, past the distant sweep of the Great Imperial Valley, which separated the Lakra Mountains from the higher Whinshan Ridge. The wyrms had seared a black wound straight through it, killing most of the season trees that dyed the land a different colour each season. The few that remained were in pink leaf, surrounded by the white leaves of winter.

The ships had taken them all the way to the southern foothills of the Whinshan Ridge – a range of steep and slender mountains, their rock a pale weathered brown, as different to Mount Ipyeda as fingers to an arrowhead. Now the court pressed ahead on foot and horseback, following the Snow Road, which curved out of the Queendom of Sepul and reached up to kiss the top of the East, where ships could try to cross a stormy neck of the Abyss. Dumai wondered if anyone would risk it, in the weeks and months to come.

Mount Ipyeda had been her life for so long. Now the world felt impossibly big.

Furtia, where are you?

Dumai followed Kanifa through watery lances of sunlight. She had not seen Nikeya since the day before. Likely she was in one of the tents – she had taken to mingling with the Lacustrine courtiers. Even after everything they had seen, Nikeya found time to laugh and flirt.

They emerged on to the Snow Road. It was at least a mile across at its widest point, paved in a smooth pale stone that countless feet had worn. This stretch bent narrower. Thick pine forest sprawled off both sides, concealing the steeds and tents, and the palanquins that bore the nobles to the mountains. For the most part, the court had been travelling by night, so they could shroud their lanterns and disappear if the wyrms flew past – which they had, several times.

The sun was high. Dumai and Kanifa walked through a line of guards and started to cross the entire road. Unlike the court, most Lacustrine seemed to wake with the sun, and the trade route was full of people, many dishevelled from walking so far, covered in soot and wounds. More and more, Dumai was starting to see Sepuli and Hüran among them.

'So many,' she said. 'How far did Taugran fly?'

Kanifa said nothing, his face drawn.

Three Lacustrine dragons circled above. They moved as if through water, still lethargic from their sleep. Dumai had listened hard, but she could not hear their thoughts, as she heard Nayimathun and Furtia. She supposed she should be grateful. It had been overwhelming in Seiiki.

'What is it the gods are waiting for?' she wondered. 'When will they grow strong again?'

Kanifa shook his head. 'Let's hope the astronomer will know.'

He led her off the road, down a steep path to a spring-fed pool. Dumai knelt beside it and drank from her hand, while Kanifa took out his knife to shear the stubble from his jaw.

'So,' he said, washing the blade, 'are we taking Lady Nikeya with us into East Hüran territory, or leaving her at court?' He shook off the water. 'She seems to be enjoying herself here.'

'I'm not sure if I admire it or not.' Dumai splashed her face. 'We've been away from Seiiki too long.'

'I agree. I still fear the River Lord has some malicious design on your father.'

'I believe Nikeya when she claims they will not harm us.' She sleeved her face dry. 'They have no need, when they control us.'

'And does she control you?' Kanifa asked her. 'Has she slipped under your skin yet, Mai?'

She wanted to deny it, but she knew him, and he knew her.

'Is it so obvious?' she said.

His face softened, though disquiet lurked in his eyes. 'I don't blame you,' he said. 'You never sought that sort of intimacy, not once. Now it presents itself to you, and so brazenly, of course you would—'

'It's weakness.'

'No.' He touched her cheek. 'I know better than anyone that we don't choose who we desire.'

Dumai moved to sit beside him, and he wrapped some of his bear-skin around her. Sometimes she wished she could have loved him the same way he loved her – but even if it was different, her love for Kanifa had always been deep as the roots of their mountain.

'Mai,' he said, 'we are so close to finding out the truth and getting home. Once we are back in Antuma Palace, you can distance yourself from her, as you did before.' He set his chin on the top of her head. 'There will be other women. Of all the people you could love, do not choose the one who is using you. You deserve more than that.'

Earth child.

A rush of wind blew overhead. They stood and ran back to the road as Nayimathun of the Deep Snows and Furtia Stormcaller soared towards it, scattering travellers as they landed.

'Furtia.' Dumai pressed her forehead to her cold scales. Furtia rumbled. 'Are you all right?'

'The fire was strong.'

For once, the dragon spoke aloud. The wound along her side had closed, leaving a ridge of melted scale. 'Will it heal?' Dumai asked her.

'Not yet. It is not our time.'

'What do you mean, great one?'

We will go north now, island child, Nayimathun told her. *The sun grows warmer, and so does their fire.*

Finally, they were a step closer to solving the mystery. Dumai sent Kanifa to wake Master Kiprun, while she sought Nikeya.

She found her in a clearing, in nothing but her underwrap, changing into fresh clothes. Dumai stopped, warmth fanning across her cheeks. Nikeya glanced over her shoulder.

'Good morning,' she said. 'Did I hear the sage tones of the Storm-caller?'

'Yes,' Dumai said. 'We must leave now.' Nikeya nodded and drew on a shirt, then reached for her hunting jacket. 'I need to give you some firm truths, Lady Nikeya.'

'A tantalising prospect.'

'Be serious,' Dumai said curtly. 'Ipyeda is a large mountain, but from what I hear, it is a hillock next to Brhazat. We face the tallest peak in the known world, and we have no time to get used to its height.'

'Very well. Educate me.'

Dumai waited a moment, to see if she would parade her wit again. Nikeya only smiled as she put on her pleated trousers.

'At a certain height,' Dumai said, 'the body starts to perish. This is the world's ceiling, beyond which only dragons can survive. The air there is too cold for us, the heart fights to beat, and in time, we drown. The second and third peaks of Mount Ipyeda are close to that ceiling. Brhazat will shatter it.' She folded her arms. 'You are resolved to follow me everywhere. I imagine you want to see this astronomer – but if you start to feel unwell on Brhazat, you must be honest and turn back, or your ambition will be the death of you.'

'Ah, but I have been such a nuisance, Princess. Surely you would be happy if I perished?'

'Your father would be angry.'

'Is that really the only reason you'd care?'

Her tone was light, but this new face she wore was her most dangerous. It almost looked fragile.

'Promise me,' Dumai said quietly. 'You must not push yourself farther than you can bear.'

'I don't mean to gasp out my last breaths on some grim mountain. I will give you the promise you seek,' Nikeya said, 'but only if you answer my question. If I am to disappoint my father, surely I deserve truth in return.' She knotted the cords at her waist before she turned to face Dumai. 'So tell me. Would you miss my company if I perished on Brhazat?'

Dumai clenched her jaw. Nikeya looked back with that strange expression, which held no trace of mischief or deceit.

Once we are back in Antuma Palace, you can distance yourself from her, as you did before.

If Nikeya was going to make her play games, then Dumai meant to be a shrewder opponent.

'Yes,' she said, making her voice hoarse. 'I would miss you.'

Nikeya smiled again, wider than the last time. 'Then I promise,' she said. 'If I am lying, let me give up water and shrivel.'

'I will gladly watch.'

Dumai walked away, leaving her to finish dressing. She was sure she heard a husky laugh. The sooner they learned the truth from the astronomer, the better – not just for Seiiki, but for her own sake.

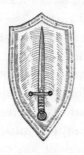

63

West

Glorian jolted awake to a realm drenched in honey. The day was mild, the sun warming to bronze as it descended, but she was so cold that fog curled through the air in front of her.

They were no longer on the sunken way that snaked through Bernshaw Forest. Now they rode on wider paths, past meadows rich and thick with flowers, and Arondine was in the distance, its castle like a white helm on the hill.

She had turned seventeen on the road, on the Feast of Early Spring. At last, she was lawfully allowed to bear the heir to Inys.

Dark seas I cannot cross, but snows I can. The words were already fading. Nowadays, each time she dreamed, she glimpsed the messenger, the woman, even if she could not always speak to her. *I have the wind and rain itself to carry me.*

Around half of the people of Ascalun followed her court. The train of thousands sprawled for miles behind, hauling carts of grain and wool and other provisions from the capital.

The Royal Guard rode in a tight formation around Glorian. Only one person had drawn their attention – a man calling her a liar and fraud, just like the one at Glowan Castle. Though her hands had trembled in their gauntlets, Glorian had not looked back, and the guards had taken him away, finding him unarmed.

Arondine was an ancient trade city. Positioned between the north and the south, it served as both a crossway and a crucible of the queendom, thronged with merchants from all six provinces. This was where Glorian meant to have her coronation – the first Inysh queen in centuries to be crowned beyond the Sanctuary of the Sacred Damsel.

Her regent had still not returned. Instead, Lady Brangain and Lord Damud rode with her, while Lade Edith had taken several hundred people towards Stathalstan to prepare its caves, clearing them of bats and bears. Glorian meant to drain the surrounding farmsteads into them, including some livestock, so the people would have meat, milk and cheese.

On the road, with nothing but her own thoughts and the scorched meadows to distract her, she had come to accept that she could not meet Fýredel in the field. Her Northern side recoiled from the prospect of hiding, but it might be their best defence. Inys was full of caves. Spineless as it seemed, the only way to triumph was to scatter and lie low, at least until she worked out how to slay a wyrm.

She had a season until Fýredel returned. When it did, she could not ask her people to fight fire. On the other hand, she could not conceal them indefinitely. Food supplies were already dwindling.

They were close to the River Tyrnan when they came across a body, sprawled under an ancient oak, legs torn off at the knee and one arm stripped to bone.

'Saint,' Lady Brangain said. Her horse whinnied as she motioned to the guards. 'Move him out of sight, at once.'

'Wait,' Glorian said sharply, and the guards stopped. 'Check his hand for the red stain.'

They did, with care. 'He's fine, Your Grace,' one of them said.

'Debatable,' Lord Damud said, eyeing the corpse. 'Make haste. We should cross the river before dusk.'

It was late in the day by the time they forded the Tyrnan and began the final approach to Arondine. A steep and narrow path led up to its first gatehouse – a misstep would send her horse slithering into the deep moat around the city. Glorian kept her eyes on the pale walls.

A city like this, built on high ground, would offer sound protection from the creatures Fýredel had left. Still, she meant to move when he returned. Arondine was too vulnerable to the sky.

By summer, she and her court would be gone again. She had Stilharrow in mind – a keep tucked into a clough in the Marshes, surrounded by wetland. If not, she might abscond to the coast, to the cliffside sanctuary at Offsay. She would have no single residence.

If only she had Ascalun, the True Sword, which had vanquished the Nameless One. It might work against Fýredel, if it had not been lost. Glorian imagined her father riding at her side.

Think, the apparition told her. *Think of other ways, dróterning.*

Arondine clambered from the foot of the shallow hill to its crest. In the distance, to the south, was the giant loaf of rock – Stathalstan Knott – that bestrode hundreds of secret caves.

'Make way for Queen Glorian,' a steward bellowed to the people as they entered. Cheers and curious murmurs filled the air. 'Make way for the Duke of Courage and the Duchess of Justice, descendants of the Holy Retinue!'

No one had expected a royal visit. Glorian tried to keep her face calm and still. She was soiled and dishevelled from the road, but she sat like a knight, with her chin high. In their faces, she saw every emotion, from joy to curiosity to fear. Most looked shocked.

They see my youth, she thought. *They see they are led to war by a girl.*

'Lord Damud,' she said, and he leaned close. 'The wyrms did not come here. I leave it to you to make these people understand the threat. All should be armed. Every blacksmith must work to that end, every fletcher and bowyer. Once the city gates are sealed, those who wish to enter must seek permission from the guards. The gates must remain locked, and all who approach should have their hands checked before they can enter.'

'It will be done, Your Grace.'

Glorian rode on, followed by her guard, her ladies, and the rest of the court. She felt every eye in the city upon her – the young queen in armour, without her regent.

Arondine Castle loomed at the crest of the hill. It had three curtain walls, each higher than the last. Once they had passed them all, crossed a bridge, and entered a large courtyard, Glorian handed her horse to an ostler and faced the castellan, Sir Granham Dale.

'Queen Glorian,' he said, bowing low. 'Your Grace, you honour Arondine by coming here.'

'I am sorry to arrive with so little warning, Sir Granham.' Glorian removed her gauntlets. 'I must take Arondine as my stronghold for a few weeks. Inys is at war.'

'I have heard the rumours that Ascalun burns.'

'They are true. The Nameless One has not returned, but the Saint has sent us a great trial. A wyrm has sown our land with a plague and sent beasts to torment our people – a black wyrm that calls itself Fýredel. I ask you to confer with the Regency Council.'

Sir Granham looked stunned. 'The Dreadmount,' he said. 'It has truly birthed more?'

'As I say.'

The old knight seemed to recover, and his face hardened. 'Your Grace, forgive me, but where is the Lord Protector?'

'He should be here within the week. In the meantime, I bid you make tallow – a great deal of it. Your people will be moving to Stathalstan, where they can be safe, and they will need light in the dark.'

'Yes, Your Grace. I'll see to it.'

'Thank you.'

Her bedchamber was in the largest tower. Her ladies helped her to remove the armour, and she sank on to the bed in her tunic, saddlesore. 'Are there any baths here?' she asked Florell. 'I have a chill.'

'I'll find out.'

'Helly, stay with me tonight.'

When the others had left, Glorian looked down at the city as the sun descended. People filed towards the sanctuary for the evening prayer.

It had not taken long for Florell to persuade the Dukes Spiritual that they had to leave Ascalun. Lady Brangain and Lade Edith had both agreed that the threat of plague was enough to break from what Lord Robart had commanded. They had ridden from the city with the creatures still hammering at the gates, chopping them down with sword and spear.

'I can't believe any of this has happened,' Helisent said, as she wrapped her hair with silk for the night. 'Glorian, are there enough caves for everyone?'

'I sent riders to scout.'

'What gave you that idea, the caves?'

'My father. Towards the end of the war, he began to use only part of his forces in battle, keeping the rest in nearby caves. Thinking him weakened, Verthing Bloodblade was emboldened to attack his war camp in the Nurthernold. That was his last mistake.'

'Then some Hróthi do know that hiding can have its advantages.'

'Yes. I mean to remind Einlek.' She looked at her friend. 'Helisent, you are a year my senior. On my commendation day, you told me you hoped to feel more settled, as you grew older. Do you?'

Helisent considered for a time.

'It feels like so long since then,' she said. 'My mother told me we are all like roses. I always thought it means that we opened our petals, took our true form, and gradually withered. But perhaps we never stop growing. If women are flowers, we are not roses, but day's eyes – blooming not once, but over and over, each time the light touches us.'

Glorian felt a tear on her cheek. She dried it with her sleeve, but Helisent had seen, and gathered her close.

'Everything will be all right, Glorian,' she whispered. 'I made sure of it.'

'What do you mean?'

A light knock at the door interrupted them, and Florell stepped inside. 'Your bath is ready,' she said to Glorian. 'Even queens must rest.'

****

At dawn, Glorian ventured back down to the overcrowded city, wearing her armour again. The Regency Council had expressed their disapproval with her excursions, but until Lord Robart returned, she meant to do as she pleased, before she was shut away.

She found Lord Damud Stillwater pacing the outermost wall, watching the guards build tall stockades and dig a trench beyond. Behind those defences, tents and rudimentary shelters huddled against the city, housing those who could find no room within.

'Your Grace,' Lord Damud greeted her. 'Good morrow. As you see, your people are fortifying Arondine. There will be stakes inside the trench, which could be set aflame.'

'More fire. Will that help?'

'The creatures that attacked Ascalun were not wholly like wyrms. They had flesh – even fur and feathers. They should burn.'

'Very good.'

'Wood is being cut from Bernshaw Forest to build catapults and springalds. Water will be placed in vats across the city, to help quench any fires,' Lord Damud went on. 'In the meantime, Baronesses Pintrow and Suthrey will oversee the retreat to the caves.' They walked along the wall. 'There is an old Inyscan tunnel that leads from the undercroft of

Hyll Sanctuary to Stathalstan, which I have set a group of flint miners to strengthening. There is room in the caves for around fourteen thousand people, as well as the supplies to keep them fed.'

'The combined population of both cities is far greater. What about the silver mines to the west?'

'Indeed. They might make a habitable shelter for the nobles.'

'The nobles?'

'Those are royal mines, Your Grace.'

'The nobles will not be hiding. The people who work those mines will have first right to stay there.'

'As you wish.'

She left him on the wall. At the bottom of the steps, she found herself surrounded by people, and tensed as her guards reached for their swords. Too many eyes were on her. They stripped away her armour, and she was young and alone again.

Then a girl of ten or so was moved forward, and shyly held out an Inyscan rose. 'For you, Queen Glorian,' she said with a neat curtsey. 'We are so happy you came to Arondine.'

Glorian took the red flower. It had been stripped of thorns.

'I am glad to be among you all,' she said, and found that it was almost true. 'I swear that I will be your shield.'

****

In the days that followed, she watched Arondine brace itself. She walked among the people, to shake her fear of them, and they seemed to grow used to her presence. The best seamstress in the city came to take her measurements, while Florell oversaw the preparations for her coronation at Hyll Sanctuary, where her namesake and two others had been crowned.

The message arrived in the small hours. Glorian was sleepless in her bedchamber, writing to her cousin, beseeching him to remember his temperance when he fought the wyrms. Einlek needed to prove the endurance of the House of Hraustr, but indulging the Hróthi thirst for war and glory would only end in scores of their people dying.

She had just dipped her quill when Florell appeared. 'Glorian,' she said, 'a messenger has come from Lady Gladwin. She has asked you to meet her at Glowan Castle.'

Glorian lowered her quill. 'Why?'

'She didn't say, but we must refuse. It's far too dangerous for you to ride in the wilds.'

'Lady Gladwin knows that, which means she would not have asked without reason. Instruct the Regency Council to hold the city in my absence,' Glorian said, rising. 'Ready my guard – and Mastress Bourn, in case we need a healer on the road. We ride at dawn.'

They set out before many people could wake. Glorian wore a plain grey cloak over her garments and kept the hood up.

As their horses galloped northwest, Glorian saw what Fýredel had left behind, a parting gift to Inys. Field upon field had been laid to waste, the farmers' bones left among their scorched crops, along with the remains of their ploughs and other tools. All the nearest settlements were abandoned. A few miles on, an orchard of apple trees, hundreds strong, had faced the same devastation.

'We are doomed,' one of her guards croaked. 'All this in weeks. What will come in years?'

'Have faith in the Saint,' Florell told him. 'And in your queen. This will not last for ever.'

Glorian herself said nothing. She nudged her horse onward, away from the ruined trees.

By afternoon, the party had crossed into the deep wilds beyond the Striding Hills. The farther they rode, the closer the air became. 'It's too quiet,' Helisent said, watching the branches. 'There are boneless souls nearby.'

'You are absurd,' Adela muttered.

'What happens to people who can't pass into Halgalant?' Helisent asked her. 'Where do they go, hm?'

'How should I know?'

'Well, I'll tell you, Adela. They linger on the clapper bridges and the bier roads.'

'Mastress Bourn,' Glorian said. The bonesetter came to her side. 'Whereabouts in Inys did you live, before you came to court?'

'Merstall, in the Fells.'

'What should the farmers in Merstall be doing now?'

'Working the fields, preparing them for seed. Spring is a busy time.' Bourn glanced at her. 'Your mother was careful, Your Grace. There should be enough grain to last at least a year.'

'And what if this goes on not for a year, but a decade, or a century?'

Glorian rode ahead before they could answer. No answer in the world would comfort her if she dwelled on that question.

****

Wulf saw the Queen of Inys crest the horizon at sunset. He waited for her at the doors to Glowan Castle.

Every time he closed his eyes, he saw the markings in the grove. *The haithwood opens only to those who know the path, like you.* He could not shake those words from his mind. *She told me about you.*

Glorian met him at the entrance and lowered her hood. 'Wulf,' she said in surprise. 'I only expected Lady Gladwin. Why are you here?'

'I didn't just go north to see my family.' He led her inside. 'Come and get warm. Lady Gladwin will tell you.'

They walked to the Old Hall, where his father and Lady Gladwin waited at the end of a long table. Under his shirt, Lord Edrick was bandaged. Wulf was glad to see the bonesetter.

'Your Grace.' Lady Gladwin bowed. 'I am sorry to call you from Arondine. Thanks to several of your nobles, starting with Lady Helisent Beck, we have made a grim discovery.'

'I fear we can bear no more grimness, Lady Gladwin. What is it you've uncovered?'

'I'm afraid that Robart Eller can no longer serve as Lord Protector of Inys. He is a heathen.'

Glorian stilled. 'A heathen.'

'Farfetched as it sounds, yes. He was seen in the haithwood, performing a ritual, dressed as if to mock a sanctarian. His followers, who fled before they could be seized, seemed to be throwing blood upon a yew. It was a hawthorn grove, Your Grace.'

'Has this been going on for long?'

'It seems he has lived a secret life as a heathen for decades.'

'I am very sorry to hear this,' Glorian said. 'My mother thought highly of Lord Robart.'

'Many did. I myself have called him a dear friend for years, and never saw his true leanings.'

'What is to be done in such a circumstance?'

'There is no precedent. I would recommend execution, but the people need hope and unity now. The last thing they need is to know that their Lord Protector disavowed the Saint.'

'Imprisonment, then.'

'Yes. For now.' Lady Gladwin paused. 'He has asked to speak with you, Your Grace. I would advise against it.'

'I have nothing to say to him,' came the tired reply. 'Thank you, all of you, for the risks you took to find this out. If you will all join me in Arondine, I would treasure your counsel.'

'You need a new regent, Your Grace,' Lord Edrick said. 'By law, you require one for another year.'

Wulf watched as Glorian seemed to ponder.

'My grandmother should be offered a chance,' she said. 'I know she is not a strong woman, but she is a Berethnet.'

'Lady Marian will have our full support, Your Grace,' Lady Gladwin said. 'I will summon her from Cuthyll.'

'One more thing, Queen Glorian, before we let you rest,' Lord Edrick said. 'While we were in the haithwood, my daughter made the decision to search Parr Castle.'

'You mean that she decided to break in.'

Wulf hid a smile.

'Yes, Your Grace. For the common good,' his father said, clearing his throat. 'In a hidden cabinet, she found evidence that Prince Guma of Yscalin – your companion – shares the same religion as the Lord Protector.' He placed a small pile of letters across the table. 'Their contents would legally invalidate your recent marriage. You could remove your ring.'

Glorian picked it up. 'These say he is a heathen?' she said. 'Was there a plot between them?'

Lord Edrick nodded. 'A plot to return Inys to the old ways, through controlling you.'

Slowly, she leafed through the pile, casting her eye over each letter. When she was finished, she said, 'No. Let him come.'

Wulf frowned.

'Queen Glorian, you cannot have a heathen consort,' Lady Gladwin said, looking stunned.

'To my understanding, we need the gold and soldiers no less than we did yesterday. Inys needs an heir no less than it did yesterday. Fear not,

Lady Gladwin,' Glorian said. 'I have a plan to make this marriage work in our favour. I hope you will trust me.'

She left with the letters. Wulf stood aside to let her pass, leaving Lady Gladwin to drink from her goblet of wine.

'A heathen for a prince consort,' she said, 'and a young girl for a queen, all at a time when we need guidance more than ever. Saint, Edrick, what will become of Inys?'

'King Bardholt always had a tactic,' came the mild reply. 'So might his daughter yet.'

Wulf slipped away to let them talk. He paid a visit to the bonesetter, who cleaned the bite wounds on his arm and dressed them with clean linen. As soon as he left, Helisent Beck waylaid him at the bottom of the steps.

'Helisent,' Wulf said, giving her a nod. 'Seems your scattered thoughts grew into quite the laidly flower.'

'You did well to watch him for so long, Wulf. I'm sorry I doubted you,' Helisent said, with the weight of sincerity. 'Was there really nothing in the haithwood but Lord Robart?'

'Other than some dancers and a pack of wolves, no.'

'That's a comfort. I feared it all my childhood, too.' Helisent leaned close enough for him to glimpse a tiny freckle in the white of her eye. 'Glorian has asked if you'd be willing to come to her bedchamber tonight. There are fewer tongues to loosen in this castle than in Arondine.'

Wulf looked up at the ceiling.

'Aye,' he said. 'I would.'

****

Glorian waited in the gloom. Her breast rose and fell, and her hands were clammy. She wrung them in her lap. Though the royal bed was close to the fire, her skin felt thin and cold.

The letters from Prince Guma had revealed the whole conspiracy. The odd pair had not meant to usurp her outright, but instead, to sway her to their religion in earnest, hoping she would renounce the Saint. Far easier to mould a monarch than force the people to embrace a new dynasty. She ran her fingers along one of them, reading its final lines again.

From what you say, I think she will be willing to hear reason. Bardholt was a licentious traitor for taking up the False Sword, like Isalarico before him — but he would have nurtured an appreciation for his world in her, and nowhere in Virtudom is more heathen, still, than Hróth. If we water that seed, I say Glorian the Third will blossom in our favour. If not, then we will let her be and quietly mould the heir. Surely five centuries of this is enough.

When her rushlight was halfway burned, Helisent arrived with Wulf. 'Jules and I will stand guard at the bottom of the stair,' she said, and closed the door.

Wulf fastened it behind her, and there was a concise silence.

'Are you all right, Wulf?' Glorian asked him. He nodded. 'Tell me about the haithwood.'

'It was a grim place. So dark and still.' A muscle flinched in his jaw. 'And I remembered it, Glorian. Not much. Just a feeling. But I knew in my soul I had been there before.'

'You are not there now. There is nothing left in those trees. It was only ever Lord Robart.'

'Aye. Likely I was born to one of his followers.'

'I was born to a heathen, too.' She sighed. 'Apparently, that's why Prince Guma sought to marry me, so we could roll Inys backwards together.'

'You're not going to dissolve the marriage?'

'No. Your sister has given me a way to make it work.' She nodded to the letters. 'These prove his intentions. Knowing those, I can keep to the contract, but also make sure he does no harm.'

'You want to do this, then,' Wulf said. 'You and me.'

They looked at each other.

'Prince Guma will know me for an adulteress,' Glorian said, 'but I already know him for a heathen. He will have to accept the arrangement.'

His expression was hard to read. 'So we'll start now?'

'If you're still willing.'

Wulf nodded, but stayed where he was, waiting for an invitation. When Glorian laid a hand on the bed, he sat next to her and took off his cloak, smelling of the applewood that had been smoking in the hall. She was more aware of him than she had ever been – his collarbone, the burl in his throat, the deep hollow beneath.

A fresh bandage wrapped him from wrist to elbow. Glorian said, 'What happened?'

'Ah, just a bite. I'll heal.' He raised a tired smile. 'I had an idea. We could handfast.' She shook her head, lost. 'An ancient custom. We wed ourselves in private, with no sanctarian, for a year and a day. You'd be lovemaking in wedlock, and then the lock would disappear.'

She matched his smile. 'You've thought about this.'

'Aye, a bit. To ease your mind.'

'Do we really want to indulge in a heathen custom, while Lord Robart rots for the same?'

'The sanctarians in Hróth sometimes allow it. They say it makes for stronger unions.'

'How do we go about it?'

'Just a few words.' Wulf clasped her wrist, and she clasped his. 'Glorian Hraustr Berethnet, I take you to be my companion. Bone to bone, blood to blood, and limb to limb, may we be bound. This night, and for one year to come, I will be yours alone.'

'Wulfert Glenn, I take you to be my companion. Bone to bone, blood to blood, and limb to limb, may we be bound. This night, and for one year to come, I will be yours alone.' Glorian could feel his heart. 'Is that it?'

'That's it.'

Glorian rose. She worked off her gold ring and locked it away, wanting it out of sight. Next, she reached for her thick braid, but found her fingers stiff and nerveless. Wulf came to stand behind her.

'Let me.'

He stroked his callused hands over her scalp and started to ravel the braid, taking with ease to the task. Each small undoing calmed and woke her, all at once.

'I suppose you laced braids for your lith,' she said.

'Sometimes. Vell always made a state of his, so I'd give him a hand.' Wulf teased a few strands apart. 'But it's working with rope that gave me the knack. You do a lot of that on ships.'

Glorian waited. By the time he was done, her hair fell to her waist.

A log crumpled in the fire, and they both looked towards it. Wulf stared for a long moment, and Glorian realised what he must be seeing. He had taken the bandages off his hands, showing burn scars.

'We can bank it,' she said, after a silence.

Wulf shook his head. 'It's the cold I usually remember, not the fire.'

'Then let us warm each other.' Glorian touched his shoulder. 'Let us try to forget, for one night.'

'You're sure?'

'I want it to be you.'

His face softened. He reached up and pulled his shirt over his head. Beneath it, he was muscular, forged over years into a weapon and a shield. Small dark hairs curled on his chest.

He took his time undressing. The Hróthi usually went naked in the hot springs and stovehouses, but that was not an Inysh custom. Wulf held out his left hand, with the palm up, and she placed her own into it, finding it steadied her.

'Have you done this before?'

Wulf nodded. 'Just with the one person.'

'At least one of us knows what they're doing.'

He smiled a little. 'It's not too complicated.'

Glorian moved a curl out of his eyes. He had a cowlick. She had never really noticed that before, not being able to look for too long. Wulf reached up to take her hand.

Even this tiny, intimate thing – even this was as a vice, with him. A Berethnet, above all others, was bound to be untouched until her wedding night. It was the only way to prove her child belonged to her companion.

Wulf ran his thumb across the backs of her fingers, as if he could hear the thought. The skin of her arms stippled. His hands were flecked with little scars from archery and sparring.

'I wish my hands were like this,' she said truthfully. 'The hands of an adventurer. A warrior. I wish I had lived the life you did, with my father. Inys is my duty, but Hróth is my heart.'

'It's mine, too.' Wulf tucked a strand of hair behind her ear. 'We can pretend we're there tonight. With the sky lights above us, the snow all around.'

Glorian pictured it. The first time she had seen the lights, she had known that she could fall in love – not with a person, but a place.

There was a strange, tight feeling in her, low down, woken by his closeness. It reminded her of her courses, except that it was painless, a sweet ache. When she opened her eyes, his were there, dark and serious in the firelight. There was a question in them now.

When she gave him a nod, he unlaced her shift and skimmed it away from her shoulders. She shrank at first, but he lifted her chin, so they looked at each other, and she nodded again. He knelt to slide the shift lower, down past her hips, and then it was on the floor.

Wulf looked up at her. Glorian shivered under his gaze. Before she knew it, she had joined him on the floor and taken him by the nape. He smoothed his hands up her waist and kissed her.

The feeling of his mouth was strange at first. She was unsure of so much – how long to kiss, how to kiss. His lips opened hers, and she tasted him, catmint and wine and an herb, rosemary. She felt a sudden whelming grief, and clutched him with a shudder, arms tight around his neck.

Wulf drew her to his chest, and she understood how deeply she had wanted his embrace, after the pain they had endured. His chin rested on the top of her head, and he kissed her there, murmuring comforts in Hróthi. His heart beat against hers.

They were each other's past. A memory of a different time, when they could laugh in plum orchards, nothing in the world to fear. She wished she could armour him, as he was trying to protect her.

Without letting her go, he moved from his knees to a sitting position and drew her into his lap. It made her shy of him again, but he cupped her face and bade her look him in the eyes.

'It's just me,' he said, his voice low.

'I know.'

'Tell me if you want me to stop, and I will.' The fire limned his face. 'Do you promise?'

'I promise.'

Wulf folded his hands at the small of her back. 'We're in the eversnow,' he murmured, 'and the hall is open to the stars.' Glorian closed her eyes, and she was there, she could already see it.

****

They stayed on the floor, with the furs from the bed under them, as if they really were in a hall. After, Glorian gazed at the ceiling, while Wulf drowsed on his back with one arm around her.

He had been slow and gentle, letting her warm to his touch. They had even been able to laugh a little, muffling the sounds with their lips.

It had been awkward and clumsy, but it was done, and without much disquiet. Just a strangeness that had waned in time.

It troubled her that sinning had seemed like the only right choice. The Saint had set her a curious test.

Wulf stirred. Glorian watched his heavy blinks, waiting for him to remember. When he did, he leaned down to kiss her forehead. 'Are you all right?'

She nodded. 'Are you?'

'Aye.' He touched her jaw. 'You know we might have to do this again. More than once.'

'Oh, no. How shall we ever bear it?'

He smiled and shifted to face her. In time, he slept again, his hand loose on her waist. Glorian lay against his chest, listening to the heart that had kept beating in the icy sea. Had she been free to choose, she would not have lain with anyone; she knew she never would again, after she got with child – but with a friend, she could find comfort in the closeness.

Helisent and Julain would sneak him away at dawn. They would keep the secret from Adela, who would collapse under its weight, but Glorian knew she would have to tell Florell.

She could not sleep, for worry, for the tenderness where Wulf had filled her. Julain had counselled her to sleep on her back, but she was never at ease that way. When the black hour came, she drew on a thick bedgown and padded barefoot from the chamber.

Her former regent had been locked into the gatehouse, where prisoners of noble birth awaited trial. When she reached the door to his cell, she found Lord Robart Eller still awake, staring at the snow moon. His red hair was awry, and he wore a simple dark tunic and breeches, which made him look much smaller than he always had in his fine garb.

'Lord Robart,' she said. 'How are you?'

He looked at her. 'Queen Glorian,' he said quietly. 'I'm surprised you came to see me.'

'I wanted to understand. I am told you performed some rite in the woods. For this, you will be stripped of everything. Why would you ever risk it?'

Lord Robart rose and came to grasp the bars. She made sure to stand just out of reach.

'For the Lady of the Woods,' he said. 'I was trying to call her back to Inysca, Your Grace. To help us. The wyrms have come to scour this land clean of Galian's vainglory. They have come because a balance of two forces is unsettled.'

'I thought you were a man who cared deeply for Inys.'

'I do,' he said, a little hoarsely. 'More than anyone. I had to try to bring this island back to the old ways.'

'The ways of witches and petty wars?'

'Not the wars. I had to give the trees their due, if nobody else would.'

'Trees are just trees,' she said, frustrated.

'And a man is just a man, yet he is worshipped. Even in death, he chains the realms to his false legacy.'

'The Saint performed a heroic deed. What is special about a yew, and why does it demand blood?'

'It was not blood, Your Grace. I swear it on all I hold dear. Go to the haithwood and taste it yourself. It was wine,' he said. 'A libation for fertility and growth – and for undoing. Galian Berethnet made this land bleed by cutting down its hawthorns. Those trees were sacred to the Lady of the Woods.'

'I do not believe in your witch. I believe in the Saint,' Glorian said. 'Surely you didn't think me so stupid as to discard my own claim to the throne.'

'Queen Glorian, I beg you, heed me.'

'Is that what Prince Guma will say?' she asked him. 'Will he beg me to listen to him as well?'

'You still mean to wed him?'

'Yes, for his gold, and all else he brings. But I will not let him mould me, as you clearly intended.'

'I admit it,' Lord Robart said. 'To have true believers in the position of prince consort and regent – that was a precious chance to effect change, by influencing you and the heir.'

'I would not have changed, my lord.'

'I think you would have, when I told you the truth, which I will now. Your ancestor was not a hero. You do not need to bear the fruit of his eternal vine. It is a lie, created to perpetuate his legacy, no more. Surely, after all that has happened, you see that you do not control the Dreadmount.'

'The Nameless One has not returned.' Her voice quaked. 'Besides, your springtime rites have not prevented this.'

'My rites are for stopping it happening again. We humans are more than ourselves, and must remember it by worshipping our world,' he said. 'You are a daughter of the heathen North. You were even born on the Feast of Early Spring, our most sacred day. We all believed you might be the one Berethnet queen who would see the truth of our cause.'

'And what would you have had me do?'

'Call her back. The Lady of the Woods. I know she can save us – her magic is as deep as the sea. Wulfert Glenn was marked by her,' he said. Glorian tensed. 'He might not have her power, but she touched him with it. He holds its remnant. He is more than he seems.'

'Wulf has nothing to do with your witch.'

'The Hawthorn Mother is no witch. She was the guardian of these isles, before we drove her far away.' Lord Robart drew back into his cell. 'Queen Glorian, I promise you, my way is the right one – but it may already be too late. I fear your reign will end in fire.'

'We cannot be sure of that, my lord.' Glorian spoke softly, sadly. 'But we can be sure that yours ends here.'

64

East

Change came like a flash of lightning. One day there was peace and stillness; the next, there was fire. The Snow Road had offered a last glimpse of safety – a pause between the loose slab and the snowslide. Now wyrms rode on the wind, and creatures hatched from rock, and not even the gods could stop them.

As soon as they smelled the tainted smoke, Furtia and Nayimathun stopped flying by day. Instead, they waited for dusk, to coast below the clouds while still avoiding the wyrms' notice.

They need the sun to see, Nayimathun informed Dumai. *They are not made for night, as we are.*

One night, they passed a burning forest, and the glow was a sinister, unnatural red, bestranging all it touched. Watching its spread, Master Kiprun muttered to himself, twisting the rings on his fingers. The alchemist was enduring the flight, though he clearly had little patience for sitting. With four riders, the saddle was crowded, but the closeness kept them warm.

Northward they went like this, slow and wary, cleaving to the Whinshan Ridge. At dawn, the dragons would find shelter in the mountains, and the humans would huddle together, trying to sleep. Dumai and Kanifa shared their pelts. They heard the calls of wyrm and tortured beast, answered by occasional explosions of black powder.

Once, they had to stay hidden for more than a day, when a flock of winged lizards circled the mountains. Furtia raked her claws and bared her teeth, while Nayimathun lay still, her tail curled around the humans. Had their mission not been too important to jeopardise, Dumai suspected they both would have flown out to fight to the death.

That night was long and terrible. They risked no light or sound. The first time Nikeya reached for her hand, Dumai pretended not to notice. The second, their fingers twined.

Let her believe you are utterly caught. Dumai kept her hand steady. *Let her think that she has won.*

When it was safe, the dragons pressed on, passing the Lake of Cold Dawns and the inland port of Pithang, where coal had once been mined. Now fire revealed the city's veins, making the very mountains smoke. Something had set the coal seams alight.

She wondered if its people had fled deeper into mountains, or chanced taking the roads elsewhere. The Empire of the Twelve Lakes was vast – too vast for Jekhen's messengers to have possibly warned everyone what was coming.

Nayimathun quenched another three fires. For the first time since the capital, Dumai prayed, placing her bare hand on Furtia. *Great Kwiriki, hear a daughter of the rainbow.* She closed her eyes. *I ask that you grant all lands your protection, and make our world a mirror of your quiet abode.*

He cannot hear, earth child, Furtia told her. *Kwiriki is beyond the bridge.*

Nayimathun spoke of a star, from the black waters of creation. What does it mean, great one?

Only fallen night can stop it.

Dumai could not persuade her to say more. As a godsinger, she knew dragons were mysterious by nature, because they were not of the world – but as a human, she wished they would speak plainly.

They were within sight of Mount Whin, the source of the River Daprang, when Nayimathun made for a low and exposed peak on the ridge. Dumai tried to call out to her – dawn was about to break, they had to hide – but days of fatigue had thickened her senses.

Furtia followed the larger dragon, down to a broken pile of stone that must have been a watchtower. From the smoking remains of three giant crossbows, and the armour on the corpses, this had been a Lacustrine military outpost. It could have been a human attack, if not for the fallen god. The dragon had been shredded as if he were paper, scales glinting like silver leaf among the ash and snow. He must have been trying to protect the soldiers.

'Taugran,' Furtia hissed aloud.

The rumble of her voice woke Kanifa. Dumai felt him tense against her back. Her own muscles were tight, her stomach baulking at the sight of a god lying dead.

'This is a border outpost,' Master Kiprun dabbed his nose. 'Built to ensure the East Hüran respect the Treaty of Shim.' He eyed the carcass of a stallion, tangled with its charred rider. 'It seems the wyrms found it.'

Dumai knelt beside the dragon and stroked the dull scales of his snout. With an aching heart, she looked north, hair ruffled by the wind. In the far distance, first light glazed the waters of the Daprang. All the land beyond that line belonged to the Bertak tribe.

'Mai,' Kanifa said.

He nodded to a soldier who could be no more than twenty. Deep gouges streaked his cheeks, and fistfuls of hair had been ripped from his scalp, scabs left in their wake. Odder still, both his sleeves had been torn, baring his forearms to the cold. Scarlet branched from his fingertips, almost to the shoulder. At first, Dumai thought it was dried blood, but on closer inspection, the redness was in his skin.

That colour was a warning – that livid red, like the flaming mushrooms that grew on Mount Ipyeda, so poisonous they could destroy the body through one touch. It woke some ingrained awareness of danger. Nayimathun leaned over them both to give the corpse a cautious sniff.

This one burned from the inside. A hiss escaped her. *Fire from the earth devours the flesh and runs wild in the blood.*

Now Dumai saw the rusty crescents under his nails. 'His face. He did this to himself,' she murmured. 'My mother said the Nameless One brought sickness to the land of Lasia.'

'I would step away, Princess,' Nikeya said.

Nayimathun got there first. Taking Dumai and Kanifa by the pelts, she picked them up with her teeth, like kittens by the scruffs of their necks, and placed them next to Furtia. She turned back to the dead soldier and breathed over him, sealing him in a mound of ice.

Dumai clambered back into the saddle with the others. As the dragons abandoned the outpost, she set her gaze on the river, trying to forget what they had just seen. Soon they would reach Brhazat, where they would find an answer. She had to keep believing it.

In the meantime, she willed her father to prepare Seiiki. It would not be long until the chaos found its way there, too.

****

The Daprang was the longest of all rivers in the East, with few kinks or turns. From above, it looked as if a warrior had run a sword along the land. In the tales, it was always frozen, but now spring was here, its waters were starting to pour strong and black, parting the deep snow.

As the cold sharpened, the dragons smelled fewer wyrms, and risked flying by day again, allowing Dumai to see the wilds beyond the Daprang. As far as the eye could see, there were no fires or smoke, despite the thickness of the forest.

'The wyrms must not have come this far,' Kanifa called over the wind. 'It's as Nayimathun said. They spurn the cold.'

'Then let us hope winter takes some time to thaw,' Dumai shouted back.

The cold will not keep them at bay for long, Furtia told her. *The tortured earth breathes hot, and burns as if with fever . . .*

It seemed like years before the northern capital of Golümtan appeared – that walled city that had been called Hinitun, its walls rebuilt after the siege that had lost it. But first of all, it was the mountains they saw, the peaks that formed one of the walls of the world.

These were the Lords of Fallen Night.

Not even her tutors knew who had given them that name, but Dumai wondered now if it had been the gods. By all accounts, it was as ancient as the range, which marked where all land maps ended in the East. The peaks were terrible, most rearing far higher and wider than Mount Ipyeda, sheared to points that looked too sharp for one coin to sit easy on them.

There was Brhazat. Dumai knew it from a single look, for it stood a head and shoulders above the line of mountains in front of it, spearing insuperably into the clear sky.

Only fallen night can stop it. She gripped the saddle. *Only fallen night . . .*

A greathorn sounded, loud and deep, as the two dragons soared into Golümtan. The archers on its walls lowered their bows. Princess Irebül must have survived the long ride home.

After four years of Hüran rule, the city still appeared Lacustrine, though the tents beyond its wall served as a strong reminder of the conquest. Furtia and Nayimathun landed near the High Perch. The stronghold bestrode a crag to the west, its sloping walls made tall and smooth. Oxen and horses, eagles and dragons pranced across its roofs, and a sun and moon gleamed on the doors, to be parted down the middle when they opened. The sheer mountains towered behind, offering an outlook worthy of the gods.

Snow blew from the mountains, smoke from fires and bloomeries. Dumai climbed down. It was far colder here than on the other side of the Daprang – and darker, too, the sky already dull at noon.

There were more horses here than Dumai had ever seen. Furtia growled at a mare, which snorted in fear.

'I think I'll wait here, to prevent a war between dragons and horses,' Nikeya said, amused. 'You can face the fearsome warlord, as your father's diplomat.'

'I am no diplomat.' Dumai reached for her pack. 'Besides, I thought charm was your area.'

Nikeya glanced at her in surprise, then smiled a little.

Kanifa dismounted. When they reached the steps to the High Perch, a group of palace guards in well-tooled leather strode to meet them. Horsehair tufted from their helmets.

'Show us your hands,' came a deep voice. 'Are you Princess Dumai of Seiiki?'

Dyed wool swathed their faces, from their chins to below their eyes, which held no small amount of caution. This far north, people might have forgotten Seiiki; certainly she doubted they had met Seiikinese merchants, or heard Lacustrine with an accent like hers.

'Yes. My father sends his respects to the Great Naïr,' Dumai said. 'May your hunts be rich in spoils, and your birds soar on the wind.' She did as they asked. 'Soldier, why do you conceal your faces?'

'The Great Naïr has been told of a sickness, carried by scaled beasts. Sickness can be spread through breath.'

'I have seen those beasts. They are burning crops and settlements, slaughtering without mercy.'

The wool hid his expression. 'Princess Irebül is hunting in the Collar,' he said. 'You may join her.' He held out a swatch of green wool. 'You are asked to wear this in her presence.'

'What of the dragons?'

'They may follow.' He noticed the alchemist. 'Master Kiprun. The Great Naïr will be pleased to see you.'

'Why is every ruler so pleased to see me this year?' he muttered. 'Shall I expect the Deathless Queen next?' Faced with stony looks, he sighed. 'Yes, yes. All under the mountains to the Great Naïr, and so on.'

A carriage drawn by snow camels bore them to a meadow that separated the city from the peaks, thick with grass and powder. This was the Collar, a stretch of land kept clear for falling rock and snowslides. Fine tents had been pitched at its western edge, where servants had gralloched a deer and set about roasting it over a fire.

Princess Irebül was some way from the camp. She wore a green coat lined with sheepskin and boots over loose wool trousers, and a quiver hung at her hip – a hunter of the winter plains, down to her ornate belt hook and the bronze eagle perched on her forearm. She beheld the Lords of Fallen Night, a tall woman rendered small in the face of them. Her people were said to have come from beyond those mountains long ago.

'Princess Dumai,' she said, seeing her approach. 'I thought you'd changed your mind.'

'I apologise for the delay, Princess Irebül. We were stranded on the Snow Road.'

'No need to explain.' She took the leather hood off her eagle. 'The wait let me escape that court.'

The bird winged towards the mountains. From what Dumai had learned, this woman had been sixteen during the conquest, spending her formative years in the wilds.

'You'd sooner be here,' Dumai said.

'That palace is a silken cage, and Hüran are not meant for walls.'

'Why did you take a city, then?'

'Necessity.' The wind had flushed her cheeks. 'Soon the days will grow colder. There will be an age of ice, of storms – a wild winter, deep and lethal. It has happened before. When a sage warned her, my mother declared we would settle, to survive the freeze.'

'I assume the North Hüran don't believe this, and that's why they stayed on the plains.'

'That was their choice. The Bertak will endure.'

'Will you fight the wyrms?'

Princess Irebül glanced at her. Her eyes were long and dark above the woollen mask she wore.

'You saw that creature,' she said. 'No bow or spear will slay it.' The eagle circled. 'We are not meant to fight this, islander. Let your gods try. What you see is the death of one age, the birth of another. Those who survive will build a new world from the ash of the old.'

The eagle swooped down on a fox and wrestled it into the snow. Princess Irebül called out to it, her voice echoing across the meadow.

'What do you know of the woman on Brhazat?' Dumai said. 'Is she really an astronomer?'

'I know only what the Lacustrine say. Some claim she is a spirit of the mountain, sent here by the gods to guard the city. They say she used to send them dreams, but it seems she no longer does. Apparently, our arrival scared her away.' Her smile was thin and frigid. 'Whatever she is, she is passing into myth. For myself, I suspect she died long ago.'

Dumai tried to conceal her disquiet. She could not let herself entertain the possibility that the person she had come here to seek might not be alive to answer her questions.

'The Great Naïr – my esteemed mother, the Eternal Sun of the North – has approved your undertaking,' Princess Irebül said. 'You have her blessing to search the mountain, in exchange for any knowledge you may find there.' The eagle perched on her arm, talons bloody, and she replaced its hood. 'Should you survive, I will ride south to inform Consort Jekhen.'

'I pray your people will be safe, whatever is to come.' Dumai started to leave, then said, 'Do you know her name, the woman on Brhazat?'

'Tonra.' Irebül stared into the onslaught of wind. 'It means *alone*.'

****

They had everything they would need on the mountain, but Dumai knew it would be wrapped in a cold she had never endured. If her mother ever learned she had climbed it, she would be speechless with anger.

'You're thinking of Unora.'

Dumai peered up at Kanifa. During the journey, his stubble had grown into the footing of a beard. 'I miss her,' she said, as she tied her spikes to her boots. 'You know what she'd say.'

'It's worth the risk.' He knelt to check her knots. 'I've missed climbing with you.'

'And I with you.' She showed him the frayed piece of their rope, tied around her wrist. 'I have always kept this with me, but we might need a little more for this climb.'

He chuckled. 'We have enough.'

They both looked up and up. Faced with the terrible slopes of the Lords, Dumai had thought she would be afraid, but found it was resolve that filled her. She could do this, of all things.

'Did you know this Tonra was almost a myth, Master Kiprun?' she asked the alchemist, who was burrowed into his furs, squinting at the mountain. 'Princess Irebül seems to think so.'

'I knew she hasn't been seen in years,' Master Kiprun admitted. 'But she probably exists.'

'What if she's just a story?'

'The Nameless One was a story, Princess,' Nikeya said, her face almost swallowed by her hood. 'We will all be stories one day, and I'd want someone to believe we existed. Wouldn't you?'

Against her better judgement, Dumai smiled, glad her face was too covered for anyone to see.

'We will go now,' she said. 'Master Kiprun, I know you wanted to join us, but—'

'No fear, Princess Fish. Now I see Brhazat, I am reminded that alchemists belong on the ground,' Master Kiprun said drily. 'I leave it to you to find any wisdom that lies on that peak.'

'I will return with it.' Dumai looked at Nikeya. 'Last chance. There would be no shame in staying.'

Nikeya shook her head. 'Where you go, I go, Princess.'

'As you wish.'

The sky remained calm as they climbed on to Furtia. She took off, following Nayimathun. Dumai narrowed her eyes against the wind. As the dragons swam up the western face of Brhazat, the incline tipped her against Kanifa, who wrapped an arm around her.

The cold had already knifed through her layers. This high, in the gods' abode, spring might well have never come.

Brhazat had four distinct sides that tapered into a spearpoint. Ice armoured its slopes, which shed white powder into the air. No life stirred. Dumai thought it was six miles high; climbing it would have taken months. On Mount Ipyeda, climbers stopped at the village for several days, so their blood could settle, but there was no time for that now.

She closed her eyes to listen to her body. By the time they were at the waist of the mountain, breathing was harder, and her head ached – but she was a kite, and the sky was familiar.

Nonetheless, she was a human, too, and soon she knew that she was past the ceiling of the world, past the point a mortal could survive for long. Her heart worked hard. They were now far higher than Mount Ipyeda, higher than she had ever been, the city a haze far below.

Earth children cannot live so high. Furtia moved slower. *The waters of creation lap against this stair.*

She breathes those waters, as we can, Nayimathun replied.

Dumai opened her wet eyes, the wind blustering in her ears. *Who, great one?*

The queen in the mountain…

The weather was starting to turn. She had never feared heights, yet her thighs gave a sudden tremor as the wind whipped into a fury, straining the saddle. Kanifa tightened his hold on her.

'There,' he called.

Dumai lifted her raw face. The dragons slowed to a drift. Some way below the top of Brhazat, where the ice was hard and pale as marble, she spied a tiny balcony, difficult to see – and a door into the mountain, perched on the very eave of the East.

She tried to blink away a sudden darkening in her eyes. Neither dragon would be able to get near it, but a wall of snow and rock led to the cave. 'Kanifa,' she said, 'we can climb that.'

'Yes,' he said.

Furtia banked as close as she could. When the dragon huffed and shook herself, Dumai slowly understood that they would have to jump between the saddle and the mountain.

Kanifa unwound the rope. He secured one end around his waist and passed the other to her, and she anchored it to the horn of the saddle. She had to concentrate until her temples hurt to do it, the knots taking longer than usual to make. Their bodies were already running out of time.

Do not goad the mountain. Her cracked lips formed the old warning, over and over. *Do not goad the mountain.*

When Kanifa loosed himself from the saddle, Dumai did the same. He took out his trusty ice sickles and set his weight against the wind before he made the leap. Once he had thrown his end of the rope to Dumai, she turned to face Nikeya, who was already trying to get up, hands clumsy in their mittens.

'I was trying to remember … if I have ever had cause to jump,' she said, with a wheezing laugh. 'I have danced and swum, hunted on horseback, but I have not jumped in a very long time.'

She barely got the words out before a coughing fit struck her. Without her hands free to smother it, Dumai heard the damp rattle in that cough. She grasped Nikeya and reached under her furs and tunic, pressing a palm to her breastbone, where her heart beat like a banner in the wind.

'Nikeya,' she said, 'you can't climb. You must go back.'

'No. I can.' Another hacking cough. 'Give me … some ginger.'

'Ginger is not a cure, you fool. Master Kiprun knew his limits. Know yours.' Dumai took her by the cheek. 'You promised.'

Nikeya looked past her, up to the door. Blood was spreading in the white of her left eye.

'Yes,' she rasped. 'I did.' She coughed again. 'If I let you send me back, then I trust that it will serve to demonstrate my honesty. Will you remember it, Dumai?'

Every word seemed to shred her throat. Dumai nodded, eyes watering in the cold. *Furtia, once I am gone, take them to the ground.* She fastened Nikeya back into the saddle. *I will call when we have what we need.*

You will die here before I return, earth child.

I am no stranger to mountains. Please, great one.

'Be careful,' Nikeya croaked as Dumai rose and turned to face Kanifa. Just as she rested her boot on the side of the saddle, a swift gust of wind threw her balance, and suddenly she was over the edge.

The rope wrenched and went taut. Shouts came to her ears, but they were garbled by the wind. Her legs hung above the black precipice; her sight darkened again. With a growl, Furtia shunted her body towards the mountain, and Dumai went soaring in the same direction.

As soon as she landed, Kanifa grabbed the back of her coat. 'Nikeya, the rope,' he bellowed up to her. He dug his spikes into the crust. 'Hurry, before it pulls us over!'

Somehow, Nikeya managed it. As soon as the rope slackened, they both collapsed into the snow.

As Furtia sank out of sight, Dumai rose and stooped against the wind, her hands tucked under her furs, and trudged after Kanifa, every step as hard as if her boots were made of stone.

Island child. With effort, she turned back to see Nayimathun. *There is a foulness on the wind. The fire comes, but the star has not. The star that brought us to this world; the long-tailed light from the black waters of creation. I must protect the land I call home.*

Thank you for escorting us. Dumai hunched into a bow. *It was a greater honour than any of us earned.*

You have the stars in you, rider. I will see you in the sky one day.

With those words, Nayimathun of the Deep Snows was gone, leaving them to stand where no human should. Dumai knew that she would never see the god of wanderers again.

Kanifa had already lashed the rope back around his waist. Dumai took out her sickles. She chipped one point into the ice, then drove her spikes in, and they began to scale the cliff.

Compared to their climbs on Mount Ipyeda, it was agony. Her weight seemed to have doubled. Each pull of her arms left her puffing and faint. By the time she edged a knee over the crust of snow at the top, she thought she would die from the burning pain in her thighs.

The door that caulked the mountainside was blocked from within. Kanifa pounded it with his fist, to no avail. Gathering their strength, they used their sickles to splinter the rotten wood, breaking and prying it until Dumai could force an arm through and wrestle the iron bars from the other side. She had never overindulged in wine, but she imagined that this was what it would feel like, as if her blood had thickened.

Inside, her knees almost gave way. Kanifa steadied her before he took out the leather pouch he had acquired on the Snow Road. Inside was a Northern firestriker. He used it to light the oiled cloth he had tied around a stick, and a small flame revealed the cave.

Tonra had built a modest home. With blurred sight, Dumai made out a hearth and three faded cushions. A pothook had been fixed above. Thick fabric draped the walls, and mats covered the floor, helping to counter the unearthly cold. Paper had piled up on a table. Dumai limped towards an opening in the rock, which led to another cave.

And there was Tonra, slumped in furs. Black hair covered her face. It had grown so long that she had wrapped herself in it, and even then, there was enough left to trail across the floor.

Dumai stepped over it and knelt. She heard no breathing. Removing one gauntlet, she took the woman by the arm, drew up her red sleeve, and pressed a thumb to her inner wrist.

'She's dead.'

Kanifa brought the light closer. 'She hasn't decayed.'

'The air is too pure and cold. Nothing rots this high.' Dumai touched a stain at her waist. 'There's blood, but I doubt she died from it.'

'More likely she starved.' Kanifa dabbed his nose. 'Or finally succumbed to Brhazat.'

Tonra was certainly thin, curled like a dry leaf in death. Dumai went to brush her hair off her face, then stopped. A corpse ought not to be disturbed. 'It is as Irebül said, then.' Her chest squeezed like a fist as she spoke. 'We cannot have come this far for no reason.'

'Keep looking.'

In the other cave, a writing brush lay on the floor, its hairs clotted into one hunk, along with the remnants of an inkstone. They sifted through rolls of fragile paper.

'Some of these are in Seiikinese. An older form, but—' Dumai paused for breath and blinked. 'Was she an islander?'

I write not of what I remember or what I have done, for that will only bring fresh torment in my exile, and already my mind is in agony. Let me dwell on that pain and sorrow no longer; let me not be overwhelmed by what I can no longer change. Instead, I mean to watch the nightly passage of the stars, as if I had no past at all. I will have no dwelling but this, and no friends but these.

Do stars go out, I wonder, in the end – those candles of the world above?

A headache was mounting. She leafed through the papers, trying to find anything pertaining to a balance.

I woke again today, against my will. This brittle air slows me, as I trusted it would. I had thought myself reconciled to this fate, but I had the world to distract me, before. Now I have no comfort.

The path open to others is not open to me. If I let myself fall, I might break into pieces, yet remain. I fear to try. I cannot try. I must do as I promised, for who better than I to do it – I who am a remnant, a firefly still aglow in amber?

Dumai had held herself together for this long. Now her stomach rang with fear. These were the ravings of a troubled mind, not the calculations of a genius. Master Kiprun had been wrong.

Kanifa was reading one. 'This seems important,' he said, showing it to her.

How you haunt me still, as I hold my half of our pact – this quickened stone that I possess, and that possesses me. It does not rest, nor let me rest, and yet I must protect it. It holds the fire at bay, but at what cost does it exist?

One day I will know, when the binding is broken. No matter how far I must go, I will know it…

'We need to find the stone she mentions,' Dumai murmured, just as she spotted another scroll on the floor, fallen with the brush. She picked it up.

The comet will pass again soon. It will mark five hundred years and six since that day on the sea, and give my enemy new power.

This time it will come on the first of the spring, in the twelfth year of the fifth century, to cool the risen fire. Perhaps it will undo the past. If not, let me not wake again.

'Kanifa. This is it.' Dumai stared at the writing. 'Tonra speaks of a comet that will come in the twelfth year of the fifth century – next year – to cool the risen fire. This must be the answer.'

'A comet.' His expression changed. 'A comet is what keeps the balance in check.'

'Father might know of it – but if this is true, this time of fire will not last for ever, just as Master Kiprun said. It is a wheel, always circling. It means we only need survive until this coming spring.'

'Easier said than done.' Kanifa coughed. 'Dumai, we've stayed too long.'

She stood without argument. *Great one, we are ready to leave,* she called, but Furtia did not reply.

While Kanifa gathered the old papers into a sack, Dumai combed the cave once more, searching every crevice, trying to ignore how fast her heart was beating. She returned to Tonra, and noticed, on her second look, that the body was curled around something.

A box.

She thought it was of Lacustrine design, hammered silver with gilding, its surface beautifully engraved. Its shape put her in mind of fruit. With care, she took it and removed its lid – and there it was, the stone. Big as a plum and smooth as a pearl, it was darkest blue, with a white glimmer at its core. Dumai gazed into those depths, finding herself entranced.

'Kanifa.'

He crouched beside her. 'This must be what she was protecting,' he rasped. 'What is it?'

'I don't know. Should we take it?'

Kanifa considered, then nodded. 'She can't look after it any more. We should try to find out what it is, and why she banished herself with it.' He pinched the bridge of his nose. 'Is Furtia coming?'

'I called her.'

Dumai cupped a hand under the gemstone, hesitating as she did it. She felt as low as a graverobber – but they needed any clue they could find.

Even through a padded gauntlet, the stone was cold to the touch. She wrapped it in a length of wool and stowed it in the pouch at her hip, pulling the cords tight before she knotted them.

An ominous sound came from outside. She joined Kanifa on the balcony to see a storm gathering over the Collar, where dusk had already fallen. As clouds enwheeled Golümtan, the whole city became a weave of burning threads, and Dumai saw a flash of gold.

'Wyrms,' she breathed.

'The gods must have summoned a storm to weaken them. We have to start climbing, Mai, to get below the ceiling.'

'We won't make it that far in this state.'

'We can try.'

Shivering, Dumai blinked against an icy blaze of wind. The sun, already tarnished, was turning red. 'All right,' she ground out. 'We go as far as we can and find shelter.'

With the rope between them, they angled themselves over the balcony and picked their way back down the ice. Descending a mountain could be far more dangerous than scaling it, and while every instinct told her to hurry, she resisted. *Do not goad the mountain*, her mother had said, but they had, by daring to climb as high as gods flew.

Furtia, please, hear me. Dumai kicked her spikes into the ice. *We can't breathe this air for much longer.*

Kanifa lost his grip and fell, and then so did Dumai, wrenched by the rope. They helped each other up and went on foot, following a ridge of bare rock. Soon it had turned steep enough that they had to sit, to stop the wind ripping them off Brhazat. Dumai tried to think of nothing but the next tiny movement. Her feet had turned numb in her boots.

They skirted a great weathered outcrop. Below, the storm thickened. A burst of lightning came, making something glint again, and then a deep rumble of thunder.

'Dumai, is it a wyrm?'

The storm had blown into them before she could reply, driving her against the mountain, hard enough that she struck her head. Freezing rain scissored her face, sharp as pottery shards, and Kanifa clasped her to him, trying to shelter her.

They kept clambering down. By the time they reached a dizzying slope covered in looser snow, it was dark enough that they could barely see a foot in front of them. Kanifa retched. Dumai breathed in shallow white puffs.

Can anyone hear me?

Silence pealed in her mind, somehow louder than the storm.

'Kanifa,' she said, in a fainter voice than she had meant, 'I taste iron. Is my nose bleeding?'

'A little.' He tried to dab it with his thick gauntlet. 'It can't be m-mountain sickness. It's us.'

Dumai managed a weak laugh, though it left her so breathless it hurt. 'Just a bad cold.' Lowering herself into the snow, she unhooked one of her ice sickles and fastened it to her arm. 'Come on. We have to slide. We'll get you down, Kan. You'll be fine.'

He took the same position. Dumai sat with her legs in front of her and shunted herself forward, using her heels and sickle to control her descent, and together they went slewing down the face of Brhazat, towards the city that lay far beneath the ceiling. She dug in just before they reached the end of the slope, a solid overhang crusted with snow.

'Dumai.' Kanifa stopped behind her. 'Can you see anywhere to shelter?'

'No.' Her heart struck her breast like a hammer. 'It's so dark. I can't think.'

Kanifa crawled to her side. As he put his hand on the edge, Dumai heard the crack, and in the terrible moment that followed, she saw what they had both failed to notice, in their blindness. This was not a shelf of rock, but ice – and when it broke away from the cliff, they fell with it.

Blackness howled around her. Instinct kicked to life, and she lashed out desperately with her ice sickle. The blade sparked and shrieked before it caught, arresting her fall. The rope went taut, almost pulling her down, but somehow, she kept her grip, cracked open her eyes, and found herself staring at her own gloved hand, wrapped around the handle.

Kanifa was some way below, saved by the rope. 'Kanifa,' Dumai cried. His entire weight pulled on the other end, pulling it hard around her waist. 'Kan, quickly, swing yourself!'

'I can't.'

She looked down in fear. Her sickle had caught on a frozen outcrop. Through the sleet, she saw that he was right – even if she had been at full strength, the rock face was too far away for her to swing him to it.

Her arm trembled. Every joint and rib was threatening to snap. She had lost so much strength at court. Calling on her deepest reserves, she reached down to detach her other sickle from her sash. With a scream of effort, she drove it into the ice. Now she could pull them both up, she could . . .

'Dumai,' Kanifa called hoarsely. 'Dumai, listen to me. You're too weak to save us both.'

'No. I can—'

The ice creaked. Her grip slipped on both sides, and she caught herself just in time, sobbing in pain.

Kanifa twisted into a new position. Dumai groaned as the rope tightened around her waist, and then she spotted the blade in his hand, twin to the one she had left in the temple.

'What are you doing?' she heaved out.

'Mai, listen to me.' He was straining to speak. 'We're both dying. If you keep holding me, you'll be too weak to save yourself.'

Dumai stared down at him. When she saw the choice in his face, she felt the blood drain from her own.

'No,' she rasped. 'Kanifa, don't.'

'I have to.' He reached up to grip the rope. 'A kite can't fly with a weight on its line.'

'You are not a weight,' she screamed in agony. 'Stop this—'

She willed the storm to freeze her hands to the sickles, to let her hold on for as long as it took.

'We fall together. Always together. It's us, Kanifa,' she sobbed. 'It's us!'

'You have to live. To see the comet.' Kanifa found a last smile for her, blood crusted on his lips and nose. 'Seiiki could ask for no better queen.'

He set the blade against their rope. Tears smeared her sight, but in that moment, Dumai saw him as if for the first time, the quiet boy who climbed the peak. He offered her the same blade she gripped now, so she could touch the sky, like him. So she could one day save herself.

He had always been there. Always with her.

And then, in one flash of steel, he was gone.

****

Later, she would not remember how she pulled herself on to the outcrop. She would not remember how she found the place where she curled up like a small hurt thing and waited for the end.

Freezing was not too cruel a death. Dumai remembered her mother telling her so, the first time she had seen a climber brought down from the mountain, unmoving. *It's like falling asleep, my kite.* Unora had drawn her close. *There is no pain. After a time . . . it begins to feel warm.*

It did. It felt like she was sitting by a stove, or tucked into her bedding on Mount Ipyeda. She started to shrug out of her furs, burning. As she dug into the snow, she thought she really could hear her mother.

Sister. Not her mother. Someone else. *Sister, I feel you fading. Don't leave me. Stay . . .*

'I can't,' she breathed.

Earth child. Voices mingled, young and ancient. She held a constellation of consciousnesses in her own. *Darkness strikes the mountain, and you with it. Find the light that touched you in the waters of the womb.*

Let me help you. Tell me how.

Somehow, Dumai reached for the stream, and the figure on the other side.

Help me find the light.

The ice was already deep in her skin, but now it branched in her blood, too. The fog in her breath thickened before a dazzling whiteness shone from her hand, lighting up the snow around her. She held it aloft until her arm lost the last of her strength, and then it went out, and she knew no more.

591

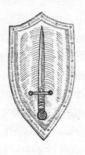

65

West

Halfway across Yscalin, the Saurga Mountains leaned apart, forming the Middle Pass, the fastest way to reach Inys. Red clay peaks climbed from its swathes of holm oaks and sweet chestnuts.

Guarding both the Middle Pass and the mine called the Ufarassus, a castle stood at monstrous height, its walls seeming part of the mountains they stood on. Poised above the largest pit, Hart Grove seemed unbreakable, its turrets all but scraping a sky leaden with smoke.

On its battlements, springalds flung bolts towards the wyrms circling the fortress, the nimble sort with only two feet. These, the Ments had named wyverns, and though others called them wingers or wyrmlings, that was the name that had spread farthest in the West.

Hundreds of miners had fled; more had stayed to fight for the nearest figure of authority. Though Tunuva held no allegiance to Yscalin, she had joined the fray when she and Canthe came on it. She would let nothing live that had been tainted by the Dreadmount.

At last, the wyverns left, their creatures routed, trees blazing in their wake. As Tunuva cleaned the blood from her spear, Canthe emerged from a mining tunnel, caked in grey ash.

'Here. You've earned it,' she said, holding out a wineskin. 'I'm sorry I wasn't any help.'

'It's all right.' Tunuva took a long drink. 'You never claimed to be a warrior.'

'True.' Canthe glanced at the castle. 'The High Prince of Yscalin descends. He's asked to speak to you.'

'I want no truck with a prince of Virtudom.'

'The ports are closed, Tuva. We will need help to get to Inys.'

Tunuva drank again.

The High Prince of Yscalin rode down from his fortress on a warhorse. A sinewy man in his seventies, he had white hair, trimmed short at the back and sides, and the bright latten eyes that ran in his bloodline. For someone on borrowed years, he looked strong.

'I hear you're a fine warrior, Southerner,' he said in perfect Ersyri. 'What brings you to these mountains?'

'We hoped to take the Middle Pass.'

'Where are you bound?'

'Inys.'

'Then your road ends here. My sister has closed the ports to stop the spread of this blood sickness.'

'I see.'

'I can help you, for a modest price. I have royal prerogative to sail to Inys,' he said. 'We've been trying to reach the port at Garazna for some time, but the wyverns keep forcing us back to these mountains. Join my escort. If we survive, you shall have a place on my ship.'

'A kind offer, Your Highness,' Canthe said. 'We are happy to accept.'

'Good. We'll leave at noon.'

As Prince Guma went to consult his soldiers, Tunuva turned to her friend. 'I will serve no prince who loves the Deceiver,' she said under her breath. 'I am not a mercenary, Canthe.'

'The Middle Pass is a toll way, which Prince Guma happens to control. It's by far the swiftest road to Inys,' Canthe pointed out. 'Tuva, if we join him, we could be there before midsummer.'

Tunuva conceded with a nod. The faster they reached Inys, the faster she could return to her sisters.

The High Prince was a man of his word. By noon, he had amassed his household, his guard, and his possessions – among them a train of huge, engraved chests – and set out northwest to Garazna. Tunuva rode with Canthe and the knights, eyes on the sky.

The Middle Pass took them through the mountains, to the seared crags and folds of the Vetalda Plain. Salt cedar and basket grass clung to its puddles and dry streambeds. They passed smouldering wheat fields and an almond grove with its trees still afire.

Tunuva could almost smell the coming of the longest day. It did not bode well. Creatures from the Womb of Fire would only stand to gain from heat, while the stout Yscali carthorses were slow and foamed with sweat.

'Do you speak Ersyri?' she asked an old soldier, who glanced at her riding coat with suspicion. A copper brooch shone on his, shaped like a sandglass. 'What is in those chests?'

'Rare crimson gold of the Ufarassus. Part of the prince's dowry for the Queen of Inys.'

'Prince Guma is travelling to marry?'

'To rule,' he replied. 'He's already married her.'

He rode ahead – uncomfortable, no doubt, in the presence of a shameless heathen. Tunuva glanced at the chests. It seemed impossible that politics should go on in a time like this. News had slowed as the world burned, since messengers no longer rode save for the steepest fees, and few ships were permitted on the waves.

It soon became clear why Prince Guma had been hounded back to his castle time and again. There was little shelter on the Vetalda Plain, and within a few days, the wyverns sniffed them out. The Yscali knights nocked long arrows and drew, but for once, the creatures withheld their fire. Tunuva saw their eyes on her and realised they must sense her magic. She shot a footed arrow at the nearest, and they left with screams that echoed for miles.

Days turned into weeks. Prince Guma drove them hard, but Canthe made a good companion. She bore the heat well, and found reasons to smile, admiring the birds and the small yellow flowers that survived on the plain. Tunuva found she liked her more and more.

No friend could stifle her ache of Esbar. She feared for her, and for their sisters – Siyu, most of all. And never had she been so far from home without her ichneumon.

They passed a farming village that had been razed to char and bones. As the sun set, they reached Garazna, where a cog with plain sails waited, and armed guards came with pots of smoke to fumigate the cargo.

Nearby, hundreds of Yscals had gathered at a barrier. Tunuva only had a little Yscali, but it was enough to understand some of their pleas. 'My son,' a man was saying, desperate. 'My son is in Vazuva. Have mercy!'

'Prince Guma,' someone else shouted. 'Your Highness, let us take our own boats, I beg you!'

'That is not in my power,' Prince Guma said, cold and firm. 'Go home. Tend your farms for as long as you can. Yscalin still needs to eat.' Ignoring the turmoil, he glanced at Tunuva. 'It seems you brought us luck, warrior – the wyrmlings smelled death on your spear. What name do you go by?'

'Tunuva, Your Highness.'

'For your trouble, Tunuva.' He tossed her a fat purse. 'And you'll join us on the ship.'

'Thank you, virtuous prince,' Canthe said with a smile, before Tunuva could object. 'Your generosity is unrivalled.'

He grunted and rode on. Tunuva offered the purse to Canthe, who tucked it away.

The guards parted to let them through. Tunuva washed her hands in a barrel of red wine and stood to have her clothes smoked before she was permitted to set foot on the ship. Canthe found them a place below deck, where they lay on their cloaks and tried to cool down.

'What I would not give for a cold bath,' Canthe sighed. 'I already miss the Minara.'

Tunuva rested her head on her arm. 'How long will this voyage take?'

'As long as it takes.' Canthe looked at her. 'Tuva, we can still turn back.'

Tunuva gazed at the ceiling.

'No,' she said softly. 'I have carried this weight in my heart for too long. In the Priory, we learn to bear pain, as the Mother did ... but mine is like a wound that never healed, never became a scar. I will exalt her by seeking the truth. Truth is what sustains the Priory.'

'She would be proud.'

With a nod, Tunuva closed her eyes. As the ship forged into the Halassa Sea, she tried to still the restlessness inside and sleep.

****

Summer had always had a smell: corn ripening in the fields, wild-flowers courting honeybees. This summer stank of wool sticking to sweat, and turning earth, and fear. Where the farmworkers of

Arondine might once have been out shearing and reaping, they dug trenches. Where blacksmiths had made nails and horseshoes, they forged swords.

At the coming of wyrms, bells would ring across the city, warning people to make for the old tunnel and flee with all haste to the caves. To avoid confusion, there would be no bells for the Feast of Early Summer. So far, there had been no sound from the wyrms, either.

Wulf visited as often as he could, and yet her blood kept coming.

As Glorian watched him train with Thrit, her thoughts drifted elsewhere. It had been weeks, but she still thought of the light she had found in her dream, and the voice that had called for it.

'Glorian,' Florell said, interrupting her thoughts. 'Lady Marian is finally here.'

At once, Glorian looked to the east, where riders flew the banners of the House of Berethnet. 'I will meet her in the throne room,' she said, walking after Florell. 'See her in.'

The Regency Council had voted, by a narrow majority, to make her grandmother Lady Protector of Inys. Though she held the position in law, it had taken a season for Marian to even set out – first because of the heavy spring rains, which had burst the rivers of the Fens, then no sooner had the waters receded than Marian had been stricken with marsh fever.

Bourn arrived before anyone else, looking exhausted. 'Mastress,' Glorian said, 'thank you. Thank you for saving her.'

'Lady Marian fought hard, Your Grace. I only had a modest supply of a bark that eases fever.'

At last, Marian Berethnet, third of that name, appeared with her small and wayworn household, all of them in grey. She walked with a cane, and Mara Glenn held her free arm.

They took one another in. Their faces were almost the same: Marian was Sabran, as Sabran had been Glorian. All that set them apart was a few wrinkles, her stature, and the grey in her hair, which had almost overrun the black. Glorian was seeing her future self.

'Your Grace,' Marian said in a hoarse voice. Mara helped her into a curtsey. 'I come to serve at your command.'

'Grandmother, please, don't trouble yourself.' Glorian took her by the elbows. 'You are welcome to Arondine. I trust you are recovered from your sickness?'

'I still have aches and chills, but your healer saved my life. Mastress Bourn is Saint-touched.' Marian managed a smile. 'Let me look at you. Last we met, you were three.'

Glorian smiled back. A pale hand came to her face, and Marian released a soft breath.

'You are so like Sabran,' she said. 'You have her strength, and your father's, Glorian. I see it.'

'Come to the keep.' Glorian took her delicate arm. 'I've had a fine chamber prepared for you, close to mine.'

'You are kind. Cuthyll was terribly cold. Poor dear Mara, cooped up there with an old woman.'

'It was a privilege, my lady,' Mara said.

Glorian shot her a grateful look as they departed. 'You will not be sent away from court ever again. You are a former queen, and a Berethnet,' she told her grandmother. 'I have not forgotten.'

A fire lit the bedchamber, and a pottage of boiled beef was steaming. The Inysh were still working the fields where they could, but the harvest had already failed. It was only a matter of time until no one in Inys – not even a queen – could eat as they desired.

Glorian helped her grandmother into a chair and draped a heavy mantle around her shoulders. 'Sweet child. Thank you.' Marian drew it close. 'All this is more than I deserve, but I vow to earn my place at your court. I find I have grown sterner in my winter years.'

'Good. We must have iron in our bones.'

Marian chuckled. 'I remember your father saying that.' She took a goblet of hot wine from the table. 'Mara tells me Robart Eller is a heathen. He always seemed kind and diligent – I trusted him to serve your mother. It sickened me to learn of his plan for your marriage.'

'I chose it. Do not fear for me,' Glorian said. 'I have a plan of my own.'

Marian regarded her. 'You have found someone else to give you an heir.'

'Do you judge me?'

'I am in no position to judge. We do what we must to serve the Saint while not destroying ourselves.' Marian paused. 'Are you with child?'

For the first time in months, Glorian wanted to break. It had been so long since anyone had mothered her. 'It's not working,' she whispered. 'We've been trying since the winter.'

'There are some days when the chances are better. Do you trust your lover?'

'Yes.'

'Good.' Marian warmed her fingers on the goblet. 'Regardless of his discretion, he must still be gone before Prince Guma arrives. The risk of someone noticing your closeness is too great.'

'I know. Mother told me all my life that I had to be perfect, to make up for the queens before us,' Glorian said. Marian lowered her gaze. 'Grandmother, was Sabran the Fifth truly so cruel?'

'Yes, though sometimes I think it was because she was in pain herself. My own mother was not evil, but consumed by bitterness.' Her face was tight. 'Sabran – my Sabran – rose above it all. She was sure in herself, even as a child. I did as much as I could to protect her.'

'You raised a great queen.'

'Sabran raised herself. But you, Glorian – you, I will help,' Marian said. 'Do you mean to rule from Arondine?'

'Not for long. I will keep my court on the move, to throw the wyrms off our scent. Fýredel seems to have made this a personal matter. Where I go, I suspect it will follow.'

'The black wyrm,' Marian murmured. 'I never thought I would live to see a creature of its like.'

Glorian sat beside her. 'Only a year ago, all my parents had to fear were the Ments and the Carmenti,' she said. 'They seem such petty concerns now.'

'Such is politics.' Marian shook her head. 'A circle with no end. A game with no victors.'

It was comforting, to speak to someone who knew. Glorian laid her head on her shoulder. 'I'm glad you're here, Grandmother,' she said, closing her eyes. 'Let us survive this together.'

Marian only stroked her hair in answer, but Glorian felt a teardrop land like a kiss on the crown of her head.

****

Weak from her illness though she was, Marian was as good as her word. No sooner had she slept a night than she summoned the Regency Council to bring her abreast of their plans.

Glorian was summoned next. As soon as she entered the room, she knew something was wrong.

'Is it Fýredel?' she asked her councillors.

'No, Your Grace,' Lade Edith said, but still looked grim. 'The High Prince of Yscalin has arrived in Inys. He rides for Arondine.'

****

The sun died like a candle, leaving a soot of night in its wake. As servants lit the torches in the training yard, Thrit notched an arrow to his bow. Wulf leaned against a pell and watched him try to lengthen the draw.

The city guards had built a crude wyrm out of wood. With his body turned to the left, Thrit took aim at its head. He had mastered all Northern weapons at Fellsgerd, but his archery had suffered in the years since he had broken his collarbone, tearing a muscle in his right shoulder. While his dominant arm healed, Wulf had started teaching him to use the other.

Thrit breathed out. Muscle swelled in his left arm, and he released the arrow. It hit the wyrm dead in the eye, but not with enough force, and they watched it tilt limply and fall to the ground.

'Well, that's it.' Sweat stuck his hair to his brow. 'I might as well just roast myself, before a real wyrm gets there first.'

'It's nerves.'

Thrit cocked an eyebrow at him.

'You've built plenty of strength in that arm,' Wulf said, 'but you remember the pain of that hurt you took, and you're afraid of it happening again. The wound has moved to your mind.' He stepped towards Thrit. 'Nock it, go on. Draw.'

Thrit sighed and obeyed. Wulf stood close beside him and cradled his right elbow with a palm.

'Here.' He guided it up a little, making Thrit grimace. 'Does that hurt?'

Thrit considered. 'No, actually.'

'Good.' Wulf moved the same hand to his waist, then to the firm belt of muscle just below his navel. 'Brace your core.' Thrit did, with a slight catch of his breath. 'You're Hróthi. You've iron in your gut and nerves, not just your bones.' He stepped back. 'Try again.'

Thrit drew farther this time, face settled into a look of determination. When he let the arrow fly, it whipped across the courtyard, and this time, it stuck in the wyrm.

'Master Glenn.' They both turned to see Helisent Beck striding across the grass. 'Her Grace wishes to speak to you.'

She took him by the sleeve and conducted him back towards the castle, leaving Thrit to set another arrow to his bow.

'Prince Guma is in Inys,' she said, by way of explanation. She waited for Julain to clear the coast before they took the stairs to the royal bedchamber, where Glorian waited in her shift, hair rippling to her waist.

'Helisent told you,' she said, seeing his face.

'Aye.' Wulf locked the door behind him. 'How long before he comes?'

'He rides from Ascalun.'

'You're still not with child,' Wulf said quietly.

Her face was careworn. 'My grandmother told me there are points in my courses when making a child is more or less likely. Today would be a good time to try. After that, you must go back to Hróth.' She closed her eyes for a long moment. 'I may have to lie with him after all. Perhaps that was what the Saint always wanted.'

'Why would he ever want that?' Wulf asked her. 'Why would the Saint want any of this?'

'A test of faith.'

'Only a cruel man would test you so.'

He joined her at the window, looking out at the city and its glimmer of torches. Glorian leaned into his chest, and as he pressed her close, he felt her shivering.

'I will miss you,' she said. 'Pray for me.'

'I will.' He gathered her to his heart. 'I'll pray for you all the way to the North.'

66

East

The longest day of summer was called the godsbane in Seiiki. In years past, it had scorched the leaves and left even Antuma dry. Now, for the first time in centuries, there was a chance it would rain on that day.

There was hope in the rain. It dripped from the eaves. The gods might be weak, but at last, they were trying to water the island. Perhaps that also meant they would be strong enough to fight for it.

Dumai followed Epabo through the palace, sweating in her grey silks. Since her return in the spring, she had been left to grieve and mend, but now the emperor summoned her.

Her memory of the mountain was vague. She knew Furtia had carried her away from Brhazat, stopping when Nikeya spied Master Kiprun and Princess Irebül riding south, so Dumai could whisper what she had seen. After that, she remembered her bed at Antuma Palace.

And Nikeya. She remembered Nikeya – holding her close, talking to her, keeping her warm, all that way.

Epabo led her towards the Water Pavilion. Despite the lateness of the hour, courtiers lingered on the walkways, admiring the rain. They muttered in her wake. She was the princess who had come from nowhere, then flown away – not once, but twice – and now her face was proof of it. While she slept on the edge of death, Unora had cut a sliver of skin from her forehead, where freezeburn had set in, shaped like the blade of a sickle.

Dumai made no attempt to hide it. It was how she would remember Kanifa, how she would carry him with her. He had told her to see the comet. She meant to grant his final wish.

Her parents waited in the gloom. Unora had returned to court not long after Dumai, to help her heal from Brhazat. She patted the cushion, and Dumai knelt close beside her.

'Daughter,' Emperor Jorodu said. 'I am glad to see you. I hope your health is still improving.'

'I feel much better. Thank you, Father.'

'I am sorry you were confined for so long. The River Lord insisted on it, given this burning sickness.'

For now, the disease had not come to Seiikinese shores – the sea was a formidable defence – but the East was aflame, and fire always spread.

'Your grief will always stay with you,' her father told her, 'but you will grow stronger to bear it. I know this from experience, Dumai.'

Dumai could not bring herself to answer, though she nodded. She had not felt strong since Kanifa had cut the rope. Unora looked weary, she who had loved Kanifa like a son.

And Osipa, loyal to the end. She had died in her sleep of her age in the spring. Just as Dumai swallowed the taste of one loss, a new cup of grief had been forced to her lips. Court had never felt so empty, nor so friendless. It would be hard to bear it when her mother left.

'It is time for you to return to your duties as my heir,' Emperor Jorodu said. 'First, I would like you to lead a ceremony to thank the gods for this summer rain. The streams flow swift because of you, and your people must remember it. Let them see your bond with them.'

'Yes, Father.'

'Before that, I have news.' He nodded to Unora. 'Your mother and grandmother may have identified the stone you took from Brhazat. If so, you have found a treasure we had long thought lost.'

Unora took a layer of cloth from the middle of the table, revealing the oily blue stone.

'Empress Mokwo wrote of a stone that could command the waters and the winds. Even the gods heeded its call,' she said. 'It was said to resemble a moon, so the Grand Empress did expect it to be pale.'

Dumai watched her face. It had been a long time since she had seen her mother look nervous.

'The moon has been known to turn blue.' Emperor Jorodu wore a strange expression of his own. 'Mokwo claimed a human could use this stone, but that only a chosen few could wake it – that for others, it would turn to dead rock. It will not answer to my touch or my wish, but I wonder if it will to yours, Dumai.'

Dumai reached out to set a single fingertip on its surface. A gentle thrum answered.

'I feel the power churning in it … but I don't know how to draw it,' she said with a small frown, trying to articulate the feeling as it came. 'As if I had the hook and bait, and the water boils with life, but no fish come to me.' She released the stone. 'Why not go to Furtia for counsel, Father?'

'You must not.' Unora spoke very softly. 'The woman who last possessed this is dead. For all we know, it could have killed her. No human should wield the gods' power.'

'Yet we must keep it, else it could be stolen again. If the Kuposa found it—' Emperor Jorodu paused. 'Dumai, does the Lady of Faces know of it?'

'Perhaps, if she looked in my pouch.'

Nikeya had saved her. She remembered a white glow shining from her hand, arms around her, the desperate pleas. Furtia had followed her light, but Nikeya had pulled her into the saddle.

'I would not have lived without her,' Dumai said. 'She could have abandoned me to Brhazat.'

'And now you are indebted to her,' Emperor Jorodu said grimly. 'That has always been their way. The River Lord will try to take advantage of it, to move her into a higher position. We must act quickly now.' Unora covered the stone. 'Dumai, your mother will protect this relic on Mount Ipyeda. In the meantime, you must be enthroned.'

Dumai glanced at her mother in silent confusion. Unora seemed unable to meet her gaze.

'Father,' she said, 'there is no time for that. Surely we should concentrate on bolstering our defences.' Seeing his expression, she stopped, heart catching. 'What is it?'

'I have faced stiff resistance on the matter from the Council of State. They remain suspicious of your motives for ringing the Queen Bell.'

He always looked tired, but she saw both his age and his pain, in that moment. 'They cannot truly fear what they have not yet seen, Dumai. I think they are reluctant to send the provinces into upheaval.'

'What do they imagine wyrmfire will do there?'

'I know. That is why we must conclude our plans soon. This stone is yet another sign that you are meant to save our house. If you are right – if a comet will stop this – then you must be empress when it does. I plan to abdicate in the autumn, at the usual time for new appointments. As your grandmother and I have planned, I will continue to hold authority from retirement. By splitting our power, we will break theirs.'

He paused to glance regretfully at Unora, who had set her jaw, eyes downcast. Dumai waited.

'I also hope to betroth you soon,' he said. 'To ensure we eclipse the Kuposa for good, it is important that we foster closer ties with the other clans. We must not leave your sister as the only heir.'

It took Dumai almost more strength than she had to keep her face steady. 'Yes, Father,' she said. 'As you command.'

****

Later, she sat on the porch, watching dawn thread the horizon with scarlet, trying not to think of what would come after the comet. It might bring the wyrms down, but she would be left with the task of saving the House of Noziken. For the first time, she grasped what that meant.

She had thought she could fly her way through this new life. In the end, she would have to lengthen the rainbow.

Sweat pricked at her brow. She looked towards Mount Ipyeda, and imagined Kanifa looking back – a ghost of him, always present, like the worn strand of rope she kept at her wrist. She thought of Nikeya, always somewhere in her mind, tucked there like a splinter.

And she knew it would rip her apart, in the end – this yearning that pulled at the seams of her being, and the duty that sewed her tighter by the day, into the robes of the Empress of Seiiki.

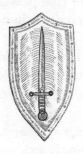

67

West

Arondine meant *eagle valley*, but the Inysh referred to it as the High City, wrapped as it was around a hill. Tunuva and Canthe joined a line at its gates with cloth over their noses and mouths. They washed their hands in vinegar before they were let past, into its overcrowded streets.

'Who's stipulating this nonsense?' someone grumbled in their wake. 'Waste of good vinegar.'

'Aye, my sleeves reek.'

Tunuva kept her hood up. She was still not used to Inysh towns – the noise and smells, the winding streets. In the South, settlements tended to be spread across more ground, allowing the buildings and people to breathe.

Only the castle rose from the crush. It must command a view of the whole valley from its height.

'Queen Glorian is here, then.' Canthe looked up at it with interest. 'I did not expect that.'

Tunuva followed her gaze. A banner flew from its main turret, white against the pall of the sky. Once more the sun looked sickly, its edge as clear as a bare rib. A match for the bruised moon.

'Clearly her consort had no idea, either,' she said. 'Did he not tell us he was bound for Ascalun?'

'He did.' Canthe grasped her hand. 'Come. I don't want to lose you in this crowd.'

It had been a hard journey from the coast. They had taken a stone causeway through the Marshes, where mist wafted off slick reed swamps, turning the sunlight to milk. Though they had faced no creatures on the trade road, fire had scarred the land. Fields and farmsteads lay in ruin; barns and granaries had burned. Canthe had eventually learned that a flock of wyverns had come in the winter, led by a great wyrm named Fýredel.

Arondine had escaped their trail of destruction. Tunuva followed Canthe along its steep and grimy streets. The castle was one of a very few stone buildings; most were black oak, roofed with straw. Small wonder that foreboding laced the city – one kiss of fire could bring it down.

It still unstrung her to be in the land of the Deceiver. From the sea it had looked bleak, but inland it was soft and green, rich in wildflowers and moss. *I always thought it must be a cold and barren place, for the Deceiver to have left it*, she had told Canthe.

Cold, yes, but not barren. Galian had a thirst for glory. A modest life on this island would not have been enough for him.

Arondine was a large city by Inysh standards, but not large enough for the sheer number of people it was trying to hold. Thousands had fled to its cobbles, choosing the fortified streets over living off the land. All wore the grey of mourning for their fallen monarchs.

Other than the castle, the most imposing structure was round and built of ivory brick, its roof an ornate dome. It must be stronger than all the rest put together. 'Hyll Sanctuary,' Canthe said, seeing her look. 'This is where the Inysh praise the Saint and the Damsel.' Tunuva clenched her jaw. 'I understand it's hard to bear, Tuva. They don't know any better.'

'Yet they happily believe an Inysh knight was the only person who could save Yikala.'

'Questioning the story is said to imperil their place in Halgant.'

Canthe stopped dead. A young woman in chainmail had emerged from the castle, riding a grey horse.

Engraved silver ringed her brow. Her skin was pale, her hair long and black. She rode up to the sanctuary and spoke to the two well-dressed men on its steps, who seemed to be overseeing an excavation.

'That can't be the Queen of Inys.' Tunuva frowned. 'She looks younger than Siyu.'

'I'd say so. That must be her grandmother, Marian,' Canthe added, when another woman came into sight. 'Each Berethnet queen looks identical to the last. It's called the Saint's Marvel.'

'How can Guma Vetalda be married to a girl of her age?'

Canthe looked at the queen, her expression clouded.

'Glorian must need an heir very quickly,' she said. 'After all, her people believe that if her bloodline should ever fail, the Nameless One will be unleashed upon the world.'

Tunuva stared at her. 'That is absurd,' she whispered. 'It's a lie.'

'Shh, Tuva.' Canthe drew her into a doorway. 'You must be careful of your words. Yes, Galian built a legacy upon the lie, and now his descendants grow it in their wombs, one after the next. The Inysh believe his blood is the fetterlock. Did you not know?'

'We knew of their belief that Galian swung the sword. Not this.'

A lie her birthson must have been raised to believe. Tunuva had never understood why so many realms clung to monarchy, but now she saw how the Deceiver had reinforced it in his land.

By the time they reached the right house, she had swallowed the knowledge, in all its bitterness. Canthe unhooked a key from her girdle. 'You still have homes across Inys?' Tunuva asked, counting thirteen keys.

'Oh, yes. Every good witch needs her lair,' Canthe said drily, and showed Tunuva through the door.

The room was cramped, with one small window to let in the light. Though the building looked humble from the outside, the rushes on the floor were fresh, mingled with herbs. Tunuva flicked a tongue of flame into the hearth.

'I'll find us supper.' Canthe set down her cloak. 'And ask in the city about Wulfert Glenn.'

'Should I come?'

'No need. You rest, Tuva.'

Canthe went straight back out. Tunuva hung her damp clothes by the fire rolled on to one of the beds. She pulled a blanket over herself and fell into a deep slumber.

She woke with a start when Canthe returned, a basket on her arm. 'I paid a considerable price for two loaves,' she said, sinking on to the bed beside Tunuva. 'Fortunately, wine still flows in Inys.'

Tunuva sat up and rubbed her eyes. 'Good. I think I need it.'

Smiling, Canthe poured them a cup each. Tunuva drank hers to the bottom, craving the warmth and softness of it. She had finished two more before she had the courage to ask.

'Did you hear anything of him?'

Canthe put down her own cup. 'Queen Sabran and King Bardholt died on their way to a wedding in Vattengard. No one knew how it happened ... until a lone survivor returned to Ascalun. A young man who somehow endured the icy waters for days before he washed ashore in Hróth, still breathing. He was the one to tell Queen Glorian that Fýredel had burned the fleet.'

'Wulfert Glenn?'

'Yes, Tuva.'

The feeling went from her fingers. 'The siden in his blood.'

'I thought the same. Even unlit, it might have warmed him just enough to keep him at the brink of death.'

'It must be him. You were right,' Tunuva said, swallowing. 'We have to find him. He could have drowned or frozen in that sea, and I would never have known. He has to hear the truth.'

'We will, Tuva. I have brought you this far.'

Their eyes met, and held.

Silence rose like unsettled dust. Canthe leaned into it, through it. The hope in her eyes was naked, tormented – a hope faced with its own demise. She still reached for Tunuva and placed a fragile kiss on her lips, and in one terrible moment, disarmed by the sweet joy of hope, Tunuva kissed her back.

The wine hung on her head and slackened everything. Canthe slid both hands up her waist, pressing their brows together, sinking into the embrace. Through a haze, Tunuva looked into her eyes. All she could see was sorrow, depthless as the midnight sky, and now it was in her as well, solitude and desolation. They bore the same pain; they shared the same loss. All they had in this place was each other. Before she knew it, she had drawn Canthe close.

The room seemed to have fallen out of time. Canthe embraced her, the green wool of her gown pleating around her hips. She wore nothing beneath. Tunuva slowly unlaced her, craving the warm comfort of skin and touch. A faint sound of relief escaped Canthe. Her hair tumbled loose, and she freed her shoulders from the gown, so it sank to her waist. Tunuva lay back, and Canthe kissed the notch at the base of her throat.

And yet Tunuva could not slip into the lilt of intimacy. The rosehip lips on hers were numbing. Her own fire burned, but she had been untethered from her senses, and no longer felt it. Canthe framed her face with those cold hands, breathing her name like a last wish.

Don't leave me again. The memory of a warmer kiss, the right and only one. *You steady me, lover.*

It woke her from the trance. She broke away. Canthe let go at once, and Tunuva closed her eyes, heart pounding.

'I can't, Canthe.'

They sat in the grip of an uneasy silence. 'Tuva,' Canthe said, 'I'm sorry. I should never have—'

'You are unattached. I am the one who is at fault,' Tunuva said firmly. 'Forgive me, my friend. These past weeks have tested my strength. I wish I could offer the comfort you seek.'

Canthe had covered her breasts. Her face was tired and guarded, the light leaving her eyes.

'Perhaps in another life.' She sat up, drawing her hair to one side of her neck. 'There is nothing to forgive. The fault is mine. I have a wont for choosing hearts … to which another holds the key.' Slowly, she stood. 'Esbar will not hear of this. You have my word.'

She lay down on the other bed. Tunuva looked at her back for some time before she turned over.

Esbar, my love, forgive me.

When she woke again, Canthe was no longer there.

****

Glorian rose from a deep sleep with the certainty that someone was inside her bedchamber.

She sat up, reaching for the sword by her bed. As she found its hilt, the darkness resolved itself into a tall figure, standing by her window, outlined by the faint light from the city.

'Don't be afraid.'

The voice was cool and soft. 'Who is that?' Glorian was shivering. 'Sister?'

'No, child. It is your mother.'

'Mama.' Ice sweated from her face. 'No. You are dead. You are in Halgalant.'

'I have descended from that hall to bring a message from the Saint,' the voice said. 'I know you long to hear his voice, and you must know he loves you, child. He sees you.'

'In spite of my vice?'

'He forgives his queens, through the merciful Damsel.' Slow footsteps. 'You cannot defeat this enemy, Glorian. But I vow to you, this age of fire and smoke will end. A star will come at morning on the first day of spring. It will be a day of fallen night, when the heavens will part for a rain from on high. The wyrms will sink into a sleep, and storms will quench the embers.'

'When will they wake again?'

'That is not for you to fear.'

The figure was close now. Her skin broke into goosebumps as a hand came to caress her cheek.

'I miss you,' Glorian whispered, tears spilling over. 'I miss Papa.'

'We have found our seats at the Great Table. There is no pain in the hall of the dead.' Fingertips came under her chin. 'You called for a sister. Who is that you see at night?'

'She has no face, but she is a voice in my head. I used to hear her often; now I hear her less.'

'This voice, does it offer you counsel?'

'Yes. I was sixteen when I first heard it.' Glorian could barely hear herself. 'I have thought all manner of things, but ... now I wonder if she was you, Mother. If she is the voice of all our ancestors. Did I summon you to me tonight by sending the light she asked for?'

'She is not you, nor me. She is a secret you must take to your tomb – a truth that can never be spoken.'

'I will not speak of her, not as long as I live. I know I must not,' Glorian whispered, 'but Mother, please don't take her from me. I never feel more alone than when she is silent.'

There was silence now, for a long time. 'Then I will seek her out for you,' the voice said. 'Only open the doors of your dream to me, daughter.'

Glorian had no idea how to obey, but she nodded. The ghostly hand came to the side of her head, giving her hair a tender stroke, and next she knew, it was morning. She sat up to an empty room, entangled in the sheets, and cold.

****

610

She broke her fast with Marian. Everything tasted sour of late, but she ate every scrap of bread and every crumb of cheese, not wanting to waste a morsel. 'We are swiftly running out of flour,' her grandmother murmured. 'I understand there will be little food from now on.'

'What should we do?'

'We can make sure what we have is shared equally. You can pass a law to restrict the raising of prices, but we cannot make grain ripen in darkness.' Marian sighed. 'It gives me no pleasure to speak of all we *cannot* do, after my reign, but I do not see how Inys will survive if Fýredel returns.'

'It will.' Glorian waited for her stomach to settle. 'Grandmother, did the Saint ever speak to you?'

'No.' Marian smiled, a little wryly. 'I was too quiet for him to notice me.'

'I had a dream last night. An apparition. Mother told me all of this would finish in the spring.'

Marian set down her knife. 'Sabran,' she said. 'She came to you from Halgalant?'

Glorian nodded. 'She told me the wyrms would fall into a sleep.'

'That gives me great heart. I only wish I knew how to explain this to the Regency Council.'

'You must not try. Mother told me I should keep my dreaming to myself.' Glorian looked at her. 'Will you find out if we can last until spring?'

'I will.'

Just then, Florell knocked on the door to the Little Hall. 'Your Grace, Lady Protector, forgive me.' Her face was pinched. 'Prince Guma has passed Bothenley. He will be here by dusk.'

Glorian found her mouth was too dry to answer. 'Of course, Florell,' her grandmother said. 'I will assemble the Regency Council to welcome His Highness.' Once Florell was gone, Marian lowered her voice: 'Glorian, have you had your blood since your lover last visited?'

'No. It would usually come in a day or two.' Glorian wrung her fingers. 'I have sent him away.'

'Good. If your efforts were in vain, we will find someone else.' Marian leaned across the table, her gaze sharpening. 'Prince Guma does not know that we have discovered his plot with Lord Robart. What do you wish to do, Glorian?'

Somewhere above the castle, a white-tailed eagle called.

'Mother told me that a queen should know the right moment to strike, and when she need not strike at all,' Glorian said. 'I believe we should let things play out with Prince Guma, and allow him to think we are ignorant. For now.'

'That guidance may have come from Sabran,' Marian said, eyes twinkling, 'but the head of a tactician sits upon your shoulders, Glorian Óthling. In this, you are your father.'

Glorian allowed herself a smile.

She busied herself for the rest of the day, riding to see the tunnel and catapults. She visited the blacksmiths at the forges, the bowyers and fletchers working in the lists. Fighters had come from all over the province, pitching camp at the walls when they found little room inside. Most had no weapons; instead, they held the tools they had once used to work the fields. Glorian supposed a well-aimed pitchfork could be as lethal as a sword.

The Yscali soldiers would be a great help. From what she knew, Prince Guma had a scrupulously trained army, to deter raiders and bandits. Soon a portion of it would be at her command.

'There is the matter of tax,' Leodyn Eller said as they inspected the ditches. She was the new Duchess of Generosity, second cousin to the heathen. 'It seems unlikely most will be able to pay.'

'My companion brings a substantial dowry,' Glorian said. 'Let him pay for those who can't.'

'Of course, Your Grace.'

All the talk of tax and weapons in the world could not stop the inevitable. At sunset, her consort forded the River Tyrnan on a destrier. Glorian watched him from the castle walls.

She met him in chainmail. Men who reached their seventies were often stooped and frail, but Guma Vetalda had been reared on mountain air and the alible food of Yscalin. Glorian stood an inch past six feet, yet he was taller, stout in the chest, with receded white hair, combed back from his brow, matching a short neat beard. Like most members of the Vetalda family, he had tawny eyes, a shock against his deep suntan, and his mouth was stern, with a scar below a thin sliver of bottom lip.

Look past all the features a person cannot help, Queen Sabran had told Glorian once. *Look at what they choose to put upon themselves.*

His finery was marked, but understated. Each fastening of his leather coat was shaped like the Vetalda pear, and his patron brooch – a shield – was cast in the same red gold. It sat discreetly on his lapel.

'Your Grace.' His voice was gruff, with an Yscali roll. 'I am Guma Vetalda, High Prince of Yscalin.' He eyed the castle. 'And now, prince of this land as well.'

'I am glad you found us, Your Highness,' Glorian said. 'I apologise for our absence from Ascalun. These are chaotic times – I fear a messenger may not have reached you.'

'Evidently.'

She sensed the Regency Council shifting, even those who had pushed for this match. Now they were faced with the royal couple, no one could deny the horrific absurdity of it.

'You are welcome to Arondine Castle,' Glorian said. 'My court will be here until the wyrms find us. Our food stores are dwindling, but we will give you what we can, after your journey.'

'We bring food of our own. Since grain now holds more immediate value than gold, half of my dowry comes in that form – I have lands the wyrms have not yet found. Our people will not go hungry, Your Grace.'

'You are most generous.' Glorian offered a smile. 'Please, rest and refresh yourselves – I have some eventide duties in the city. Sir Granham Dale will see your retinue settled.'

'Where is the Lord Protector?' He searched the faces behind her. 'I expected Lord Robart.'

'Sadly, Lord Robart is unwell. We fear he has the blazing plague,' Glorian said. 'While he is confined to his castle, my grandmother, Lady Marian Berethnet, acts as my regent.'

He was too well-trained to betray himself. 'I wish Lord Robart a swift return to health, though I fear he will not recover. There seems to be no cure.' After a pause, he said, 'The journey was long – I will speak to your castellan, to find my own chamber tonight. Goodnight, Your Grace.'

Glorian watched him leave. Whenever he was ready, she was.

68

East

'Princess.'

Dumai stirred with a faint headache. 'Juri. Is it time?' she said, hoarse. 'Have the wyrms come?'

'No, Your Highness.' Juri faltered on the threshold. 'Are you well?'

'Yes.' Dumai sat up a little, rubbing her eyes. She had not meant to sleep. 'What is it?'

'Her Majesty has sent you a message.'

Juri held out a knot of fine paper, which Dumai opened with care. *For the attention of the Crown Princess, whose sister is eager to see her*, it read. *Please come at the hour of the conch.*

Osipa would have told her to make an excuse, but Dumai could not bring herself to turn her back on Suzumai. The child was only eight, as innocent of politics as she remained of wyrms.

'Very well.' Dumai pushed the bedding away. 'Will you help me dress?'

'Yes, of course.'

The rain had lightened to a mist, sometimes fattening to drops. On her flights, Dumai dressed almost as she had on Mount Ipyeda, but now she found herself enclosed in heavy robes again.

Yapara was even rougher than usual, combing as if she wanted to rip out a hank of hair, and now there was no Osipa to stop her. 'You seem troubled, Lady Yapara,' Dumai said. 'Unburden your mind, if you wish.'

Yapara upheld her indifferent expression.

'This gentle rain is beautiful,' she said, 'but it reminds me that the gods are not yet as strong as they were. One can only wonder why they had to be disturbed.'

'I assure you that the gods know my reason.' Dumai looked at the window. 'I fear everyone will know it soon.'

Nothing more was said. Until the wyrms came, she would be an object of ridicule or misgiving at court, warning of an enemy no one could see. It would end, but it would be a bitter triumph.

As she crossed the palace, she tried not to look for Nikeya. Instead of dulling the ache, a season of separation had richened it. Each time Dumai did catch a glimpse of her – always at her periphery, usually with her fellow Kuposa – it stayed with her for days, like a bruise.

Nikeya had saved her, yet suddenly they were apart. The will of the emperor, perhaps. She ought to be relieved.

Nights offered some reprieve. She was haunted then not by a woman or wyrms, but a vision of a snowbound valley. It reminded her of her flying dreams, the ones she had often dreamed at the temple. Her mirror sister had reached out while she lay on the brink of death, and after – but Dumai could not remember their conversations, or even if she had answered.

It was time to face her other sister. The one she had usurped.

Suzumai was in her nightclothes, watched by the chief Lady of the Bedchamber as she played on the floor, absorbed in a story she was mumbling to herself. When Dumai stepped into the room, the woman retreated with a small bow, and Suzumai looked up.

'Dumai?' she said in wonder. She rushed to her and wrapped her arms around her waist, pressing her face there. 'I missed you so much. You were away for such a long time.'

'I hope I will not go away again.' Dumai knelt in front of her, brushing a tear from her cheek. 'Don't be upset, Suzu. I am here now. We have not spoken in some time, have we?'

Suzumai shook her head. 'You fly away so often with the great Furtia. One of my uncles says it is because you have grander concerns than Seiiki,' she said. 'I didn't understand. You are to be empress, and I am going to help you. You must not *want* to go so often.'

Which uncle she meant, Dumai had no idea. The empress had several brothers. 'Your uncle misunderstands why I leave,' she told Suzumai. 'I go to help Seiiki, not to run from it, Suzu.'

'Could a dragon take me over the sea?' Suzumai said, drying her tears. 'Then I wouldn't have to swim. I could see everywhere, the whole entire world. Do you think I could ride one, like you?'

'I hope you can.' Dumai looked at the floor. 'You have so many fine toys.'

Suzumai nodded earnestly. 'Would you like to see my dollhouse?' she asked, taking Dumai by the hand to tug her to it. 'My granduncle gave it to me. He makes it better every year. Do you like it?'

'The River Lord is very generous.' Dumai crouched with her, seeing that it was a miniature recreation of Antuma Palace, perfect in every detail. 'Did he give you the dolls, too?'

'Yes.' Suzumai gathered them up. 'He made sure all of us are here, all safe and together. This one is me,' she said, showing Dumai the smallest doll. 'Here is Father and Mama, and my nurse, and my cousins – and you. He made you, Dumai.' Suzumai showed her. 'I kept her with me all the time when you were gone. I thought if I looked after her, then you would be safe, too.'

'That was very thoughtful of you, Suzu,' Dumai said, touched. 'You did keep me safe.' She studied the wooden figure, its fixed and placid smile. The hair was real. 'I see many great and noble people in your dollhouse, but not the River Lord. Did you lose him?'

'He never gave me a doll of himself. I wanted one – he is so generous and clever,' Suzumai said wistfully, 'but he said he felt silly, giving himself to me as a present. He's funny.'

Dumai looked down at her doll self again. 'Yes,' she said. 'Where is your granduncle now?'

'I think he went away. Will you play with me?' Suzumai asked her. 'Just for a little while?'

Dumai forced another smile, even as her insides soured. 'I will stay for as long as you like,' she promised, and when Suzumai embraced her again, she held the child as close as she could.

****

Suzumai soon tired of the dolls, and they sat on a garden porch to star-gaze and keep watch for dragons. Their patience was rewarded when Pajati the White appeared, silent and beautiful, swimming through the hazy sky as if it were the sea. Suzumai gazed after him in amazement.

Comes the star of life and balance, now the sower of cold chaos . . . closer by the night, not yet here . . .

Dumai tensed, eyes closing. His voice washed right the way through her, surprising her with its clarity. He sounded even closer than Furtia. Then again, Pajati was an ancient elder dragon, who was thought to have come from the sky.

Exhausted by so much excitement, Suzumai fell asleep, clutching the dolls representing both of them. Dumai gathered her into her lap and looked back to the sky, wondering.

'She loves you.'

Empress Sipwo had stepped on to the porch, hair cascading to her waist. She came to stand beside Dumai.

'Even when your father told her she would not be empress, she never stopped,' she said, gazing towards where the mist hid the mountains. 'She said it was right that you ruled Seiiki, because you were her big sister, the eldest, a rider. Not once did she resent you for it.'

'She is a very kind child. It must have been hard to keep her that way.'

'That is why I am grateful you came. Suzu is too small for that cold seat.' As the empress leaned down to take her, she said in a low voice, 'I believe you struck the Queen Bell with reason. I believe the gods speak to you, and through you. My uncle is wrong to deny this.'

'Then will you persuade him to listen to me, if I speak of what I have seen on my travels?'

'He has gone to attend to his estates in the northern wetlands. When he returns, I will try to open his ear – but this world is his world, Dumai. It may be his world for a long time yet.'

Not if it ends, Dumai thought. *Then it will not even be the gods' world.*

'Your Majesty,' she said as Empress Sipwo turned to leave. 'When I came back from Sepul, the River Lord sent my parents a sorrower. He said you killed it.'

'I did. I fear those birds,' came her soft reply, 'but I never asked him to send it to Jorodu or Unora.' She gave Suzumai a kiss on the top of her head, where a crown would sit the heaviest. 'I will not keep you, Dumai. Thank you for seeing Suzu. She has missed her big sister.'

****

It came on her as brutally as a snowslide – the feeling of being shut in a box, pressed into a space that had never fit her. Suddenly her layers were

617

smothering, and the air weighted not with rain, but with dread. As she walked back to her own quarters, the dollhouse locked itself around her thoughts. By the time she reached her bedchamber, she was breathless and clammy.

'Juri, please, help me out of all this,' she said. The handmaiden rushed to assist her, leaving her in her underrobe. 'I need nothing else. You may do as you please this evening.'

The girl shepherded the others away. Dumai sank to the floor. There was no Osipa to guide her, no Kanifa to make her smile. *I do not want this.* Panting, she pressed a hand flat to her stomach, the other to the mats. *I have never wanted this. This is not me . . .*

Brhazat had been in the spring. Now it was deep into the summer, and she had done nothing for Seiiki. Kanifa had let go of his life to save hers, yet she was still a wooden doll, waiting to be picked up and placed. Not until this moment had she understood, in full, what Princess Irebül had said in Golümtan. *That palace is a silken cage, and Hüran are not meant for walls.*

Neither was she. She was meant for the sky. Was that not where a rainbow belonged?

It took her time to think clearly again. When she did, she was ashamed, sitting there with her fine clothes and fresh water, squandering her salt. Her mother had not been able to cry at all when she lived in a dust province, even when death had surrounded her.

Dumai blotted her face with her sleeves. She was a fool for weeping. Exhausted, she undressed to her skin and crawled to her bedding, where she slid into a light and fitful sleep.

There you are.

At once, she was in the dreamers' land – but this time, it was as sharp as the waking realm. Above, the fog had thinned, and she made out a silver net over the sky, stars glistening at its crossways, most of them almost too faint to see. She could hear the stream so clearly.

On the other side, the figure had solidified. She stood with uncharacteristic stillness.

Sister. Dumai turned to face her fully. *I am so relieved to hear your voice. I have never felt more alone in my life.*

You are not alone. You have not been alone for a long time.

You saved me. She found she could open her eyes and still just about see it all. *You feel . . . different.*

So do you. I feel your pain, your restlessness. You feel trapped. That is why you reached for me again. The voice rang clear and calm, all wariness

618

gone. *And yet I also feel a great power from you. I sense that something lost has finally been recovered.*

You know. Dumai shifted on to her side, moulding herself back into the fragile boundaries of the dream. *If you know what I have found, then you know how to use it, too. It will not answer my call, as you do.*

That is because it has another half, which I possess.

You. Her eyes darted beneath their lids, matching the thunderstrokes of her heart. *You have a stone, too?*

A piece of the star was broken in twain. The star that will calm the fire back into the deep earth, for a time.

I feel it coming. Above, the stars glowed. *Is this why the gods brought us together?*

My sister, it must be. I understand now. We must join our two halves, to hold off this destruction. The figure walked towards their stream. *Your dreams have shown you where I am. Come while we still have time.*

I still do not know who you are, or where that valley lies.

I am your friend. Now we are both stronger, you can follow our bond all the way to my side. A bridge appeared. *Do not be afraid. Let me show you the naked truth of our power, given to us by the sky.*

She stepped straight over the stream, and touched Dumai.

That touch ripped away her illusion of dreaming. She knew, she *knew* she was awake – and yet the dream went on, bridge and bedchamber entwined, and the figure rose before her, still faceless.

It was dark in the room. A weight crushed her chest. Her body trembled, naked and clammy. A hand made of shadow had come to her cheek. She smelled and tasted icy steel, pierced with a sweet bitterness.

The cold washed from her face to her palm. She stared at the hand with shortened fingers, where a light had danced to life, a flickering star. *All of this is real*, the voice said, as the figure released her. *Leave now, and you will reach me in time.*

The vision disappeared. Seized as if by a water ghost, Dumai bolted upright, as chilled as if she had eaten snow. Sweat dripped from her hair, slicking her wet and cold as a dragon.

At the entrance to the Water Pavilion, the guards' spears blocked her way. 'I must see His Majesty at once,' she said.

Her apprehension must be burning like a fever in her eyes. When she was finally shown into his quarters, she found Emperor Jorodu beside a hearth.

619

'Dumai.' He beckoned her towards a cushion. 'You look shaken, daughter. Sit with me.'

She could hardly get the words out. 'Father, I know this will sound reckless, given what remains at stake, but I must beg your leave to depart. I must fly.' Kneeling, she looked him in the eyes. 'A messenger has come to me. It is the culmination of many dreams – those I had on Mount Ipyeda, and after, when I came to court.'

She told him all of it. He listened without interrupting, fervour quickening his gaze.

'Such dreams are a rare gift, but they run in our house,' he said, when she was hoarse from talking. 'Dumai, do you think this figure is a messenger spirit, sent by Kwiriki?'

'Or someone touched by the gods' power, as we are,' Dumai said. 'The Grand Empress believes the stone our ancestor sought was white. What if she is not mistaken?'

'You mean you think there are two stones?'

'They might help us to fight the wyrms.' Dumai removed her gauntlet. 'See for yourself that this is real, Father.' She held up her hand, with the palm facing him. 'A remnant of the dream.'

'I needed no convincing.' Her light floated in his eyes. 'You think she will give you the other stone?'

'Or show me how to wake mine, at least.'

'But the wyrms, Dumai – it's too dangerous.'

'I have survived before.'

Emperor Jorodu seemed to think. 'You are supposed to be visiting the Grand Empress soon,' he said, with a growing smile. 'That gives you an excuse to leave court. I could even send a cart to Mount Ipyeda, as if it had you in it. All of this would buy you time.'

'You will let me go?'

'Your grandmother would insist I did. Clearly she saw your affinity with the gods, and even the emperor must heed their call. Your mother may not understand, but we do,' he said. 'We are Noziken.'

Dumai watched him rise and cross the room, opening a hidden compartment in the floor.

'I entrust the blue stone to you.' He took out a small box, for preserving woodfall. 'You will also need protection, if you are to fly into the chaos beyond our island.'

She waited. He turned back to her with a sword in his hands. Its openwork pommel formed a leaping golden fish within a circle, and studs ran the course of its single-edged blade.

'This sword belonged to Queen Nirai. It is called Nightborn,' he said, 'and soon it will belong to you. Take it, to defend yourself.'

It looked a heavy thing to wield. Dumai started to reach for it, then lowered her hand.

'Your Majesty, it is too magnificent a gift. I have not the skill or stomach to use this,' she said. 'I am content with my ice sickles. Kanifa made them for me. I know they will keep me safe.'

Emperor Jorodu smiled again.

'Perhaps this is a wise decision,' he said. 'You should be free to make your own legacy, Dumai – but you must take armour this time, for your mother's sake, and mine. You ride into a war.' He set the sword down, and presented her with the small box instead, a cover for the stone within. 'You have been a gift to me, daughter. Bring us the sum of all your dreams, so we may win the battle to come. The battle that may yet decide if any of us will be left to remember.'

****

Epabo brought the armour from where the saddle had been found – a fortified jacket, broad plates of iron sewn on to cloth. In the Rain Pavilion, Dumai tied back her hair and covered it with a hood that fastened under her chin, reinforced with twisted metal rings. Heavy sleeves for her shins and arms came next, then her furs and riding boots.

Furtia, do you hear me?

The dragon sounded distant: *The air thickens. This way comes the fever of a shattered earth.*

Great one, I must ask for your help once more. She retrieved her ice sickles. *Will you come to me?*

Careful not to wake her handmaidens, she took her secret way into the Floating Gardens and waded out to the nearest island, as she once had to meet Kanifa. This was the only part of the palace where a dragon might land without being seen. She took a lantern from the bridge and carried it with her, into the dark.

'Dumai?'

She turned with a hand on one of her ice sickles. When a figure stepped into her light, she breathed out.

'Nikeya,' she said, releasing the handle. 'What are you doing here?'

'I came for a late walk.' Nikeya took Dumai in, from her boots to her hood. 'Dumai, the heir can't keep flying away. If you leave a third time, the Council of State will think you are disloyal to Seiiki. The River Lord has already sown that particular seed among the nobles.'

'May I not visit my own grandmother?'

'I had no idea the Grand Empress was so dangerous that you need armour,' Nikeya said in amusement.

'My armour,' Dumai said, 'is none of your concern.' They both stopped to watch Furtia soar overhead and descend, the light from her scales bobbing on the black water. 'I will return before long. Do not speak to anyone of this, if you value your position here.'

'All this time at court, and you still can't make a threat. Or tell a lie.' Nikeya raised her eyebrows. 'There is a way to guarantee my silence. Let me come with you.' When Dumai looked away, Nikeya lost patience and took her by the chin. 'Wherever you are going, you might need help. Why should I have saved you if I meant you harm?'

'To win my trust.'

'Frankly, I think I deserve it. And I find that I have dreamed of flying.'

Dumai had little time to decide. In that moment, it was simpler to take her than to leave her.

'It will be a harsh ride,' she said. 'I do not plan to stop often. There is no time to retrieve your furs.'

'No need. I stored them here, in the gardens.' Nikeya released her. 'I always knew we would ride again, Princess.'

****

The Sundance Sea washed a long grey beach on the northern coast of Seiiki. It had no formal name, for the fishers' huts there were rotting, and its salt kilns had not burned in years.

As dawn broke, a boat struck out from its shore. The man inside sculled away from the cliffs, nets and pot traps clustered around him, tears slick on his face, his fingers red around the oars. He would make his way to a physician he knew, at the busy port of Cape Ufeba.

69

West

The young Queen of Inys rode among her people again. Tunuva watched from the steps of Hyll Sanctuary as Glorian Berethnet offered them comfort, nodding to her guards to give them bread or coin.

She claimed descent from Cleolind, but that could not be. Yet there must have been a Queen Cleolind of Inys – someone who was not the Mother, but had stolen her identity. Tunuva might never know who it had been, for that woman was long dead.

Glorian disappeared into the throng. Tunuva looked up once more at Hyll Sanctuary, which now served as the main entrance to a siege tunnel. Galian Berethnet gazed down from its walls, holding Ascalun. No sign of his queen consort.

Canthe had been away for days, seeking news of Wulfert Glenn. Fortunate, since Tunuva had wanted time to herself. She had never learned embarrassment or shame, but she did know remorse, and it filled every day.

She made her way back to the cramped room, where she poured herself a measure of sour Inysh wine, more than she would usually drink. Every day Canthe was gone was another day her sisters needed her spear.

Mother, she prayed, *let me see him, just once. Let it be enough.*

At midnight, Canthe finally returned. 'How was your journey?' Tunuva asked her.

'Hard. I am sorry for the wait, Tuva. Many roads are closed to hinder the plague.' Canthe lowered her hood. 'I was able to speak to a servant from Langarth. Wulfert Glenn has returned to Hróth.'

'Hróth?'

'It seems he was a retainer to the Hammer himself. Now he is pledged to the new king.'

'When did he leave?'

'Not long ago. If our luck holds, he will not have gone any farther than Eldyng. It's not far to sail, if we can find a ship.' She sat beside Tunuva, keeping a respectful distance. 'Tell me, Tuva. Will we go?'

Tunuva finished her drink. In this cold place, she found it warmed her.

'We have come this far,' she said. 'I suppose the North is but a little farther, Canthe.'

****

Glorian walked through Arondine Castle as if to her own execution. Her guards followed. For the first time since his arrival, Prince Guma had asked to join her in the royal bedchamber.

A fresh ripple of nausea made her swallow. She had the letters – they were sealed in a strongbox, hidden at Offsay Sanctuary – but her nerve could not fail. She could not show fear.

Prince Guma waited for her. He wore a quilted bedgown, the crimson and gold of his crest.

'Your Grace,' he said, with a polite dip of his head. 'Thank you for joining me.'

'Your Highness.'

The fire snapped as their eyes met. *To freeze is an instinct shared by all living things. Think of how a deer stills when it scents a threat*, her father reminded her. *There is no shame in it, Glorian.*

'Do your guards know Yscali?' he asked in that tongue. Glorian shook her head. 'I presume you do.'

'Yes.'

'Good. Then we may speak in private.' His voice softened a little. 'You need not be afraid, Queen Glorian. I do not expect this marriage to be consummated, now or ever. It represents a new era of fellowship for Yscalin and Inys, but be assured, it will be chaste.'

Glorian nodded without speaking. *A queen should learn the ways of watching.* She remained as still and poised as her mother always had. *Like a falcon, she waits for her moment to strike.*

'Your Regency Council must be pressing you for an heir,' he said, reaching for a goblet. He spoke with a distinct northern inflection. 'I pity you that burden. This is no time to bear a child.'

'It is a sacred burden, which I carry with joy,' Glorian said in the dialect she had learned since childhood, for use at the court at Kárkaro. 'It is what the Saint expects of me.'

'Yes, the Saint expects a great deal of his descendants. A great deal.' He drank. 'Those expectations are why I will sleep here tonight, so we may say the marriage has been consummated.'

He did not believe in the Knight of Fellowship. She wondered what the faith of trees said about marriage.

'Choose whomever you please to get you with child, if that is what you desire,' Prince Guma said. 'I only ask that you are discreet, Glorian. I will respect your dignity; I ask that you also respect mine.'

'I would not risk my heir being known as a bastard.'

'Good. In return, I will be a loving father to that heir. A father in all ways but blood.'

I see what you are doing, she wanted to tell him. *I see you trying to twine your roots around my unborn child.*

'Hart Grove is your home,' she said instead, walking towards the fire. 'A beautiful name for a castle. I suppose there are many trees in its grounds.'

Prince Guma looked at her with fresh interest. 'There were far more before my ancestors began to mine the mountains,' he said, 'but yes. Your own ancestor, Glorian Hartbane, was courted there by King Isalarico. They carved their names into an oak, which can still be seen today.'

'Yscalin gave much for that marriage. Now it gives much for ours.' Glorian formed what she hoped was a tentative smile, the smile of one who could be led. 'I am grateful.'

Her companion nodded. 'You will have to forgive me. It would be courteous of me to offer to sleep on the floor,' he said drily, 'but I fear these bones could not withstand it.'

'Fear not. Mine are made of iron,' Glorian said. 'Even queens sleep on floors in the halls of Hróth.'

Prince Guma passed her some of the bedding and waited for her to arrange it before he blew out the candles, leaving the fire to burn. Once more, Glorian Hraustr Berethnet fell asleep in furs on her own floor, warmed by the same hearth that had smouldered as she lay with Wulf.

And the secret in her womb seemed to whisper: *I am here, too. I am here.*

70

North

The midnight sun gilded the calm waves of the Ashen Sea. Blood mixed with its waters on the shore, where Wulf wrenched his spear from a corpse with coiled horns and metal hooves. As the wound smoked, he watched the glow leave its eye, an ember turning cold in its socket.

His own eye had puffed shut. What had struck him, he had no idea. He had lost count of the talons scraping at his mail, the beaks striking his helm.

He planted the end of his long axe in the sand. Wheezing from the smoke, he scraped his hair from his eyes and peered towards Bithandun, so tired he was almost drunk with it, swaying. The Silver Hall had not yet fallen, but its roof glowed with fire, and no amount of thrown water could quench it. The wyrms had come for Virtudom, as Fýredel had sworn.

When your days grow long and hot, when the sun in the North never sets, we shall come.

A soldier ran into the sea to put out her burning clothes. For three days and nights, they had battled an onslaught from the Iron Mountains: housecarls, raiders, people of every trade and rank. All Hróthi were expected to be fighters, for theirs was a cruel land, a hard one.

The creatures of the Dreadmount could be slain, but not with ease. Scale like tuff enclosed their bodies. Some had vulnerabilities – places where the flesh gaped, often at the shoulder of the wing – but some were so encrusted, it was hard to find a weak point for a spear or sword to pierce.

He pulled off his helm and cloth mask to breathe, sweltering in his mail and wool. Einlek had commanded everyone to cover as much of their skin as they could, and even Wulf had not been given leave to break the rule. *If you go about like some bare-chested berserker, so might others*, Einlek had warned him. *Set an example.*

Wulf had told him about the Inysh plan to move people underground. Einlek would not brook it in his kingdom, except for bairns and those who were too old or frail to fight.

We do not hide in the dark in Hróth. No one sings songs of trembling in tunnels. If we die, we die with blades in hand. We die in a way that will be remembered.

So they fought for their lives in their burning capital, hardly able to tell day from night. They fought, and they fell, and they died by the hundred.

As Wulf tried to rally his strength, a lesser wyrm – a wyvern – swooped along the beach, unleashing fire. He lunged over a wattle fence and landed in a crouch, his body acting before his mind had grasped the threat. The fence burst into flame just as he rolled away from it, and the wyrmling swept its wings, lifting itself back towards Bithandun. Spears went sailing after it, and hails of arrows flashed from the walls.

A gasping cry drew his attention. A woman in mail was running towards him, drenched in dark blood and heaving for breath, with three serpents – lindworms – slithering after her.

'Thella,' Wulf bellowed at her, 'drop!'

The housecarl pitched to the ground. His axe hit a lindworm in the breast, making it howl. Wulf drew his sword and charged.

The shrouded sun was still afloat. No day or night, and no reprieve.

His boot caught on a heavy softness. He fell into a pile of bodies. He was on the flaming deck of the *Conviction*, and Vell lay there, with tallow flesh and hair like tinder, a melted man...

Thella sprang back to her feet and kicked the lindworm with a shout, startling it away from Wulf. It tangled around her ankles and sank its teeth into her thigh as she fell. Grabbing hold of her spear with a furious scream, she plunged the head deep into its body, right through a break in its crust of scale. It bled gouts of steaming tar and

628

collapsed, still coiled around her limbs. She made a small, wet sound as its weight crushed her.

Wulf tried to shake the memories off. Teeth clenched, he wrestled an arm around the beast, trying to heave it off Thella, but the other lindworms were enraged. He wrenched her spear free and swung it wide, almost blind from the soot and dry heat. The lindworms recoiled, only to slither towards him again with hisses like raw meat hitting a pan.

'Wulf!'

Thrit ran towards them with a throng of housecarls. Mustering a war cry, they circled and harried, striking with axe and shield and spear until the two lindworms lay dead, steam curling from their injuries. Between them, the housecarls got the third off Thella, who coughed blood.

'Warriors of Eldyng,' came a familiar voice, pitched at a bellow. 'All who remain, to me, at the gate!'

A war horn blew. 'I'll take Thella,' Thrit said, pulling her arm around his neck. 'Get to the king!'

Flame erupted across a roof. Wulf ran towards the blast of the horn, his limbs acting before his mind again. Beneath his mail, sweat drenched his tunic.

The fallen lay thick on the narrow streets, charred and mangled – barely human in death, as on the white ship. (*Saint, you have kept me alive, let me crush them.*) He picked up a spear, hurled it at a monstrous bird, stopped to reclaim the weapon, kept running.

Einlek was near a gap in the wall. Bardholt had built it with stone, even if Bithandun was timber. He had seen enough forts burned in the war to know when a little more gold was worth spending. The high-ranked housecarls – those who had served Einlek before he was king – had herded the beasts together and found a battering ram to force them out. Not all of them had wings; not all could surmount the wall easily. More survivors were waiting to block the way with whatever they had been able to salvage.

Wulf went to the battering ram. He threw his back into helping wheel it towards the creatures, building up speed until the ram hurtled of its own will to its mark. The din was enough to shatter the ears and daunt even the stoutest heart.

'Shields,' Einlek ordered, joined by others, as creatures flocked to attack from the sides. Wooden shields came up to give them something else to gnaw on. A united shout, and Wulf helped drag the ram a second time, first away from the wall, then towards it.

As soon as they had forced the beasts out, the battering ram was wedged into the gap, and the people found barrels, even brought corpses, stacking up as much as they could from the ruins of their capital. Wulf grabbed whatever he could throw: weapons, two oars, a rack that must once have held meat, a table with a broken leg. With so many hands working together, the pile was soon high enough to give the creatures trouble breaking through. Fire archers came to set it ablaze.

'It's coming,' a voice cried. The wyvern was back, and it had them all caught like fish in a net. Wulf looked up, his knees turning to slurry as he remembered Fýredel.

A harpoon ripped into it.

The sound of its screech jolted him free. He stared as it rolled, like a foundering ship, and crashed down on a line of houses, blood spraying from under its wing. A rain from above should have smothered the fires, but where the blood struck, flame sizzled and abounded. On the city walls, a giant of a man took up another harpoon, lips skinned back.

'Slay it,' Einlek bellowed, as howls of triumph shook the street. He thrust up his iron arm. 'For the Saint!'

'The Saint,' came the answering roar.

With that command, the Hróthi fell upon their foe, hitting with hammers and stabbing with staves and swords and pitchforks, drunk on their rage and the taste of revenge. They sawed and prised away its scales to reach the sweltering flesh beneath. They swarmed, like the bees that had haunted Wulf for a lifetime.

Yet it was not the bees he recalled as he climbed on to the wyvern. It was a tale he had once heard of needlers, fish that ate flesh, which lurked in certain Southern rivers. A single needler was no threat – but together, they could strip a lion to bone.

****

After that, the fight was over, for a time. When a wyrm fell, it seemed to strike panic into its followers. By dawn, they had all disappeared from Eldyng. In their wake, they had left hundreds dead, and thousands more grievously wounded. The wyvern was decapitated, its head paraded through the streets and mounted on the gate of Bithandun.

The king summoned his housecarls that night, along with those Hróthi who had shown the highest courage during the attack, including the whaler whose harpoon had struck the killing blow.

They ate beneath the broken roof of Bithandun. It might have collapsed altogether if not for a bold group of carpenters, who had climbed up to smother the blaze using the heavy banners from its walls, desperate to save the hall Bardholt built. It was disquieting to see it without the royal heraldry, but at least some of the roof remained.

Ash wafted like snowflakes across the tables, which had seen endless feasting not so long ago. By the light of the low-burning fires, they shared tales of their deeds, raising their cups to those who had ascended to Halgalant.

Hunger was the unwelcome guest. Where food had once been rich, now there was only simple fare, even for the king and his guard.

'You all fought like the Saint himself today,' Einlek said, when they had scraped every plate. 'None more than Góthur Wyrmkiller, whose harpoon felled the beast.'

For the first time, the guests raised their voices in a cheer. Góthur was pounded on the back.

'In the past, our people longed for a glorious death in battle,' Einlek called. 'Now we can only hope to die well for the Saint, and for our best patron, the Knight of Courage, who smiles on us tonight. This may seem a small victory in a rumption, but remember what we did today. We slew a wyrm.'

The cheers rose. Wulf smiled at Thrit, who hitched up a weak one in return.

'I might replace this throne with that foul creature's head,' Einlek said, to raucous laughter. 'Though he'd kill me for saying it, I think my uncle would agree that a wyvern is a finer trophy than a whale.'

'Finer,' someone agreed, 'but not finer than Fýredel!'

Cups banged on the tables. 'Aye, his head would make a dread throne.' Einlek lifted his own cup. 'We will drink from that horned skull before I sit upon it. I will carve my uncle's name into his bones.' The din that ensued would have raised the roof, had there been much of a roof left. 'Now,' he declared, 'a song, to exalt those who dine in Halgalant this night.'

More cheers. Wulf slipped his last scrap of gristly meat to the hound under the table, scratching between its ears. When he looked up, Einlek beckoned him with a raised eyebrow.

He sat alone on that cold skull. As always, his mother was absent. Ólrun Hraustr had fought in the war, but had since become a recluse, tortured by a belief that she was made of ice.

'I hear you killed many,' Einlek said, when Wulf was close. 'I would keep you at my side, but I have another task for you – one that must be yours alone, Wulf. I must send you away again.'

'I'm starting to think you don't like me, sire.'

'Unfortunately for you, I only send people I like into danger. Those are the people I usually trust.' He flexed his fingers on his battle axe, which leaned against the throne. 'Have you ever ranged on the Northern Plain?'

'No.'

'We have an outpost there, in the Oxhorns. It serves as a waystop for those going east, a safe place to trade with friendly Hüran, and a last defence against those who would encroach into our territory. The Yscals gave us two springalds to defend it,' Einlek said. 'Among those who hold this outpost – Járthfall – are many strong warriors. We need every fighter back in our cities.'

'You want me to get them.'

'You would have to go through the Barrowmark, but the plague cannot kindle your blood. We also know you can survive the very hardest cold. No doubt there will be wyrms there, too.'

'I'll manage.'

'Good man.'

The task was as a relief. A long ride would test him, but he could escape the fire and foul smoke, if only for a while.

'I will spare you as much food for the journey as I can,' Einlek said, watching the others. 'I would offer you a knighthood on your return, but it seems my cousin has already promised that you will receive one when the war is over.'

'You've heard from Queen Glorian, then?'

'Yes, a few days ago. She asked me to thank you,' Einlek said. 'For the gift of your loyalty.'

Wulf stood very still, realisation unfurling its feathers.

'She plans to be crowned soon, now the heathen Eller is gone.' Einlek smiled coldly into his goblet. 'My cousin is a Hraustr. If that

Yscali greybeard thinks he's going to gain any power over her, he will taste both our blades.'

'Aye, sire.' Wulf cleared his throat. 'When should I set out?'

'Dawn will do. I want those fighters back as soon as possible. The whaler struck a lucky blow today, but if there had been more than one wyvern, we may not have saved Eldyng. Our foe was also not as large as Fýredel, or its heinous siblings.'

'Siblings?'

Einlek drank from his cup of mead. 'Heryon Vattenvarg wrote to me,' he said. 'There are at least two other great wyrms – one like iron-stone, one grey. The Southerners call the former Dedalugun; the other, the Ments call Orsul. There is also at least one that crosses between the North and the East, which we Hróthi have named – Valeysa. I suspect they fly here as we speak.' His knuckles blanched. 'Meet me in the stables. For now, Wulf, drink your fill, and laugh. This day will be a song.'

Wulf nodded. As he turned away, he concealed a smile. He had never expected to be a father, least of all to a daughter he could never claim, but the thought still made him warm.

Glorian must be relieved, but nervous. The thought made his smile fade. Happy though he was that none of it had been in vain, he already feared for her, being with child in a time like this.

When the healers arrived, the drunk housecarls bedded down for the night, weary to the bone. An unconscious woman was borne in, her insides peeping out of her belly. One man had an unhinged jaw, and another had been so deeply clawed that he screamed as the healer dabbed honey on the ruin of his skin. Thella coughed into a rag.

Thrit was in the corner with one arm under his head, clean bandages around his middle, two fingers splinted. 'How's your shoulder?' Wulf asked, sitting beside him.

'Fine.' Thrit was looking past the ceiling. 'Calling this a war is like a lamb calling the shambles its battlefield. It's dead before it even smells the blood. Queen Glorian is right – we should be finding places to hide.'

'You know that's not the Hróthi way.'

'If this goes on, there won't be a Hróthi way.'

Wulf agreed, but in silence. He could no more convince Einlek to hide than he could tuck the midnight sun beneath the sea.

They slept under the sky. Wulf woke to almost the same light, finding Thrit still asleep. The cocks never crowed in the summer, but he had trained his body to know when it was morning.

Outside, the welkin was a queer yellow, the sun washed pale. In the silence, people were no longer celebrating, but loading corpses into carts that had once burst with fish and cloth. Einlek met him at the stables, where his ostler was tending to a muckle Inysh destrier, white with a grey mane

'So many dead,' Wulf said. 'Will you burn the bodies, sire?'

'They'll be weighted with stone and dropped in the sea. Their bones will endure, but the plague will not spread.' Einlek patted the destrier. 'Wulf, this is Prúth, one of my uncle's favourite steeds. He has been to Járthfall before, and his coat should help you pass unnoticed. You have as much food as he can carry. He's yours when you return.'

'My king.' Wulf took the reins. 'This is too generous.'

'Just come back alive. If you meet the Hüran, be wary. Some tribes are affable enough; others will attack on sight.' Einlek gripped him by the shoulder. 'Get my fighters back.'

'And just where in Halgalant are you going?'

Wulf turned to see Thrit stood at the door, arms folded.

'Thrit,' Einlek said. 'Wulf is leaving us for a time.'

'Forgive my intemperance, sire, but fuck that,' Thrit said grimly. 'We're down to four in our lith. Where Wulf goes, I go.'

'Thrit, you can't,' Wulf said. 'I'm going through the Barrowmark, to the Norther—'

'I don't care if you're going through the Womb of Fire,' Thrit told him, eyes flashing.

'Let him go,' Einlek said, before Wulf could gainsay. 'Thrit, you made an oath to your lith, and I'll respect it – but if you catch this bloodblaze, I do not expect you to return. We can't have it spreading any farther than it has.'

'It will never enter Hróth through me.'

'Good.' Einlek nodded to the ostler and gave Prúth a last stroke. 'Perhaps this is a task from the Saint, so you can all be reunited.'

'Sire?'

'Karlsten and Sauma are both at the outpost,' Einlek said. 'I sent them to bolster the ranks.' Wulf and Thrit exchanged a surprised look. 'Saint go with you. When you return, you will find me still fighting.'

He left in a sweep of cloak. Wulf mounted Prúth, while Thrit was handed another horse, grey as fog.

'Can't believe you were trying to sneak off without me, Wulfert Glenn,' he said darkly. 'Don't you know by now that a lith belongs together?'

'If I ever forget, I have you to remind me.'

They rode out of the city, side by side. Had they looked back, they would have seen a small Inysh ship on the horizon, fighting against the Ashen Sea to reach the smoking shore.

71

North

Her first sight of Hróth was a burnt city, a headless wyrm draped over its roofs, scales ripped from its flesh and passed like hot loaves in the streets. On a hill stood the feasting hall of the Hraustr, where the Hammer of the North had ruled from his seat of carven bone.

Of course, Canthe spoke Hróthi. She had a gift for uncovering secrets – her silver tongue charmed people into loosening theirs. After two days in Eldyng, she knew Wulfert Glenn had ridden away with another house-carl, bound for the wilderness. She had spent more of her gold on thick bear pelts, doughty Hróthi steeds, and boots with teeth to grip the ice.

Soon they were back on his heels, riding faster than Tunuva ever had on horseback.

They took the ancient road the Hróthi used to transport amber, which slunk through leaning pine forests and forded dark and brutal rivers. Waterfalls fell white and glittering, showers of shattered glass, from cliffs so high the water barely touched the ground.

Even as the days slipped away, the sun never departed. Tunuva had always thought the eversnow must be a fable, and there was greensward here and there – but even deep in summer, Hróth was cold and hard.

Siyu had wanted to live here. Tunuva wondered if she would ever have been happy. *Do not think of her.* She spurred her mount. *Think only of him. Find him, so you may find her again.*

Canthe stayed just ahead, seeming to know her way, as always. In time, they reached the marchland known as the Barrowmark, and there, they saw the first birds circling.

A body lay on its side in the snow, dead perhaps three or four days. Farther on, they found two more, each holding an axe.

'The Barrowmark is where it started,' Canthe said. 'In a village to the far north, called Ófandauth.' Threads of snow crowned her. 'We should keep riding. Only death lies here.'

She was right. From then on, there was no end to the bodies. Hundreds or thousands, all dead of plague – Tunuva had lost count by the first night. Carts laden with corpses sat abandoned on the wayside.

When their waterskins ran dry, they stopped at a frozen lake to fill them. Tunuva knelt in the snow and crunched a fist through the ice, misted black water welling up to greet her. She had just dipped the mouth of her waterskin when she saw another corpse.

The man had crawled headfirst into the shallows. From the waist down, he was bone and rot, slim pickings now even for crows – but the lake had tightened around the rest of his body, preserving his screaming head and red hands.

By the time a tall ridge covered the horizon, Tunuva could not think beyond the endless drumbeat of hooves. They galloped northeast until the mountains parted.

'The Vathuld Pass,' Canthe said. 'Here, Hróth ends, and the cold wilds begin.' She looked at Tunuva. 'Last chance to turn back, my friend.'

Tunuva gripped the reins. She was a warrior born in fire, and all that lay beyond was snow.

'Eastward, then,' she said.

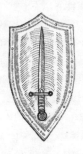

72

West

Once more the sun had darkened in the eastern sky. Standing at the window to her bedchamber, Glorian gazed at it, wrapped in her mantle. The Dreadmount must be smoking.

Perhaps it was the sight of it that twisted her insides yet again. As she heaved over her chamberpot, Helisent rushed to her and held back her hair. When Glorian had spat out the last of it, Helisent locked a hand over hers, over her womb and the green shoot within it.

When her blood failed to appear a second time, she had known. Her grandmother had advised her to wait until at least the third month before sharing the news with the Regency Council. She would be further along than they knew.

On the surface, her body was unchanged. Newness surged within. She was exhausted. Her teeth hurt to their roots. All she could imagine was the sort of world her successor would inherit, dead and scorched and grey.

There was another grief, for herself. Her father had fought so hard for her to have a childhood, and here she was, at seventeen, a new Berethnet in her belly.

Papa, you tried.

Helisent took her to the only bath in the castle, where Julain and Adela were waiting. 'Is he kind to you, Glorian?' the latter said as they rinsed her hair. 'Prince Guma. He's so old and stern.'

'Hush, Adela.' Helisent collected the linen. 'Glorian had little choice. Things are as they are.'

'Why are you not upset by this, Helly?' Adela demanded. 'And you, Jules – doesn't it trouble you?'

'Adeliza.' Glorian caught her hand. 'You and I are milk sisters. We must trust one another, always,' she said gently, 'so you must believe me when I say it's all right. I have everything under control.'

Adela frowned in confusion, tears in her soft brown eyes. Glorian pressed her hand.

In the solar, she picked at her supper, willing herself not to be sick again, and waited for her hair to dry. It seemed heavier on her back. When a knock came at the door, Helisent let Marian in.

'Glorian,' her grandmother said with a sigh. 'Forgive me, child. It seems I am condemned to be a bearer of bad news.' Glorian stood. 'I have yet to establish how, but Robart Eller escaped Glowan Castle. A forester found his body in the haithwood, hanged from the branch of a yew, drained of blood. From what they could tell, he cut his own throat.'

'Saint save us,' Julain murmured. 'What sort of madness could have seized his mind?'

Glorian quelled an absurd twinge of sorrow. He had seemed kind, all that time he was plotting.

'We will tell Prince Guma that it was the plague,' she said. 'The Ellers may choose what to do with the body. I suppose he would not have wanted to enter Halgalant, so we need say no prayers for his soul on its journey. I do not know where heathens go when they die.'

****

Inys seemed too still. Too quiet. A queendom with its breath held and its eyes for ever on the sky. As the days wore on, heat enclosed it in a clammy fist. Tempers flared in the city; a riot in the market square, another in a line for bread. A baker was accused of using bone instead of flour.

Glorian could not sleep, so she paced. She was sick, and her chest burned. When she woke, she could never remember her dreams, though she was sometimes filmed with ice. Robart Eller haunted her. His family had chosen to burn his body, to bolster the lie that he had died of the plague.

Your ancestor was not a hero. His words gnawed at her mind. *You do not need to bear the fruit of his eternal vine. It is a lie, meant to perpetuate his legacy, no more.* Still those words refused to leave her.

The next time she was sick, threads of hair clung to her tears and her mouth. As soon as they knew she was pregnant, the Regency Council would lock her away from the world. When she could stand, she picked up the mirror her mother had given her, and panic gripped her with such force that she almost retched again. Her face was the truth. Her face was her crown.

Her supper had gone cold. She took the knife in one hand and grasped a lock of hair with the other – her black hair, one aspect of the Saint's Marvel. The hair of a Berethnet queen.

All her life she had worn it to her waist. She pulled the knife through the gathering of strands, watched her hair drift to the floor, and the world did not end. All lay quiet. Now exhilaration stole her fear. She cut and cut, wrenching the blade through all that heavy darkness, and the more she hacked away, the lighter her breathing. This small thing, she could still control. Her womb was not her own – but her hair, surely that could still be hers, surely.

By the time the first bell clanged, she was slumped on the floor, surrounded by tufts and reels of black, her hair scruffy around her face. Florell came straight in.

'Glorian—' She stared down at the floor, the knife. 'Sweeting, why have you done this?'

'To remind me that I am still mine.' Glorian looked at her. 'Tell the Regency Council it's time.'

****

They had been packed for weeks. In the gloom, Helisent and Adela helped with her armour. On the streets, torchbearers flocked out to guide the people to Hyll Sanctuary. Many wept and protested and tried to fight their way ahead, too fear-stricken to keep their retreat calm. Others waited with grim acceptance for their turn to descend into the mining tunnel.

Glorian watched the sanctuary devour one candle after the next, then scores at once. She buckled on her scabbard and sheathed her sword. Finally, Lady Gladwin arrived.

'Your Grace,' she said, 'I bid you come with me at once. The wyrms will be upon us soon.'

The Regency Council and some of the other nobles formed a restless gathering in the courtyard, where Sir Granham Dale stood ready to lead them to the tunnel. Prince Guma was among them, armoured in mail and a breastplate, a gold circlet above his brows. Glorian wore hers, too, thanks to Marian reminding her of its importance at the last.

'Are you well, Your Grace?' he said in his usual steely tones, speaking over the bells.

'Yes, Your Highness. Thank you.'

'I heard what happened to Lord Robart,' he said, keeping pace with her. 'Perhaps he is fortunate. He sleeps peacefully tonight, while we must face the fire of the Dreadmount.'

'That fire was in his blood. I do not envy him.'

The castellan led them into Hyll Sanctuary. In the undercroft, he ushered them down a steep set of steps, which led into the base of the hill. From there, they strode through the utter blackness of the escape tunnel, where the air was thick as unwashed wool. Dry stonework lined its battered walls, where the Inyscans had burrowed through the earth.

Sir Granham went at the front with a torch. All the way, Glorian expected the ancient tunnel to collapse and bury them, but its walls held fast. The miners had worked hard to strengthen it.

It was two miles' walk to Stathalstan Knott. By the time they reached it, Marian was weak with exertion, and even Prince Guma could no longer hide his fatigue. Some of his Yscali guards slowed to wait for him. Keeping hold of her grandmother, Glorian stepped into the first tall cavern, taking in the limestone that had lengthened into long knives overhead.

It smelled of tallow and livestock. She was already sweating under her mail and gambeson. City guards and Yscali soldiers were shepherding people into the deeper caverns, but some had clustered near the entrance to wait for their loved ones, either in small groups or alone. Glorian watched them from under her hood. Somewhere in the dark, chickens fluttered, and cows lowed their disquiet, while conversations joined into a hum. Bourn knelt beside an unattended child, who had skinned her knee and wept pitifully.

'This was a better choice than trying to fight,' Helisent said under her breath to Glorian. 'You know that, don't you?'

'My heart is Hróthi,' Glorian replied, 'but my wits are more Inysh, I think.'

'The Saint is merciful.'

'I only hope my cousin relents and sends his people to safety. There are no caves near Eldyng, but—'

'Queen Glorian.' Lade Edith appeared from the shadows. 'Welcome to Stathalstan.' They bowed. 'We've prepared a cavern for you and your ladies.'

'Thank you, my lade. Does all go to plan?'

'So far, thank the Saint,' they said, glancing at the tunnel. 'Now everyone is here, I will order the undercroft sealed. We do not want any creatures following our scent.'

'No one was left behind?'

'No one. The guards were thorough.'

'Good.'

Glorian heard a short gasp. The nearest people had realised who she was. She watched them, just as they watched her – searching for any trace of anger or hatred in the haunted eyes that reflected the candle-light, like that in the man who had wanted to kill her.

But none of them moved; none of them spoke. They were waiting to be addressed.

'Do not be afraid. The Knight of Courage is with you,' Glorian said. 'We are as safe in here as we can be. Together, I believe we will survive what lies ahead, as my ancestor survived, against all odds, on the red sands of Lasia. Trust now in the Saint, who watches us in darkness.'

Her voice was so much louder in the cave. So were their voices as they echoed: 'Who watches us in darkness.'

Glorian nodded to them all. Only then did she follow Lade Edith away from the whispers, up a creaking set of steps the miners must have raised. The caves grew colder by the step.

Lade Edith had tasked their personal servants with escorting the nobles. When Glorian was shown to her makeshift chamber, the relief was immense. Her cave was warm and silent, lit by fine wax candles that burned without the smell of tallow – a mercy for her unsettled insides.

'Sir Bramel will be just outside,' Lade Edith told her. 'If you will excuse me, I must see to the people.'

'Thank you, my lade. You have gone far beyond the duties of the Duchet of Courtesy.'

When Lade Edith had gone, Glorian sank on to the bed. Her grandmother had the next cave, with Mara Glenn to attend her.

'Adela,' Glorian said, 'will you try to find me some warm milk and honey?'

'Yes.' Adela looked at the dark way out and swallowed. 'May I take a candle?'

'Of course you may.'

Julain watched her leave. 'You'll have to tell her,' she said to Glorian. 'When you start to show.'

'Adela knows nothing of childing. She won't be able to tell I'm further along.' Glorian unlaced her boots. 'This is already too much for her.'

Once her ladies had extracted her from her mail, Marian came in to sit beside her on the bed. 'How is the sickness?' she said, feeling her brow and cheeks, tucking her short hair behind her ear. 'Ah, yes, this is practical for war. You look just like your namesake.'

Glorian managed a smile. 'The sickness is the same. My teeth ache,' she said. 'Saint, all of me aches.'

'It is hard, but it will ease. I remember how it was with Sabran. Around the fourth month, I felt stronger.'

Julain said, 'Does Wulf know?'

'I sent him a message, of sorts.' Glorian glanced at the mouth of the cave. 'It's Fýredel that flies this night. I know it in my ribs.'

'He will find nothing in Arondine.' Helisent sat on her other side. 'Thanks to you and the miners.'

'But he will not stop.' The candles flickered. 'Death comes for Inys.'

Marian stroked her hair. 'You must stay as calm as you can, Glorian. For the child.'

Adela hurried back with fresh milk and a pot of broth. Glorian drank, then let her grandmother tuck her in, as if she were still a small child. There could be no fires in such a cave, so her ladies crowded into the bed, for warmth – all three of them, their arms around each other, around her. One of the mousers found them, too, and joined the pile of limbs. Adela tucked the mewing bundle of fur against her chest and fell asleep.

For the first time in days, Glorian felt safe. *They will hold you as well,* she told her belly. *You will never be alone, even if the world is bleak.*

Her body was exhausted, but her mind refused to quiet. She dared not reach for her mirror sister – her ladies would feel the chill on her skin. At length, she rose, careful not to wake them, and walked to where Sir Bramel Stathworth was on guard. He blinked at the sight of her.

'Sir Bramel,' she said, 'will you take me to the lookout?'

With a torch in hand, he strode through the tunnels, where the rock seemed to keep narrowing. He helped her reach the uneven inclines, leading her to where the caves rose into the knott itself.

They emerged through a crack in the stone, finding Lady Gladwin alone on a hillside nook, exposed to the elements, tending a small fire. It seemed like the only light in the world.

'Who is that?' she said sharply.

'Only me, Lady Gladwin.' Glorian stepped into the light. 'If you'll forgive the intrusion.'

'Queen Glorian.' Lady Gladwin recovered. 'You should stay below ground.'

'I must see.'

Glorian stood by the brazier and gazed towards Arondine. The bells had stopped – the ringers had been last to flee – and every torch had been put out, the better to keep it from the wyrms' sight. The night was black as the inside of a blindfold.

They waited. A breeze whipped at her hair, and she nestled into the mantle, shivering.

She somehow felt the wyrms before they came. A warning prickle at her senses. When their wings could finally be heard, Lady Gladwin went straight to the brazier and folded cold ashes over the hot, plunging them into absolute darkness. Glorian closed her eyes, listening to the *rush, rush, rush*. This must have been the sound her parents heard before the end.

Fýredel might not see the city. She opened her eyes, finding that she remained blind, and too aware of her own blood.

Fire tore the night asunder.

Glorian sat in silence, rooted to the rock. She watched as Arondine was swallowed into a red furnace, high enough to singe Halgalant. By its light, she could just make out wings. Each primal scream raked her spine. As buildings bowed and thatch burst into flame, she prayed no one below could hear, that the rock was thick enough to keep her people deaf to it.

She watched until dawn peeled open like a wound, to bleed its light across the sky.

When the smoke cleared, Fýredel was enthroned on Hyll Sanctuary. He looked towards the knott, and Glorian could have sworn those eyes met hers. His fiery throat opened, like the gate to the Womb of Fire itself.

'So,' Glorian said softly, 'here you are, wyrm.'

73

North

O nce, a barren ridge of land had joined the northern East and eastern North. The brave had been able to cross it on foot. According to *The Epic of the Seas*, the Abyss had devoured it, estranging the two continents.

That stretch of the Abyss was called the Broken Corridor, and Dumai was sure she was looking at it. These were the northern shallows of the Abyss, where ice erupted like cracked teeth from under the waves.

High above it, dragons floated – strange, vast guardians of the heavens, gazes blue and void. Some looked down when Furtia passed, while others seemed blind to her, silent and remote, waiting for something. There was no other life. Here, it was as if there was no war.

Yet Dumai had breathed in the smoke above the Queendom of Sepul. She had heard the wyrms' calls as Furtia flew across the Empire of the Twelve Lakes. Each night revealed hundreds of fires. Now she knew why the sun was black, giving forth a light without brightness.

She had wanted to keep to the coast, but it was a feeling that she followed, not a path or map. The figure in her dream had been right. Their bond was pulling at her now, even when she was awake. Furtia seemed to sense it, too, when Dumai laid a bare hand on her scales.

The dark sea should not be crossed, Furtia told her. *Chaos slumbers in its depths.*

This is only a short stretch. We need not cross the deep waters – only the remnants of the land. Dumai kept a hand pressed to her scales. *I have no choice but to follow, great one. Something is calling me.*

The stone was tucked against her chest. Even through its box and her layers, she could feel a chill from it. *That which is like a thing will always call to it,* Furtia replied, *but so can that which is unlike a thing.* She banked a little. *Its voice will be the loudest, the voice of the unknown.*

Dumai could not tell what she meant, but she knew by now that asking would be no help. The gods would have their secrets, and not even the Noziken were always meant to understand.

Nikeya slept against her, arms around her waist. Despite the distance they had covered, they had barely spoken – Furtia flew so swiftly that the wind roared over their voices, and on the rare nights she stopped to swim and rest, they were so hoarse and windbeaten that they fell straight to sleep.

Riding was no longer a discomfort. Dumai was part of the saddle now, as if it had been made exactly to her measurements. Even as she watched for wyrms, she savoured the scalding cold, the gusts of wind, the openness. This was where she belonged – not at court.

She still ached for Kanifa. Sometimes she would glance behind her, expecting to find him there.

At the end of the Broken Corridor, the waters rushed against a steep headland, crusted with snow. All that lay ahead was pallor. If Dumai had it right, she was no longer in the East. Snow ran thin as spilled milk over the eroded rock and earth. Trees reached through like fingerbones, with bundles of brown grass and sedge here and there.

With the other stone, they might be able to hold off both the wyrms and the intrigue until the comet arrived. If not, she would know the cause of her dreams, and that might be enough.

I feel you. As if to crush any flickers of doubt, the voice came again. *You are almost here.*

Yes. Dumai smiled until her cheeks hurt. *I look forward to embracing you, after all this time, my sister.*

****

The sun never set in this land – a peculiarity of Northern summers. Its rays were tarnished. On the third day of dim light, a river cracked the land open, dark as a spill of ink. Furtia descended and let down her riders, then slid into the water to refresh her scales, eyes closing in contentment. Dumai stripped to her underclothes and waded into the shallows to wash.

'You are headsick.' Nikeya knelt to fill her flask. 'Do you mean to almost freeze again?'

'The cold spring on Mount Ipyeda built my endurance. It sharpens the senses.'

'And dulls the wits, apparently.' Nikeya watched her. 'They didn't let me see you when you were unwell. I couldn't tell you how sorry I was, about Kanifa. I tried to look for him.'

'You could not have saved him.'

'He was good and kind, even if he didn't like me. I confess that I envied your friendship.'

'You have plenty of friends. I see you with them at court, where everything seems to amuse you.'

'They're family.' Nikeya stoppered the flask. 'At court, family is not always a comfort.'

She was more beautiful than ever in the cold, with a flush in her cheeks, eyes warmed by the sun.

She is still silver. Dumai went underwater, hoping the icy burn would scour her thoughts. *She will always be silver.*

They lit a fire to warm themselves and ate some of their salt-dried stores. Once Furtia was rested, they clambered back into the saddle, where the drift of flight soon lulled Dumai into a doze. She reached for her mirror sister again, hearing no answer but the pull, which was taking them west.

She was slipping into a deeper sleep when Furtia shuddered, jolting her wide awake.

Furtia, what is it?

The scream of a god was a terrible thing. When Furtia swung her head, Dumai glimpsed a huge shaft of wood in her crest. She looked down in horror, seeing nothing but snow.

I am stricken . . .

They were under attack. She untied herself from the saddle, ignoring a protest from Nikeya, and lunged for the cascade of manehair in front of her. She had to get that spear out, or Furtia would be unable to fly.

The wind tore at her hair and numbed her ears as she reached a horn, the gauntlets helping her keep a firm grip. She hooked a leg over

647

it, panting with the effort of holding on, but Furtia was losing height by the moment, heading straight towards the ground. At once, Dumai was pulled back to the day she fell off the dragon. She cleaved to her now with both arms, unable to think or breathe, nor see more than a sickening whirl of black and white.

'Dumai!'

Barely clinging on, she craned her neck. Nikeya had abandoned the saddle and somehow climbed halfway to her. 'Take my hand,' she shouted, holding it out. 'Come on, Dumai!'

'Nikeya, go back—'

'Shut up and take my hand!'

Dumai loosened her grip and slid towards her. Just before the collision, Furtia pulled up, stripping away snow, her underside scraping the rock beneath. Nikeya lost her footing just as Dumai grasped her, and they fell together, into the screaming white.

Hitting the ground beat the breath from Dumai. Her teeth cut her tongue. Cold soaked into her clothes. When she was sure she could move, she sat up to find that she had fallen into soft snow.

Furtia?

Only the wind answered, moaning low and haunted through the bareness of the Northern Plain. She spat out blood and looked for Nikeya, finding her pillowed in thick snow nearby, hair over her face. Dumai crawled to her and turned her over, cupping her head with care.

'Nikeya.' She felt for breaks. Nikeya lay still, not breathing. 'Nikeya, stay with me, please—' Dumai wrestled with the collar of her tunic, trying to find a pulse. 'Can you hear me?'

At once, Nikeya coughed out fog, and Dumai froze.

'Yes. I hear you pleading with me to stay with you, Princess,' she said, lashes flickering. 'I must be dreaming.' Dumai stared at her. 'Finally, you admit you like me. If I'd known all I had to do was fling myself off a dragon, I would have tried that a long time ago.'

'That was not funny or clever,' Dumai said, furious. 'Did you get out of the saddle just to play this trick?'

Nikeya sighed. 'I know this threatens your mulish belief that every Kuposa is a duplicitous sneak,' she said, 'but I got out of the saddle to get *you* back into it. To save you, again.'

Dumai took a slow breath, relief washing away her irritation. Snow rolled out for about a league, tufted with yellow grass, before it met a steep ridge.

'Those mountains – Furtia would have taken shelter there. Dragons heal in high places, if they can't find water,' she said. 'Did you see where the spear came from?'

'Yes. A watchtower,' Nikeya said. 'There was a fire.' She nodded to a distant column of woodsmoke to the east. 'It could be a signal to others to find us. We should leave.'

'Why would anyone hurt Furtia?'

'Because the sky rains death, Dumai. The Northerners would have long since forgotten our dragons, if they ever saw or heard of them at all. They've been asleep for so long.'

'They think she's a wyrm.' Dumai looked back towards the smoke. 'We have to explain.'

'I don't know about you, but I don't speak a Northern tongue, and I doubt they speak ours.' Nikeya stood with difficulty, holding her side. 'I can't tell which part of the Northern Plain we've fallen on, but neither is good. If it's the Hróthi side, they'll kill us for being unbelievers. If this is North Hüran territory, they'll kill us for being strange island people who have not sought permission to cross their land. I don't know which is worse.'

'We'll find Furtia,' Dumai said, 'but first we need to find shelter.'

'If you say so.' Nikeya held out a hand again. 'Are you starting to hate mountains yet?'

Dumai grasped it. 'That would be to hate a part of my own heart.' Seeing Nikeya grimace, she said, 'Are you hurt?'

'I think I've bruised my ribs.' She puffed out a little fog. 'I'm fine. Shall we get to shelter?'

Reaching the ridge was hard. The snow remained deep, making each step laborious, and Nikeya had soon paled from the cold.

'Dumai,' she said. 'Do you see that?' She pointed as best she could with cloth mittens. 'That break in the mountain. It's small, but it could be a cave, couldn't it?'

It was low down enough that they could climb to it. 'You have sharp eyes.'

'It's the archery.'

They were almost to the cave when Dumai sensed a change on the wind. Somewhere far behind, a horn blew, and she turned to see a flock of winged creatures, flying straight towards them.

She grasped Nikeya by the arm and pulled her up the last steep boulder. Seeing the danger, Nikeya scrambled after her, and no sooner had they ducked through the opening than red fire exploded in their wake. As they ran into the darkness, a wyrm roared after them, then took off, back into the sky.

They were quiet for a time, catching their breath. 'They're everywhere,' Nikeya said, her voice thin. 'Dumai, they must be in Seiiki by now. We should never have left when we did.'

'We can't turn back yet.' Dumai glanced at the entrance. 'The horn. Was that the Hüran?'

'If so, let's hope they didn't see us come in here.' Nikeya braced her side. 'If you can make that light again, now would be the time.'

Dumai had already closed her eyes to find it. Seeking the same part of herself that she had touched on Brhazat, she called the white glow back to her palm, casting shadows on the walls.

'I saw it on the mountain. It was how I found you,' Nikeya said, the light dancing in her eyes. 'How do you do that?'

Dumai shook her head. She could not have explained it, just as she could not explain how she told different parts of her body to move, or how a thought was formed. It simply was.

They walked deeper into the mountain, sidling through narrow clefts in the rock, working their way downward. When they came across a dry chamber, Dumai collapsed against the wall, so tired that her legs trembled. Nikeya sank down beside her.

'All our blankets are in the saddle,' she said, past a rattling jaw. 'I know you will think this another courtiers' trick, Princess, but ... I fear I may freeze if you don't hold me now.'

Dumai wearily opened her pelts. Nikeya huddled against her, resting her head on her breastbone, and Dumai folded the furs around her in return, unsettled by the violence of her shivering.

'This armour is an uncomfortable pillow,' Nikeya said. 'Are you planning to do battle with the wyrms?'

'I can't fight.'

'That makes two of us.' Nikeya closed her eyes, as if she were listening for a heartbeat. Dumai willed hers to slow. 'I've always hated the cold. Numbness is death to the poet.'

'I wonder that you insisted on joining me again.' Dumai set her chin on the top of her head. 'You were not made for this life, Nikeya.'

'Perhaps you should ask yourself why I still follow you.' She shifted closer, sniffing. 'Why have you come to the North?'

'To meet someone. I think it's best for both of us if you don't know anything more.'

Nikeya suddenly moved away, pushing off the pelts. 'What must I do to earn your trust?' Her words shook with cold and frustration. 'I saved you. I kept you alive on our way home. I have crossed half the world with you, and I have yet to cut your throat. You don't want to lose me – you said it, I heard you – and yet you don't trust me. What more can I do?'

'Enough of this. It has been two years since we met, and you are still the Lady of Faces.' Dumai was too drained to raise her voice. 'I may be naïve and sheltered to you, but I am not blind.'

'I know that.'

'Then do not play at innocence. You say you have not cut my throat, but that is not how your family works. Your family operates just as you do – by keeping the Noziken in your debt,' she said. 'Have you not seen the dollhouse your father gave Suzu?' Nikeya looked away. 'There is no doll in his image. He is the one who plays.'

'If you saw that, you would have seen me in there.' She wrapped an arm around her knees, her gaze hard and distant. 'My place in his life is more complicated than you know, Dumai.'

'Explain it to me, then.'

She sat there for a long time. 'I will,' she said, 'but not now. We're both tired.'

'Then come here.'

Nikeya seemed to give up the fight. She pressed close again, and Dumai wrapped both arms around her shoulders.

'I am only doing this to keep you warm,' Dumai told her.

'Of course,' Nikeya murmured. 'If that is all I ever have of you, I will accept it.'

74

North

The North shone like crushed diamond beneath the midnight sun. Wulf had no idea how long he and Thrit had been riding. They slept when they were tired, in the few shelters they could find in the wilds: hollows behind waterfalls, ledges fringed with dripping ice. No summer could melt the eversnow – not even this summer of fire – but it could soften it.

Járthfall was a long way into the Northern Plain. Still, all housecarls learned to live off the land. There were bear grapes sleeping under the snow, speckled clutches in low nests, animals and birds to hunt.

For a time, all that lay before them were steep bluffs of rock that knuckled from snow. They breathed cleaner air than they had in weeks. The horses fought their way on to higher and higher ground, hooves sinking deep, while Thrit tried to keep their spirits up, singing when there was no quarry to scare.

It was only on their second week of riding that they saw a wyvern for the first time – heading south, uninterested. This must be a poor hunting ground when feasts of flesh were piled elsewhere. Still, they were more careful after that. One night, they woke to see a creature pass below, a huge scaled elk with embers for eyes.

The next day, they saw one of the great wyrms, the one Einlek had called Valeysa. Tawny all over, the beast flew straight overhead, like the wyvern, heading for Eldyng.

Next came an ancient forest of blood pines, which seemed tall enough to brush the clouds, snow tumbling from their branches. A carpet of dark needles hushed the hoofbeats.

When Wulf and Thrit emerged, they beheld a lake, and mountains blocked their way eastward – one with two peaks, draped in snow. These were the Oxhorns. On the far side of the greenish water, a shelf of rumpled ice slouched over a sheer wall of rock, shedding grey waterfalls. White rubble had calved into the lake. Its shore housed the bones of a camp, with a firepit and a rack for stretching hides.

'This is too small to be the main camp,' Wulf observed. 'Must be for bathing and the like – but we're in the right place.'

'Aye. This is Járthfall.' Thrit eyed the hanging ice. 'I really don't like the look of that.'

'The outpost won't be on it.'

'I wager we'll still have to cross it to get there. An ice helm is an excellent defence against unfriendly visitors.' Thrit turned in his saddle, searching the valley, then nodded to a faded path that disappeared into the mountains. 'That should be our way in. Looks like a steep ride.'

'You wait here, if you need a rest,' Wulf said. Thrit rubbed his eyes. 'I can head up alone.'

'I believe I made myself very clear, Wulfert. You go nowhere alone.' Thrit gave his horse a pat. 'Up to the outpost, then. Let's warm our bones and think of some way to embarrass Karl.'

****

Her light kept the darkness away. Dumai watched its flicker, the way it revealed the veins in her hands.

It had also revealed the paintings in the cave. They could have been recent or very old, but she felt it was the latter. She took in the rough figures, the runes – things she was certain she had no hope of understanding.

The largest of the images was a circle with lines streaming out from it, surrounded by stars. It crossed the whole ceiling before curving down into the wall opposite Dumai. This could be an ancient hand trying to capture a shooting star. She had wished on many of those as a child, lying on the temple roof with Kanifa.

Or it could be the great comet Tonra had believed would come.

Below, hundreds of handprints overlaid one another, pressed into the wall with many shades of paint. The red ones troubled her. They all seemed to be reaching for the star, or warding it away.

Is this Kwiriki's Lantern?

Nikeya slept on at her side. They had to find Furtia, but they were both bruised and exhausted, and Dumai knew better than to goad another mountain. Brhazat had reminded her of the importance of that lesson. Let Nikeya sleep in peace for just a little longer.

She had not heard a word from the inbetween, though she sensed they were in the right place, or close to it. The silence was starting to trouble her.

When Nikeya stirred, she looked around and blinked, as if she had forgotten where she was. Seeing Dumai, her face softened into an unguarded smile. A moment later, her brow pinched.

'My fingers.'

Dumai took off her mittens for her. When she saw, her chest tightened. 'You have frostnip.' She blew warmth on to her fingertips, which had turned pink and swelled a little. 'You must keep your hands moving as we go on.'

'Will I lose the fingers?'

'Not if you keep them out of the cold.'

'What happened to yours?'

Dumai curled them in her gauntlet. Nikeya reached for the cord around her wrist, asking permission with her gaze. When Dumai nodded, she unwound it and eased the armoured glove off, so she could see the remnant fingers.

'I was ten,' Dumai said, letting her touch them. 'The snowstorm came out of nowhere, while we had climbers on the peak. The sky had been clear all morning, but a mountain makes its own weather.

'When they brought the first man down, one hand frozen solid, I ran out, certain I could find my mother. In my haste, I forgot my gloves.' She almost shivered, remembering. 'It was like ... falling inside a pearl. In moments, I had lost my bearings in the snow. Mother found me just in time. I lived, but my fingertips died. She trimmed them with a blade.'

'That must have been terrifying, for a child. I never knew such hardship.'

'It taught me to keep my guard up, even when I think I know exactly what I'm doing. And to raise it higher when I have no idea.' Dumai looked at her. 'Did the River Lord tell you to seduce me?'

Nikeya kept hold of her hand.

'Of course he did,' she said, very softly. 'But you've always known that.'

'How can I ever trust you, then?'

'You already do. You were not made for artifice and intrigue, Dumai. It's what I've always liked about you. You trust people, because you want to see the good in them. Even me, in spite of yourself.' Nikeya traced the line of her jaw. 'I know I have tested your patience, but I needed to see who you were, to make sure Seiiki had a ruler who would protect its people. I think you could be that ruler – born to a mother from the dust provinces, raised on a mountain to cherish the gods.'

'My father loves the gods, too, and the people. It is yours who stops him knowing them.'

'Dumai.' Nikeya cupped her cheek. 'I know I am a Kuposa. I know you see me as his instrument, a bird who sings only his songs, but I told you. I am my own woman.' Her voice caught. 'I can't deny that I am like him. But I am also like my mother, and she taught me to love the gods. So I will stand with you ... and I would be your comfort. If you let me.'

When Dumai drew back to look at the Lady of Faces, she found her gaze as bright as tumbled stone, her lips a silent invitation. This was her true face, vulnerable in its nakedness.

Her fingers were still cold. Dumai almost closed her eyes when Nikeya brushed her cheeks, her lips – except she never wanted to stop looking at her. In this glow, she was painted in moonlight.

'I don't watch to watch you fade on that throne,' came her whisper. 'Look at my cousin. Sipwo is a ghost of her old self, starved of love. You'll suffocate without it, Dumai.' She was so close. 'It's just us here. No one will know.'

Seiiki was so far away. Dumai touched her wrist – and it was all of it, all of her, her cleverness and her smile and her laugh, her fearless resolve, her warmth in the iron cold of the North.

It was her loyalty, which could be a trap, but could just as well be real, in this place.

It was two long years and thirty years. It broke her guard. It broke the lock. She let go of her last shred of resistance, and it floated away, lighter for having been released. Nikeya leaned into her, holding her face as if it were unbearably delicate, fingertips light as breath. Dumai grasped her in return – and then Nikeya kissed her, soft as the first rain of spring, washing the rest of the world away.

All her life, she had buried the part of her that longed for an embrace like this. There had been little room for softness on the mountain, where survival and ritual had been all that mattered.

But this mattered now. Within that kiss, nothing else did. Seiiki was gone, and so were the intrigues of court and the lure of the sky, and anything else that would keep them apart.

Nikeya drew back to whisper her name. Dumai breathed her in, a wingbeat between her legs. When their lips met again, warmth filled her throat like a long drink of sunlight.

Daughter, have you lost your senses?

No, she thought. *No, I have found them.*

A memory welled, of the first time she had seen another woman naked – a young widow of Ginura, warming herself in the hot spring after her climb. Her hair down her back, long dark brushstrokes of it, and her hip, curving like a shell from the sea.

The woman had caught her looking and smiled, and Dumai had rushed off to finish her chores, face on fire. Later, the woman had caught her in the corridor and kissed her on the cheek, leaving with a wisp of laughter. It was all she had thought about for a month.

She had not understood her feelings. Not then. She had tucked that morning and that sweet kiss away, to cherish only in secret, in darkness – but from then on, her senses were sharp around women. A sharpening not like the tip of a blade, but like music soaring to the height of its power, or an unexpected chill, making her breath catch and her skin awaken. Some women left her with the thought that everything was new and bright.

Kuposa pa Nikeya had made her world so bright it hurt.

Now the hurting ceased. Nikeya threaded both arms around her, and Dumai pressed her as close as she had always yearned, and it made sense, it had always made sense.

You are near.

Dumai broke the kiss, chest hitching. 'Dumai.' Nikeya touched her cheek. 'What is it?'

'The messenger.' Dumai was already on her feet, delving into the mountain with a laugh. 'She's here.'

Wait for me, sister. The voice coursed through her mind, drowning Nikeya. *Go to the place I showed you. I will meet you there.* This was why she had come here. The small glow in her hand lit the way.

She emerged from another crack in the rock, a different flank of the mountain, where two peaks walled a small, deep valley. The sun had bronzed the sky.

Nikeya stepped out, too, blinking against the light. Dumai crunched uphill, through untouched snow. 'I must say, this is a first, Princess. I have never kissed someone and had them run away at once,' Nikeya remarked, trudging in her wake. 'Usually they wait a few hours.'

'Please, Nikeya, be quiet.'

'I'll be quiet as a pond if you tell me what's happening. I don't see a map in your hand.'

'I hear her. Just like I hear Furtia.'

'Who?'

'The woman in my dream.'

'Wait.' Nikeya was already out of breath. 'You're telling me we're here because you had a dream?'

At the top of the slope, Dumai stopped. Before her lay another field of snow, and across it was the mountain she had seen, with twin peaks. The sight of it made her laugh again, in sheer relief. It was real. Her sister must be here. She stepped forward, and then straight back.

Something felt wrong. She took stock of the scene, the long downward course of the snow from elsewhere in the mountains. To the west, it suddenly fell away, as if cut with a knife. Dumai knelt to scrape the top layer off, finding dense ice beneath, pleated and wrinkled like cloth left to dry, shaded with blue. Somewhere below, she could hear water rushing.

'It's a glacier. A climber told me about them,' she said. 'The ice moves too slowly to see, but it is always moving. Always melting.' She straightened. 'These can be very dangerous.'

'Then let's not cross it.' Nikeya grasped her elbow. 'Dumai, answer me. You really came to the North ... for a dream?'

A thread of black was rising farther down the glacier. Without replying, Dumai started towards it, then passed her other sickle to Nikeya. 'In case you slip,' she said, and headed for the smoke.

Close to where the ice ended, a crag of weathered rock carved free, long and flat enough that several wooden buildings had been raised on it, not like any she had seen in the East. That must be where her sister was waiting.

They picked their way along the thick ice. At one point, Nikeya strayed too far, and her boot punched through a rotten spot. Dumai steadied her, and Nikeya clutched at her sleeve in return, breathing out long sashes of fog. After that, they tried to keep to solid ground.

When Dumai saw the dark mounds on the snow, she paused, instinct rising. Taking a deep breath, she risked the glacier and walked slowly towards the nearest.

A young woman lay dead, brown eyes iced open. Her hands were red, and blood had soaked into the snow, from the gash that lined her throat from ear to ear.

Nikeya caught up. 'The sickness.' She took a step away, covering her mouth with her sleeve. 'We should not be here.'

Dumai counted the bodies. Most of the twenty she could see were almost naked, despite the perishing cold, and long cuts streaked their limbs, like those on the young soldier near the Daprang.

It only occurred to her that there must be at least one survivor – the person who had lit the fire, who had cut the others' throats – when a bellow of anger came from the outpost, and a man with a sword was running towards them.

75

North

They made their way up a long mountain pass, where the Hraustr crest was emblazoned on teal banners. Wulf could smell snow on that wind, a skill known to most Northerners – an early promise of autumn. He stopped to wait for Thrit, who trudged up to join him.

The pass opened straight on to the ice helm, which looked about a mile wide, filling a deep valley between two sides of the Oxhorns. Snow covered its gaps, like butter smoothed with the flat of a knife. That made it far more dangerous than if it had been naked. Wulf swung his longaxe into his hand, watching the ground for the shadows and tucks that boded a hidden crack in the helm. At least the layer of snow was thin.

About halfway across the ice, an isle of rock hunched free. Hróthi buildings huddled on it, flying the same banners. Wulf tested the ice underfoot before he took the first step, Thrit at his side.

'I used to have nightmares about falling into a break,' Thrit said. Their cleats rasped through the snow. 'Vell always said they were bottomless.'

'Don't talk about it.'

'Fine. I'll think about it.'

Wind whistled along the frozen valley, battering their cloaks. Wulf let himself imagine a merry hearth, a song or two to cheer the soul. He stopped when he saw movement, expecting a scout. Two figures were on the ice, and seemed to be fighting.

'Now, what could that be about?' Thrit said, nose pink with cold.

Wulf shook his head and kept going. As they got closer to the outpost, he slowed again.

He recognised one of the people on the ice.

Karlsten was near as white in the face as his surroundings. Gaunt and filthy, in greasy furs, he swung his greatsword at a small woman with dark hair, who was narrowly keeping out of his reach.

'Get away,' Karlsten roared at her, the words almost snatched by the wind. She parried with some manner of blade, but the shock of it almost felled her. 'Wyrm-loving witch!'

'Karl.' Wulf cupped his hands around his mouth to bellow it. 'Karlsten!'

He was too far away. Wulf threw himself into a run. He spied a tell-tale crinkle in the snow and jumped it without breaking pace.

Now he was closer, he could see a third person, sprawled on her side. Straight black hair swung off her shoulders, damp with snowbrowth. She shouted in a language Wulf had never heard.

As he approached, her eyes locked on to his. They were dark and wide, their lashes speckled with snowflakes. She was not a Hüran rider. The Hüran did not wear armour like hers – in fact, he had never seen clothes like hers, except for the pelt. She had to be Eastern.

Wulf raised his axe a little. Since she was in armour, she had likely come to raid Járthfall. She held up a sickle with a fortified handle, face hardening around her pain. Blood smudged the snow where she had been, and her free hand was pressed to her waist.

The injury would keep her down. Wulf ran past her. 'Karl,' he shouted again. 'Karl, it's us!'

Karlsten let the blade fall, panting. The other woman stole the chance to run towards her fellow raider. Her weapon was an identical sickle, and she wore no armour at all.

'They're all dead,' Karlsten said, with a hoarse laugh. Under the sweat and blood, his face was tearstained, eyes raw. Red sleeved him almost to the elbow, but not the red of the plague. 'I had to kill Sauma, our Sauma. She wouldn't stop screaming. None of them would.' He pounded the side of his own head. 'No place in Halgalant now.'

'Karl, come here. Let's go home.' Thrit held out a wary hand. 'These women are no threat.'

'I'm not going anywhere.' Karlsten spat on the ice. 'No surprise that you turned up, Wulfert Glenn. Did you summon this pair of witches here, too?'

Wulf chanced a look at the women, who were backing away.

'I don't think they're here to fight,' he said to Karlsten. 'Scavenging for food, maybe. These are brutal times.' He widened his stance. 'I can't let you kill innocents, Karl.'

'Innocents.' Karlsten let out a bitter laugh. 'Those two rode here on a wyrm. I saw it.'

'No one can ride a wyrm.'

'The Saint didn't bury the old world deep enough. Its vice must burn away.' His face lost all mercy. 'This is the way I take back my seat. I should have done this years ago.'

'I don't want to fight you, Karl,' Wulf said, 'but I will.'

'Good.'

Karlsten swung up his bloody sword. Wulf stood his ground, and raised his own weapon.

Almost in the same moment, darkness unfurled across the ice in the near distance.

Wulf stared, fingers turning bloodless on the axe. A great black lindworm had appeared at the top of the valley, near as large as Fýredel. In unison, he and Thrit went for their bows.

The ice creaked and strained under the sheer bulk of the creature. Its eyes were blue, like the seat of the hottest flame, and icicle teeth glinted in its maw. Wulf blinked away a sudden wash of memories.

'Saint's bones,' Thrit said, voice fainter than its wont. 'Wulf – I think that could be a dragon.'

And then, with a howl of pure rage, Karlsten charged up the snow towards it.

****

Dumai ran after the Northern warrior, fighting the pain where his sword had caught her. She pitched over the ridges and swells of the glacier, using her sickle to surmount the larger surges.

Ahead, the Northerner leapt across a deep blue rift, while Dumai was forced to stumble around it, the deep wound in her thigh pulling. *Furtia, get away*, she tried to call, but her leg seared like hot iron, yanking her focus off her mind. She tripped and fell hard on her knee.

Furtia watched the enraged human run at her, baring her teeth. He swung his enormous sword, slicing through scale and flesh in a spray of white sparks and silver blood, and the dragon screeched, twisting away from him with a swing of her tail. Dumai heard herself cry out in anger.

He was going to kill a god. The sight brought tears to her eyes. Furtia snapped at him, and her clawed foot broke straight through the ice, making her blunder.

Dumai reached the Northerner just as he raised his blade again, and blindly drove her sickle at him, punching it between his shoulders. She wrenched it free, finding blood on its tip.

Her hand shook. She had never *attacked* anyone, never wanted to. The Northerner rounded on her, hate oozing from every crease of his face, and dealt a sickening blow to her stomach. Before she had even felt the pain, he had slammed his head into hers and shoved her away from him, down a steep icy slope. She heard Furtia roar before she hit a solid fold.

Earth child. Dumai tried desperately to get up, her spikes grating. *I cannot fly . . .*

Come to me, great one . . .

'Dumai—' Nikeya reached her, turning her on to her side. 'Are you hurt?' Dumai could only cough in answer, agony flaring in her middle. The other Hróthi overtook them. 'Stop him,' Nikeya shouted at them in Lacustrine. 'Is this how Northmen treat a god?'

The pale Northerner was driving Furtia up the glacier, hacking at her with his heinous sword. The other two men went after him, wielding axes. Dumai could only slump on her side.

'Help Furtia,' she wheezed at Nikeya, who snatched up the sickles, face set in resolve, and ran towards the dragon. Dumai felt a strange twinge of recognition and looked towards the outpost, far away – to where two figures had appeared on the frozen river.

One was slightly ahead of the other, closing in at a tremendous pace. Whoever the woman was, she ran faster than anyone Dumai had ever seen. Greying curls sprang around her brown face, flecked with snow, and she dressed like the Hróthi. She held a jointed spear in one hand.

Furtia caught her attacker with the slender end of her tail, whipping him away from her. He flew backwards, struck his head, and lay still, while the dragon pried her leg free of the glacier. Dumai struggled towards her, leaving a smear of blood in her wake.

Furtia . . .

But Furtia was not looking at her. She was looking at the woman with the spear.

Something changed in the dragon. Dumai stared up at her, feeling a crackle through the hairs of her arms, tasting metal. Furtia reared over them all with a deafening rumble, and when she crashed on to the ice again, her foot came down hard on the murderous Northerner.

Dumai muffled another cry with her fist. Not once in her life had she heard of a dragon killing a human, intentionally or otherwise. One of the Hróthi men let out a wordless bellow, but Furtia ignored it, her gaze nailed to the newcomer, tongue rattling.

The tall woman stopped and took up a defensive stance. She regarded Furtia as if she were a wolf or a bear, the barest shadow of caution in her gaze. Furtia roared, eyes flashing bright as lightning, a storm on earth. Rushing straight past Dumai, she charged the woman, forcing her into retreat. Dumai crawled in their wake.

Furtia, we have to leave, now!

SHE HOLDS THE RISEN FIRE.

The words were a thunderclap in her skull. Whiteness frosted her sight. She looked up just in time to see Furtia bearing down on the woman, who threw up her hand, palm facing the dragon. Fire exploded from her, a swathe of red and smokeless flame. It seared through her glove and melted the snow in one sluff, revealing the thick ice beneath.

Dumai stopped with a gasp. She had seen many bizarre things in a year, but her mind could not make sense of this. This woman had just made fire out of nothing, as a dragon summoned rain. Furtia screamed in fury. She blew a stormwind at the enemy, who slid back and dug her boots into the ice, her fire still leaping forth.

For the first time since Furtia had emerged from the lake, Dumai saw her as she was – inhuman and wild, an ancient celestial.

Someone grabbed her from the side. For a moment, she thought it was Nikeya, but Nikeya was still coming back down the ice. This face was unfamiliar, cowled in a hood, framed by golden hair.

And she knew. Looking at her, touching her, Dumai knew.

'Sister,' she breathed. 'Is it you?'

There was no more pull. They were together. Dumai laughed in relief, but the woman only tightened her grip.

'The stone,' she said in Seiikinese, her voice deep and cold. 'Did you bring it?'

'Yes, but—' Dumai looked harder, chilled. 'Are you the voice from my dream?'

There was no recognition or love in those eyes, none of the tenderness of their dreaming.

I am one of them, came a whisper in her mind.

Dumai stiffened, the joy freezing inside her. 'No.' She tried to get loose, but the woman had an iron hold on her. 'This stone is mine. Where is yours?' she rasped. 'Who are you?'

She could not think clearly before this icicle of a woman, whose gaze was flat and terrible. A blade flashed, and then she was cutting at Dumai, into her coat. They grappled for the box, thrashing like two fish on land, Dumai trying to kick away.

'I don't want to hurt you, Easterner.' A hand fastened on her throat. 'Give it to me now. It is not yours—'

Then the weight was off her. Furtia had seized the woman between her teeth. She flung her down the ice, towards the fire-wielding one, who had buckled to her knees.

Furtia was bleeding from the old wound in her side. The red fire – wyrmfire – had melted another slew of scales. As Dumai shuddered with uncontrollable cold, Nikeya wrapped an arm around her, pulling her on to Furtia.

'Furtia, go,' Dumai gasped, reaching out to touch the dragon. 'Go, now. Get away!'

She clung to a frond of manehair as Furtia turned, splintering the ice. The sound of churning waters grew louder.

I will find it, sister. Dumai risked a look back, and there was the pale woman, staring at her. *Do not think that you can hide it for ever. Only one of us will live that long.*

Nikeya dragged her into the saddle. As Furtia clawed up the weakened glacier, it heaved and cracked wide in her wake, and the whole valley broke in two.

****

Tunuva forced her hands closed, smothering the wyrmfire she could only just control. It had never blazed so hot, so red, as when she turned it on that wingless beast. Her fire had retaliated in a way it never had to other wyrms, licked out of her like sap from a tree.

664

Though it had resembled a horned serpent, it had not been like Dedalugun. Neither was it an amalgamation of animals; it was too large for that. It had not tried to breathe fire, and had not been redolent of siden, not at all – it had smelled of the sea, and the way it plucked her senses had reminded her of Canthe.

The glacier had yawned open, a split that ran from the Hróthi outpost almost to the top of the valley, too wide to clear with a jump. Canthe had been thrown a long way, and was sprawled on the ice, her hair tangled around her.

'Canthe,' Tunuva said, giving her a hand. 'Are you all right?'

'I'm fine.' Canthe looked different, her gaze hard and her white face stiff. 'Tunuva—'

Tunuva followed her line of sight. With her last strength, she ran towards the point of the breach where one of the three Northerners had been standing. His friend was on the other side.

He had fallen into the glacier as it broke. Gripping the wall with gloved hands and spiked boots, the young man tried to lift his weight, but he was too far down. Tunuva swung off her cloak and tossed one end to him, and she reeled him up, muscles working.

As soon as she pulled him to safety, he crumpled into her, shaking all over, and slowly he opened his brown eyes. Tunuva stared into them, and he stared back.

She had seen those eyes in mirrors for half a century. She had seen his face in a dream of bees.

And a name escaped her before she could stop it.

'Armul.'

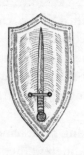

76

West

Arondine had burned for days. Its proud castle had crumbled into a midden, a tragic mockery of itself.

Hyll Sanctuary had suffered, but Fýredel had left some of it standing. The people gathered in the ashes outside it. They parted for Glorian Berethnet as she rode through the city.

Her mare whickered. Draped over its hindquarters, her cloak was the red of the Inyscan rose. Against the snow of ashes, it was a defiant reminder of the Nameless One – not of his coming, but his defeat. Inys might yet fall to his servants, but there would be no red wings in the sky. There was only the red of the blood royal, the blood that kept him chained.

The horse wore steel barding over its face. The silver keys of the House of Hraustr dotted its heavy black caparison, and the sword from her father hung at her hip. She spurred the mare up the steps to the sanctuary and dismounted. Part of the wall had fallen here, so they could all see inside, to where an ancient throne remained, blackened but intact.

As she walked to it, Glorian slowed, the coldness blooming. *Only one of us will live that long.*

She could not possibly be dreaming now. The voice was so distant, she could barely hear it – but hear it she did, in her waking mind.

But the Arch Sanctarian was nodding to her, and she continued towards him, tamping the echoes until they fell silent.

Somehow, she made it to the throne. Before her people, Glorian took her rightful place, and the Arch Sanctarian lowered a crown on to her head – spiked like golden teeth, a war crown.

'Glorian, third of that name, daughter of the House of Berethnet, Princess of Hróth, true descendant of the Saint,' the Arch Sanctarian shouted for all to hear, 'I crown thee now the Queen of Inys, twentieth to sit her throne, head of Virtudom – Glorian Shieldheart.'

Glorian grasped its arms, and they knelt to her.

She walked back into the dark light of the sun, and mounted her horse again. The people looked up at her – drained and grieving, but alive.

'I come before you,' Glorian said, 'among you, a woman of Inys. My mother was of royal blood, but my father was a bastard son, born in poverty in Bringard, nothing to his name. When war called, he answered – for freedom, for justice. He taught me to do the same.'

A wind rushed through the ruins, carrying the scent of smoke.

'Good people of Inys,' Glorian called, 'this is not a war like that which my father won in the North. We cannot raise our shields against the sickness ravaging our lands, nor fight with iron swords an enemy whose hide is iron. Though we are all warriors for the Saint, he will not smile to see us die for him in vain, trying to slay an army he cannot mean for us to vanquish. Though we are brave, we Inysh are also temperate. Without caution, without fear, courage is but folly by another name. A warrior who means to win knows when to save their strength.'

Her father, smiling at her, his face dappled by the light from the water.

'My friends, this is a test.' Glorian raised her voice: 'A new world *will* come from this fire, but for now, we must wait – wait for the Saint to scour our sins clean, and to judge the virtue in our souls.

'For now. And yet, should a time come when we do need to fight, when steel is the only way to survive, I will ask you to join me on the battlefield – and in return, I vow to you, I will give you a Princess of Inys, fruit of the unending vine, to shield you from the Nameless One. I carry her now; she grows in my womb – Sabran, seventh of that name!'

This time, they roared in triumph. Behind her, Glorian could feel Prince Guma gazing at the back of her head.

'Will you come when I call?' she shouted, raising her sword. 'Will you fight for Inys, for the Saint, for me?'

'Shieldheart,' someone bellowed, and they all took up the cry, the guards beating their shields. 'Shieldheart!'

Shieldheart.

Shieldheart.

Shieldheart.

77

North

His chest was on fire. He had swallowed all the water in the sea, and suddenly he woke – in Halgalant, now, in the hall of the Saint. Surely he could have that, this time. Let it be the end.

When he had dreamed of the heavenly court, he always hoped it would be warm. Instead there was a deep chill in his body, even though a fire rustled nearby. He peeled open his eyes, finding himself in a lumpy bed, bandages around his chest. Beneath them, his skin burned.

Memories formed a cracked mirror: a warrior devoured by hatred, hacking at the wyrm, at him. The greatsword slashing his chest. A scaled hide crushing Karlsten of Vargoy.

A hand stroked his brow. It belonged to a woman, sitting on a stool at his bedside.

He guessed she was about fifty, perhaps a touch younger or older. Tight black curls tumbled almost to her broad shoulders, rippled with grey, and her skin was a warm dark brown, freckled across her neckline and nose. A sole one sat on the bow of her lips, right where an archer would hold it. She wore a collared linen shirt tucked into trousers.

'Who are you?' Wulf said hoarsely. Her gaze was tender on his face. 'Do you speak Hróthi, or Inysh?'

'Neither.'

The words came from a pale woman, also tall, her golden hair in a long braid. She wore a gown of grey wool, kilted up to the thigh, showing calfskin breeches and fur boots.

'She is from Lasia,' she said, stepping into the room, 'and has learned only a scantling of Inysh.' She came to sit on the edge of his bed. 'You must be Wulfert Glenn.'

This one did speak Inysh. She had one of those rare ageless faces, though he doubted she was much older than forty.

'Aye.' Wulf wet his lips. 'You know me?'

'I know many things.'

'You'll know where Thrit is, then.'

'Your friend is keeping watch outside. We are in the outpost at Járthfall,' she said. 'We stopped so you could rest a little. One of the wounds you took went deep into your chest.'

'Karl.' Another memory caught up with him. 'Those women. They … rode a wyrm.'

'Peace, Wulfert. Everything is all right.' She placed a calming hand on his shoulder, as if she could hear the dunt of his heart. 'They are both gone. So is their beast.'

Her touch raised an odd feeling. Even though he was sure he had never seen her before, something was familiar. The other woman had not once taken her eyes off him.

'I assume you're raiders,' Wulf said, searching the room for his weapons by sight. 'Were you after food?'

'No, though the supplies here will be useful for our onward journey. My name is Canthe. And this,' the towhead said, 'is Tunuva Melim. She's your mother, Wulfert.'

Wulf stared at Tunuva, and Tunuva gazed back. Her thick lashes were damp.

'Armul,' she said, very softly.

He sensed its significance in her tone. This must be the name he was given at birth.

'This can't be right,' he said. 'I was found in Inys.'

Yet he did see a convincing resemblance. They shared the same high cheekbones, the same chin and strong jaw, and there was a certain likeness in their eyes as well.

'Yes,' Canthe said. 'Tunuva has long thought you dead.' She folded her hands in her lap. 'I am Inysh, like you, but also a traveller. A long time ago, I saw you at Langarth with your adopted family, the Glenns. Years later, I met Tunuva, and we fit the clues together. We set out to find you at once.'

'To find *me*. While the world is burning.'

'Tuva has walked through fire and plague to do just that, Wulfert.'

Wulf glanced again at Tunuva. He could see the grief and hope etched into her brow, smelted from the darkness of her eyes, laid so bare it almost hurt to look her in the face.

His thoughts were a strand picked loose from a cloak, unravelling into disorder. He found his anchors in her face, clinging to every detail: the empty piercings in her nose and earlobes, a faint birthmark near her temple, the places where lines had started to set in. Sad and tired though she seemed now, tiny dents were smiled into the corners of her mouth.

He was looking at his mother. He had a mother. After all these years, she had come searching for him, as he had always dreamed she might.

'Wulfert,' Canthe said, 'there will be time for explanations.'

She wore a gold love-knot ring on her forefinger. It looked old. *Gold*, he thought, distantly. *For royals*.

When he faced Tunuva again, a muscle clenched in his cheek. 'I want one explanation now,' he forced out. 'Ask her how I came to be alone in the woods, with no one on earth but a wolf to protect me. Ask her why I had to live thinking I might be cursed.'

Even if Tunuva had no Inysh, it was clear she heard his bitterness. Pain showed on her face. Canthe translated, and she answered in a soft voice.

He wished he understood her. Every time he had imagined meeting his first family, he had imagined them Inysh, too poor to have ever fed another mouth. Not once had he thought he might come from else-where. Not once had he pictured a woman like this, hale and strong.

'Wulf, I'm sorry,' Canthe said, 'but Tunuva has no idea how you got to Inys. We think you were abducted. She will tell you all she knows, but it is a deep wound you ask to tear open.' Wulf gave her a stiff nod. 'For now, may I ask why you were this far east?'

'Thrit and I were sent to bring the Hróthi from this outpost home.' He started to get up. 'Sauma and Karl, the others. I have to bury them.'

He tried not to think of the broken mess of Karlsten, or Sauma with stained hands. He wondered if the plague seeped through the skin, so even the skeletons would have red fingerbones. Now there were only two in their lith. *Eydag and Vell and Regny, dead,* Karlsten hissed into his ear, as if from Halgalant itself, *and all they have in common is Wulfert fucking Glenn.*

'We have already laid your friends to rest, in a cave not far from here,' Canthe said.

'You touched them?'

'Not with our bare hands … but the plague cannot take root in witches. Not you, either, I suspect.'

'You admit to being a witch?'

'It is the only word you know for what we are – but there are others, Wulfert. We can teach you.'

Wulf narrowed his eyes.

'Tunuva would like to take you to the South, to show you where you come from,' Canthe said, her tone gentle. 'She will tell you about your family and its purpose – the heritage that kept you from a cold death in the Ashen Sea. The part of you that you have always feared.'

'How do you know anything about me?'

'I am Inysh. Of course I know of the witching.'

'I can't go with you. I am sworn to the House of Hraustr,' Wulf said curtly. 'Einlek King needs all our blades.'

'Tunuva is a great warrior. She can teach you how to fight wyrms, and slay them. You can return to Hróth with even greater strength.' Canthe raised her eyebrows. 'Do you not want to know who you are?'

Wulf drew a deep breath. Sooner or later, Einlek would find out about the outpost and assume he was among the dead.

If he went, he might finally understand why he survived and others perished. He would know the answers he had sought all his life. The prospect lured and chilled him in equal measure.

For the first time, Tunuva spoke in Inysh.

'Please come,' she said quietly. 'I will tell you.'

He did have a memory of her. Not quite a picture in his head, but a feeling – the same feeling that had fretted at him as he ran through the haithwood. A love that had surrounded him. A low, calming voice, and a laugh in the sunlight. Those had belonged to her.

Salt tanged in the corner of his mouth. Seeing it, Tunuva stroked her thumb along his cheek.

'Armul,' she said again, in a whisper.

Einlek needed him. Thrit needed him. But when Tunuva called him by that name a second time, he accepted defeat. He had to go with her – to hear, at last, the tale that had been kept from him for twenty years. The secret that had stalked him all his life.

He owed it to himself. He owed it to Tunuva, if he really had been stolen from her arms. He owed it to the bairn inside Glorian, who might yet inherit whatever curse or gift was in him.

So he said, 'Where is it you want to take me?'

'To Lasia,' Canthe said. 'To see the truth.'

****

The outpost was two days behind them when Furtia Stormcaller collapsed. Dumai slid from the saddle and trudged up to her head. Her own skull hurt for lack of sleep; her face was swollen on one side. At least her waist had stopped bleeding.

Furtia flicked her tongue over the snow. Blood smeared her claws where she had blindly crushed the Northerner, and patches of dark scale had been misshapen, melted and warped by red flame again. She had not said a word since they fled the valley.

Dumai knelt before her and reached out to touch her claw, head dipped in deference. She needed to open her mind to the gods again, but now she was afraid, not knowing what poison might drip into her dreams. She had to make the waters of her mind freeze over, stopping any voices from entering.

'Great one,' she said, slow and clear, 'please, let me try to take the spear out.' A briny huff whipped her hair back from her face. 'Furtia, you need to heal.'

Mist curled from the dragon. Pain must have defeated her, for she finally lowered her enormous head to the ground. Dumai took hold of the spear and heaved at it with all her might. Furtia hissed as her crest squelched and clenched, and blood dribbled down her snout.

Dumai blew out a breath. Nikeya came to grasp the haft, and together they wrenched it clear. When the rest finally came free, they both fell into the snow in a heap.

'The only way this could be worse,' Nikeya said, puffing fog, 'is if a wyrm appeared and ate us.' Furtia shook herself, growling at the spear. 'Do you have anything resembling a plan?'

Furtia laid her head back down and closed her eyes. Dumai leaned against her, her stomach aching. 'We need to find a mountain or a lake. The sea would be best,' she said, her breath freezing in front of her, 'but I don't think we're anywhere close to it.'

'The glacier would thaw into a lake, wouldn't it?'

'We can't go back that way. Not when one of them could conjure wyrmfire.'

'Six met on the ice, not counting Furtia.' Nikeya reached up to stroke her. 'Which was your messenger?'

Dumai swallowed, her throat tethering. 'The one who attacked me. The pale woman,' she said, with difficulty. 'It must have been her, because she knew me, but ... she was not like she was in my dreams. She lured me here. I always thought she was my gift from the gods, but her words were a hook on a line, drawing me in.'

'Our gods have butterfly spirits to serve them. Master Kiprun said all things had their equal and opposite. Perhaps the wyrms have spirits, too, sent to trick and misguide us.' Nikeya knelt in front of Dumai, taking a knotted wrap from her coat. 'She wanted this, didn't she?'

Dumai watched her undo the wrap, revealing the stone. Furtia shifted in her sleep. 'What do you know of it?'

Nikeya wore a face Dumai had never seen on her, and did not understand. 'I heard an old story of a blue stone that could raise the sea,' she said, turning it over. 'Did you take it from Tonra?'

'Why are you asking me this?'

'Because it was not yours to take. Surely a godsinger knows better,' Nikeya said, her brow creased. 'Would you steal bones from a dragons' grave, or goods from a funeral boat?'

'You presume too much.' Dumai grasped the stone back from her. Furtia twitched again. 'Kanifa told me to take it. He trusted me to care for it, as you must not.' She lifted her chin. 'I am under no obligation to explain or justify myself to you – you who dare to speak of taking what was never yours. A kiss does not make you my consort.'

Nikeya flinched.

'No,' she said. 'Of course not. After all, I am a devious Kuposa, and you, a perfect Noziken.' She stood. 'We should find our way back to the river, Your Highness.'

As she returned to the saddle, Dumai pressed her brow against her knees, gnawed by remorse. She had not meant to be cruel to Nikeya.

Furtia gave her the gentlest nudge in her sleep, but even with a god at her side, she had never felt more forsaken.

At least there was the stone, tucked into her glove. It was all she had to show for her journeying.

'Great one,' Dumai said, touching Furtia, who cracked one huge eye open. 'Do you know what this is?'

She held it up. Furtia smelled it, light waxing beneath her scales.

The star shed this. It should have been swallowed into the waters. The words broke through the ice Dumai had tried to layer on her mind, giving her a sudden headache. *It holds a great and terrible power.*

I can't use it.

It drinks from somewhere far away. It drinks, and it binds, and it does not sleep. Furtia gave it another sniff. *It has little more to give, but it sings to me. I am of the star, and so is this – and so are you.* She touched the very tip of her tail to it, and the whiteness at its core shone like a tiny moon. Dumai breathed fog as it turned colder in her hands. *With this, we will be stronger, earth child. It will lead us back to the salt waters; it will lead us home.*

78

North

'I still don't like it, Wulf,' Thrit said.

They stood on a cobbled beach near Eldyng, Thrit shouldering his pack.

'We've talked about this,' Wulf said quietly.

They had argued about it, in fact, as they sculled an abandoned boat along the coast – one oar held by his mother, and the other by the Inysh woman, Canthe. She had been the one to offer the bones of an explanation to Thrit, which had not been received well ('This all has the smell of a cult, frankly, and I don't think Wulf should go near it'). She had explained that Thrit could not go with them, which had caused a little more arguing.

'I understand why you need to do this. I do.' Thrit sighed through his nose. 'But the two of us are all that's left.'

'That's why you should be far away from me.'

'Not this again.' Thrit grasped his nape. 'Listen. Karlsten died because he saw danger in difference. He saw it in those women; he saw it in their dragon. Some people *need* to call others evil, so they can seem pure and righteous in comparison, or to purge contempt they hold in secret for themselves. Karlsten gave in to that. In the end, it swallowed him.'

'He could be good. I remember.'

'Believe he was born rotten, or that something rotted him. Either way, he was a churl – but it might help if the world was different. We could start by not scorning one another for our beliefs, or lack of them,' Thrit said, with a bitter flinch of his mouth, 'but perhaps it's too soon for that. Perhaps it will take the end of the world.'

'Aye.' Wulf paused. 'You really think that was a dragon?'

'Like I told you, it's been centuries since anyone last saw one.'

'It attacked Tunuva.'

'I know.' Thrit looked grim. 'That isn't the story my grandparents told.'

The waves kept a tense silence from falling. Wulf thought of the road ahead, long and unknown.

'I'd best be away,' he said. 'Will you stay in Eldyng?'

'I think I'll go to Inys, if Einlek will let me. Someone needs to make sure the Yscali heathen doesn't get his teeth into Queen Glorian.'

'I'll meet you there, when I can. Look after yourself, Thrit.'

'Wulf—'

Thrit clasped his arm, hesitating. His grip was firm, then gentler.

'Thrit?' Wulf said, only for Thrit to take him by the jaw and kiss him.

It was the swiftest press of lips, delivered almost in one breath. Wulf had just enough time to feel the softness and warmth of it. Before he could so much as close his eyes, or even understand what had just happened, Thrit took a full step back, looking shaken by his own boldness.

'Sorry,' he said, with a nervous laugh. 'I did try to hint, quite often, but—' He cleared his throat. 'If I didn't do that now, and you got yourself killed, I'd never forgive myself.'

Wulf knew he needed to speak – perhaps more than he had ever needed to speak in his entire life – but all he could do was stare. By the time he woke his tongue, Thrit was halfway up the beach, muttering curses to himself.

'Thrit,' he called, hoarse as a parched crow. Thrit stopped at once. 'I'll come back. Don't ... die.'

Wulf glimpsed a sweet and unexpected future, far away. Then he turned around and walked towards his past.

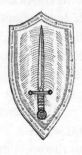

79
West

The Harmur Pass remained shut, but no soldiers defended it now. They swam around the locked gates, hauling their horses through the shallows of the Gulf of Edin.

When they reached the Ersyri side, Tunuva knelt on the sand and gathered it between her fingers, breathing in the scent of the desert. She was back in the South. Every day moved her closer to home.

She watched Wulf as he took it in. He must never have imagined a place like this, with sand to the horizon. Even after weeks of travelling with him, Tunuva could not stop stealing glances at his face, hoping for another shift in his expression, a detail she had missed.

In some ways, he was Meren: thick stern brows, a bony nose. It ached to see those again, in their child – but Wulf was also her. They shared the same narrow ears, the same cheekbones and jaw and chin. His eyes reminded Tunuva of herself, but also of her own birthmother, Liru.

He was no longer the smiling boy she had fed and rocked and sung to sleep. No, those eyes spoke of terrible hardship. He was quieter than she had expected – but then, she tended towards reserve, too. Meren had been more expressive, as free with his laughter as his gestures.

Their child should have learned to speak Selinyi. Instead, Wulf had been taught the harsh language of the Hróthi and the rolling lilt of northern Inys. Each time he fell asleep, Canthe taught Tunuva a little more Inysh, but a few sentences would not make her fluent.

There had been no mother in the house he grew up in. Tunuva was ashamed of her relief. It would have pained her so much more, to know her place had already been filled.

'What is that?' Wulf said. His hand strayed to the axe at his side. 'Canthe, is that a ... lioness?'

Tunuva followed his line of sight. In the middle distance, a pale shape was kicking up dust.

'No. Far better,' Canthe said warmly. 'It's Ninuru.'

When she reached Tunuva, the ichneumon pitched her off her feet and licked her face raw. Tunuva flung her arms around her friend. 'Nin,' she said, laughing. 'How did you know?'

'You fed me.' Ninuru licked her once more. 'You left.'

'I know.' Tunuva pressed her face into sleek white fur. 'I'm sorry, honeysweet. I won't go again. Will you take us home?'

Ninuru looked to Wulf, who was staring at her in amazement.

'He smells of you,' she told Tunuva.

80

East

Ever since the gods had woken, they had carried a thick haze of sleep on them. The blue stone ripped it clean away. With Dumai pressing it to her scales, Furtia had sniffed out a deep black lake in a valley, strewn with the remnants of a North Hüran camp, and broken a hole in the ice.

Once she was submerged in water, the wound in her crest had started to heal. She caught them silver fish between long sleeps.

Dumai spoke to Nikeya only when necessary. For once, Nikeya returned the favour. She disappeared for hours into the forest by the lake, hunting what deer and birds remained. When she came back, she skinned and roasted her spoils in silence, no spark in her eyes.

Each time they lay down to sleep, Dumai wanted to ask her forgiveness. Each time, stubborn pride strangled the words.

It was better this way. She had trusted the voice in her dream, and it had betrayed her. It was a sharp reminder not to trust Nikeya, either. No matter how sweet her kiss, she was silver.

No matter that she saved your life.

Seiiki was all that mattered now. This journey had been a terrible mistake.

On the seventh day, Furtia was healed enough to fly, and they left the North behind them. The dragon took them back across the Broken

Corridor, then followed the coast of the Empire of the Twelve Lakes, knowing her way home. Dumai slipped in and out of sleep. Her physical hurts were mending, but they tired her.

Sister?

Dumai woke halfway to the inbetween. Her exhaustion had softened the dark ice of her mind, letting a voice from outside flow again.

You would still dare to call me sister?

I . . . don't understand. Her breath knotted in her chest. *You haven't spoken in so long. I felt alone without your voice.*

Do not think to deceive me with yours again. For the first time, she turned her back on the stream. *You will take nothing more from me.* Before the trickster could answer, she shook herself awake, the tears cold on her cheeks. One day, she might think of the betrayal and not weep.

The Grand Empress would know how to cut what had tethered her to the dreamer.

She had to do it soon.

****

A dark smog lined the Sundance Sea. As it refined into a coastline, Dumai gazed towards it. She felt and smelled the smoke before it came in sight – piled over the island, smothering the sunset.

Seiiki was on fire. It blazed with such a fury that the flames made their own wind and cloud.

Dumai watched a herd of deer stampede from a roaring wall of light. She saw a single wolf, its pelt ablaze. Hot ash made her cough until she tasted her insides. She leaned to the side of the saddle and saw two dragons in a meadow, broken and tangled in death.

No.

Nikeya woke with a dry cough of her own. Seeing the conflagration, she made a faint sound against her sleeve.

Now comes the fire beneath, the swollen earth. Furtia spoke for the first time in days. As she passed through the black smoke, her crest flickered. *The star has not yet wept, earth child.*

I know, great one. Dumai swallowed, tears running again. *I know.*

The wyrms must not have been in Seiiki long. Past the coast, Furtia flew over unscathed fields and trees. Below, people were fleeing towards the capital. Dumai realised why when Furtia came within sight of

681

Antuma. Several dragons had formed a circle of protection around Mount Ipyeda and the Rayonti Basin, including Tukupa the Silver.

Furtia sailed between them, towards the palace, and landed in its main courtyard. Dumai dropped to the ground.

The walkways rushed past. A few courtiers were outside, wet cloths pressed over their mouths, but Dumai paid them no heed. Reaching the Inner Palace, she stopped, giving Nikeya time to catch up. The guards wore grey tunics beneath their armour, masks of iron and leather over their lower faces.

'Stay back.' One of them reached for their sword. 'The Inner Palace is sealed.'

'Where is my father?'

'Princess Dumai,' another said, eyes shocked above the mask. 'You're ... alive.'

'Why should I not be?'

'You must see the River Lord. He is in the Throne Hall,' came a muffled reply. Dumai marched in that direction, though not before she heard someone mutter, 'Great Kwiriki, what is to be done now?'

Nikeya followed her. 'Dumai,' she said, 'grey is for mourning at court.' Dumai shut her mouth tight. 'His Majesty—'

'Do not say it.'

Nobles thronged the Throne Hall, traced by the dim reflections off the water. Dumai shouldered through their ranks. When they realised who had come among them, their mutterings sharpened into chatter, and they parted to make way, so she could see the Rainbow Throne.

The throne, and her sister, sitting on it.

Suzumai wore paling layers of grey. The mantle that swamped her was almost black, a silver crown teetered on her head, and her hair was combed to her waist, laden with dancing pearls. Seeing Dumai, she stared at her damp furs and dishevelled hair, the bruising on her face.

'Suzu,' Dumai said, just as stunned.

'Princess Dumai,' came a familiar voice, before her sister could utter a word. 'Can it be you?'

Dumai stiffened. She had failed to notice him beside the throne, a shadow by her sister.

'It is. And you, Nikeya,' the River Lord said, his face a picture of relief. 'I never thought to see you again.' He wore a small crown of seashells. 'Thank the great Kwiriki.'

'We are both very well, Father.' Nikeya came to stand beside Dumai, sliding on her court self like a sleeve. 'But this is a disturbing sight indeed. Where is Emperor Jorodu?'

The question covered the hall, silencing every whisper.

'Tragedy has struck our court. A band of murderous provincials infiltrated the palace,' the River Lord said, his voice breaking the utter quiet. 'They were demanding retribution for an outbreak of sickness on the coast – a sickness that turns the hands red and boils the blood. They believe it arrived with a Lacustrine ship, which brought a crossbow for you, Princess Dumai.'

'Consort Jekhen offered it to me in exchange for my assistance,' Dumai said. 'To help us fight the wyrms.'

'Unfortunately, provincials are of a crude and rustic mindset, thinking of little beyond their fields. They saw an arrival from the mainland and blamed it for their suffering. It was dismantled in a riot, and the Lacustrine soldiers who brought it were killed.'

'What?' Dumai whispered.

Out of sight, Nikeya gripped her wrist, hard enough to hurt.

'By the time the guards cut them down, the intruders had breached the Inner Palace, infecting His Majesty. He fought very hard ... but he was the Son of the Rainbow,' the River Lord said heavily. 'His body could not withstand such pain, such fever.'

Dumai looked between the River Lord and her sister, her stomach warning her of a trap.

'I'm sure this must be a great shock, Princess,' the River Lord sighed. 'I offer my sincere condolences.'

'What was done with his body?'

'We had no choice but to burn it,' said one of his many cousins. 'We do not yet know how this sickness spreads. It was all we could do.'

No Seiikinese ruler had ever been burned. He should have been laid in a river barge, on a bed of pearls, sung to the sea without end.

'Since you could not be found anywhere, we feared you had been captured and killed,' the River Lord said, wringing his hands in a show of distress. 'The Council of State made the difficult choice to enthrone your sister – the heir apparent – as Empress Suzumai.'

He could make anything sound reasonable, even usurpation. The gift of his silver tongue.

'I am a dragonrider – a woman, firstborn,' Dumai managed to say. Nikeya tightened her grip. 'Suzumai is a child of nine.'

'Your father was the same age, and he was a splendid ruler, as were many children of the rainbow before him. All of us are here to help and guide Empress Suzumai. I hoped you would join us.' His voice was the gentlest reproach. 'Princess, as a former godsinger, would you truly ask us to unravel the sacred rites of an enthronement?'

Discordant murmurs filled the hall. Suzumai looked nervously at her new subjects. 'I'm sorry, Dumai,' she said. 'I didn't mean to take your throne. I thought you were dead.'

'As you all see, I am alive,' Dumai said coolly. She had to maintain her composure. 'As my father informed the Council of State, I was making a private visit to my grandmother.'

Years of work and planning. All the groundwork the remnants of her family had carried out in secret, undone in a few days. With Emperor Jorodu dead, there could be no shadow court.

She had been a naïve fool, to leave at such a fragile time. Nikeya had been right to warn her.

'Now you have returned,' the River Lord said, 'I would like to address some matters of great import, Princess.'

'Let us address them. Here, my lord,' Dumai said. 'In the open.'

'As you wish. First, I must dispute your belief that your age prepares you to rule. Suzumai has lived at court all her life, while you spent yours on a mountain. You have no particular knowledge of Seiiki. You have been to Mozom Alph, but not Ginura.'

'Father,' Nikeya said, with a feather of laughter, 'surely you know that Furtia Stormcaller summoned Princess Dumai on her journeys. Would you ask her to ignore the gods?'

'Never, daughter, but it does not change the fact that the heir to Seiiki abandoned it in a time of need. We cannot live in fear of that. Second is the delicate matter of how this red sickness entered Seiiki,' the River Lord said, after a polite hesitation. 'Princess, before your journeys into the world, we were safe. Now we are not. It pains me to do this – but I must, for the sake of Seiiki. Will you please show us your hands?' Dumai did it without question. 'Ah. Your fingers. Does the sickness not begin there?'

Dumai frowned as voices bristled again. 'Lord Kuposa, I have lacked these fingers since I was ten.'

'It will raise questions among the people, Princess Dumai,' the River Lord said, sighing yet again, as if all this sent him into despair. 'These wyrms have set their minds to fear. I think it best that you leave once more, for your own protection ... to Muysima.'

Dumai held his gaze. 'That is the place of exile.'

'That is not true, Princess. It is somewhere you will be safe for a time, where you may know contentment.'

'No,' Suzumai cried. 'Granduncle, please, don't send Dumai away.'

'Now, Your Majesty—'

'Please.' She was suddenly in tears. 'She is my sister, my only sister. I want her to live here.'

The River Lord knelt beside the throne.

'Your Majesty, I serve at your command,' he said. 'I think we could find a way to let Princess Dumai stay. I know it would comfort you.' Suzumai nodded at once, making her crown quiver. 'But your big sister is in grave danger. She must not keep flying away from court. She must respect my place as regent and obey, or there will be quarrels, and she must always show you deference. Do you understand that, Your Majesty?'

'Yes,' Suzumai said shakily. 'Please, Dumai. Say you will.'

For nine years, the child had been kept docile and dependent, in awe of her granduncle.

Another silver Noziken.

Dumai looked at them all, the whole belfry of courtiers. Her father had summoned her because she owed allegiance to no one. Now she saw that no one owed allegiance to her, either.

I am alone. She stood at a great distance from herself. *I am alone, with my foot in the fishnet.*

No, not alone. Outside, a dragon waited for her. The stone was tucked between her breasts. And when she heard the words in her head, they did not belong to a god, or a woman in a dream. It was her own voice.

What are you doing?

As that question filled her mind, a weight lifted.

She did not have to fight this battle. She did not have to stand here and try to outwit the River Lord. She did not have to become like him – and she had come so close, some days. This court had made her reckless, untrusting and hard; it had almost made her cruel.

Now she remembered the godsinger of Mount Ipyeda, who had wished for nothing more than the life she already had. That godsinger had needed no throne to serve Kwiriki, or to help the people of Seiiki. After all, she had known Kwiriki before she ever set eyes on his throne.

You are a kite, a rainbow, a rider. The realisation tilted the corners of her lips. *Where have you ever belonged but the sky?*

Before she could think better of it, she walked towards the throne and knelt, taking Suzumai by the hand. 'Your Majesty,' she said, 'I love and respect you, as your big sister. I will not ask for the Rainbow Throne. You have every right to sit on it, too.' She touched her cheek. 'I must leave again, for a little while, but I will always come back.'

Suzumai swallowed, eyes shimmering. 'You promised you wouldn't go away again.'

'I know.' Dumai tightened her hold on her hand. 'I'm sorry. Will you keep me safe?'

'Yes,' Suzumai whispered.

Dumai looked at the River Lord, whose face betrayed his curiosity. He was trying to predict her next move.

'I do not wish to fight you when an enemy threatens our island. I would not seek to divide it from within,' Dumai said, rising to face him. 'My mother was once a ... provincial, as you say. She worked the barley fields of Afa. Her father was its governor, long ago.'

At last, understanding barbed his gaze. She wondered if he had ever guessed who Unora was, or if she had disappeared from his notice as soon as she was stripped of her nobility.

'As a godsinger, as a rider, and as a princess, I serve them,' Dumai told him. 'It is they who will suffer most in this time of fire. I have the means to defend them. I must use it.'

Beside her, Nikeya released a breath. The River Lord watched Dumai without speaking. She could see him preparing to reshape her words, the busy work behind his eyes.

'I will go into exile, but not to Muysima.' Dumai faced the nobles. 'Emperor Jorodu wished for power to reside in two places. The Grand Empress will attest to this, as will my mother, the Maiden Officiant.' Hundreds of eyes stared at her. 'I will honour his wishes. I will go beyond this court and establish my own, in the provinces – to protect our island, to give hope to the people, until the coming of the comet that will end this.'

Before the River Lord could steal the final word, she strode from the hall to immediate shouts of indignation, taking the path the nobles cleared for her, blocking out their voices as best she could.

Nikeya came after her. 'Dumai,' she called. Dumai kept walking. 'Do I really mean so little to you that you would turn your back on me altogether?'

Dumai slowed, and looked her in the face.

'Tell me the truth,' she said. 'Did you know he meant to enthrone Suzu in my absence?'

Anger tightened her face. 'You *still* think I am his to wield?'

'Please, Nikeya.'

'I did not know,' Nikeya said, flushed. 'I don't even know if he arranged the attack on your father. We both know that isn't his way. Whatever happened, you have given him exactly what he wants by leaving. You've lost.' She reached for Dumai, holding her face. 'I know how much you've suffered in such a short time, but to challenge him like that, before all his allies – do you not see?'

'Perhaps not,' Dumai said. 'I was not meant to see, Nikeya. This is not who I am.'

'Listen to me. Leave now, and Suzu will spend the rest of her life in the dollhouse. You can still feign submission,' Nikeya said. 'You can find ways to exert your will.'

'My father tried that for a very long time. He thought he was winning until he was dead,' Dumai said wearily. 'The River Lord plans to exile me. Better that I exile myself, on my own terms, for the good of Seiiki.' She looked towards the mountain, the wooden city in front of it, the forest on its slopes. 'I have not lost the game. I simply withdraw from it.'

'You are a Noziken. You cannot withdraw.'

'You believe that because you have played all your life, because you once knew no world beyond his world – but I have seen you outside it, Nikeya. There is more. Just come with me.'

Nikeya had worn more faces than Dumai could count, but never all at once. Her features were not a mask now, but pure embroidery, made up of the finest stitches of emotion: surprise, tenderness, sorrow, too many shades and myriads of feeling to be picked apart.

'It means so much that you would ask,' she whispered, 'but we both know I'm not meant to fly at your side. My power stems from him.'

Her smile was small and pained. 'Consort Jekhen was right; so were you. I am beautiful and silver, and nought else. I am a flower grown for court.'

Dumai might have agreed once. Instead, she took Nikeya by the hand and pressed one brief kiss to it.

'I am sorry for what I said in the North,' she said softly. 'Please watch over Suzu.'

She strode back across the courtyard, to where Furtia Stormcaller waited for her, and climbed into the saddle. Nikeya stood alone and pale, holding herself as if she would break.

Furtia, take us to Mount Ipyeda.

Dumai gripped the horn. Furtia rose, and then they were gone from the palace at last, soaring towards the mountain that was home.

She did not look back.

81

South

With Ninuru, the ride to Lasia was swift. Wulf sat behind Tunuva, his arms around her waist, while the ichneumon cleaved to the Spindles for as long as she could, so they had cover when a wyrm passed. There were fewer in the Ersyr now – they must have moved on. In their wake, they had left bodies rotting in the sun, settlements in ruin, and naked wanderers, their arms red.

Wulf shot each one down, stopping their screams. He had a good eye.

When they reached the Lasian Basin, Ninuru stopped, and Tunuva slid off to collect water from a broad pink leaf. When she returned, she found Wulf gazing up at the trees.

'You remember,' she said, summoning her Inysh.

Wulf nodded. 'Yes. A bit, I think.' He breathed in through his nose. 'It smells so green.'

In his fleeting smile, she caught a glimpse of her child, burbling as he took his first steps.

Ninuru forged her way into the trees. As they drew closer to the old fig, Tunuva began to feel perturbed. The thought of facing Esbar clenched her chest. Her sisters might not even be there. More likely they had been called to a city far away, to defend its survivors.

Wulf followed Tunuva through the roots of the fig. She lit the tunnel with her flame, seeing it fascinate and unnerve him. He looked more like Meren when he was curious.

'Your birthfather,' Tunuva said slowly in Inysh. 'Do you remember him?'

'No.' Wulf glanced at her. 'Who was he?'

'Meren.'

'Meren.' His pronunciation was careful. 'I'm sorry he's dead.'

Tunuva dropped her gaze with a nod, wishing they shared a larger trove of words.

On the other side of the tunnel, she removed the saddlebags from Ninuru and kicked off the sheepskin boots that had roasted her feet for leagues.

'Tuva?' She turned at that whisper of her name, and then Siyu was in her arms. 'Oh, Tuva,' she said thickly. 'You're home.'

'Siyu.' Tunuva grasped the back of her head, warmth flooding her heart. Siyu clutched her in return. 'It's all right, sunray. I'm home. I missed you.'

'I missed you, too.'

Tunuva framed her face, shocked by the change in it. Months of battle had sheared her cheeks thin and hollowed her eyes, making her seem older than her nineteen years, and scars laddered her arms, which were lined with new muscle. She had cropped her hair from her waist to her shoulders, strengthening her resemblance to Esbar.

'Esbar said you'd left,' she said quietly, a remnant of pain in her voice. 'Why, Tuva, when we needed you?'

Tunuva circled her cheekbone. 'I did have reason. I will leave you to judge it.' She hesitated, glancing towards Wulf. 'Siyu, this is ... my birthson, Armul. Wulf, as he was named in Inys.'

Siyu looked at him in disbelief. Wulf eyed her with wary interest.

'Your birthson,' Siyu said. 'Is it true?'

'I think it is.'

'I am so pleased for you, Tuva. Now you have your own child back.' Siyu smiled bleakly. 'You need not have your name disgraced by a poor fool like me.'

'Oh, Siyu – no, no.' Tunuva drew her close again. 'Having you carry my name is the great joy of my life. You are as much mine as you ever were. I just had to know.'

690

Siyu nodded into her shoulder. Tunuva suddenly remembered the day Esbar had told her birthdaughter the whole truth, and Siyu had come running, clambering into her lap to embrace her.

Tunuva, I love you. I'm so proud I have your name.

'I would do the same for Lukiri,' Siyu told her. Seeing Canthe, she went to kiss her on the cheek. 'Canthe, you're all right as well. I'm so happy you're all home.'

'Hello, sweet Siyu.' Canthe smiled. 'It's good to be back. Is Lukiri well?'

'Yes, she grows strong.'

'Siyu,' Tunuva said, 'is Esbar here?'

Siyu turned back to her with a guarded expression. 'Yes,' she said. 'We've been in Isriq, but Esbar said we should return, to replenish our magic and supplies. Those who were waiting here have gone out in our stead. Should I find ... Wulf somewhere to sleep?' she added, sounding out the Inysh name with interest. 'You must have had a hard ride.'

'If you could. Thank you, sunray.'

Siyu took him by the arm. Wulf let himself be shepherded away, still drinking it all in.

A lamp burned in her sunroom. It touched Tunuva, to see it lit and warmed. Even though she had abandoned the Priory, her chamber had been kept ready. She opened her chest of garments and changed into a fresh robe, resisting the urge to lie down and sleep.

'Tunuva.'

Esbar was in the doorway, dressed in pale apricot silks that fastened at her waist.

Her hair curled past her shoulders, tucked back to show her amber earrings. Like Siyu, she had new scars, thicker muscle. Strong as ever in body, but her face – her face betrayed the burden of leadership. Small dents undercut her eyes, which were dull and hard as stone. Tunuva closed the chest and stood.

Esbar confronted her with a clenched jaw. Not once in more than thirty years had Tunuva not known what to say to the woman she loved – but they had said so much, and not enough.

'Did you find him?' Esbar said at last. She stayed on the threshold. 'Your birthson.'

'Yes. He was in the North.' Tunuva mirrored her, holding her posi-tion. 'Esbar, before I say another word, you must know that at least

691

some of the Easterners are assisting the wyrms, and have wyrms of their own. One of them attacked us in the mountains, and two women rode it. Clearly it is an established alliance – they even had a saddle.'

'Did either of them have magic?'

'I couldn't tell. The wyrm attacked me on sight. It was not like any other I have seen,' Tunuva said. 'I think it had the same magic as Canthe. My red flame leapt to repel it.'

Esbar nodded. 'We'll consider the implications later,' she said. 'For now, we have enough to face.' She folded her arms. 'You are certain the person you found is Armul.'

'His Inysh family called him Wulfert Glenn, but I know he is the child I birthed. I see myself in his face. I see Meren.'

'Canthe was right, then.' Esbar stepped into the firelight. 'You were gone for a long time. I was afraid you had died.' She sat in the chair beside the fire. 'And then I was afraid you had decided never to come back.'

'Surely you know me better than that.'

'I thought so.'

Tunuva drew up the other chair, keeping the small table between them. 'Siyu tells me you have been in the Ersyr.'

'Yes. I have done as much as I can for Daraniya, but there are so many of these creatures, bent upon our destruction. I fear that this will only end when there is nothing left of us,' Esbar said softly. 'I cling to faith as flame clings to a wick already curled and black.'

'The Mother will see us through this, Esbar.'

'The Priory, perhaps. What of you and I?'

Tunuva had never thought she would feel truly cold again, until Esbar uq-Nāra asked her that question.

'That decision must be yours.' Her throat constricted as she spoke. 'Nothing has changed for me.'

Esbar sank deeper into the chair. 'All these years I have watched you grieve,' she said, 'and when you had hope, I failed to fan it. I was only afraid it was false hope, Tuva.'

'You thought you were doing the right thing. Desperation made me foolish.'

'We can all be foolish when it comes to love.' Esbar breathed out. 'Armul – Wulfert – is welcome here. I must confess, I am curious to see him. And glad to have a little more of you.'

All at once, her eyes were brimming. Esbar had not wept in so long. Tunuva reached across the table and took her by the hand, interlocking their fingers.

'Is it enough?' Esbar asked her in a strained voice. 'Is our life enough for you now, Tuva?'

'It was always enough. I just wanted the truth.'

Esbar tightened her grasp. 'I would not live another day without you by my side,' she said in a whisper. 'Be with me. Forgive me, and I will give you the same grace. Let us do what we were born to do.'

Tunuva leaned across to her, setting their brows together. There they sat, for a long time: breathing, staying.

82

East

The sun rose cold and grim above Mount Ipyeda. Each day, more smoke was darkening the sky.

'So you have all but declared war on the Kuposa,' the Grand Empress said. 'Well, granddaughter, I suppose that was one way to handle them. I expect the River Lord – the regent – will retaliate.'

She sat with Dumai and Unora in her quarters, just as they had all sat on the night Dumai learned who she was. Two years later, they were almost back to where they had begun.

'He has what he wants. A meek child on the throne, and the regency. There is no reason for him to attack me,' Dumai said. 'The River Lord may be concerned with his own power, but even he must see now that the wyrms and the sickness are more important. I have seen the destruction they have already wreaked in the rest of the East. Even in the North.'

'Perhaps. Or perhaps he will now see you as the only real threat to his dominion. After all, a Noziken has never defied him so openly, nor established a rival court.' The Grand Empress gazed towards the window. 'Unora, what do you say to all this?'

'I am no child of the rainbow, Manai.'

'You bore one, and she will need you. Dumai has no knowledge of the provinces. You do,' the Grand Empress said. 'You know how to survive in times of scarcity. That will be useful.'

Dumai said, 'I have your blessing, then?'

'My son wanted a shadow court. A rival court is . . . less subtle, perhaps, but this is no time for subtlety, and we are the rightful monarchs. We do not need to stoop to smiles and puppetry.' The Grand Empress looked at Unora. 'Prepare to leave. Help your daughter.'

Unora nodded and left, her face set in determination. Dumai knew her mother was angry with her for absconding to the North, but she also knew she was already forgiven.

Her grandmother set a taper to the woodfall.

'Osipa used to light this. I keep forgetting to do it myself,' she said, with a thin smile. 'She became my handmaiden when I was six, still the disregarded princess. Without her, I am having to learn new ways to live. I imagine you have these moments, too, when you trip on the spaces Kanifa filled.'

Dumai nodded. Being in the temple without him already hurt almost too much to bear.

The Grand Empress returned to her stool. 'Tell me your dreams, as you once did.'

Once, the dreams had been all that unsettled her. Dumai wished she could go back.

'For almost two years, I have dreamed of a voice, and a figure, standing by a stream,' she said. 'I have thought of her as many things: a reflection of myself, a sister and a friend. I have spoken to her, and confided in her. She helped me. And yet she betrayed me.'

As she told her grandmother everything, the Grand Empress seemed to grow more and more troubled.

'A shared dream,' she said, when Dumai was finished. 'Yes, child, I have heard of this. A thread between spirits, like dust between stars. Queen Nirai wrote of it. It is a rare and sacred thing . . . but even the sacred can be profaned. I cannot say who this woman is, but clearly we are not the only people in the world the gods have touched.' She shook her head. 'I sometimes wonder if Kwiriki even knows who sits upon his throne. All he wanted was for Seiiki to be strong, regardless of who ruled. Perhaps it matters less than we have all believed.'

Dumai watched her. 'Are you giving up hope that we can survive this?'

'Only questioning the price of survival. If the House of Noziken is ever to recover, you would have to bear an heir, Dumai. I sense your path does not lead you to motherhood. Should I – your grandmother – force you to go against your nature, all for the sake of preserving a name?'

'But we are the link to the gods. If the House of Noziken falls—'

'Snow Maiden herself had no special gift. The gods would choose again.' The Grand Empress sighed. 'Let us wait for this comet to pass. Then we will see what Seiiki decides. I will remain here, to pray for you, while your mother helps you establish your court.'

'You may not be safe so close to the city.'

'An old woman is no threat to the River Lord. Besides,' she said, with a touch of satisfaction, 'the gods linger close to the mountain. I do not think they will let me come to harm.' She took Dumai by the chin. 'Fly now, my brave granddaughter. Be who you were called to be.'

IV

The Long-Haired Star

CE 512

someone will remember us
I say
even in another time

                                                   – Sappho

83

South

A fire kindled by magic flickered in the hearth. Wulf watched it, wishing he could sleep a little longer.

Today was the day he would tell Tunuva. For weeks, he had considered whether to stay or leave, torn between two lives.

He was still a curiosity here. An outsider raised to worship the enemy. A noble in a place with few titles. A man better with blades than bread. In the Priory, war was the domain of women, who lived to exemplify and honour its founder, while men took care of the home.

But he was also an anointed brother, odd fit though he was. His head had been daubed with the sap of the tree when he was just an hour old. In the end, he had found a sense of belonging.

He still had to go back to his family in Inys. After the *Conviction*, they could not bear his loss again.

He would miss Siyu. She had given him the strongest welcome to the Priory, taking him under her wing in all things. Of the many women he now called *sister*, she felt most like family – never more so when she had told him why she was named after Tunuva.

He would miss Esbar, even if she had taken most of the autumn to warm to him. After all he had learned of the Priory – the truth of what had happened here, and who the Saint had been – he supposed he might be suspicious of armed Inysh outsiders, too, if he were her.

The men's quarters encircled a round chamber for rest and study. The walls were thick enough to dull the sounds of the nursery. Wulf walked along the corridor, where large vases overflowed with flowers, tended by the boys. He had never so much as watered a plant, but Sulzi, who was three years his senior, had taught him a little of how to care for them.

Wulf was glad. In the wake of so much fire, knowing how to nurture would be useful.

Tunuva had told him what had happened to his own birthfather. Now he knew why he heard the bees in his sleep. Now he would always know.

It was not quite sunrise. Tunuva would still be in the burial chamber, so he descended to the hot spring. A soak always fortified him. Perhaps it spoke to the magic slumbering in his veins.

He was still absorbing all of that: the orange tree, and Galian and Cleolind. The Priory itself was proof, or he might never have believed.

It should have hurt. This place should have confirmed his fears that he was the child of a witch – but acceptance was soft, and bitterness shrank the heart. He refused to be like Karlsten.

At last, he had the missing threads of the tapestry. He knew how old he was. He knew he had been born in winter. He knew why he was still alive. Since he was born, magic had slept in his blood, no more dangerous than warm oil or wax. It was no curse. All it had ever done was keep him safe, both from the plague and a death by cold water.

Tunuva was no witch. She was a warrior, and a woman of honour. He was proud to be her son.

He found her in the armoury, polishing one of her blades. Usually the men did such work, but she seemed to find peace in caring for her weapons.

She noticed him and smiled. 'Good morning,' she said. 'How are you?'

'Well,' he said in Selinyi. 'Just sore.'

In the months he had spent here, he had done his best to learn her language. Unlike Hróthi, Selinyi shared no roots with Inysh, but with help from Canthe, they had managed.

'It was a long journey,' Tunuva said, keeping her answer slow for him. 'You fight very well.'

'Thank you.'

Throughout the autumn and winter, he had helped the sisters defend the South from the two wyrms roaming there: Dedalugun and Fýredel. He had been the only man among them, but Esbar had refused to squander a trained warrior ('If you're staying here, boy, you can make yourself useful'). For the most part, they had been protecting the Wareda Valley.

He had only seen Fýredel once. It had made him sweat, as he did when he saw the white ship in his dreams.

'Can I help you?' he said to Tunuva.

'Yes.'

Wulf stood beside her. She nodded to her clever spear, and he started to scrape the dry blood from its engravings.

'I have to leave.'

It came out low and hoarse. Tunuva stilled for a moment, her lips tightening.

'I know,' she said, this time in Inysh. 'I know … you would say.'

He placed a hand over her wrist.

'I'm sorry,' he said quietly. 'For all of it, Tunuva. I'm sorry I was stolen from you. I'm sorry for Meren. I'm sorry we'll never know how it happened, and that we lost so much time.' He swallowed past the dryness in his throat. 'I'm sorry I can't stay with you.'

Tunuva forced a smile. 'You are a strong warrior, in the bone. Men, they are not the warriors here.' She grasped his hand. 'You have a life in Inys, in Hróth. Your family. Thrit.'

'I have a family here, too.'

Now her smile reached her eyes.

'Come.' She placed a hand on his back. 'We will find Canthe, and speak with Esbar.'

Canthe was reading in her room, dressed in sleeveless gold silks. Unlike the other women, she had no cloak, and Wulf had never seen her fight. She haunted this place like a ghost.

Still, he sensed a power in her. Not the comforting warmth he felt from Tunuva. No, whatever lurked in Canthe was strange, and struck him as familiar, in some distant way.

'Hello, Tuva. Wulf.' She closed her book. 'Imin told me you had returned. You must be tired from the road.'

'I'll be back on it soon,' Wulf said. 'I must speak with the Prioress. Would you help?'

'Of course.' Canthe rose. 'I take it this is not a private matter.'

'I'm leaving.'

'So soon?'

'For now, my place is in Virtudom.'

'I understand. The Priory is not an easy place for outsiders.' She gave him a wry smile. 'As I have learned myself.'

They found Esbar on her balcony, watching the sunrise. In the Lasian Basin, one could almost think the world had not come to an end. Several wyverns had flown over the valley, but the women had brought them down.

Esbar turned. Her gaze darted first to Tunuva, as always. It would be a comfort, to know they had each other here. Esbar was sharp as a thistle, but any fool could see that she would die for Tunuva – for anyone born into the Priory.

'Prioress.' Wulf inclined his head. 'I've come to take my leave. I must return to Virtudom.'

Canthe translated into Lasian. Esbar listened, arms folded.

'We knew your time here would not last. You are free to leave, as a brother of the Priory,' Canthe said, pausing when Esbar spoke again, 'but you will keep the vow you made when we showed you the tree. You will never utter a word of this place, nor tell its truth to anyone.'

'The Inysh should know,' Wulf said, looking at Esbar. She narrowed her eyes. 'Everyone in Virtudom should. They should know what Galian Berethnet was. Who really swung the sword.'

When Canthe had translated, Esbar shook her head, and this time, Wulf understood her reply.

'One day,' she told him in Selinyi. 'Not today.'

Wulf lowered his head a little. 'Tell her I swear it on my honour,' he said to Canthe. He went to one knee. 'Prioress, before I leave, I would ask a last favour of you.'

At this, Esbar stepped forward. 'Get up,' she said, in barbed Inysh. 'Here we do not bow or kneel.' She took him by the elbows, and Wulf rose, surprised. She must have learned from Tunuva. 'What do you ask?'

He took a deep breath. 'First, there's something you should know. About the Queen of Inys,' he said. 'She's with child.' He looked Tunuva in the eye. 'The child is mine.'

Tunuva stared at him. Beside her, Canthe was a statue, every feature still.

702

He had hoped not to confess it, but something in him felt he should. His child, the future Queen of Inys, might have magic of her own, even if no fruit would kindle it.

'She is your friend, this queen,' Tunuva said.

'Yes. I understand you might resent her, but she doesn't know the real history, Tunuva,' Wulf said. 'I'd like to go back, to see her safe. She'll be close to giving birth by now.'

Esbar closed her eyes and pinched the bridge of her nose.

'I'm sorry, Prioress,' Wulf said. 'If I've complicated matters.'

'I'm sure it's just a shock,' Canthe said gently. 'Tell us, Wulf, how will you return to Inys?'

'I'll have to risk the sea. That's where my request comes in,' Wulf said. 'I wondered if I might take an ichneumon to the coast. They're faster than any horse I've seen.'

Esbar seemed to consider, then nodded. 'One of the unclaimed ichneumons will take you as far as the Yscali coast,' Canthe translated as she replied. 'From there, you must go alone.'

'Thank you, Prioress. Canthe.'

With a bow that made Esbar sigh, he left. On his way out, he extended a cautious hand to her black ichneumon, who gave it a sniff before licking it.

On his way back to the men's quarters, Wulf slowed in a wide and windowless corridor, seeing the Priory as if for the first time. This was his birthplace. It should have been his home. As he took in every detail – the tiles on the floor, the ornate pillars – he felt a sudden sorrow for the life he could have led, for the boy who had been named Armul.

He opened his hand on the wall, committing its strength and coolness to memory. As he pressed his brow to the old stone, he yearned to drag his lost home into his soul, make it stay with him. He would carry this place through fire and ruin, across the remnants of the world.

'Wulf.'

Siyu had appeared behind him, Lukiri on her hip. 'Siyu,' Wulf said, clearing his throat. 'How are you?'

'I wanted to spend today with Lukiri. I am afraid she will forget me, next time I leave.'

'You never really forget your mother.' Wulf paused. 'You're young to have a child, Siyu.'

'It was not planned.'

'Do you ever regret it?'

'I was careless,' she said quietly. 'Her birthfather paid for it. But Lukiri is a blessing.' Lukiri laughed at the sound of her own name. 'Why did you see Esbar?'

'I'm going back to Inys, to fight with my family.'

'This is your family.' Siyu creased her brow. 'It will hurt Tuva.'

'I'd like to come back, but this war isn't over yet. I have people who need me in Inys.'

Siyu sighed and held out Lukiri. Wulf took her, confused.

'Come with me,' Siyu said. 'You should see, before you go to the Deceiver.' Wulf turned Lukiri to face him with care, and she looked up at him with huge brown eyes, blinking.

He would never hold his own daughter like this.

Siyu took him to the splendid War Hall. This was where Tunuva had shown him her magic and taught him new ways to fight. It made him proud that his mother was the best warrior he had ever faced. Now Siyu walked to the pillars at its end, all capped with sculptures.

'These hold the names of all the women of the Priory. The sister lines,' Siyu said. 'They go back to the handmaidens of the Mother.' She pointed at a neat inscription. 'Here is Tuva.'

Wulf studied all those centuries of names. A small number had been chipped away.

'So many,' he said. 'Where are the men?'

'Not in here. Come.'

They descended again. As it turned out, the men had chosen a wall in their quarters as a memorial.

'The brother lines,' Siyu said, placing a hand on it. 'Here is Meren, your birthfather.' She took a pouch from her belt and handed it to him. 'Your name should be here, too.'

Wulf opened the pouch to find a small hammer and chisel. With resolve, he chose a place close to his birthfather, and he carved his birthname in Selinyi, the way Tunuva had taught him.

****

Siyu had stolen an evening with Lukiri in the valley. The child wobbled on her stout legs, heedless of the destruction beyond the Lasian Basin.

Wulf sat nearby, the corners of his mouth curled up. Lukiri squealed for joy as she fell against Siyu, bubbling with laughter.

Tunuva watched them from a storeroom, aching with love. She could still not believe Lukiri was almost two, or that her birthson was twenty. She watched and watched, wanting to preserve this perfect day in amber, wear it like a pendant on her breast.

Soon it would be a distant memory. Wulf was leaving. Esbar had called a retreat to the Priory only to gather more supplies, to renew their siden and whet their blades, before they set out to protect the survivors – however many might be left. This was a dream within a nightmare.

'Our children.'

Tunuva looked back. Esbar had found her.

'I wondered where you were.' Esbar cast her gaze about. 'I don't think I've been in here since—'

Tunuva nodded, remembering. Their hungry kisses on the straw, before Saghul knew. Every night they had found a new place to make love. Esbar came to join her at the window.

'I don't want him to go,' Tunuva said, very softly. 'But he would not be at peace here.'

'He was too long in the world.' Esbar sat on the sill. 'There is my grandchild, Tuva. The Queen of Inys carries yours – the Deceiver's bloodline, for ever twined with the Priory.'

Tunuva had not allowed it to sink in. Her unborn grandchild was already doomed to the fate of a queen, condemned to bear fruit no matter the cost, and all she would know of the Mother were lies.

'There is no longer a siden tree in Inys. The child will never know the truth; I doubt any of her descendants will,' Tunuva said. 'But what does this mean for the Priory?'

Esbar continued to look at the valley. Even in perfect stillness, she was graceful. Tunuva sat beside her and reached for her hand. She feared Esbar might pull away, but she let Tunuva hold her, even if she made no move to tighten the grasp, as she usually would.

'For now, I think it best if we keep this between the two of us – and Canthe,' Esbar said, a cool afterthought. 'Many of our sisters would resent an Inysh queen with mage blood. They might even want her dead, for fear she would use her powers to honour the Deceiver.'

'I agree.' Tunuva glanced at her. 'Where will we go next?'

'Wherever duty calls us. We will stay here long enough for our sisters to eat of the tree, to recover from the fever – and then we ride, to protect our world. To give what hope we can.'

Tunuva nodded. 'I am with you.'

'Good.'

Esbar pressed their hands together – a tiny, precious folding – before she left in silence. Tunuva returned to her watching, knowing this was the last night she would have everything she wanted in the world, all in one place.

84

East

For the first time since they withdrew from the world, the gods were shedding rain across the harbour city of Ginura. As people ran into the spray to quench their clothes and hair, steam churned from creatures with fire in their blood, water sizzling on their armour.

In a mighty twist, Furtia Stormcaller swept over the old castle. Her roar carried like thunder across a ravaged sky.

Dumai clung fast. When she leaned to the left, Furtia moved with her. Other dragons flew in their wake: Burmina the Splendid, Pajati the White, others whose names she had not yet been granted. Their voices rustled in her head, Pajati always louder than the others.

The star approaches . . . the sky rings of its coming . . .

. . . star, she holds a fragment of the star, it calls to us . . .

Chaos reigns . . . chaos on chaos . . .

Winged beasts circled the harbour. Taugran the Golden had arrived in Seiiki shortly after midwinter, and from its lair on Muysima, it had set about devastating the island.

Below, screams and shouts filled a city that had once been peaceful, which now blazed like a forge. Its people fought a throng of desecrated creatures. Once the wyrms had found Seiiki, they had set about binding its animals to their will, giving them iron hooves and teeth, enkindling their eyes. The Ginurans threw nets at them, beat them with tools and shot them with arrows. Some of them were likely fighting their own livestock.

She had to get them all to safety. If she could save the granaries and storehouses here, all the better.

Mounted warriors charged the creatures, swords glinting under the dark sun. Clan Mithara had mustered them in her name. The head of the clan had pledged her loyalty to Dumai, as had those of the Eraposi and Tajorin families, who had been outraged by her exile. So far, the rest had clung to the hem of Clan Kuposa, with only a few minor nobles defecting.

It mattered little to Dumai. Only when the comet had passed – if it passed – would she think of the fate of the Rainbow Throne. For now, the River Lord could keep it.

Sparks blew in the wind. Everywhere they landed, fire burst like black powder, destroying houses and temples. Dumai shielded her face as a granary exploded. Furtia poured more rain from her flanks, her scales turning icy. Pressed against her, Dumai shivered, jaw rattling.

The stone was cold on her breastbone. She had ridden barefoot and without a saddle. If the stone touched her skin, and her skin touched Furtia, the dragon could reach for its power with ease.

A roar sounded behind her. From beneath the brim of her helmet, she glimpsed a wyrm ram into Burmina the Splendid. The green dragon hit back with a thunderbolt, and the wyrm folded.

The world split again and again. Threads of white and blue, red and orange seamed her eyelids. *We should begin leading people to the forest, and leave the others to fight,* Dumai told Furtia. *This city is too vulnerable.* The dragon rumbled her agreement.

Ginura stood on the cliffs above a bay. Thousands of survivors had run to its beach, sheltering beneath the natural arch that swept out from the cliff to the shallows. Some had fled into a tidal cave, while others made the desperate swim to the Dragon's Tooth. All there was to eat was moss on that towering stack of rock, but it was safer than the city.

A group armed with spears had gathered in the surf, herding something that could have been a wyrm – except that its head was birdlike, and its front limbs had split into metal pincers. Furtia swooped towards it. Lightning crackled in her mouth, raising every hair on Dumai.

Furtia landed hard enough to shake the beach. She snatched the monster, jaws crunching around its body. With a swing of her head, she flung it into the sea, where it thrashed in a fury of steam and spray, sinking out of sight. All along the shore, people shouted in triumph.

Dumai wiped her face on her sleeve. Through a blur, she tried to count the bodies, stopping when panic thickened her breath.

She pulled off her helmet and raked back her dripping hair. Though she still wore the armour her father had given her, months of war had not turned her into a fighter. She carried no weapon. All she could do was fly – but perhaps that was enough. It had to be enough.

The survivors gathered around Furtia, reaching for her scales. Furtia huffed in disquiet. Dumai calmed her with a stroke. Not long ago, touching a dragon would have been punishable by death. In a time like this, she could not blame the terrified people for seeking comfort from a god. Steeling her nerves, she climbed up to where they could see her.

'People of Ginura,' she called, loud enough to burn her throat, 'I am Noziken pa Dumai, daughter of the Maiden Officiant and the late Emperor Jorodu.' Above, a wyrm let out a hideous screech, seeding panic through the crowd. It passed overhead without seeing them. 'You must not stand against the enemy any longer. Too many have fallen here.'

'We have nowhere to go,' a young woman protested. She was crouched by a dying man. 'This red sickness ravages every city. The River Lord has left Seiiki to burn.'

'There is a place where you can take refuge.' Dumai spoke over a tide of agreements. 'Make your way to Mayupora Forest. The gods will defend you until you reach the cover of the trees, where Lady Mithara will meet you. If you can find useful supplies, bring them, but do not risk your lives for possessions. Help those who are frail and injured.'

'Queen Dumai,' one of the soldiers cried, thrusting up his sword. 'Guardian of Seiiki!'

She had first heard those words in a dust province to the east of Basai, where Furtia had poured rain on the fires, and the villagers had danced in it. Now the whole beach clamoured with her name, thousands of voices rising together. Furtia rumbled her satisfaction, but all Dumai could see was a ghost of Kanifa, standing among them, smiling.

Seiiki could ask for no better queen.

****

Mayupora Forest covered most of the north of the island. Mount Tego guarded its eastern reaches, and its western flank broke against the ridge called the Bear's Jaw. As Furtia flew over the sea of ancient trees, Dumai wished she could have left court sooner, to see more of Seiiki.

Not long ago, fields of swaying feather grass had formed a pale golden hem on the forest. Those were gone, leaving nothing but ash.

So much had burned in so little time.

Dirty snow fell, mingled with soot. For months, the wyrms and their offspring had slaughtered without mercy, while the red sickness had ravaged the coast, originating from a tainted stream near Mount Izaripwi. The sun remained dim, the harvest had failed, and the winter had been long and harsh. All of this was too much for one island to bear.

Dumai had done her utmost to hold off the attacks. When the blue stone was near, the gods were stronger, able to summon water and thunderbolts – but she could not be everywhere at once. Several dragons had already fallen, and more had retreated back into hiding.

Seiiki was breaking. By Winterfall, there would not be much left for her sister to rule.

So far, Mayupora Forest had escaped the devastation. At first, Dumai had thought it an absurd risk to send the survivors into the trees – one tongue of fire could doom them all – but the wyrms had avoided torching the greenwoods. Instead, they seemed bent on destroying every human settlement that had the misfortune to draw their attention. Isunka and Podoro, both large and thriving cities, had collapsed in a matter of days.

Now the wyrms had spread everywhere, to pick off towns and farming villages, and the people had almost nowhere to run, trapped as they were by the seas around Seiiki. Some had taken up arms to defend themselves, but the creatures' hides were hard to break. As far as Dumai could tell, the River Lord – the regent – had made no attempt to help.

Waiting for the comet was the better choice. The deep forest would give them protection.

Furtia came to drift over a grove of season trees. She curled the end of her tail around Dumai, lowering her gently to the ground, before she floated back towards Ginura.

I will keep watch over the earth children.

Thank you, great one.

Dumai turned north and crossed the grove. Several white leaves had dropped early, making room for tiny pink sprouts. Winterfall would come in a few weeks, and with it, the first day of spring. She began her footslog through the depths of the forest, along the path trodden by hunters and foragers, following the subtle markers to her court.

Hemlocks, chestnuts and bear pines grew tall enough to conceal other life. Thick green moss swallowed all sound, except for the occasional, familiar call of a sorrower. Dumai barely heard. Her ears were aboil with the din of the battle, her head sore from holding so many voices. Her boots seemed ironshod. Her nose ran and her body trembled.

Her mother waited by an ancient beech tree. Months in the forest had changed her. She still wore grey, her layers practical and warm, and kept her hair out of her face with a cloth.

'Dumai.' She released a long breath. 'Are you hurt?'

'No.'

'And the Ginurans?'

'On their way to the northeastern camp. Lady Mithara will show them the path,' Dumai rasped, her throat raw from the smoke. Unora wrapped her in a mantle and pressed a warm flask into her hands. 'Mother, there is so much sickness. So much death.'

Unora touched her cheek, smearing ash from it. 'I know,' she said. 'I know, my kite.'

Dumai followed her to the camp that served as her court. It sprawled from the mouth of a cave, the former retreat of Tukupa the Silver. A healer checked their hands for redness.

Some of the Seiikinese had risked staying in their homes, tarring their windows to hide their hearth fires, while others had fled to the mines or dug their own shelters. Dumai had decided on a different way to protect the people under her care, directing them to places where the gods had slept on land. Such places were usually sheltered, with a source of fresh water and a prayer bell, which could be used to signal to other camps.

They could not hide in the wilds for ever. The wyrms had not attacked the forest, but their earthbound creatures might yet sniff the survivors out. If not, starvation would waste them away, or the red sickness would slip through their defences and force them out of hiding. So many granaries had burned, and livestock had either perished or turned monstrous. By summer, all that would be left was ash, unless Kwiriki's Lantern calmed the chaos.

The dragons seemed to think it would be soon. Dumai hoped they were right.

Small cookfires smoked across the camp. Unora led her past the tents and into the spine of the limestone cave, which ran deep, its ceiling toothed by seeping water. Hundreds of people were hidden where Tukupa had once slumbered, their weary faces lit by oil lamps. Dumai stopped to check on three people without families, who she had rescued from the salt road.

In a cavern for the sick and wounded, the outlaw named Rituyka was waiting, sipping from a flask. One of his three brothers lay beside him on a mat, sleeping off his burns.

'Queen Dumai.' Rituyka gave her a nod. 'We brought millet and barley. Some wine, as well, to warm and cheer us.'

Dumai nodded. Until she had met this wily reed of a man, she had not grasped how little sway the palace held over the provinces. Even before the wyrms, Rituyka had lived as a bandit, stealing from store-houses and mansions. Like Unora, he had grown up in Afa Province.

'I am glad to hear it,' Dumai said. 'Where from?'

'Purinadu.'

'That estate belongs to Clan Kuposa.' Unora used her rural accent when she spoke to him. She checked her store of foraged herbs, for use in salves and tisanes. 'You must be careful, Rituyka. Your work is important, but we don't want to draw their eye to the forest.'

He gave her a crooked smile. 'They have larger concerns. For once, they are like the rest of us.'

'Do not underestimate the regent. His palace is safe while the gods protect it, and this turmoil gives him the perfect cover to get rid of Dumai. He will seize every chance he can.'

'We will not let anything happen to our queen.'

Dumai stifled a dry cough on her gauntlet. 'Did anyone see you?'

'No. There was evidence of an attack. The River Lord has called all of his private forces to Antuma.' Rituyka raised his eyebrows. 'There's something else, Queen Dumai. The siege engine the Lacustrine gifted you, the bed crossbow – we found it on the grounds of the estate.'

'The River Lord told me it was destroyed.'

'It's certainly in pieces. Looks to me as if it might be mended, but I'm no woodworker.'

'He hid it away for himself,' said Unora, her voice thin with anger.

'He is so determined to weaken me that he would withhold a strong means of defence,' Dumai said softly. 'With that weapon, how many more lives could we have saved?'

'Now you taste the unwatered poison of his ambition.'

Dumai tried to quell the storm in her mind. It grew harder by the day – to be calm, to think clearly.

'We might still use this to our advantage,' she said. 'Rituyka, I want you to inform Lady Mithara and Lord Tajorin. I believe they each have a number of blacksmiths and carpenters at their camps. If they can work out how to put the crossbow back together, we might still build more, to defend the remaining settlements. We have plenty of wood.'

Rituyka stood. 'At once, Your Majesty.'

'I'll join you. We need more moss.' Unora gathered her pouches before she followed him. 'Dumai, you rest. I'll return before dark.'

****

In her tent, which was pitched at the mouth of the cave, Dumai took the stone from around her neck. After months of examining it, she still could not use its power herself, but Furtia could. That was all that mattered.

Exhaustion made her want to lie straight down and sleep. She removed her armour, then peeled off the damp clothing beneath, taking stock of her injuries. With every flight and battle, she earned more. A burn mottled her thigh, knotted with weeping blisters. Small cuts flecked her face where rubble had struck. Then there was the cough that wrenched her chest. Even if she wore a wet cloth over her face, the smoke got through.

She had no mirror, but she knew she must resemble a ghost. A woman drawn with a drying brush, the ink straining for the strength to complete her, leaving her faded at the edges. Her hair was grey with ash, as if she had aged a century since leaving court.

She still felt more alive than she ever had in Antuma Palace.

The snow kept falling. She washed in the icy stream nearby, then returned to her tent to warm herself, and to comb the tangles from her hair – always a painful task after flight.

At dusk, she went to sit outside, among her people. A man gave her a generous helping of millet, topped with bracken shoots and mushrooms, murmuring his thanks for her courage. Another pressed his bowl on her, insisting that she would need the strength.

713

The stolen wine was passed around. A woman who had lost her arm was roasting chestnuts on a fire. As Dumai chewed the taste from the shoots, she listened to soft conversations between friends and strangers alike, sharing in their memories and losses. She heard their fires crackling, the merciless cough most survivors brought with them, the creak of the trees. It had been a brutal winter, but she felt calm for the first time in days, wrapped in her mantle, surrounded by life.

A girl of twelve stared into the nearest fire, bundled in a pelt. Dumai moved to sit at her side.

'Iyo,' she said, 'have you eaten?' The girl shook her head. 'It's cold. You need to stay warm and strong.'

'My sister was the strong one.' Her eyes were vacant. 'Not me.'

'She is safe now, with the great Kwiriki. Nothing can hurt her.' Dumai nodded to the man beside the fire, who brought another bowl. 'I miss my sister, too.'

Iyo looked up at her. 'Why is your sister not with us?'

Dumai mustered a strained smile. 'That is a story too long to tell.'

'Let me tell you another,' an elderly woman said to Iyo. 'To give us hope on this cold night.'

A hush fell as people turned to listen. Iyo leaned against Dumai, who held her close.

'Since we have Queen Dumai among us,' the woman said, 'I will tell you a tale of another great queen. A queen who wanted to grow a greener world for her people, and loved them all the same, whether they were born in a dust province or a harbour.' She paused, and the silence became absolute. 'Let me tell you a tale of the Mulberry Queen.'

A few people glanced at Dumai, their expressions hard to read. Dumai had the sense that she was being let into a secret.

'Long ago, in ancient days, there lived a girl of Ampiki, which lies at the very end of this island – almost as old a village as the rock of Seiiki itself. She lived as we do now, always in fear of hunger and thirst,' the storyteller said. A few children shuffled closer to her. 'In the tales, she has no name, like too many women in stories of old.'

'Dumai.'

A hand touched her shoulder. With a last glance at the storyteller, Dumai sent Iyo to the young couple who had been caring for her, then followed her mother back to her tent.

'That story sounded familiar,' she said.

'It is a favourite in the dust provinces. A poor orphan who made herself a queen of outcasts.' Unora lit the lamps. 'Lady Mithara is safe. Rituyka will take her to see the crossbow, but they will need a great deal of wood. Will you help me collect some in the morning?'

'I can't stay.'

'You can.' Unora knelt before her, eyes hard. 'Listen to me. You have been away for days, in all that smoke and soot. For the time being, you have done all you can.'

'I carry the stone. Without it—'

'You cannot always be with the gods. They know that you are bone and flesh.'

'I woke them. When they die, it is because of me.' Her voice broke. 'The stone lends them strength.'

'Stop this.' Unora held her face. 'I know I can't keep you from leaving. But if you refuse to heal and rest, you will be too exhausted to fly with Furtia. You will make bad decisions. Never forget what you learned on the mountain. Remember and respect your limits.'

Dumai knew she was right. Her legs shook, her eyes stung, and her throat was sore.

'I will stay,' she said. 'To recover my strength.'

'There is much you can do to help us here.' Unora sat beside her. 'The comet will come soon. We must trust in the gods. Have you thought any more on what you want to do when this is over?'

'No. All of this has proven that the River Lord should not be regent,' Dumai murmured, 'but how can I ask our people to fight for me in another war, after so much violence?'

'They may be willing to try, for all our sakes, to place a kinder leader on the throne. I still believe the gods will help you over him.' Her mother stroked her hair. 'You have time to decide, Dumai. For now, rest and heal. We will face each new day as it comes.'

Dumai nodded. By now she was so tired she could hardly keep her eyes open. As soon as her mother had left, she crawled into her bedding and slept, too soundly to hear the voice in her dream.

****

She woke to a light touch, in darkness. 'Dumai,' Unora said, her voice low and strange, 'a survivor has reached us.'

715

Dumai rubbed her eyes. 'Are they from Ginura?'

'You should see for yourself.'

They walked between the tents and a solitary fire, back to the old beech. Beside that final marker, a horse had collapsed, close to death. One of the hunters had its rider in his arms.

The young woman was covered in filth, dressed in farmers' clothes she must have worn for weeks. Ash smirched her short hair. When her eyes flickered open, Dumai could only stare at her.

'Dumai,' Nikeya whispered. 'I found you.'

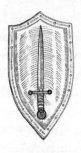

85

West

Once, Stilharrow Deep had breathed a gentle mist at dawn, as the eastern light lifted a veil from its waters. Now smoke coughed from the many fires that licked between the corpses there. Wind ripped through its skeletal trees, scissored with dirty sleet, reeking of death and smoke.

From under an outcrop, Glorian watched her knights and soldiers fight with creatures stitched from nightmare.

A torn bedsheet of ice covered the steep and narrow valley. A horse slipped into a break and thrashed in fear, snorting fog, before a scaled wolf fell upon it and tore out its throat, darkening the blood that washed the ice. The rider went crashing into the water, shout muffled by their closed helm. Arrows rained down on the wolf from the castle.

Glorian shifted in her saddle, an ache budding in the small of her back. Over her red gambeson, a sleeveless coat of mail sheathed her from neck to thigh, covering the huge shelf of her belly. She was far above the battle, beneath a snowy overhang that kept her out of sight.

Nearby, a waterfall remained frozen, like the shroud on a great candle. She watched the stakes of ice weeping.

Inys would not survive for long after the thaw. Winter had bought a period of grace – Fýredel had disappeared, presumably to the warmer South – but his scores of foul creatures had stayed to carry on the slaughter, butchering thousands of her people by the day.

Carmentum was already gone. Whispers of its fall had finally reached Inys. One day it had been a thriving republic, and then it had ceased to exist, scattering its people to the wind.

'Your Grace.'

Lord Damud approached on a destrier, snowflakes caught in his short curls. Behind him, the last few creatures screeched as her soldiers rode them down with lances.

'Are they routed?' Glorian asked. Her breath ruffled white. 'For now?'

'For now.'

Corpses littered the valley. Largest was the wyvern that had led the attack, grey from its snout to the barb on its tail. A boulder from a catapult had struck it from the sky.

'No sign of Fýredel,' Glorian said.

'I've no doubt he'll soon find us, if this is one of his.'

She nodded. It was clear that what the wyverns saw, the great wyrms came to know.

As far as the Regency Council could tell, there were three of them, each named by a different region. Orsul was harrowing the North, Dedalugun was in the South, and the last sighting of Fýredel had been in western Yscalin – yet reports claimed five had emerged from the Dreadmount. Glorian could only assume the other two were in the East.

When they came, there would be no warning. Those tending the signal fires had long since forsaken their posts for the caves.

'We should decide where to move next,' Lord Damud said. 'I will summon your council, and the Lady Protector.'

'Very well.'

Glorian glanced at the castle, where her consort was overseeing the catapults, and then back at the ice. A man crawled towards his fellow soldiers, bleeding from what remained of his body. One of them nocked an arrow and sent it straight into his skull without flinching.

The archer glanced up at Glorian. She nodded, absolving them of the sin, and turned her horse around.

****

In her bedchamber in the castle of Stilharrow, Glorian stood before the hearth. Her ladies lifted the mail from her shoulders and unbuckled the gambeson.

The firelight cast her shadow on the wall. It shook her, to see how swollen she was.

Helisent brought her a fresh tunic. 'Glorian,' she said, 'how are you?'

Glorian could have wept in relief. It had been days since anyone had asked how she was and looked in her eyes, not at her belly.

'I'm tired.' She cradled its weight with both hands. 'She's so heavy.'

'It will be done soon.'

And I may be dead.

The thought was distant and numbing. Several of her ancestors had died in childbirth, and she knew what had killed at least one of them. The tyrant had been sliced out of her mother.

Helisent guided her to a stool. Julain kneaded a few precious drops of lavender oil into her hair, smothering the smell of smoke. Glorian could feel herself nodding off. Such gentling lulled her back to easier times.

Her dreams had been silent and empty of late. The voice in her head had pushed her away, and now she could not find their stream at all. A terrible darkness had clotted between them.

Two years had passed since the voice had first spoken, and still she could not ravel out this weave of dreams, nor grasp if it was earthly or divine. Now it seemed to have disappeared.

It pained her, to be without that small comfort.

'Glorian.' Julain touched her cheek. 'Glorian, you're exhausted. Let me tell Lady Marian.'

'No,' Glorian said.

'You barely slept last night.'

'I will have all the time in the world to sleep when this is over.' Softer, she said to herself, 'In the spring.'

The Regency Council sat at a round table. Shutters had been locked against the cold, and a fire snapped in the hearth, but the councillors still wore the same layers they had outside. They watched Glorian like eagles, as if the weight of her belly could topple her.

'May I help you, Your Grace?' Lady Brangain asked, rising.

'No need.' Glorian took a seat. 'I rode a horse today. A chair is less likely to throw me.'

More than one jaw clenched, though Lade Edith cracked a smile. None of them liked her riding, but her grandmother had allowed it, so long as she kept out of sight, and ostlers were on hand to calm her mount.

Marian soon arrived with Bourn. After Forthard and the bonesetter had disagreed yet again on how to deal with the plague, Glorian had separated them, sending Forthard to the north and keeping Bourn at court. Bourn helped Marian into her chair before leaving.

'Are you well?' Glorian asked her grandmother.

'Yes. Just old and stiff.' Marian patted her hand before addressing the Regency Council: 'Since a wyvern has now seen us at Stilharrow, we can assume Fýredel will soon know our whereabouts. The time has come to choose another stronghold. What say you all?'

'My ancestral seat would shelter us,' Lade Edith offered. 'Strathurn Castle is far to the north, in a valley not unlike this one, easy to defend. We should chase the cold for as long as we can.'

'Queen Glorian can't possibly ride to the Fells in her condition,' Lord Randroth spluttered.

'And the sea is too dangerous,' Lord Damud said, calmer. 'Better to keep to the southern provinces, though I do understand your thought about the cold, Edith. Ought we to consider a cave shelter this time?'

'Yes. Selverpit, perhaps,' Lade Edith mused. 'Though the entrance is said to be so hidden that people have fallen into it.'

'Then the wyrms won't see it, either.'

'Hm.'

Lady Gladwin considered the map. She had cropped her grey hair close to her skull.

'The Dowager Earl of Goldenbirch is presently at Hollow Crag, with many people of the Leas. At last count, that was the single largest gathering of survivors,' she said. 'A visit from their queen would surely cheer their hearts, after so much darkness and uncertainty.'

Glorian said, 'How many are there?'

'Fifteen thousand souls, or thereabouts. It may be more by now.'

Marian looked unsure. 'Do you really think it safe there, Gladwin?'

'Nothing has caught their scent, to my knowledge. Lord Ordan has been careful.'

Glorian reached for the map and found the place on Cenning Moor. 'Fifteen thousand,' she said. 'I would like to give them comfort.'

'Absolutely not.' Lord Randroth dabbed his red nose. 'Offsay is close, and safe.'

'And nowhere near my people.'

'It is very late to ride so far, Your Grace,' Lady Brangain said. 'You could give birth any day.'

'Yes, to the heir you enjoined me to conceive at only seventeen,' Glorian said quietly. 'I suffered the touch of an old man to make her.' That shamed most of them into looking away. 'Nowhere in this queendom is safe any longer. I will not tremble on the coast. If Hollow Crag has protected those souls, then it is good enough for me – and for my daughter, who may yet be born there.' She met each of their gazes in turn. 'I will go to them.'

A tense silence reigned. Then Marian said, 'We ride for Hollow Crag.'

86

East

Nikeya slept, as she had for two days. Unora had cleaned her wounds, daubing a resin salve on the burns, while Dumai had combed the ash from her hair and washed more from her face.

On the night she arrived, she had been cold and confused, her lips splintered by thirst. Now she slept in the warmth of the tent, breaths scratching into coughs. Dumai checked her fingers and felt her fore-head, finding no fever or chill, or any stain of the red sickness.

She had never thought she would set eyes on this woman again. Nikeya was part of the life she had relinquished.

As night drew in, Dumai emerged from her tent, into a red and shad-owed light. It was cruel that evenings should be so beautiful in this time of death, the sun a glowing coal.

'Queen Dumai.'

Dumai turned. 'Lady Mithara,' she said, joining her by the hitching post. 'I did not expect you so soon.'

Lady Mithara wore a coat of iron and stiff leather over hunting clothes, the breastplate marked with the stork of her clan. This was her paternal grandaunt – a proud and gentle woman who had lived in the region for decades, since the Kuposa had taken steps to erode her influence. As head of the Mithara, it was she who had pledged their loyalty to Dumai.

'I am glad to see your feet on the ground for a time, niece. It is good for you to be among the people,' she said. 'But I understand a certain Kuposa found your camp. Unora told me, in confidence.' Her gaze was piercing, wary. 'What do you mean to do with Lady Nikeya?'

'I have yet to learn why she is here.'

'Presumably as a spy for the regent. She has been his instrument since her mother died.'

'Only since then?'

Lady Mithara gave a curt nod. 'I knew Tirfosi. A good woman.'

'I owe Nikeya my life,' Dumai said. 'She has had many opportunities to hurt me, and took none of them.' A sharp breeze ruffled their furs. 'Have you come about the crossbow?'

'I had the parts brought to my camp. Once we understand how to piece it together, we will be able to build more. The people will know they are from you, not the River Lord.'

'So long as they have protection, it doesn't matter to me where they think it came from.'

'It should. You must be formally enthroned after this chaos, and my clan means to see it done.'

'Seiiki cannot bear a civil war after this, my lady. We will wait and see what the gods decide.'

She went to the nearest cookfire and opened a pot of venison stew. Lady Mithara fastened her horse to the post before entering a tent, while Dumai returned to her own with a bowl.

Inside, Nikeya was awake.

They looked at each other for a long time. Nikeya swallowed, deep shadows under her eyes.

'I thought I would die before I reached you,' she said.

Dumai slowly became aware of the bowl scalding her palm. She moved it to the other.

'You could have,' she said, kneeling beside Nikeya. 'Here. You should eat.'

'Thank you. I tried to hunt on the road, but so many animals have fled into the forests, or been . . . remade.'

'I suppose a noble lady never learned to forage.'

'I risked it once, in desperation. I was sick for a day,' Nikeya said, with a bleak smile. 'Later, a farmer told me it had been a godslight mushroom.' They had glowed throughout the forest in the early winter, clustered on the dead beeches. 'He showed me some grasses I could eat. The next morning, he tried to take my bow as payment for that service.'

'Our food is humble, but sweeter than grass.' Dumai set the bowl down. 'The horse died. I'm sorry.'

'Better than living as a beast of anguish.'

Dumai helped her sit up. Nikeya caught her gaze. Just that one touch, that meeting of eyes, brought back all the wants she had tried to forget.

'This camp is not easy to reach.' Dumai let go. 'How did you get here?'

'I was so tired. I needed water, so I made for a city. I was almost to Ginura when I saw Furtia – finally, after months of following every whisper of her,' Nikeya said. 'I rode to this forest with the Ginurans, and happened to see an old friend from court, who now serves as guard to Lady Mithara. He described the markers I would need to follow to find you.'

'You should have rested first.'

'I feared I would be recognised.' Nikeya picked up the bowl, resting it on her knee. 'Your camp has kept you alive, but it is a far cry from court. How have you withstood this winter?'

'The forest provides.' Dumai watched her as if she would disappear. 'When did you leave?'

'Autumnfall. You were hard to find.'

'Lady Mithara and Lord Tajorin will be glad to hear that.'

'Even my father could not conceal his ire at their defiance.' A coldness washed over her face. 'He has done nothing with his power as regent, even as our island burns. I stayed as long as I could, to watch over Suzumai, but when I uncovered the truth, I could not stand the sight of him a day longer.'

'What truth?'

'The attack on the palace. It was him.'

Dumai waited for the knowledge to set, like dye into cloth. 'Is my grandmother in danger?'

'Tukupa the Silver protects the temple. For now, the Grand Empress is safe.' Nikeya looked at her with disquiet. 'I didn't know, Dumai. He must not have trusted me. I never thought he would go so far as to plot the death of an emperor.'

She coughed again, so hard her eyes welled. Dumai gave her a cloth and a flask of water.

'I believe you,' she said. 'He had the crossbow destroyed, too.'

'I know. There was always cruelty in him,' Nikeya said, 'but he killed in softer ways than murder.' Her fingers tightened on the flask. 'I almost lost you to him. He has wielded and worked me for thirteen years, using me to realise his ambitions at the cost of my freedom to choose. I am his daughter, not his doll, and I have served his interests for too long.'

She took a long drink.

'You found the crossbow, then,' she said, when the cough had calmed. 'At Purinadu.'

'Yes.'

'Look in my saddle, and you will find the plans the Lacustrine brought with the weapon. I stole them from his study. They should help you put it back together, and build more.'

'That must have been a risk. Thank you,' Dumai said quietly. 'It will help us protect the survivors.'

'I hope it will prove to your mother and allies that I am not a spy.'

'My mother knows you saved my life. Others may not feel warmly towards you.'

'I am confident that I can win them over.'

Dumai smiled, in spite of herself. 'That is one of your gifts.'

Nikeya looked at her for a long time, the flicker of the oil lamp in her eyes.

'Suzu,' Dumai said. 'Is she safe?'

'My father has shut her away. She knows little of the conflict beyond the palace, and trusts in her regent to rule in her stead. It hurt to leave her, but she still has the Dowager Empress.'

'You wish to join my court, then,' Dumai said, holding her gaze. 'To sleep in the wilds among outlaws and paupers, led by a queen without a throne. Are you certain, Nikeya?'

'A flower grown for court might yet thrive in a forest.'

'You had better not tell anyone your name. Lady Mithara knows, but your clan is not popular here.'

'I like to think I am not a fool.' Nikeya motioned to her own hair, which now fell just past her chin. 'Observe my cunning disguise. Do I not look provincial?'

Before she could stop herself, Dumai reached out to brush it behind her ear, lingering on her jaw for a moment.

725

'Make sure this face is convincing,' she said, very softly. 'So you can stay at my side.'

Nikeya nodded, reservation clouding her face.

'There is another reason I came. I have a proposal that may help us protect Seiiki,' she said. 'And I must keep the promise I made in the North. I must tell you the truth, as best I know it – about our families, and the reason they are intertwined.'

From one look, Dumai knew that what she was about to learn would shake her world to its foundations.

'Not here,' she said. 'I know a safer place to speak.'

****

Rituyka believed the forest was haunted by those whose remains had not reached the sea. Like many from the region, he refused to leave the camp after dusk. Dumai lacked his fear, but night did bestrange the stillness beyond, where the silence was so deep and empty not even the wind could break it. She walked between the towering pines, a lantern held in front of her.

Perhaps her father lingered here, waiting for her to redress his murder.

Kanifa would not be among these ghosts. He had lost his life a long way from their island. She prayed her friend was content with his fate, his spirit rooted to a mountain – but sometimes, when her courage failed, she wished he would find his way back to her.

Snow pattered from the branches, which grew dense as a roof, so they could hardly see the sky. Nikeya carried the other lantern, dressed in borrowed clothes and deerskin boots that were too big for her.

'I'm not sure I like that I have no idea what you're plotting. No wonder I had to leave the palace,' she said drily, stepping wide across a log. 'I must be losing my flair for intrigue.'

Her voice broke the smothering quiet, nerving Dumai to use her own. 'Your place was once at court,' she said. 'Mine was on the mountain.' She searched for the next marker, a branch twisted into an arch. 'A forest is new ground for both of us.'

'If we lose our way, the ground is exactly where we are heading.'

'I have yet to lead you astray.' Dumai held out a hand, helping her over a fallen tree. 'I'll show you how to forage soon. In return, you could help me improve my archery.'

'At least I bring one useful skill.'

They climbed a rugged cliff that carved a rare gap through the canopy. A hot spring pooled a short way up, overhung by a snowy branch, and Dumai placed her lantern beside it.

'No one should overhear us here.'

'Or see us.' Nikeya looked back at the trees. 'We didn't have to go nearly so far.'

'I'm told these waters are healing. You're still weak.' Dumai sat beside the hot spring. 'And you did say you hated the cold.'

'How thoughtful.' Nikeya gave her a smile. 'Will you join me this time?'

Dumai raised a faint smile of her own. 'I like the cold.'

'You're learning.' Nikeya held her pelt close, mischief in her eyes. 'Perhaps I feel shy this evening.'

'I can always turn away.'

'No.'

The silence closed in again. Trapped by it, Dumai was all too aware of her heart, thick and slow.

Nikeya loosened the sash at her waist. One by one, her layers rustled to the ground, until she stood naked, barely lit by their two lanterns. Dumai kept her eyes on her face.

'You can look at me,' Nikeya said softly. 'I want you to.'

'I am looking at you.'

A small smile touched her lips again. 'I love that you've never mentioned my beauty. I was taught to wield it without mercy,' she said. 'It is the first thing people see. It is what they remember.' She glanced down, arms crossed over herself. 'Beauty requires no talent.'

'Sharpening it to your benefit does,' Dumai said, 'but that is not how you won me over.'

'What did?'

'Everything else, in the end.' Dumai held her gaze. 'You don't have to share your secrets, Nikeya. The conflict between our families, the regencies – they matter less now than they did before. It took me a long time to trust you, but I do. I trust that you want to stand at my side.'

'Our world floats on secrets, as I told you once. I want you to know all of mine.'

Nikeya waded into the warmth and sank under. She surfaced with a deep sigh of relief, scraping her short hair away from her face. Dumai glimpsed several cuts and grazes, and a swathe of faded bruising on her shoulder. She had fought hard to reach this place.

Once Nikeya had washed off the last dirt and soot, she came to rest her elbows on the side.

'There is a legend in my clan. About our origins,' she said. 'A secret told to certain heirs. Before we saved your dynasty, one of our ancestors served the Mulberry Queen. Do you know her story?'

'The bones of it,' Dumai said. The name raised bird skin on her arms. 'They tell it in the camp.'

'She was a poor woman who discovered an island in the Unending Sea. A mulberry tree grew there, and it gave her a remarkable gift. She could make fire without spark or tinder,' Nikeya said. 'At first, she was alone on her green island, Komoridu. Over time, others flocked to her shores, for she welcomed those who were needy and outcast.

'But when her tree finally died, so, too, did her will to live. By then, she is said to have drawn breath for centuries. She sent her loyal subjects away. Though her queendom had withered, she wanted the best for its people, most of whom had come from Seiiki. She asked my ancestor to infiltrate the nobility, to maintain the balance between two forces.'

Dumai thought back to the chart, in the chamber of life.

'Yes,' Nikeya said, reading her face. 'What we learned from Master Kiprun fits exactly with all this. You see, before the tree died, my ancestor was permitted to eat its fruit, and take its fire into herself.'

'How were you to keep this balance?'

'You're clever, Dumai. Think on it. The stars run in your family, as fire runs in mine. Our bell should be gold, really – like flame and sunlight – and your fish should be silver.'

Two years ago, Dumai might not have believed any of this. Now it made a certain sense.

'Your line once had formidable powers. Empress Mokwo could make storms and inflict dreams on her enemies – even bend the waters of the mind, draining out the will. The Kuposa were meant to temper that unearthly power,' Nikeya said. 'We lost our fire, but a residue still runs like oil in our blood. We only lack the tree to rekindle it.'

'Your father does not seek mere balance, does he?'

'No. Like his recent ancestors, he sought to control and dominate the Noziken, taking his chance while the gods slept. Instead of advising your relatives, he preferred to steal their authority.'

'You are different.'

'I like to think so.' Nikeya lowered her gaze. 'I wasn't. My mother tried to keep me kind and devout, but when she died, my father shaped me into his agent, the silver needle that embroiders his world. I took quickly to intrigue. I always strove to impress him, so I went to spy on your grandmother – he liked to stay abreast of what the Noziken were doing. When I saw your face at the temple, I rode to warn him, but your father got to you first. One of my rare failures.

'Then you were at court, and you had Furtia. My father claimed you would bring chaos, and that I must rule you, for the sake of everything we held dear. Your magic is awake; ours is not. That threatened his sense of security. For a year, I was torn between loyalties.'

'That's why you insisted on flying with me,' Dumai said. 'You wanted to see who I was.'

Nikeya nodded.

'I never expected to like you so much,' she said. 'I have played with many hearts, but with you, it was all too real. For the first time in years, I nurtured a wish of my own. A wish that lived beyond his shadow.' She looked up at Dumai. 'I would have explained it all sooner, but I didn't think you would believe me. I have no fire, no real proof.'

'Then how do you know this is true?'

'I don't. These are ancient hearth tales, and all clans like to give themselves impressive origins. But my father believes it.' Nikeya paused. 'And I can resist the red sickness.'

'What?'

'I helped a dying woman on the road. I took her hand before I realised it was red. Mine never changed.' Nikeya showed her. 'The wyrms breathe fire. It seems they cannot sicken me.'

The quiet deepened again, broken by the lap of water and a nightingale. Dumai circled a thumb over her own palm, where the white light had risen. Her vivid dreaming, the gods' voices – they were only the first steps on a long path to grasping all she could do.

What she still failed to understand was why these abilities had appeared in her, and not her father or grandmother.

'You told me you had a proposal,' she said.

'I'm afraid to say.'

'Why?'

'Because even letting it pass my lips could shake your trust in me, and I can't bear that, Dumai.'

'No. You can speak your mind.'

Nikeya seemed to weigh her sincerity. Dumai watched her throat working, her chest rising with breath.

'Join me first,' she said. 'I want to hold you as I say it.'

Dumai glanced away. She had bathed in front of others many times, including Nikeya, but this was different. Taking off her gloves, she undid the clasp of her hunting coat.

The hot water took the chill from her skin. Nikeya drew her close. She kissed her fingers, lingering on the remnants, and Dumai shivered at the intimacy of it. After so much hardship and mistrust, there was nothing between them.

'Heat and water,' Nikeya said. 'A little of both of us.' She looked up at Dumai. 'In the North, you reminded me that I was not your consort. What if I was?'

Dumai just kept from embracing her. Even one movement could fracture this dream.

'My father would see it as a victory,' Nikeya said. 'He would think he had won – that I had succeeded in sculpting you into our grip. In secret, you and I would be a true partnership. Together, we could chisel away his influence. You have the love of three clans, at least, and I have the Nadama, through my mother. We might still balance the court, Dumai.'

Her hands slid down, taking Dumai by the hips.

'If I were to be empress,' Dumai said in a whisper, 'I would need an heir of my own.'

A picture came, unbidden, of a stranger crushing into her. Her body taken over, laden, stretching and filling beyond her control, growing a seed that unfurled in the darkness. She knew that bringing it into the light would rip a deep scar through her mind, even if she recovered in body. It would all pull so hard on her line that it broke her, leaving her to sink. She had known for many years that she would not do it by choice.

'Dumai.'

Nikeya pressed their damp foreheads together. Her face, her voice, banished the picture.

'There is another way,' she said. 'Suzumai is your sister and my cousin. We could make her strong and brave, bolster the rest of your family – and you and I could rule as the Mulberry Queen would have wanted, with the people as our guide. All we need do is trust one another.'

Dumai touched her then – just barely, with her fingertips, stroking along her jaw. Nikeya watched her with aching, restrained hope.

'It's a good idea. It could work,' Dumai said, and realised it was true. The relief was enough to bring a smile back to her lips. 'We must wait for the comet, but … I will think on it.'

Nikeya framed her face. 'I will think on it, too,' she said, almost too soft to hear. 'I will think of being yours.' Their noses brushed. 'I will think of having you in my arms every night.'

Dumai could hardly think at all. Her heart was beating at her breastbone. When Nikeya kissed her, all else faded into the dark, even the rock beneath them.

She was soaring.

Nikeya walked them farther into the spring. Dumai hitched her into her arms, feeling a tireless pull between her thighs, a call to draw Nikeya close. (*No*, she reminded herself, drunk with need. *No, I am the one at the end of the hook*.) Nikeya grasped her hair, and the strength of her touch was a confirmation.

The spring washed around their waists, reaching their shoulders. Dumai longed to touch her as the water did, covering all of her, all at once. Nikeya sighed into her neck. Even wordless, desire lay thick on her voice, and Dumai imagined her in bed – their bed, for a ruler and consort. A bed that was also a harbour. The thought pushed away the other picture, made her deepen the kiss. They lost their footing, and Nikeya laughed against her lips. It had been so long since she had heard a laugh like that, sweet and carefree.

Somehow, they reached the shore, and Dumai laid her on their clothes. Nikeya gazed up at her, the love so clear in her eyes that Dumai wondered how she had ever missed it.

'I had a dream,' Nikeya whispered, 'that you were still a godsinger, and I was your shrine.'

I had the same dream, Dumai wanted to say, but her throat was dry from wanting. Instead, she spoke with touch. She cradled a breast as if it were sacred, a river pearl in the shell of her palm. Nikeya pressed her close, one hand on her shoulder and the other on her waist.

Time lost all boundaries, all meaning. Dumai had never done this, except in sweet and secret dreams, but Nikeya was the silver moon that told her where to go. The undertows of her body, her small and tender sounds, her limbs – those were the only guides Dumai needed. She watched pleasure wash over her, break on her, and it was a sight more breathtaking than dawn on Mount Ipyeda. Dumai kissed her once more, and though she had never bathed in the sea, she knew how the waves would taste in her mouth.

Dumai smoothed a strand of hair from her brow. Nikeya smiled, her eyes sparkling in their old way. She draped a leg across Dumai, tipping her on to her back, and sat across her hips, hand sliding low, the touch a startling promise. With the other, she interlocked their fingers.

'Do you trust me?'

Her voice was soft as evening prayer.

'Yes,' Dumai told her. 'I trust you now.'

Nikeya lifted their twined fingers to her cheek. These might be the very last days of the world – they had no time to waste on waiting. Nikeya captured her lips once more, and there was nothing else.

She drowned in the ruthless sea of Nikeya, and she longed for the whole burning world to drown with her.

87

South

Night had not yet fallen, but the Priory was silent, save their footsteps. Wulf walked with Tunuva and Siyu, to the tunnel that would take him outside, back into the death throes of civilisation.

'I do not want you to take an unclaimed ichneumon,' Tunuva told him. 'They can be stubborn.' Lukiri tottered beside her, gripping her fingers. 'Ninuru will keep you safe. She is waiting outside.'

'Ninuru is yours, Tunuva.'

'She will return quickly.'

As soon as they reached the tunnel, he caught the faint smell of the smoke beyond. Siyu wrapped him into a tight embrace. 'Armul,' she said, her voice faint. 'Be safe, brother.'

'And you.' He placed a kiss on her head. 'Treasure your family, Siyu. All your days.'

'I do.' Siyu reached up to grip his chin. 'Do not worship the Deceiver. Even if you keep our secret, know the truth, here.' She placed a hand over his heart. 'Do not be an Inysh fool.'

Wulf gave her a grave nod, then crouched in front of Lukiri.

'Goodbye, Lukiri,' he said. Lukiri glanced up at Tunuva with a frown. 'I have to go now.'

Her frown deepened. 'Go now,' she echoed. 'Looky-yee.' She reached out to pat his face. 'See soon.'

'I hope so, wee one.'

Lukiri nodded, but her lip quivered. Siyu picked her up and walked away, leaving him alone with Tunuva, who held out the wide leather sheath she had been carrying on her shoulder.

'I made this for you,' she said. 'I know you prefer the sword, but a spear is the best weapon, for wyrms.'

Wulf opened the case. Inside was a beautiful Kumengan spear, like hers, with hinges so it could be folded away. His Selinyi name was carved into the handle, small enough to be discreet. 'Thank you,' he murmured. 'It's a bonny weapon, Tunuva. I'll take good care of it.'

'Be happy. After all of this, I hope you can.'

'I will, I think. Now I know who I am.'

A painful silence descended. Looking at her, Wulf thought he might never find the strength to leave.

'I am sorry,' Tunuva said, her voice straining. 'I looked for you. For so long—'

'It wasn't your fault.'

He wished he had more Selinyi. As her jaw shook, he prayed she understood what he said next.

'I envied Mara and Roland, knowing their mother, even if it was just for a short time,' he told her. 'I would cry myself to sleep, trying to remember you. And I did. I remembered your voice. I remembered your arms, and your love, in my heart. I never imagined my mother was a great warrior, who loved me so much she would cross the world to see me one more time.' He tried to smile. 'You are more than I could ever have dreamed.'

Tunuva stood there, eyes lined with tears.

'I will miss you,' she whispered. 'You are welcome here, always. You can come back.'

'I'd like that.'

'Then I will see you again.' Tunuva held him close. 'Goodbye. My brave son.'

Wulf clasped her as near as he could. He tried to fix the moment in his memory – the scent of the girin flower, her sturdy warmth, her breathing.

He would never dream of bees again. The sound of her voice, the feel of her arms, had silenced them for ever.

'I will honour the Mother,' he said. 'And you. As long as I live.'

'You already have.'

Tunuva clutched him, trembling. When they parted at last, Wulf pressed a final kiss to her forehead. She let her breath go in a shudder and watched him stride into the darkness.

Only when he was out of her sight did he let the tears seep down his cheeks.

****

She wept until her voice burned through, until her joints hurt and her eyes scorched, and her head was thick with pain. Curled beneath the orange tree, she sobbed her joy and sorrow to the night.

You are more than I could ever have dreamed.

Beneath the stars, the fruits glimmered like candlelight, as if to comfort her. *You are always here.* She pressed her cheek to its trunk. *You are too rooted to run from this place.*

She grieved for Armul, alone in the valley. For years of lost memories. For the boy he might have been, and the lies he had been told, and all he had suffered outside of the Priory. Tears flooded her cheeks. She gasped for breath, a hand pressed between her womb and her heart.

He was proud to be hers. He was proud.

And gone. Gone into the forest again, out into the maw of the world. She would always carry the pain of his loss, even if its weight was lighter. It was hers to throw like clay on a wheel, to be turned and worked and smoothed into a shape she might one day be able to hold within herself.

But she also felt relief. He had believed her story, not condemned her as a witch. He knew the Mother. He had grown up to be a warrior, as kind and gentle by nature as Meren.

And she loved him just as much now as she had when she held him for the first time.

88

East

Dumai lay in a nest of bedding. In her arms, Nikeya rested, engold-ened by the faint glow of a candle.

Outside the tent, all was dark. They had set out into the forest at dawn, as they had every day since Nikeya had come, and helped Unora and the others chop wood for the crossbows. Later, Nikeya had helped Dumai refine her archery before shooting down a deer for supper. To hide her clan, she had named herself Tonra, after the woman on Brhazat.

'Do you think it belongs to the gods?'

Dumai glanced at Nikeya. She was studying the dark stone, tilting it into the light.

'Furtia said it was a remnant of the star,' Dumai said. 'That it held a great and terrible power.'

'It unsettles me.'

Nikeya stifled a cough. Dumai stroked her hair, taking a deep breath.

'I have thought on your proposal,' she said.

'At last. I was almost starting to feel embarrassed. A rare experience, for me.' Nikeya sat up. 'What was the outcome of all that rumination, wise sage of the forest?'

'I am sorry it took so long. I have never been with anyone, the way you and I are—'

'Dumai, I know. I'm teasing. Have you not met me?'

736

'Fortunately.' Dumai traced the line of her back, stroking the last of the bruising there. 'I was born into a temple. I know the bones and stomach of every ritual of Seiiki, from the ancient to the new.' She met that bright and curious gaze. 'We pledged our love by water, under the night sky. If you still want to be wed to me, then you already are, Nikeya.'

Nikeya linked their fingers.

'Then I am.'

Dumai smiled back, brushing the start of a tear from her cheek. Nikeya lay at her side again.

'Of course, the courtly tradition is that one is always discovered in bed, the morning after a secret marriage,' she said, a coy light in her eyes. 'Sooner or later, the world comes to know.'

'We should keep it a secret for now.'

'Queen Dumai, are you ashamed of your silver consort?'

'I simply want to treasure these hours, with no one to remark on us. Besides,' Dumai said, reaching up to tuck her hair behind her ear, 'a clever woman once told me that our world floats on secrets.'

Nikeya laughed at that. 'You are sweeter with your words than you were. I credit myself.'

'As you should.'

Dumai kissed her, breathing in the smell of woodsmoke from the fires. 'Furtia has been gone for some time,' Nikeya said, when their lips parted again. 'When will you fly next?'

'When I am called.'

'But you'll come back.' She was serious now. 'Promise me, Dumai.'

Dumai looked at her, into those troubled eyes, and said, 'I promise I will always try.'

Later, she was close to sleep when the sweat turned cold on her skin. *I feel as if you are at peace.* The voice she had held at bay for so long. It felt like its old self. *It warms me, sister.*

Dumai could almost see her, the figure in the mist. *It will not last*, she sent back, before she could think better of it. She let herself sink into the black sea of slumber, twined around the woman she loved. *No peace can last in this great sorrow.*

89

South

Time passed, and the world kept burning. Tunuva fought beasts in the Crimson Desert. She shot wyverns and winged snakes from the sky. She and Denag rode east together, delivering a precious bottle of plague remedy to Queen Daraniya. Soshen and Siyāti had been right.

At last, Esbar summoned them all back to their home, for the Priory had been called.

Gashan had been in Jotenya, that mighty stronghold of the march-lands, when its walls had fallen to the servants of Dedalugun. Now she and the other survivors rode for Nzene. She meant to mount a defence of the capital, and Esbar was resolved that they would help her.

The night before they set out, silence lay upon the Priory. Only Tunuva was awake, standing at a window. It was rare that the stars could be seen through the smog, but tonight they showed themselves.

Somewhere beneath them, Wulf was making his way back to his Inysh family. The spear had been all the protection she could grant him, and even then, it might not be enough.

She had not expected him to smile at the prospect of returning. Now the possibility was a seed, buried deep, already reaching out tiny green shoots. They would never reclaim the time they had lost, but to see him again in her silver years – that would be a gift.

'Tuva.'

Canthe had appeared without a sound. She stood at the end of the corridor, all in blue.

'Are you all right?'

'Yes.' Tunuva tried to compose herself. 'Forgive me, Canthe. I just … thought of Wulf.'

'You never need to conceal that from me. I can't imagine how I'd feel if I saw my daughter again.' Canthe joined her at the window, touching a cool hand to her arm. 'Are you glad to have seen him?'

'More than I can express. I never had a chance to thank you for reuniting us,' Tunuva said. 'If there is anything I can give you for your kindness, it is yours, sister. Only ask.'

'I hear you are leaving for Nzene tomorrow.'

'Yes. I think you should come with us – Siyu tells me you have done well with your archery, and it might be a good way to prove yourself to Esbar. I know she will reward your patience.'

Canthe glanced down at her own hand, turning the gold ring on her forefinger.

'If I am to fight,' she said, 'I do have something I would ask of you, though I know you may be obliged to refuse.'

'Name it.'

'To see the Mother's tomb.' Canthe kept her gaze low. 'After so long in Inys, under the yoke of the Deceiver … I would like to pray before her bones. It has haunted me, Tuva, to know I was chained for so long to a lie.'

It was the most sacred place in the Priory, and Canthe was not even a postulant. Tunuva knew Esbar would never allow it.

The refusal was almost to her lips when she drew it back. Canthe had done so much to help her find Armul. In exchange for that, a private visit to the tomb seemed a small request, a modest one.

Easy to grant, on the spur of the moment. Not so easy to forget. Tunuva was already carrying the secret of that foolish kiss in Inys; she could not conceal another from Esbar.

'I'm sorry, Canthe,' she said quietly. 'Even the initiates cannot set foot in the chamber.'

'I understand.' Canthe closed her eyes. 'But no one would have to know, Tuva. It's just us.'

When she turned to face Tunuva, two tiny stars had risen into the sky of her pupils. Their gazes locked. Tunuva slackened, tasting steel.

A heaviness came over her, and the darkness of the corridor seemed to thicken as Canthe took her by the hand.

'Thank you, my friend,' she said. 'I know it will help me, to see the Mother.'

Her fingers were as cold as death. Tunuva frowned at them, trying to remember what she had just said.

Next she knew, she was in the deserted corridors, down the stairs to the burial chamber. At its doors, she reached for the key around her neck, as she did every morning.

'Wait,' she murmured. 'We shouldn't be here.' Her voice was slow. 'How did we get here?'

'Tuva.'

She flinched. Now it was Esbar holding her hand, a look of concern on her face.

'Esbar?' Tunuva tried to blink the shadows from her eyes. 'I thought you were Canthe. Am I dreaming?'

'You've been so tired, my love.' Esbar touched her shoulder, turning her back towards the door. 'It's been a hard day, but we must see the Mother, before we leave for Nzene.'

'Yes.'

Inside, the dark was crushing. Tunuva lit a flame and sleepwalked her way around the chamber, igniting the lamps, as she always did. When she turned back, it was Canthe who stood before the coffin, both hands on its cover. Her hair gleamed like beaten gold in the glow.

'Help me open it.'

Tunuva could hardly keep her eyes open. 'Canthe,' she said, 'what is happening?'

Canthe looked up. Tunuva stared at those eyes, into some primordial absence.

'Please, Tunuva, help me open the coffin,' Canthe said. 'I mean no harm.'

No harm, Tunuva thought, nodding.

She decided she must be in a dream. Her legs waded through dark water, and her skin was hot and cold by turns, her heart beating too hard. Nothing in the room held a firm edge.

The coffin had not been disturbed for centuries. Strong though Tunuva was, it wrung sweat from her, to shift the cover from its place. Canthe joined her, heaving with all her might, and slowly the cover rasped aside, revealing her: Cleolind Onjenyu, Princess of Lasia.

Not a skeleton, but a woman, entire.

The Mother, incorrupt.

Her body was whole. No decay, nor signs of age. Skin of darkest brown, smooth with youth. Hair trimmed close to her skull. Her lashes curled against her cheeks; her lips sat just apart. Tucked into the crook of her arm was a figurine of Washtu, who pulled hair from the sun to give fire to the world. Her hands were folded over one another, gilded with rings.

She did not breathe. She did not move.

'Cleolind.'

A pale hand gripped the side of the coffin. Tunuva looked up hazily to see Canthe, her face expressionless.

'There you are,' Canthe said, almost tender. 'You always were so beautiful. He would have liked you like this. The Damsel, waiting for a knight.' She leaned close, almost close enough to kiss those lifeless lips. 'Do you dream of him, in your own abyss?'

'You knew her,' Tunuva breathed. Now she knew she was dreaming. 'You knew the Mother.'

Canthe only had eyes for the body. 'I was sure you would have it, Cleolind. I came so close to holding its twin – the one Neporo hid away.' She closed her eyes and breathed in. 'But yours *is* here, within my grasp. I have heard its starlight whisper. Where did Siyāti hide it?'

She stepped away from the coffin, leaving Tunuva to gaze in reverence at the Mother. Decades of imagining what she had looked like, and here she was, as if in amber.

This is a strange dream.

Canthe knelt at the foot of the coffin. 'There,' she said, amusement in her voice. 'I believe I know where your mysterious key fits, Tunuva. Saghul asked you to protect more than a corpse.'

Tunuva saw what she had seen. The seams in the dais, and the keyhole set into it, which a gold cover had concealed.

She slid the key into its lock. When it had turned all the way, she pulled, and with a rasp, a chest came with it, a chest that had been set into the dais. Nestled within was a white gemstone, a glow shimmering at its core. A star contained in cloudy glass.

'Tuva?'

Canthe tensed. Esbar came into the chamber, fire in her hand. She took it all in – the open coffin, Tunuva, and Canthe – and her face went colder than Tunuva had ever seen it.

741

'Canthe.' Her voice shook with restrained anger. 'How dare you set foot in this chamber?'

Tunuva watched the fire in her hand turn red. At once, her mind sharpened, and the shadow was blown from her eyes, leaving her disturbed and nerveless. It had not been a dream. She looked back at the pale stone. A hook of temptation caught on her, the selfsame pull that had drawn her to Canthe, and before she could doubt herself, she grasped it.

White light flared at her fingertips. She reeled away from the coffin and fell hard against the floor.

'Tuva,' Esbar gasped.

'No.' Canthe was staring at her. 'Tunuva, what have you done?'

All was dark. The stone clung to her fingers. Her siden withered away from its chill, which bladed through her blood, locking her limbs as it went.

'Tuva, you fool,' Canthe said, starting towards her. 'You have doomed yourself—'

Before she could get close, Esbar slammed her into a wall. Tunuva retched. She had fallen through ice, into water that seared like thousands of swordpoints. Her hand was clenched around the stone, her skin frozen to it, and for all she tried, she could not let go.

'I knew you came here with some foul purpose, Canthe – if that is your name,' Esbar bit out. 'No more lies. What are you doing here, in the Priory?'

'Do not fight me, Esbar,' Canthe said, eyes watering as Esbar tightened her grip. 'All I need is the waning jewel. I sensed it, when the Dreadmount opened.'

'What is it doing to Tuva?'

'It is not your—'

'This is why you've been sniffing around her. Because she's the tomb keeper. You never cared about her,' Esbar said, hatred creasing her face. 'You just wanted to gain her trust.'

'Oh, you don't know the half of it, Prioress,' Canthe said, the cruelty as sudden as it was soft. 'Did she tell you I know the taste of her lips?'

Tunuva tried to get up. She was weak enough to faint, her breath trapped in her throat, but she could still hear Esbar: 'Enough of your hissing. What is that thing, and why do you want it?'

'None of you even knew it was there. Surrender it to me, and I will go in peace, just as I came.'

'Never. I might not have any idea what it is, but it belongs to the Mother. You think I would give anything of hers to another Inysh deceiver?'

'Let me do this without violence,' Canthe said, a fraught note to her voice. 'I cannot leave the Priory without it. It is more dangerous than you could ever comprehend.'

Tunuva managed a groan as her windpipe thawed. Esbar looked towards her, face lit by her flame and her eyes deep as wells, stowed with fear.

Canthe used the distraction to twist her wrist. Esbar gave a tortured sound, a sob caught in a scream, and collapsed to the floor. She had never made a sound like that.

'Esbar,' Tunuva rasped.

'Illusions, Tuva. Esbar is seeing many things. All the nightmares she's had, and more,' Canthe said. 'Visions of you embracing me; of Siyu and her baby, eaten by wyrms; of her birthmother on a pyre; of her ichneumon caught in a trap, whimpering for her. Everything that Esbar fears, I can make her live.'

Dark magic rippled through the burial chamber. A power that stank of iron, laid over a sharp, sour base.

'You gave me those dreams,' Tunuva said, bitter remorse filling her. 'It was you.'

'It was necessary. Your living siden gives you some resistance to this magic, but in your sleep ... you were easier to mould. I needed you to trust me, Tuva.'

'So I would let you into this room.' Tunuva pushed herself from the floor. 'You said your sterren was spent.'

'This is but a shadow of the power I once had.'

'Let her go.' Tunuva held out the stone, the waning jewel. 'Take it, Canthe. Take whatever you want.'

Esbar arched in agony, staring at the ceiling. Canthe stepped over her. As she approached Tunuva, the stone glowed.

'I don't understand,' Tunuva said, trying to slow her. Somehow she needed to protect both the stone and Esbar. 'Who are you?'

'Oh, I have had many names: Hertha, Jórth, the Hawthorn Mother. I was the Witch of Inysca. I was the Lady of the Woods.'

And Tunuva realised, as she looked up at this woman who had been her friend. Every piece of her shattered heart came together – not smoothly, but like broken teeth, the shards piercing.

743

There is a forest there, wild and dark and beautiful, that crosses the whole island, shore to shore. A place feared without cause. At last, after twenty years, she understood. *They call it the haithwood, and as the story went, a witch lived there . . .*

'You.'

Canthe stopped in front of her.

'It was you.' It burned her throat as she said it, like a curse. 'You are the one who took my child.'

Tunuva thought she would deny it. Until she said in a whisper:

'Yes.'

Tunuva stared up at her. Her body was bloodless. A ghastly laugh escaped, boiling up from her vaults like a poison, some runoff of the agony she had kept chained down there for years.

She had let this woman comfort her. She had laughed with her, ridden with her – kissed her, fool that she was. She had bared her heart, because they had both survived the same pain.

The honey and the blood, the bees, the ditch, the wanting to be dead – at last, Tunuva knew the cause of it, all of it. She knew whose arms had carried Wulf to the land of the Deceiver.

'Tell me why.' It was all she could say, all she could think. 'Why, why?'

'Tuva—'

'You should have ripped the heart from me. It would have hurt me less, Canthe.' Vines of fire snaked around her fingers. 'What did I ever do to deserve this?'

'Nothing,' Canthe said thickly. 'Please. Give me the waning jewel. Let it be over.'

Tunuva shook her head and pressed it to her throat, where hot defiance welled. When that power benighted her mind, she firmed her eyes shut and held her flame, trying with all her might to resist.

Canthe cried out. Tunuva looked up to see an arrow buried in her shoulder. On the threshold, Hidat stood with her bow, a second arrow nocked and drawn. This one struck Canthe in the thigh. As she crumpled, Tunuva dived past her, to Esbar.

'Ez,' Tunuva whispered, cupping her face. 'Esbar—' Esbar recoiled from her touch. 'Shh, my love. It's me.'

Esbar blinked away tears. Tunuva helped her up, while Hidat sent a golden blaze into the chamber, brightening all the oil lamps at once. Canthe shielded her face with one arm. The fire seared her sleeve away, but the skin beneath was unburnt.

'Get out. We outnumber you.' Esbar wiped sweat from her upper lip. 'Begone from here, witch.'

'Witch,' Canthe said, her laugh almost desperate. 'Yes, Esbar uq-Nāra. I am always the wicked witch in the end.'

The gemstone shone on the floor. Canthe moved towards it, and time narrowed as if through the waist of a sandglass, and Tunuva reached for her siden, breaking into that forbidden reserve. An overwhelming rush of heat swallowed her body whole. She mustered it into her palm and unleashed a searing flash of wyrmfire, turning the chamber red.

Hidat flinched back. The sandglass burst. Canthe hit the coffin and crumpled like paper, the ends of her hair charred, skin raw from the heat. Before she could recover, Esbar charged to the coffin, took hold of its lid, and heaved it aside with a scream of exertion.

Tunuva clenched her burning hands. Canthe choked out a ghastly sound that flecked her lips with blood. The lid had staved her ribs in, almost breaking her in half. Eyes glazed by pain, she lifted a shaking hand off the floor, towards Tunuva, before her arm fell limp.

Silence returned to the burial chamber. Hidat broke it first. 'Is she dead?'

Esbar knelt beside Canthe and took hold of her wrist. 'I don't feel a heartbeat,' she said hoarsely, 'but we will lock her in. I trust nothing I see around her.'

'I was so blind,' Tunuva whispered.

Esbar glanced up at her. 'These nightmares that have plagued me for months. It was her,' she said. 'Hidat, it must have been Canthe who made you see Saghul, tricked you into killing Anyso.'

Hidat looked shaken. 'Why?'

'To drive a wedge between Esbar and me,' Tunuva said. 'She knew Siyu would run. She knew I would go after her, and Esbar would not, as Prioress.' Esbar met her gaze. 'All of it was to isolate me, to worm her way into my heart, so one day I would unlock this chamber for her.' She retrieved her key from the lock. 'Because I am the tomb keeper.'

'How did you make wyrmfire, Tuva?'

'I will explain.' Esbar picked up the stone. 'This feels wrong. It feels ... like Canthe. But the Mother was protecting it.' She looked at the other body. 'How is she like this?'

Hidat followed her line of sight. Seeing the Mother, she went to one knee, gripping the coffin. Esbar walked to Tunuva and handed her the stone, which glowed.

'We should bury her deep,' she said. 'Help me, Tuva.'

90

West

Winter still held in the north. Glorian kept her gaze ahead, as she had every day since they had left Stilharrow, shivering as wind carved through her heavy wools and mail. At last, they had crossed into the Leas, once golden with wheat and orchards. Now her horse scuffed through blackened stubble.

Smoke rose in pillars in the distance. The sky was dim, the sun a glob of melted fat. She might have thought it was snowing, but she knew the difference between snow and ash by now.

All she smelled was death, and death. Inys wore grey, to mourn itself.

'Glorian.'

Helisent passed her a waterskin. Glorian pulled down her cloth to drink, soaking the scratch from her throat. Florell sat in a pillion behind her, to keep her from taking a fall, and Bourn stayed close, riding beside Marian. The Regency Council had pressed her not to come, preferring she retreat to Offsay – then at least one Berethnet was safe – but she had refused to leave Glorian.

For weeks, the royal party had travelled northward at a cautious pace. Avoiding open fields, they took sunken ways and twittens and drovers' paths, deer trails that wound like thread beneath trees. When they slept, it was nestled under bridges, in caves or ruins.

For days on end, they met no one, heard no one. No candles or watchfires flickered in the night. When they did see flame, they fled, knowing the smell of wyrm.

Now Lady Gladwin brought them to a copse of oaks, where they found a clear pool. 'We'll stop here,' she called. 'Fill your skins and water your horses. This may be the last time you can.'

Glorian let Florell help her down. Her belly made her awkward. While the party rested, she ventured into the trees to find a secluded place. Sabran was sitting so hard on her, she was about to burst.

Her ladies stood guard while she unlaced her trousers – no easy thing, when she could see nothing south of her belly – and took off the clout she had taken to wearing. She tensed when she saw the thick yellowish wad on it, marbled with a thread of blood.

Glorian glanced over her shoulder. She had no idea what it was, but if Bourn saw it, they might try to stop her riding any farther. She buried the clout, as if it had never happened.

****

They struck out again, into the first grass they had seen in days, grown thick without livestock or sickles to trim it. Lady Gladwin led them to an ancient barrow, the tomb of an Inyscan princess, no more conspicuous than a hill. Hoping to sleep there, they slipped through its entrance – only to find two families huddled inside, sharing a brace of thin rabbits. Seeing Glorian, they made room in the burial chamber, and the royal party slept among strangers. For the first time in weeks, Glorian almost felt safe, curled inside the mound.

That evening, they set out again, taking the two families with them.

Great swathes of land were still ablaze. Even now, after months of the wyverns' onslaught, Glorian could not fully accept what she was seeing. None of the devastation looked real.

The sun disappeared. By the glow of their saddle lanterns, they followed Lady Gladwin to a coppice of pines, moving at a brisk canter. Glorian felt a sudden twinge. All she wanted was for Sabran to stay inside, away from the dying world, safe in the snug of her womb.

'Lady Gladwin,' she said, swallowing a cough. 'How are we to approach Hollow Crag?'

'Under cover of darkness.' A cloth muffled her reedy voice. 'We don't want to draw anything there.' Seeing Glorian rub her belly, she said, 'We can rest again, Your Grace.'

'No.' Glorian breathed in. 'Keep the pace, my lady.'

By sunset the next day, they were fording the River Went, which had started to thaw. From there, the horses trotted between hedges, long since overgrown, and at last, they reached an outcrop overlooking Cenning Moor. It rolled towards an isolated rock in the near distance, which knuckled up from the grass and snow, shaped almost like a cockscomb.

Hollow Crag.

Everywhere, people were running towards it.

Prince Guma rode forward, eyebrows beetling. 'What do those fools think they're doing?'

'Saint. They'll draw attention.' Lady Marian looked in shock at the councillors. 'Gladwin—'

A terrible sound made the horses snort. Glorian stiffened. 'Wyverns,' Sir Bramel roared, just as a pair of them swept overhead.

'Ride,' Lady Gladwin barked at the party. 'There's no other shelter. Ride for Hollow Crag!'

All obeyed, the guards closing ranks on either side of Glorian. Florell wrapped an arm around her waist, holding her close, but dread almost throttled her. This choice might yet have killed them all.

The wyverns torched through the survivors. Glorian set her teeth. As their horses galloped across the snow, they overtook the thousands of people making the desperate run to the rock. She looked over her shoulder, smothering a cry when she saw another three wyverns.

'Don't look,' Florell shouted over the wind. 'Glorian, don't look. We're almost there!'

Glorian forced her gaze ahead as they thundered into the shadow of the rock. Its yawning was low down, almost hidden from the sky. As soon as they reached the shelter of its overhang, she was helped in a great rush from her horse. Sabran kicked and kicked within her.

Several gloved hands ushered her into the depths of Hollow Crag. Lady Gladwin marched ahead, past those who were collapsing, out of breath, or sobbing in relief. Even the Queen of Inys could go unnoticed in this crush.

Lord Ordan Beck, the Dowager Earl of Goldenbirch, was ensconced in a warm cave that rang with worried voices. When the guards let his daughter through, he looked up, fear leaping into his dark eyes.

'Helisent?'

'Papa.' She went to him. 'You're all right.'

'You have to go. You can't be—' Seeing Glorian and Marian, and then the Regency Council, he croaked, 'No.'

'By the Saint's holy bones.' Lord Edrick Glenn stared at them all. 'Lady Protector, what are you doing here?'

'Before we submit to questioning, I might ask what in Halgalant is happening,' Marian said, holding on to Glorian. 'Lord Ordan, I was assured this place was safe. Now I have brought my granddaughter here, I find scores of people in plain sight, and wyverns on the wing.'

'Madenley came under attack. The survivors fled in a great panic,' Lord Ordan explained. 'Hollow Crag is the nearest cave, but in their terror and haste, they were not careful. They have led the entire flock to Cenning Moor.' His eyes were bloodshot. 'A few people got away time, but it's too late for the rest of us. To leave would be to walk into death.'

'We are trapped here.'

'Yes. They would surely have seen the entrance by now, and if not, they'll follow the scent.'

'Tell me you have not brought the entire Regency Council,' Lord Edrick said, ashen.

'All but Lord Randroth, who rode to Offsay,' Marian said shortly.

Lord Ordan let out a weak laugh. 'Oh, Saint forbid we're left with that pompous sack of bluster.'

'So every member of the House of Berethnet is in here,' Roland Glenn said, raising an eyebrow. 'Forgive my crudeness, Lady Protector, but you really did choose a shite place to visit.'

'Roland,' Lord Edrick warned.

'No. We can survive this,' Glorian said. They all looked at her. 'The entrance is a chokepoint. It's low and small, difficult for the wyverns to reach. They will have to send their beasts to force us out, and those beasts have weaknesses. We can defend Hollow Crag.'

'We've hardly any weapons, Your Grace,' Lord Ordan said.

'When Verthing Bloodblade marched on Vakróss, he needed to get his forces over the river. There was just one bridge, which my father defended. He alone killed seventy warriors, giving his allies time to prepare – and I am certain we have more than one fighter. It can be done.'

'With respect, he was fighting his fellow humans, not wyrms.'

Glorian laid a hand on her belly.

'I am likely to give birth in this place,' she said. 'I want my child to have a queendom left to rule. I want her to taste apples still crisp from the orchard. I want her to see the green of Inysh spring; to know the scent of wildflowers, the taste of bread, the sound of laughter. I do not want her life to end at her first breath, her voice strangled away by smoke.'

Several glances were exchanged, doubts and hopes delivered without a single word.

'The Saint is with us,' Glorian told them. 'Let us give these foul things one last cry before the end. Let us give the world a reason to remember us.'

A long silence descended.

'King Bardholt was a great warrior,' Prince Guma said, concluding it. 'I say we lead by his example.'

Glorian thought of his letter, keeping her face blank. *Bardholt was a licentious traitor for taking up the False Sword.*

'I agree,' Lady Gladwin said. 'We ought to send the strongest fighters on to the moor, to try to thin their forces before sunrise. Once they have enough light, the wyverns will make things harder.'

Lord Ordan seemed to steel himself.

'Some of those who fled in time promised me they would bring help,' he said. 'Paupers' Henge might yet answer the call – that's the nearest refuge – but if not, we have arrows, the guards from Madenley and Arondine, and anyone who can lift a blade or sharp tool. We could mount a defence of the entrance, for a time. Perhaps long enough to discourage them.'

'Those beasts never give up,' Lord Damud said. 'Whatever happens next, there will be death.'

'Forgive me,' Bourn intervened, 'but the queen needs somewhere to rest. It was a hard ride from Stilharrow.'

Glorian wanted to gainsay, but she did need to sleep, or she would be more of a danger than a help to the Regency Council. 'Aye. Follow me, Your Grace,' Roland said, taking a lantern from the table. Glorian walked after him with Julain and Adela, while her grandmother stayed to confer with the nobles.

'Master Glenn,' Glorian said, taking the arm he offered her, 'have you heard from your brother?'

'He's still in Hróth, fighting with King Einlek. So his lithsman tells me.'

'Thrit or Karlsten?'

'Thrit. He arrived a few weeks ago.'

That troubled her. Surely Thrit would not have wanted to leave the rest of his lith, or his king.

Roland avoided the large caverns. The newcomers from Madenley were crowding into those, raising a commotion among the thousands of northerners who had been living there peacefully by candlelight for months. He took Glorian past a buttery and a hospital, where sanctarians and healers were tending the sick. Water rushed down a wall, misting them all with spray. There was no sign of the plague, save the smell of vinegar.

A small cave had been made up as a bedchamber. Its pallet was humble, but after weeks on horseback, it was better than a featherbed. Glorian lowered herself on to it, wishing she could sleep at once, but she was filthy.

'I'll leave you, Queen Glorian,' Roland said, 'but we'll keep you abreast of the situation.'

'Thank you, Master Glenn.'

He pulled a drape across the entrance in his wake, giving her a semblance of privacy. 'What do we do?' Adela said, wringing her hands. 'Glorian, are we going to die?'

'Do not speak of death again, Adela.' Julain looked hard at her. 'Find a basin of clean water, please. Glorian can't sleep like this.'

Glorian just sat on the pallet, too exhausted to answer. Julain tried to get the ash from her hair.

Outside, the wyverns must be mustering.

Bourn soon came to see her. 'Your Grace, if I may, I would like to ensure your wellbeing before you sleep,' they said. 'It was a hard ride.'

'Of course,' Glorian said. 'Julain, Adela, you should try to find something to eat. Be careful, please. There may be a crush.'

Once they were gone, she rolled up her layers and beckoned Bourn, who knelt in front of her. They placed their cool, smooth palms on her belly.

'On the road,' they said, 'did you notice any pain or bleeding, or other changes?'

'Something like ... what you cough up with the throttle.'

'The unsealing of the womb.' Bourn looked grim. 'Your time draws near, Queen Glorian.'

'Then I will have my daughter here.'

'I fear so.'

Bourn pressed their fingers to her wrist. 'We can hold the entrance. Just like my father,' Glorian said. Bourn nodded slowly. 'Is all well, with the child?'

'As far as I can tell.'

Glorian glanced at her belly, swallowing.

'Mastress Bourn,' she said in a whisper, 'I know that birth can go awry. If my daughter and I are both in distress, you know you are bound to choose her over me. I cannot make another child.'

'I was told.' A twinge of sorrow crossed their face. 'I should not say this, Queen Glorian.'

'Please.'

'I grieve for you, that you should have to do this. I also grieve for Carmentum. They found a different way. Any order of succession that demands a child bear a child … I find it hard to stomach.' Their jaw ground like a mill. 'I know that it keeps the Nameless One fettered. I only wish the Saint had not made this the price of his protection.'

Her father would have punished this. It was blasphemy, a lack of faith. Glorian searched herself for anger, and found none.

'Thank you, Kell,' she said. 'For your honesty.' She covered their hand. 'Will you help me?'

Her voice shook a little. Bourn grasped her hand in return.

'I will.'

Glorian let them go and turned on to her side, unable to stay awake. In the distance, she heard the seeds of realisation in the other caves, bursting into cries of fear. Just before she slipped into the darkness, she reached for her sister, and in that moment, she was almost at peace.

****

When she woke, it took some time to remember where she was. Once she did, she wished she could forget again.

'… has the baby here, what will we do then?'

'Hollow Crag will keep us safe,' Helisent said under her breath. 'Glorian is right. With that small entrance, it could work.'

752

'Not once the wyverns can see,' Julain told her. 'Our fighters are hungry, weak, and poorly armed. Half of them are not even soldiers. Others are drained from the fight at Madenley. You know this as well as I do.' Fear clipped her voice. 'We should have gone to Selverpit.'

'Too late now, Jules. The milk is spilled.'

'Is there no chance we can slip away with her, while it's still dark?'

'I fear to try. What if she goes into labour?'

Julain made a low, strangled sound. 'Either way is death, unless our fighters hold the line.'

Glorian felt a rippling cramp. Eyes closed, she waited, willing it to pass. *Not now.* She pressed her eyes tighter. *Not yet, Sabran. It's not safe.*

As if the child had heard, her womb quietened. She propped herself on her arm.

'What is happening?'

Helisent and Julain both started. 'Lord Ordan has mustered the defence,' Julain said. Ash still smudged her face, and her braid was windswept. 'You should not think of it, Glorian.'

'I must.' Glorian sat up, her belly heavy in her lap. 'What time is it?'

'It's just turned dark. The wyverns won't see much for tonight,' Helisent said, 'but their creatures have followed the scent from Madenley. They will be here before the hour is up.'

'How many?'

Helisent swallowed. 'I don't know.'

'Tell me, Helisent.'

'Hundreds of creatures attacked Madenley.' Julain was hoarse. 'Some witnesses think it was far more, according to Roland Glenn.'

'How many do we have?'

'My father anticipates a force of a thousand or so – that's if Paupers' Henge doesn't answer the call,' Helisent said. 'He will position most of them beyond the entrance, and the rest just inside, to finish any beasts that succeed in breaking through the vanguard.'

A thousand Inysh fighters against the offspring of the Dreadmount. Once the wyverns had daylight, her forces would have to pull back to Hollow Crag, or they would be burned alive.

'Saint be with us,' Glorian whispered.

'Your Grace.' Roland knocked on the wall. He seemed to have been given the role of royal caretaker. 'I promised Kell Bourn you'd eat, before I ride out to defend the entrance.'

'You mean to fight, Roland?'

'Aye, I can use a sword well enough. Not as well as my brother, alas, or I might stand a better chance of surviving.'

He took her to a nearby chamber. Glorian was slow and breathless, listening to the din in the dark.

She found a table piled with a feast she would never have thought possible for one person in a time of famine: salted meats and cheese, fresh salmon, and a hot stew of rabbit, shank mushrooms and garlic. There was even bread. It was more food than she had seen since Offsay, a sanctuary on the coast, where there had been fish and scallops aplenty.

'I presume the people do not eat so well,' she said.

Roland shook his head. 'Every three days, if that. A group of scavengers slips out to bolster our stores with pignuts, weasels and hares, and so on. They've had it far worse farther north, where the frost is thicker. I heard the people of Calthorn had turned to eating one another by the time it fell.' Seeing her stricken face, he said, 'Likely just a rumour.'

'Do they blame me?'

'They know you're growing our protection.' He glanced at her belly. 'Most blame each other, for their sins. I'm just glad Wulf is far away, or they'd have pointed the finger by now.'

'Yes,' Glorian said. Sabran gave a tiny kick. 'How many people are with child in these caves?'

'Twenty, I think, at last count.'

'Are there any who are in the last days, as I am?'

'I've seen a couple who look as if they could burst any day. Begging your pardon, Your Grace,' he added, running a hand through his hair. 'I've lost my manners in this hole.'

'I would like them to share in this food. Would you invite them here?'

Roland eyed her, curious. 'We've not much food left, and we can't gather more now.'

'Bring them.'

It took him some time to find the nine women, in the darkness of the caverns, among the sixteen thousand people who now filled Hollow Crag. One of them had swelled so big that she waddled – twins, perhaps. They were all older than Glorian, one with grey in her hair.

'Your Grace,' they all said.

'Good evening.' Glorian found a smile for them. 'You are all great with child, as I am. My councillors believe my body should be well-nourished. It stands to reason that yours should be as well.' She motioned to the bench on the other side of the table. 'Please, eat with me.'

The women were silent. She could see the craving in their dull eyes, their hollow cheeks.

'Queen Glorian,' the eldest of them murmured, 'you are so generous, to invite us to your table.' She lifted her chin. 'But for myself, I'll not take one scrap of food from the heir.'

The woman with the largest belly licked her lips, glancing at the others. 'Neither will we, Your Grace,' she said, after a hesitation. Her voice cracked as she spoke, the desperation clear.

One by one, they curtseyed, turned away from the feast, and left Glorian alone. Her belly gave a pang. Through a blur, she stared up at the ceiling.

Is this what you wanted? As she wept for the first time in weeks, she willed the words to Halgalant. *Is this what you wanted your kingdom to be?*

****

She slept with one arm over her belly, curled like the cup of an acorn around it. A hand on her shoulder drew her awake.

'Glorian,' Julain said, 'it's started.'

The words took a moment to sink in. Clumsy with sleep, Glorian pushed herself upright. 'I want to see the Regency Council.' She breathed deep, grasping her belly. 'Let me—'

As she stood, she felt it: a tiny break in the vaults of her body, and then an uncontainable surge between her legs, and water puddled at her feet. She stared at it, then at Julain.

Bourn had told her this would happen. It would happen when Sabran was ready to come.

'Oh.' Adela had turned very pale. 'Oh, no—'

'Get Mastress Bourn, now. Tell the Lady Protector,' Helisent said to her. 'Hurry, Adela!'

Adela rushed away. Helisent guided Glorian back to the bed, and Julain held her by the shoulders. 'It seems my battle will be here,' Glorian said, through gritted teeth. 'So be it.'

91

East

Dumai woke deep in the night, to find the oil lamp burning low and Nikeya still asleep. Still in her arms, and safe.

There was so much they had yet to learn. It must reach back for centuries or more, this intrigue of the Mulberry Queen.

As for the balance, that was far older. She would have to look far and wide to understand its implications, and even then, it could take more than a lifetime.

But what she felt for this woman, who had ridden through fire to hold her again – that was as good a place as any to begin. Dumai drew her close, pressing the gentlest kiss to her shoulder.

As she drifted back off, a coldness washed over her. She tried to see into that realm of stars and running water.

I feel your fear, your pain. Like nothing I have ever felt. Her eyes closed. *I see you, sister. Was it really you I met in the snow?*

I opened the doors of my dream to another. The figure was so faint. *Sister, be with me. I need your strength.*

'Dumai.'

Unora was at the entrance to the tent, a flicker of shock on her face. When Dumai sat up, careful not to wake Nikeya, it softened into quiet understanding.

'You knew,' Dumai said.

'I always did.' Unora was holding a candle. 'I'm sorry, my kite. Someone has arrived.'

'Who?'

'Epabo. He has found you again.' She looked gaunt. 'He fears your sister is in danger.'

92

South

Ninuru raced towards the city, her paws kicking up dust. Tunuva held on to her fur with one hand, the saddle with the other, as they followed Jeda. Siyu clung to her waist. Other ichneumons ran behind them, each carrying a warrior. All of them thundered past Lake Jodigo.

To the west, wyverns flocked. A distant black cloud marked the pyre that was Jotenya. No sign yet of Dedalugun.

Ahead, Esbar made straight for the Godsblades.

For weeks, Kediko had refused to fortify Nzene. Only when the Lasian ambassador to Carmentum had arrived at his court, months after Tunuva had first warned him of the threat, had he finally seen fit to act. High walls had been constructed, blocking the narrow passes between the mountains. In front of each one, a ditch bristled with sharpened stakes and kindling, and behind, rows of towers had been raised for archers.

Apparently, Kediko could be resourceful when it pleased him.

Thousands of shaken and injured survivors were waiting to enter through the only wall with a gate, beside Mount Dinduru, largest and most sacred of the Godsblades. At any other time, they might have stared at the sight of so many ichneumons. Instead, they made way without protest.

'State your names, and your business in Nzene,' an official shouted down from a tower.

'Esbar uq-Ispad,' Esbar called back. 'I bring warriors for the High Ruler, at his invitation.'

Gashan must have told the official that name. With a nod, she motioned to the guards on the ground, who stood aside as one for the ichneumons. Tunuva rode Ninuru through.

Nzene was preparing for war. Heat fanned from the ironworks. Mounted warriors held lances and war shields, gilded with the pomegranate of the House of Onjenyu. Some people were making for the mountain caves, or barring themselves into their homes, most of which were tile and stone. Far more prepared to fight for the city, grasping all manner of weapons, from swords and bows to any tool they could turn to their advantage: sickles, hammers, hay forks. Some had shrewdly painted their skin with clay, to stave off fire.

Esbar marched them up to the palace. Gashan Janudin awaited them with folded arms, her masked ichneumon at her side. Barsega had run far ahead to reunite with her little sister.

'Prioress,' Gashan said.

'Royal Treasurer.' Esbar stopped in front of her, mirroring her stance. 'You called.'

'The High Ruler of Lasia called.'

Esbar nodded to the ichneumon. 'Barsega managed to find you, I see.'

'She was always faster than your Jeda.'

'But not half as good at menacing growls,' Esbar said, giving Jeda a stroke. Jeda growled.

Gashan looked her former rival in the eye, her lips twitching into a smile. She wore the white cloak of an initiate over her armour.

'Esbar, I know you and I have never precisely been friends,' she said, 'but I ask all of you to stand with me now, to defend the Domain of Lasia, as the Mother once did.'

'For that,' Esbar said, 'I am willing to forget the past.' She grasped Gashan by the arm, and Gashan gripped hers in return. 'Tell us what's happening, sister.'

Gashan beckoned. Leaving their sisters and ichneumons in the Inner Court, Esbar and Tunuva followed her.

'Dedalugun will be here soon,' she said. 'I did my best, but Jotenya was too exposed, in the marchlands – when its wall fell, the battle was lost. The Godsblades offer more protection.' They rounded a corner. 'Many people have risked the copper road, hoping to reach the Spindles in time, though I hear there are wyrms there as well.'

'There are,' Tunuva said.

'Everyone else is trapped here, on the streets – about two hundred thousand people.'

'The High Ruler praised his army when I met him last. How many soldiers are here?'

'Four and a half thousand. The others are fighting across Lasia.'

'Which means you don't know if they're alive or dead. They're probably dead,' Esbar added, pursing her lips. 'Can you assure me that the High Ruler approves of our presence?'

'His Majesty has remembered the importance of the ancient bond between his bloodline and the Priory.'

'It only took the end of the world to remind him,' Esbar said under her breath. 'Take us to him, Gashan, if you would. I wish to hear this revelation from his own mouth.'

'I have a revelation for you first.' Gashan faced them both. 'Something may be about to stop all of this.'

'What?'

'I've been combing the library for any knowledge that might help us. I found an ancient tablet in the royal archives. I believe it is from across the Eria, brought here by Suttu the Dreamer.' She showed it to them. 'It took me some time to interpret the script – portions of it are worn off, as you see. But it speaks of a comet, which has passed this world before.'

The tablet was round, made of clay. Esbar shook her head. 'How will a comet help anyone?'

'It is due to come again soon – now, at any moment. Surely the timing has significance.'

'That sort of thing was always your area.'

'Wait,' Tunuva murmured. The stone was turning colder. 'Ez, Canthe spoke of a comet. She claimed it was the source of her other power – sterren. That magic weakened my fire in Carmentum. What if it can do the same to the beasts of the Dreadmount?'

Gashan raised an eyebrow. 'Who is Canthe?'

'No one you need to worry about,' Esbar said, giving Tunuva a nod. 'Gashan, have you told Kediko?'

760

'No.' Gashan tucked the tablet away. 'He believes in the significance of the celestial bodies. I feared he might not prepare Nzene if he thought an answer would fall from the sky.'

'So you did notice his flaws.'

'Not now, Esbar,' Gashan said curtly, marching on. 'What is this about another magic?'

'Not now, Gashan. If a comet does come, so be it. If not, we will need to fight for our lives.'

Kediko Onjenyu was dressed for battle, but seated in comfort, with a goblet and a bowl of fruit. Seeing Esbar approach, he winched his features into his usual smile, but Tunuva saw what two years of chaos had done to him. His war crown failed to conceal his grey hairs.

'Leave us,' he told his servants, who departed. 'Esbar. I hear you are now Prioress. Congratulations on your promotion.'

'Congratulations on your survival, High Ruler. We are honoured to have spent the last two years keeping wyrms away from your fine palace,' Esbar said, with a tight smile. Kediko broadened his. 'At your invitation, I have brought my daughters to Nzene, to fight for the House of Onjenyu – but before we raise our blades, I wish to reassure myself that you have not mistaken this for an invasion. I understand our presence has unnerved you recently.'

'If I gave Tunuva that impression, I apologise. You are welcome here. After all, we are all humans, born of flowers, bound together in the shadow of the Dreadmount.' Kediko drummed his fingers on the throne. 'I relish this opportunity for the Priory to prove its prowess.'

'I believe we have proven our prowess already, in several of your cities,' Esbar said, her smile turning dangerous. 'We drove Dedalugun away from Jrhanyam.'

'Driving him away is one thing. Slaying him would prove my doubts wrong, once and for all. If you cannot slay a wyrm, what edge has the Priory over a conventional army?'

'Will you be joining us?' Esbar asked, still with that smile. 'I hear you were a fighting man in your youth.'

'I would. Gladly,' Kediko said, 'but I would hate to take that Mother-given duty from you. After all, you have waited all your lives for something to protect me from.' He sat back. 'Good luck to you, Esbar.'

Before Esbar could kill him, Gashan led her away.

'I swear by the Mother,' Esbar bit out, 'I will humble that smiling fool if I have to personally chew Dedalugun to death, picking off each scale with my teeth. I should let him burn.'

'He wants this, Esbar.' Gashan steered her up the stairs. 'He wants to goad you into slaying Dedalugun.'

'I would hate to disappoint.'

On the terrace, they looked out across Nzene – the sky, the tarnished platter of the sun. Tunuva reached for Esbar, and Esbar looked at her, her eyes speaking a lifetime of words.

Dedalugun would fall. If not, they would die together, under the Lasian sun, doing what they had been born to do.

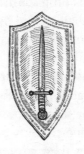

93

West

On Cenning Moor, soldiers fought by wyrmfire. In the depths of Hollow Crag, thousands of survivors listened to the clash, knowing well that if it stopped, their lives would be snuffed out next.

Enwombed in her chamber, the Queen of Inys laboured – her body opening by increments, for hours. Her grandmother prayed at her side. Bourn waited at the end of the pallet, while her ladies hovered nearby. No one else. The birth of a Berethnet was sacred, to be witnessed only by a few.

Candles melted into stumps. Past the thick walls of Hollow Crag, half of the nobles were on the moor with the soldiers and knights, fighting the onslaught of creatures. This deep in the cave, Glorian could hear nothing.

'The battle,' she blew out. 'Tell me what's happening.'

'You mustn't think of it,' Florell told her. 'You must only think of this, Glorian.'

'I want—' Another pain struck her. When it had passed, she gasped for breath. 'How many have come?'

'Sweeting, please.'

'I am almost eighteen,' Glorian ground out. 'Helisent, ask your father.'

Her mind went white with the next cramp. After an eternity, Bourn gave Marian a nod.

'Your Grace, you have opened enough,' they told Glorian. 'When you feel ready, you can start to push.' Glorian braced herself on her elbows. 'Since there is no birthing stool, I would urge you to kneel for this part of your labour.'

'You ask her to bear a child on her knees?' Florell said, stunned. 'This is the Queen of Inys.'

'The pain is in her back, my lady,' Bourn said in clipped tones. 'Lying on it will not help. An upright position is far more—'

'No, Mastress Bourn,' Marian cut in. 'It would be unbecoming for a queen. I gave birth to a strong child on my back. So did the Damsel.'

The Damsel died, Glorian tried to scream, but pain stripped those words away. Her body moved with a will of its own.

She closed her eyes, trying in vain to escape her straining flesh. She pictured the sky lights, the calming blue and green of them. Her mother after the attack, gentle for the first time in years. Her father sitting at her side, the sun reflecting off the water in the queenswood.

That is the hardest part. Knowing that you embody a realm, he whispered. As her womb tided, so did all of Inys. *That your eyes are its vigilance; your stomach, its strength; your heart, its shield; your flesh, its future.*

A sudden tumult roused her. 'What is it?' she said. Julain mopped her brow. 'Who's there?'

Julain swallowed. 'Prince Guma.'

'Send him away,' Marian said, her face stark with anger. 'Sir Bramel, keep him out.'

Glorian glimpsed his face, the flash of tawny eyes, before her guards wrestled him back. She gathered her belly into her arms.

I will not let him get to you.

A deep burning between her legs, far stronger than before. She gripped her ladies' hands as if she would break them, a cry scraping from her throat. She thought of praying, or dreaming, but she could do neither. In the haze of the next push, she thought of Numun of Carmentum – ash now, perhaps, along with her republic. It made no sense to envy her.

And yet Numun never had to rip herself asunder.

Damn you. A low sound, her own. *Damn you, Galian Berethnet. Why did you not have to suffer, but each of your descendants did?*

When the tightening was over, she slackened, eyelids heavy. 'Glorian, don't give up,' Julain urged.

Why is this the only way?

Glorian let her head sink into the pillow. She was tired – so tired. She imagined Fýredel before her, waiting to eat her child alive.

****

The Womb of Fire had spilled into Inys. Wulfert Glenn saw it from a distance, his eyes watering from the wind and the smoke. It had taken him weeks to make it this far, but at last he was here, on Cenning Moor.

His steed galloped for Hollow Crag, where Riksard had said his father was hiding. The wyverns and their beasts had found it first. Blood and filth turned the ground to a slester, and fires roared all over the moor, turning the night red. They lit the creased face of the rock.

He rode towards where the fighting was thickest, clad in his chainmail. 'Stay in formation,' a voice bellowed to his right.

Wulf stopped his horse. He knew that voice. Just as he thought he saw Roland, fire erupted across the grass, flames as tall as the giants of Northern lore. He shielded his face.

Cries of pain and fear were pealing. Three wyverns lit the moor with their own fire, making it easier to see their prey. Whatever way he turned, there was madness: horses rearing and whinnying, corpses on corpses, moving nightmares.

'Wulf!'

He coughed his guts up as ash filled his mouth. Yanking his swatch of wet cloth back over it, he took out the spear from Tunuva and unfolded it the way she had shown him. As soon as the hinges were locked in position, he wheeled around, searching for the source of the voice, and saw his brother, filthy and bleeding, hacking at the beasts from horseback.

'Rollo,' he roared into the din – then something slammed into him, and he fell into thick mud.

The shock of the blow left him winded. He twisted on to his side to see a monstrous thing, like an ox. It rammed its horns into his horse, then lunged for him, sparks blowing from its nostrils. Wulf wrestled free of the mud and gore, just as teeth plunged into his shoulder. Shouting in agony, he made a grab for the spear, seized the beast by its bare animal halse and drove the point into the roof of its mouth.

'Wulf!'

Drenched in sludge, Wulf wrenched his spear free and crawled through the crush, trying to get back to his feet. His shoulder burned. 'Thrit—' The clangoring swallowed his words. 'Thrit!'

He buffeted through the soldiers, ducked away from a lindworm. A wyvern swooped low, and he rolled under it, and next thing he knew, he had crashed straight into Thrit.

'Wulf, where the fuck did you come from?' he shouted through his cloth. 'How long have you been here?'

'Lasia. Not long.' Wulf let go of him to take a shield from a dead knight, hefting it on to his arm, and they turned their backs to each other. 'I take it we're defending Hollow Crag.'

'Apparently.' Thrit dashed the sweat from his brow. 'Queen Glorian is in there. There's word she's in labour.'

Wulf stared towards the rock. 'What is she doing here?'

'Unhappy coincidence.'

'I should go in there, to help guard her—'

'Yes, by all means, barge in and show Prince Guma the face of the man who made him a wittol,' Thrit barked at him. 'Don't be a fool, Wulf. Her battle is in there.' He nocked two arrows. 'Ours is out here.'

Wulf nodded, and raised his spear.

94

East

The first time Dumai had met Epabo – her father's mysterious ally – he had been coughing blood on the snow of Mount Ipyeda. Now he was even weaker, coughing soot into a cloth.

His left arm had been bitten off at the elbow. The healers at the southernmost camp had done their best, cleaning the remnant and burning it shut, but Epabo had walked a long way with that injury. Even if he had not bled so heavily, the limb had already festered.

He had been carried through the forest on a stretched hide. Now he lay in a small tent, dying. Dumai watched him wake from a fitful drowse.

'Can you hear me, Epabo?'

Epabo managed a nod. 'Princess Dumai.' He wore a thick cloth mitten on his remaining hand. 'I beg you, come no closer. The red sickness may be in me.'

'What happened?'

'A winged creature on the road, in the night. I didn't see until its iron teeth were in me.'

Dumai glanced at her mother, who knew how much a body could endure. Unora gave the barest shake of her head.

'Such beasts roam wild in every province. Seiiki is on fire,' Dumai said. 'Why risk leaving the Rayonti Basin?'

'I had to see you. To tell you what the River Lord has done.'

She knelt where she was, disquiet lining her stomach. 'When you came to the temple, you changed the course of my life,' she said. 'Tell me. Will your tidings change it again?'

'I fear so. It seems our story is to end as it began.'

'Did you find me by following Lady Nikeya?'

'I had been watching her closely, but when she left the palace, I saw no need to follow. Not this time.' He grimaced in pain. 'I'm not sure how long I have to explain. You should summon Furtia Stormcaller.'

'Does Suzu need help?'

'Yes.'

Dumai nodded, closing her eyes. The stone was at her neck, bolstering the bond.

Great one, I need you. Can you come?

The fire is strong, earth child.

I think it rises high enough to threaten my sister at court. Dumai concentrated. *If you are near me, please come.*

I am coming.

Epabo wet his chapped lips. Sweat shone on his collarbones and ran in raindrops down his face. Unora left the tent and returned with a cup of clean water, placing it within his reach.

'The River Lord has always shown little care for the provinces,' Epabo said, 'but his failure to defend our people has confused and disturbed the nobility, including his fellow Kuposa. Even the cities have been left to burn. Only you have protected us, Queen Dumai.

'After Lady Nikeya absconded, I decided not to pursue her. Instead, I remained in the palace to watch over Empress Suzumai,' he continued. 'One night, the River Lord left on horseback, which threw the court into disarray. I assumed he was trying to find his wayward daughter. When he returned, he was … different, quieter. He refused to see the Council of State, secluding himself into the Water Pavilion. Still he made no move to stop the burning of our island.

'When he finally emerged, the River Lord announced that he had worked out a way to end our suffering. He had discovered a precedent, in an old Western tale – the tale of the Nameless One.'

Dumai looked at her mother.

'I left the scroll there, with your father,' Unora breathed. 'It would have been in the Water Pavilion.'

Epabo nodded. 'In the tale,' he said, 'a great red wyrm descended upon the city of Yikala, in a land named Lasia. Its ruler, Selinu, found a way to appease the creature. First, he sacrificed the livestock to its jaws; then he sacrificed the people, drawing a lot each day to decide who would die. One day, the lot fell upon his own daughter, a princess.'

'Our livestock has already been taken,' Dumai said hoarsely. 'Epabo, where is the River Lord?'

'Taugran has made its lair on Muysima. The nearest city is Uramyesi, which still holds many thousands of survivors. The River Lord declared that he would go there, to treat with the beast and save what remains of Seiiki. He would also take Empress Suzumai.'

Dumai swallowed.

'As soon as I heard, I reached out to Lord Tajorin through his friends at court. They have been helping those who would defect to your side. I sent a message to your grandmother, to warn her of the danger,' he said, 'and then I followed the web of whispers across Seiiki, north to Mayupora Forest.'

'What is it you fear?'

Unora grasped her own arms. The cloth she wore concealed her expression, but her eyes were enough to betray her foreboding.

'Why would he take the young empress to Muysima, knowing Taugran is there?' Epabo said. 'I believe he means to be rid of her, under the pretence of saving Seiiki. He will offer her to the beast, just as the High Ruler of Lasia surrendered his own child.'

'Suzumai is under his control. Why would he harm her?'

'To consolidate a House of Kuposa.'

The voice made them all look. Nikeya had appeared at the entrance to the tent, a hunting coat thrown over her shoulders.

'I'm sorry to interrupt,' she said. 'Hello, Epabo. You've looked better.'

'As have you, Lady of Faces.' Epabo managed a smile. 'I am glad that we find ourselves on the same side.'

Nikeya nodded. 'We all know my father has changed,' she said to them. 'His need for power has grown in this chaos. This fire will have convinced him that Clan Kuposa must seize its chance to rule, while the gods are at their weakest. I can imagine him performing a noble sacrifice of the Noziken.'

'Epabo,' Dumai said, 'thank you, for everything. I will lead the gods to avert his folly.'

She marched from the tent, into the freezing night, to collect what she would need.

'Dumai.' Unora caught up to her, Nikeya just behind. 'You mustn't go. It could be a trap, a way of drawing you into the open—'

'I can't leave Suzu at his mercy,' Dumai said firmly. 'Furtia and I will get her away.'

'Taugran is much stronger than Furtia,' Nikeya protested. 'You know this, Dumai.'

'Not for long. I feel the coming of the star.'

It was true. Her awareness of it was taut and strong, a string pulled along the neck of a lute, tuned to something that moved closer by the hour.

'Nikeya,' Unora said quietly, touching her shoulder, 'will you leave us a moment, and watch over Epabo?'

'Of course.'

Nikeya dealt Dumai a concerned look and went back to the tent. Unora took Dumai by the cheek.

'Do not go to Muysima.'

'I have to—'

'I wished, Dumai. When I was twenty.' Her voice strained. 'I asked a wish of Pajati the White.'

Dumai stared at her.

'I wished for a way to reach the court, so I could save my father. Sipwo dreamed of me that night.' Unora spoke in little more than a whisper. 'Pajati is an elder dragon – born of the stars themselves, not the sea. His light was still within me when you were conceived.'

'How do you know?'

'He told me it would last one turn of the sun.' She pressed one hand to her stomach, low down. 'I think it woke the old gifts of your line, in the waters of my womb.'

'You could have been executed. It was forbidden.'

'A blade would have been kinder than a death by thirst, or a wasting sickness. I had nothing left to lose, but now I do.' Unora kept hold of her face. 'Muysima is where my father perished. A curse lies on that island. Please, my kite – stay here, where it's safe.'

Unora was no longer the hardened woman who had survived a hostile mountain. One mention of that island, and she was the dying girl from a dust province, alone in the world.

Dumai drew up her sleeve. 'You must stay here. The people in this camp need a leader they trust.' She reached for the fraying strand at her wrist and worked it off. 'Kanifa gave this to me, from our rope, before I left for court. Hold it for me, like the end of a line. Take it and know I am your kite.'

Unora clasped the strand between their hands.

'I can never regret that wish,' she finally said. 'If I had not gone to the great Pajati, my bones would lie in the dusts of Afa, and I would never have had you.' Dumai pressed their foreheads together. 'I will let you go, as your grandmother taught me. I will keep hold of this line and wait for your return to me.'

'As soon as I can,' Dumai whispered to her. 'No matter how long I am gone, I am coming.'

****

Dumai prepared herself in her tent. She wove a rainbow through the darkness of her hair, cords in every colour she had worn when her father brought her to Antuma. Once she had fastened her armour, she picked up her ice sickles and made to secure them to her hips.

'When do we leave?'

She turned. Nikeya was already dressed for the saddle, bundled in thick furs, eyebrows raised.

'You must stay here,' Dumai told her. 'My mother will need help.'

'So will you.'

'Nikeya, if anything happens to me, you will be the only one who might be able to temper or defeat the River Lord. Only you know his true motivations. You must remain the Lady of Faces.'

'She is dead, Dumai.' Nikeya held her gaze. 'I told him I loved you. I have chosen a side.'

Dumai shook her head, torn between frustration and tenderness.

'You can pretend you were lying,' she said, even as Nikeya came towards her. 'Tell him you were hunting me for him, or trying to finish your seduction – anything, Nikeya. You must be able to slip back into his circles. I need you to leave that way open.'

'I am still his only child, his legacy within our clan. I could persuade him to stop this without violence.' Before Dumai could argue her case, Nikeya said, 'Muysima smokes with hot springs. While the gods slept, that isle became restless. The early Kuposa used its heat and waters in their metalworking. In recent years, my father sent all exiles there, to mine it.'

'Why?'

'Looking for ways to quicken our fire.'

'You said the gift came from a mulberry tree.'

'There must be another way to reclaim it, somewhere in this world. The woman we saw in the North, on the glacier – she could make fire from her hands,' Nikeya reminded her. 'But my father has lost his senses to this pursuit. I might be able to help him recover them.'

If Dumai had any fight left in her, it disappeared when Nikeya wrapped both arms around her neck, pure resolve in her eyes.

'Our plan hinges on Suzu. She is our future. I want to help,' she said. 'I know part of you still lives on the mountain, where you were the one who took all the risks – but we are married now, Dumai. Even if it's still a secret, we are meant to face all fights together. Let us start by saving the child who is to be our heir.'

I am almost here, Furtia said, making Dumai shiver. *The star will light the sky erelong, and fallen night will quench the fire.*

'A true partnership.' Nikeya kissed her, just softly. 'Remember?'

Dumai grasped the hand on her chest, defeated. 'Furtia is here.' She took a deep breath. 'Are you ready to fly?'

'Yes.'

'Then come with me.'

95

West

Glorian lay on her pallet, breathing slow and deep. She could hear echoes and voices from the other chambers, mutterings just outside. Once there was a howl of grief, and she knew a body had been saved from Cenning Moor. Julain held her hand and prayed for deliverance.

Still there was no child.

Some hours into her labour, hundreds of fighters had arrived from Paupers' Henge, answering Lord Ordan. That was the last news she had heard. No one would tell her more of the battle.

'Helly,' Glorian breathed, 'what time is it?'

Helisent pressed a kiss to her forehead. 'I'll try to find out.'

She left, passing Bourn and a gaunt Marian. Julain and Adela had been sent to fetch boiled water and cloths. Glorian touched the brink of sleep again, the earthen smell of unbirth in her nose.

Bourn had explained that her labour had stalled. She was supposed to feel calm and safe, but she knew there was no safety here, and her body had locked in the face of that truth, refusing to relinquish Sabran. How could she send a child towards a world on fire?

I'm sorry. Her legs gave a tremor. *I can't help you . . .*

When Helisent returned, she said, 'It's almost dawn, Glorian. Happy birthday.'

773

Glorian opened her eyes. At the stroke of midnight, she had turned eighteen, ending her minority.

Now she was truly Queen of Inys.

'Remember your fourteenth birthday?' Helisent whispered. 'We spent the whole day under the sun, running through the wildflowers.' Glorian smiled. 'We swam in the lake and ate on its shore – honey cakes and gingerloaf, apples so crisp you could cut them like snow.'

'I remember.' A tear leaked into her hair. 'I wish we could go back there, Helly.'

'We will, Glorian. I promise.'

'Lady Protector, they're overwhelming our forces,' Sir Bramel shouted from the chamber beyond. 'Too many have died on the moor. Even with the swords from Paupers' Henge—'

'Join them now, Sir Bramel. Take all the guards,' Marian ordered. 'Do whatever you must.'

They were coming, and Glorian was helpless, as trapped in suffocating darkness as her child. Inys could have had one more sword, if only she could have been free to fight.

Bourn appeared at her side. 'Queen Glorian,' they said, their tone calming, 'Your Grace, I need you to push, just once more. The princess has been long in coming, but she's almost here.'

Julain hurried into the room, her apron smudged with blood, and set down a ewer of boiled water. 'They're back at the entrance,' a voice cried. 'Oh, Saint save us—'

'Sir Bramel will drive them out,' Marian barked at the guard. 'Help him, now. Your queen is labouring.'

Glorian took hold of her belly with both hands. *I see now*, she thought. *I see now, Papa. All those who give life are warriors.*

She felt a sudden, desperate fury. Her heart pounded not only with fear, but overwhelming frustration. If she could do this, the price to Inys would be paid. Her body would be hers at last, as it had never been. She moved from the pallet to the floor, lifeward.

'Glorian, what are you doing?' Florell asked as she shifted on to her knees, hands braced on the floor.

'I am Queen of Inys,' Glorian ground out. 'Even I kneel before the Saint.' She reached back, panting. 'Hold me. Helisent, Florell, help me.'

A warrior possesses her own body, she had once told her father. *Inys has mine.* She had to possess her own body in this moment – for Sabran, and for Inys.

Helisent and Florell flanked her. She hooked her arms around their shoulders, and they grasped her waist, holding her up, and Bourn crouched in front of her, a mantle at the ready. She drew a huge breath, then strained with all her might. The child forged down.

The one duty she could never refuse. This had been her only purpose, from the cradle – to yield more life, even though she was alive. To give more than herself, because she alone was not enough. She saw the cruel truth of it now. The relentless, violent circle of monarchy.

One day, you will sit across a table from your own daughter and tell her who she will wed for the realm, her mother called from her memory, *and you will remember this night.*

A scream ripped up her throat, hot as wyrmfire, like the place where Sabran crowned. She broke open the very last store of her strength and poured it into that one blind command and then her child was out, and it was done. All Glorian saw was a blur of purple before Bourn wrapped the child, and she folded over herself, heaving. Helisent and Florell embraced her and kissed her, shaking so hard that Glorian rattled, too.

At last, a wail came. 'She's here,' Marian called, her voice hoarse with relief. 'Princess Sabran is here!'

Other voices took up the tidings. Glorian slumped against Helisent. Red smeared her inner thighs, her calves.

There, now, Numun, she thought. *Here is the sacred blood of the Saint, blood you never had to spill.* Tears mingled with the sweat on her face. *You were right, and you are dead.*

Bourn returned to her, their hands washed clean. 'My baby,' Glorian murmured. 'Is she all right?'

'She's perfect, Your Grace.'

'They'll smell the blood.' Her lashes fluttered. 'I want to hold her.'

It took so long for them to prepare her. Every moment of waiting hurt. When Glorian thought she could bear it no more, they placed the child in her arms. Sabran was rumpled from the birth, with wisps of black hair.

Now I am free, and she is bound.

Marian came to sit beside Glorian, kissing her on the temple before she beheld the child. 'Oh, there she is.' She traced the sign of the sword on her forehead. 'Bless you, Sabran.'

Sabran lay quiet and fragile. A tiny nose and tiny lips. Tiny fingers, each with a tiny fingernail.

Another perfect sacrifice, chained to her legacy.

'Lady Marian.' Sir Bramel had come back, bloodied. 'My lady, the Dukes Spiritual would see you.'

Marian nodded and kissed Glorian once more, on the top of her head. 'Brave, brave girl,' she said hoarsely. 'Rest, now, Glorian. We'll keep you safe for as long as we can.'

When she was gone, Glorian gazed at her daughter. The others kept a respectful distance.

'Sabran,' she said, too soft for them to hear. 'You are Sabran Berethnet, seventh of that name. Your grandmother was sixth. She was a great queen, who healed a queendom, as you must.' She pressed a tearstained kiss to her brow. 'And all the while, I will love you. I love you. You are perfect and complete, exactly as you are – and you are enough, now and always. Even if Inys never tells you so, you are already enough to me.'

Sabran peered towards her face. Though she had been bathed, her eyes were still sticky with wax. Glorian used a gentle fingertip to clear them, finding them already green as spring.

Bourn severed the slick cord between them. If this were any other time, a milk nurse would be called, but instead, Glorian fed her daughter herself. When the afterbirth came, she hardly noticed, wrapped up in the quiet wonder of her newborn, the life she had knitted with Wulf. In that gloom, she could imagine there was no one else.

It was Julain who broke the illusion. She came to sit with Glorian.

'The sun has risen.' Her voice was bereft of hope. 'The wyverns can see the moor clearly now. I don't think it will be long before our soldiers are dead.'

'Even with the ones who came from Paupers' Henge?'

'It's not enough, Glorian. They're so tired.' Tears streaked her cheeks. 'I feel just as I did when you fell off your horse. You're in danger again, and I can't save you. I can't save Sabran.'

'It's my fault. I should not have insisted on coming here.'

'You did it for Inys.'

Adela brought fresh candles. Glorian slipped into a weary doze, Sabran gathered to her heart. She skimmed a strange and terrible dream, a sandpiper wetting her wings on the sea. She flew over a burning isle, and a need pounded her chest, hers and not hers: *save her, save her.*

When she woke, she knew where she would go.

Sabran grizzled at her breast. Glorian held her close, breathed in her sweet milky smell. 'You and I have something to do,' Glorian told her. Then she looked at Florell. 'Ready a horse.'

'A horse.' Florell shook her head. 'Glorian, you just gave birth – what do you mean?'

'I am Queen of Inys,' Glorian reminded her, 'and I no longer require a regent. With my Saint-given authority, I charge you to bring me a horse, and a cloak.'

'Queen Glorian.' Bourn looked speechless, but managed to say, 'Your child needs her mother.'

'Fear not.' Her legs trembled, but she stood. 'Sabran is coming with me.'

****

Cenning Moor glistened as the sunrise touched it. Wulf fought on, Thrit at his side, over bodies and lost weapons.

Deep in the night, an army in the hundreds had arrived from Paupers' Henge. That had strengthened them, for a time, but most had come on foot from their shelter, leaving them exhausted before they had even joined the fray. Hours later, there was no sign of a reprieve.

Thrice the wyverns' forces had breached Hollow Crag. Thrice they had been forced out. When the new fighters arrived, the Duke of Courage had led a foray from inside, scything down beasts and driving them back to the drystack wall that crossed the eastern stretch of the moor. The Duchess of Temperance had come next, with Lord Edrick at her side, and then Sir Bramel and the Royal Guard.

All that had been when they had darkness to obscure their movements. Now the sun was laying their position bare.

Wulf had stopped trying to keep count of the creatures. Each time he thought their ranks had thinned, they thickened anew. The wyverns must be calling them from all over the queendom. Each time they soared overhead, they somehow found more ground to burn.

He tried to surrender to the flow of the fight, using skills he had learned in both Hróth and Lasia. The Kumengan spear was the perfect weapon for fighting the creatures – its long reach kept him out of theirs, and its head could pierce the weak points in their armour. Tunuva had made it strong.

But he was not a spear. His body trembled with fatigue; his sight darkened with it. His movements were slowing, and had been for hours. Even killing one creature took sweat and blood.

No one was meant to fight so long. The Inysh troops were flesh and bone, and what they faced was iron.

Hollow Crag had been lost from the start.

'Nock,' Lady Gladwin commanded. From the shelter of an outcrop, her archers aimed at the sky. 'Draw!' Wulf plunged his spear through a lindworm and wrenched it back out. 'Release!'

Scores of arrows flew at a wyvern. Bristling with wood and steel, it crashed headfirst into the moor, its scream deafening. Its kin flocked above, breathing fire at the lancers who rode to finish it off.

Wulf had fought with his brother all night, trying to protect him. Roland had only received the paltry instruction of most Inysh nobles – some lessons from a local knight, odd friendly spars with friends. He had done his best, but exhaustion had forced him back to Hollow Crag. Most soldiers had withdrawn from the moor at least once, then returned to fight again, but without food, they could only recover so much of their strength.

Thrit had stayed, determined to help the Inysh forces hold the line. Now, at last, he crumpled.

'Get up,' Wulf wheezed, gripping him by his chainmail. Thrit shook his head. 'Come on, man, up.'

'Leave me.'

'We'll get you inside—'

'I'm finished, Wulf. Can't make it.'

Wulf was too weak to carry him to the entrance. The battle had drawn them too far away. Instead, he hauled Thrit under an isolated boulder, where several men had collapsed, and a woman bled from a grave wound to her side.

'I wish I'd had the backbone to tell you earlier,' Thrit said, panting. 'I suppose I hoped you'd see.'

Wulf dashed the sweat from his upper lip. 'I think I did,' he rasped. 'I just couldn't—' His throat burned. 'I was scared, Thrit.'

Thrit swallowed. Wulf grasped his hair and kissed him on the lips, and Thrit slung both arms around him and dropped his head on his shoulder, each heavy breath nearing a sob.

'Queen Glorian,' a voice bawled. 'The queen!'

Wulf looked towards it. Over the clash of blades and teeth, the inhuman screeches and yawps of the enemy, he heard shouts as Glorian Berethnet rode out from the caves, war horns sounding in her wake, a red cloak wrapped around her.

What is she doing?

'Warriors of Inys.' Glorian held her sword aloft. 'Hearken to me!'

Somehow, she made herself heard. Wulf struck out from the shelter, staring towards his childhood friend.

'You have fought through a night of fire and terror. There has been no greater courage since the Saint vanquished the Nameless One,' Glorian declared. She was white as a bedsheet, hair stuck to the sweat on her face. 'It is the first morning of spring. The Saint told me in dreams that there would be a holy sign this day. I vow to you, it will be soon!'

Iron teeth, scorching eyes. Wulf sensed the beast before he felt the hot snort of its breath. He slewed through the mud and carved its belly with a knife, blood and guts soaking the grass.

'There are sixteen thousand people inside Hollow Crag. You are all that stands between them and death. You held these vile wretches at bay while I gave birth,' Glorian cried. 'Behold – this is Sabran, Princess of Inys and Yscalin, who shields you from the Nameless One!'

That was when Wulf saw. Tucked into the crook of her arm was a swaddled bundle.

Glorian threw off her cloak, to a great clamour from her people, heard even over the ring of steel and the garbled shrieks. Beneath it, she was still wearing a bloodstained shift.

'Here is the heir I promised you, the chain upon the Nameless One. Here is our first victory,' Glorian roared. 'The Saint has delivered me of a daughter!'

Her hair was still lank from the childbed. Thousands of stricken faces gaped at her, while the creatures bayed.

'All through the night, I have bled for this queendom. See here, the sweat of my labour, the blood of the birthing bed,' Glorian called over them. 'Now I charge you to protect the child I have borne, as she protects you! Hold the entrance. Defend my family and yours!'

Sabran, Sabran, Sabran.

'Fight for our queendom, warriors of Inys!'

Shieldheart, Shieldheart, Shieldheart.

She had shocked or shamed them well enough. The cry went up across the moor. Thrit joined his voice to it; so did Wulf. He felt the change in the air: resurrection, rage, resolve. This might be the end of the world, but if the heir died, so would all that remained.

He saw bone-weary soldiers rise. Spears were wielded, blades retrieved from the mud, axes raised to hew at wing and horn and scale. War horns resounded. Arrows soared high as song.

'Go to her.' Thrit gripped Wulf by the shoulder. 'Wulf, get her inside.'

'Don't die on this moor. Swear it, Thrit.'

'Sworn.' Thrit gave him a shove. 'Go, Wulf, now.'

Wulf ran. The world was a blur. Halfway there, he grabbed the reins of a riderless horse and threw himself across its saddle.

'Glorian!'

She heard. Across the bloody, smoking battlefield, their gazes clapped.

That was when Glorian Shieldheart did something even her father might have thought was a tad reckless. Wulf saw the decision on her face – and then she spurred her own mount.

Her mare came galloping towards him, clearing a line of fire with a whinny. Panic erupted in her wake, and Lady Gladwin bellowed new orders at the archers. Wulf rode all the faster, heart almost pounding out of his chest, his only thought to reach her side.

When they met, Glorian pressed their child into his arms. 'What are you doing?' Wulf asked over the din. 'Glorian—'

'Take her. Take her away from here,' Glorian cut in, breathing hard. 'Go south over the river. Follow the drovers' path until you find the hill like an upended bowl, the tomb of the Inyscan princess. Take her to it, Wulf, to the barrow. Wait inside until it's safe.'

'Glorian.' Wulf stared from her to their wailing bairn. 'I can't.'

'Hollow Crag is lost. Fýredel will come for me. See her safe, Wulf. Someone will find you both.' She bent to kiss the child, and Sabran screamed. 'She is the chain upon him now.'

Cupping her with one hand, Wulf reached for Glorian with the other, grasping her arm. 'Come with us,' he urged. She shook her head. 'Glorian, you'll die here. Everyone will die on Cenning Moor.'

'So be it. I have done my duty. I would gladly give my life in battle, as my father would have. I am free to do as I choose. I choose to die with courage.' She held his cheek and smiled, looking straight into his eyes. 'Live, Wulfert Glenn, my dearest friend. I will see you in Halgalant.'

She wheeled her horse, and charged to war.

96

East

Muysima lay close to Uramyesi, the city built where Snow Maiden was said to have sung her lament. This late in the evening, the island for exiles was hard to see. No lighthouses ever burned on that forsaken shore.

Furtia flew with seven other dragons, tiny stars twinkling in the seams where her scales met. Dumai watched the streets of Uramyesi, finding glimmers of light between its rooftops – pyres, for those who had died of the sickness, each one creating sleepless ghosts. Her grandfather must been brought to this city. A boat must have taken him to his end.

Uramyesi ended in a sheer drop. There, the black waters of the Abyss shattered against a wall of cliffs, each of monstrous height. The highest leaned some way over the water, an arrowhead pointing at the island, threatening any exile who dared to dream of home.

The last glow of sunset reddened the horizon. A row of tall fires, just as red, lit the end of that particular cliff. Dumai narrowed her eyes, the blue stone cold against her breast.

Furtia, those fires. That way.

The beast of the deep earth is close, Furtia told her. *The one we saw before.*

I know, great one. Dumai placed a hand on her scales. *We must not let it harm my sister. She was born with the star, too.*

Furtia growled a reluctant agreement. Nikeya kept both arms around Dumai, tight enough to hurt, as the dragon began her descent to those cliffs. Dumai glanced up, finding the sky dark and clear.

One of the Four Gates of Seiiki stood at its end – the Western Gate, the youngest. Thousands of people had gathered before it. Seeing Furtia and the other dragons, they parted, voices rising in relief. Furtia landed among them with a rumble. She lowered her coils, and Dumai stepped down with Nikeya. When the other dragons surrounded Furtia, their presence strengthened her resolve, and quenched her fear.

The fire has risen high, but its time is almost passed. Pajati the White spoke, the one who had illuminated her. *Step forth, you who hold the star. You will grow strong with us . . .*

Chaos bends now in our favour . . .

Dark flakes tumbled around them all, a fine ash that fell just like snow. Dumai touched the stone. An inexplicable detachment had come over her, as if her mind had floated some way above her body.

'Take it,' she said, handing it to Nikeya. 'If I have to fly against Taugran, and I fall, it will be lost for ever to the sea.'

'You need this, to defeat Taugran.'

'No.' Dumai breathed the night in deep. 'The comet is so close, Nikeya. Don't you feel it?'

Nikeya looked nervous. Reluctantly, she passed the cord over her head, tucked the stone under the high collar of her tunic, and took Dumai by the jaw, looking her straight in the eyes.

'Don't fall,' she said. 'I have waited all my life for you, Noziken pa Dumai.'

Dumai gathered her close, allowing herself to be moored by her, her warmth and weight. In that long moment, all her senses sank back towards earth and settled within her. She smelled the fires and pines of their forest. She felt Nikeya shivering against her, the mittened hands pressed to the small of her back.

Then they turned together, and walked towards the Western Gate.

It formed a perfect frame around the sunset. Twisted from drift-wood, it stood as tall as a black pine. After Kwiriki had made her a throne, Snow Maiden had raised the first of these gates, to show the other dragons that they were welcome to return. It had taken her years to win their trust, and she had faced many trials to convince them, but it was the gates that had finally worked.

Come back, the doorways whispered. *Come back to our isle, lords of the water. Make a home with us.*

No offering bowl hung from this one. Instead, there was a different shape.

Sobs came from the crowd. Dumai could not make out individual features, in that terrible light. Most people were shrouded with damp cloth to keep out soot and sickness. When she reached the Western Gate, she frowned at the black lake beneath it, lit by braziers of wyrmfire.

The star comes ... but too late for them ...

Their blood is spilled, the light extinguished ... the light of Kwiriki, the first, who lit the waters of their minds, made them one with us ...

'Nikeya,' a voice croaked. Dumai turned to see Sipwo, restrained by armoured men. 'Is it you?'

'Sipwo.' Nikeya tried to go to her cousin, only for more guards to point spears at her. 'I would be fascinated to know what you all think you're doing,' she said, unflinching in the face of their weapons. 'This is the Dowager Empress of Seiiki. Who are you to hold her?'

'Her uncle's sworn protectors,' one of them said. 'Step away, Lady Nikeya.'

'Ah, the silly boys who protect his estates,' Nikeya observed. 'Stop playing at warriors, you fools. I doubt you've used those spears in your lives, except to fend off desperate farmers.'

'Dumai, I beg you.' Sipwo was almost as grey as her robes. 'Stop him. Dumai, tell Furtia, stop him—'

Arrows were nocked and trained on Dumai. She turned back to the Western Gate, searching for sense, just as he stepped through it – the man who was now emperor in all but name, unless she stopped him.

Kuposa pa Fotaja, the River Lord, had always been brazen. Not so brazen as to walk through a gods' doorway.

'Princess Dumai.' His voice was deeper, throaty. 'I am pleased you could join us tonight.'

Dressed in scarlet robes, lined with black, he looked nothing like a courtier. His large eyes were no longer brown, but grey all the way to their corners, consuming the white.

He is warped by the fire. Furtia rattled her loathing. *Taugran works him to his will, like iron in the forge ...*

Dumai had no idea what it meant, but a whimper distracted her. She looked up to see a familiar child, suspended by her arms from the shrine. Suzumai stared down in terror, and Dumai stared back.

'Suzu—' Her voice snapped in her throat. She strode towards the River Lord and grasped one of her sickles, her hand trembling around the handle. 'Release her, Fotaja, now.'

'The Empress of Seiiki must die this day, Princess.'

The words boomed in her, as loud as his bells.

'You know the legend of the Nameless One, who broke the mantle of the world, who sleeps beneath the cold black sea.' His tongue lingered on every word. 'He flew first to the land of Lasia, where the sun burned hot, and the risen fire had warmed the ground.'

'What has this to do with Seiiki?'

'He whispered to me. Taugran the Golden,' the River Lord said. 'I searched for him on Muysima.'

'What lies did the wyrm tell you?'

'The House of Noziken must be the sacrifice. You have the star in your blood, and the dragons' favour,' came the soft reply. 'They, too, must fade into chaos.' Furtia bared the full length of her teeth. 'The Noziken are one with them. Now only three of you remain: your grandmother, your sister, and you.'

The Dowager Empress was trembling, gaze pinned to her last surviving child. Dumai looked again at the darkness on the ground, beneath her boots, and saw it for what it was.

'No,' she whispered.

'Yes. I had all of your remaining relatives brought here,' the River Lord said, 'to be devoured.'

Anger gripped her throat, anger she had never realised she was capable of feeling. 'You fool.' She started towards him, only for Nikeya to pull her back. 'You have lost your mind to a story!'

'Rich words,' he said, a sliver of his old self breaking through, 'from a Noziken.'

The sun had disappeared. For the most part, the crowd had been silent, held by a fear beyond words, but a few people were weeping. Sipwo wrestled against her captors again.

'Stop this, Father,' Nikeya said, forcing on her calmest face. 'Empress Suzumai is your grandniece – a Kuposa, as well as a Noziken. Would you feed your own family to the wyrm, too?'

'Ah, my heir, my sweet daughter.' His eyes turned dark again, the whites returning with his recognition. Dumai sensed it would not last for long. 'Did you abandon me, in truth – you, with precious kindling in your blood, who could burn just as strong as I do?'

'So could Suzu.' Nikeya held still. 'Father, there is another way, I know there is. I saw a woman in the North.' Dumai could see her thinking on the spot. 'She had the fire as well. She could make her own fire, like the Mulberry Queen. Let me pursue her for you.'

The River Lord shook his head.

'You have chosen your side. When Kwiriki's Lantern comes, its power will ignite this Noziken you love so much. She will outshine your faded light. She will seek to conquer you, as the sea conquers flame. Even the waters of your mind will be at her command.' His gaze fixed on hers before the grey overtook his eyes again. 'Taugran sees you, Princess Dumai. Through my eyes, he sees.'

Furtia. Dumai called out to her, feeling the dragon uncoil with her rage. *Furtia, can you reach my sister?*

Taugran is coming, earth child . . .

'Take me,' Dumai said, desperate to distract the River Lord. 'Take me instead of Suzu. I don't carry the flame.'

'No,' Nikeya said hotly.

'It is too late,' the River Lord said. His face went slack as rotten fruit. 'But fear not. You will die this night, and I will bring your grandmother from the mountain. She is the end of the rainbow.'

'Not if I stop you.' Dumai summoned the white glow, letting it pool into her hands. 'Show me your light, my lord, and I will show you mine.'

'You will lose.' When scarlet fire sprang from his palms, the people cried out, and Nikeya stiffened, staring at her father. 'The wheel will turn your way, Princess. Chaos will make you bright.' He stepped towards her, into the white glow. 'Yet I still have a little time.'

Sister, I need your help, Dumai thought, but she was too awake to dream.

Suddenly the gods were roaring. The River Lord raised his hands, full of fire, and with them came a mass of golden scale, pitted and tarnished, coming up from beyond the cliffs. Screams erupted from the crowd. Half stampeded to the city or down the steep path to the beach, while terror held the rest in place, as if moving could draw its eye.

Taugran the Golden opened its mouth, black as depthless chaos, teeth like mountains spearing from his jaws. They clanged together. With a jerk of its terrible head, Suzumai was gone.

There was a moment – an hour, a year – in which no one breathed. Then the Dowager Empress let out a strangled howl, the sound of a mind severed from reason. She clawed free of her guards and threw herself into the blood, soaking her sleeves in it, her hair.

Dumai could only watch, her mind unmoored again. She looked at the place where her sister had been. She looked at the fresh blood on the ground. She looked at Sipwo, deranged by anguish. She looked at Taugran. A whiteness screamed over her senses. She was on the mountain, climbing to the summit. She was lost in the night with the storm all around her.

She ran straight at the wyrm.

Time slowed like a stone through water. She did not think of her mother, or Nikeya, or even Suzumai, for something else had consumed her. She shoved past the River Lord. He was nothing. Now he was the wooden doll.

An arrow pierced deep into her side.

'Dumai,' Nikeya screamed.

But Dumai felt no pain. She was too cold. Rivers of unearthly light were shining through her skin. She was a star sleeved in quick flesh, fallen to earth to temper the fire, and death was nothing, if she did what she was meant to do. She ran across the blood of the rainbow (*only red, only red*), straight for the edge of the cliff, flinging her body after Taugran – and then she was alone in thin air, and the black waters were roaring up to meet her.

You are a kite. She saw the slick teeth in the waves, rocks that would crack her head like a shell. *Take to the sky.*

Before she could strike the sea, Furtia swept beneath her. They flew with shared fury into the night, after the beast of the deep earth, the gods of the island rising behind them.

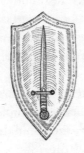

97

West

Blood was threading down her legs, but Glorian fought on. Since her first breath, she had been bound, fettered to something else – but no man could restrain her now, by no law, mortal or divine. Not now the holy toll was paid. Not now she was free of it. She was eighteen, and Queen of Inys.

In birthing, she was finally born.

Shieldheart, Shieldheart, Shieldheart.

A rage that was both hers and not hers pounded in her gut. She hefted a shield and swung with the sword, hacking at the beasts on Cenning Moor, still in her bloody shift. She slashed it away at the knee and kept fighting, barefoot in the mud and slaughter – daughter of bone and iron, born to be a warrior queen. When a monstrous cockerel ran at her, she mustered all the anger she had ever held, and she hacked off its head.

This was a battle to the death, yet she was utterly alive.

Shieldheart, Shieldheart, Shieldheart.

At last, a muscular arm came around her waist, wrestling her on to a horse. 'Let me go.' Her voice broke against her anger. 'Let me fight—'

'You are Glorian Shieldheart,' a muffled voice told her. 'You can't die yet. Inys still needs you.'

Glorian writhed against the grip, but her body refused to be strong any longer. All she could do was cling to her sword as a helmed rider took her out of the battle, back to Hollow Crag.

Inside, the shadowed chambers wrapped her, and then she was laid in a fresh bed, blood seeping. Bourn was nearby, and her baby was gone. Wulf would get Sabran away, to chain the Nameless One again.

And so it went, on and on.

Glorian closed her eyes, her brow torching. Perhaps this was not a bed, but her bier. Inys had filled and emptied her. It was all done. Her purpose served. If she wanted, she could die.

She drifted again – in her dream, she was flying. *Sister, cut your line and soar.* The stream was churning, the figure in and out of sight. *I wish I could. I wish I had. I wish I could wing all the way to your side.*

If her sister replied, it was too quiet to hear – but another voice encroached in her stead, silencing all others. Glorian opened her eyes as it reached into Hollow Crag. The voice that had haunted her for two years.

The voice that had begun all this.

'Shieldheart,' it hissed, and she knew it was Fýredel.

****

Wulf rode like the Nameless One flew behind him. His horse galloped away from the thawing River Went, the hoofbeats as hard and fast as his heart. He gripped the reins with one hand and his daughter with the other.

Three wyverns were in swift pursuit.

They swooped low over the frosted grass. Wulf glanced over his shoulder and cursed. He had to lose them before he reached the barrow, or they would see him go into it.

He knew the tomb of the Inyscan princess. As a child, his family had made many visits to the Leas, and Lord Edrick had shown his children the barrow. *We must know the secrets of our pasts,* he had told them, *to understand the future.*

The drovers' path was overgrown, passing under oaks and birches. As soon as the horse burst free of it, the wyverns were on top of them again, and when the barrow came into sight, he knew he had failed to save his daughter – not just her, but all of Inys.

Sabran was going to die in his arms.

Fog escaped his lips. His inner wrist suddenly hurt. Some force was building in his hand – a sharp point, like a shard of ice, numbing his fingers. Instinct drove that arm up, and a white bolt came forking from his palm, hitting a wyvern in the joint of its wing. Sabran went just as cold in his arms. He felt it even through her swaddling.

The wyverns screamed and swung away. Looking back at them, Wulf glimpsed it – a comet, high above Inys. Not a shooting star, but a queen of the heavens, with a long silver beam that streamed in its wake. It had appeared as if from nowhere.

Shaken, he rode on. In some tales, comets were a promise of doom, but nothing could be worse than what they had already suffered.

By the time the wyverns had wheeled about for a second attempt, only the horse remained, charging back towards the drovers' path. As they soared after it, Wulf crawled into the barrow, the heir to Inys still snug in his arms, not knowing what in Halgalant had just happened to him.

****

Glorian dressed herself, for once. Her quilted red gambeson and dark breeches, with boots. Anything else would only make her die more slowly. Better to burn fast and bright.

Fýredel had made an offer, as she had known he would. If Shieldheart surrendered, he would lead his forces away from Hollow Crag, allowing those trapped inside to escape. They could find some other hovel to cower in. He would take the Queen of Inys as his trophy and be gone. There would be no more blood on Cenning Moor.

Glorian had always known a wyrm could bargain. Selinu the Oathkeeper had made a deal with the Nameless One. She belted on her scabbard and sheathed her sword.

'I don't want you to see,' she told her ladies. 'Stay inside.'

'Glorian.' Adela had not stopped weeping. 'You can't.'

'I must. I have continued the bloodline of the Saint,' Glorian said quietly. 'That was my bounden duty as a Berethnet. The other, as a queen, is to protect my realm.'

'You are not a wretched duty to us. You matter – for you, not just for giving us an heir,' Julain said, her voice cracking. 'Don't you understand?'

Glorian set her jaw. 'You have all been so good,' she said, her voice a whisper. 'The sisters a Berethnet cannot have. I will save you all a place of honour at the Great Table.'

Helisent embraced her first, with a muffled sob. They all clutched her close, and Glorian held them back, just as hard, before an ashen Florell led them away for the last time.

'Glorian, let me go in your place,' Marian said hoarsely. 'Fýredel may not see the difference.'

'It will.' Glorian kissed her on the cheek. 'I am so glad we reunited, Grandmother. Please take care of Sabran.'

Marian pressed a kiss to her hands, wordless with grief. Glorian hefted on her shield and turned to meet her fate.

She walked through the caverns of Hollow Crag. The survivors made way for her, some openly weeping, others grim and silent. Glorian looked straight ahead, trying to conceal her fear.

The moor was deathly in its stillness. A tomb for the unburied dead. Char and ash blew over corpses. Her remaining knights and soldiers were empty-handed, their weapons on the ground. They had all known the fight was lost when Fýredel arrived.

Glorian had almost forgotten the horror of Fýredel in the months it had been gone. Here was the very spit of the Dreadmount, waiting for her on Cenning Moor, to burn her as it burned her parents. Its creatures gave it a wide berth, heads bowed in submission.

'You waged a fine war against Inys, Fýredel. Against the world, it seems,' she said, trembling against her will. She prayed no one could see. 'Let there be no more violence. Here I am.'

'You come alone, with useless steel,' Fýredel said. 'No metal of the earth can stand before its purest fire.' Its gaze flicked to the fullness of her belly. 'You are with child. It will not live.'

Glorian mastered her expression, the way her manners tutor had trained into her. She could still feel herself bleeding.

'If my house ends here, so be it. Kill me, if you will. Kill us both,' she said. 'Only leave my people be.'

'You will not die, Shieldheart.' Fýredel lowered its head, so its eyes looked straight into hers, two hot brands on her soul. 'The flame of the deep earth that forged us lives in you, with your vile cold. The fire shall warp and work it. You shall bend to a new shape.'

Glorian could see her own reflection in its iron teeth. There was no divine protection. No sign from Halgalant. Fýredel was speaking in riddles, but they were a promise that she would suffer.

Mother, Father, give me courage.

All at once, Fýredel looked up. The creatures stamped and bayed. Too afraid to move so much as a finger, Glorian followed its line of sight – and saw the comet in the sky, wide and long, its tail splitting in two.

But I vow to you, this age of fire and smoke will end. A star will come at morning on the first day of spring.

Glorian jerked her attention back to the wyrm. Fýredel hauled in its breath and screamed at the sky. She dropped her shield to cover her ears, but her eyes were already back on the comet.

She watched as the second tail splintered apart. It was shedding countless spears of starlight, bright enough to see by morning, each charting a course towards the blazing world.

It will be a day of fallen night, when the heavens will part for a rain from on high.

This was it.

It must be now.

A high, wild laugh escaped her lips. Fýredel dropped its gaze back to her, as if remembering she was there. It reared for the kill, its jaws yawning wide as the neck of the Dreadmount – and then its flame died, withering back into its throat, and it blew only wind.

The wyrms will fall into a sleep, and storms will quench the embers.

'Wretch of cold and ardent blood. Bearer of the star.' Its eyes were still afire. 'From the darkness comes a doom.' A rattle of its cloven tongue. 'We will return. Be certain, Shieldheart. When the fire rises anew, when our master stirs in the Abyss, when another wears your crown, we will return. Breathe in your ruin and your ashes. Live in fear.'

All across Inys, the creatures of the Dreadmount howled, their calls rising to fill a morn as blue as ancient ice. Fýredel opened its wings, the heralds of death. It returned to the sky.

And then it was gone.

98

South

Smoke blurred the sun above Nzene. Though it was a stone city, the wyrms had found plenty of kindling. The thatched roofs in the outskirts, the storehouses, the gardens and the cloth markets, the sacred groves, the palms that lined the widest streets – all burned with a livid fire.

Gashan had been right. Dedalugun was too immense to slice with ease between the Godsblades, the way the limber wyverns could. It had wings big enough to darken the city. Time and again it flew over the sun.

Tunuva defended the temple quarter. As she sank her sword into a giant serpent, she smelled the cedars blazing in the House of Edina, saw two orchardists tow out a basket of rare seeds. Now and then, she would glimpse a familiar cloak in the red fug of smoke and brick dust and sand. The ground shook as a grey winger brought down a statue of Gedani.

Esbar was nowhere to be seen. For a time, they had guarded an enclosure where several nobles had taken shelter in their manses. They had worked together, slaying anything that came near, until a hulking wyvern crashed between them, a harpoon in its belly.

The lesser wyrms had destroyed one of the city walls, letting a flood of creatures past. Now they rampaged throughout Nzene. Tunuva carved her way towards the rampart closest to Mount Dinduru. Though the gate was still barred, it remained a weak point. She sensed a shudder of power – one of her sisters, mantling a street or a square with a warding.

Kediko could explain it away later, if anyone cared. Tunuva sincerely doubted they would.

A burning tree crashed across the path in front of her. Ash choked her, hot cinders fluttering past her eyes. She sheathed her bloody sword and snapped open her spear, using it to skewer a beast and shove it off a soldier, whose gut was frayed open.

To her right, she saw Gashan wielding her own spear, as if she had never put it down.

The Mother had lived in Yikala, but she must have set foot in Nzene. She had loved all Lasians as her own, and Tunuva meant to defend them, for the woman who lay in the coffin.

Blood smeared her tunic from wounds that had already closed. Tunuva mopped her brow, breathing hard, alert for any glint of golden hair, or a cold white face. They had buried Canthe, and yet.

And yet.

War horns blared out. Tunuva flattened herself to a wall as the Royal Guard came thundering on horseback down the street with swords and crescent blades. Archers shot at the winged snakes that flapped over the city, each arrow flashing dull gold in the sunlight.

High on the slopes of the promonotory, with creaking groans, lines of catapults slung huge blocks of sandstone into the air. Three wyverns fell upon the highest, smashing its long arm to splinters, torching the remains.

'There,' a man roared.

Tunuva looked up when rubble came tumbling on to the streets. Dedalugun had landed on Mount Dinduru.

'Come forth, Kediko Onjenyu.' Its voice rumbled across the city, carrying the dark resonance of an earthquake. 'Come forth for the reckoning, blood of the vanquisher.'

Gashan was overseeing the springalds. They slanted towards the great wyrm and released hails of bolts towards him. The catapults tried next, for good measure. Slabs of stone crashed into the mountainside below him, each with a sound like a thunderclap, loosening a thousand rocks, raising screams of horror far below. Dedalugun winnowed its wings.

It was a terrible fiend to behold. Not as large as Fýredel, but every scale and sinew spoke of chaos and a shattered world. Thick black smoke vented from its jaws, its nostrils.

'Tuva!'

She turned. Esbar forced her way through the crowd, drenched in blood.

'Did you see?' she shouted. 'Mulsub is still in its breast. See how it catches the light?'

Tunuva craned her neck, narrowed her eyes against the sun. When Dedalugun leaned out from its roost, she saw the glint. The spear was stuck there like a thorn. 'What are you thinking?'

'We can use it to wrench off a scale.' Esbar drew a blade and knifed away a beast that must have once been a goat. 'That was how the Mother defeated the Nameless One. She broke a gap in his armour with Ascalun, so she might pierce the flesh beneath. If we can ground Dedalugun—'

'The siege engines can't reach it. How can we?'

Jeda ripped the head off a winged lion. Close by, Ninuru was so drenched in blood, her fur had turned pure red.

'The stone,' Esbar said over the din. 'It feels like Canthe, calls to her magic – the same magic that drove Dedalugun away in Carmentum. Do you think you can use it against him?'

Tunuva groped for it. 'It may speak to water,' she said. 'If we lure the wyrm to Lake Jodigo—'

'It's worth a try.'

They charged in the same direction the warriors had gone, their ichneumons running beside them.

The mudbrick wall was the thickest the Nzeni had built. Beyond, the creatures screeched for blood, trying to claw and smash their way through the gate. Hundreds of people had thrown their weight against it, their shoulders bracing splintered wood. Guards formed up to kill whatever might break through. Tunuva slipped between them and climbed the ladder to the top, where archers released flaming arrows. Other soldiers hurled rocks and spears, or poured hot sand from massive urns. The bridge across the ditch had been cut down, but still the monsters came.

A red cloak caught her eye. Yeleni Janudin lay dead, her lifeblood dying the cloak darker.

Behind the archers, Siyu danced with lethal grace. Her foe had the face and paws of a wildcat, grown into the body of a wyrm. Twisting to elude its claws, she flung up her spear to block a bite, and when it sank its teeth into the haft, she drew a curved Eyrsri knife, one made for cutting through armour, and sliced across its throat, spraying blood. It slumped before her, twitching.

Dedalugun let out a horrendous roar. From here, the beast was nothing but sound, too high to see. Tunuva realised it had put the sun behind it, so no archer could take clear aim.

Siyu stepped away from the corpse. Tunuva reached her just as she sank to her knees beside her sister.

'Siyu,' Tunuva said, 'we will bury her in the valley. I swear it.' She grasped her by the shoulder. 'Keep defending this last wall. Esbar and I must get through that herd.'

'No.' Siyu caught her wrist. 'Tuva, don't leave—'

'We go only as far as the lake, to slay Dedalugun.'

'How?'

'I think I know a way.'

They both looked up when the wyrm trumpeted its dominance again, making the entire city tremble in its shadow.

'Let me come.' Siyu wiped her face with her cuff. 'Dedalugun killed Lalhar. I will avenge her.'

There was no time to argue, so Tunuva nodded. She watched Esbar soar from the wall, and then leapt herself, into the moil of monstrosities. Together, they ran straight at the ditch and dived across. Siyu landed beside Tunuva, still gripping her slick knife.

They sliced through a thousandfold horde, the world narrowed to glimpses, parts: dripping teeth, the gleam of claw, the haunches and heads of too many creatures, cruel beaks tearing at their cloaks. More than once, Tunuva saw human limbs mangled into scale and iron, just as she had in Jrhanyam, faces moaning at her. Her mind locked them all out.

Ahead, Esbar wielded twin swords, using her fire to burn open a path when none appeared. Whatever she hit, Tunuva dealt it another blow, and Siyu handled whatever was left. A wyvern flew over their heads and blasted flame across the wall. A second torched it again, baking the bricks so dry that cracks spread and splintered across them.

The third wyvern swooped low. With a scream, it drove its entire body into the wall, breaking it down, its head shattering what remained of the gate. War horns sounded a warning as the creatures stampeded over the ruins and poured into Nzene.

Tunuva grasped Siyu by the hand. They vaulted the breastworks the Lasians had built to make the creatures' advance more difficult.

Without stopping, Tunuva climbed on to Ninuru, pulled Siyu with her, and rode straight after Esbar, who had already mounted Jeda.

Lake Jodigo was untouched. During the summer, it could appear as thin and clear as glass, a mirror lying flat against the sunburnt earth. Now the winter rains had swollen it, the water deep and dark. The closer Ninuru came to its shore, the harder the stone hummed against Tunuva, chilling her.

They were far away from the city now, though not too far to stop hearing the screams, human and animal and wyrm. Dedalugun sat on the mountain as if it were his throne, a giant of ancient lore. Its scales could have been hewn from the same rock.

Esbar swung off Jeda and looked towards the wyrm. Tunuva watched as she held up both hands. Her fingertips turned gold.

And then she let her fire erupt.

In more than fifty years, Tunuva had never seen a sister of the Priory unleash her earthly fire with such power. It blazed towards the sun in two pillars of ferocious light, which twisted into one, roaring like wind. Her hands spread wide, the tendons straining in her neck.

Tunuva gazed at her in wonder. It was as if Esbar was drawing the Womb of Fire through her body – as if she herself had become the Dreadmount. Washtu, come again.

Saghul had chosen well.

Siyu summoned natural flame and laced it through the firestorm. It was bright enough to be seen from the city, even in full daylight. The smell of siden soaked the air.

At last, Dedalugun turned. It saw the beacon in the desert, fire not breathed by any wyrm.

'You see us,' Esbar hissed. 'We see you.'

Dedalugun launched himself off Mount Dinduru, displacing snow and rock, and came soaring towards the lake. Tunuva took the white stone from under her tunic. It was cold now, glowing bright, a full moon in her hand.

'Tuva, hurry,' Esbar shouted, her hair blowing about her face.

Tunuva held the stone towards Lake Jodigo. An unseen cord tightened between it and the lake, as if she were holding a fishing line. She willed the water to rise from its bed.

Ripples spread across the surface. Not enough, but even that small tug had sapped a great deal of her strength. Dedalugun was hurtling towards them, descending enough that its underside almost grazed the ground. Tunuva clenched her teeth and tried again.

Esbar and Siyu both quenched their flames. Breathing hard, Esbar nocked an arrow to her bow, turning from fire divinity back to human. Except for a glaze of sweat, she looked almost unmoved.

Her arrow struck Dedalugun straight in the eye. Its claws ripped trenches through the earth. Landing hard enough to break the ground, it poured its red fire on Esbar and Siyu, and they wrapped themselves in wardings.

Tunuva gripped the waning jewel. The water stirred, heaved, fell out of her grip. She almost fell with it, shuddering. Dedalugun rounded on her with a roar.

Just when she thought the lake would never move, something drew her gaze up. Flecks of silver rained through the sky, weeping and darting from a broad streak of light – a bearded star with a split tail, longer and brighter than any she had ever seen.

In her hand, the stone turned brilliant white, so cold she almost dropped it in agony. A cold that hurt her fire. Dedalugun had looked skyward as well, but now its fiery gaze returned to her. Tunuva tried to weave a warding, only to find her magic frozen. In all her life, it had never failed to answer her call. Fear stoppered her throat. Her hand ached and shook around the stone. Suddenly it weighed as much as a boulder.

Before she could so much as reach for a weapon, Siyu was there, wrenching at the spear in its breast. She kept hold of it as Dedalugun reared, lifting her from the ground. Siyu braced her boot on its scales and pulled, and when she fell, the spear came with her.

She landed in a crouch. Dedalugun made a sound like the earth grinding. In freeing the spear, Siyu had opened a hole in its armour. The wyrm struck her away, and she lay still on the sand.

'Siyu,' Esbar screamed.

Her cry sliced into Tunuva, even as she echoed it, agony clenching her chest. Siyu did not move.

Dedalugun turned back to Tunuva, blood leaking from its eye. It sizzled where it hit the ground. Tunuva backed away. All around her, the world smelled different, like metal. Her own magic was shrinking in her veins, cowed by the comet, but the stone was shining bright enough to come near blinding her. This time, the need to pull was overwhelming.

Lake Jodigo shivered in anticipation of her touch. She looked at Siyu, then the comet.

Smell of iron. Smell of blood.

She remembered pushing, bearing down, as Armul emerged from her, the bricks underfoot, her body toiling. All the while, Esbar had stood at her side, never once letting her go.

Tunuva remembered that feeling with her whole heart, allowing it to fill and wake her every sinew, and turned it on itself. She drew, as if to drag a twisting fish from the Minara. As if to take her child back into her womb, where he could never have been lost.

She drew, and with one mighty pull, Tunuva Melim lifted the lake.

At once, her body ached to its joints, and she would have given anything to sleep. Instead, she imagined the water as the fire she could no longer touch, drawing and gathering it to her will.

At first, it was like lifting a weapon too heavy for arms.

And then, as the stars fell, it was as easy as breathing.

The lake had too much salt in it to sustain any life. She swept it over Dedalugun, and all that heavy water shattered on its wings. She drove it deep into its maw and down its burning throat and right the way through its foul entrails, willing the water to ice. Dedalugun tried to beat its wings, then crashed to the ground, steam venting between its scales, boiled in the furnace of its own belly, its roars and screams drowned by bubbling water.

Esbar ran to where Siyu lay. She snatched up the enchanted spear and charged towards Dedalugun, boots splashing through the flood. Tunuva kept forcing the lake through the wyrm until that loose scale broke away altogether, snapped off by the torrent of lakewater – and Esbar plunged the spear into the flesh beneath, right to its heart.

Dedalugun screamed. With the last of her will, Tunuva lifted what remained of the lake away from Esbar and Siyu before letting it crash back into place, water spraying and roiling. When she looked up, the wyrm lay still, steaming.

By the time Tunuva got to her, Esbar had cradled a soaked Siyu in her arms. She reached for Tunuva, and they wept beneath the bearded star – holding each other, holding the child they both loved.

99

East

She no longer remembered a time before the storm. It had overspread the dark sky above Uramyesi, stemming from the mouths of dragons. On the ground, far away, the slaughter went on.

In the sky, there was war.

The crack and crash of thunder filled the night. Taugran had summoned its wyrmlings, which besieged the city, circling like gulls. Lightning flashed from the stormclouds that rose to meet the flock. Below, the Abyss threw itself against the cliffs of Uramyesi.

Everywhere, Seiiki roared.

Dumai watched the world turn stark, then black again, over and over. There had been a moon once, long ago, but now it was gone, swallowed by the storm. Even with the blue stone far below, the gods' power was growing stronger, unlocked by the very air.

Rain drenched Dumai to the skin, so she was as cold as Furtia, skin and scale becoming one, and the wrath of the dragon tightened her chest, and she no longer knew whose anger it had been first. All she knew was the need to destroy the creature that flew before her, that breathed flame from its loathsome maw, making the dragons call out in fury.

The fire. The thought coursed through them both, Dumai and Furtia. *The fire of the deep earth, arisen.*

Dumai buried her bare hands in manehair. She had danced with silver bells and golden fish, drawn a rainbow through a dollhouse, and never understood what mattered. The fire had risen.

A fire that must be quenched.

Yes, they hissed together. *Yes*.

Taugran flew past, its golden scales reflecting the fires it set below. Furtia snapped for its tail. Once more, Taugran eluded her. For a creature so enormous, it moved like water. When Dumai snarled in frustration, so did the dragon, and with their voices came a roll of thunder.

Lightning forked from sky to earth, setting a fleet of boats alight. Furtia twisted in the air, pursuing Taugran. Dumai clung to her mane, teeth bared.

Far below, more dragons had come. They blew stormwinds towards the wyrms, keeping them away from the people, who were fleeing inland, away from the battle. A harpoon from a bed crossbow whistled past Furtia, striking a wyrmling in the breast. Dumai hardly noticed. She had eyes only for Taugran. She wished she could hear its voice in her mind, as she could hear the gods. She wanted to hear the voice of chaos.

She wanted to hear chaos scream.

The chase went on and on. The wyrm, unleashing turmoil on the land, burning it. Furtia, soaring after it, battered by the scorching wind from those wings. Other dragons wound about them, surrounding Taugran with lightning.

All the while, Dumai turned colder and colder. In a dark corner of her mind, she knew she had already bled for too long. The arrow was between her ribs, tearing through the inner softness of her body.

The River Lord had killed her. He had set her a trap, knowing someone would tell her that Suzumai was in danger. His guards had been there to make sure she died, whether by arrow or by wyrm.

The Noziken and the Kuposa. So much time wasted on a rivalry that meant nothing. She should have been trying to heal the tortured earth. She should have searched every text in the East until she understood why this had happened, to stop it from ever happening again...

She threw the thought off. Her human recollections warred with dragons' instincts. She clung to the memory of Suzumai, her mother and grandmother, Nikeya, and all the dead Noziken. The Grand Empress would bear no more children, even if the River Lord let her live.

The rainbow had finally come to its end.

Darkness gathered. Her breaths came short. Still she held on, the wind ripping back her hair. She imagined the cold was not death at all, but the great Kwiriki, singing to her.

Taugran released its fire across the shore, torching every boat. And Dumai thought it would never end: the suffering, the dread.

Kwiriki had made a young woman a throne and told her to protect this island. Dumai would honour that bargain, struck long ago in the eye of the storm. She would save Seiiki, at the cost of the House of Noziken. She would keep the promise for as long as she breathed.

Furtia emerged from her own clouds, into the clear night. For a beautiful moment, there was quiet. No rain or thunder or fire. Dumai looked over her shoulder, searching for Taugran. Rain dripped from her lashes. The storm had beaten her skin numb.

It is here, earth child. The star has come. Furtia raised her head. *Our time is now.* Dumai looked up to see light in the darkness – a gleam of pure silver, flawless and clear.

The star that brought us to this world, Nayimathun had said. *The long-tailed light from the black waters of creation.*

There it was. White needles were streaming in its wake, falling towards earth like rain.

Kwiriki's Lantern.

Beneath her, Furtia glowed as she never had. Now every scale was clear as water, so her light came gleaming through. She was a mirror of the star, her crest the moon itself. Dumai laughed for joy and let the magic wash her clean.

We are strongest as the star falls from the black waters. Stronger than the risen fire. Furtia spoke in her mind. *For a time, it will be as it was long ago, when water could still conquer flame, as water always should.*

Dumai held on to her. She smelled the sea, and rain, and something else.

The fire will die away beneath the star. It will wither back into the earth, but if Taugran sleeps, it will wake again, when the fire rises anew. Furtia swam through the chilled air. *You will not be here, but others will.* Dumai breathed fog. *Taugran should not sleep. All of of our light may quench it. Its heat may scorch us, in return.*

Taugran swung over the rooftops, wings gleaming, its wyrmlings breathing fire below. Nikeya could be anywhere down there. Dumai willed her to run, to be gone with the stone.

Earth child, do you see?

Blood leaked from where the arrow had punctured her. The darkness thickened once more, but there was no more pain. She had lived well for thirty years.

Yes, Dumai told her. *Yes, great one. I am with you.*

She remembered:

Seven dragons, gods of water, circling the beast of the deep earth. The dragons she had rung awake, flying towards chaos. Once she had feared that she had woken them for no purpose, but this must be it. Together, with the comet, they could destroy Taugran.

To make sure the people of Seiiki survived.

To make sure that Taugran never returned, even if others did.

Furtia reached the monster first. The dragons coiled themselves around those tarnished golden scales, sizzling at their touch, and their inner light erupted into whiteness. The comet was in all of them, and they were all soaked in it, as the stars descended.

Drenched in fallen night.

Dumai watched her palms brighten. The light had always been in her. It was how she could speak to the gods. How she had survived Brhazat. At last, she knew the truth, cupped it between her hands – the secret her mother had kept all her life.

That night, long ago, Unora of Afa had swallowed a star, so her daughter could give birth to one. Pajati had given Unora a gift, and now Dumai would give it back to the gods.

Mama, I forgive you. I forgive you all of it. I love you as the rain loves the earth. As the mountain loves the sky. I will love you when the star returns, and when the black waters swallow the world.

Taugran the Golden screamed into the dark. Wrapped around its monstrous bulk, the gods withered like paper over burning coals. Still they held on. They imprisoned Taugran. Blinded by their glow, Dumai heard them all tighten their coils, tighten and tighten and tighten once more, until they had smothered the furnace in the wyrm.

Taugran the Golden was dead before it even started falling.

Red fires blew out across the island. Light turned to darkness, pierced by the tempest of stars. Furtia slid away from Taugran, and Dumai went tumbling with her, into the endless black of the sea.

****

She sank, a woman made of stone. Her bones must have broken when she hit the water, but the pain was distant, shapeless. She opened her eyes. Perhaps it was a dream. Perhaps she was already dead, and this was her peaceful descent to the deep, to the Palace of Many Pearls.

Her mind was at rest. She let herself drift, the sound of her own heart slowing, slowing.

She thought of Nikeya and wished.

She wished they could have had more time.

Lights knifed into the sea. They cooled the fire in her bones, in her side, and then she felt nothing at all.

****

She woke alone on cold grey sand, smelling blood and dragon. The Abyss had pushed her back to shore. Unable to feel, she rested on her side, her hair spread under her cheek.

Beside her, Furtia Stormcaller was silent and still. She lay on the sand like a kite without wind, scales burned so dry they flaked away like dead leaves when a breeze sighed past.

It had taken seven dragons to extinguish Taugran for good. The others must be nearby. This shore would be their resting place, and hers.

Dumai reached out to touch the god that had chosen her. More scale crumbled off beneath her fingers.

I'm sorry.

Dawn bloomed on the horizon. The light revealed that the wyrms were gone. Dumai could no longer see their wings, or hear their calls over Seiiki.

On the contrary, there was a terrible silence, away from the roar of the sea.

Kwiriki's Lantern was still in the heavens, trailing stardust. She could die well, to a sight like this – the sky alive with flecks of silver, and the comet, the sign of the gods' protection and love.

For a time, she slept, or slipped into unconsciousness. When she stirred again, she was much colder, her hand clammy beside her face. She had become a water ghost. Her side stung where the water lapped it. She could no longer move, so she knew it would be soon.

At first, she thought the pale dragon was a vision, or a dream – the spirit of the great Kwiriki, coming to lead her away. It drifted to land beside Furtia, and then turned to Dumai.

You have fallen like the star. Pajati the White nudged her with his snout. *And yet I heard you wish, and I came.*

'Wishgiver.' Her voice was barely there. 'I see now … that I was a wish.'

She called me from my sleep, and you were formed in starlit waters. Pajati huffed at her. *You still have time, though it grows short. While the star is in the sky, its light can mend your flesh, your bones. You hold enough of its remnant … but you must use all you now possess, all I gave the dying woman. I cannot offer more, earth child. Not now it is our time.*

Her breath came slower. Her heart was a crushed moth, just barely fluttering.

Dream well, for you can choose just once.

If she returned to Antuma, there would be civil war. Seiiki would not survive that bloodshed.

The sea washed around her, fanning her hair. She pictured Mount Ipyeda, the painting on her mother's wall – the Palace of Many Pearls, and all the blissful people tucked inside. And then she pictured Nikeya.

Nikeya.

As she closed her eyes, she saw the hidden stream one more time, and the figure in the fading distance, still without a face.

I wish I had known who you were. She sent the words across the ashes of the world. *Goodbye, my sister, my mirror. My friend.*

It was better that she disappear. At last, she saw a way. She reached for the light deep within, and darkness accepted it, like an offering.

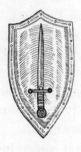

100

West

Deep in the barrow, all was quiet. Wulf waited inside with Sabran, watching as she dozed against his thighs. She slept with her legs tucked up, as she must have in the womb.

It was spring, but inside the false hill, winter clung. He had moved his cloak to cover Sabran. For hours, he had not thought of anything but her. Not the light that came from his hand, or the comet. Just the child he had never expected.

Daylight strained into the barrow through a smokehole. By that faint glow, Wulf drank in the sight of his newborn daughter, so he would remember every snuffle, every feature. He ghosted a thumb over her cheeks, her threads of hair, her ears. Best of all were her delicate black lashes, strokes of the finest brush.

Sabran slept like a small bear, lips apart, breathing from her belly. 'Aye,' Wulf murmured, giving her a gentle pat. 'Must be a tiring affair. Born at the end of the world.'

It was the first time he had spoken, and his voice made her stir. She paddled her feet against his middle.

'Hello,' he said.

Sabran made a little sound. He looked into her eyes, green as withy leaves.

'Where did you come from?' he asked her. 'Who is it you all look like, hm?'

She wrinkled her brow.

'You'll be all right, you know. I wasn't raised by my birthfather, either. He died a long time ago. I turned out reasonably well.' Wulf tucked a fold of his cloak under her chin. 'Now, I don't know if the Prince of Yscalin will love you, but don't fuss, wee one. Others will.'

Glorian must have managed to feed her, between giving birth and inspiring the troops. Her belly was warm and swollen. He leaned in closer, so he could hear her tiny breaths.

'I suppose I'd better tell you something about me. While we have time,' he murmured. 'I was born in a bonny valley in the South, to a kind warrior and a man the birds trusted – birds that sang him to his doom, which only the bees saw. I was stolen over sand and sea, deep into a louring wood, where a wolf carried me away from a witch to a man who loved me like his own. I fled from my past to the eversnow, where the sky ripples with light. I stood on a white ship that burned, but I didn't, because I had a secret in my blood.

'We've something special in us, you and me,' he told her. 'Sabran Melim Berethnet, you are descended from a man who built a kingdom on a lie. He told the world he had vanquished a monster, but in truth, it was a great princess who did it. Her name was Cleolind. She built a house to guard the truth – not for glory, Sabran, but because the truth matters. You will be the first Berethnet queen who has that truth within her.

'It's just an ember. Less than that. It's more a candle, I suppose, a light you'll never feel or see. You might not be the one who tells it – but it will live in you, all your days, and keep you very warm.' He placed a fingertip on her breastbone. 'Just here.'

She peered up at him. Wulf smiled at her, a tear seeping down his cheek.

'You are a secret, like my mother. Like our sisters. Like me.' He kissed her soft head. 'And I love you.'

Sabran yawned with a squeak like a mouse, heedless of it all. Wulf shook with the sudden force of his tears. He pressed her to his heart, and he willed her, in some small and hidden chamber of her own, to remember how his love had wrapped her. How his voice had sounded, here in the strange womb of the barrow.

And he prayed, not to the Saint, but to the Mother. He prayed no bees would haunt her dreams – that instead, she would whisper her secrets to them, tell them of the memory of him. He prayed her days rang with laughter and song.

He stayed that way until he heard the hooves coming towards the barrow, crying of victory.

****

Cenning Moor had erupted into cheers. All across Inys, the people were emerging from their hideouts, to stand in the sun without fear of the fire.

Only the Queen of Inys still wept. She held herself inside her cave, alone for the first time in years. A silver thread had unravelled within her, and with it, the voice in her dream disappeared.

Epilogue

Tunuva

The Lasian Basin had started to wake. For a long time, the birds had been silent, sensing the change in the world.

Now the honeyguides warbled again. Tunuva Melim followed one.

It had been many years since she last visited the clearing. The men had decided to bury Meren there, in a place he loved, where the honeyguides had led him on that fateful day. Tunuva had not been able to face the body – once had been enough – but Esbar had told her later that the birds had come to mourn him, singing a sweet dirge over his grave.

Beyond the Lasian Basin, all was quiet. No wyrms howling in the night. No screams.

When she reached the place, memory struck with the force of a warhammer. The smell of blood on sweetness. The taste of fear in her craw. Her own cries. There was the tree the bees had hummed in, broken open with an axe, honey still glistening on its bark. *Honey never rots away*, Meren had told her. *You could wait a thousand years and still eat it.*

The men had planted sunbreath. Meren had loved those flowers, which opened each summer, bright as his smile. Tunuva knelt and placed her palm where his face had been.

'Meren tried to protect him.'

The stillness of her body felt primal. She sensed unearthly magic, far stronger than before.

'I did it quickly, if it comforts you,' Canthe said. 'Wulf was looking at the bees – Meren was trying to teach him not to fear them. He never saw the body.'

Tunuva remained where she was. Somehow, she was not surprised that Canthe had survived.

'You never told me why,' she said. 'Why you killed Meren. Why you took my child from me.'

'The world is broken, Tunuva. You have seen that now, all of you,' Canthe said. 'Long ago, the balance of two magics was disturbed – the balance that once held our world in harmony. All this suffering and death was a disastrous consequence.'

She stepped into the clearing. Tunuva could not look yet, but her body was aware of every footstep.

'I once tried to teach a man to love my tree as well as I did. I tried, but he turned away from it. He turned away from me as well,' Canthe said. 'Bereft of my daughter, I longed for a child with mage blood, one I could teach from the cradle – an heir to help me heal the earth. A guardian for the forest, in case anything should happen to me. I went to the Priory.'

'How did you know about it?'

'I was alive when it was founded. When I saw Wulf, I knew. A sister is not supposed to cleave too close to her own flesh, after all,' she said. 'I thought a boy would not be missed.'

'He was. Every day. Every moment,' Tunuva said quietly. 'But you know that now.'

'I do.'

Tunuva remained on the ground. Her breath was bundled at her breastbone, like something trapped inside an egg that was about to crack.

'Tell me,' she said, 'after all the trouble to steal Wulf, why allow the Inysh baron to take him?'

'My enemies found me. I knew they would kill him, and I was too weak, by then, to keep him truly safe. I gave him to someone who could, but I always hoped to return for him, one day.'

'Then why did you not?'

'Because I saw that he was happy.'

'He would also have been happy with me, as he was before.' At last, Tunuva rose, her movements slow, and faced the woman she had once called her friend. 'Why are you here?'

Canthe wore only a fishnet, knotted at her shoulder. Her wet hair trailed to her waist.

'You know why,' she said.

'You are never entering the Priory again.'

'The Long-Haired Star grants many gifts to those who know its secrets. Now my sterren is renewed, I can take any form I wish. You will never know if I am there.'

'You became Saghul, to trick Hidat. You changed your shape and walked in hers.'

'No. That would have taken more than I had. I only cast an enchantment. When Hidat looked at me, she saw and heard Saghul Yedanya. An illusion, not a change – but yes, it was all me. I knew it would drive Siyu away. I knew what that would do to you and Esbar.'

'So you not only took my birthson, but almost estranged me from the two people I love most in this world.'

'I do not expect your forgiveness, Tunuva. I already know that is too much to ask.'

All was too still, the air as thick as the honey.

'Did you come here for the fruit,' Tunuva said, each word a fresh pain, 'or the jewel?'

'The latter.' Canthe cast her gaze southwest. 'I know it is here.'

'The key no longer is. I sent it far away.'

'Tunuva, I have lived for a long time, but my patience is not boundless where that abomination is concerned.'

'What is it, that is raises such fear in you?'

'That knowledge is not your burden. The duty to right this is mine, no matter how low I must sink.' Canthe took another step, her bare feet silent on the earth. 'Tell me where the key is. I can make you.'

'You can't, because I don't know where it is. And I am not afraid of you, Canthe.'

'Why?'

'You could have stolen the key while I slept. You could have killed me for it,' Tunuva said. 'But you wanted to earn my trust.'

'I needed your trust. My sterren was too weak to keep a firm hold on your mind without it.'

'That is not the only reason. You stayed for two years, because you wanted to belong in this family. You were careful. You reunited me with Wulf, despite the risk.' Tunuva held her gaze. 'You say you lost a child.'

812

'That was true.'

'Why did you help me find mine?'

A honeyguide sang.

'I think you did it,' Tunuva said, 'because you love me.'

Canthe lowered her gaze.

'When I realised the tomb keeper was the same woman whose child I had taken, I wasn't sure if I could stand to cause you pain again. After all, I am also a mother, though my daughter is long dead,' she said. 'And then you were kind and gentle with me, and it was worse. I have more regrets than you can ever know, Tunuva Melim, but this is my greatest – that it was your child I took. That it has cost me a place in your family. I would offer you my life in penance, but you could not kill me. I fear nothing can.'

'Knowing you walk alone is enough.'

Canthe closed her eyes. Tunuva watched her pluck a glass bottle, about as long as a thumb, from her sleeve.

'Take a drop when you feel weak,' she said, holding it out. 'It will stop the stone draining your magic too quickly.'

'Why would I accept this from you?'

'The stone will always be hungry, Tuva. You will not hold a flame for long. The strain may even kill you,' Canthe said. 'Please. Your family needs you strong for a long time yet.'

After a rigid silence, Tunuva took the bottle, careful not to let their fingers touch.

'If you truly love me,' she said, voice knotting in her throat, 'do not return here – not in any guise – until you are certain I am dead. It will hurt me too much, to know you are close. I will remember your betrayal every time I taste honey or hear bees. I will remember when I see the flowers on this grave.'

Canthe looked at her. Where her eyes had been depthless wells, there was a flicker of despair.

Then all emotion disappeared, like dust blown from a sketch.

'I will walk the world alone, as you desire,' she said, her voice low. 'I will wrap myself in lies, so none will offer pity or succour. I will be the Witch of Inysca. I will make myself as monstrous as you see me now. I will inflict my own punishment, for the loss of you.'

Tunuva returned her gaze with a clenched jaw, unshed tears building in her own eyes.

'One day, I will find the key. I will take the waning stone and hold it close, until its song quietens,' Canthe said, soft as sleep. 'Then I will know. I will know you are dead.'

She melted back into the forest, gone the way she came. A crow winged away from the Lasian Basin.

****

The same hour Dedalugun was slain, its beasts had lost the fire in their eyes. As the bearded star wept streaks of light, they had all retreated from the city, leaving its people to grieve their dead.

Across the South, every creature with the stain of the Dreadmount had started to weaken. First, the wyrms could no longer breathe fire. Soon their wings no longer held them. Within three days, they had all crawled away, to sleep or perish. The world lay devastated in their wake, but they were gone. The comet had lingered for a week – Esbar and Tunuva had charted its course – before it faded back into the far depths of the sky.

Kediko was a shrewd man, despite his years of doubt in the Priory. He had already used the comet to explain away the moving lake and the unseen force deflecting the fires, claiming it had been a spectacular gift from the divinities of night, to persuade Abaso to quench the wyrms' fire. Whether the survivors believed his story, Tunuva had no idea.

She rode Ninuru back to the Priory. Imsurin worked in the scullery, making bread. Hidat was instructing the girls in the War Hall. For the first time, Lukiri sat with them – young though she was, she could watch and be curious.

After they had returned from Nzene, they had found Canthe gone. Blood had stained the floor beneath the stone, but there had been no sign of her. No one had seen her leave.

No one would ever see her again, for as long as Tunuva drew breath.

Smoke no longer dulled the sun. For the first time in months, it blazed hot enough to make her sweat. There would be hunger for a long time, but new crops would soon have enough warmth and light to ripen.

She found Esbar near the orange tree, basking in the rays. Tunuva lay beside her, and Esbar took her by the hand, intertwining their fingers.

'I saw Canthe.'

'We knew she would show her face in the end.' Esbar opened her eyes. 'She came for the stone.' Tunuva nodded. 'She will never reach it. Why does she want it so badly?'

'I don't know, but I think she fears it.'

Their ichneumons wallowed in the Minara. Barsega had whelped. Her brood of pups squeaked and capered around her, practising a war dance. When Siyu returned – and she would return – she would be granted another pup, to raise as she had raised Lalhar. Hundreds of birds chirruped in the forest. Tunuva slowed her breaths and let the sounds of home soak in.

Above, the oranges were flickering, dimmer than their wont. The comet seemed to have dampened all fire in the world, both on the surface and beneath. Last time Tunuva had eaten, there had been far less magic in the fruit. Now each flame she conjured left her wick too short.

She had noticed, however, that Esbar could sustain one for much longer. So could everyone else.

For you, only death will break the connection. The bottle was cold at her side. *It will feed on your magic.*

After a long time, Esbar turned on to her hip and looked Tunuva in the eye. When the sunlight gleamed in her hair, Tunuva recalled the sheer power and splendour of her in Nzene, unleashing enough fire to burn the sky. Now she was all softness, her gaze tender.

'Tuva,' she said, 'I have thought long on whether to ask you this, but you and I have never had secrets.' She kept hold of her hand. 'Was Canthe telling the truth, in the tomb?'

Tunuva let her memory stray there. The night she had locked at the back of her mind.

'She kissed me. And I kissed her,' she murmured. 'I looked in her eyes, and I saw something worse than death. She had felt so much, for so long, that all of those feelings had lost their individual strands, the way even the brightest dyes can blend into a grey.

'And when she embraced me, it spread in me, too, the dead grey of her solitude. Had I kissed her for the rest of my life, I could never have broken free of that tangle, that mass she held within. I had never felt more alone, in that moment, seeing so much loneliness.'

Esbar was silent, listening.

'I wanted no rancour between you and Canthe. That's why I hid it,' Tunuva said, 'but for me, there has only ever been you.' She turned to face Esbar. 'Can you forgive me?'

'I forgave you before I asked.' Esbar touched her cheek. 'You are a sun to people like Canthe. It is your nature to warm all you see, and the sun does not ask forgiveness for shining.'

Tunuva pressed a kiss to her palm, releasing the burden she had carried all those months.

'We know the truth now. Canthe can never deceive us again,' Esbar said with resolve. 'I have left a warning for our sisters in the archives, telling them to be wary of strangers.'

'What of the Inysh matter?' Tunuva asked. 'Will you leave word of that in the archives, too?'

'Yes.' Her gaze turned distant. 'I will leave a tablet there, stating that the Queen of Inys is always to have a mage as her protector; that this is my ruling as Prioress of the Orange Tree – but I will allow our future sisters to interpret my reasons as they see fit.'

'Thank you,' Tunuva said.

'I do it to protect a part of you that will live on,' Esbar told her, 'but also because a position in Inys will always be of value to us. We can see into the land of the Deceiver.'

'I agree. Let our sisters know what he did to the Mother, so they might always guard the truth.'

The Red Damsels needed no flame to fight. Each sister was a living blade. They would hunt the wyrms now, to the same places they had forced humans into for almost a year. They would stalk them to the deepest caves, the highest roosts and farthest wastes, to ensure they never rose again.

An ichneumon pup snuffled towards them. Esbar nudged Tunuva with her shoulder.

'Go to the Mother,' she said. 'She must miss your voice.' With her old smile, she took Tunuva by the chin and drew her in for a kiss. 'And then come to my bed, my love, and warm me until dawn.'

****

The blood had been scrubbed off the floor, and the coffin sealed with a new lid. On top of it, a statue had been placed, watching over the burial chamber. Kediko had sent it himself, as a gift to the Priory – a standing effigy of Cleolind, based on a carving in his palace.

It was, Tunuva had to admit, a reasonably close likeness. Still, the High Ruler would have to work for several more years – possibly for the rest of his life – before Esbar warmed to his overtures.

Tunuva lit a tiny flame. She used it to light the lamps in the chamber, all one hundred and twenty of them. There were not enough candles in Lasia to mourn all those who had fallen in the slaughter that did not yet have a name.

She knelt before the tomb of Cleolind, and she sang, as she had many times. She sang in love and worship. She sang of grief and fear and loss. She sang as if the Mother could hear every word – and perhaps she could, in her bed of stone. Perhaps she would smile in her sleep.

When she could sing no more, Tunuva Melim rose and placed a kiss upon the coffin.

'Mother, we are your daughters,' she said softly. 'We remember. We remain.'

Wulf

A rooster crowed beyond the windows of Langarth. Unlike many Inysh buildings, the manor had withstood the devastation. The plague had never breached its walls; no flame had ever caught the thatch.

Langarth would stand for centuries yet, in the shadow of the haithwood.

Wulf lay abed in his old room, where the shutters were open to let in the sunlight. He listened to the birdsong that drifted from the ancient oaks, along with a great flaught of leaves.

According to the foresters, most of the haithwood had been left untouched, as if even the wyverns had dared not shed light on its depths. Just like the house, the trees had survived, to watch a new age dawn on Inys.

Thrit slept beside Wulf, one arm slung across his waist, head on his chest. Wulf lifted a hand to stroke his tousled hair.

Even in the wake of Cenning Moor, it had taken him a long time to decide. After all they had lost and endured, he had been afraid to risk his friendship with Thrit, the last of his lith.

Three years before, he had promised himself he would needlebind his heart, and so he had. Unpicking those tight stitches had been a complicated task, but Thrit was patient. All through the spring and into the summer, he had never once mentioned the matter.

After the Dukes Spiritual had found Wulf in the barrow and taken his daughter into their custody, he and Thrit had gone straight to Calebourn, to await the first ship that would bear them to Hróth.

Einlek Ironside had survived another war, and had welcomed them back with open arms, to serve for as long as they wished.

Einlek had made brutal choices. Shrewd as he was, he had spied an advantage few others had – that the wyverns and their servants did not appear to see those with the plague. Gathering a large group of people in the final stage, before the blood caught fire, he had offered them a chance for a glorious ascent to Halgalant. They had walked straight into a flock of small wyverns, armed with every tool and weapon that could be spared, and butchered them by surprise. Most others with the plague had chosen to jump from the Hólrhorn, their bodies left to rot on the beach.

Wulf tried very hard not to think of that place. The skeletons on the black sand of Márevarr.

For weeks, he and Thrit had ridden with Einlek, to help gather and burn the dead and start to rebuild homes. Wulf had spent that time as more of a carpenter than a housecarl. Meanwhile, Einlek had managed the politics that would help Hróth survive until the next harvest.

In his bones, Wulf knew Sabran would be part of them. He said nothing. A single protest would betray her bastardry. All he could do was trust Glorian to protect their daughter.

Thrit had always slept like a rock. Today was no exception. Careful not to wake him, Wulf sat up and dressed.

By the Feast of High Summer, he had made his choice. He meant to let himself be loved, and to love in return.

He had thought for days on how best to resurrect the subject. Thrit was fond of romantic gestures. In the end, Wulf had decided to take him to Averóth, a cliff that commanded a dazzling prospect of the longest firth in Fellsgerd, where they had first met. On a clear day, it was beautiful.

Naturally, the sky had opened as they climbed, rain turning the ground slack. Naturally, Wulf had fallen arse over chin, making Thrit cry with laughter. It was the first time either of them had truly laughed since Cenning Moor. Only once they had reached the top – covered in mud, still chuckling – had Wulf finally kissed him. It might not have been elegant, but Thrit had been overjoyed, and that had been worth the pain in his tailbone.

Now he fastened his belt and walked from the bedchamber, down the stairs and into the gardens. The sun was almost back to its old self, though it might take years for the harvests to recover. The dead were still being counted, but Inys had lost at least half of its people, with more still falling prey to the plague. Finding enough hands to work the fields would not be easy.

Wulf splashed his face with water from the keg before he went to the rose garden. Riksard had returned to Mentendon, and their loyal gardener had died at Cenning Moor, leaving the flowers untended. Taking up a pair of scissors, Wulf started to clip away the faded heads.

His family had already left for the capital, so they could stop to visit Caddow Hall. Tomorrow, he and Thrit would follow them to Ascalun.

'You did learn some lessons from us.'

The voice was familiar. Wulf turned to see a young woman, hair curling around her face. It took him a moment to recognise Siyu uq-Nāra, the last person he had expected at Langarth.

'Siyu,' he breathed.

Siyu laughed and ran into his arms. Wulf held her close, shaking his head in amazement.

'I didn't think I'd see you again for a long time,' he told her. 'Least of all in Inys.'

'I am trying to like this place, but these clothes are so dowdy, and they itch,' Siyu sighed, huddling into her cloak. 'Is the wind always so hard and cold?'

'You've not seen the half of it,' Wulf said. 'I'm afraid this is a bonny autumn day, by Inysh reckoning.' She looked in dismay at the sky. 'How long have you been here?'

'Some weeks. I came to learn more Inysh. I knew you would come back to see your family, so I waited for you.'

'Why do you need to learn more Inysh?'

'The Prioress sent me. I will explain.' Siyu nodded to the trees. 'We should go out of sight. Your angry knight would not want you to meet a strange girl in your garden.'

His mouth twitched. 'Which one is the angry knight?'

'The one who thinks people must all be married, or he is very upset.'

'Ah, that'll be the Knight of Fellowship. You'll find they're all a wee bit angry.' Wulf hung the scissors up. 'Come on, then. Let's go for a stroll. Thrit is here, but he's still asleep.'

Siyu went to collect her horse. Leading it by the reins, she walked with Wulf along the boundary of the haithwood.

'You've been wounded,' he said, noticing a stiffness to her posture. 'Did it happen in battle?'

'Yes, at Nzene. Is this it – the wood where you were left alone?' she added. 'It is beautiful.'

'Aye.' Wulf glanced at it. 'How is Tunuva?'

'Very well. The Priory is trying to find where the wyrms have gone to sleep. That is our important task now – to hunt them, and make sure they do not return,' Siyu said. 'Tuva told me to send her love to you.' She linked his arm. 'You know, our birthmothers slew Dedalugun.'

'They did?'

Siyu nodded. 'No one else will ever know, but it was Esbar and Tuva.'

Wulf smiled. 'Dedalugun is the one who hurt me. I can't fight while I heal. Esbar sent me here, so I could be useful, now I am an initiate.' She stopped beside a gnarled oak. 'But I need your help.'

'I'll do my best.'

'Esbar has two favours to ask. The first is that you find somewhere to hide this.' She detached something from her saddle and removed the cloth that covered it. An iron box of unusual shape. 'One of my sisters forged it. It can only be unlocked by a mage, and contains a key that cannot stay any longer in the Priory.'

'Why?'

'Canthe wants it, and we must keep it from her, Wulf.' When he furrowed his brow, Siyu said quietly, 'It was Canthe. She took you from Meren. She was the witch in the wood.'

Wulf stared at her in disbelief.

'Canthe,' he said. He thought of the white light that had come from him, the one the comet had seemed to awaken. It had never returned. 'Do you know why she did it?'

'No, and Tuva is afraid she will return. She has a magic we do not know.' Siyu grasped his elbow. 'The box must be put somewhere very safe. You must tell its place to me, and I will tell Esbar, so if we ever need it, our sisters in the future can bring it back to Lasia.'

'What if Canthe comes for me?'

'Better not to find out. You should leave Inys.'

Canthe had laughed with him, translated for him, reunited him with Tunuva. All the while, it had been her.

Wulf said, 'Is there anywhere she won't find me?'

'Perhaps not,' Siyu conceded. 'But the Priory will help you. There is safety in a family.'

Wulf thought on the matter of the box for a time, taking the weight in his hands.

'The Sanctuary of the Sacred Damsel,' he murmured. 'The false tomb of the Mother. It's a meaningful spot – that's where we could put this. What was the other favour Esbar asked?'

'It is a gift to you, in a way. Now the Berethnet queens have Melim blood, the Prioress has decided they will have the protection of the Priory, like the Southern monarchs. Since you are friends, can you ask Queen Glorian to give me a place in her court?'

Wulf realised what she was saying. 'You'd stay in the Deceiver's land just to protect my daughter?'

'I have always wanted to see the world. It will help us, to know what the West is doing, and what they say of the Mother,' Siyu said, eyes full of resolve. 'Esbar did this for Tuva, to protect her grandchild, but I do it for you, too, Wulf. I will try to help Sabran.'

'Thank you. I know this must have shaken the Priory.' Wulf grasped her elbow. 'I'm leaving for Ascalun soon, to be knighted. Let's see if there's an opportunity. Come with me.'

'I will,' Siyu said, 'and on the way, you must tell me all I should know of Queen Glorian.'

****

Months after the coming of the comet, Ascalun was still a skeleton of its old self. Pale rubble had piled up around the castle. Houses had burned to the ground or been pulled down to stop the fires. The Sanctuary of the Sacred Damsel was missing the bulk of its roof. Every building in sight had signs of damage. It would take decades to undo the destruction.

Still, the wealth of the Ufarassus was helping, so Wulf had heard on the road. He had no idea how Glorian was handling the marriage, but she must have kept the upper hand over Prince Guma.

Ascalun Castle was full to bursting. The Queen of Inys had summoned many people to be knighted, from all across Virtudom. In the vast white hall that was the throne room, a crowd had gathered to watch the first accolades. Wulf washed his hands in a stoup of vinegar before he entered, earning a nod from Kell Bourn, who still wore a thick cloth over their nose and mouth.

His fathers were both inside, as were Mara and Roland. Returning their smiles, Wulf waited for his turn with Thrit, Siyu just behind him.

'Góthur of Eldyng,' the steward called, and the slayer marched forward, chest puffed out.

Glorian stood before her marble throne. It was the first time Wulf had seen her since Cenning Moor. Then, she had worn her bloody shift, a fearsome warrior. Now she was arrayed in red silk, intricate needlework along the sleeves and neckline. Her hair was still short beneath her gold crown, and a scar curved across her forehead from the battlefield.

Glorian the Third, saviour of Inys.

Glorian Shieldheart, who had sacrificed herself to Fýredel, only for its flame to wither before her. Some said her willingness to die had called the comet from the heavenly court – the light of Ascalun, sent by the Saint, to cut down the servants of evil once more.

Wulf risked a glance at the people closest to the throne. No sign of Prince Guma, which made him breathe a little easier. When he saw Lady Florell Glade, his heart soared.

In her arms was a baby girl, wrapped in a crimson mantle. A baby girl with tufts of black hair, her cheeks rounder than they had been. Florell patted her back as she looked about the hall with big green eyes, silent and curious. He tried his best to hide his smile.

Sabran.

Each knighting was a long affair, with readings from the Arch Sanctarian. Wulf watched his daughter until a voice called, 'Wulfert Glenn of Langarth, housecarl to Einlek King.'

Wulf stepped forward, to murmurs of interest, and knelt before Glorian. Some of them must have heard about his ride from Cenning Moor, the newborn princess in his arms. Glorian kept her face expressionless throughout the readings, but her eyes smiled. Wulf hitched up a tiny smile of his own.

There were so many things he wanted to say to her. He wanted to ask if she was happy, now she had fulfilled the duty she most feared. He wanted to tell her that she had never had to do it, because her house stood on a lie. Perhaps he would, somehow, one day.

They could not meet in private for a very long time. To keep Sabran safe, they would have to be strangers.

The Arch Sanctarian closed his prayer book, and Glorian said, 'Wulfert Glenn.' She was still eighteen, but spoke with authority, as if she had aged a decade since their last meeting. 'You are called to knighthood for your deeds in the Grief of Ages. You saved Princess Sabran from the Siege of Hollow Crag. In doing so, you protected Inys from the Nameless One.'

Wulf bowed his head. Glorian took her Hróthi sword and set the flat on his shoulder.

'In the name of the Saint,' she said, 'I dub you Sir Wulfert Glenn, a knight of Virtudom.'

The sword touched his other shoulder. Two years ago, this would have meant everything to him, when he still craved acceptance. Now he had it, the title sat heavy on him.

All of it was a lie.

'Thank you, Your Grace,' was all he could say.

The Arch Sanctarian presented him with his golden spurs, and a girdle lined with green cloth, its plaques inscribed with the representations of the Virtues of Knighthood. Wulf ran his thumb over the wheat of generosity, the virtue he had shared with Lord Robart Eller.

'For your courage in saving Princess Sabran,' Glorian said, 'I will grant you any gift in my power, Sir Wulfert. Tell me, what do you desire?'

Wulf stood, holding the trappings of his new rank.

'Your Grace,' he said carefully, 'I would ask you to take a lady into your household.'

Siyu came forward with a smile. They had chosen a fine ivory gown, a pair of earrings, and a bonny necklace at Langarth – Mara would understand – and a seamster in Wulstow had taken the gown in for her. Wulf had to admit that she made an excellent show of being a noble lady.

'This is Siyu uq-Ispad, a distant cousin of Queen Daraniya of the Ersyr,' Wulf said. 'Lady Siyu once followed the Faith of Dwyn, but during the Grief of Ages, she saw the light of Ascalun.'

'Your Grace,' Siyu said, 'it would be my honour to serve you and your daughter, Princess Sabran, so I might follow the Six Virtues.'

Giving Siyu a noble background, to protect her, was an easy lie to uphold. Glorian would never confirm it with the Ersyri queen. In the unlikely event that she did, Apaya uq-Nára would smooth it over.

Glorian glanced once more at Wulf. He raised his eyebrows. 'If you are sure this is all you want, Sir Wulfert,' she said, 'then your request is granted. Lady Siyu, if you will come to the Queens' Tower this evening, my First Lady of the Bedchamber will see to it.'

'Thank you, Your Grace,' Wulf said, rising with Siyu, who echoed him. 'Your generosity is unrivalled.'

'Farewell, then, Sir Wulfert Glenn.' Now Glorian did smile, small and faint. 'Fire for your hearth.'

'Joy for your hall.' Wulf looked her in the eyes, one last time. 'Goodbye, Queen Glorian.'

****

Fire had torn through the Sanctuary of the Sacred Damsel. Swathes of floor had shattered beneath its fallen roof. While the sun was up, an army of stonemasons and glassworkers had made it impossible for them to enter, but once night fell, it was left in silence.

Siyu had made short work of the lock. She wore trousers and a shirt now, and a hooded cloak, like Wulf. Inside, they walked through the rubble and dust, which had been swept into mounds.

'Why are there no statues of her?' Siyu asked him. 'I saw in other places – the Deceiver is never shown with his queen.'

'The Saint destroyed all images of the Damsel personally, they say. In Inysh history, she died giving birth to Princess Sabran. He was too lost in grief to ever look upon her again.'

'So he erases her, to protect his own feelings?'

'His own legacy.'

Siyu pressed her lips together, looking at the remains of a plinth. 'Cleolind Onjenyu sleeps in Lasia,' she said. 'Whose bones lie in this tomb?'

'I doubt we'll ever know.'

The coffin was a block of unadorned marble, with no apparent lid or seam. All the dust had been swept off the baldachin that covered it.

'She's meant to be in a vault underneath that,' Wulf told Siyu. 'You'll be all right, finding somewhere to put it?'

'Yes.' Siyu cradled the iron box to her chest. 'You go, Armul. I will find my way back to Ascalun Castle.'

'If you ever need help in Inys, my family will give it. They won't ask questions. Just go to Langarth,' Wulf murmured. 'I'll see you again one day, I hope. In the Priory.'

'You will come back to us?'

'I don't know when,' he said. 'Thrit wants to travel, once the world stops smoking – maybe to the East, if we can get there. I don't know if the Priory would ever let him in. But if they can set their minds to it, then I'd like that, Siyu. I'd like to come home.'

'I hope to see you there.' Siyu freed an arm to embrace him once more. 'Goodbye, brother. Live well.'

'May the Mother always protect you, sister.'

Wulf kissed her brow before he turned to face the doors of the false tomb, a monument to an ancient lie. As he walked towards them, he unclasped the heavy girdle from his waist and let it fall into the dust.

Thrit was waiting outside, and so was the world.

Glorian

It had taken the best part of a year to muster the courage to sail. Until then, parting from Sabran had been too terrible a prospect. She had dreamed of foundering on the waves, leaving her child alone. Those were the only dreams she had now – nightmares that knit the past and present.

She woke from one, snapping up straight as a nail in her bed. Fýredel had sunk its teeth into her belly and torn her baby out, swallowing Sabran whole, and Inys with her.

Glorian stared at the window, remembering where she was. She curled back into the furs, touching the brink of sleep again.

Sister.

The only answer was the moan of the wind through the mountains, shot with snow. She knew by now that the voice in her dream was gone, like Fýredel.

Flames snapped in the hearth. Shunted back to wakefulness, she pushed away the furs.

When Einlek had written to invite her to Hróth, she had thought of refusing him. Inys needed its queen more than ever, in the aftermath of the Grief of Ages. She had not wanted to part from Sabran, even though she had milk nurses now, and could hold up her own head.

By the Feast of Late Summer, her ladies had encouraged her to go. Helisent had seen it first – that she found it harder and harder to rise, as if her bones were not just lined with iron, but with stone. Siyu had warned her that some mothers experienced a deep sorrow after pregnancy, but Glorian had refused to accept it. She had no time or room for that.

Yet her own mother had carried a certain darkness, even years after being with child. King Bardholt had called it *unmód*, when the mind seemed to detach and sink. The Virtues Council had finally agreed that it would be good for Glorian to visit her cousin, to recover from everything.

She had arrived in Eldyng as the sky lights began their dance. Einlek had taken her to Isborg and Askdral, and then to the bleak towers of Vattengard, to finally meet the Sea King. Glorian had floated like a dead fish through that day. Einlek had been there to support her, but when she had clapped eyes on Magnaust Vatten, with a reserved Princess Idrega, her thoughts had come untethered, and she remembered little after that.

Now she rose and went to the window. Her bedchamber had a breathtaking view – the snowbound trees of a drunken forest. Once the royal visits were over, Einlek had brought her to his hunting lodge in the Nithyan Mountains, where all was quiet, and she could rest.

Outside, the daylight was still low, the moon out with the dawn.

When she stepped into the snow, her breath froze before her. Hróth was always crisp in late autumn, but this depth of cold was unusual, even in the mountains. The passing of the comet had somehow quenched the Womb of Fire, but in its wake, the cooling had gone on.

Glorian had always weathered the cold well, and walked in only her shift and fur boots. When she saw the woman sitting under an ash tree, a streak of white in her hair, she stopped.

'Aunt Ólrun,' she said, after a moment. 'Are you all right?'

'You feel it, niece,' Ólrun Hraustr said, eyes closed. 'The great chilling – the Vildavintra.'

Glorian stepped a little closer, wary. Her aunt had always been troubled. 'Vildavintra?'

Wild winter, it meant.

'We will survive it.' Ólrun had the same eyes and nose as her dead brother. 'You and I are touched by night, as Bardholt never was. Einlek will see, in the Vildavintra.'

Unsure of what to say, Glorian continued through the snow. Her aunt had survived two wars. Of all people, she needed peace.

The stovehouse was a short walk away, tucked among the firs. Once she had hung up her clothes, Glorian shut herself inside and ladled water over the hot coals, listening to their sizzle. She sweated for a long time on the bench, breathing in the scent of pine.

There was only one way to banish the feeling that had clung to her in Inys. Today was the last time she could use it.

Near the stovehouse, a waterfall had frozen stiff, and a door had been cut through the ice on its pool. Before she had given birth, Glorian would never have been allowed to sink in, for fear the cold would harm her womb.

Now she stood before the black water, belly still thick, ice underfoot. She took a slow breath and slid into the darkness, quicker than she had last time. Over three weeks, she had learned to endure. Pain came first – a bitter fire – and then complete relief. Like heavy bedding after sleep, the shadows were ripped from her mind, leaving her raw and stinging and new. She ducked under and surfaced again, her whole body ablaze with cold.

A thread of green light crossed the sky, then another. Leaning back into the water, Glorian closed her eyes and laughed – for she was awake, and her soul was alive, and her body was hers, it was fully hers now.

****

Einlek was breaking his fast on his balcony. Food remained scarce, but here in the wilds, there was game to be hunted, and fish to be hooked from the rivers. Glorian joined him, hair dripping.

'How was the water today?' Einlek asked her. 'More bracing than your balmy Inysh lakes?'

Glorian nodded. 'I have felt well for the first time in months here, Einlek. Thank you.'

'You needed to stop for a time, to collect yourself. We both did, after so much tragedy.' He passed her a bear pelt, which she wrapped around her shoulders. 'It has been good to have you here, Glorian. I'm only sorry that I have to send you back so soon.'

'Inys needs me. So does Sabran.'

His jaw tightened at the mention of her. Glorian laid a hand on his iron arm.

'Prince Guma never touched me, Einlek. He never will,' she said. 'Sabran is not his.'

He narrowed his grey eyes. 'Whose, then?'

'I will not tell you, for his sake. Or hers.' She looked away. 'I know I shamed the Saint.'

Einlek snorted. 'You gave Inys an heir, and spared us all from the Nameless One. I would not call that shaming the Saint.' His warmer hand came to cover her fingers. 'I am glad you told me. These last years were a trial from Halgalant. We did what was necessary.'

He served her a cup of hot wine, and she drank, letting it warm her all the way to her middle.

'Aunt Ólrun mentioned something,' she said, after a long moment. 'The Vildavintra.'

'A foolish tale from the heathen days. A time when the spirits will break free of the ice and kill the world.' He swallowed his venison. 'Pay her no heed. Her war days still wilder her mind.'

'It does feel colder than usual, Einlek.'

'Hróth has been on fire, like everywhere else. Anything would feel cold in comparison.' Einlek glanced at her. 'Before you leave, I have to ask you something, Glorian.'

'Yes?'

For a time, her cousin looked out at the sunrise on the mountains, his face hard to decipher.

'The House of Hraustr is young,' he said. 'At present, there are only three of us in the family, not including you. My queen wants many children, but I have no siblings, in the meantime.'

Einlek had married not even a month after the wyrms fell. Surviving his second war must have driven his mortality home. Instead of a foreign consort, he had chosen the iron-willed Chieftain of Vakróss, who was almost as wealthy and admired as Skiri Longstride.

'It is a small family to rule after such a tragedy as the Grief of Ages,' he said. 'If Hróth is to remain at peace, and in Virtudom – which we know it must – I need to strengthen it.'

'I will do all I can to help.'

'Vattenvarg,' he said. 'He has a marriage to Yscalin, with Princess Idrega, but he still wants the foothold he almost had in Inys. He wants to betroth his younger son to your Sabran.' Glorian watched him. 'Haynrick is five. It would not be like your situation, a rush to the bedchamber. They would not have to wed until Princess Sabran is ready.'

'Einlek, must we really appease the Vatten again?'

'That has not changed. My wedding may have pleased my chieftains, but if we want to keep Mentendon in the fold, we should placate the Sea King. I wanted to plant the seed.'

Mentendon had to stay in Virtudom, or her parents' legacies would be undone. Glorian could not allow that.

Yet she thought of her baby, and her hand trembled around her cup.

'Sabran is not even a year old,' she said. 'It is hard to move my mind that way, Einlek.'

'I understand, after everything. Nothing is yet set in stone.' Einlek patted her hand. 'Let me know when you are ready to leave. I will take you to your ship myself.'

****

Fýredel had made trophies of her parents' bones. Glorian knew this, yet she always imagined her mother and father wandering over the Ashen Sea, trapped by the eternal fog.

She watched as an ice mountain appeared for the first time since she was a child. When her hands shook yet again, she clasped them on the wale.

She was Glorian Shieldheart. She was exactly who her parents had always needed and wanted her to be, and had to remain so – for Sabran, for Inys. Hróth had scoured the rust from her iron, lifting the heavy shadows off with it. They would not return.

They could not return.

The *Steadfast* docked at Werstuth. Once Glorian had loved to sail. Now she had to wait for a time at the port, so her legs would stop trembling, before she could climb into a saddle.

She rode with her guards through the snow, back to Drouthwick Castle. It was one of the few strongholds that had been left untouched during the Grief of Ages. More than once, she had to call them to a halt, her body pressing her for rest or attention. Sometimes it forgot that she had paid the tax on it, and sought to remind her of Hollow Crag.

She knew it would pass. Of course it would pass.

Her ship had arrived a day sooner than anyone expected. Upon reaching the castle, she started up the stairs to see Sabran.

'Glorian.'

She turned. Prince Guma stood at the door, immaculately groomed, as always. 'Your Highness,' Glorian said, with her customary reserve. 'I thought you would be at Glowan.'

'No. I have been here for two weeks,' he said. 'Your grandmother and ladies have just settled Princess Sabran. It may be best to let her sleep. Will you join me for supper?'

Reluctantly, she nodded. Sabran was a fretful child, and had not slept with ease since the day she was born.

In the Dearn Chamber, supper was served. 'I trust you enjoyed your visit to the North,' her companion said.

'Yes, thank you.'

Prince Guma did not touch his meal. He clasped his hands on the table, his rings glistening.

'I have been made aware that certain letters were discovered at Parr Castle.'

Glorian stopped eating.

'Yes,' she said.

It seemed their confrontation would be now.

'Any fool could see that Yscalin brought far more than Inys to our marriage,' Glorian said, keeping her voice as low as his. 'At first, I thought you agreed to the match because I am the head of Virtudom. A place at my side brings you the power and standing you have always craved, deprived of a throne by your twin as you were – but when Lord Robart Eller was arrested for performing heathen rites, your letters were found in his study. I learned that the two of you conspired to sway me to your hawthorn faith.'

'Not just hawthorns,' Prince Guma said. 'In Yscalin, those of us who remember more often worship the yew.' He reached for his cup. 'When did you discover these letters?'

'The Feast of Early Spring.'

'Before my arrival.' When she gave him no reply, he said, 'You could have dissolved our union when you learned of my beliefs, since it was not consummated. You still could. The Saint forbids divorce or remarriage, but I'm sure your sanctarians would make an exception, in this case. How can a royal consort not believe the royal lie?'

Treason and blasphemy, laid in the open.

'You are more than aware of our precarious situation in Inys,' Glorian said. 'I need the Ufarassus.'

'As you needed an heir. It would have been hard to find a new consort at that time. Better to marry me and get with child by the barons' son.'

He caught her expression. 'Yes, I know who it was – Wulfert Glenn. Your ride at Hollow Crag was hardly subtle, Glorian.'

'I had no choice.'

'No.' He returned his knife to the table. 'You know what I plotted, yet we are still wed, because you need my gold. I applaud your attempt to outflank me. No doubt your father would be proud.' His thick fingers pleached. 'Did you execute Lord Robart Eller?'

'He took his own life.'

Prince Guma closed his eyes, regret pinching his forehead and the corners of his narrow mouth.

'He was the most devoted,' he said. 'The plan was his idea – to convert you to our faith. You see, he believed you were meant to help us, born as you were in the spring, to a heathen. He hoped you were our Green Lady, who would bring Inysca back to the true way.'

'A vain hope, for I believe in the Saint. Did you not see the sign that came from Halgalant?'

'You can believe it was from your Halgalant, or you can see it as an act of unconquerable nature. Perhaps it was our ancient rites that called the comet, not your prayers.'

Glorian managed to hold his gaze, even as her heart surged into her throat.

'You are aware that I went to Ascalun, before Arondine,' he said.

'Yes.'

'That is because I sent my servants to Arondine first. I had thought your people might have rallied against our marriage, you see, and wanted to be assured of my safety. I believed I was risking both my reputation and my life.' He raised his white eyebrows. 'Imagine my surprise when I saw how deeply your people had come to believe the Berethnet lie. All they wanted was the heir. You were but a womb to them; so will your daughter be.'

Glorian clenched her jaw to stop it trembling.

'Your cousin, Einlek. His dynasty is young and fragile,' Prince Guma said. 'How long will it take him to want to barter Sabran?'

'I know Halgalant is real,' Glorian whispered. 'I have met the dead who dwell there.'

'They cannot protect your daughter. If you stay this course, you will doom her to a life of sorrow and servitude. I would not trade her like horseflesh. Let her become a true Queen of Inysca.'

'Inysca is gone.'

'You believed you had no choice but to bear a child. Will you take hers?' His voice had gone flat and cool as a knife, working deep under her skin with each word. 'Or will she be allowed to listen to both my beliefs and yours, and decide which she prefers?'

'For a Berethnet, there is but one path.'

Prince Guma regarded her. With shadow filling the lines of his face, his eyes were cabachons of amber, petrified on the bark of a tree.

'I pity you,' he said. 'It was unthinkably cruel of Galian, to build a legacy upon the wombs of his descendants.' He returned to his meal. 'Allow me to show you the way of the groves, and you could save more than your throne, Glorian. If not, I will go back to Yscalin – but even when I am returned to the earth, others will rise to take up the mantle. After this Grief of Ages, our numbers will only grow, along with doubt in your Saint.'

'Take the blinders off your threat, so I may look it in the eye.'

'The raiders know I make no threats.' He held her gaze. 'We, the believers – our roots go deep. They may yet tangle around your loved ones. Keep me from Sabran, and I will not stop them.'

Glorian scented the threat, but this time, it did not freeze her.

'Tell me,' she said, 'do you know how my late father executed Verthing Bloodblade?'

At first, the question went unanswered, and the only sound in the room was the fire.

'He kept his enemy alive for a long time, bound in chains. He thought for many days on how best to kill Verthing, who had murdered his brother and so many others,' Glorian said. 'Then the Saint came to him in a dream – though he did not know his name – and told him how it should be done.'

Prince Guma did not betray a flicker of fear, but even her blood had run cold when she first heard the rumour, whispered by two servants who had thought she was asleep.

'Yes,' he said. 'I heard what Bardholt did.'

'I am Marian the Less – but I am also the Hammer of the North, and I am the Malkin Queen. They live in me, too. I am not the soft creature you hope to mould. Not any more,' Glorian said. 'Threaten my family again, and you will remember, as I give you wings.'

Prince Guma raised his goblet in a wry toast.

'I do hope you enjoyed your visit to Hróth. How sad that your daughter will not have the same freedom,' he said. 'My faith accepts her as she is. Yours demands that she be ploughed and sown.'

Glorian broke a sweat at those words. The earthen smell of the cave filled her senses – smell of iron and unbirth, the reek of wyrm. Holding her silence like a shield, she rose from the table and left.

She had no memory of starting to run, but she must have, for suddenly she was in the nursery, where Siyu watched over the crib. 'Your Grace, I thought you were coming back tomorrow,' she said in surprise, but Glorian had already gathered up Sabran. 'Queen Glorian—'

'No.'

It was all she could say, all she could think.

She passed her startled guards and hurried down the stairs, along the torchlit passages. Heaving for breath, she unlatched a door and ran into the night, straight for the queenswood. The pines were so tall, and so terrible, and yet they seemed to call to her.

Her boot caught on her hem, and she fell hard, a cry escaping. Sabran screamed awake.

Glorian tried to rise. When she looked up, Inys was still everywhere, surrounding them.

Sabran bawled as if her heart was broken. Strips of linen swaddled her, tucking her tiny arms to her chest. In desperation, Glorian tried to tug them off, but Sabran only screamed louder, and Glorian stopped, realising she had no idea how to do it, how to unbind her.

'I'm sorry.' She forced the trembling words out. 'I'm sorry, Sabran. We have to protect them. We can't let this happen again, can we, all this death?'

Sabran stared at her in accusation, crying.

We do not break. We do not falter. Glorian choked out a bitter, tearless sob. *One day, you will sit across a table from your own daughter and tell her who she will wed for the realm, and you will remember this.*

At last, someone knelt in the snow beside them. Glorian flinched in anticipation of a touch.

'Queen Glorian,' Siyu said, 'I have a small daughter, too. Her name is Lukiri, and I would do anything in this world to protect her.' Her voice was very soft. 'You won't always be able to. This world is not always kind. But we will try, as long as we can, all of us. All women can be sisters. We will be yours.'

Glorian looked up at her, tears leaking down her face. 'Why are you being so kind?'

Siyu just smiled at her. She gave Sabran the gentlest touch on the cheek, and at once, the child stopped crying.

'I will tell them you ran out because you thought you saw a fire.' She held out a hand. 'Come, Your Grace. Come inside, where it's warm. Princess Sabran does not like to be cold.'

Glorian looked down at her baby, and a tear dropped on to her brow. Then she reached out, and took the other woman's hand.

Nikeya

Mount Ipyeda watched over the ruins of Antuma. For the first time in three years, Kuposa pa Nikeya made her way up its stepway, eyes watering from the cold. She had waited until spring to climb, in the safe part of the year, but the snow had shown little sign of relenting.

It had been tempting to try sooner, but she would not goad the mountain. Dumai had warned her against that, as they lay together in the depths of Mayupora Forest. Nikeya still knew precious little of mountains, and had almost no tolerance for them. Her ascent had been slow and careful, much like the dance of politics – one step, a wait, another step.

Always slow, daughter, her father had taught her, in one of his gentler lessons. *A flame that burns too quickly lives a short and senseless life.*

Nikeya stopped to brace her ribs. Each breath threatened to splinter them. Inchmeal, she pressed on, drawing on her last reserves – lifting one boot, then the other, each step harder than the last. The first time she had done this, she had brought servants and a guide. This time she had refused all help. The villagers had warned her to reach the temple by dusk at the latest, or the cold would freeze her.

The sun had just disappeared when she got there. She slid to her knees, gazing at the High Temple of Kwiriki, the place where she had met the woman she would come to love.

How long had she waited for Dumai since then, watching the sky for the ghost of a dragon?

Nikeya hardly remembered. Those first days had rolled like smoke over fog, hard to distinguish from each other. She still wore grey, as everyone did, to mourn the thousands of dead. Seiiki had been found later than the mainland, but on an island, there had been nowhere to run.

Unora came to meet her at the entrance. 'Nikeya.' Her face was thinner, weary. 'You're alive.'

'Maiden Officiant.' Nikeya held her furs close. 'May I come in?'

Silence lay on the temple, much as it did on the city below. Unora led her to the Inner Hall, where the Grand Empress of Seiiki sat beside a sunken hearth. Nikeya had never seen her, despite many attempts. She was small and pale in the grey folds of her mantle.

'Your Majesty.' Nikeya bowed, her stiff body protesting. 'It is my honour to meet you in person.'

'I am hardly a picture of majesty now,' the Grand Empress said in a dry tone. 'Only the rotten stump of a tree.' Her hair was white. 'I wondered when you would return here, Lady Nikeya. Did your father send you to finish the undoing of the Noziken?'

'Kuposa pa Fotaja is dead.'

Unora stood in the corner, watching.

'My father went to Muysima, the isle of exiles, where Taugran the Golden filled him with a strange form of the red sickness. The wyrm saw through his eyes.' Nikeya forced the words past her trembling lips. 'After Taugran fell, my father declined at once, and soon died.'

'You were with him?'

'Yes.'

She could have killed him when he started to howl. A blade would have been a kinder fate, but he had taught her to savour all poetry. He had been the one who sought to set his blood on fire.

'A year has passed since then,' the Grand Empress stated. 'Where have you been?'

'I have been searching for Dumai, as have many others.'

'And did you find my granddaughter?'

Nikeya clenched her jaw.

'No,' she said. 'Only the great Furtia.'

That first long walk along the coast still lingered in her dreams. A mist had swathed the island the day after the comet appeared, and she had entered it alone, carrying a lantern.

Seven dragons she had found along Muysima Bay, their scales curled away and scattered like leaves, the waves breaking against their hides. Furtia Stormcaller had been the last. When that giant body had emerged from the mist, she had run to it. She could still hear her own desperate screaming. Her calls of a name – all in vain, all unanswered.

'I am told my other granddaughter was devoured,' the Grand Empress said, 'along with the rest of the House of Noziken.' She looked at Nikeya. 'Dumai rode against Taugran.'

'Yes.'

'Tell me how it was.'

'Sit by the hearth first, Nikeya,' Unora said quietly. 'You should warm yourself.'

Nikeya knelt on one of the cushions. The exhaustion was catching up with her, making her thighs shake. Unora steeped a pinch of ginger as she told them everything.

She had locked it all into a box in her mind. There were fingerprints on its lid, from the nights when she had woken alone, and the days she had spent trying not to look back.

'Furtia and the others surrounded Taugran,' she said, once she had shared the rest. Her mouth moved without the thoughts fully joined to it, so she could speak the words, but not quite feel them. 'A brilliance came. It was all of their light – a blinding glow, like thousands of light-ning bolts. Then all that remained in the sky was the comet.'

It had stayed there for several days. Nikeya had barely looked up while she trudged along the coast, each day smothering hope. The sight of it had been too much to bear.

That final light was seared onto her eyelids for all time. The light that had consumed Dumai, and the utter silence that had followed, the dark made deeper by the glare before it.

'The comet ended it all.' Unora filled her cup again. 'Dumai knew it was coming.'

'Yes.' Nikeya swallowed the knot in her throat. 'One of my father's soldiers loosed an arrow at her. Even if she survived the fall, she would have been too weak to swim.'

'And yet you searched,' the Grand Empress said.

'She may have decided to leave me behind, but I was not so willing to give up on our dream.'

Nikeya lowered her head as soon as she said it. She had held down the bitterness for so long.

'Dumai may not have been fully herself,' the Grand Empress said. 'I am sure she never meant to abandon any of us, but when that comet appeared, she had no choice. You see, the great Pajati gave Unora a gift – a drop of his light, which woke our old power in the child she conceived, a child of the rainbow. Dumai was called to be with the gods.'

'They saved everyone on the beach. Everyone in the city,' Nikeya said. 'Including me.'

As she spoke, she tasted salt. Her father had always told her not to trouble him with tears; to use them only to further the cause – but her father was dead, and she had survived, and now she could weep for all of her losses.

'Lady Osipa wrote to me, before her death,' the Grand Empress said, watching as Nikeya brushed the tear away. 'She told me of your blatant designs on my granddaughter. You must have thought it an amusing game.'

'I will not deny that it started that way. My father asked me to govern her.'

'At least you admit it.'

Nikeya reached into her coat and took out a case, for preserving woodfall.

'Dumai entrusted this relic to me.' She presented it to the Grand Empress. 'Since I failed to find her, it belongs to you, Your Majesty. You are the last of the House of Noziken.'

The Grand Empress opened it. The glow from the stone was brighter than ever, bestranging her features.

'I had thought this was lost to the sea,' she murmured. 'You came here to return it?'

'Yes.'

'And what do you plan to do next, Lady Nikeya?'

'I don't know. My future has always rested on others. Now those others are all gone – my father, Suzu, Dumai.' Her voice tapered to a whisper. 'What now for the shining court?'

'Dumai told me you held a water marriage,' Unora said.

Nikeya glanced between them, and nodded.

The memory warmed her like another pelt. Even now, she smiled at the rightness of it, the feeling of certainty when their lips met. She could see Dumai smiling at her, lifting the tiny freckle on her cheek.

'Then you, Lady Nikeya, are Dowager Empress – or Dowager Queen, as you like – of Seiiki.'

The soft words like ink into paper, indelible. Nikeya stared at the Grand Empress.

'No,' she said hoarsely. 'Your Majesty, I know how this must appear, but that was never my intention. All I wanted was Dumai, and for her to rise as queen, after all this.'

'I hear they are calling *all this* the Great Sorrow – the loss of the fleeting world we once loved, a world that burned away like dew. How fortunate we were to touch it.' The Grand Empress looked hard at her. 'You are convincing, Lady Nikeya. I see your father in you, staring out of those bright eyes. Part of me wonders if even your grief is part of a long and elaborate performance, designed to win you a right to the Rainbow Throne.'

Nikeya shut her eyes. Even in death, her father possessed her, kept her locked inside his dollhouse.

'I told you, Grand Empress,' she said, with all the dignity she could muster. 'I do not want it.'

'And yet,' came the mild reply, 'someone must take it. Someone must step forth to rule Seiiki.'

As silence returned to the darkening room, the Grand Empress closed the case.

'Dumai told us about your meeting with Master Kiprun,' she said. 'If he was correct, then what we just experienced was an Age of Fire. We ruled in that time – we, with the gods' starlight in our blood. But even if any Noziken remained, I would desire change.'

Nikeya dared not speak.

'Sooner or later, Dumai would have needed an heir. We all know she could not have borne that. She would have drained herself to dust, just to paint the rainbow farther. Even if your plan had worked, she would only have passed the expectation to Suzumai. Unora and I both wanted children, but what if neither of my granddaughters had?'

Dumai had been afraid of that outcome. Nikeya had embraced her, as if they could press the fear smaller between them.

We'll find another way.

'History may record the end of my line as a tragedy,' the Grand Empress said, 'but a house that crushes its own daughters beneath its foundations – that is no house at all. Better it burns with the rest. A different world must be drawn from the ashes. Who better than you to build it, heir of the secret flame?'

Nikeya furrowed her brow.

'Yes,' the Grand Empress said, her smile as tight as a seam. 'I know the story your father believed. If we are to keep the balance of the

Mulberry Queen, I believe it is your turn to rule. In a time of starlight, fire must rise.'

'Me.' Nikeya whispered it. 'After all of this, you would relinquish it to me, of all people?'

'I didn't say it wouldn't sting. But I have had enough.' Faint shadows undercut her eyes. 'I would still not want you enthroned, for fear you had manipulated Dumai. Except that Epabo – my son's mysterious servant – came to see me, before he left for Mayupora Forest.

'Prior to your departure, Epabo had been keeping an eye on you. He told me that the River Lord had visited his daughter one night, to give her a task. She was to help him destroy Princess Dumai, to turn back the great tide of love she had found in the provinces. She was to spread lies about the princess, sow the seeds of scandal, coax or coerce others to speak ill of her – to light whatever fires it took to burn her reputation to the ground.'

Nikeya tried to keep her mind from that room, even as she listened to her own story.

'At first, Lady Nikeya tried to resist him discreetly. She proposed that, instead of trying to discredit an imperial heir, her father simply bolstered his own reputation, by helping the provinces himself,' the Grand Empress said. 'The River Lord accused her of caring for the exiled princess. He told her it made her useless to him – as useless as her dead mother.

'Of course, once he had struck that blow, he tried to soothe the bruise. Epabo had seen him do that to his daughter before – a cruelty, then a kindness. After all, Lady Nikeya was his heir, his only child. His legacy. He needed her, of all people ... but the next day, she was gone, and the bell in Belfry House had been brought down.'

Loathing had scorched her every vein that night. She had almost believed that was how it must be – that the flame of hatred could spark the sleeping magic in her blood, and she could burn him to the ground, as he had commanded her to burn Dumai.

'I am not some carven thing that is incapable of love,' Nikeya could hardly speak. 'He tried to make me so, but he failed. Because of my mother. Because of Dumai.'

'Then rule for her, exactly as you planned. I believe you did love her, and that she loved you,' the Grand Empress said. 'Let the House of Noziken fade, like the comet. Let now be your time.'

Nikeya could only look at her.

'It is not a gift I give you, but a heavy burden,' the Grand Empress said, her tone gentling. 'Seiiki is devastated. Many of our people lie dead. The red sickness will linger for a long time yet, even as the gods find their strength again, and rains fall once more on our land. It will take a confident leader to light the way now. But someone like you could do it, I think – a woman with a flair and a liking for intrigue, but also a heart as soft as a song. A woman who has the support of a clan that I doubt will want to let go of their power.'

'But the Tajorin and the Mithara—'

'—are loyal to me. This is the best way to bring peace.' The Grand Empress lifted an eyebrow. 'Dumai said you were once called a flower grown for court. I do not see that as an insult, but an endorsement. A flower in a world of ash is proof that life endures.'

Nikeya could not stop the tears now, even if she made no sound.

Silence fell like night. At last, she pressed her forehead to the floor before the last Noziken.

'If you believe me worthy, then I must obey,' she said. 'I will not rule as a queen or an empress, or even a Kuposa. I will not sit on the Rainbow Throne. That belonged to your house, not mine. I will rule as Nadama pa Nikeya – Dowager Queen, and Warlord of Seiiki.'

After a hesitation, Unora said, 'Nikeya, surely war is the last thing the people can bear.'

'Not war among ourselves, but against the wyrms. Should they ever return, I mean for us to be ready. Seiiki must be strong, so there will never be another Great Sorrow.'

The two older women exchanged a long look. One look to decide the future of an island.

'I will come down the mountain and intercede with Tukupa the Silver,' the Grand Empress concluded. 'Should she accept you as my successor, then it will be so, Warlord of Seiiki. Unora and I will remain here, to support you as you establish your rule. Where is the Council of State?'

'Ginura,' Nikeya said. 'Furtia and Dumai saved its castle. The nobles wait to hear from you.'

'Hear from me they shall. But first,' the Grand Empress said, 'let us see to the Rainbow Throne.'

****

It stood in the ruins of Antuma Palace, the place Nikeya had called home for a decade. She watched as the godsingers broke it apart, using a blade forged in the old foundries of Muysima. When it splintered, it sounded exactly like ice. Most of the shards would be enshrined in Seiiki, but two would go to Queen Arkoro and Consort Jekhen, if they had survived.

Tukupa the Silver watched the breaking. She was the descendant of Kwiriki, and now she was stronger than ever, her eyes brightened and wildened by the comet. All the others had woken.

Beside her stood the Grand Empress, off the mountain for the first time in decades.

'You will have to learn to sign, if you are to intercede with the gods for your people,' she told Nikeya, leaning hard on Unora. 'Dumai could speak to them in her mind, but that is not an art known to most of us. I will teach you a different way.'

Nikeya nodded.

'There is something else I would like you to ask the great Tukupa,' she said to the Grand Empress. 'I have thought for some time, about how best to honour Dumai. She loved the people. I saw that every day in Mayupora Forest.' Unora swallowed. 'During my search for her, I saw many orphaned children, left alone by the Great Sorrow.'

'What do you ask, Lady Nikeya?'

'It should not be just one family – not mine, nor yours, nor any other – who truly know the gods. I would like to train some of these orphans as riders, to help defend Seiiki.'

Unora smiled. 'Dumai would have liked that very much, I think.'

The Grand Empress glanced up at the dragon, who returned the look, blowing fog through her nostrils.

'You should be patient, Lady Nikeya,' the Grand Empress said, the corners of her mouth tweaking. 'My granddaughter may yet guide you herself. The dead whisper through the crash of the waves. Sometimes, they may even choose to return to us – we, who are left on the shore.'

****

Thanks to Clan Kuposa, the House of Noziken had lived a long way from the coast. Nikeya would make no such mistake. Ginura was the last place Dumai had visited, apart from the city where she had fallen.

Once they had received the order in person from the Grand Empress, the few surviving members of the Council of State – most had been in the palace when it burned – had confirmed her as Warlord of Seiiki. Nikeya knew she would have to work hard to win over Lady Mithara and Lord Tajorin.

That is one of your gifts, a distant impression of Dumai reminded her.

The Nadama were flocking to her court at Ginura Castle. Nikeya meant to bring greater change to Seiiki, as the years went on – but she would still have to be slow, always slow. She would rule for a time as if she were queen, and see what other ways opened for her.

The remaining Kuposa had not been pleased with her choice of name. Still, without her father, they were already proving less of a force. Most of them wanted to distance themselves from the man who had betrayed Seiiki. She could work them to her will, now they were shaken from his web of intrigue. Soon she would spin a web of her own.

The wyrms and their creatures had gone into a deep sleep, as the gods once had. Every last one would need to be hunted, to ensure they could never rise again. The red sickness would not only have to be forced out, but kept out. As for the imbalance that had caused it all, that would need to be rightened, and soon.

Nikeya meant to righten it.

She was Dowager Queen and First Warlord. For her crest, she took the golden fish with the rainbow arching over it, and two swords to defend them, as if the bell had been reforged – silver, to balance the gold. She would not let anyone forget the House of Noziken.

She would not let them forget Queen Dumai.

Her throne overlooked the sea without end. By day, she was the iron leader, laughing and strong. At night, she wandered alone through her castle, listening to the waves, dreaming of what could have been. For the rest of her life, she would be wrapped around an emptiness.

I will see you in the Palace of Many Pearls, she thought. *Wait for me, Mai. I will not be long.*

****

Months into the Age of Starlight, the First Warlord of Seiiki pored over her latest edict. Outside, snow fell where thick ash once had. Eyes dry from reading in the gloom, she glanced up from her work.

A figure stood in the corner of her study, wearing the robes and veiled headdress of the Maiden Officiant.

'Unora,' Nikeya said in surprise.

'No.' The visitor inclined her head. 'Please excuse my unannounced arrival. I know you have a duty of great import to perform tonight.'

'Indeed, which is why I ordered my so-called guards to let no one into my private study. Yet here you are.' Nikeya tapped the end of her brush on the table, too intrigued to mind the intrusion. 'Still, plenty of time to admonish them later. Who are you?'

'Unora of Afa has withdrawn from her duties as Maiden Officiant, to devote herself to caring for the Grand Empress. I am her successor.'

'It is a long road to here from Antuma. Why come so far from the mountain, godsinger?'

'To wish you a long and prosperous rule,' came the soft answer. 'And to give you a token of my regard.'

The visitor came forward. Her right hand remained beneath her sleeve as she laid something on the table.

A comb, adorned with a gold butterfly.

'You will find me on Mount Ipyeda,' she said, 'should you ever require counsel. Or comfort.'

Nikeya slowly looked up, finding the pair of dark eyes behind the veil. Ripples had been moving through her marrow since she heard that voice.

'Thank you,' she said, hitching up a smile. 'I look forward to seeing you soon, Maiden Officiant.'

She could have sworn the godsinger smiled back. 'Not too long, Dowager Queen.'

As silently as she had come, she was gone.

Nikeya stared at the place she had stood, with the sudden and terrible sense that she had just met a water ghost. If not for the comb, it would not have seemed real. She was rising to follow, to ask for a name, when her Chief Minister appeared on the threshold.

'Warlord,' he said, 'it's time.'

She composed herself.

'So it is,' she said, fastening her armour. 'Fear not. I am ready.'

The truth would have to wait, for Tukupa had brought the eggs to Ginura – eggs that had stayed underwater for centuries, biding their time while the fire rose. In the sight of her gods, the Warlord of Seiiki laid a hand on the smallest, listening for movement.

'Come, now.' Her whisper misted its surface. 'Come, now, and let us make the world bright.'

Beneath her fingers, the egg cracked.

THE PERSONS OF THE TALE

THE STORYTELLERS

Dumai of Ipyeda: A godsinger at the High Temple of Kwiriki in Seiiki. Born and raised on Mount Ipyeda, she is the daughter of Unora of Afa, the Maiden Officiant.

Esbar du Apaya uq-Nāra: Munguna – presumed heir – of the Priory of the Orange Tree, nominated to succeed the incumbent Prioress, Saghul Yedanya. Esbar is the birthmother of Siyu uq-Nāra, bonded to the ichneumon Jeda, and has been in a relationship with Tunuva Melim for thirty years.

Glorian Hraustr Berethnet (Glorian Óthling *or* Lady Glorian): The only child of Sabran VI of Inys and Bardholt I of Hróth, making her a princess of both realms. She is heir to the Queendom of Inys, first cousin of Einlek Óthling, and niece of Ólrun Hraustr.

Kuposa pa Nikeya (the Lady of Faces): A Seiikinese noblewoman and courtier. Nikeya is the sole child and heir of Kuposa pa Fotaja, the River Lord of Seiiki. Her mother was the poet Nadama pa Tirfosi.

Sabran VI Berethnet (Sabran the Ambitious): The nineteenth Queen of Inys and head of the House of Berethnet, daughter of Marian III of Inys and the late Lord Alfrick Withy. Sabran is companion to King Bardholt I of Hróth, and mother to their daughter, Glorian.

Tunuva Melim: An initiate of the Priory of the Orange Tree, a secret society founded by Cleolind Onjenyu. Tunuva is the tomb keeper, guardian of the remains of Cleolind, who oversees funeral rites in the Priory. She is bonded to the ichneumon Ninuru and has been in a relationship with Esbar uq-Nāra for thirty years.

Unora of Afa: Maiden Officiant of the High Temple of Kwiriki. She is the daughter of Saguresi of Afa, who served briefly as River Lord of Seiiki before he was sent into exile on Muysima.

Wulfert 'Wulf' Glenn (the Child of the Woods): Adopted son of Lord Edrick Glenn and Lord Mansell Shore, the Barons Glenn of Langarth. His adopted siblings are Roland and Mara. Wulf was a foundling, thought to have been abandoned in the haithwood as a young child. He now serves as housecarl to Bardholt I of Hróth, in a lith headed by Regny of Askrdal.

THE EAST

In Seiiki, the particle 'pa' between the family and given names – thought to originate from Old Seiikinese – indicates that the individual is a member of a noble clan. It fell out of use around CE 620. Most of the East Hüran go only by personal names, but may use a matronymic to help clarify their specific relationships, e.g. Moldügenxi Irebül means 'Moldügen's [child] Irebül.

*

Arkoro II (Queen Arkoro): Queen of Sepul, head of the House of Kozol, and granddaughter of the final Autumn Queen, who reunited the Sepul Peninsula after the Age of Four Queendoms. Arkoro is said to be a descendant of Harkanar, a woman who grew from the bone of a dragon.

Consort Jekhen: Empress Consort of the Twelve Lakes through her marriage to the Munificent Empress. Jekhen was born in poverty in Kanxang, later securing a post as a chambermaid at Black Lake Palace. Her storytelling caught the attention of the young Princess Tursin, who fell in love with her.

Epabo: A servant to Jorodu IV of Seiiki. Epabo often acts as his spy.

Eraposi pa Imwo (Lady Imwo): A handmaiden at the Seiikinese court.

Jorodu IV (Noziken pa Jorodu *or* Emperor Jorodu): Emperor of Seiiki and son of Manai III. He is married to Kuposa pa Sipwo and father to her three children, of whom only one – Princess Suzumai – survives. He was enthroned at the age of nine, after his mother fell ill, and spent most of his minority under the control of a regent, Kuposa pa Fotaja.

Juri: A handmaiden at the Seiikinese court.

Kanifa of Ipyeda: A godsinger at the High Temple of Kwiriki in Seiiki, whose principal duty is to care for the Queen Bell. He lived in a dust province before his parents entrusted him to the care of the Grand Empress.

Kiprun of Brakwa (Master Kiprun): Court alchemist to the Munificent Empress of the Twelve Lakes. Kiprun has been on an extended trip to the Nhangto Mountains, trying to finish an ancient recipe for explosive powder.

Kuposa pa Fotaja (Lord Kuposa): River Lord of Seiiki and head of the formidable Clan Kuposa, which has controlled Seiikinese politics and court affairs since the defeat of the Meadow King. He was regent to Jorodu IV and is the maternal uncle of Empress Sipwo, making him granduncle to Princess Suzumai. He has one child, Nikeya.

Kuposa pa Sipwo: Empress consort of Seiiki through her marriage to Jorodu IV. She is the niece of Kuposa pa Fotaja and mother of Suzumai.

Kuposa pa Yapara (Lady Yapara): A member of Clan Kuposa and a handmaiden at the Seiikinese court.

Lady Mithara: Head of Clan Mithara. She was harried from court by Clan Kuposa and has since chosen to remain at her home in the forested northern reaches of Seiiki.

Lord Tajorin: Head of Clan Tajorin. He nurtures a dislike of the Kuposa.

Moldügen the Provident (Eternal Sun of the North *or* the Great Naïr): Elected leader of the Bertak tribe, and, by extension, the settled East Hüran. Moldügen led the conquest of the Lacustrine city of Hinitun, believing her nomadic people required a stronghold to survive a severe and imminent winter.

Moldügenxi Irebül (Princess Irebül): A warrior princess of the Bertak tribe and daughter of its leader, Moldügen the Provident. In accordance with the Treaty of Shim, Princess Irebül was sent to live with the Munificent Empress in exchange for the Lacustrine heir, Lakseng Dethwan, to ensure a lasting peace.

Mithara pa Taporo (Lady Taporo): A member of Clan Mithara, and cousin once removed to Dumai.

Manai III (Noziken pa Manai *or* the Grand Empress): A former Empress of Seiiki, now Supreme Officiant of the High Temple of Kwiriki, located on Mount Ipyeda. Following a mysterious illness, she was forced to abdicate before her son and sole heir, Jorodu, was old enough to rule alone. She was married to a member of Clan Mithara.

Noziken pa Suzumai (Princess Suzumai): The only surviving child of Jorodu IV of Seiiki by his empress consort, Kuposa pa Sipwo. At the beginning of *A Day of Fallen Night*, Princess Suzumai is heir presumptive to Seiiki.

Padar of Kawontay: King consort of Sepul through his marriage to Queen Arkoro.

Rituyka of Afa: A thief and bandit.

Tajorin pa Osipa (Lady Osipa): A member of Clan Tajorin. Osipa was, and remains, a loyal handmaiden of the Grand Empress of Seiiki – the only member of her entourage to have followed her from court to Mount Ipyeda.

Tonra: A woman who lives near the summit of Mount Brhazat, in the Empire of the Twelve Lakes. She was said to have once sent dreams to the people of Hinitun.

Tursin II (the Munificent Empress): Empress of the Twelve Lakes and head of the House of Lakseng. Her spouse, Jekhen of Kanxang, often acts on her behalf. Since the Lacustrine defeat at the Battle of Hinitun, the Munificent Empress no longer controls any territory north of the River Daprang. Since this territory includes three of the Great Lakes, the East Hüran often refer to her as the Empress of Nine Lakes.

DECEASED AND HISTORICAL PERSONS
OF THE EAST

Harkanar: The first Queen of Sepul, who grew from the mislaid bone of a dragon. After chasing the dragon for many years, Harkanar finally caught her attention, and the two of them founded the Queendom of Sepul.

Kuposa pa Sasofima: The founder of Clan Kuposa, who betrayed the Meadow King. Her family used the forges of Muysima to create the prayer bells across Seiiki.

Lightbearer: Later known as the Carrier of Light, this is an epithet given to the first dragonrider in Lacustrine history, from whom the House of Lakseng claims descent. Since there has been significant disagreement over the identity of the Lightbearer, and rumours that they were a shapeshifter, their appearance has been presented differently over time. They founded the city of Pagamin.

Mokwo I (Noziken pa Mokwo *or* Empress Mokwo): Thought to have been the first Seiikinese ruler to style herself *empress*, said to possess formidable powers.

Mulberry Queen: A Seiikinese woman who is said to have ruled an island named Komoridu in the Eternal Sea.

Nirai III (Noziken pa Nirai): A former Queen of Seiiki. She was a gifted dragonrider, whose favoured mount was Tukupa the Silver.

Saguresi of Afa: A former Governor of Afa and father of Unora, raised as a farmworker. After passing the necessary examinations to become a scholar, he was awarded the position of governor from Manai III of Seiiki. Thanks to his diligence in bringing water to Afa, he was raised to the prestigious role of River Lord under the young Jorodu IV. After Clan Kuposa took issue with this, they arranged for Saguresi to be exiled to Muysima, accusing him of having woken a dragon.

Snow Maiden: The legendary founder of the House of Noziken, whose personal name has been lost to history. Following the rejection of dragonkind by the early Seiikinese, Snow Maiden would walk along the cliffs of Uramyesi, singing a lament to the sea. She found a wounded bird and nursed it back to health, and the bird transformed into a dragon, Kwiriki, who cut off one of his horns and gave it to her in gratitude. Due to its iridescence, the horn was known as the Rainbow Throne, and Snow Maiden became the first Queen of Seiiki.

THE NORTH

Most Hróthi do not use family names. Like the Bertak tribe in the East, the North Hüran mostly keep to personal names and matronymics.

*

Bardholt I (Bardholt Hraustr, Bardholt Battlebold *or* the Hammer of the North): The first King of Hróth. Bardholt was born into a poor family in Bringard as the second child of a boneworker. After defeating Verthing Bloodblade in the War of Twelve Shields, Bardholt united his country under one crown, founded the House of Hraustr, converted his people to the Virtues of Knighthood, and married Princess Sabran of Inys, who was later crowned Sabran VI. Since Clan Vatten submitted to his authority, he is also King of Mentendon. Bardholt is the father of Glorian Hraustr Berethnet, younger half-brother of Ólrun Hraustr, and maternal uncle of Einlek Óthling.

Eydag of Geldruth: A housecarl to Bardholt I. She is the eldest of the seven in her lith.

Einlek Ólrunsbarn Hraustr (Einlek Óthling *or* Einlek Ironside): Nephew of Bardholt I. Since his cousin Glorian was duty-bound to rule Inys, Einlek was made óthling (heir) of Hróth. He earned the moniker *Ironside* after he cut off his own hand to escape captivity during the war, replacing it with an iron arm after losing most of the limb to infection. His mother is Ólrun Hraustr, Bardholt's elder half-sister.

Heryon Vattenvarg (the Sea King): A raider and chieftain of Hróth, who led the conquest of Mentendon after the Midwinter Flood. He submitted to the authority of Bardholt I and now rules in his stead as Steward of Mentendon. He is father to Magnaust, Brenna and Haynrick.

Issýn: A former snowseer of Hróth, who helped persuade its people to embrace the Virtues of Knighthood and became a sanctarian in the wake of the conversion. She now lives in the remote village of Ófandauth and counsels Bardholt I.

Karlsten of Vargoy: A housecarl to Bardholt I, orphaned during the War of Twelve Shields.

Ólrun Hraustr (Ólrun Icebound): A Hróthi boneworker and runesmith who fought alongside her brother, Bardholt, during the War of Twelve Shields. In recent years, she has rarely been seen in public. She is mother to Einlek Óthling and paternal aunt to Glorian Hraustr Berethnet.

Regny of Askrdal: Chieftain of Askrdal and niece of Skiri Longstride, whose murder began the War of Twelve Shields. Until she comes of age, Regny is serving Bardholt I of Hróth as a housecarl, overseeing her own lith: Eydag, Karlsten, Sauma, Thrit, Vell and Wulf.

Sauma of Vakróss: A housecarl to Bardholt I. She is a daughter of the Chieftain of Vakróss.

Thrit of Isborg: A housecarl to Bardholt I.

Vell of Mágruth: A housecarl to Bardholt I.

DECEASED AND HISTORICAL PERSONS OF THE NORTH

Skiri Longstride (Skiri the Condoler): A former Chieftain of Askdral, who was known for her compassion and tolerance. She sheltered Bardholt of Bringard and his family from persecution by those who believed they were cursed by the ice spirits. After her murder by Verthing of Geldruth, Hefna of Fellsgerd – her closest friend – declared war on Verthing, beginning the War of Twelve Shields. Skiri's only surviving heir is her niece, Regny.

Verthing of Geldruth (Verthing Bloodblade): A deceased chieftain of Hróth, who wanted the wealthy province of Askrdal. After Skiri Longstride refused his offer of marriage, Verthing murdered her, sparking the War of Twelve Shields. Bardholt of Bringard eventually defeated him in single combat. He was later executed.

THE SOUTH

The Ersyri particle 'uq' is used across the South to indicate birthplace. 'Du' is an ancient matronymic of Selinyi origin. Some women of the Priory – particularly those who descend from Siyāti, the second Prioress – use both particles, e.g. Esbar du Apaya uq-Nāra means 'Esbar of the Orange (Tree), daughter of Apaya.'

*

Alanu: An anointed brother of the Priory of the Orange Tree.

Anyso of Carmentum: A baker from the Republic of Carmentum. He is the son of Pabel and Meryet, and has two sisters, Hazen and Dalla.

Apaya du Eadaz uq-Nāra: An initiate of the Priory of the Orange Tree, who holds a long-term post at the Ersyri court, protecting Queen Daraniya. She is the birthmother of Esbar and maternal grandmother of Siyu.

Arpa Nerafriss: Chief advisor to Numun, the present Decreer of Carmentum.

Canthe of Nurtha: A Western newcomer to the Priory of the Orange Tree.

Daraniya VI (Queen of Queens): Queen of the Ersyr and head of the House of Taumāgam, who chiefly resides at the Royal Fort of Jrhanyam. Apaya uq-Nāra has been her personal bodyguard for decades.

Denag uq-Bardant: An initiate of the Priory of the Orange Tree. She has a gift for healing, and has overseen childbirth in the Priory for many years.

Ebanth Lievelyn (the Briar Rose of Brygstad): A Mentish noblewoman and former courtesan. After the Vatten forced a mass conversion to the Virtues of Knighthood and outlawed her profession, Ebanth helped organise an ill-fated revolt before fleeing to the safety of Carmentum. She later became the consort of one of her clients – the ambitious politician who became Numun, Decreer of Carmentum.

Gashan Janudin: A kindled initiate of the Priory of the Orange Tree. Gashan was posted to the Lasian court in Nzene to defend Kediko Onjenyu, but accepted a place as a treasurer on his Royal Council, angering the Prioress. She is bonded to the ichneumon Barsuga.

Hidat Janudin: An initiate of the Priory of the Orange Tree, bonded to the ichneumon Dartun. She is a close friend of Esbar and Tunuva.

Imsurin: An anointed brother of the Priory of the Orange Tree. He is the unofficial leader of the men, and birthfather of Siyu uq-Nāra.

Izi Tamuten: A kindled initiate of the Priory of the Orange Tree, who teaches the sisters how to care for their ichneumons.

Jenyedi Onjenyu (Princess Jenyedi): Daughter of Kediko VIII, and sole heir to the Domain of Lasia.

Kediko VIII: High Ruler of the Domain of Lasia and head of the House of Onjenyu. Unlike most of his predecessors, he has a tense relationship with the Priory. His heir is his daughter, Princess Jenyedi.

Lukiri du Siyu uq-Nāra: Birthdaughter of Siyu uq-Nāra and Anyso of Carmentum.

Mezdat uq-Rumelabar (Mezdat Taumāgam): Eldest daughter of Daraniya VI, formerly Princess of the Ersyr, who was the favourite to inherit the throne. During a visit to the Serene Republic of Carmentum, Mezdat became disillusioned with monarchy and renounced her titles. Upon her return, she married a politician who later became Numun, Decreer of Carmentum.

Numun of Carmentum: The Decreer of Carmentum, elected as leader of the republic. She is married to Mezdat uq-Rumelabar and Ebanth Lievelyn.

Saghul Yedanya: Prioress of the Orange Tree. Her munguna – presumed heir – is Esbar uq-Nāra.

Siyu du Tunuva uq-Nāra: A postulant of the Priory of the Orange Tree. Birthdaughter of Esbar uq-Nāra by her friend Imsurin, though named after Tunuva Melim. Siyu is bonded to the ichneumon Lalhar.

Sulzi: An anointed brother of the Priory of the Orange Tree.

Yeleni Janudin: A postulant of the Priory of the Orange Tree and hunting partner of Siyu uq-Nāra. She is bonded to the ichneumon Farna.

DECEASED, LEGENDARY AND HISTORICAL PERSONS
OF THE SOUTH

Butterfly Queen: A semi-mythical figure. She was a beloved queen consort of the Ersyr who died young, plunging her king into unending grief.

Cleolind Onjenyu (Princess Cleolind, the Mother *or* the Damsel): Princess of the Domain of Lasia and daughter of Selinu the Oathkeeper. In the year BCE 2, Cleolind was chosen to be sacrificed to the Nameless One, but fought

854

and vanquished him with the help of an orange tree and the enchanted sword Ascalun. She relinquished her claim to Lasia and created the Priory of the Orange Tree, to ensure the South would be prepared if the wyrm returned. The religion of the Virtues of Knighthood professes that Cleolind wed Sir Galian Berethnet after he defeated the Nameless One to save her, becoming queen consort of Inys, and later died in childbirth. This story is disbelieved by members of the Priory, who believe Cleolind died after leaving the Priory on unknown business not long after its foundation.

Gedali: High divinity of doorways and passage in the Orchard of Divinities, the predominant Lasian pantheon. Gedali is often invoked during childbirth. Their own child was Gedani, the creator of humankind.

Imhul: A Lasian divinity of the wind.

Jeda the Merciful (Queen Jeda): A queen of the former Taano State in Lasia, who welcomed Suttu the Dreamer and her people after their long journey over the Eria. Esbar uq-Nāra named her ichneumon in honour of Queen Jeda.

Liru Melim: Birthmother of Tunuva Melim, who was killed defending the House of Taumāgam from a surprise attack.

Melancholy King: A semi-mythical figure, said to have been an early king of the House of Taumāgam. He wandered into the desert, following a mirage of his bride, the Butterfly Queen, and died of thirst. Ersyris use him as a cautionary tale, most often to warn against blind love.

Meren: An anointed brother of the Priory of the Orange Tree and close friend of Tunuva Melim, who fathered her birthson. He was killed in an apparent wildcat attack.

Old Malag: A Lasian trickster divinity.

Raucāta: A seer of the ancient Ersyr, who prophesised the fall of Gulthaga.

Selinu Onjenyu (Selinu the Oathkeeper): High Ruler of Lasia when the Nameless One attacked the city of Yikala. After sending all the livestock to placate the wyrm, he organised a sacrifice of human lives, including his own children in the lottery. When his daughter, Princess Cleolind, was chosen to die, he honoured his promise and sent her to her doom, gaining the epithet *Oathkeeper*.

Siyāti du Verda uq-Nāra: An Ersyri handmaiden of Cleolind Onjenyu, born to a family of perfumers in the Wareda Valley. She became the second Prioress after Cleolind left the Priory. She is a direct ancestor of Apaya, Esbar and Siyu.

Soshen of Nzene: One of the nine handmaidens of Cleolind Onjenyu, and an early pioneer of alchemy and chemistry. She created the limbec, which she and Siyāti uq-Nāra used to distil a cure for the Curse of Yikala, the plague breathed by the Nameless One.

Suttu the Dreamer: The legendary founder of the House of Onjenyu, who led the Joyful Few over the Eria – the great salt desert, still thought to be impossible to cross – from a distant civilisation named Selinun. Queen Jeda of Taano State welcomed them to Lasia. Suttu carried a spear, Mulsub, which she claimed was dipped in starlight.

Washtu: The Lasian high divinity of fire, believed to have pulled hair from the sun to bring heat and light to the world. She is both the enemy and lover of Abaso, the high divinity of water. The Priory of the Orange Tree assigns particular importance to Washtu.

THE WEST

Adeliza 'Adela' afa Dáura: A lady-in-waiting to Glorian Berethnet. Daughter of Liuma afa Dáura.

Annes Haster: A woman of the Leas, married to Sir Landon Croft.

Bramel Stathworth (Sir Bramel): A knight of Inys and guard to Glorian Berethnet.

Brangain Crest (Lady Brangain): Duchess of Justice, head of the noble Crest family, and a descendant of the Knight of Justice. She is mother to Julain Crest.

Damud Stillwater (Lord Damud): Duke of Courage, head of the noble Stillwater family, and a descendant of the Knight of Courage.

Doctor Forthard: Royal physician to the House of Berethnet.

Edith Combe (Lade Edith): Duchet of Courtesy and a descendant of the Knight of Fellowship.

Edrick Glenn (Lord Edrick *or* Baron Glenn): Baron Glenn of Langarth, and adoptive father to Roland, Mara and Wulf. He is married to Lord Mansell Shore. He is responsible for the haithwood north of the Wickerwath, keeping it on behalf of the Countess of Deorn, who lives some way from the forest and reports to Lord Robart Eller, the highest authority of the Lakes.

Erda Lindley (Dame Erda): A knight of Inys and guard to Glorian Berethnet.

Florell Glade (Lady Florell): First Lady of the Great Chamber to Sabran VI of Inys.

Gladwin Fynch (Lady Gladwin): Duchess of Temperance, descendant of the Knight of Temperance.

Guma Vetalda (the Hermit of Hart Grove): High Prince of Yscalin and Duke of Kóvuga, and twin brother of Rozaria III of Yscalin, born a few minutes after her. Uncle to the Donmato Alarico and granduncle to Princess Idrega and Prince Therico. He rules from the stronghold of Hart Grove and is the wealthiest man in Yscalin, thanks to the mines known collectively as the Ufarassus.

Helisent Beck (Lady Helisent): A lady-in-waiting to Glorian Berethnet. Daughter of Lord Ordan Beck, the Dowager Earl of Goldenbirch.

Idrega Vetalda: Princess of Yscalin and only daughter of the Donmato Alarico and his companion, Thederica Yelarigas. Sister to Therico, grandniece of Prince Guma, and granddaughter of Rozaria III.

Julain Crest (Lady Julain): Principal lady-in-waiting to Glorian Berethnet, and daughter of Lady Brangain Crest, the Duchess of Justice.

Kell Bourn (Mastress Bourn): A bonesetter and assistant to Doctor Forthard.

Liuma afa Dáura: A lady-in-waiting and former tutor to Sabran VI of Inys, who taught her Yscali. Liuma is now Mistress of the Robes. She is from minor Yscali nobility, the daughter of a knight, and is mother to Adeliza afa Dáura.

Magnaust Vatten (Lord Magnaust): Firstborn child of Heryon Vattenvarg, the Sea King, making him heir to the Stewardship of Mentendon. Brother to Brenna and Haynrick.

Mansell Shore (Lord Mansell): Baron Glenn of Langarth through his marriage to Lord Edrick Glenn, and adoptive father to Roland, Mara and Wulf. He is the younger brother of Baroness Shore of Caddow Hall.

Mara Glenn: Niece and adopted daughter of Lord Edrick Glenn, born to his sister, Rosa. Mara is the middle child, sister to Roland and Wulf.

Marian III (Marian the Less): A former Queen of Inys, the third and final monarch of the Century of Discontent. Daughter of Jillian III and mother to Sabran VI. Following her abdication, she retired to the coast with her companion, Lord Alfrick Withy, and now resides at Befrith Castle in the Lakes.

Mariken: A servant of Florell Glade.

Ordan Beck (Lord Ordan): Dowager Earl of Goldenbirch, responsible for the haithwood south of the Wickerwath. Father to Helisent, his heir apparent. He reports to Lady Gladwin Fynch, the highest authority of the Leas.

Robart Eller (Lord Robart): Duke of Generosity, head of the noble Eller family, and a descendant of the Knight of Generosity. He is the Lord Chancellor of Inys – ceremonial head of the Virtues Council – and the highest authority in the province of the Lakes, as well as a trusted friend of Sabran VI of Inys.

Randroth Withy (Lord Randroth): Duke of Fellowship, head of the noble Withy family, and a descendant of the Knight of Fellowship.

Riksard of Sadyrr: An ostler at Langarth.

Roland Glenn: Nephew and adopted son of Lord Edrick Glenn. He is brother to Mara and Wulf, and heir apparent to the Barony of Glenn.

Rozaria III: Queen of Yscalin and head of the House of Vetalda, one of the three sovereigns of Virtudom. Elder twin sister to Guma Vetalda.

Therico 'Theo' Vetalda: Prince of Yscalin and younger son of the Donmato Alarico and his companion, Thederica Yelarigas. Brother to Idrega, grand-nephew of Prince Guma, and grandson of Rozaria III.

DECEASED AND HISTORICAL PERSONS OF THE WEST

Alfrick Withy: Companion to Marian III and maternal grandfather to Princess Glorian.

Carnelian the Peaceweaver: A former Queen of Inys.

Galian Berethnet (Galian the Deceiver *or* the Saint): The first King of Inys. Galian was born in the Inyscan village of Goldenbirch, but rose to squire for Edrig of Arondine. The religion of the Virtues of Knighthood, which Galian based on the knightly code, professes that he vanquished the Nameless One in Lasia, married Princess Cleolind of the House of Onjenyu, and with her founded the House of Berethnet. Worshipped in Virtudom, but reviled in many parts of the South, Galian is thought by his followers to rule in Halgalant, the heavenly court, where he awaits the righteous at the Great Table.

Glorian II Berethnet (Glorian Hartbane): A former Queen of Inys, whose love marriage to Isalarico the Benevolent brought Yscalin into the Six Virtues of Knighthood.

Isalarico IV Vetalda (Isalarico the Benevolent *or* Isalarico the Betrayer): A former King of Yscalin, who abandoned the old gods of his country to marry the spirited Glorian II of Inys.

Jillian III Berethnet: The seventeenth Queen of Inys and second monarch of the Century of Discontent; daughter of Sabran V and mother of Marian III. She was murdered shortly after being crowned.

Sabran I: Daughter of Sir Galian Berethnet by his queen consort.

Sabran V (the Malkin Queen): The sixteenth Queen of Inys, and the only tyrant of the House of Berethnet, known for her cruelty and greed. Her reign began the Century of Discontent. She had a daughter, Jillian, by her Yscali consort, who died under suspicious circumstances.

NON-HUMAN CHARACTERS

Barsega: An ichneumon, bonded to Gashan Janudin.

Burmina the Splendid: A Seiikinese sea dragon.

Dartun: An ichneumon, bonded to Hidat Janudin.

Dedalugun: One of the five great wyrms – later known as the High Westerns – that emerged from the Dreadmount in CE 509.

Farna: An ichneumon, bonded to Yeleni Janudin.

Furtia Stormcaller: A Seiikinese sea dragon, who went to sleep in a lake in Nirai's Hills, so she might counsel the imperial family.

Fýredel: One of the five great wyrms that emerged from the Dreadmount in CE 509, generally agreed to be the dominant of the five. Fýredel was first seen in the Queendom of Inys.

Imperial Dragon: Leader of all Lacustrine dragons, elected by arcane means, who once chose the heirs to the Empire of the Twelve Lakes. Like the majority of dragons, she has been asleep for centuries.

Jeda: An ichneumon, bonded to Esbar uq-Nāra, named after Jeda the Merciful.

Kwiriki: Believed by the Seiikinese to have been the first dragon to take a human rider, worshipped as a deity. He carved the Rainbow Throne out of his horn and gave it to Snow Maiden, who had nursed him back to health after an injury, making her Queen of Seiiki. Kwiriki is thought to have left for the celestial world, sending butterflies as his messengers.

Lalhar: An ichneumon, bonded to Siyu uq-Nāra.

Nameless One: An enormous red wyrm, thought to have been the first creature to emerge from the Dreadmount. His confrontation with Cleolind Onjenyu and Galian Berethnet in Lasia in BCE 2 became a fundament of religion and legend the world over.

Nayimathun of the Deep Snows: A Lacustrine dragon associated with the Lake of Deep Snows, worshipped as a god of wanderers.

Ninuru: A white ichneumon, bonded to Tunuva Melim.

Orsul: One of the five great wyrms – later known as the High Westerns – that emerged from the Dreadmount in CE 509.

Pajati the White (Pajati the Wishgiver): A Seiikinese elder dragon and a guardian of Afa Province. Before the Long Slumber, Pajati was known to grant occasional wishes to the people of Afa.

Taugran the Golden: One of the five great wyrms – later known as the High Westerns – that emerged from the Dreadmount in CE 509.

Tukupa the Silver: A Seiikinese sea dragon, believed to be the offspring of Kwiriki.

Valeysa: One of the five great wyrms – later known as the High Westerns – that emerged from the Dreadmount in CE 509.

Glossary

Banewort: Deadly nightshade. Despite its toxicity, it is often used as a surgical anaesthetic in Inys.

Commendation: The formal introduction of an Inysh noble into society, held at any point between their fifteenth and sixteenth birthday.

Cutter: A type of ornate Ersyri sailing ship. They are mostly used as coasting vessels, but are capable of sea travel.

Dróterning: A Hróthi term meaning *little queen*.

Drape: A loose sleeveless garment, made of silk or linen, which fastens at the nape.

Edin: A continent of unknown extent. Its northernmost regions are divided into the Ersyr, Lasia, Mentendon, the Serene Republic of Carmentum, and Yscalin.

Eke name: Nickname or epithet.

Faith of Dwyn: An ancient religion originating from the continent of Edin, which advocates for a state of perfect balance in all things. It is the predominant religion of the Ersyr.

Feather death: Death from old age (on a featherbed), feared by most Hróthi.

Godsinger: A position in certain mountain temples of Seiiki. Among their duties, godsingers perform rituals and prayers intended to wake dragonkind from the Long Slumber.

Herigald: A garment worn by sanctarians in Inys, usually made of green and white cloth. Apprentice sanctarians wear brown.

Ice helm: A Hróthi name for a glacier.

Ichneumon: A quadrupedal mammal native to the continent of Edin, once considered sacred in some parts of the South, particularly the Taano people of Lasia. Ichneumons have been hunted for their pelts and strong bones throughout history. Wild ichneumons now largely dwell in mountainous regions to avoid human contact, but some have formed an age-old alliance with the Priory. Each postulant bonds with an ichneumon by weaning it with its first meat, which causes the pup to imprint on her for life

Lerath: A tree native to the Northern Plain. They have thick boughs and black needles, and their sap can be drunk.

Lith: An organisational unit for housecarls (armed retainers) in the service of the King of Hróth. Each lith has seven members to mirror the Saint and the Holy Retinue. Bardholt I has twelve liths, largely headed by relatives of his wartime allies.

Mage: Someone who has eaten the fruit of a siden tree and absorbed its terrene magic. Mages can conjure and deflect fire, and may exhibit a range of other abilities, such as heightened vision and hearing, resistance to cold, or an aptitude for metalworking.

Mirrorfolk: A word referring collectively to teachers, followers and scholars of the Faith of Dwyn.

Munguna: Approximately translating to *favoured sister* in the Yikalese dialect of Old Lasian, this title is bestowed on the woman the incumbent Prioress wishes to succeed her.

Needletooth: A carnivorous Southern fish. They are scavengers by nature, but may swarm in large numbers if they sense blood or thrashing prey.

Orchard of Divinities: The afterlife in the dominant polytheistic religion of Lasia; also, a collective term for its pantheon of gods.

Óthling: The preferred heir to the Hróthi throne. It was previously used for individual chieftains' heirs.

Palanquin: An enclosed litter.

Pearl mantle: Nacre

Sax: A large Hróthi hunting knife.

Sheepsbane: A tickborne illness, common in the Fells of Inys.

Siden: Also known as terrene magic. A power that stems from the core of the world, the Womb of Fire, and can be absorbed by anyone who eats the fruit of a siden tree.

Skin fighting: A Hróthi term for unarmed combat.

Sorrower: A black Seiikinese bird with a call like a grizzling infant. Legend has it that an Empress of Seiiki was driven insane by its cry. Some say sorrowers are possessed by the spirits of stillborn children, while others believe their song can bring on a miscarriage. This superstition has resulted in them being hunted sporadically throughout Seiikinese history.

Sterren: Also known as sidereal magic, this mysterious power comes from the Long-Haired Star.

Sun folly: A mood disorder common during the months of the midnight sun, when true darkness never falls in the North. Its main symptom is insomnia, occasionally leading to poor judgement, irritability and erratic behaviour.

Sunset Years: A later Seiikinese term for the years preceding the Great Sorrow. CE 509, specifically, is called the Twilight Year.

Salt warrior: A Hróthi raider.

Taano State: One of the Five States of Lasia before their union into a single domain. Taano is now the most widely spoken dialect of Lasian, closely followed by Libir.

Throttle: An Inysh name for inflammation of the tonsils; also used more broadly for any illness that causes a sore throat.

Winter gripe: An Inysh name for an illness similar to influenza.

Womb of Fire: The fiery core of the world, and the cradle of *siden*. The Nameless One is thought to have been formed in the Womb of Fire.

Woodfall: Wood that has lain on the seabed. If this occurs in Eastern waters, where dragons once swum, there is a chance the wood will burn with a clean, sweet scent. Coastal villagers can often make a living from selling woodfall to temples.

Timeline

EARLY HISTORY

Suttu's Crossing: In the legendary civilisation of Old Selinun, a young girl named Suttu declares that she has dreamed of a way to survive the Eria. Guided by an enchanted spear named Mulsub, she leaves, bringing with her around a thousand believers, the Joyful Few. They miraculously survive the inhospitable and arid salt flats. Arriving in southern Lasia, they are greeted by Queen Jeda of Taano State, later known as Jeda the Merciful, who takes them in.

Union of Lasia: The Five States of Lasia are united into one under a single dynasty, the House of Onjenyu. Its first High Ruler is descended from Suttu the Dreamer and a noble family of Libir State.

The Arrival of the Hüran: A group of stragglers arrive in the Empire of the Twelve Lakes, claiming to have come from a land called Brhazat across the Lords of Fallen Night. They call themselves the Hüran and become nomads in the North; the largest mountain of the range is named in honour of their lost home.

BEFORE THE COMMON ERA (BCE)

BCE 2

The First Great Eruption of the Dreadmount. The Nameless One – a red wyrm – emerges from the Womb of Fire and settles in the Lasian city of Yikala, bringing with him a terrible plague. Selinu the Oathkeeper, ruler of Yikala, organises a lottery of lives to sate the beast.

Hearing of the plight of the Yikalese, an Inyscan knight, Galian Berethnet, rides into their city and promises to kill the Nameless One. In exchange, he desires the conversion of Lasia to his new faith of the Virtues of Knighthood, and Cleolind Onjenyu as his bride.

Princess Cleolind vanquishes the Nameless One with Galian's enchanted sword, Ascalun. She rejects his offer, relinquishes her claim to Lasia, and founds the Priory of the Orange Tree.

In the months following the eruption, the moon often appears blue.

BCE 1

Selinu the Oathkeeper offers land to a group of bereaved Yikalese. They discover a ruined settlement named Karana, which will later become the Serene Republic of Carmentum.

CE 1

After two years of the moon appearing blue, it returns to its usual colour. The Empire of the Twelve Lakes, the Ersyr, the Kingdom of Inys and Yscalin take this as a sign of great significance and reset their calendars. This way of reckoning time eventually spreads across the entire world.

In Inys, Galian Berethnet founds the new city of Ascalun and a royal dynasty, the House of Berethnet. He is crowned King of Inys and marries a woman calling herself Cleolind Onjenyu.

CE 4

The real Cleolind Onjenyu leaves the Priory without clear explanation. Her beloved friend Siyāti attempts to find her, to no avail.

Galian Berethnet dies, leaving his infant daughter as Queen of Inys.

CE 6

A significant disturbance is observed on the Abyss.

CE 12

A comet passes the world.

CE 13

The Hüran record a 'winter of chaos' on the Northern Plain.

CE 248

After a period of great power, the dragons of the East begin to retreat into the Long Slumber, a sleep from which they will not awaken for over two hundred years.

CE 279

The Chainmail of Virtudom is formed when Isalarico IV of Yscalin weds Glorian II of Inys.

CE 301

A revolt against the House of Noziken begins in the provinces of Seiiki, led by the Meadow King. A metalworker named Sasofima kills him and is rewarded with a title and a clan name, Kuposa.

CE 333

The Lacustrine city of Hitanin receives a foreign traveller who uses the alias Tonra. She ascends to Brhazat and is never seen again, but a handful of people of the city begin experiencing strange dreams.

CE 370

Sabran V of Inys is born. Her mother, Marian, dies shortly after the birth, making her queen on her third day of life.

CE 416

Princess Jillian – the future Jillian III of Inys – is born to Sabran V and her Yscali companion, Prince Alarico.

CE 434

Princess Marian – the future Marian III of Inys – is born to Jillian III and her companion.

The Serene Republic of Carmentum is officially established.

CE 459

Tunuva Melim is born to Liru Melim.

CE 462

Unora of Afa is born to Kiywo and Saguresi.

CE 465

Princess Sabran – the future Sabran VI of Inys – is born to Princess Marian and her companion, Lord Alfrick Withy.

CE 480

Verthing of Geldruth makes an offer of marriage to Skiri Longstride of Askdral. When she refuses, he murders her, claiming her domain for his clan. Her closest friend, Hafrid of Fellsgerd, declares war on Verthing, who becomes known as Verthing Bloodblade.

Hróth erupts into a blood feud, the War of Twelve Shields.

The catastrophic Midwinter Flood strikes the northern coast of Mentendon, drowning thousands and destroying its capital, Thisunath.

CE 481

With his fellow Hróthi occupied with the war, the raider Heryon Vattenvarg takes advantage of the Midwinter Flood, which has destroyed Mentish coastal defences. His aim is to settle the country, claiming it for himself and his clan.

Taken by surprise and unsupported, the Mentish are soon forced to give up their fight and submit to Vattenvarg. He founds a new capital, Brygstad.

CE 482

In Hróth, the war continues. Verthing Bloodblade recognises the threat of Bardholt of Bringard – a young commander chosen by Hefna of Fellsgerd – and resolves to force him into surrender, capturing his adopted brother, Hýrri, and his seven-year-old nephew, Einlek Ólrunsbarn. Einlek severs his own hand to escape, while Hýrri is murdered.

Unora of Afa arrives at the court of Antuma and becomes pregnant by the Emperor of Seiiki.

CE 483

On Mount Ipyeda, Unora of Afa gives birth to a daughter, Dumai.

The War of Twelve Shields ends with the defeat and execution of Verthing Bloodblade. Bardholt 'Battlebold' Hraustr is declared the first King of Hróth. Sabran Berethnet proposes to him, and he converts to the faith of the Virtues of Knighthood to marry her.

In exchange for the betrothal of his daughter Brenna to Einlek Óthling – the heir to Hróth – Heryon Vattenvarg pledges his loyalty to Bardholt I and is named Steward of Mentendon. He also converts to the Virtues of Knighthood, bringing Mentendon into Virtudom. Both the Ments and the Hróthi are forced into conversion.

CE 492

Tunuva Melim gives birth to a son, Armul, by her friend Meren.

At nine months old, Armul disappears, and Meren is killed. The incident is blamed on a wildcat attack.

CE 493

Siyu uq-Nāra is born to Esbar uq-Nāra by her friend Imsurin.

CE 494

On the Feast of Early Spring, Glorian Hraustr Berethnet is born to Sabran VI of Inys by Bardholt I of Hróth.

CE 509

A Day of Fallen Night begins in late autumn. Glorian is 15, Dumai is 27, and Tunuva is 50. Wulf does not know his exact age.

Acknowledgements

I started *A Day of Fallen Night* in early 2019 and finished it in the summer of 2022. It was written through bereavement, a pandemic and a long battle with endometriosis – I could never have done it without my own Priory.

Thank you to my agent, David Godwin, who continues to be the best possible champion of me and my work, and to the teams at DGA and Peters Fraser & Dunlop, including: Amandine Riche, Heather Godwin, Jonathan Sissons, Lisette Verhagen, Lucy Barry, Philippa Sitters, Rosie Gurtovoy and Sebastian Godwin.

To my wonderful editor, Genevieve Herr, for tackling another doorstopper with me; to Sarah-Jane Forder and Sarah Bance, for combing through the details of this giant book in record time; to my extraordinary publicist, Philippa Cotton; and to David Mann, Emily Faccini and Ivan Belikov, who have turned *A Day of Fallen Night* into another work of art.

My debut, *The Bone Season*, came out in 2013. I'm so happy that *A Day of Fallen Night* is out in 2023, to coincide with my ten-year anniversary as a published Bloomsbury author. Thank you to everyone on the global team, including: Alexis Kirschbaum, Allegra Le Fanu, Amrita Paul, Ben Chisnall, Beth Maher, Callie Garnett, Donna Gauthier, Elisabeth Denison, Emilie Chambeyron, Grace McNamee, Joe Roche, Ian Hudson, Kathleen Farrar, Laura Meyer, Laura Phillips, Lauren Dooley, Lauren Molyneux, Lauren Moseley, Lauren Ollerhead, Lauren Whybrow, Lucie Moody, Marie Coolman, Marigold Atkey, Meenakshi Singh, Nancy Miller, Nigel Newton, Paul Baggaley, Phoebe Dyer, Rachel Wilkie, Sara Helen Binney, Suzanne Keller, Trâm-Anh Doan, Valentina Rice and Valerie Esposito.

A particularly special thanks to Alexandra Pringle, the Prioress of Bloomsbury, who acquired my debut in 2012 – and, in doing so, made all my dreams come true. Alexandra, thank you for believing in me from the beginning, and for always being there to encourage, reassure and inspire me. It's been such a privilege to be one of your authors, and

I'll always be very proud that an editor of your brilliance saw potential in *The Bone Season*. I hope all my future books will be the sort of books you would have chosen.

To my publishing teams and translators all over the world, including Benjamin Kuntzer, Sam Souibgui, and the rest of the magnificent team at De Saxus.

Due to timings not quite matching up, I wasn't able to express my gratitude to the audiobook narrator of *The Priory of the Orange* Tree in its acknowledgements, so a huge thanks to Liyah Summers for bringing the story to so many more people than it would otherwise have been able to reach.

To the people who have kept my spirits up, helped and supported me over the last three years of work on this book, including: Alwyn Hamilton, Claire Donnelly, El Lam, Harriet Hammond, Helen Corcoran, Holly Bourne, Ilana Fernandes-Lassman, John Moore, Kat Dunn, Katherine Webber, Kevin Tsang, Kiran Millwood Hargrave, Krystal Sutherland, Laure Eve, Leiana Leatutufu, Lisa Lueddecke, Lizzie 'Hux' Huxley-Jones, London Shah, Melinda Salisbury, Molly Chang, Nina Douglas, Peta Freestone, Richard Smith, Saara El-Arifi, Tasha Suri, Vickie Morrish and Victoria Aveyard.

This book is dedicated to my mum and best friend, Amanda Jones, whose fierce love and strength has worked its way onto many pages of *A Day of Fallen Night*. Mum, Dad, Alfie: thank you for always being there, through all the tough deadlines and worries and days of self-doubt. I love you all so much.

Finally, a heartfelt thanks to the international book community, including librarians, booksellers, reviewers, bloggers, authors and everyone on the powerhouse that is BookTok. Since *The Priory of the Orange Tree* was published, your support has grown beyond anything I could possibly have imagined. I hope you've enjoyed returning to this world, and that you love the new characters as much as I've loved telling their stories.